**AREA MANAGERS OF SWANN-ON-WHEELS,
1878-1889**

WESTERN WEDGE	(1) HAMLET RATCLIFFE
	(2) ALBERT ('BERTIEBOY') BICKFORD
SOUTHERN SQUARE	'YOUNG' ROCKWOOD
KENTISH TRIANGLE	GODSALL
THE BONUS	VICARY
CRESCENTS SOUTH AND CENTRE, MERGED	TOM WICKSTEAD
CRESCENT NORTH	MARKBY
BORDER TRIANGLE AND SCOTLAND, MERGED	(1) FRASER
	(2) JAKE HIGSON
THE POLYGON	(1) BROADBENT
	(2) JOHN CATESBY (FORMER MANAGER)
MOUNTAIN SQUARE	BRYN LOVELL
NORTHERN AND SOUTHERN PICKINGS, MERGED	MORRIS
TOM TIDDLER'S LAND	DOCKETT
IRISH BRIDGEHEAD	(1) O'DOWD
	(2) CLINTON COLES
LONDON H.Q.	KEATE (WAGGONMASTER)
	TYBALT (CHIEF CLERK)
	STOCK (ADJUDICATOR)

Cal Sachs

R. F. DELDERFIELD

—

Theirs
Was the Kingdom

SIMON AND SCHUSTER · NEW YORK

The author gratefully acknowledges the encouragement given him by the old-established firm of Messrs. Pickford. The decorative drawings are reproduced from contemporary prints lent by the Mary Evans Picture Library and the National Freight Federation.

For my old friend and colleague
Eric McKenzie, as enterprising
as any Swann. Salesman and
cheer-leader extraordinary

THE SWANNS OF 'TRYST'

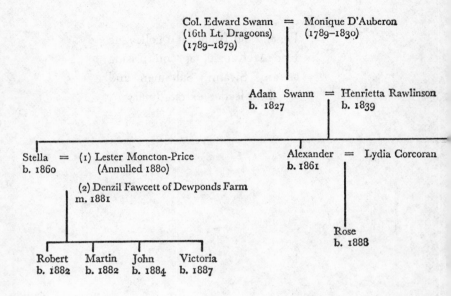

Col. Edward Swann = Monique D'Auberon
(16th Lt. Dragoons)   (1789–1830)
(1789–1879)

Adam Swann = Henrietta Rawlinson
b. 1827   b. 1839

Stella = (1) Lester Moncton-Price
b. 1860   (Annulled 1880)

(2) Denzil Fawcett of Dewponds Farm
m. 1881

Alexander = Lydia Corcoran
b. 1861

Rose
b. 1888

Robert   Martin   John   Victoria
b. 1882   b. 1882   b. 1884   b. 1887

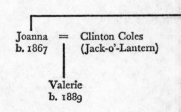

Joanna = Clinton Coles
b. 1867   (Jack-o'-Lantern)

Valerie
b. 1889

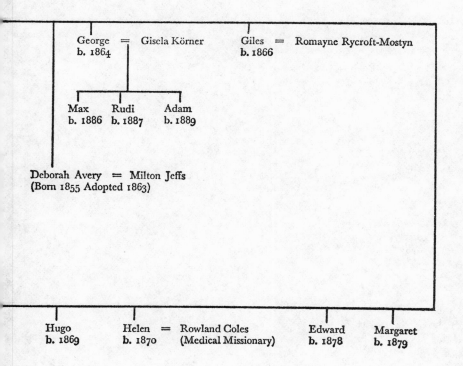

George = Gisela Körner   Giles = Romayne Rycroft-Mostyn
b. 1864   b. 1866

Max   Rudi   Adam
b. 1886   b. 1887   b. 1889

Deborah Avery = Milton Jeffs
(Born 1855 Adopted 1863)

Hugo   Helen = Rowland Coles   Edward   Margaret
b. 1869   b. 1870   (Medical Missionary)   b. 1878   b. 1879

Contents

THEIRS WAS THE KINGDOM

VIEW OF THE RIVER
December, 1878

TOWARDS noon, when Swann's carters, stablemen and vanboys gathered in the yard and about the sprawl of sheds and warehouses, munching their bread and cheese and spilling shards of pastry from penny pies bought at the stand lower down Tooley Street, cohorts of London sparrows attended them. But when dusk fell, when the gates were locked after the last homing waggon and the only men inside the enclosure were watchmen, the sparrows, most knowing of London's cadgers, flew west to scavenge Covent Garden, abandoning Swann's Bermondsey headquarters to a pair of robins. The robins then assumed private ownership of the rectangle and were always in hopes that the tall, broad-shouldered man with the friendly eyes, and the curious rolling gait, would stay overnight and be on hand to provide breakfast at first light, pushing wide the tower casement and calling them to perch on the sill of the old belfry.

Often enough he appeared, having slept on the camp bed he had there, and they heard his cheerful shout this morning, as the grey light probed the swirling river mists, so that they took off from the warehouse gutter, dropping down within pecking reach of his large, horny hand.

He called, as always, "Hello, you two! Help yourselves. Take the chill off the morning": and grinned as they advanced warily to feed from his hand, paying no heed when he cleared his throat, threw up his head and sniffed the damp air, accepting him as one of the regular early risers hereabouts, with time as well as pasty crumbs on his hands, and a geniality he would shed once the working day had begun and he had opened his newspapers and settled to his desk.

His presence there, at this hour, was irregular. In spring and summer he might watch the dawn from the tower casement no more than once a fortnight but at this season of the year, coming up to Christmas, he was sometimes there for days at a stretch, a strongly-made, shambling man, who seemed to enjoy his isolation high above the wilderness of slate and tile, a man who had a word for them even when that great desk of his was spread with papers and he seemed absorbed in a never-ending task.

*   *   *

In summer and early autumn, between late May and mid-October, the sour whiff of the river predominated, a compound of bilges, decaying flotsam, spoiled vegetables, drowned cats and half-starved, ownerless dogs, spread across a twenty-foot margin of hard-packed bluish mud that was the permanent residue of Plantagenet, Tudor, Stuart and Georgian sewage. A miasma so focussed, and so indigenous, that it sometimes seemed to enfold the entire South Bank in a fond, foetid embrace, like a cloud of marsh-gas stealing up river from the wastelands of both sides of the estuary. But that was the summer scent of the yard.

In mid-winter, as now, the river whiff moderated, taking a modest fourth place to the reek of the adjacent soap factory, the more pungent stink of the tannery nearer the bridge, and the sharp, acrid smell of innumerable horse-droppings in the clubbed approaches to the tideway.

Adam Swann was never conscious of the reek, summer or winter, having had twenty years to get acclimatised to it. On a morning like this, for instance, when he had been up here a day and a night summarising his annual reports and assessing the turnover of his regions in order that he could apportion the Christmas bonuses, he thought of the long river reach, stretching from London Bridge to the forest of masts marking the most westerly moorings of the Surrey Commercial Dock, as his private demesne, something peculiarly his, like the queer, octagonal tower he had used as his office ever since he settled here in the autumn of 'fifty-eight. Vast business expansion had never tempted him to shift his headquarters to a more salubrious spot and he could have told you why. Indeed, he occasionally did tell customers, family and underlings why, whenever he saw them wrinkling their noses beside his open casement.

He would say, with a hard grin, "Where else could I keep finger

2

and thumb on the pulse of the nation? Look at that string of barges, those lighters and wherries making rendezvous with the ocean-going shipping lower down the river. Why, dammit, I can stand here taking stock of my own concerns and everybody else's at one and the same time! Could I do that anywhere else in the city at seventy pounds a quarter?"

And those among them who fancied they knew him well would shrug at his conceit and descend the spiral staircase to the teeming yard where his waggons came and went and his horde of retainers heaved and cursed and pottered, reflecting that Adam Swann was a queer chap, an amateur who had outdistanced all the professionals in the square mile, a man who took more pleasure in the cut-and-thrust of commerce than he had ever taken as a mercenary in the field. And that despite the fact that he had been present at battles which had now taken their place in the history primers at every redbrick board school in the country.

Invariably he forgot his visitors as soon as their steps had died away on the stone stairway, lunging back into the embrasure and slowly massaging the muscles of his thigh where the straps of his artificial leg had chafed during a long session at the desk. But before he addressed himself to his work again he would glance out across the river at the Conqueror's tower, far higher, bulkier and more majestic than his but not all that much older, for the Carmelite convent that had preceded the brewery, the livery stables and the waggon park here was twelfth-century, or so they told him, and the beam that had supported a bell that summoned the sisterhood to prayer was still there as a bulge in the plaster ceiling of the eyrie.

That was usually how he thought of it when he was up here alone at first light, with the river mists shredding and the blurred outlines of the bridge taking shape before his eyes. An eyrie, owing absolutely nothing to anyone else alive, a place where he could assess his personal destiny in terms of past, present and future, so that his review sometimes took the form of a jaunty, self-congratulatory circuit of the octagonal room, where everything he saw and touched was part and parcel of his odyssey. The walls up here were plastered with maps representing every square yard of his territory, and sometimes it seemed to him they trumpeted an astounding achievement, not only on his part as creator, but on the part of the handpicked men who staffed the fifteen regions known by a string of odd, quirkish names—The Border Triangle, The Lancashire Polygon, The Mountain Square, The Western Wedge and so on; names his fancy had found for them when he slashed his territory into a dozen different slices, drew up his maps and pinned them to the wall.

He thought of them now as children, with characteristics and idiosyncrasies far more diverse and far more interesting than the eight children he had sired on his eighty-acre estate fifteen miles to the south and he supposed there was a logical reason for this. For the Swanns of 'Tryst', from nineteen-year-old Stella, now off his hands, to the family postscript whose arrival last January had astonished him, owed no more than a small segment of their individual egos to him, whereas the segments of his wall-maps had been a conscious act of creation on his part and had been nurtured, over two decades, on a diet of edicts emanating from this tower and directed by his hand and brain.

The view of the river was one thing—his private 'Peak in Darien', from which he could feel the nation's pulse. The regional maps, proclaiming the steady growth of his enterprise, were something else. But there were other random features of the tower that were permanent reminders of the stages in his twenty-year haul and when the stocktaking mood was on him he would review them severally and collectively, making a kind of mosaic of a life he always saw as beginning the day he came here in his thirty-second year.

He discounted the wasted years prior to that. His childhood and boyhood were dim now, a period spent in preparing himself for a career that had become, over the centuries, obligatory to a male Swann, one of following the drum across the world until sword, bullet, arthritis or half-pay cut the process short, leaving survivors to feed on their memories. The years that mattered had been his middle years, from his thirty-first birthday onward, and he was fortunate in that he could calculate to the exact minute the turn of the tide on the littered field of Jhansi at the very end of the Sepoy Mutiny, when he had fallen beside the Ranee's necklace, reached for it and stuffed it into his sabretache before losing consciousness. From that moment he regretted nothing. From then on, buttressed by the yield of the rubies, he had groped his way forward with a definite sense of purpose, making his mistakes certainly but profiting

4

by the least of them and, just occasionally, when challenged by a
fortuitous set of circumstances, propelling himself and his enterprise
forward in a series of prodigious leaps. The evidence was all around
him. It warmed his heart to contemplate it piece by piece.

In a wall niche directly opposite the window was the silver frigate
with its commemorative plaque, a craftsman's scale-model of one of
his two-horse, medium-weight vans, presented to him on his return
to work after eleven months' absence learning to walk on a tin leg.
He never looked at it without recalling the moment, thirteen years
ago, when he had limped in here, making heavy weather of that
spiral staircase, and read the little pyramid of names inscribed below
the Swann insignia, a swan with a wheel where the port wing
should have been. It was a trophy that would never leave here while
he lived. It did not belong anywhere else, only here, where the argosies of the men whose names it bore came and went. It represented
not merely loyalty on the part of sixteen men and one woman, but
the thrust he had transmitted to them as they wrestled, year by year,
to build something out of nothing. The Ranee's necklace, his starting capital, had been valued at nine thousand pounds. To Adam
Swann the price of the silver frigate was incalculable.

Above it was another, very different trophy, a map less than half
the size of the other seven and the only one hanging there that had
been drawn by another hand. A railway map, antedating his enterprise by a few months and given him, half in jest, by a man called
Walker, erstwhile depot manager of the Great Western at Plymouth,
who had sparked off the entire adventure by a single, casual remark.
Over the years Swann could still hear Walker's bantering voice—
"Don't invest a penny in railways, your own or anyone else's. If I
was your age, and I wish to God I was and starting all over again,
I'd do something better. Study that map and fill in the blank spaces."

Well, he had done it within months and the process had led him,
more or less directly, to the most ungainly trophy in the room, an
object—it defied a more definite name—that made every stranger
who crossed the threshold cock an eyebrow, and wonder what a
transport magnate could want with a huge costumier's display stand,
that spun on a pivot and seemed, in motion, to take on limited animation, as though it was a cross between an anarchist's infernal
machine and a pot-bellied robot. They were not so far wrong. In a

way it was a robot, at least, it had a robot's name and was known to everyone familiar with Swann's methods as 'Frankenstein the Fact Finder'. He spun it now, smiling a little at his own cleverness and eccentricity, and recalling the night he had sat up here inventing it as a short cut to milking facts and figures from his head clerk's canvass of their first four regions. He did not use it overmuch now. Most of its data was filed inside his head, but he was always eager to demonstrate it to anyone politely interested and whenever his captive audience included a hard-headed businessman he knew, somehow, the thoughts he took away with him. Swann, of Swann-on-Wheels. A very warm man, it was rumoured, with a streak of originality that somehow had established him as the fastest and most reliable transporter of goods in the country. But still, somehow, an amateur among professionals.

He did not quarrel with that, having long since decided that the country was thronged with amateurs, that the Empire had been acquired and administered by amateurs, that, but for amateurs, the industrial revolution would have been stillborn a century ago and some other tribe would have cornered the world's trade.

Up here, whenever he was camping overnight, he lived rough, bivouac fashion. Creature comforts made no appeal to him and he had never cared a straw what he ate or drank, or where he coiled himself under a horse-blanket borrowed from the night-duty stableman. He lunged past Frankenstein, giving it a final spin, and paused at the end of his great oak desk, piled with the results of his twenty-four hour foray. A foolscap sheet lay there, covered with his neat, angular writing, a list of fifteen regions with the area manager's name in brackets alongside, and underneath the calculated bonuses based on their individual turnover. He gave the sheet a long minute's study, comparing it, in his mind's eye, with the previous year's list and noting that Fraser, away up in the Borderlands and beyond, had at last overhauled his nearest rivals, Godsall, of the Kentish Triangle, and Rookwood, of Southern Square. Well, he was glad of it. The circular that his head clerk Tybalt would send out as a result of his night's labours would keep those comparative youngsters on their toes and this would be Fraser's last full year before retirement. Fraser was a trier. Runner-up for six years in succession and now top of the list, with the whole of Scotland under his thumb. Experience counted for something after all.

He laid aside the list and picked up the only item on the desk that had no commercial significance, a heavy silver frame containing two photographs, one of his wife, Henrietta, the other of his four eldest children, booted and spurred on the terrace of 'Tryst' before setting off to a meet of the West Kent foxhounds. It was full day now, crisp and clear over the river, the heatless sun level with the spars of the furthermost vessels in the dock. Noting this he ceased his prowl and stood propped in the alcove waiting for his coffee to warm on the iron stove, his mind occupied with a kind of equation that an idle moment like this encouraged. Where, if truth were known, lay his loyalty? To those grimed maps, to Frankenstein and the fifteen names on the foolscap sheet? Or to this woman and those striplings and the other four out of sight? He had found answers to all his sums over the years but never an answer to this one, perhaps because a photograph was never a true likeness, never told you anything important about the sitter.

Henrietta, for instance. Here she was, her plump, pert, pretty self, and yet it wasn't her at all, or not as he had come to know her since the day he rode over the moor and hoisted her on to the rump of his fagged out mare. The camera had reproduced her fussy get-up in the greatest detail but where was her sparkle? And underneath all those yards of draperies where were the factors that had kept him faithful to her all these years?

It was the same, to a degree, with the children, although here he was less dogmatic, for he was always ready to admit that he did not know them and was never likely to know them. There was his first-born, Stella, named for a star he once saw over that well at Cawnpore in 'fifty-seven; his eldest son, Alexander, proud as a peacock in his first hunting topper and obviously impatient to stride out of the picture and throw his leg across that mettlesome young gelding the old Colonel had bought the boy on his seventeenth birthday. There was young Giles, standing slightly apart, and looking his usual solemn self, as though, instead of the prospect of a day in the saddle, he was going in search of martyrdom. And finally, there was that merry rascal George, the only one likely to follow him into the hurly-burly of the city with any prospect of relish.

7

What the devil did he know about any of them? How and when should he have learned? This room, these maps, had sucked him dry over the years. Nine-tenths of his time and nervous energy had been expended here, calculating the profit on a haul of slate from Llanberis to Swansea, or a thousand gallons of milk from Wiltshire farms to city dairymen. Playing one lieutenant off against another. Scratching round for a new capital to replace worn-out teams and vehicles. Exploiting a new idea that would tap a fresh source of profit. His family had been an afterthought, a spare-time hobby, like chess or croquet, and inevitably, as the years hurried by, Henrietta had usurped his place as master of 'Tryst', reducing him, little by little, to the role of a privileged lodger, or a favourite uncle whose prerogative was to spoil rather than guide the thrusters who kept his home in a permanent uproar.

With a final glimpse at the river he turned away, replacing the heavy silver frame on the desk and wondering, incuriously, if increasing age and girth would encourage him to live on his fat, to turn his back on this stinking, clamorous stew and spend more of his time at home enjoying the fruits of all this toil and turmoil. He doubted it. If an artificial leg had not slowed him down would age and the indifference to money that marched with age? In all the time he had been here money had not troubled him much. His sense of drive derived from other things—a consciousness of contributing, of playing a part in the burgeoning of the nation, in a search for perfection within the limits of the profession he had chosen and the path he had marked out for himself when he was fighting other people's battles on the other side of the world. Everyone worth his salt cut his own swathe. The only useful thing you could do for fellow-travellers was to encourage them to stand on their own feet and find their own way through the jungle. The names on that presentation frigate proved that if nothing else. Each of them owed his opportunity to Swann-on-Wheels so that his real family was listed there and would doubtless remain his sole concern until they carried him away in a box and his son George, or someone else, took his place at that desk.

The thought made him grin as he lifted his coffee from the stove and sniffed its fragrance. Whoever it was would not waste much time vacating this slum and seeking more comfortable quarters.

8

North of the river perhaps, within easier reach of the big railway termini and the new trunk roads they were laying down. Or a few miles south, in one of the semi-rural suburbs, where a man could breathe clean air. The enterprise would surely recast itself in the decades ahead. New and faster methods of transport would be devised. Railways would improve and so would roads, even country roads, whereas manufactories, now concentrated in the North and Midlands, would lap into the southern shires, proliferating like flies as more and more markets were opened up overseas by the imperialists and the missionaries.

He thought about the Empire for a moment. Where its frontiers would be drawn and which tribe, if any, would overhaul it and challenge its supremacy by the time the old queen died and that plump, racketty Edward mounted her throne. The gloomy Germans, possibly, who had given the yammering French such a thrashing a few years ago. Or the Yankees, who were not likely to stay minding their own business. How much longer had he got to watch the merry-go-round? Ten years? Twenty? Perhaps even a few more, for somehow, after so many adventures, he felt marked down for old age. More than that he could not see himself retiring while there was breath in his body.

*   *   *

He was sifting through the morning mail when Tybalt, his head clerk, poked a bald pate into the tower, holding a buff telegram as though it was liable to bite. He was familiar with Tybalt's ranges of expression. The one he wore now was almost surely associated with bad news of one sort or another. He said, irritably, "Well, come in man and give it to me. Don't stand there looking so damned apologetic. Which of 'em is in trouble this time?" and Tybalt replied, morosely, "It's personal, sir. From 'Tryst', prepaid. The boy's waiting for an answer."

He took the telegram and opened it, recalling as he did that he had told Henrietta he was likely to move north to confer with her father Sam and Catesby of the Polygon before he came home for the Christmas break. The telegram said: *Colonel much worse. Doctor Birtles says matter of days. Think you should come. Love, Hetty.* He said, with a grunt, "It's the old Colonel. Wire Catesby and my

9

father-in-law, and tell them to hold over that mill business for a week or two. It's not all that urgent. I'll have to go home and wait. There's nothing else to keep me. I've worked out the bonuses and the annual summaries are in draft. You'd best have them copied and circularised," and he rose, swinging his tin leg in a wide arc to clear the end of the desk.

Tybalt said, with a rich gravity that suited him far better than elation, "I'm very sorry, Mr. Swann. He was a dear old gentleman. I got to know him very well when I was down there a great deal at the time of your accident. You'll miss him very much, I'm sure."

"He's had a damned good innings," Adam said, unsentimentally. "If he lives on into February he'll be eighty-nine but I hope, for his sake, that he doesn't. However, I should want to be there," and Tybalt murmured "Of course," gathered up a sheaf of papers and left, as though he disapproved of his employer's cavalier reception of such grave news.

Adam followed him down, his nostrils tingling in keen morning air only marginally tainted by the whiff of the soap factory. He crossed the yard and lifted his hand in greeting to the giant waggon-master Keate, who was conferring with the master smith. The place would have to get along without him for a spell but it might be some time before he was back. Old men who had suffered two strokes sometimes took their time dying. And then, as he passed through the gates and hailed a four-wheeler, to take him to London Bridge Station, he had another thought. It was how this side of the bridge must have looked when his father was born in 1789, a decade or so before the sprawl of factories had penetrated beyond Rotherhithe and long before the docks were built, a time when every vessel that entered the river rounded North Foreland under press of sail. The interval between then and now appeared to him then as a millennium rather than the better part of a century, and his mind leaped forward another span of years, so that he tried to picture what it would be like when he, in his turn, lay dying. Unrecognisable again he wouldn't wonder, with that new bridge they were always talking about down the river a reach or so, and God alone knew how many tunnels burrowing under the slime of the Thames. Places and people had that much in common. They sprang up, preened themselves in the vigour of youth and the fancied permanence of maturity and then, almost overnight if one reckoned in terms of history, either crumbled or took on an entirely new form. Nothing lasted all that long and it therefore followed that the world would always belong to the young. To lively sparks like his son Alex, to his daughter Stella who would soon, he supposed, come to him with talk of grandchildren, to George who would inherit his packload sooner or later, and to young Giles with his serious eyes, eyes that would never make much of a balance sheet but would always look sympathetically on the derelicts that, even at this early hour, were scavenging among the rubbish tips outside the biscuit factory.

Part One

SWANNS AT LARGE

1

Thoughts at a Funeral

THE old Colonel died at five minutes to three, on the morning of January the nineteenth, 1879.

His son, Adam, who had been taking a turn at sitting up with him for almost a week now, did not witness the death. He was dozing in the armchair beside the leaping coal fire and the cessation of the long, rasping breaths alerted him in the way a sudden change in sound pattern had broken his bivouac sleep in his campaigning days. He rose without haste, massaging his thigh where the support straps of his artificial leg had chafed during the long vigil, lifting the old man's hand and waiting, aware of the contrast between the stillness of the room and the tumult outside, where the wind soughed in the stripped branches of the avenue beeches, as though the Colonel's spirit had taken flight among them, rejoicing in release from the withered old carcase on the bed.

After a few moments he released the hand, closed the eyes and gently pressed the jaws, remembering, as he did this, that he had performed the same office for a score of men young enough to have been the old man's great-grandsons. But that was long ago, at Balaclava, Inkermann, Cawnpore and Lucknow, places and occasions rarely remembered in the last two decades.

Even now he felt more relief than regret. The dear old chap, who looked so small under the blankets, had been dead to him, and to everyone else at 'Tryst', since the night in June last year when those lively young sparks of the Sixteenth had brought him home after his collapse at his final Waterloo anniversary dinner in Apsley House. They were hardly more than boys, the aides of paunchy, mottled, bewhiskered old veterans attending the dinner as guests, but they had handled the old man with reverence and this, Adam supposed, was understandable. To them he would be a museum piece for only that week *The Times* had reminded them that the

15

Colonel had served under Old Beaky, the Iron Duke, twenty-eight years dead, and was, moreover, the only man sitting around that table who had helped to drive Ney's storming party down the steep escarpment at Busaco, in September 1810. He had thus attended more than fifty Waterloo dinners and was a legend in his own right.

Adam paused a moment, wondering whether to summon the male nurse they had engaged and then wake Henrietta and tell her the news but he decided against it. It was not a moment for family clamour. He preferred, for the time, to marshal his own thoughts and walked stiffly to the window, lowering the sash an inch or two to freshen the air of the sick room, letting his mind explore his relationship with the old man, a very unusual one, he would say, especially over the last twenty years, when it had been that of a father and son in reverse. But it had suited them both since the latter had turned his back on the Swann military tradition and gone into trade.

The old man had been very happy down here, pottering about in the sun and the wind, spoiling and being spoiled by a flock of grandchildren, by Henrietta and all the servants, who thought of him as a family heirloom embodying the prestige of an era that seemed to Adam as distant as Agincourt. Born soon after the storming of the Bastille, he had taken the field at eighteen and spent the next seven years riding and fighting for his life in Portugal, Spain, Haute Garonne and Flanders, hectored by men whose names would forever be associated with the Iron Duke—'Farmer' Hill, Tommy Picton, Sir Joseph Cotton, red-headed Craufurd, darling of the Light Brigade, and a hundred others. A splendid company, no doubt, but as irrelevant as mediaeval pikemen in an age of breechloading rifles, the Gatling, and four-funnelled iron-clads capable of projecting twelve-inch shells.

He retraced his steps to the bed, still flexing the muscles above the joint in the leg and staggering a little on that account. The coals in the grate shifted, the pendulum of the small French clock spun under its glass dome, and outside the wind gusted breathlessly across the bleak winter landscape. He looked down at the rigid, angular features, trying to see the old man as he had been all those years ago, a pink-cheeked, curly-haired lad, with brown, laughing eyes, cantering through the passes of the Pyrenees in pursuit of that wily old rascal Soult, beating the dust from Johnny Frenchman's knap-sack all the way from Torres Vedras to Toulouse. Four years it had taken them, six if you counted the two abortive campaigns, but the Colonel had found his pot of gold in the first French town they had captured. Not loot or promotion, but a pretty brunette, dispensing cakes in a pastry-cook's kitchen, one of the French mademoiselles who welcomed the English dragoons as liberators. And that was odd in itself, for pot-bellied Bonaparte was now even more of a legend than his rival, the Duke, and was regarded by many as a martyr to British bureaucracy after he had died on an Atlantic rock, denied the title of Emperor. But time had put that right. Adam himself had seen Napoleon's splendid tomb at Les Invalides.

The train of thought led him, logically enough, to Waterloo, and his glance moved from his father's face to his right hand, marking the bluish stumps of the two truncated fingers, the result of a wild slash by a French cuirassier who had died a moment later, struck through the throat by his nimble little opponent. After that nothing very much, or nothing to fill the history books. Service on a few fever-infested islands; half-pay retirement; a young wife to mourn and a troublesome son to rear; tranquil years in late middle age be-side Derwentwater with his crotchety old sister, Aunt Charlotte and, in the long evening of his life, twenty years in the Kent countryside, reproduced in a hundred of his laboured water colours, three of which hung in this room, conflicting oddly with other trophies that hung there, the sabre, the dragoon's helmet in need of a polish, a posed photograph of a Waterloo dinner, and the telescope through which the old man had once watched Marshal Soult ordering his outposts across the Bidassoa.

Well, as he had indicated to Tybalt when the telegram arrived, the old chap could count himself lucky. How many of his contem-poraries had lived to see a grand-daughter in her bridal veil? How many had been given the chance to grow old gracefully in pleasant, comfortable surroundings, with a dozen women to wait on him, and a tribe of children to listen to his stories? Not one in twenty, Adam would say, with bitter personal experience of war wastage. Possibly not one in a hundred when you thought of the slaughter at places like Badajoz, Ciudad Rodrigo, Salamanca and Waterloo, or the ransom of a thousand wet nights in Spanish bivouacs and long stretches of service in murderous tropical climates.

He squeezed the maimed hand, tucked it under the bedclothes and drew the sheet over the face. "I hope to God I'm half as lucky," he said aloud and stumped from the room, seeking his own quarters.

2

Henrietta wept when he told her, and thirteen-year-old Giles, who had been a close confidant of the old man, turned pale but said nothing, slipping away to commune with himself in the winter woods while they discussed funeral arrangements. Stella, eldest of the brood, would not know until they sent word to Courtlands, her new home across the county border, whereas Alex, the eldest boy, would be unlikely to learn of his grandfather's death for weeks, for God only knew where he was at the moment, with his unit poised to cross the Tugela and slaughter Zulus. The younger children, taking their cue from George, now sixteen, assumed lugubriously pious expressions that failed to conceal their secret relish at being the centre of attention at a military funeral. Adam noticed their sternly repressed exuberance and smiled grimly. It was the prerogative of the very young to feel smug in the certainty of immortality, but he had looked for tears from Henrietta. She had never made the least secret of her belief that, but for the good offices of the old man, she would have been denied the splendid fulfilment of the last twenty years. Adam, left to himself, she said, would have handed her back to her father after her flight from home in a thunderstorm, despite the truculent showing he made at the confrontation when Sam Rawlinson had appeared with a writ. He had not been in love with her then, and had no thought for anything but his improbable dream of a nation-wide waggon service. But the old man had enlisted with her the moment Adam ushered her over the doorstep, a scared, bedraggled fugitive in a tattered, cageless crinoline, and in the end Sam had taken himself off grumbling and swearing, cutting her out of his will and leaving the reluctant White Knight no alternative but to marry her and found a family here in Kent. There was more than

18

that to their relationship, as Adam well knew, although he had never exhumed that ridiculous involvement with that popinjay Miles Manaton, who had come so close to raping her on the islet in the river that ran within sight of 'Tryst'. Luckily for everyone the Colonel had been on hand that day, had mounted her on his skewbald, packed her off home, and briefed her on a story to explain her disarray and hysteria. And afterwards, intercepting Adam at the yard, he had spoken up for her so that the whole stupid affair had passed effortlessly into limbo. Adam, remembering all this when he saw the glitter of tears in Henrietta's eye as she bent over the bed and kissed the old man's brow, thought: "She's regretting him a damned sight more than she would her own father. Now why should a woman with her lust for life carry a grudge down the years, for it's clear she's never really forgiven Sam for trying to barter her for a piece of wasteland adjoining the old devil's mill in that foul little town where I found her." He said nothing, however, except a word or two of perfunctory comfort about the old man's death in life since his stroke and perhaps she shared his relief. What man in his senses wanted to survive as a hulk?

*   *   *

They buried him in Twyforde Green churchyard three days later, where the Swann family was, as the younger children had anticipated, on show for everybody in the county. A sober-faced row of them, occupying the full length of the second pew, the front pew having been surrendered, by protocol, to the officer commanding the Colonel's old regiment, and the dragoons of the Sixteenth who travelled over from Hythe to see the doyen of their regiment accorded the honours due to a man who had lost two fingers at Waterloo.

Military display did not impress Adam Swann. It never had much, not even when he was a serving officer himself, and now that part of his life was as far behind him as his boyhood. He did not begrudge the old man his colourful requiem, with six scarlet-coated troopers as bearers, and the reigning Colonel and Adjutant as pall-bearers. It flattered Henrietta, who still cherished the conceits of her youth concerning soldiers, and it obviously impressed the younger children, who listened far more attentively to the military chaplain's windy eulogy than they listened to sermons delivered from the same pulpit during their Sunday church attendance. For himself he found his mind ranging on other, irrelevant subjects. Whether or not to take Tybalt's advice and sink more money into the Dublin branch; whether Lawyer Stock was right or wrong to urge the purchase of a fleet of Swann coasters to haul goods by sea as well as road; whether John Catesby, his northern manager, and a fervent trade unionist, would cross the floor and manage Sam Rawlinson's mill, now that the indefatigable old rascal had made another fortune on the Stock Market, based on his holdings in the Suez Canal Company.

"Our brother-in-arms, privileged to shed blood at the most famous engagement in history . . ." The florid old chaplain droned on and Adam, hunched in his pew, his gammy leg at an awkward angle, spared a speculative thought or two for his eldest son Alex, who had rejected the offer of a junior partnership in the most prosperous haulage firm in the country, to play soldiers with Lord Chelmsford and his legions in Zululand. And he only eighteen, the age when the old man and a score of long-dead Swanns had ridden off to the wars. He wondered if the presence of so many uniforms in the little church would promote anxiety in Henrietta for her eldest and favourite son, away seeking his baptism of fire, but thought it very unlikely. She was still extraordinarily naïve about soldiers, and what was expected of soldiers once the bands had stopped braying. Nothing he had ever told her about war had succeeded in moderating her girlish obsession for scarlet and gold, for the swagger and glitter that she had found so attractive in that idiot Miles Manaton until he grabbed her and tried his damnedest to peel the drawers from her backside. An incident like that would have induced most women to look beyond the uniform at the man inside but it had not taught Henrietta anything very significant or why would she have urged him to let Alex sail off to Natal in October, the moment he was offered a commission in some tinpot local levy?

"Did his duty by Queen and regiment . . . upheld the honour of the flag on foreign fields . . ."; the mottle-faced, port-punishing old chaplain was clearly enjoying himself so that Adam, catching up on sleep, rose rather jerkily when the final hymn was announced and everybody fumbled for hymnbooks. He shot a half-mischievous, half-rueful glance at his wife but she avoided his eye. She looked

pre-occupied, he thought, so the old man's long-awaited death had been a shock after all. Well, he fancied he knew a way to restore Henrietta to her customary high spirits before another dawn and promised himself that there would be no mourning the far side of the bedroom door. A few hours in his arms, a little flattery, a shared joke or two, and she would be herself again, with the pleasant rhythm of their lives restored. There was, he assured himself, very little he did not know about Henrietta Swann, née Rawlinson, the artful little devil he had plucked from a moor all those years ago, and this despite the successive layers of camouflage she had donned since he had saddled her with a family and installed her in a mansion standing in an estate of eighty acres. She could persuade most people, no doubt, that she was gently born, and liked to observe the proprieties. He knew better.

*   *   *

For once, however, he was wrong about her, as wrong as he could be. Henrietta Swann, standing demurely beside husband and children, trilling out the verses of the familiar, full-blooded hymn, was not, as it happened, thinking of the old Colonel, the occasion, or the obligatory proprieties it demanded of her. Instead she was trying hard to arrive at a conclusion concerning the marriage of her daughter Stella, now standing three children away from her, and sharing a hymnbook with her well-bred, impassive husband, Lester Percy Maitland Moncton-Price, heir to Sir Gilbert Moncton-Price, Bart., of Courtlands, in the county of Sussex, whom she had married quietly late the previous summer. Quietly, because at that time the old Colonel was expected to die at any moment; and quickly because Lester had been a serving officer when they became engaged and was anticipating a posting to the Cape to join his unit.

The girl had been in a rare tizzy to see herself installed as chatelaine of the great, draughty place the Moncton-Prices maintained just across the county border but there had been no occasion for the hurry after all. The moment Stella's settlement had been agreed Lester Moncton-Price threw up his commission in the Hussars and joined his father in what he advanced as a filial endeavor to recoup the summer's flat-racing losses on the autumn steeplechases. Henrietta had not been informed whether their string of successes had resulted in keeping the creditors at long range but she was in no doubt at all as to what had induced the Moncton-Prices to marry into trade. That much, she supposed, must be general knowledge in the area but nobody, seemingly, found it degrading, not even Adam, who argued that men like Sir Gilbert, whilst they were almost always short of ready money, could never be hounded beyond a certain point, so long as they owned land and had family ties with influential people at Court and Westminster. On the whole, he told Henrietta privately, he approved the match. Marriages of this kind, he said, were recognised as a means of national compromise now-adays and Stella, a tradesman's daughter, would be unlikely to do better down here in the country if that was the life she hankered after. It was out of the question to give her a season, like that ac-corded the daughters of deeply-entrenched county families. In twenty years or so seasons would be obligatory on the part of suc-cessful tradesmen's daughters but changes of this kind took time. As it was they were still the prerogative of people who inherited money.

So they were married in this same church in September and Stella, pink with triumph, drove away behind a pair of matched bays to Courtlands and Henrietta, thereafter, held her peace. She did not even inform Adam that he had entirely misunderstood her concerning her doubts. They had nothing whatever to do with the mountainous losses of the Moncton-Prices at Newmarket and Epsom, and even less with young ladies' seasons, and the rituals of husband-hunting in London drawing-rooms. They were instinctive and deeply personal, arising out of her own discoveries concerning the nature of men and marriage, that told her good manners in public, a generous settlement, and the prospect of a title, were threadbare substitutes for a shared sense of humour and the prospect of a romp down the years with a lusty, tolerant husband. She would have been more likely to make a determined stand had she not long since made up her mind that Stella, whilst undeniably pretty, grace-ful, and an expert in croquet, dancing and small-talk, was very short on humour and therefore unfamiliar with the hidden meaning of the word 'romp' as applied to marriage. Had she not been she would have shied away from a mincing, rather effeminate beau like Lester, and possibly gone as far as climbing out of the bedroom one night and running off to Gretna Green with someone like that lumping great farmer's son, Denzil Fawcett (or Follett was it?) who had been mooning after her, poor, deluded oaf, since she had put her hair up when she was thirteen. For that, or something like it, was what Henrietta would have done in her shoes, but mother and daughter had very little in common, and perhaps Stella did not deserve anyone better than Lester Percy Maitland Moncton-Price and the clutch of long-nosed children he was likely to give her. She was certainly not equipped to appreciate the fearful ecstasies of near-abduction, shared adventure and breathless submission to a man like Adam Swann, who had shed a family tradition like a housewife discards an empty peapod and gone about making his own way in the world with a gusto that would shake the dust from any number of Moncton-Prices. It was very difficult, she supposed, to view this kind of thing through another woman's eyes. For herself, looking back, she would have felt cheated had she been denied the pleasure of finding a man for herself and learning for herself how to anchor him.

She stole a cautious sidelong glance at daughter and son-in-law, seeking confirmation of her suspicions that some of Stella's colours were beginning to fade and found it, or thought she found it, in appraisal of Stella's waistline. It was still as slender as the day she married, eighteen inches or a little less, and that after five months as a bride! She noticed something else too and it seemed to her even more significant. Man and wife were sharing a hymnbook but their fingers were not touching. They were singing listlessly, without physical awareness of one another, and Lester's face wore its customary expression, the carefully-measured arrogance of the privileged and well-britched. The family look, Henrietta told herself, was already beginning to transfer itself to Stella for she too looked impassive. Impassive and a little wan.

The appraisal had the power to depress Henrietta so that she at once sought to restore her spirits by transferring her glance to the rest of her flock, deliberately repressing thoughts of the Colonel, whose presence at 'Tryst' all these years had been a benediction. There was surely no profit in mourning such a gentle, whimsical creature for, as long as she lived, she would never forget him, and whenever she remembered him it would be with gratitude. But he had been old and feeble whereas her brood, ranged on either side of her, were young and full of promise. Without the necessity to follow the close print of 'Onward Christian Soldiers' she let her discreet glances range left and right whilst she continued to sing lustily, first in the direction of that ebullient rascal George, who was looking as merry as a cricket, notwithstanding the solemnity of the occasion, then towards Giles, who she felt sure would miss the old man more than any of them, then to the three post-crisis arrivals. Joanna, almost twelve, Hugo, ten, and Helen rising eight, and finally to the tall, dark, self-contained man who had sired them so absentmindedly, with more than half his mind on his waggon routes over the Pennines, and the rate of haulage from Grimsby quays to the fish-markets of cities south-west of the Humber.

She contemplated them all severally and collectively, her heart swelling with pride, as it always did when she saw them assembled together. George who, as Adam always declared, had been born laughing; Giles, the solemn, gentle one, who sometimes seemed so much older and wiser than any of them; Joanna and Helen, as pert and pretty as a pair of wedding posies, and Hugo, who shared her passion for soldiers, and was obviously enjoying every moment of this colourful occasion. As splendid and individualistic a bunch as you could find singing 'Onward Christian Soldiers' in any pew in the land. The eldest married and off her hands; the next, Alex, at this very moment calling the Zulus to account for daring to reject the benefits of absorption into the Empire, and the long tail of the procession right under her hand. Seven in all—no—whatever was she thinking of?—*eight*, counting the one-year-old surprise packet at home with Phoebe Fraser, the nursery governess. And all in twenty-one years.

Did she want to add to the tally? Was it even likely, with herself entered upon her thirty-ninth year, and Adam coming up to his fifty-third birthday? She didn't know and she didn't care. For herself she was as strong as a horse, and for a matriarch approaching her forties still in possession of a surprisingly good figure, the legacy, she assumed, of her father's splendid health and any number of Irish peasants on her mother's side.

At times like these she sometimes caught herself feeling as smug as the ageing Victoria, seen in garlanded magazine illustrations, palisaded by a tribe of royal descendants but it was not, she reminded herself just in time, a day for smugness. They were here to say a final goodbye to the Colonel and she would have to master the impulse to blubber at the graveside when those six dragoons lowered him into Kentish soil. She knew, of course, that women were expected to blubber at funerals but it was a concession she was not prepared to make, not even for decency's sake. All her life, even before Adam found her, whisked her on to the rump of his mare, and carried her off like a freebooter's prize, she had taken pleasure in standing on her own two feet, and looking the world in the face with a judicious mixture of pride and impudence. The approach had served her well and was, she knew, wholly approved by Adam, himself as proud as Lucifer and as daring, in his quiet, deliberate way, as Mr. Stanley in search of Dr. Livingstone. Besides, nobody would be watching *her* at the graveside. Their eyes would be for the panoply out there among the leaning tombstones of so many homespun Kentishmen . . . She hoped the snow would hold off a little longer. Not merely for the sake of so many bareheaded mourners but for the sake of Giles' cough and her own devastating bonnet, arched high over the forehead and crowned with three cunningly-wrought cloverleaf bows. Even two yards of crepe could add elegance to a bonnet if it was artfully trimmed, and why not? The old man had always had an eye for a well-turned-out woman.

The hymn came to an end and she gave Adam a nudge, lest he should disgrace them all by nodding off again during the final prayer. Then, as the dragoons clumped forward to lift the coffin, she straightened her long, black gloves, tucked her arm through Adam's and took her appointed place immediately behind the pall bearers.

3

His drowsiness left him as they moved into the open. There had been a light fall of snow during the service and the path beside the yews lay white as a freshly-laundered sheet until it was soiled and scuffed under the bearers' jackboots. The coffin, he thought, looked ludicrously light, not much heavier, he would judge, than that fancy casket the Ranee's steward had carried on his saddle bow during the ambush at Jhansi. He thought about the casket as his senses absorbed the timelessness and essential Englishness of the scene, a starveling crow lumbering out of a bare-branched elm, the nostril-stinging crispness of the winter's day, the long, winding procession with the big blob of scarlet at its head, the fruity tones of the chaplain, intoning English cadences. It wasn't really a solemn occasion. No more than the passage of a tired old man moving his last few yards over powdered snow in a box like the one that had held the nucleus of Swann fortunes, a thirty-stone ruby necklace that had provided the capital for the first fleet of Swann waggons.

He wondered why he should think of that at this moment and then he knew, for as they approached the junction in the paths the slim figure of Deborah Avery slipped from behind a yew to take her proscribed place in the string of immediate mourners. Behind the youngest, bonafide Swann as befitted an adopted daughter, but ahead of the staff and the old man's intimates, for in everyone's mind Deborah ranked as family. He smiled at her and she smiled back, probably the only person here who shared his doubts concerning immortality, and that despite her youthful sojourn among all those French nuns, while her father, his former partner Josh, was racketting about in the company of whores and blackguards of one sort or another. They had formed an understanding, he and Deborah, soon after she had returned from that fancy school of hers in Cheltenham, pledging herself to a life of thankless social work in the stewpots of the wealthiest civilisation in the world. He tolerated her obsession with the unwashed and underprivileged, whereas she, for her part, accepted his dedication to commerce to the exclusion of all other claims on his conscience. He liked Deborah. She had brains and charm and was a credit to him and to that rascally father of hers who hadn't been seen or heard of in years.

Beyond the row of elms, no more than a few short miles across the Kentish ploughland and coppice, stood Charles Darwin's many-windowed house at Down. Deborah would probably see Darwin as a pioneer in the nonstop war on cant, the man who had made nonsense of Genesis and plunged all England into a welter of doubt but for himself he did not give a damn about the authenticity of the

Scriptures, or whether he was cast in the image of God or an equatorial ape. His watchword, now and always, had been 'sufficient unto the day . . .', and the only parable that made commercial sense to him was that one about the steward who buried his talents. Life was for living and money was there to be made and spent on comfort and material progress. And after comfort and progress, he supposed, compassion, so that he saw himself as occupying a halfway-house between the advocates of laissez-faire and the swarm of clamant reformers in which his adopted daughter had enlisted. Change was inevitable but it would stem from capital not consciences. Recent history proved as much. Shaftesbury, crusader extraordinary, wouldn't have saved a single seven-year-old from slow death in the mines and factories if he had not been able to launch his crusades from a base of privilege and wealth.

*   *   *

The Guard of Honour's volley, when it came, startled everyone but Adam, whose eye had been on the angled carbines and contemplating—of all things—the curious phenomenon of smokeless powder. A volley like that, fired over a grave twenty years ago, would have produced six puff-clouds of sulphurous gas. Now there was nothing to be seen above the raised barrels but a thin film of impurity, that hung for a matter of seconds in the keen, frosty air. He saw the massed ranks of the mourners waver and then the gleaming barrels came down in concert, and the chaplain folded the Union Jack and tucked it under his surplice, as though he feared it might be mislaid in the dispersal and he would be asked to account for it by his quartermaster at Hythe. He looked at Henrietta again, surprised to find her dry-eyed, and then at George and Giles, standing close together, looking down into the open grave. Their dissimilarity struck him again, the older boy relaxed but absorbed, as though witnessing an interesting bit of pageantry, his younger brother caught up in the glum finality of the ritual. He thought, idly, "What the devil do any of us know about the chemistry of the body? Two lads, with common parents and common ancestors going back to the year dot, but they come from different planets", and then his daughter Stella touched his elbow, and his sense of detachment left him to make room for sympathy, for she was shedding the tears he had expected of her mother and seemed, indeed, devastated by the ordeal.

He remembered then that she too had been very close to the old man before she realised she was pretty and had a flair for fine clothes and twittery small-talk, so that she learned to think of herself as the most eligible filly in the county. Well, that was all behind her now, he supposed, taking some satisfaction in the fact that she had turned instinctively to him for comfort, instead of drooping on the arm of that sulky-mouthed husband she had cornered. He experienced a fleeting, insignificant qualm as he looked over her shoulder at Lester Moncton-Price, noting an impassivity amounting almost to boredom in the young coxcomb's expressionless eyes, and the immobility of the fleshy red lips—woman's lips he thought of them— but then Henrietta was patting her, and George was piloting mother and sister to the path leading to the lych-gate, and he heard Henrietta say, in a tightly-controlled voice, "He wouldn't want you to feel sad, Stella . . . I confess I don't, although I thought I should. He had a good life, and a very happy one with us. Thanks to Papa . . ."

It was generous of her to say that, he thought, especially when it was she rather than he who had done the fussing over the last few years. Then he understood her line of reasoning. Comfort and security, of the kind the old man had relished, would have been denied him in his old age had his only son lacked the initiative to slough off that fusty Swann military tradition and concentrate on the business of making money. He studied her approvingly then as they settled themselves in the carriage for the two mile journey back to 'Tryst'. There was an overall word for her and it eluded him for the moment, as a familiar place-name would sometimes escape him when he was working out a waggon route in his belfry overlooking the Thames. 'Staunch' was it? 'Stalwart'? 'Intransigent', 'Tempered', 'Resolute'? He ran it down as they left the last of the cottages behind —'Indomitable'. She met every new circumstance indomitably and it had been this rather than her looks and figure that had singled her out from the very beginning of their association. Ordinarily, he had very little patience with the kind of woman they had been breeding over here while he was campaigning across the seas in youth and early manhood. But Henrietta was singular; had always been singular.

He thought, as the carriage ran under the edge of the silent woods and over the hump of Twyforde Bridge, "She always thought of herself as lucky but I'm luckier. Suppose I'd latched on to a pretty little girl like Stella, instead of to the offshoot of a man with vigour and enterprise in his bones, like that rascally old father of hers? Odds on I should be a widower by now, what with all these children. Suppose I had left her to dry out in the sun on that moor the night the little devil ran away from home in a thunderstorm? Where would I have chanced on a woman capable of showing the fortitude and resource she demonstrated thirteen years ago, when I lost my leg, and she found herself saddled with a leaderless business, a sprawling great house, a young family, and a fourth child in her belly? I'll stake every penny I possess that there isn't another Henrietta between the Channel and the Pentland Firth and be damned if I don't tell her so before we douse the lamp tonight."

4

He did, in so many words. In his own deliberately possessive way, the way he invariably went about the business of promoting their moments of intimacy. And she, for her part, made no more than a token show of being shocked. After sharing his bed for twenty years she could read his intentions like nursery print.

Through the half-open door of his dressing-room she could hear the steady rasp of his razor as he sheared his strong, bluish bristles, and she wondered, smiling at her reflection in the dressing-table mirror, if he was aware that she always recognised an after-supper shave as a preliminary to tossing her about on that great four-poster they had inherited from the Elizabethan occupiers of the house. She went on combing her hair, rehearsing a formal protest that she knew would not have the least effect on him, but in a way she misjudged him. He was much gentler than usual, at least in his initial approach.

He came stumping out of his room and moved across protesting floorboards to stand behind her and the ungainliness of the movement told her he had already loosened the master strap of the harness that held his artificial leg to the knotted, bluish stump she had insisted on inspecting the first night he was restored to her after that long, dismal interval that followed the Staplehurst railway crash. The wound had no power to shock and dismay her then and in the thirteen years that had passed since his discharge from the Swiss convalescent hospital she had come to equate the mutilation with the glory that had attached itself to him at the time. She never saw him as a cripple, or thought of him as even marginally handicapped. The leg was just a specifically-fashioned boot he lugged around, not out of necessity, but on account of a caprice that matched all his other caprices, singlemindedness, sustained personal initiative, iron nerve and a surprising tenderness at moments like this.

He took the brush from her hand and rested half his weight on her shoulder, studying their faces in the mirror, and they remained a moment like this, cheeks touching, and the scent of his shaving-soap in her nostrils. He said, quietly, "Tell you something, Hetty. I was damned proud of you today," and when, mildly surprised, she asked why; "I expected a scene and there wasn't one. The old man would have hated a graveside sniffle on your part. Were you thinking that?"

No, she said, she hadn't even felt like sniffling, or not once they were clear of the church, where she had had time to marshal her thoughts and remind herself of the old man's pitiful helplessness since June. How could anyone who loved him want that prolonged indefinitely.

"Young Stella came near to making a scene," he said, absently.

"Stella has her problems. But I daresay you realised that today."

"Yes, but they aren't insurmountable," he said. "She'll handle them, given time." And then, almost irritably, "Neither you nor I would have had a moment's peace if we had insisted on second thoughts and held out for a long formal engagement. She's not got your strength of mind but she can be damned obstinate."

It was true, of course, but there was rather more to it than that and she was resolved to pursue the subject but not now. There were more immediate matters on hand. She had not been a wife to him all these years without learning to recognise priorities and said, with a shrug, "If she wants advice I hope she'll have the sense to ask for it," and was surprised when he laughed and demanded, in that shameless way of his, whether Stella had been given any in advance.

"Far more than anyone gave me."

"Aye," he said, goodhumouredly, "I'll warrant that's so. And more than most brides get this side of the Channel. Let it ride then. These things have a way of working themselves out."

She knew from his tone that he was not disposed to stand there half the night speculating on his daughter's problems. At times like this, when the great house was still, and they were alone together in a room lit by the single dressing-table lamp and the flicker of the coals in the high grate that had replaced the great open hearth, she was able to isolate herself from the complexities of family life and revert to the mood of their earliest days together, before they had assumed such a packload of responsibilities. As always his heavy masculinity enfolded her like a many-caped mantle, so that she would have liked very much to have flattered him by a show of impatience but his weight pinned her to the stool and she could do no more than take his hands, pressing the palms to her breasts. It was enough. He tweaked the ribbon bow of her nightdress and bared one shoulder, kissing it lightly almost perfunctorily, but when she responded to his kisses with an involuntary flutter, of the kind she experienced on every single occasion he had laid hands on her over the last twenty years, he became his usual purposeful self, as decisive about love as he was about trade and barter down at the yard. Without more ado he slipped the nightdress from both shoulders and cupped her breasts in his hands, lifting their fullness to his lips so that his posture increased his weight and she cried out, laughingly, that this was more than she could bear and he should show a little patience, tonight, of all nights.

It was a familiar pattern, a game they had played longer than she cared to remember now that the streaks of grey in his hair were past ignoring. He said, lifting her bodily from the stool so that her nightdress slipped to her thighs, "When I show patience this side of the bedroom door, my dear, you can begin wondering what I'm about in the regions. You're not always on hand, remember. Damn it, we've not gone the rounds together since the Colonel took to his bed."

She remembered then, as he carried her across to the four-poster, recalling a moment in their marriage that had been etched in tragedy, for it had occurred no more than a few hours before the incident that cost him his leg and come close to costing her sanity. It was the day Giles had been conceived during an absurd, bucolic tumble down in a pheasant hide at the foot of the drive, whither she had hurried in the hope of intercepting him on his return from one of his free-ranging visits to his widely-scattered depots. In one way it seemed a lifetime away, but in another only the day before yesterday. The years had done nothing at all, thank God, to moderate the extreme pleasure she derived from his physical dominance that invariably laced their moments of intimacy with good humour and a sense of renewal, converting their concourse into a kind of frolic that slowed the march of the years. Reminded of this she felt impatient with her doubts about Stella's happiness, Giles' cough, and George's restlessness, and the pettifogging demands of the younger children. They were nothing and he was everything. She did not put them out of mind exactly—she particularly wanted to discuss with him the possibility of getting Alex into a good regiment—but, as always when they were alone, and he was in one of his possessive moods, she could stack them like a jumble of parcels waiting to be posted. Her arms went round his neck so eagerly that she forgot about his leg, an essential preliminary to any embrace of this kind and her impatience must have pleased him for he said, chuckling, "Wait, the lamp . . ." and left her for a moment, not merely to extinguish the light but also to avail himself of the opportunity to turn his back on her while he unbuckled the side-straps of his leg. It was his one concession to modesty, or possibly an intensely-felt masculine pride. In thirteen years he had never learned that the act of removing that ungainly contraption was incapable of invoking the smallest stirring of revulsion in her.

He was beside her in a matter of seconds, pulling her half-shed nightgown clear of her legs, so that she lay naked on the quilt, revelling in the warmth of the room, congratulating herself on her foresight in instructing the maid to build a good fire up here as soon as they returned from the funeral. He took his place beside her but propped on an elbow so that he could watch the firelight play on her body. This was an important part of the pattern of their ritual on these occasions, and had been ever since he had succeeded

32

in exorcising the last of her conceits concerning personal privacy within a marriage to a man of his temperament. Tonight, however, he seemed in less hurry than usual but lay looking down at her, with that half-smile of his tinged with gentle mockery, one hand engaged with her hair still half-imprisoned in the ribbons she had been removing when he came in, the other playfully gyrating her nightdress, as though it was a flag he had captured in a skirmish. His playfulness, at such odds with the solemnity of the day, infected her, and she said, with a giggle, "That reminds me of Arabella Stokes."

"That old trout over at Tithebarrow? Why?"

"She isn't as prim as she looks. Or behaves, when you men are guzzling your port. The last time we were there to dinner she made everybody blush. Everybody but me, that is, for I've forgotten how, married to you."

She had caught his interest in a way she seldom succeeded in doing by daylight, when, as like as not, his mind was engaged with his work, or one of the dozens of newspapers he brought home to study.

"You only listen to me when I'm undressed," she said, pretending to pout. "I'll tell you some other time."

"You'll tell me now," he said, tossing aside the nightdress and throwing his arm about her waist. "What the devil has this night-dress to do with that wizened old woman at Tithebarrow?"

"It was Arabella's nightdress I was thinking of. She's a bawdy old gossip, and was telling me and the other wives about old Mr. Stokes' demands, when they were first married. About a hundred years ago."

"It must have been. Well?"

"Whenever he wanted to make love to her he would turn facing her and say, 'Lift your linen, Arabella.' Just like that. Nothing more. And always on a Saturday."

The laugh it drew from him surprised her. It was really a very small joke and had elicited no more than giggles from herself and Mrs. Stokes' toothy niece at the time, but he seemed to find it very rich indeed. More than a minute passed before he could say, "Always on Saturday? How was that possible?"

"If it wasn't she had to say so, and then he'd grumble and go to

33

sleep without another word. Oh, it's funny enough, I suppose, especially knowing her, but I remember thinking how awful it would be to be married to a man like that and from what I gather there are plenty about, even now."

"Far more than there were in Arabella's young days," he said, "for cant of that kind is a national disease. It was one of the first things that struck me when I came back from the East. The really damnable thing is the double standard. More than half those Holy Joes keep a buxom little doxy tucked away in a love-nest within a cab-ride of their counting-houses."

The wonder that she could talk to a man on this level never really left her, not even now, after more than twenty years as his bedmate, and recognition of this intensely private and personal boon moved her to reach out and stroke his freshly-shaved cheek. "I've never stopped loving you, Adam. Not from that first day on the moor. I was remembering it in church this morning, when I should have been thinking of the Colonel."

"So was I," he admitted, surprisingly, "and with it the time we said 'Enough' before we have to take a lease on another pew." He hoisted himself half upright and she seemed to detect in his calm, speculative expression a special reason for his torpidity, for although his love-making, up to a certain point, was often leisurely, it was unusual for him to gossip until he had spent himself. She said, defensively, "You don't want more children? You've made up your mind to that?"

"It occurred to me that perhaps you had."

She sat up, so abruptly that she startled him. "Why? Did I ever say so?"

"No, you never did, Hetty, but I daresay you thought it when that last little bundle turned up after a seven-year interval."

She said, deliberately, "You're quite wrong. I never did think it. As a matter of fact I was very relieved when Doctor Birtles told me there wasn't the least doubt about it."

He turned his head and stared at her with amused exasperation. "Dammit, woman, we have eight. And you'll be thirty-nine in July. Eight, not counting Deborah, and as healthy and handsome a string as I've ever seen anywhere. Don't you ever give a thought to my pocket or your figure?"

34

She said nothing immediately but he knew somehow that this was not, in her estimation, a fit subject for joking. Begetting children was, but not subjecting them to a kind of arithmetic, in the way he sometimes did when presiding over the brood at breakfast-table on Sundays and holidays.

Her silence puzzled him a little.

"Well? What do you say to that, my love?"

"Nothing," she said, carefully, "providing you're joking. *Are* you?"

Faced with that he hardly knew if he was or he wasn't but then the tinge of asperity in her voice told him, reversing the judgement he had made of her in the course of that old chaplain's mumbling obituary. It was wrong to assume you ever came to know any woman, particularly a febrile, impulsive little madcap like her. Not a day or a night passed when you failed to discover something new and unpredictable, an impulse, an artifice, a prejudice, a conviction based on instinct, or a fleeting facet of character that she had kept well-hidden for reasons known only to herself.

"I'm not joking," he said, and she replied, briskly, "Then I'll tell you what I say. That 'string', as you call it, is my stock-in-trade. Like your teams and depots and annual turnover. You don't stand still up at that Thameside slum of yours, so why should you expect me to? I'm as strong as a horse and you've already as much money as you can hope to spend. You preen yourself on having made your mark in trade and I'm every bit as proud of having been the means of bringing you healthy children. But there's another side to it, apart from sound investment in sons and daughters."

He was grinning now. "Go on. Tell me, Hetty."

"You'll grant I was able to help—with the important part of your life that is—when you were hurt in that smash, and you were considerably surprised and very pleased, I think, to find the business much as you left it when you came home."

"I've told you as much, many times."

"I know. But what I did then wasn't important to *me*. It was just something that came out of an emergency. What I've found much more important most of the time we've been married is—well—that you've enjoyed me as a woman, and haven't ever stopped wanting me this way. No matter what you had on your mind I was always

35

able to make you forget it, if only for an hour or so. The business is vital to you, and the children are just as important to me. Of course they are. I never made the least secret of wanting a large family, that went out into the world and did all the things you and I would never have time to do in one lifetime. But what happens in this room, when we're alone at night—that's really mine, you understand? Any fool can have children but I like to think I've done far better than that, giving you something no one else could have given you, not even those women nobody mentions but everyone knows about, whose business it is to please men for money. Do you think I'd risk losing that?"

He was touched but astonished. It seemed to him strange and wayward that she should interpret a light-hearted remark concerning the length of their family as a broad hint that they should deny themselves the indulgence they had enjoyed over the years.

"I'm not suggesting I should stop loving you in that sense, Hetty. You must know there are ways and means . . ."

"Don't tell me about them!" she snapped, "for I don't want to hear and I certainly don't want to practise them! I've heard other wives mention 'ways and means' aimed at not having children and to my mind it entails . . . well, cheating, if you like. There's only one way for a woman to love a man, and show that she loves him, and I learned that from you, years ago."

There was no kind of answer to this, or none that he could think of. Pride in her, and gratitude too inflated him, so that he saw her as someone infinitely more complex than a sensual, buxom wife, a hit-and-miss mother, and the exasperatingly immature fugitive from reality that she had sometimes shown herself to be over the dips and peaks and levels of their marriage. Clearly she was a far more introspective person than he had imagined, for all his smug, masculine certainty that he knew every curve and cleft of her body, and every variant of her quicksilver temperament. He sensed, vaguely, that he had just learned something new about her secret evaluation of the partnership, an aspect she had succeeded in concealing over the years. She saw the row of children in that pew as her profits in an enterprise but they were incidental to its main purpose, a purpose as well-defined as that which had translated him from mercenary to creator and driving force of a gigantic enterprise in a period of twenty-one years. Her essential purpose was to adjust to him, in all his changing moods, boosting him when he stood in need of a boost, sanctioning his erratic flights from the cares of office. It was to spend herself keeping age and self-doubt at bay and moderating the inevitable loneliness of a man who spent most of his waking hours among subordinates, using her body as an instrument trained and tempered to absorb his essential egotism, a task she not only relished but would share with no one, physically or spiritually. He thought, with an inward chuckle, "By God, it's lucky for both of us I've found all the solace I ever needed right here in her company. I wouldn't care to find myself in a rival's shoes if she ever got to hear about it."

Suddenly he tired of the game of tinkering with the machinery of their marriage and drew her close to him, seeking her mouth and letting his hand slip the length of her back to caress the soft roundnesses of her buttocks, after which he addressed himself to the task of demonstrating that he not only understood her line of reasoning but wholly endorsed it. Presently she stirred within his embrace but it was only to enfold him with her legs and hold him there until he was spent and mocking the small glow of vanity his ardour invariably promoted on these occasions, particularly since he had passed the fifty mark and should, he told himself, have outgrown a young man's pride in performing so simple a function. The sensation of wonder persisted, however, long after they had pulled the blankets over them and she was asleep, her head turned to him, her left hand resting in the hollow of his hip, the truncated hip that represented, for him, his own invincibility and his wife's inexhaustible reserves of pluck and versatility, reflecting that she had never really extended herself until he was converted, in a single moment of time, from man to hulk during that shambles over at Staplehurst.

He lay awake a long time, expressing his supreme satisfaction in her by stroking her disordered hair under his hand, thinking back on what she had said and on the units that had resulted from momentary encounters such as this, and it was a chain of speculation that led him, rummaging haphazardly among his thoughts, to that curious remark of hers about creating children who would—how had she put it?—'go out in the world and do all the things we could never hope to do in a single lifetime'. What had prompted that, he wondered? Was it the fact that one son and one daughter had al-

ready launched themselves, Alex halfway across the world to fight
a few thousand savages, Stella into life-partnership with a man
who might or might not know the art of training a vain, ignorant
girl into a wife of Henrietta's calibre? Well, as to Stella, he was
content to reserve judgement. No marriage was a cakewalk until
years had passed, and two people had learned the art of tolerance
and the tricky business of adjusting to one another physically, an
aspect of marriage of the first importance.

As to how Alex was faring, he could make a few guesses, based
on his own experiences as a soldier. He would have learned by now
that there was more to soldiering than dressing up and looking fierce,
that to make headway in that field one needed more luck than ability.
He thought of all the young men he had seen riding out to war in
the wake of the old Colonel and in the moment before sleep came
to him a stab of anxiety steered him into a brief disquieting dream,
in which he was whisked back to the plain beyond Jhansi and had
been unhorsed within inches of a fortune in rubies, the luggage
of a man he had killed. Then, because he was essentially a man of
action, who rarely dreamed and never recalled dreams, he slipped
the extra notch or two into a deeper, more timeless sleep, with his
hand still buried in his wife's hair and her limbs moulded to his
in a pattern of sleep they had formed over the years.

2

To Kill a Zulu

THE rough track curved east across the lower shoulder of the plateau under a blue and cloudless sky as wide and empty as the Pacific. Over to the left, where the heat haze shimmered and lapped the sandstone base of the giant outcrop that broke the surface of the plain, the little white tents stood in trim rows, with here a red or a black dot moving to and from the waggon park, and there the lazy spiral of a cooking fire, where men of the South Wales Borderers and their native allies were preparing their midday meal.

The scene, Alex Swann thought, glancing over his shoulder as he followed the trundling rocket-battery out of camp, was like a parody of war, the neatly ordered spread of soldiers and conical tents he had so often set out on the nursery floor at 'Tryst', a picture-book war that could easily end in the clamour of Phoebe Fraser's lunch bell, and a meal of cold beef and green salad, after which he would wander away with young George or Giles to the paddock to catch the ponies, forgetting the martial array on the floor upstairs.

It was a time and a place for day-dreaming. A wide, dusty plain under an incredibly tall sky, where the mind made a compound of past, present and future so that it needed conscious effort to see oneself as a real soldier, with a real Martini-Henry in his saddle bucket, and a real six-chambered revolver slapping his thigh as the lean pony picked its way among the cracks and boulders of the make-shift track. Back at Helpmakaar, where the settlement had been thronged with soldiers, and native levies like his own, the Natal Native Contingent, the feeling had grown on him that everyone there, from Lord Chelmsford downwards, was engaged in a gigantic game, for although newcomers like himself had been assured by Boer farmers that a brush with the Zulus was unlikely to prove a picnic, it did not seem credible that a nation of savages, notwithstanding their warlike traditions, could stem a three-pronged invasion across the

Tugela and Blood Rivers for more than a week or two. After that, he assumed, it would be a kind of hunting foray among the drifts and kopjes, ending in some sort of truce dictated from London, and before the English spring came round they would all be back in Natal, swapping tall stories of their experiences, and looking about for new adventures in another continent, service with his father's old comrade, General Roberts, perhaps, currently grappling with Afghan tribesmen in the passes of the North West Frontier, or possibly further east, in Burma or Borneo. Thinking this he reviewed his luck at getting here before the advance began, and enlisting under a man of Colonel Durnford's reputation, wondering whether he owed his good fortune to his own unrelenting pleading or to his father's influence with South African merchant houses. Whichever it was he would have missed the boat if he hadn't decided to go aboard with the minimum luggage, and most of that was now stored at Durban, so that his possessions, accoutrements aside, were limited to a razor that he only needed to use twice a week, a Bible his former governess, Phoebe Fraser, had pressed on him, and ten sovereigns, the gift of his practical mother, snug inside the lining of his tunic and excess weight out here where the nearest store was thirty miles back along the route.

The sun was blisteringly hot and sweat built a crescent of beads under the blunt peak of his pith helmet, plastering shirt and tunic to his back, like a football jersey after an early autumn game on the pitch at Mellingham. He thought about Mellingham, his mind dancing away into the heat haze, of old Greenacre, who had been so eager to accompany him but had gone, instead, into his father's scent factory, poor devil, and of old Jumbo Bellchamber, his study-mate, cramming for the Foreign Office exams. He was, he supposed, unique in possessing folks prepared to give him his head in these matters, to let him discover for himself what he wanted to make of his life. He was luckier still in having a mother predisposed in favour of the military life, even though he was not absolutely decided on it as yet and was still, in a sense, experimenting. There was no question of going into a scent factory, like poor old Greenacre, or mugging for an office life, like Bellchamber, but there were any number of choices open to him, anything, say, from a permanent commission in the cavalry, to trying his luck as a planter in one of the scores of new colonies where Victoria was God's vicereine. The choice, at all events, was his and that was what mattered. Most chaps' mothers, he imagined, would have made a frightful scene over his abrupt departure in October, within a month of his sister's wedding to that flabby-looking hussar with the fancy name.

The pony was making heavy going of the track, and so was the rocket battery team up ahead. He could hear the harsh clatter of its undercarriage, the slither of the mules' hooves on sun-slippery stones, the apathetic shouts of the drivers. A dozen lengths behind him, jogging along two by two, rode the Basutos, as unlikely a set of soldiers as he had ever seen, notwithstanding their fancy get-up and martial frowns whenever they remembered to stop grinning. It was a pity, in a way, he had not arrived in time to sign on with a trained European unit, where troopers took a pride in their appearance, people who could have taught him something about native warfare, but he assumed that could be remedied as soon as Cetywayo had sued for peace. He could then assess the prospects of a real military career, using his experience out here as a door-opener.

The sun was a ball of bedstead brass and he was almost asleep in the saddle when Lieutenant Copland came spurring back, reining in level with him and shouting something about the Colonel wanting the Basutos to ride up on the plateau and see if there was any sign of Zulus or Zulu cattle beyond the ridge. He shouted an order and extended his left arm, reflecting as he did so that this was the first order he had issued since he had arrived in Africa, the first he had ever issued to grown men. The thought brought a faint blush to his cheek and he kicked his pony ahead across the scrub in case the natives should notice his callowness. In less than ten minutes he was a hundred feet above the track, with a clear view of Isandlwana, the great sandstone outcrop, on his immediate left, and the skyline of the plateau right ahead. Six Basutos had followed him, in very leisurely fashion he noticed. No one would ever make soldiers out of such material and it occurred to him that Lord Chelmsford would have been well-advised to mount the invasion with European troops and use the local levies as drivers and carriers en route, leaving a majority back at the mission station at Rorke's Drift. In another moment he had topped the rise and could enjoy a magnificent view of the entire plain, forty miles of it he would say, and all as empty as a moon crater, despite the crawling passage of Durnford's pigmy column a mile ahead, and two thousand other pigmies back at the camp on the lower slopes of Isandlwana. Then, recalling his purpose up here, he waved to the Basutos to close up, at the same time unslinging his binoculars, the loan of that affable regular, Lieutenant Melville, whom he had met back at Rorke's Drift two days ago. He lifted the glasses, sweeping the broad declivity north of the track.

Something moved down there and he paused to wipe the sweat from his eyelids. A cow or a bullock, then two, then a dozen, browsing along the gentle slope about eight hundred yards to the north, where there was the long downslope of a shallow valley, a *donga* they would call it here, with waist-high scrub growing on it, and a boulder-strewn bed like the surface of the track he had just left.

He was still watching the cattle when he heard the high-pitched scream from the nearest Basuto, level with him now but fifty yards or so nearer the camp. For a second or so he thought the man must be clowning but then two other troopers scrambled up beside him and at once all three were gibbering and gesticulating, jabbing their fingers down towards the herd, indicating a dark, motionless blur that spread itself across the scorched landscape from a point just north of the cattle, and on beyond them, as far as the eye could reach. He wondered vaguely what it could be, his mind conjuring with a variety of improbable alternatives, a vast spread of tarpaulins, or acres of plum jam, or a wilderness of ripe blackberries, if blackberries grew on African plateaux. And then he saw that the patch was formed by a mass of densely-packed men, thousands and thousands of men, squatting on their haunches, or sprawled at ease in the spidery grass of the donga and other dongas further afield, relaxed but watchful, statuesque but somehow projecting a terrible menace.

He could see them clearly now, a dense and utterly silent mass, and it was hardly necessary to fumble with Melville's binoculars and identify them as a Zulu impi, or a dozen impis, with yet another vast column in motion over to the far left, moving at the double to encircle the lion-shaped hill where the tents were pitched and the blobs of scarlet still moved leisurely to and fro between tent-lines and waggon park.

*   *   *

His immediate reaction was to lug his pony round and ride pell-mell down the slope towards the track and the security of the column but then, hard on the heels of this thought, was another that kept him sitting there, gazing down at what looked to be the entire Zulu nation. His immobility had to do with years of automatic responses to raucous-voiced seniors at Mellingham, cries that insisted he passed the ball, or added his weight to the scrum, or looked up into the sun to judge the flight of a spinning cricket ball arching its way towards the boundary. With a tremendous effort he braced himself, hearing his breath wheezing in his throat, and feeling his right hand falter as it reached out and grasped the scorching butt of his bucketted rifle. The Martini-Henry came out but at that moment the nearest Basuto galloped past, whirling his arms and still screaming, so that his pony swerved and almost unseated him and he cursed the man in a shrill voice and spurred after him, grabbing his bridle and pulling him to a halt.

He could have spared himself the effort. The man, and the others behind him, were all but incoherent, eyes rolling wildly, blunt fingers stabbing in the direction of the donga, so that he sought to steady them by raising his rifle and firing down into the silent black mass, then wheeling and spurring his pony back along the ridge, with some idea of despatching one Basuto west to warn the camp and the others north-east to overtake Durnford and the rocket battery that he could just see lurching round a bend in the track.

Someone, the N.C.O. probably, anticipated him. Before he reached the eddying group a horseman detached himself, shooting off towards the tent-lines like a whipper-in heading a pack of hounds from a false scent. Then, riding in a tight knot, the rest of the patrol went skittering down the slope uttering shrill cries that were lost in a low, reverberating hum that rose from the donga on the other side of the crest. It was a very curious, inhuman sound, a low, sustained buzz, like the sound that might emerge from a gathering of all the hornets in the world, and it was the hum rather than the certainty that he was in the presence of an army of trained spearmen that terrified him. It was as much as he could do not to follow the Basutos but some instinct, deeply-rooted in his personal past, or in the ancestral tug of a dozen martial Swanns, held him to the crest, rifle in his hand, binoculars thumping on his chest, and as the sustained groan

43

of the Zulus rose in pitch he kicked the pony a few yards higher up the slope and forced himself to look down the further side.

What he saw there now amazed him, amazement succeeding terror, for the scene in the donga had magically transformed itself in a little over a hundred seconds. All the men he had seen down there were now in motion, loping up the gentle slope towards him and moving in superbly dressed lines, plumes nodding, braced assegais flashing, oxhide shields thudding as they swung up and down in a kind of devil-dance on the forearms of the warriors. The thrum of their naked feet made a background music to their hideous humming and suddenly the whole plain was filled with the sound, so that men pottering about that camp two miles or more away must have been alerted.

The nearest ranks were perhaps four hundred yards distant when he fired again, and then again. It was like peppering the wall of a castle with a reed pea-shooter, of the kind he had used to tease old Melroy's cows grazing beside the river at 'Tryst'. He did not know whether either of the bullets found a mark but the recoil of the weapon struck his shoulder like the blows of a club and he heard the shots, tiny, popping, irrelevant sounds in all that uproar. Then he swung away and went cantering down the southern slope at breakneck pace, aiming to strike the track some half a mile ahead of the point where he had left it. As he rode he saw that the strung-out column was already alive to its terrible situation. Groups of men, in advance and in rear of the rocket battery, were falling back at an oblique angle making for a rocky ridge that ran out from Isandlwana at an angle of about forty-five degrees and would afford some kind of rallying-point for a fighting withdrawal to the camp.

Copland met him on the track, Copland, the superior, bewhiskered lieutenant, who had patronised him all the way from Helpmakaar. But there was nothing patronising about the young colonist now. His mouth was open like the jaws of the village idiot at Twyforde Green, and his pale blue eyes, already prominent, seemed to project from the sockets like the eyes of a grasshopper. Bringing his horse up on its haunches, he shouted, "How many? How far off?" and Alex, without pausing in his dash for the ridge, shouted, "The whole Zulu army . . . thousands . . . right on your heels!"

He did not wait to see what Copland made of that but galloped on, heedless of boulders, to the highest sector of the ridge that lay within a mile or so of the camp that was, he remembered, occupied by a few mounted Kaffirs under a sergeant of G Company, 2/24th Regiment. Durnford's column must have moved and regrouped at fantastic speed, for already a mob of men had gathered there, more than half of them Europeans, with the rocket battery in their midst. He rode in with Copland hard on his heels and as he threw himself from the saddle, and dragged the pony behind a boulder as high as the pommel, he saw Colonel Durnford, pith helmet pushed back on his high, balding forehead and his soft, Dundreary whiskers giving him the aspect of a Sunday School superintendent rather than a man of action. He was saying, quietly, "Steady, there . . . steady, boys . . . hold them off . . . independent firing . . . pick your man . . ." and then moved on, passing slowly along the line of rocks behind which men were already kneeling, or lying prone and firing into the south-facing slope of the plateau.

Alex saw then that the impi had advanced with the speed of cavalry and that the slopes were black with running, crouching men, half-hidden behind a rippling line of ox-hide, and also that the effects of the scattering fire were already showing in the occasional stumble and a general slowing-down of the onrush. Here and there the ordered ranks were dissolving into knots of men, seeking the sparse cover of the scrub across which he had just galloped, but there was no sign of a check further back towards the crestline, and seemingly no end to the swarm of men scrambling over and converging on them from the plain. From here they looked like millions of ants, hedged about by a halo of winking lights centring on the broad blades of their assegais, a great wall of ants a mile deep, flowing down on to the plain in a tide that nobody could hope to stem for more than the time it took to mount a concerted rush of the kind he had witnessed when he fired his first shots. The natives among the rocks already understood this and were bolting in batches but the Europeans and some of the N.N.C. hung on, trying, between scattered volleys, to form some kind of continuous line among the rocks and stumbling about between a swirl of riderless horses with trailing reins and lathered bits, everyone getting in one another's way and cursing as they groped in their pouches for ammunition. And all the time Durnford walked erect, chiding and encouraging, the Sunday School teacher soothing an unruly class.

They were moving back now, two hundred yards, three hundred yards, firing as they dodged from boulder to boulder and made for the open ground at the extreme eastern edge of the camp. Somewhere out ahead, now deep in the heart of the impi it seemed, a single rocket soared before the battery was engulfed and then, clubbed into a single, struggling mass, black and white, horse and man, the shattered column spilled into the perimeter of the camp, its onrush carrying the double rank of G Company a hundred yards nearer the base of the rock, where men were already forming in lines about the waggon park, and the bark of commands cut through the din and confusion that stunned the senses and made concerted action even more difficult than it had been out on the ridge. For here everyone was impeded by tents and the tripwires of pegs and guyropes, and nobody seemed to know at which point to rally or, for that matter, which way to face. A long eddy of scarlet in the west indicated that the impi Alex had seen on the move had already encircled the mountain and was boiling through the saddle of Isandlwana.

2

So many times in his childhood and boyhood he had seen himself engaged in a battle, sometimes as a front-ranker, engaging the enemy with a sword, pike and battleaxe, more often as an aloof, unruffled general, directing stolid troops from the eminence of a dappled grey as tall as his father's. But the factors here had nothing in common with anything within his experience in the nursery or the world of books, of the kind Mr. Henty wrote. Battles were set-pieces, with infantry in the centre, cavalry on the wings and artillery, where it was present, posted between, or playing on the enemy from a safe distance. Here, ringed by thousands of humming savages, there was no order and no plan, strategic or tactical, only a vast, heaving scrimmage in an ever shrinking perimeter under the towering peak of Isandlwana.

Up to the moment of the wreck of Durnford's column, breaking through the lines of G Company and carrying them back in their rush, the camp itself, with its neatly-pitched tents, its bivouac fires and horse-lines, had represented sanctuary but this was now seen to be a mirage. No kind of safety was available here. Everybody and everything was at odds, as though the onslaught of the impis had been a violent thunderstorm breaking over the heads of a crowd at a garden fête, and to Alexander Swann, milling about aimlessly in the midst of it, the frantic scene resolved itself into a series of unrelated cameos, like pictures flashed on the magic lantern screen his brother Giles had been given by the old Colonel on his seventh birthday. He saw G Company reform and begin steady volley-firing. He saw a huge black trying repeatedly to mount an unsaddled horse. A drummer boy ran past, carrying a cap full of cartridges and it was the child's stumbling passage that reminded him he had fired the last of his bandolier cartridges back on the ridge and was now humping a useless rifle. He knew where the reserve ammunition was housed in the regimental waggons across the compound and began to run there instinctively. On the way he passed Lieutenant Melville, the young regular who had lent him the binoculars forty-eight hours before, but this was no time to return them. Melville, mounted on a big horse, was encumbered with the regimental colours, a heavy pole and yards of emblazoned cloth, an impossibly clumsy burden for a mounted man, however good his horsemanship. Then Melville was obscured by a mob of hysterical Kaffirs, plunging away to the south-western angle of the perimeter, where the track to Rorke's Drift crossed the saddle, and he thought, fleetingly, "If they're bolting they'll run themselves right against a forest of asse-gais . . ." for he remembered the encircling impi that had moved round the mountain, obviously with the idea of sealing the road back to Natal. Then the bark of artillery from higher up the slope told him guns were in action and he would have rallied on them, as the one reassuring sound in the midst of all this welter and babble, but between him and the isolated puffs of smoke were the tent-lines, milling with natives, all trying to catch riderless horses. He turned away and went at a stumbling run towards the two regimental wag-gons, to find each of them beset by boys, cooks and bandsmen, all clamouring for ammunition stowed in heavy wooden boxes bound with copper bands and fastened, it appeared, by any number of deepset screws. Two bearded men were at work on one box, trying to draw the screws with a single screwdriver, but even here, four hundred yards from the firing-line, they were getting in one another's way and the screws remained motionless as they clawed and scrabbled at the half-buried heads.

Around him men began to curse and prance, like amateur fire-walkers walking a trench of live coals, and all the time the sense of unreality enlarged itself so that he wondered if what he was witnessing was a purely personal experience, brought on by a touch of the sun, and the illusion continued until, miraculously the lid was torn from the ammunition box and the men and boys fell upon it like starving beggars at a soup kitchen.

As a latecomer in the queue he had no hope of getting his share so he abandoned his rifle and pulled out his revolver, turning to run back across the perimeter with some half-formed notion of re-joining what was left of Durnford's column. But in the time it had taken him to cross the camp and watch the quartermasters wrestle with the row of screws, the scene inside the tent-lines and waggon park had changed utterly. There was no longer any semblance of a defensive formation and what had been ranks of red-coated Borderers were now knots of struggling men, exchanging bayonet thrusts with five times as many Zulus, each armed with his stabbing assegai. He understood then, with a terrible certainty, that the battle was lost, that all of them would die here in a cloud of red dust raised by a hundred independent scuffles reaching all the way across the camp to the impassive, sphinx-like peak silhouetted against the cloud-less sky.

The very certainty of this steadied him a little and he plunged towards an isolated waggon, against which a few N.C.O.s and privates of the 2/24th were braced, holding off a mob of blacks with their bayonets. He was no more than ten yards distant when all but one of the Europeans went down, the survivor, an extremely tall sergeant, saving himself by leaping on to the flat surface of the vehicle and standing there very coolly eyeing a ring of savages. Then, taking his time, the man began to shoot at point-blank range, and at every shot a Zulu pitched on his face or leaped spinning into the air to fall flat on his back, until the press around the waggon was eased and only the dead, black predominating, lay there in grotesque attitudes.

It was curious what a single man could achieve, Alex thought, as though he was no more than a privileged spectator to the scene, and he would have remained watching until an assegai entered his own back had not another riderless horse, saddled and bridled, and still carrying a rolled cape and empty carbine bucket, trotted slowly across his line of vision, momentarily blotting out the sergeant standing on the waggon and the sprawl of dead about its undercarriage and broad-spoked wheels.

He was never able to remember catching the horse, mounting it and joining the thin stream of fugitives making for the steep, stony track that led down to a ravine south of the made-up road they had used two days before when they bivouacked here after marching out from Rorke's Drift. He must have done these things instinctively, vaulting into the saddle in the fashion of old Yorker, the groom at 'Tryst', whose boast was that he could mount a sixteen-hands horse from a standstill although in his late fifties. The stream of horse and foot carried him along at a plunging, loping pace, and as he rode another set of pictures stamped itself, magic-lantern-like, upon his memory and were to remain there, chronologically arranged, for the rest of his life. He saw a bay horse immediately ahead carrying two Colonials, and on either side of the horse ran six-foot Zulus, thrusting up at the riders with broad-bladed assegais, so that first the pillion-rider fell and then the rider himself, the latter slipping sideways and somersaulting with two spearpoints protruding from his chest. The horse pounded on and when Alex was aware of it again it was carrying a trooper of the N.N.C., bent low over the mare, his heels flailing the animal's flanks.

Down at the approach to the ravine men were dismounting, shouting that it was impossible to cross on horseback, but one Colonial tried to jump from lip to lip, falling far short and crashing down the furthermost slope. A man with a face the colour of cheese clutched at Alex's bridle, shouting a question in Afrikaans, but then he too fell away, transfixed by a flung assegai thrown from the camp side of the steep depression, and a moment later Alex was down there himself and leading the horse up the far side where he saw an artilleryman sitting on a rock bandaging a great gash in his forearm that was spouting blood in a thin jet. At the crest the rout began to sort itself out, for of the mob that descended into the donga not one in ten emerged on to the winding track beyond, but a few Zulus were still keeping pace with the stampede, scrambling among the rocks in frantic efforts to get ahead of the stream of fugitives and cut them off before they could converge on the nearest river crossing. There were, he supposed, no more than thirty or forty survivors, all thundering along at a breakneck pace and sometimes loosing off revolver shots at Zulus who drew level with them. The magnitude of the disaster pressed on his temples like the copper bands that had enclosed those ammunition-boxes, preventing logical thought and relating everything he did to the struggles of an animal in a trap.

He could still see Melville up ahead, distinguished by his clumsy seat on the bay dictated by the double armful of colours he was carrying. He had shed the pole apparently and even as he rode it struck Alex as astounding that a man should encumber himself with such an impossible burden at such a moment. Another officer about Melville's age was with him, turning in his saddle every few seconds and keeping the tireless Zulus at bay with his revolver. Between them ran two men of the N.N.C. both unarmed, and then a string of horsemen, one carrying a bayoneted rifle like a lance.

In this way, pell-mell, and without the least semblance of order, they came to the bluff that overlooked the Buffalo River, now in spate and rushing down the gorge at a tremendous pace, the volume of water breaking on a thousand half-submerged rocks, and the low hills on the further bank lying empty and grape-blue in half shadow. For the first time since he had turned away from the regimental waggons Alex identified himself as a unit in all this chaos and with identification came hope that he might, with any amount of luck, cross over into Natal and survive this appalling catastrophe. He saw at a glance that it would be suicidal to attempt to ride down to river level so he threw himself out of the saddle, abandoned the horse and ran down the rocky path with men on either side of him, each jostling for elbow room, pitching, stumbling and cursing one another, and the Zulus who ran among them, lunging at any uniformed man within stabbing range. In the shallows he saw a Kaffir killed with a thrust through the throat but the man's death meant nothing to him and he splashed past the Zulu in the act of withdrawing his assegai, as though they had all been rabbiters killing for sport on the banks of the river that ran within a few hundred yards of 'Tryst'.

The water was ice-cold and the current murderously swift. Here and there the heads of men and horses bobbed and swirled as the flow caught them and tumbled them downstream. Melville had disappeared, drowned no doubt, or killed on the bank, but the officer who had been with him was breasting the current and still erect in the saddle, so that Alex, whirled within reach of the tail, grasped it, and was trailed slantwise across the channel between two projecting rocks, each big enough to rank as an islet. On the furthermost of them he saw Melville again, lying face downwards half out of the water, his legs enveloped in the sodden folds of the colours. Then, losing his grip on the tail, his knee brushed a submerged rock and his feet found shingle, so that he was able to stagger up the far bank in the wake of the horse and discover, to his amazement, that he was still in possession of his revolver that swung by a lanyard from his neck. He stood there a moment dazed, unaware at first that the man who had crossed on the horse was now spurring it back into the water and striking out for the rock where Melville still lay inert, his feet shrouded in the flag he had carried all the way from the camp. The man's action struck him as so nonsensical that he cried out, urging him to return before the Zulus got across, but his warning was lost in the continuous roar of the torrent and he remained standing there, watching the current catch the trailing end of the colours, lift it from the rock and carry it away downstream.

A few men, almost all of them native auxiliaries, scrambled up the bank higher up the river and as Alex watched shots came from the bank they had just left and he saw a party of Zulus standing at the head of the path down which he had run and firing the width of the stream. He turned to run but at that moment Melville or his comrade called to him from the shallows and he saw that the officer who had re-entered the water had succeeded in dragging his friend clear and regaining the bank. The horse, mortally wounded by shots from across the river, threshed its way ashore and died in an eddy, almost at his feet. He waded in up to his waist and grasped the elbow of the half-conscious Melville, the first action he had performed since he rode down from the plateau that was not directly concerned with his own preservation. Then all three of them, clinging together like home-drifting drunkards, made some kind of attempt to climb the rocky slope directly ahead, pushing up into a trackless area of scrub and boulder that would afford some kind of protection against the scattering fusillade across the river.

They had climbed no more than a couple of hundred yards when Melville fell forward on his knees and his companion said, "Can't . . . not without a breather . . . they'll come across . . . mean to get every man . . . warn Natal . . . my damned leg . . ." and Alex saw that the man's breeches were bloodied and that his foot was turned outward at an awkward angle. The subaltern turned away, now addressing himself to Melville, "Did what we could . . . rest here and hold 'em off a spell . . ." and Melville, retching, nodded but seemed unable to do more.

Alex said, carefully, "A few got across, one or two mounted. They'll make for Helpmakaar and raise the alarm. We could go along the bank to Rorke's Drift . . ." but the man said, "Not me . . . couldn't walk another step, or Melville either. We'll stay here and watch out for a stray horse. We've got revolvers." And then, in the authoritative tone all the regulars used towards auxiliaries like himself, "Make your own way upstream. Tell Chard at the mission house to evacuate the sick, loophole the place, and hold on as long as he can. That's an order. You've got ammunition for that revolver?"

"Six in the chamber and a handful of spares."

"Give me the spares. Go inland beyond the ridge, then strike west and follow the river. Don't stop."

Alex groped in his tunic pocket, his fingers searching out the elusive cylindrical bullets embedded there. He found nine and passed them to Melville, now sitting up and making some attempt to dry the mechanism of his revolver. Alex said, falteringly, "I lost your binoculars . . ." and Melville said, with a grin, "We don't need binoculars," and pointed towards the river, clear of fugitives now but dotted with Zulus gathering in a group on the bank about the carcase of a horse. "Name's Cogshill," the other man said, briefly. "My respects to Chard at the mission house. Get going, for God's sake, get going . . ." and Alex turned away, setting his face to the lower slopes of the hill. Before he reached the crest he heard a volley of shots and looked over his shoulder. Melville, and his friend Cogshill, were seated back to back in a small, open patch of ground. Between them and the bank were a swarm of Zulus.

3

It was only when he was well clear of the river, and relatively secure from pursuit he would judge, that he could make some attempt, however imperfect, to come to terms with the chaotic events of the last three hours. In that brief interval an army of upwards of two thousand men had been eliminated. Wiped from the face of the earth. Slaughtered piecemeal by a race of men he had thought of, up to that time, as sub-human, equating approximately with aboriginals. It was the shock of their vast superiority in field tactics, in mobility, in physique, stamina and courage, that made the greatest impact on his mind, far greater, at that time, than his own miraculous escape. The heat had gone from the sun and the sky began to cloud over after he had put a mile or more between himself and the clearing, where Melville and Cogshill awaited death with a sangfroid that he did not find so awesome as the matchless hardihood of the humming savages, charging into a crossfire of Martini-Henry bullets and field-gun shells, overturning everything in their path and running on, heedless of loot, to account for fugitives who had stampeded across the *col* south of the camp. Even a river in spate had not checked their onrush. They were back there now, spearing men like Melville and Cogshill, and after that, he supposed, they would sweep on to overwhelm the whole of Natal, utterly defenceless since the departure of Lord Chelmsford's widely-separated columns. It was an astounding performance on the part of savages and a humiliation on the part of trained and disciplined Europeans that could never be expunged, and he wondered briefly what Cetywayo's triumph might mean in wider terms and whether, from this day on, the Cape itself was safe from the converging horns of those charging impis. Helpmakaar, a few miles inside Natal, was surely doomed, and so was the hospital and storehouse at Rorke's Drift, towards which he was supposed to be heading. Perhaps, warned of the Zulu's approach, Durban might be put in some kind of defence, but the mission station on the river, garrisoned by a single company of 2/24th, would be overwhelmed and squashed like a matchbox, so that there was surely no profit in risking one's life a second time to bring word to that fellow Cogshill had mentioned . . . what was his name? 'Chown', 'Chartwell', 'Chart'?

The reflection checked him in his stumbling passage along the hillside and he sat down on a spur of rock, realising how utterly spent he was, and how many hours had elapsed since he had eaten or drunk. His mouth, dry with terror and exertion, was like a sand-pit and his limbs, now that he ceased to employ them, began to shake like those of a terrified child. Fleetingly, but with a kind of self-punishing relish, he reviewed his debut as a soldier and found, in the survey, a degree of shame that brought tears to his eyes. From the moment he bolted down from the plateau beyond the sandstone peak he had not shown a single spark of courage or enterprise, save the bare minimum required to save his hide. He had emptied his rifle haphazardly in the general direction of the enemy, had helped the terrified Basutos to break the lines of G Company on the edge of the perimeter, had fiddled about during the brief battle and fi-nally, at the first chance, grabbed somebody else's horse and fled for his life. It was no consolation to remind himself, as he did at once, that almost everybody else had behaved in precisely the same way once the Zulus were inside the camp, or that things had hap-pened with such stunning speed and fatality that there had been no time to shape an alternative course. Examples of courage and self-sacrifice had not been entirely wanting on the lost field. There had been that chap Melville, encumbering himself with his regi-mental colours all the way to the river and beyond; there had been Cogshill, who had made good his landing but sacrificed his horse and chance of escape by riding back into the river to drag Melville from the flood. But above all there was the memory of the tall ser-geant who had scrambled up on the waggon and remained there, ringed by savages, shooting down at his assailants as though he had been at target practice on an English range. His mind had recorded these things at the time but they had done nothing at all to check his headlong flight. It occurred to him then that he might be the sole survivor of the rout. Perhaps, like General Johnny Cope, he would be the first man to carry the news of his own cowardice to Helpmakaar, so that the name of Swann would become as infamous in Africa as it was famous among the merchants of English shires. For a moment the naked prospect of this did battle with the residue of terror that had outlasted his dash for the river and self-respect won. He stood up, half resolved to retrace his steps and add his six revolver bullets to the tiny arsenal of Melville and Cogshill. Then he remembered the latter's laconic instructions—"My respects to Chard at the mission house. Get going, man . . . that's an order . . ." and a flicker of purpose stirred in him, so that he got up and ploughed on, picking his way among the outcrops and listening to the whistle of his own breath and the dolorous squelch of water in his boots.

*   *   *

He had been walking about an hour when he first saw them, a long, long line of blacks, moving along the bank at a steady, mile-consuming trot and strung out, it seemed, for a mile or more as they headed upstream at roughly twice the speed he could expect to move over this kind of ground.

At first, catching his breath, he thought it was the entire Zulu army but then, ducking swiftly between two upright stones, he estimated the force at about three thousand, an impi perhaps, and without the least doubt making for Rorke's Drift.

The sight, far from appalling him, did something to restore confidence in himself for up here, three to four hundred feet above the level of the river, he had the edge on them, inasmuch as he could see without being seen, so long as he kept his head down. It occurred to him then that no other survivor, given that there were other survivors, would be as well placed to observe and report upon the arrival of at least one impi on Natal soil and understanding this he made a long, careful scrutiny of the moving column, noting that less than one man in twenty carried a firearm and that most of them seemed older and scrawnier than the leaping young bucks that had overwhelmed the camp at Isandlwana.

Their heads, he noticed, were ringed. He remembered something a Boer had told him about this ring signifying maturity and old blood on spears carried by men who had gained their battle experience ten or twenty years ago in wars with the Matabele and other tribes. He watched the tail of the long procession disappear round a wide bend in the river and its head reappear a minute later some way inland, as though another encircling movement, of the kind he had observed when he saw the first impi in motion, was already in progress, with Rorke's Drift as the target of the centre or 'chest' of the formation.

He knew his duty then and was resolved to do it, even at the risk of his worthless life. It would be to keep the column under observation, to overlook its attack from the high ground further south, then strike out the moment dusk fell for Helpmakaar. Only by doing this could he hope to outbid General Cope and at least bring information of some importance to Helpmakaar. But before he set off, moving at an angle of forty-five degrees to the river, he spared a moment to clean his revolver, ejecting the cartridges and drying each chamber and the hammer with shreds of cloth torn from the lapel of his tunic, now as dry as tinder where it did not touch his skin.

The first shots came about an hour later, when he had covered, perhaps, four miles on his new route, and they seemed to come from the north-east so that he changed direction again, moving swiftly but carefully in case the Zulus had thrown out flank guards. It wanted no more than an hour to sunset then and the sky in the east was already appreciably darker than overhead. The going was a little easier here, drystone terraces, almost free of scrub, rising to a summit that he judged was the height overlooking the mission station on the Natal side of the Buffalo. He even recalled the name of the map— 'Oscarberg'; the Oscarberg Heights, or the Oscarberg Terrace, and it was ideally situated for his plan. From its elevation he could look right down on the mission house and any Zulus occupying its lower slopes would necessarily have their backs to him. Then the sound of firing began again, increasing in intensity until it became almost continuous, and he abandoned his cautious approach and broke into a run, scrambling from ridge to ridge until he gained the summit and flopped, gasping, in a patch of scrub that sprouted from a spider of small crevices that formed a shallow cave. Inching forward on his belly he moved towards the rim of the little crater and what he saw, peering down, astonished him as much as or more than his initial glimpse of the squatting army in the dongas behind the plateau.

Rorke's Drift was already beleaguered but it seemed to be giving a far better account of itself than the camp at Isandlwana, for the nearest Zulus were pinned down on three sides of the string of buildings and the men down there seemed to have anticipated attack for they had converted what he remembered as a huddle of shacks and half-built kraals into a tiny, improvised fortress, buttressed with a rampart of biscuit boxes and mealie bags and strengthened, in the section facing him, by two laagered waggons. The regularly spaced flashes from the mission itself, and from the storehouse further east, told him that both buildings had been loopholed and whoever had improvised the fortification had clearly made provision for a last stand, for the compound was sub-divided by another wall of biscuit boxes, and a tiny citadel of mealie bags had been erected inside the eastern section behind the storehouse, adjoining the smaller of the two kraals. He knew that the mission was being used as a sick bay and that two days ago there had been no more than a dozen or so men detained there, but he had no means of knowing the strength of the garrison, except by trying to count the flashes, or estimating the number of men moving about inside the compound. There could hardly be more than a couple of hundred, he would say, and that made the odds around fifteen to one, too heavy he would have thought, despite the obvious advantage to men firing from behind shoulder-high ramparts.

Almost at once he had an opportunity of gauging the garrison's chances of survival for within minutes of his arrival at the summit of the terrace the Zulus advanced in waves against the mission house and once again he heard that unearthly humming sound, that seemed to do duty for a battle cry so that the crackle of musketry seemed insignificant. Yet a surprising number of Zulus fell, the nearest less than fifty yards from the breastworks, and soon the survivors retired, falling back among the scrub and the station ovens that offered cover within close range of the buildings.

He was watching them gather there, massing for a renewed attack, when he became aware of a slight movement immediately below him, on a lower spur of the terrace, and looking down he saw a small group of Zulus armed with flintlocks preparing to snipe at the garrison from the elevation overlooking the buildings. Their presence alarmed him. From up here, notwithstanding the antiquity of the weapons they brandished, redcoats inside the compound were easy targets and some of them, manning the far wall, had their backs to the riflemen. He could not watch them for more than a moment, however, for soon, as the humming rose in pitch, his attention was riveted to the new assault, hundreds of leaping figures running directly on to the rifles of the garrison, and sometimes coming to grips with the defenders over the rampart of bags and boxes.

He could judge now the terrible inequality of the struggle. The redcoats, no more than a few dozen of them, were evenly spaced along the walls, whereas the Zulus seemed without number, and were reckless of life in their attempts to clamber over the obstructions and spill into the compound. Prodigies of valour were performed down there, the attackers reaching over the barriers and grasping at the jabbing bayonets with their bare hands. He saw Zulus using the dead as footholds and one warrior, erect on the barricade, grab a bayonet and wrench it from its socket before he was shot down at pointblank range.

The struggle seemed to go on a long time, half-obscured in trailers of smoke, the din rising as a continuous clamour, but then, once again, the Zulus fell back, and he saw a few wounded inside the compound being carried away to the mealie bag citadel adjoining the smaller kraal. He thought, wretchedly, "Next time they'll do it . . . I'll sit here and see every white man down there slaughtered . . . If the Zulus had the least sense they'd wait until dusk . . ."

He was wrong, however. Seemingly they did not possess that much patience, or were maddened by their losses, for soon a new attack developed, this time against the barricaded doors and windows of the hospital where the dead already lay one upon the other. The leading Zulus, now using their dead as shields, penetrated to the porch where they were mown down in dozens by the concentrated fire of the defenders, and the sun was a red crescent on the ridge before the attack eased off and he saw that someone inside the compound was organising a withdrawal from that section of the defences and attempting to concentrate the garrison into the smaller area behind the storehouse.

Then, with a soft puff, the hospital roof took fire from a flung torch and a line of violet and scarlet flame began to lick its way along the length of the reed thatch, the smoke rising in a great grey spiral, the glow of the flames casting a lurid light on the embattled rectangle, playing on the buttons, badges and rifle barrels of the defenders and over behind the oven ditch, where the Zulus were rallying opposite the laagered waggons, on the blades of their assegais and the metal ornaments they wore.

The scene was so absorbing that he completely forgot his own involvement in it, only remembering it when he heard a scatter of shots from immediately below and isolating them in his mind from the sharp, decisive crack of the Martini-Henrys the defenders were using. The snipers he had seen there were at work, using the lull to pick off figures moving about in the compound, or standing to at the breastworks. Three Borderers fell as he watched and were carried away by their comrades but most of the shots went high, passing over the enclosure walls to raise little spurts of dust in the trampled ground beyond.

He had to make a decision then, whether to risk all in an attempt to extricate himself, crawl out of range and start out for Helpmakaar with the news that the Zulus were this side of the river in force, or stay hidden above the mission house and witness the final overrunning of the defences and the massacre of every man in the garrison. For he could not see how the defenders could hope to hold on through the night and reasoned that if he left now he might manage to find his way down on to the plain in the last glimmer of daylight, making a wide sweep to avoid running into stray Zulus at the foot of the terraces.

He had almost decided to take this course when a fresh spatter of shots rang out from the rocks and one seemed to come from very close at hand. He pulled himself forward an inch or so and was just able to see the barrel of an antique sporting gun, of the kind Boer hunters must have used a generation ago, and his familiarity with firearms told him that up here, firing heavy slugs from a greatly depressed angle, the marksman had a fair chance of hitting someone and ought to be silenced if that was at all possible, notwithstanding the terrible risk of betraying his own position.

He drew back and began to work his way round the larger of the rock buttresses that screened him, moving with extreme caution and taking the greatest care not to dislodge small fragments of rock

that would alert the sniper immediately below. Presently he could
see him clearly, a warrior in his late forties or early fifties, with a
red ostrich plume fixed to his headband and, cradled in his shoulder,
a wide-barrelled sporting gun of the type hunters still used in the
coastal belt above Durban. At that moment, yet another attack developed below, the tireless Zulus swarming out of cover and moving,
in obedience to what looked like a concerted plan, on the hospital
from which the sick and wounded were still being evacuated in the
light of the flames. The renewed uproar gave him the cover he
needed and he raised his revolver, steadying it against a small spur
of rock and firing from a range of about twelve yards.

The bullet must have struck the sniper in the temple, killing him
instantly. He uttered no sound and made no movement beyond a
single convulsive jerk. His museum-piece clattered down, alerting
another man posted below, but the fellow, after a casual upward
glance, turned back to watch the fight, so that Alex made up his
mind to try and account for him while the attack lasted. He rose
half upright in the rapidly fading light and worked his way round
the vertical stone and between two rounded boulders, deliberately
sealing his mind against the hellish uproar coming from the direction of the hospital, where the Zulus had at last made a lodgement
and were scrambling through the shattered door and windows.

It was fortunate that the sniper's attention was riveted on the
battle. Had it not been, he must have heard movement among the
loose shale on his immediate right. As it was he rose excitedly to his
knees when a shower of soaring sparks rose as a result of the storming party's rampage through the hospital and Alex was able to shoot
him at leisure, the impact of the bullet pitching him forward and
over the flat stone he was using as an elbow rest. He went on down,
head over heels, for twenty yards or more before his body became
lodged in a crevice, and as he fell two other snipers rose out from
the line of rocks below and began to scramble down to the barricade,
evidently satisfied that the post was now enveloped and on the point
of falling.

He loosed off two random shots at them but almost certainly
missed, for by now his attention was deflected by the garrison's un-
hurried withdrawal behind the reserve defences bisecting the compound, and by the maddened rush of the Zulus from the western

door of the burning building into the open ground beyond. Here they were cut down in swathes and only a few reached the line of biscuit boxes before the attack faltered and shredded away. In less than five minutes from the tumble of the second sniper the space between the small kraal and the blazing hospital was empty of living Zulus, apart from the odd one or two who were trying to drag themselves out of range.

It was astounding, he thought, that the post had not been overrun. Whoever was directing its defence down there must have possessed iron nerve and a great deal of imagination, for the garrison was now firing from behind stone walls and for the first time since he had looked down on the scene Alex had hopes that the place would hold out until Chelmsford's main column could return via Isandlwana to its relief. He took refuge, meantime, on the little shelf of rock where the dead sniper lay, reflecting that here was the first man he had knowingly killed, but feeling no pride in the achievement. The fellow was grey-polled, wrinkled and scrawny, a great contrast to the young giants who had run beside the fugitives all the way to the Buffalo River, and as he crouched there, looking at the small, round hole made by his bullet, he remembered a friendly Boer's parting quip as they shook hands, preparatory to his departure from Helpmakaar with his squadron of the N.N.C. He had said, in his guttural English, "So, my young friend, you're off to kill a Zulu. How old are you? Eighteen? I killed my first when I was thirteen and out with Retief."

To kill a Zulu. This, then, was war, not as he had imagined it, turning the leaves of the illustrated magazines his father introduced into the house, not even as it was portrayed by men like Henty, who had actually served in wars and should have known better, but real war, where it was a straight choice of kill or be killed, and in response to a curious impulse he turned the man on his back, closed his eyes and loosely folded his arms.

Down below all was relatively quiet. The hospital roof still glowed red and clouds of heavy smoke, caught in the night breeze, rolled towards the river where it could not obscure the garrison's aim. He had a feeling of near certainty now that he had witnessed the final attack and that all the Europeans who had survived down there would live to boast about their part in an epic. For it was an epic, of a kind that far surpassed anything he had ever read about battles; a few score men, responding to discipline and years of routine training, holding off a mob of gallant savages throughout hours of unremitting pressure, fighting calmly and steadily in the light of a burning building and inflicting losses, he would guess, at a ratio of about ten to one in the process. He thought about that for a moment, relating it to his own childish resolve to follow the career of a soldier and found that it fused, despite the pity he felt for the ageing Zulu beside him. To become equipped for a performance of that nature; to stand there without losing one's head or taking to one's heels, and fight it out against odds. He thought again of Melville and Cogshill, sitting back to back without hope but without fear either, and then of the tall sergeant at Isandlwana, aiming and firing from the eminence of the waggon. Training, inducing that kind of pride and that kind of coolness, was everything and you never heard much about it. The emphasis was always on flags and drums and horses.

A terrible drowsiness stole upon him and he crawled deep into the recess behind the ledge, spreading his legs, propping his back against the cool surface of the rock and pointing his revolver at the oval aperture lit by a rosy glow. And suddenly, without knowing it, he was asleep.

3

Change of Landscape

THE paddock oak came cracking down a few minutes before five, the rending, whickering *snack* of heavy timber rocketing her from sleep much shallower than the sleep she took for granted when he was beside her and her fears and frustrations were subject to his jocular analysis.

Whenever he was absent for more than a few days, however, submerged worries, no more than vaguely bothersome by day, would rise to the surface of her mind when she was lying in what seemed to her—in his absence—about an acre of bed.

Then, as now, sleep would either evade her altogether or she would drift into a series of muddled dreams, rising at odds with herself so that the business of the day would tend to clog, reminding her of her wifely inadequacies in the very earliest days of their marriage when she had no clear idea at all how to run a place like 'Tryst' or hold her own with a pack of quarrelsome servants.

Her current disquiet was uncharacteristic of the mature Henrietta Swann. In the last few years she had adjusted to the uneven rhythm of her life and even when hedged about with a variety of problems had been able to enjoy long periods of tranquillity in the midst of a domestic turmoil that less experienced women would have mistaken for anarchy.

Sometimes she let him persuade her to allow house and family to take care of themselves and accompany him on one of his periodical migrations that took her as far north as Edinburgh and as far west as Plymouth, and when this happened she saw herself as the wife of a prosperous sea-captain, with business in every corner of the world, so that her 'shore' problems seemed trivial and remote. She had not accompanied him on his latest odyssey, however, and the weeks following the Colonel's death were unlike any she could recall, if one excepted that awful interval following the Staplehurst rail crash, before absorption in his business had proved such a splendid antidote for fear and loneliness.

Her mood was linked, she supposed, to the old Colonel's elimination from the family circle, to the sour knowledge, whenever she wandered into his former quarters, that everything was in its place but he, the quiet, watchful, ever-tolerant presence, for so long attuned to her doubts and misgivings whenever she was thrown on her own resources. She told herself, repeatedly, that it was high time she adjusted to his death and to the absence of Stella and Alexander, reminding herself that, with George and Giles away at school, she still had more than enough to supervise, with the three younger children, a fifteen-month-old baby, a house of nearly fifty rooms and a staff of eight, three of them less than half-trained.

Reassurances, although well enough in daylight, brought no more than marginal peace of mind by night, especially as she was passing through one of her sleepless spells that was due, she decided, to the abominable weather they had been having since the snowfalls of late January and early February.

The head gardener told her it was seasonable and perhaps it was, sleet showers that lashed the mullioned windows, and a string of south-westerlies that stormed into the hollow like a stampede of wild horses and set everything billowing and rattling until they threatened to strip pantiles from beams where they had rested for three centuries and send the sugarloaf chimneys tumbling over the eaves and down into the forecourt.

At the height of such a commotion it was like living on a ship, for up here the entire structure creaked and groaned and stirred and whispered, as though it shared her lifelong detestation for wind and would have welcomed a thunderstorm that neither she nor 'Tryst' minded in the least.

The wind had been particularly tiresome tonight, one of the last nights of winter she supposed, for she always assumed spring was on the doorstep when the hateful month of February was out. Outside, where the double avenue of copper beeches divided the paddocks and ran down to Twyforde Lane, the gale was baulked by rising ground so that having arrived there in such a prodigious hurry it recoiled, not knowing how to circumvent the obstacle, roaring all the way round the house and finally doubling back on the triangular cleft in which 'Tryst' stood under the tall, wooded spur. And here, wretchedly indecisive, it would eddy about restlessly and menacingly, as though searching out an unsuspecting victim, finding none and hurling itself at the chimneys or mounting a fresh assault on the bluff.

She heard the grandfather clock on the landing strike two and then the half-hour, after which she abandoned all attempts to sleep and sat up, slipping into the quilted bedgown Adam had brought her from Paisley and lighting the bedtable lamp that needed trimming and smelled abominably but offered some kind of anchorage in this tempest of sound. Then, soothed to some extent by the familiarity of the room, she set about marshalling the identifiable sources of her unease, arranging them in order of precedence as she had once approached the complexities of his leaderless waggon service during the sombre winter of 'sixty-five/'sixty-six.

The most obvious of them, of course, was concerned with Alex, who might or might not have been involved in that shameful battle at a place with an unpronounceable name, 'I-say' or 'E-saw' something, a word that ended, she recalled, in a whistling syllable, like 'wonna' or 'wanna'. There had been a great deal about it in the papers more than a fortnight ago and even Adam, whose involvement with Imperial affairs was always superficial, had seemed disturbed, muttering that Chelmsford, the general the papers seemed to hold responsible, was no better than the old fossils who had bungled the Crimean campaign and the events that resulted in the Sepoy Mutiny. "The chap they need out there is Roberts," he told her, grumpily, but she remembered then that the Indian general had been a classmate and war comrade of his before he left the army, and therefore assumed this to be prejudice on his part. It did seem, however, that something was amiss in Zululand, where a few thousand savages were said to have won a decisive victory over half as many Europeans. She had been an attentive reader of war despatches since girlhood and could never recall this happening before. It was always the other way round. As to Alex, Adam had assured her she had no need to worry on his score. Had he been killed or even wounded, they would have been informed before casualty lists were telegraphed to the War Office and printed in *The Times*. There was provision for this kind of thing nowadays, he told her, far more than had existed in his day, when upwards of a year could elapse before people at home were notified that a son or a husband had died in some footling skirmish in a jungle or river-bottom. He despatched a wire to his Capetown agents, however, and asked them to make enquiries concerning volunteer officers of the Natal Native Contingents, and after that, or so it seemed to her, had forgotten Alex in the flurry that attended the opening of his Irish branch, a circumstance that whisked him away to Dublin more than a week ago.

She continued to dream about Alex, however, seeing him dishevelled and distraught, as he poked aimlessly about a great, treeless plain, and whenever she came downstairs after one of these unsettling dreams she would enquire sharply if there had been any post other than business mail and would be glum and tetchy when Stillman, the Colonel's old batman who did duty for butler at 'Tryst', said there was not.

Thus, getting on for three weeks after the news of Lord Chelmsford's defeat (the newspapers referred to it as 'poor Durnford's disaster') her eldest son qualified as the first of her worries, but those of the eldest daughter were also clamouring for priority, particularly since she had talked with her at the Colonel's funeral tea.

Clearly all was not well over at Courtlands. Any mother with half an eye could see that, but it was quite another thing to run down the cause or causes of Stella's lack-lustre expression, her reluctance to communicate and her overall listlessness, for these might stem from a variety of reasons, anything from a clumsy husband's bridal-bed fumblings to his father's debts, or possibly the desire of an inexperienced girl to bring some kind of order into that place of theirs across the county border.

She wished then, and with all her heart, that she had insisted on a much longer engagement, if only to give her time to assess Lester as a husband, and the Moncton-Prices as a family. She wished also that she had been more specific with Stella in the one wary discussion they had had on the subject of marriage, for it seemed to her, in retrospect, that she had done the girl an injustice by not giving her the benefit of her own experiences of twenty years ago, when she had married at approximately Stella's age.

At this distance it was difficult to recollect the gist of such advice as she had given her. Something along the lines of keeping a sense of proportion, she fancied, a hint or two that most people talked a great deal of nonsense about sharing a bed with a man and having babies and that, once one adjusted to it, it could be both rewarding and amusing. She had to admit, however, that these hints had not had much effect on the girl, who really could be extraordinarily stupid concerning everything outside fashions and horseflesh. They said she had a wonderful seat on a horse but that was no qualification for marriage. Or was it, if one was marrying into a horsey family like the Moncton-Prices? It was all very frustrating, this lack of news about Alex, and this fog of uncertainty surrounding Stella and that dandified husband of hers. And then, as if all this was not enough, there was Giles' cough and Giles' martyred expression when the Christmas holidays ended and he was packing his boxes for school.

Giles had gone to Mellingham as a matter of course. No one, least of all Giles himself, had questioned the wisdom of sending a very sensitive child of thirteen to a Spartan establishment that catered, she was told, for embryo soldiers. Alex had been happy there and so, it seemed, was George, but then Alex had more or less set his mind on soldiering whereas George, confound the boy, would be happy upside down in a barrel of treacle and had learned the trick of infecting everybody around him with his own high spirits before he was three. Giles was not remotely like either of them, lacking Alexander's heavy predictability and George's gaiety and ebullience, so that he had always seemed to her to live a private, self-contained life, thinking his own thoughts, making his own judgements, drawing on reserves of wisdom, distinctions that set him apart as a kind of pocket soothsayer so that it was very difficult to treat him as a child in need of a child's protection.

She was aware, of course, of the reason for this. It was not Giles' gravity or the sense of stillness that set him apart in her mind, but the memory that he had, as it were, registered himself as an adult before he was born, for she had been carrying him through all those wretched months when Adam was dead to her and later, when he was learning to walk again in that Swiss hospital across the sea.

In those days the child in her womb had been a source of enormous comfort to her, a part of Adam left behind to sustain her but this, of course, she had later come to regard as pure fancy. It was daunting, over the years, to watch fancy resolve itself into fact.

She made a decision then and it helped to settle her mind. The moment he returned she would consult Adam about finding Giles a smaller, less prestigious school, where they would foster his individuality instead of trying to mould him to a pattern. She would also consult Doctor Birtles about that cough of his, for what the boy needed was bracing, upland air which he was unlikely to find in Berkshire.

She was getting her bothersome problems into some kind of order now. Alex and Stella were old enough to look to themselves. Giles should have her championship the moment Adam returned. And as soon as it was light she would address herself to the minor irritations—that new girl's dreadful memory concerning the weekly laundry cycle, the increasing slovenliness of Stillman now that the Colonel was not there to keep him up to his duty, young Hugo's habit of talking with his mouth full, the frequent squabbles of Joanna and Helen over the ownership of hair ribbons and the like; the small change, she supposed, of any woman with a growing family, a husband who spent most of his time out of reach, and a house the size and age of 'Tryst'. The landing clock struck half past three. She turned down the lamp, wriggled lower in the bed and slept.

But then, as though circumstances were sworn to deny her a night's rest, the paddock oak came crashing down fifty yards from her window, and the uproar brought her bounding out of bed and peering into the windy darkness, half expecting to hear the house erupt behind her and see Stillman or Phoebe Fraser, the governess, light the downstairs lamps and run out to discover what was amiss.

Nothing happened and she could see no evidence of the damage, although she was absolutely certain it was the oak, one of her favourite trees that stood only a few yards beyond the paddock rail, a veteran all of three hundred years old that must have seeded itself from the spur above the house about the time that old pirate Conyer made up his mind to build a house for the Cecil girl, forbidden the company of a penniless suitor.

The prospect of seeing the great tree prone and splintered saddened her. All the time she had lived here it had been a symbol of permanence, a reminder that she and that Cecil girl had a great deal in common, both having married the same kind of man in the face of parental opposition. She knew she would not sleep now although the gale was slowly blowing itself out, satisfied, no doubt, now that it had inflicted permanent damage on the old place. She lit the lamp again, looked at her watch and found it was just after five. Slipping into her woollen bedgown she went out on to the landing where there was a candlestick left for emergencies, reasoning that it would be light in an hour or so and she could make herself tea in the kitchen and pass the time doing a laundry check while she waited to review the storm damage from the drawing-room windows. She lit the candle and carried it, guttering madly, down the broad staircase and through the swing door that led to the big stone kitchen.

It was far more cheerful in here. A log glowed fitfully in the downdraught of the chimney. The old iron kettle, hanging on its spit above the grate, held water that was close to boiling so she tipped it, filling the smaller kettle and balancing it on the log while she fetched tea, milk and sugar from the pantry. The kettle lid was rattling before the cup was set and it was whilst carrying kettle to teapot that she first heard the rattle of the door latch.

The sound startled her until she remembered that the gardener's boy slept in the loft over the stables and had therefore almost surely been roused by the crash of the oak. She called, sharply, "Is that you, Philip?" and crossed to the door, laying her hand on the bolt. But the voice that answered was not Philip's but a deeper one, charged with agitation and calling urgently, "No, ma'am, it's me! Denzil Fawcett, from Dewponds. May I speak to you, ma'am?"

Dewponds was the farm a mile or so up the river, the nearest to 'Tryst' of a spread of farms occupying a ripple of hollows this side of the woods and Denzil, she recalled, was the only son of Stephen Fawcett, the farmer, a rather morose man, who was on guardedly friendly terms with Adam, both having served in the trenches before Sebastopol. She guessed then that the gale, as well as bringing down the Conyer oak, had inflicted more serious damage on the farmhouse, and that Denzil had been sent for help. She called, "Wait, I'll open up!" and drew the bolt, using her shoulder to prevent the heavy door opening its full width.

He slipped inside quickly, a wildly dishevelled young man about Stella's age, running his fingers through dripping hair and blinking nervously in the light of the kitchen lamp. He was, she could see, not only soaked to the skin but very embarrassed at finding himself in the presence of the mistress of 'Tryst' in her bedgown and night-dress. She pushed the door to and he hastened to help her, silencing the long, whistling sough of the wind.

"I saw a light," he said, breathlessly. "I was going to shelter in the stables until someone stirred and I could ask for Mr. Swann . . ." and then a flush spread across his moist, tanned cheeks and she hit on a deeper reason for his obvious embarrassment. It was no secret at 'Tryst' that he had been madly devoted to Stella ever since he brought her home with a bruised backside after a toss she had taken in the hunting field. That, however, would be years ago, when Stella was rising fourteen and the boys made far more of the incident than it merited, teasing Stella unmercifully about her straw-chewing swain until Adam had put a stop to it at Stella's request.

She said, "Has anything happened at the farm? Has the river flooded again?" and he said, avoiding her eye, "No, Mrs. Swann, nought like that. Maybe it's best I talk to *Mr.* Swann."

"You can't," she said, suddenly glad of his company, "Mr. Swann is in Ireland, and you're soaked through. Here, have some tea, I've just made it. The big oak came down and woke me up. Nobody else heard it but they'll be stirring in an hour, so tell me what brought you here at this hour and in this weather?"

He said, with a great effort, "Your daughter did, ma'am . . . Miss Stella . . ." and then, sullenly, "She isn't that now, is she? Not since—marrying!"

She learned something from the difficulty he had in getting that last word out, as if it pained him as much as losing a bad tooth. It also occurred to her to wonder if that calf-love episode, that had been the subject of so much family laughter, was as innocent as she had supposed at the time, but then, studying him closely, she noted his increasing embarrassment and decided that it must be, for a lad like him would hardly presume to make a bid for a girl with Stella's background. And even if he had entertained such a grandiose notion Stella was not the kind of girl to give him the slightest encouragement.

She said, sharply, "My daughter sent you? At *this* time of night?"

"She's . . . she's at our farm. She didn't want me to come, or not

70

yet. But I thought . . . mother thought . . ." and he stopped his big hands seeking an anchorage on the mug she had placed in them a moment ago.

Henrietta experienced an unpleasant shrinking sensation in the pit of her stomach. If Stella was at Dewponds Farm, within a mile of home, then she was in some kind of trouble. Bad trouble she would say having regard Denzil's presence here at five in the morning. She said, carefully, "How does my daughter come to be at your farm? Don't stand there fiddling with that mug. Drink it, lad, then go over by the fire and tell me exactly what's happened."

The edge on her voice helped him to make the effort. He took two great gulps of tea and drifted over to the hearth, setting the mug down on the slate chimney-shelf and rubbing his great, freckled hands one upon the other. "I found her," he said, finally. "She saw my lantern up in Carter's Copse when I was out with the lambs. We had trouble and I was sitting up in the spinney hut . . . She came over the gate and called . . . She was in a bad state . . . she'd walked, you see, in all that wind and rain."

"*Walked?* From Courtlands? Good heavens, it's twenty miles, isn't it?"

"Not the way she came, across country. It's far enough though. She was about done and soaked through and through."

"But why? In God's name *why*, boy?"

"She ran away. She was making for here I suppose but then . . . well, she changed her mind and asked me to take her in. I roused Mother and the girls and they dried her off, gave her some soup and put her to bed in Dulcie's room. She's there now. Asleep, I reckon."

It was as wild and improbable as one of her dreams about Alexander. As improbable, in its way, as her own mad flight the night Sam tried to marry her off to Makepeace Goldthorpe in exchange for a piece of land between mill and railway line. But Stella wasn't being married off, and she had always thought of her as a weak-willed character, so that it astounded her to discover that the girl had the spunk to run away and make her way home, irrespective of what had prompted the flight.

She found herself looking at Denzil more sympathetically. Perhaps it wasn't calf-love that had prompted him to take charge of the drenched fugitive, to abandon his lambs to rain and wind and hurry her back to what must surely be a very startled and embarrassed family. She said, fighting her impatience, "Did she *tell* you anything, Denzil? Any reason why she should *do* a crazy thing like that?" and watched him carefully, interested to see the way he flung up his head, not perhaps defiantly but resolutely. "That rake Moncton! He's been treating her badly. His father, too, from what I could learn." And then, dismally, "You won't send her back, will you?"

It was a direct appeal and she was glad it had not been made in the presence of anyone else, who would be unlikely to acknowledge chivalry in a lumpish farmer's boy. She was grateful then to the wind for bringing down the oak and rousing her while everyone else slept. She said, quietly, "Finish your tea, lad. Dry yourself off a bit. Then tell me everything. *Everything*, you understand?"

He seemed to consider this a moment and the air of distraction that had attended him ever since he crossed the threshold moderated. Deliberately he squared himself, so that she was surprised to notice that he was as tall as Adam and even more strongly made. His rough clothes steamed as they clung to him and she thought, involuntarily, "Why the devil do we halter ourselves with all the fancy conceits that go along with money? He would have made a perfectly splendid husband for the girl, and taught her something worth knowing while he was taking care of her and giving me grandchildren I could be proud of . . ." but she said, prompting him, "I'm waiting, Denzil."

"She didn't say much, or much that made sense any road. She was fair worn out, and her clothes was in tatters. Besides she was crying, and it wasn't easy to follow her in all that wind."

"But you heard enough to decide to take her home instead of bringing her here."

"Aye, I did that, Mrs. Swann, and she can stay at the farm as long as she's a mind to. With your permission that is."

"We'll come to that. Meantime I'll have to know at least as much as you know."

"It fair beats me how she could marry a man o' that sort," he burst out. "Or even if she wanted to, why you and Mr. Swann didden stop her, seeing she's not of age. They're trash, for all that great place they live in, and all those fine horses they breed. People like us have always known it, but you wouldn't, seeing you weren't raised about here. I was near out of my mind when I first heard about it . . ."

He stopped suddenly, the flush returning to his cheeks. "I'd best hold my tongue," he concluded, "she's in enough trouble a'ready," but then, reading her expression, he went on, desperately, "There was never the least thing wrong about me and Stella. We'd meet from time to time, over on the downs, when I was ditching, or fetching the cows from pasture. She was always on her mare, and mostly she'd do no more than lift her crop and go her way. Not always tho'. Sometimes she'd rein in and pass the time o' day. One time . . ." and he stopped again, glowering down at the smouldering log in the hearth.

"This is between you and me, Denzil. I said I must know everything but I give you my word it won't go beyond these four walls. What happened that one time?"

"Nothin' really. I was mad enough to tell her what was in my mind, that she was just about everything to me. More'n Dewponds if the truth's known."

"What did she say to that?"

His head came up again. "She just laughed and made me see what a dam' fool I was, so I started walking off, but she slipped off the mare and called me back. She said she was sorry she'd laughed that way and she was too, otherwise why should she . . . She come right up to me then and kissed me. Just that once. Then she got up again and rode off without a word. That was the summer before last and whenever I saw her after that she was with one of the others. Mr. Alexander, mostly."

"And that's all?"

"That's all, Mrs. Swann. I'll swear on the book if you ask me to."

"That won't be necessary, Denzil. Thank you for telling me."

She had a picture then of their association over the eternity of adolescence, a pretty, impossibly remote little madam, buttressed by wealth and a new social position, and a great gallant oaf like Denzil Fawcett, mooning his life away as he trudged about his tasks, lifting his head every now and again in the hope that he would catch a glimpse of her, perhaps exchange an odd word with her, a crumb of dry bread that would keep him going for another week or so. *Any* kind of crumb, a wave, a smile, or an odd word or two if she was in the mood to bestow such favours. And then that single moment of declaration, greeted by derisive laughter and after laughter, no doubt, a flash of compassion on her part, followed by a lightly bestowed kiss, as though that would last the poor devil a lifetime. Anger rose in her, not for him certainly but for Stella, for the cold fish she had married and that rackety old father of his. But mostly for herself and Adam, who had let things drift to this pass, a daughter of theirs who had supposedly made a good match, running off into the night after six months as a bride and making for the one person from whom she could expect aid and comfort without conditions to go along with them.

She said, "Wait here, Denzil. Pour yourself some more tea and give yourself a rub down with that towel while I'm dressing. We'll roust out young Philip and he can harness the trap but, while I'm gone, think of some excuse for my going with you, something the servants will likely believe."

He looked surprised and then hesitant so that she added quickly, "Don't fret. I'll not send her back but there's no point in her coming here either, for this is the first place the Moncton-Prices will look when they discover she's gone, if they don't know already. I'll bring some things she can change into, and I know a place where she can hide while Mr. Swann and I sort this out one way or another. Do you trust me that far?"

"Why shouldn't I? You're her mother. You'd surely know what's best for her."

"Yes, I do," Henrietta said, and left him, going through to the hall and up the stairs and noting, on the way, that the first glimmer of dawn was showing on the edge of the downs.

2

The vault-like stillness, the enduring silence of the house, and the terrible sense of timelessness it brought was not fully apparent to her until the January frosts had stopped the hunting and she lost contact with everyone she knew save Lester and his sharp-featured old father, and even their company was hard to come by, particularly when Lester's crony, Ralph Ponsonby, was about the place.

Nobody save the old man ever addressed her unless she began

the conversation and when she did they seemed to listen with ill-concealed impatience, so that they could get back to their racing gossip, or exchange one of their mysterious male jokes that made no kind of sense to her.

She and Lester were never alone, not for a single moment, for he had a room of his own along the corridor and had used it every night, even his wedding night, when he had shipped so much wine at dinner, and during the billiards match he played with Ponsonby later, that the head stableman had to be summoned to put him to bed.

The old man had stayed on, playing interminable games of patience on a board that rested on his knees, and in his gruff way had been considerate towards her, suggesting that she had a brandy and some of his shelled nuts before retiring to the great, dilapidated bedroom they had given her, where her trousseau was still waiting to be unpacked. She had no maid to help her. Women, if any were allowed above stairs, never seemed to come to this part of the house and that in itself was strange, for who made and aired the beds, and carried coals and hot water upstairs?

The bleakness and anonymity of the house had pressed hard upon her that first night and even now she had not adjusted to it. She never ceased to compare its austerity to the warmth and cosiness of 'Tryst', with its gleaming surfaces and smell of age, its continuity that did not run contrary to the vitality of newcomers like the Swanns but somehow enfolded them and coached them in its ways, graciousness, and durability. Courtlands was old, though not so old as 'Tryst', but its smell of the past contained elements at odds with these things. It had never, it seemed, been loved and cared for and in the lower rooms old dust had gathered in the fabric, so that instead of pleasant smells, like lavender and resin that pervaded 'Tryst', there was a whiff of mildew and damp rot. There was no kind of scheme inherent in the fittings and furnishings, for here and there pieces had been sold off to pay racing debts and their removal had never been camouflaged, as where the wallpaper that had once backed a picture or a Welsh dresser remained its original colour, in contrast to grimed sections that had been exposed since they were pasted there a generation ago. The gardens were neglected too, for the entire household revolved around the stables, the only part of the mansion in good heart.

Loneliness, and a kind of dragging apathy engulfed her from the first moment of coming here. The servants were mostly broken-down old horsemasters and ostlers, who seemed to regard the living quarters as a camp, and a temporary camp at that. But it was not the outward aspect of the place that troubled her so much as her isolation, an eighteen-year-old girl set down among so many ageing men, who paid her scant deference and seemed in fact to regard her as one of the young master's doxies temporarily lodged in the house and likely, at any moment, to move on bag and baggage, to make way for a replacement.

She was not much given to self-pity and throughout those first few months had made a great effort to adjust to the translation from a background of cushioned comfort and hilarity, to one of near squalor and overall drabness, her happy childhood buttressing her against despair. But for all that, week by week, she sensed she was losing ground. Even Lester who, now that he was her husband paid her no attention at all, admired her horsemanship, and was amiable enough when they were mounted, but once the horses had been off-saddled and rubbed down he drifted off somewhere, either to supervise the training of one or other of his entries in the big steeplechase events, or to play billiards, or to drink and consort with his inseparable companion Ponsonby, a young man concerning whom she could discover nothing, beyond the fact that his stepfather had owned a horse that won the Derby and had once trained Lord Rosebery's racehorses, but who seemed now to have latched himself on to the Moncton-Prices.

She had recognised Ponsonby as the major impediment to the marriage on that first, disconsolate night. It was Ponsonby, she was certain, who had talked Lester out of their honeymoon trip to Biarritz, now postponed indefinitely, for the flat season would open in a month or so and it was well known that the Moncton-Prices had entered their colt, Figaro, in the Epsom classic. She could forgo a cross-Channel trip in winter but it was humiliating to hover on the extreme edge of this tight family circle waiting and waiting for Lester to use her as she had been led to believe all young men used their brides, particularly in the early days of marriage.

She was by no means entirely ignorant of men and men's ways, having been raised in the company of two lively brothers not much younger than herself, and had thus come into contact with any number of their high-spirited friends at garden-parties, birthday gatherings and Christmas celebrations at 'Tryst'. At least a dozen of these young sparks had embraced her in odd corners of the house, and two or three of them had tried to adventure a little further but had been rebuffed, for Stella Swann had never, since putting up her hair more than five years ago, failed to put a realistic price upon herself as the eldest daughter of a man whose name was a household word and thought herself as fetching as any of the models used by Mr. Millais or Mr. Burne-Jones, or even Mr. Rossetti in their annual Academy exhibits.

Sometimes, once she had passed her fifteenth birthday, and was beginning to think of herself as eligible, she would compare herself with one or other of the willowy heroines in these highly-publicised paintings, telling herself that most of them, notwithstanding abundant tresses and large, soulful eyes, looked anaemic, whereas she, for her part, had just as much hair, a much healthier complexion, and curves in all the right places, so that it did not surprise her in the least that she was very popular in the ballroom, and much sought after at soirées and garden-fêtes organised by people like old Mrs. Halberton, the social lioness of the district.

She knew that she was not in the least clever, like her courtesy-sister, Deborah, whom she had always admired and continued to admire, even though Deborah now showed unmistakable signs of turning into a blue-stocking. But men were supposed not to love clever women so with her looks and her figure, to say nothing of her skill in the hunting field, she did not think she would have the least difficulty in catching a young man who would adore her, and pay her far more attention than her jovial money-grubbing father paid his wife, who nonetheless continued to look at him (on those occasions when he was there to be looked at) like a spaniel bitch hoping to be taken rabbiting on the downs.

One man did look at her in that way. Poor, lumpish Denzil Fawcett, the farmer's son over at Dewponds, who had rescued her after a tumble in a soggy ditch the far side of Cudham one autumn morning, carried her all the way home and then succeeded in making a great nuisance of himself when his sheep's-eyes informed her brothers and sisters that she had made a conquest. But poor Denzil,

who was really rather like Jan Ridd in Mr. Blackmore's highly recommended but tedious novel, did not qualify as a beau in the way
Alexander's friend Bellchamber did, for Bellchamber père owned
a scent factory, whereas Roger Stanton, one of the subalterns of
the Sixteenth Light Dragoons, who had brought her grandfather
home after the Waterloo dinner, had an uncle in the House of Lords.
She was rather sorry now that she had not encouraged Roger and
used him as a foil against Lester when the latter began to pay regular
visits to 'Tryst', but he had arrived rather late on the scene, when
she was more or less committed, and the prospect of being Lady
Moncton-Price had put everything else out of her head.

Well, it was now far too late to ponder strategy and it was up to
her, she supposed, to overcome what she could only assume to be
Lester's shyness as regards his role as a husband. She had always
assumed, up to that time, that conquest was the male's prerogative,
and that a woman's duty was to remain mysterious and elusive, even
after she was 'claimed' as they said. But where was the profit in being
elusive when nobody came looking, and shyness on the part of one's
husband sometimes seemed to amount to a kind of panic, as when
she had gone to the door and called him by name on the fifth night
of her marriage, and asked his assistance in freeing the top hook of
her corsets that had become entangled in a loose thread of the brace?

Even now she did not know what to make of his attitude on that
occasion. He had appeared almost instantaneously, looking very red
about the face, and had remained standing just inside the door, a
door he seemed reluctant to close, while she had recrossed the room
to stand before the spotted mirror of her dressing-table in a half-shed
corset, voluminous white drawers and a rucked-up chemise she had
been pulling over her head when the hook had caught on the thread.

Attempting to make allowances for his obvious embarrassment
she had said, over her shoulder, "Please, Lester . . . the top hook,
it's caught . . ." and had waited, almost willing him to make a joke
about it, as Phoebe Fraser or one of her sisters would have done and
then, who knew, to embrace her from behind, and lower his lips to
her shoulder, so that she would at least *feel* married, even if what
he did afterwards was frightening or a little painful, as her mother
had hinted during that one rather embarrassing conversation they
had had a day or two before the wedding.

But when she felt no touch and heard no movement she turned to see that the door was shut, and that he was on the far side of it and scuttling along the corridor to his own quarters and she had felt so rejected that she tore the corset free, burst into tears, and sat half-undressed on the lumpy, uncomfortable bed, admitting to herself that he was as much a stranger as he had been when Mrs. Halberton had introduced him to her at the fête organised in aid of Polynesian lepers, although what a man like Lester could have been doing there was more than she could say.

After that things had drifted from bad to worse. Ponsonby, whose very presence she came to detest, was hardly ever absent from the house, a tall, foppish ever-smiling young man about Lester's age, with a very fresh complexion and mocking greenish eyes that played over her with a kind of contemptuous amusement, as though she had been an awkward puppy continually falling over its own blundering feet. Every night about ten ennui would drive her upstairs to bed and she would lie awake, listening to the rustlings in the house and the owls hooting in the limes about the lodge gates until, around midnight or later, she would hear Lester's boots clump past the door to his room down the corridor and once or twice, when they had been drinking too much, the honking laughter of Ralph Ponsonby.

Once or twice she half made up her mind to go to him and force him to discuss this curious and altogether unprecedented situation but she never quite summoned enough courage, knowing that another rebuff on his part would drive them even farther apart, or that he might read into her approach experience with men she did not possess. Then again, when the cheerless Christmas had passed, she toyed with the notion of seeking Sir Gilbert's advice, but soon realised that it would prove impossible to bring herself to the point of asking the leathery old man what a bride was expected to do in these circumstances.

When the old Colonel died, and they had travelled over to 'Tryst' for the funeral, she almost brought herself to the point of raising the matter with her mother, who did give her some kind of opening just before they parted after the funeral tea. It was not fear or embarrassment that checked her but pride, so that she went home without, she hoped, having betrayed the fact that marriage to Lester

Moncton-Price was a permanent twilight of expectancy, a waiting around for something ill-defined, nebulous, depressing and utterly baffling in every single respect.

3

The climax came one blustery night in late February, about a month after the Colonel's funeral, when the four of them, herself, the old man, Lester and, of course, Ralph Ponsonby, had dined together and later adjourned to the only room in the house with the least pretensions of comfort, the big drawing-room with heavily brocaded curtains and a great open hearth before which Sir Gilbert sat with his board on his bony knees and the little stacks of miniature playing cards that he used for his nonstop games of patience.

Lester and Ponsonby lounged in some thirty minutes later, their faces flushed with the port and brandy they had been guzzling, but soon they excused themselves and went off into the billiards room, where she could hear the monotonous snick of balls whilst she pretended to be engrossed in Surtees' *Jorrocks's Jaunts and Jollities*, one of the few readable books in the musty library at Courtlands.

About ten she said goodnight to Sir Gilbert and went to bed, taking her time about undressing and dawdling in front of the small coal fire, one of the few luxuries she had secured for herself and she was sitting here, her toes on the fender, when she heard a prolonged rustle that seemed to come from behind the wainscoting, left of the fireplace, the side nearest the corridor where it turned a right angle to the stairhead.

She had heard pattering noises there before but had assumed it was caused by mice and there were wainscot mice even at 'Tryst'. This sound, however, was caused by something bulkier than a mouse and she at once thought of rats and moved in stockinged feet a few steps closer to the wall angle, at the same time grasping the heavy brass-handled poker. Rats were unpleasant bedroom companions, but she did not fear them any more than she feared mice. She had often joined Alex and George in a rat-hunt in the stabling area at 'Tryst', and had even killed one on occasion. She meant to kill this

one if she could. It would give her something to do as well as something to talk about in the morning.

With her ear pressed to the panelling, however, she thought she
detected another sound, together with a smell that did not suggest
rats. It was the sound of suppressed breathing and the smell that
came to her, faintly but unmistakably, was that of cigar smoke. After
a moment or so she was quite sure of it, sure enough to cross the room
and put on her bedgown and slippers, but as she groped for the gown
in the dark closet she heard a click and a scurry beyond the door,
as of someone passing swiftly along the corridor towards the stairs.
She went out then but the corridor was dark and she could hear
Ponsonby's high-pitched voice coming from the stairwell, calling
out something to Sir Gilbert. She went back to her room for a candle
and then returned to the spot where the corridor turned, opening
the door of a large broom cupboard and holding the candle high,
the poker still grasped in her right hand. Then she lowered it for
inside there was no mistaking the whiff of tobacco and holding the
candle at floor-level she could see flakes of cigar ash among the handles of the upended brooms. She saw something else too, a small
circle of light in the lowest section of the recess where it sloped away
to meet the crossbeam of the bedroom wall. The light centred on
a very small knothole and by stooping low she found she could see
more than half her room, including the fireplace, the armchair she
had been sitting in and even a pile of underclothes on the chest
beside the bed.

It took a moment or two to absorb the implication of her discoveries. Somebody, certainly a man, had been making a habit of
following her upstairs, crouching in this cupboard with his eye to
the knothole, and watching her undress, and the Peeping Tom could
only be one of three, for whilst it was entirely possible that one or
other of the broken-down old racing men about the house was capable of such an act, none of them would be likely to smoke a cigar
whilst engaged upon it. That left Sir Gilbert, Ralph Ponsonby and
Lester himself.

She went out, closing the door, and returned to her room, sitting
before the fire and forcing her mind to study the problem objectively, as though she was solving someone else's dilemma. She kept
the burning shame and indignity of her discovery at arm's length,

as something not to be contemplated, for she realised now that whoever had used that cupboard on successive nights during the winter
must have seen her mother-naked not once but a score of times. She
thought, with relief, that she had never once used the close stool
they provided, but had preferred to walk the length of the draughty
passage to the huge, high-seated water closet, the only privy that
existed in this primitive house, but it was bad enough to know that
the wretch, whoever he was, had been able to study the most private
areas of her body when she was washing in the footbath. The
thought made her flesh crawl, as though she was being marched
over by an army of bedbugs.

She pondered the suspects one by one. Sir Gilbert? Lester? or that
ever-smiling hanger-on Ralph Ponsonby, and she decided at once
that Ponsonby was the most likely, although she could not be sure.
There was a factor here that made it possible the culprit was Lester.

She concentrated on him first, wondering if there was a link here
with his deliberate avoidance of her, that might be due to a terrible
shyness, camouflaged by truculence. She remembered how unwilling
he was at all times to be left alone in her company. There was something to be said for this theory. It was all of a piece with his baffling
elusiveness, his obvious reluctance to consummate the marriage and,
above all, his near-panic when she had summoned him on the occasion her corset hook caught in the thread and had asked for help.
He had appeared, on that occasion, almost instantaneously, and this
might well mean that he had been concealed in the cupboard when
she called and would assume, for a few seconds at least, that he had
been discovered. All three of them smoked cigars but somehow, although he had the reputation of having been a rakehell in his
younger days, she could not imagine the old man hiding in a broom
cupboard and squinting through a knothole at his nineteen-year-old
daughter-in-law. He would be more likely, she thought, to do something more positive, pinch her behind, perhaps, or convert a paternal
kiss into an embrace, letting his hands stray down the front of her
bodice in the manner of some of the younger men who had embraced
her.

Finally she eliminated him and that left her a choice of two, one
who might prefer spying from ambush rather than taking what he

had a perfect right to take, the other a man capable, she would say, of any small infamy that did not require courage.

It was a delicately poised balance, about fifty-fifty she would say, and she realised then that the identification of Peeping Tom was of terrible importance to her. If it was Lester then one could find, within his odd conduct, reason for hope. At least it showed that he was interested in her as a woman and might, with careful handling, be coaxed to claim his rights as a husband. She wondered wretchedly if she was equipped to perform so delicate a task, regretting that she had not availed herself of all the opportunities she had had of learning more about men. Obviously they were not, as she had assumed, uncomplicated creatures, but could be even more devious than women. She remembered then, with a sudden insight into the sex, whispered talks among the girls at a party she had attended a year or so ago, concerning Mr. Ruskin's recent divorce from the beautiful Effie Gray, who had subsequently married the famous painter, Millais.

She had forgotten the details, unfortunately, but remembered it had something to do with Ruskin's inadequacies as a husband and that Effie had been a virgin after years of marriage. There had been a great deal of giggling concerning this, and the divorce had been a forbidden subject. So proscribed, in fact, that one of her friends, a very forward young lady called Caroline Coutts, had been put across her mother's knee and slippered for daring to mention the subject at the breakfast table.

Perhaps Lester was like Mr. Ruskin? Perhaps he had something wrong with him, an injury from childhood possibly, that made him different from other men, and as she thought this there came to her, unbidden but vaguely welcome, a feeling of compassion for the sulky, elusive, boorish man she had married in such a prodigious hurry. If, indeed, it was Lester who followed her upstairs, then she could find it in her to be sorry for him, although she understood now that it was a situation that would have to be resolved one way or another. She could hardly continue like this, a married woman who was not married, deprived of all prospects of babies, and the companionship of a husband. If, on the other hand, it was Ponsonby who was doing the peeping, then he had put a weapon into her hand that would surely lead to his instant dismissal from the family circle, even if exposure resulted in a scandal. In the meantime she had to be sure and she suddenly saw a way, or fancied she saw a way, to tip the balance one way or the other. She would go down the backstairs, looking in at Lester's room en route to make sure he was not there. If he was then it surely followed that he was the one who had scuttled down the corridor when she had advanced, poker in hand, against the imaginary rat. If he was not then she was still left with the choice of two Peeping Toms and would make an innocent suggestion about putting down rat poison in the stairhead broom cupboard when they were all assembled at breakfast-table. It should be very easy, by studying their expressions, to decide who was the guilty party.

She went out and along the corridor to Lester's room, tapping on the door, getting no response, opening it and glancing inside. He was not there and she felt a slight stab of disappointment, closing the door again and standing, indecisively, at the top of the backstairs. She was still there when she heard the rumble of voices from the kitchen below and it occurred to her then that she might, conceivably, have been mistaken in eliminating the staff, for it was unusual for any of the servants to be up and about in the kitchen quarters at this hour.

Treading very carefully, for the old stairs squeaked abominably, she went on down, pausing at intervals to listen in the hope that she could identify one or other of the voices. At the bottom of the staircase, where a short stone passage led directly to the kitchen, she realised they were not those of the servants but of Lester and Ralph Ponsonby, the former's voice predominating, with only the odd word or two contributed by Ralph.

If it was unusual to find servants in the kitchen after midnight it was even more unusual to discover either one of the menfolk in the rear quarters of the house at night, or indeed at any other time. She knew that they very rarely penetrated there, leaving the entire management of these regions to the slatternly cook, Mrs. Wighouse, and her motley staff of men and boys who had direct access from kitchen to stables.

Standing quite still in the passage she realised that someone was eating at the kitchen table, for she could hear the scrape of knife and fork on pewter and this again struck her as odd, so that she advanced a couple of paces and, holding her breath, stooped and peeped through the giant keyhole. What she saw in the first glance made her gasp, so that instinctively she drew back, pressing herself hard against the stillroom door, her hand to her mouth, her body shaking and quivering.

Ponsonby was seated at the table, demolishing the remains of a cold duck and being waited on by Lester, whose attentions were those of an obsequious servant in that he bobbed and grimaced as he moved to and from the larder with pickles and potato salad and finally, a tankard of ale drawn from the barrel on the lowest of the slate shelves. Ponsonby, she noticed, was entering into the game, if game it was, acting out the part of the master as he flourished his knife and fork in a gesture that was half jocular, half menacing, and whenever he did this Lester cringed and smirked. Then, as he set down the beer mug, Ponsonby did something more positive, grabbing Lester round the waist and pulling him towards him, so that they stood for a moment pressed together, grinning at one another like a couple of sportive Cheshire cats.

The tableau was so bizarre, so out of key with all she knew of both men, that it was then Stella drew back, not knowing what to do yet realising instinctively that to intrude would provoke a scene she would be quite unable to sustain in the presence of Ponsonby. Intense curiosity, however, brought her back to the keyhole almost at once but, although prepared for almost any development, what she saw now had the power to shock her half out of her wits.

Lester had a long sliver of duck protruding from his mouth and as she watched he bent within close range of his friend's face and Ponsonby seized the loose end of the meat in his teeth and began to nibble so that their lips met in a kiss and Lester's hand went round Ponsonby's neck so that they remained in a loose embrace, exactly like a pair of lovers, and unsavoury lovers at that, with that scrap of half-chewed meat linking them.

Suddenly she felt violently sick, pushing herself clear of the door, groping for the handrail of the stairs and somehow negotiating the stairway as far as the closet before she vomited, holding herself half erect, one hand encircling the rusty pipe connecting the closet to the cistern in the loft. What she had witnessed had no precise meaning for her. It was outside the range of her comprehension and yet she knew, somehow, that it represented the end of her involvement with this man, this family, this house, that it was absolutely imperative that she should leave it and them at once, before association with them involved one more night under their roof. She saw, too, dimly but with a curious certitude, that here was the real reason behind her isolation and deprivation, for she was not married to a man at all but to some poor creature who was neither man nor woman but a kind of freak, with tastes and habits that were foreign to every other male she had ever met or heard about.

The prospect of immediate escape braced her, at least momentarily, so that she put off thinking where she might go at this hour of the night and in a raging gale that was shaking the house. She only knew that she must put distance between herself and the two young men downstairs so that she was startled, on entering her room, to find Sir Gilbert sitting in her basket armchair, warming his slippered feet on the hob, just as she had been doing when the scuttle behind the wall launched her on this sickening adventure.

She had entirely forgotten Sir Gilbert but at first it did not seem odd that he should be sitting there in his shirt and breeches, with his cravat removed and his sinewy old throat exposed, his lined face wearing a paternal expression and his silvered hair newly dressed with a pomade that emitted a scent that she associated with lavender soap Phoebe Fraser had introduced into the nursery when she was a child.

His presence there, serene and relaxed, caused her to falter on the threshold, but he rose at once, extending a thin, blue-veined hand as though to welcome and reassure her, and his voice carried reassurance as he said, gently, "My dear . . . you're unwell . . . something you've eaten . . . Take a tot . . ." and he lifted a wine-glass and a bottle of his favourite table wine, producing both as though by magic from somewhere near the fender.

She accepted the wine gratefully and without uttering a word but when she had emptied the glass, and set it down on the night table, she said, in a voice that did not seem to be hers, "I . . . I must go . . . Go home . . . At once! *At once*, you understand?"

He did not seem in the least surprised by the statement but replied, taking her hand, "There now, my dear, don't talk of such things. Give the wine a chance to settle your stomach. Come over here by the fire," and very courteously he made way for her so that her wits, so widely scattered, began to remuster and she looked at him closely for the first time, noticing not only that he was half-undressed but was studying her in a curiously intent manner, as though making some kind of assessment of her panic. She said, stifling a hiccough, "Was it *you* in the cupboard?" and he said, with a look of surprise that was obviously genuine, "In the cupboard? In what cupboard?" and she pointed in the direction of the wainscot so that he rose and went over, his keen eye raking the scarred surface of the panel and coming to rest on the empty knothole that was barely noticeable from this side. He turned then, looking thoughtful but still very composed.

"You heard someone behind there? Is that what made you ill? You were frightened?"

"No," she managed to say. "Not of that . . . something else . . . downstairs in the kitchen."

"Tell me. I'm your friend here. Your only friend."

It was strange, she thought, that he should say that and in that level tone, precisely and carefully as though he had rehearsed it for a week, and her eyes darted about the room, now seeking a means of escape. He noticed the glance and repeated, insistently, "Tell me, my dear. Tell me what frightened you," and when she made no reply, "You heard someone in the cupboard? Well, that's possible. It's what one might expect, I imagine. One of their more extravagant outlets, providing they were well bottled in advance. But I'll put a stop to it. You can be quite sure of that!", and suddenly, to her intense surprise, he raised his clenched fist and struck the panel a violent blow so that it split around the knot and fell inward in two even halves.

"I'll have Danvers replace it in the morning," he added, as though, instead of punching a hole in the wall, he had soiled a table napkin or broken the stem of a wineglass.

She continued to stare at him, waiting for the next sequence in this progressive nightmare and presently it came as he flexed the knuckles of his hand and crossed over to her where she stood with her back to the fire. He said, in the same level tone, "Go to bed. I'll stay with you. You can tell me your story in the morning," and reached out with both hands, grasping her bedgown at the shoulders.

She knew then precisely what he intended and although panic rose in her throat, bringing on another volley of hiccoughs, the prospect did not frighten her in the way that the incident in the kitchen had. For here was something inside the context of her experience, a lecherous but vigorous old man, lusting after a woman young enough to be his grand-daughter but determined, if he could, to demonstrate his vigour in a way that would feed his pride. She understood too that she was cornered and could look for no rescue from the two men downstairs, and also that, unless she kept her nerve, and temporised whilst her mind explored the chances of tumbling into her clothes and slipping down into the hall, she was lost, cut off for all time from the safe, familiar world outside where she might, in years to come, succeed in persuading herself that everything that happened here tonight was part of a confused dream.

She said, clutching her gown about her, "You shouldn't be here . . . I'm not frightened now . . . it was just . . ." but then his expression changed, and he looked at her bleakly, saying, "I can guess what you saw, child. You don't imagine I'm unaware of that relationship do you? That's *why* I'm here. I should have made it my business to tell you long ago. But it needn't matter, I can assure you of that."

She managed to say, "But *why*? Why did he marry me?" and at that he laughed, saying, "Well, that's a tomfool question, I must say. You brought him a thousand a year, didn't you?"

"But I couldn't stay now. There wouldn't be any difficulty about the money if I explained . . ."

"Explained? To whom? To your father, so that it became gossip in all the Cheapside coffee houses? To your mother, who would relay it to every tittle-tattling woman within twenty miles of your home? Do you *want* that kind of scandal? Do you *want* every thruster in the West Kent hunt tittering every time you appear at a meet or a steeplechase? No, my dear. There's a simpler way than that. We go our path and they go theirs and no one a penny the wiser."

She looked at him with a kind of wonder. "*We*? You and me? You mean Lester would agree to that?"

"Why the devil not? He isn't in the least interested in you as a wife, and only as a woman so long as he can snigger about you with that lover of his. They see *you* as a freak. As the bearded lady at a fairground booth, if you like. Don't you understand even now

what they've been about, pushing one another into that cupboard
and taking turns at the peephole?"

"You mean Ponsonby is a . . . a . . . kind of wife? That he'll
always be here?"

"He or someone like him. You can never tell with a relationship
of that kind. It might go on for years. It might end in a woman's
quarrel, in screams and accusations and even violence of one kind
or another. He's Stukeley blood, piss-thin this side of the country.
Stukeley and Everard on his mother's side, God rot her, for bringing me such a brat! However, it's not past mending. You could manage something better I'll warrant," and he reached out again, his
arm encircling her waist.

She knew then that her only hope was to play for time. A few
minutes would do, enough to hustle into a few clothes and run.
Run anywhere. Out into the dark and wind, where they couldn't
find her and drag her back to make her choice between living out
her life with a wretch who preferred fondling a man, and took his
pleasure in a woman through a chink in a broom cupboard, or being
seduced by this pomaded old roué, who seemed long ago to have
made up his mind to get an heir from her, as though she was one
of his fillies brought to stud. She said, trying with all her might to
keep her voice steady, "You would be kind to me? You'd drive that
man Ponsonby out of the house?"

He looked at her speculatively. "I'd be kind, yes. You could have
anything you fancied providing you were a sensible gel. Lester
would have to stay on for appearances' sake, and it could take time
to prise Ponsonby loose. Might be done tho'. We should begin casting
around for a substitute, someone more manageable, a stableboy possibly, someone who could keep his mouth shut."

"Get rid of them now, then. Get them clear of here for a spell
. . . for an hour or so . . . while . . . while you're here. Invent something. Say there was trouble in the stables. For I couldn't stay here
another minute if I thought there was the least prospect of their
spying on us . . . if they weren't at a safe distance this first time, you
understand?"

He seemed to consider this a long time, finding it extravagant
but perhaps understandable in view of the shocks she had suffered
in the last hour. Finally he said, with a sigh, "Very well, if that's

what you want. I'll go down and turn one of the mares loose and start a hullabaloo. It's a wild enough night to set a door swinging," and he smiled, as though relishing the hoax. "But I make conditions too. As proof of the bargain do something for me. A very small thing. Take off those things and warm the bed, for I won't be gone more than ten minutes."

She knew there was no alternative yet the effort of parting with her gown and nightdress was more than she could manage, so that she remained standing against the night table, her hands clutching the quilted material of the gown. He said, very sharply, "Come now! They've looked you over times enough, damn them. Why should I be denied the pleasure?" and at that she shrugged herself out of the gown and let it fall, kicking off her slippers, loosening the neck ribbon of her nightdress and turning her back on him as she pulled it over her head.

She could feel his glance playing over her, all the way from her plaited hair to her heels, and again she felt the terrible flesh-crawling sensation she had experienced in the cupboard. He said, hoarsely, "Don't be shy, my dear. I've seen a thousand women in my time but none prettier than you. Turn around. You shouldn't be ashamed of a body like that," and she turned, her hands drooping at her sides, her eyes on the threadbare patch of the stained strip of carpet beside the bed.

She expected then that he would seize her but he did no more than look her over, much as she had seen him look at a new horse brought in by one of the many nagsmen he dealt with. Finally he got up, patted her shoulder and moved across the room, saying, "Don't worry if you hear shouting and running about. I'll be back in a few minutes," and she heard him turn into the corridor and stalk towards the backstairs with firm strides.

It took her less than a minute to scramble into her shift, drawers, dress, stockings and boots. She did not bother with her corset but stumbled over to the closet, wrenched it open and grabbed a riding-cloak lined with heavy, waterproofed material. Then, no more than seventy seconds after she had heard his step descending the back-stairs, she flitted out into the corridor and along it to the head of the main staircase that led directly into the great, draughtswept hall where a single oil-lamp burned on a half-round table just inside the great door, with its complicated array of locks and bolts, as formidable as the fastenings of a gaol.

She had no intention of wrestling with them but ran down the stairway and into the big drawing-room, where tall French windows gave on to the flagged terrace overlooking the lawn. The bolts on the windows were stiff and rusty, like every other piece of metal-work in the house, so that she broke a nail drawing them from their sockets but the air that rushed in when the wind caught the frame and flung it back on its hinges was as exhilarating as the first gulp of air sucked down on surfacing after swimming underwater in the pool above the islet at 'Tryst'. She went out into the blackness, groping her way to the balustrade and then, turning hard left, moving its full length to the door in the brick wall that led into the greenhouse and beyond that to the kitchen garden. By the time she had reached the five-barred gate opening on to the lane her eyes had grown sufficiently accustomed to the darkness to make her way without stumbling but the wind tore at her hair and cloak, blinding her with its folds so that she had to tug them free to see the surface of the lane and fight her way down to the open ground where the road passed about a quarter-mile east of Courtlands.

For some time, for the better part of an hour it might have been, she battled along mindlessly, unable to accept the reality of her escape. It was only when she paused, gasping, in the lee of a Dutch barn short of a village, that she was able to form some coherent pattern of flight, her intimate knowledge of the paths, bypaths, and gaps around here coming to her aid, and her instinct as a horse-woman telling her to keep the south-westerly at her back in order to head east over the crown of the moor, down through Bletchley Green and over the watersplash at Cooper's Corner, where the tor-rent rose to her thighs before she reached higher ground and found the dust road that wound south-east between clumps of wind-whipped larch and spruce.

With the wind to boost her along she moved at five miles an hour, despite the darkness and intermittent slashes of rain. Then the weather began to moderate a little and she wondered whether she was far enough on her road to find a sheltered place to hide and catch her breath but thought better of it and pressed on until her head spun and her feet began to play her false, so that she thought,

"I got away from them but I shall die out here, sure enough, and somebody will find me in a ditch when it's light and wonder how I came to be there . . ." But the prospect of dying out on the high-road, like a used-up tramp, did not strike her as so bizarre as that nibbling exchange between Lester and Ralph Ponsonby, or the determination of that scented old reprobate to take his son's place in her bed in order to ensure the continuity of the Moncton-Prices. It did not seem to matter now what happened to a body that had been so defiled and she could even feel a spurt of malice at the manner in which she had tricked the old roué, who would doubtless be hunting for her high and low when he found those French windows banging in the drawing-room and guessed she had escaped.

It was about then she saw the light, a yellowish speck that glowed, went dim, and glowed again over on the crest of a field to her right. Instinctively she made for it, turning off the road to cross a hundred and one furrows of heavy clay that plucked at her boots and caused her to stumble half-a-dozen times, so that she was soon plastered with mud, her cloak and dress heavy with the stuff. But little by little the speck of light enlarged itself and presently she saw that it was a lantern swinging over the entrance of a doorless hut on the edge of a copse crowning the field.

She called then, shouting into the wind, and the light was momentarily obscured by the passage of a figure who advanced down the last few yards of the field towards her, calling out something she could not understand. Then she fell flat yet again and felt herself lifted as easily as if she had been a shopping basket but after that there was no sequence to events, for images came and went, caught up in a tumult of wind and whirled away over the tossing trees of the copse. She identified the figure as Denzil Fawcett, the farmer's son from Dewponds, when they were less than a mile from home and was able to answer some of his questions, but very impatiently for she had an overwhelming desire to escape into sleep and never wake again, for her mind was more exhausted than her body so that she would not have objected to sharing a bed with a dozen old men so long as she could stretch her limbs, get warm and feel a pillow under her head.

She had a confused impression of stumbling along, supported by Denzil and after that standing mute in a small circle of bustling women, who spooned broth into her and began peeling off her clothes and rubbing her with a rough towel, but after that came a moment of triumph for she was inside the warm bed with a soft pillow and the sound of the wind was muted and finally heard no more.

4

Henrietta as Bailiff's Man

THERE was time to ponder her strategy during the longish jogtrot
through the maze of intersecting country roads that retraced, in a
westerly direction, the route Stella had travelled in the wind and
darkness twelve hours before.

As to tactics, she had, in reserve, Denzil Fawcett in the driving
seat, and his presence, although glum and uncommunicative, indicated in some way that he was hoping to exploit his entirely unforeseen advantage and this made him a useful ally. She sensed this
from the first, and that was one reason why she had invited him
to help her resolve this highly unsavoury business after Stella had
awakened to find her mother sitting at her bedside, sympathetic
but as relentless in her catechism as a New Scotland Yard detective
extracting a deathbed confession from a felon.

It had not been easy to assemble the minimum information needed
for a confrontation of the kind she had in mind but Henrietta,
having decided that her life would need a great deal of unravelling,
persisted and as the story unfolded she was astounded, not so much
by Stella's blindness but by her own and Adam's in allowing the
wretched girl to expose herself to such dreadful risks and humiliations.

True, she had never much cared for a match based on hard cash
and an admitted hoist up the social ladder, had never looked with
favour on that sulky-mouthed Lester, or his rackety old father, but
it had never occurred to her that the son might be thoroughly vicious,
or the father a wicked old satyr, of the kind one might meet in a
German fairy-tale featuring ogres who breakfasted on children.
Shame, dismay and rage succeeded one another as the girl's broken
sentences acquainted her, piecemeal, with the facts but it was the
climax that shocked her beyond belief, for she realised that, but
for good luck, and a display of hardihood and desperation on Stella's

part, the Swanns of 'Tryst' might well have been saddled with a grandson begotten by that old rake in circumstances that were too disgusting to be contemplated.

It was this, above all, that made her resolve to deal with the situation personally, without waiting for consultation with Adam or Lawyer Stock, who handled all their legal affairs. For here, surely, was something that had to be settled at once and with finality, for she made up her mind on the spot that nothing—*nothing*—would induce her to sanction the return of the girl to that house of infamy. Simultaneously she made up her mind about something else. Somehow Stella's tracks would have to be obliterated, if only to avoid a scandal that would drag the family's name through acres of filth and bid fair, if it got abroad, to damage the business. This meant that under no circumstances should Stella return home, where, as like as not, that old devil or his son would come seeking her within hours, primed with some cock and bull story of hysteria on the girl's part, that had sent her flying into the night like a mad woman, babbling a story that no one was likely to believe.

Yet Henrietta believed it, every single word of it, although she did not make the mistake of confiding more than was absolutely necessary to the Fawcetts, merely hinting that Stella had been cruelly served by the Moncton-Prices, father and son, and that she was resolved to take what steps she could towards achieving a permanent separation. She did not say upon what grounds, reasoning that a bucolic family like the Fawcetts would be unlikely to know how the quality went about annulling their failed marriages. She did ask, however, for the loan of the Fawcetts' trap, and for Denzil's services as escort, saying that a man of Sir Gilbert's temperament was likely to be offensive and obstructive when she called for her daughter's belongings.

She told Denzil rather more, saying that she intended to whisk the fugitive clear out of the county and hide her where her husband and father-in-law would be unlikely to find her. And as anticipated she found him a willing ally, prepared to involve himself further by escorting Stella all the way to the Midlands, where Henrietta had decided she could find a safe, if temporary, refuge with Edith Wickstead, former vicereine of the Swann territories in the eastern counties and wife of the present manager, Tom Wickstead, one of her husband's most reliable lieutenants.

Her mind flew to Edith instinctively. Long ago, before she had even met the woman, Edith Wickstead, then Edith Wadsworth, had been madly in love with Adam and had admitted as much when challenged by Henrietta at the time of the Staplehurst train crash. But despite this, or possibly because of it, the two women had become very close friends during the crisis period and now Edith was safely married to that merry-hearted, black-eyed Tom Wickstead and had three children and a pretty home in the wooded area between Peterborough and Oundle. It would not be necessary to do more than telegraph in advance, asking for hospitality for a week or so, and Edith was perhaps the only person in the world whom Henrietta could confide a matter of this delicacy.

The wire and following letter could wait. Her first priority, as she saw it, was to head off any possible attempt on the part of the Moncton-Prices to enforce the return of her daughter. With this intention uppermost in her mind she ordered Denzil Fawcett to harness his trap for a drive to Courtlands that same afternoon. Stella, he assured her, was welcome to stay at the farm for as long as she wished, and he told her privately, as he was harnessing up, that his father had ordered the family to say nothing concerning her presence there. As regards this, he added, they were lucky. His father had had unsatisfactory dealings with the Moncton-Prices over horses, and had long since formed the opinion that they were gentlefolk in name only. They had not only cheated him but insulted him into the bargain and Fawcett senior, a dour, unforgiving man, of strong Methodist persuasions, disapproved of them root and branch.

Reassured on this point Henrietta set out in the Fawcett trap, having dispatched a message to 'Tryst' by one of the farm lads to the effect that she was dealing with unexpected business on her husband's behalf, and was unlikely to be home before dusk.

*   *   *

He said little as they jogged along and Henrietta, for her part, was glad of it, for her mind was in a turmoil from which only one hard line resolution emerged. Sir Gilbert Moncton-Price was to be confronted and no promises made to bring about Stella's restoration to her husband. For the rest she would have to rely on her wits and, if necessary, on bluff.

They had covered perhaps two-thirds of the distance before Denzil voiced the thought uppermost in his mind.

"What's to become of her, ma'am? Suppose he claims her in a court o' law? He could, couldn't he? Wouldn't she be forced to go back there, and be whipped by that brute she married? I've heard of such cases, and if it happened I'll make no bones about telling you what I'd do if I came to hear of it. I'd break his damned jaw, and that's a fact. Aye, an' wring his neck too, if I had to!"

"You can leave threats to me," she told him, with an approving sidelong glance at his heavy, glowering face. "Meantime you'll be pleased to give me your promise to remain outside with the trap while I go in for her things. This is a matter for lawyers, Denzil. You've already done us all a better service than we've a right to expect."

He said, scowling, "I done nothing, Mrs. Swann. Or nothing I woulden do fer any decent young woman, lost in open country of a night. But there's nothing I woulden do for Miss Stella." He paused for a moment before adding, unhappily, "Can't never think of her as Mrs. Moncton-Price. Or Lady Moncton-Price or whatever it's proper to call her now."

"Well, we think alike in that respect," said Henrietta, grimly, "and she'll not be that much longer if I have anything to say in it."

She noticed then that he seemed to cheer up as he said, passing his horny hand over his brow, "Can you . . . well . . . cancel *out* a marriage? I mean, without one party taking it into their heads to get clean out o' the country, along o' someone else?"

"I'm told that it can be done," Henrietta replied, and left it at that but he was obviously exploring a variety of eventualities and behind them all, buried in a fog of uncertainty, was a tiny flame of hope. Hope of that kind, she supposed, never really died and after all why should it in his case? Stella, in a moment of mischief, had once blown upon the tiny spark, making it glow a little.

She said, carefully, "Will your family think it a scandal, you travelling with her to Peterborough? I'd take her myself, of course, but that might put the Moncton-Prices on her track," and he replied, staring straight at her like a great, moonstruck ox, "Me? I'd take her to Timbuctu if need be. Not that it'd advance me in her eyes, but then, I woulden expect that. Me and Miss Stella, it was all . . . well . . . something I liked to think on when I was going about the work. You woulden ever tell her what I told you, back at the big house, ma'am?"

"No," Henrietta said, "or not without your permission," and then, responding to a stab of irritation that a man as huge and loyal and capable as Denzil Fawcett should be at the mercy of a silly girl's caprices, "I'll tell you what I think, Denzil, and it's something else that will remain a secret between us. I wish she had taken it into her stupid head to run off with somebody like you and it's not the first time I've thought it."

To her surprise the statement did not embarrass him but rather the opposite, restoring to him something of a countryman's pride. He braced his wide shoulders, flicked his whip, and said, stubbornly, "At least I'd ha' taken good care of her. She wouldn't have had to run from *me* in the middle o' the night! Will she ever get over what happened to her over there?"

It seemed to indicate, she thought, that he was not quite so bucolic as he looked, and might well have been putting two and two together, distilling something approximating the truth from Stella's talk on the way from his spinney to the farm. She said judiciously, having decided to take one fence at a time, "She's young, Denzil, and the young can put most things behind them. She'll soon be herself, providing that I can get it into her head that she won't have to return there."

"Ah," he said, guardedly, "but Mr. Swann might take a diff'rent view," and she replied, sharply, "In matters of this kind Mr. Swann will take my advice!" and it seemed to comfort him.

They turned in at the drive about four in the afternoon and the forecourt of the long, rambling house seemed deserted. She told Denzil to wait under the stable arch and got down, returning to the front of the building, climbing the four steps and giving the bell pull a resolute tug. The bell did not seem to work, so she rapped defiantly on the door with her umbrella handle and continued hammering until the door was opened by a shambling old servitor, who asked her, none too civilly, whom she sought. She thought, "This place is a ruin, lived in by creatures who belong on a race-track rather

than in a respectable household", and once again it occurred to her
that Adam's habitual judgement must have deserted him altogether
when he capitulated to Stella's importunities to become Mrs.
Moncton-Price.

"Who do you suppose I'm here to see?" she demanded, tartly. "Not
you or one of the stablemen. Tell Sir Gilbert Mrs. Swann is here,
and wishes to speak to him at once!" and she pushed past him and
swept into the hall, taking a seat on a worm-eaten stool that stood
there, very insecurely she thought, like the rest of the fittings and
furnishings she could see.

The man mumbled something and wandered off. Left to herself
she sniffed the air, wrinkling her nostrils with distaste. "There's
damp rot hereabouts unless I'm mistaken," she said aloud, and the
sound of her voice was like a whistle in the dark. Her resolution
faltered a little, however, when the man returned with the old villain
in his wake. She gave him a swift, interrogatory glance, deciding
at once that he was unlikely to show the least embarrassment at
meeting her and would almost surely exchange bluff for bluff when
confronted with his villainy. He seemed outwardly courteous,
however, for he said, with a small bow, "My respects, Mrs. Swann.
We'll go into the drawing-room. Will you take tea with me?"

His cool impudence took her breath away but she replied, quickly,
"No tea, thank you. I've a trap waiting and I shan't keep you long,"
and he said, with the ghost of a smile, "At your service, ma'am,"
and then motioned her into a big room with French windows, the
windows, no doubt, from which Stella made her escape.

There seemed no profit in bandying words with him so she said,
as soon as the servant had closed the door behind him, "It won't
surprise you to learn I've come for my daughter's things. Not all of
them, of course. I'll make do with some of her clothes and necessi-
ties so have somebody pack them. The rest can be sent on later."

His pepper and salt eyebrows rose an inch as he said, "She arrived home safely? I'm glad to hear of it. I wasn't deeply concerned,
except for her foolhardiness. A lass who can sit a horse as she can
would be likely to know every gatepost between here and Twyforde
Green, by dark or daylight. Did she explain her extraordinary conduct?"

She could have fallen on him then with her umbrella. In a way he was already putting the onus of this ridiculous situation upon her. She had expected extreme truculence, icy politeness, violent abuse even, but not a mixture of irony and forbearance from a man who, twelve hours before, had plotted to deflower his own daughter-in-law. For a split second, no more, she questioned the truth of Stella's rambling story but then her mind cleared and she realised he had had plenty of time to rehearse his approach, and had probably coached his son into the bargain. She said, flatly, "Of course you'll deny everything. You would have to. Anybody would, unless he was mad as well as unspeakably vile! Ring for somebody to get me those things . . ."

But he interrupted her, saying, very reasonably, "Come, don't be in such a hurry, Mrs. Swann. I haven't the least idea what your daughter told you concerning that silly escapade of hers and you don't have to confide in me unless you wish. All I'm concerned with is that she should return here before tittle-tattle gets about. That won't serve your family or mine, Mrs. Swann. You surely agree with me as to that."

She realised then that her position was not quite as strong as she had assumed it to be. The bare bones of Stella's story concerning both him and his son were barely credible to anybody who had had a Christian upbringing and had been raised, moreover, in the south country, where life was softer and more civilised than in her native north. On the other hand there seemed no other course but to lay down her entire hand, and let him make what he could of it.

She said, clasping her hands on her lap, as though to prevent them doing violence on him, "See here, Sir Gilbert, there isn't going to be a scandal if I can help it, but that doesn't mean I'm prepared to expose my daughter to the risks any decent girl would run in your house and company. As to getting her back here, you can put that out of mind. Before we let that happen my husband would fight you and yours through every court in the land, and I dare say we should come out of it with less mud on our backs than you or your precious son— She's *never* coming back, you understand? *Never*. I haven't digested everything she told me, for much of it seems to me as dirty a story as one would be likely to hear outside of a brothel. But I've heard sufficient, and *believe* sufficient, to understand this marriage never was a marriage, and the law has a way of meeting that contingency. Or so my attorney assures me!"

She was relieved to note, in the blankness of the expression his seamed old face at once assumed, that she had rattled him, and went on, more confidently, "You see, Sir Gilbert, you've taken altogether too much for granted about us—my husband and me, that is. He's well known and well respected in the city, whereas I'm not the ninny most women of my kind are, or like to pretend they are. I was brought up in a mill town thirty years ago, when things were far rougher than they are today. Neither am I the kind of person to be imposed upon, for ever since I married Mr. Swann he's encouraged me to look things in the face, and call a spade a spade when necessary. That girl of mine isn't going to drag out her life tied to a man who isn't fit to be anybody's husband. Neither is she going to be at your disposal as a brood mare. You talk of scandal. Well, nobody wants it, and everyone in our position hopes to avoid it, but there are limits to the price one is prepared to pay for hushing things up. Your price is far too high. You follow me so far, I hope?"

"Perfectly," he said, and although she could not have sworn it there was respect in his voice. "There is one aspect, however, that you appear to have overlooked. Would anyone believe a story like that without proof?"

"The latter part of it? Perhaps not, for it's hard to believe any man who sits on a magisterial bench would seduce his nineteen-year-old daughter-in-law. They would have to believe, however, that my daughter was still a virgin and that after more than six months as your son's wife. That would go some way, I think, towards getting her an annulment."

He seemed to consider this a long time. Sitting there, with the sour whiff of damp rot in her nose, Henrietta began to wilt a little but she hoped she did not betray it and waited patiently until he said, reaching over her shoulder for the bell-cord, "You're a remarkable woman, Mrs. Swann. Quite remarkable, if I may say so. Very well, I won't fight, providing the case is handled with discretion and that can be done with your husband's kind of money. Just keep my name out of it, that's all I ask. For if you don't I'll hit back at you somehow, you can depend upon it. It's bad enough being saddled with a son like mine, without having to pull his damned chestnuts out of the fire in public. I'll send the rest of her things over by carrier, unless your husband would prefer fetching them in one of his . . . er . . . carts!"

He could not have said anything more calculated to make her master her nervousness, or add fuel to her extreme indignation. A tradesman's daughter herself she had always taken pride in the name of the man she had married, a name, she calculated, that was not only more honourable than his, but went back a good deal further into the social roots of the nation. She stood up, meeting his bland stare unflinchingly and saying, "I don't think you're in any kind of position to insult us, Sir Gilbert. My husband's in trade now but neither one of us has to apologise for that. Our money comes to us honestly, hauling goods about the country. Your kind live off the poor, generation by generation, without putting a penny piece back into the country. How did you come by this house, I wonder? Not by hard work, certainly. More probably by shipping negroes to the plantations. Or by taking the winning side in some quarrel between two sets of thoroughgoing rascals centuries ago! Maybe that's why you think you can treat everybody but your own kind as if they were animals. Maybe that's why you produce children who can't even reproduce themselves, something any peasant in the land can do without much difficulty. I'll tell you something else while I'm here. I never did like the idea of having grandchildren derived from your kind of stock and opposed it from the start. Well now, praise God, it can't happen, and I'd see my daughter dead before I gave you a chance to alter that. Either you get those things or I walk through this ratty old house and help myself. And if you or any of those broken-down old wretches of yours try and stop me I'll bring charges against you for common assault. And don't think I couldn't either. There's a young man awaiting me outside who could break everyone's head in this place and would take pleasure in doing it at a word from me."

His expression had not changed, or not much. He was still looking at her now with a curious intentness, his bloodless lips creased in a half-smile. Then, quite suddenly, his frame lost its rigidity and he looked, she thought, incredibly old and tired, as though all his years of dissipation had caught up with him in a single moment, causing him to lose interest in the game he had been playing with her up to that moment. He approached the bell-rope with queer, shuffling steps and tugged it half a dozen times. She heard a cracked bell echo somewhere in the house as he went towards the door and threw it open.

"Danvers will get your daughter's trunk," he said, as the old man came hobbling to answer the summons. "You there—" he addressed the old ruin as though he were a dog "—take Sopworth up to Madam's room and tell her to pack what she finds in a bag and bring it out to the forecourt." The old man nodded and disappeared again and for a moment Henrietta thought he would follow and took a step towards the main door but he hurried past her to open it, holding up his free hand in an arresting motion, so that she paused near the threshold.

"I said it once and I'll say it again," he said, getting hold of himself, so that his bearing was now that of a stiff, rather courteous old man, showing a guest to her carriage. "You're a remarkable woman, Mrs. Swann, and a credit to that husband of yours. You're right about one thing but wrong about another. We did make a fortune in the slave trade, but there was a time when my side of the family was capable of breeding women with your kind of sparkle. We lost the knack, somehow, inbreeding with the wrong sort. You'd show more care with horse-flesh, unless you wanted a string that looked well in the paddock but couldn't last the distance, or fell at the first fence. For all that I meant what I said about hitting back at you if you cause a stir. I've got my pride too, or what's left of it," and he nodded briefly and turned away, leaving her to descend the steps and cross the forecourt to the trap. A few minutes later the old servitor Danvers came out carrying a pigskin holdall and Stella's reticule, that he placed in the back, whereupon Henrietta said, "That's all, Denzil. Drive me home, please," and was ashamed to realise that she was trembling so violently that he must have noticed her extreme agitation although he had the sense not to comment on it.

They were more than a mile away, descending the dip to the watersplash before she spoke again, saying, between her teeth, "Don't lose touch with me, Denzil. And don't continue to think of yourself as something beneath my daughter's notice. You aren't and won't ever be. It's all a question of time, you see. Families like ours and his go up and come down, sometimes in a generation. Maybe your turn is out ahead."

2

The two letters were lying on a silver tray on the side table when she let herself in. A bulky package, with coarse, travel stained wrappings, and a smaller, thinner letter, sealed with a thumb print impressed on red wax. She knew at once that the fat letter was from Alex and her heart, that seemed almost to have stopped beating after the terrible pounding it had taken during the day, gave a great, joyful leap as she shut the door on the darkness and carried the letter into her sewing-room, without bothering to ring for the tea she so badly needed.

Her hands shook so much that she had the greatest difficulty in removing the complicated wrappings but she got them off at last and found a much-folded newspaper, printed in coarse, heavy type and inside its folds a five-page letter from Alexander, headed, 'January 29th, Durban'.

She turned up the lamp and let her eyes run swiftly over the lines of sloping, boyish handwriting, absorbing the general drift of the letter before going back to the start and reading each successive sentence, word by word.

Its gusto, lightly camouflaged under a deliberately laconic style, took her breath away, so that for a moment she completely forgot where she was and joined him in his stupendous adventure thousands of miles away, spurring with him down the hillside with twenty thousand savages at her heels, swept along in the flight of a disintegrating army and then riding pillion with him on that hell-for-leather gallop for the river. Some of the episodes he recounted seemed familiar—that bit about the two young officers who had saved the colours for instance—and she had to think a moment before remembering that there had been a piece describing this single cheerful aspect of the lost field in the *Pall Mall Gazette* only a few days ago. The realisation that her flesh and blood had actually witnessed

it acted upon her like a powerful stimulant and she read on, to learn
how he had found his way along the river to a place called Rorke's
Drift, a name that already wore the halo of battles like Blenheim
and Waterloo, so that the awful disaster preceding it was automatically downgraded to the status of a skirmish. Then, with rapt attention, she read of his part in that battle and how, when the Zulus
had been driven off, he had gone down to the charred building to
meet its defenders, including the famous Lieutenants, Chard and
Bromhead, and how Lord Chelmsford's relieving force had appeared
that same day and Alex, along with other survivors, had been sent
back to the coast to form the nucleus of a new army for the protection of the colony.

He was likely to remain there, it seemed, until reinforcements
arrived and the Zulus were called to account, and learning this she
felt relieved. It must mean that he would be denied any more blood-
curdling adventures, at least for the time being. Then she readdressed herself to the lengthy postscript, written, it seemed, just
before he got the letter aboard a fast packet-boat for England. It
puzzled her at first, for it did not seem to have been written by the
boy she remembered, a lad who had never had the capacity to look
inward like his father or young Giles, and yet was able to tell her
precisely how he regarded his miraculous escape. He had added,
in pencil, "I don't mind admitting there were times when I thought
myself an idiot to have let myself be drawn into a thing like this,
especially when I was hiding among the rocks and watching the
battle for the mission house. But things looked different in the morning, with the Zulus all gone, and that splendid chap Chard counting
the dead and rebuilding the barricades in case Lord Chelmsford
didn't show up. He didn't seem to think he had done anything very
remarkable, fighting off that horde with less than a hundred men at
his back, but everyone here regards him as a real hero, and so do I,
for he's helped me make up my mind on one thing. I mean to go
through with it. I can't imagine settling to anything less after this
and wondered if you could estimate my chances of getting into a
decent regiment, where chaps don't run away like my lot did, and
like I did until I saw what could be done with a few trained men and
a chap like Chard to lead them. In short, sir, it's the Queen's shilling
for me from here on, but I shall, of course, have to see this through

to the end until Cetywayo's kraal goes up in smoke, and those beefy lads of his dip their plumes to us. You can write care of 'Post Restante, Durban,' and letters will find me, but now, as you can imagine after such a drubbing, we shall be at sixes and sevens until reinforcements arrive. Your loving son, Alexander."

There was, of course, the inevitable P.P.S. It read: "The newspaper enclosing this letter is a Durban account of both affairs, garbled but true in substance. Post it on to old George and get him to hand it on to Jumbo Bellchamber as a change from cramming for F.O. exams, poor beggar."

She knew him well enough to read more into the letter than he had intended. He had been scared, very badly scared, but the events of the day had predisposed her in favour of people scouting around for enough courage to keep them at their posts, and anyway, being Alex, he was over it now, and looking ahead to the next fence. She smiled the secret smile reserved for all male vanities and opened the slim letter, overlooked in her brush with the Zulus, seeing that it was only the usual Sunday-duty-scrawl from Giles who, as the younger of the Swanns at Mellingham, was now saddled with the job of writing the compulsory bulletin to his parents.

They had told her that new boys' duty letters were censored by the house-captain or a junior master, presumably to prevent the spread of despondency, common among first and second termers. The final paragraph of this one indicated that Giles had taken artful precautions against the censors. After half a sheet of well-spaced gossip concerning games and health, he had written; "I am looking forward to the Easter break, Mamma, but it will be strange to be home with grandfather not there." Then followed the piece in code, concerning matters he would not want generally known; "I miss you all very much on Sundays, when we aren't kept so busy with prep, games and fagging. And that reminds me to tell you I am not fagging for George's friend, Smithers, as I had expected this term. Another new boy called Burke (I think I told you about him) very much wanted me to exchange and I did because his fag-master, Gifford, left last half. I now fag for Quentin, a cricket-colour who has promised to coach me at wicketkeeping when summer half comes round. That's all the news. Your very loving son, Giles."

In their first, hard-driven years away from home both Alexander and George had sprinkled their duty letters with comments on schoolfellows whose names meant nothing to her, but these names did. They also made his letter more revealing, and infinitely more poignant than Alexander's dramatic dispatch. She remembered Smithers as one of George's closest friends and on this account unlikely to use Giles harshly. She remembered too that Burke had been a very timid boy, scared half out of his wits during his first term. It was demonstrably clear what had happened. Giles, a candidate for martyrdom if ever there was one, had moved over on Burke's behalf, and prevailed upon his elder brother to keep an eye on the poor little toad.

The letter made her reflect, for a moment, on the tyranny of men's schools that all males, Giles included, were at such pains to defend. It also reminded her of her resolve to talk Adam into making that change she had been contemplating before Stella's trouble had driven everything else out of her head. She wondered how many years would have to pass before she could resign her position as caretaker of the family, reckoning it at about fifteen, the period that would elapse before baby Edward was as old as George, but then, recollecting Stella's troubles, she did her sum again, concluding that her stewardship was more likely to last a lifetime. One or other of them would always stand in need of her, whether or not they were prepared to admit it. In most marriages, she supposed, the protective role would be that of father and husband. In others it would be shared. In her case it was an exclusively maternal responsibility, for Adam's real children, although sporting the Swann insignia everywhere they went, did not reside at 'Tryst' but were scattered all over the islands. She was considering whether she resented this or whether, deep down, she enjoyed the responsibility, when Phoebe Fraser, the Scots governess, appeared with tea and crumpets, listening gravely to the account of Alexander's adventures. She did not pry, thank God, into what her mistress had been about all day. There had been times when Henrietta (who liked a gossip when Adam was away) had resented Phoebe's Lowland dourness but today she welcomed it. Phoebe, a strict Calvinist, would be unlikely to take an objective view of Stella's flight unless, of course, the reasons were explained to her. And there could be no question of that.

Phoebe said, unsentimentally, "Well, it's a relief to learn the laddie is sound in wind and limb after all we've read about in the papers," and then, dismissing the Zulu war as an irrelevancy, "The younger bairns will soon be awa' to their beds. Will you go up and bid them goodnight?"

No, Henrietta said, she would not for she had had a very exacting day and was quite tired out. In her absence, however, Phoebe could read them their brother's letter for that would give them plenty to talk about among themselves. Phoebe took the letter and went, leaving her mistress to luxuriate before the sewing-room fire and dispose of four butter-soaked muffins before recollecting one small duty remained before she could put her feet up, read a chapter of *Silas Marner* and make an early night of it.

She went over to her little bureau, took a sheet of notepaper and wrote to Adam's head clerk, Tybalt, the only man in the world who could be relied upon to know where her husband was at any given moment. She wrote,

"Dear Mr. Tybalt, You would oblige me by sending this telegram to Mr. Swann *at once*. Certain urgent matters require his attention in Kent. Thanking you, Henrietta Swann." Then, before sealing it, she took a plain sheet of paper and wrote, "Come home wherever you are stop Alex safe stop Other matters requiring urgent attention stop Love Henrietta."

She smiled as she licked the envelope. It occurred to her that she had just struck two telling blows against the towering edifice of male complacency. Tybalt would lay awake half the night wondering what could possibly have gone adrift in the Kentish Triangle, and why Godsall, the manager there, had consulted Mrs. Swann instead of himself. Adam, the moment the telegram reached him, would be obliged to occupy the journey homewards making even wilder guesses at the nature of the domestic crisis.

There was no malice in Henrietta Swann but there was still, for all her thirty-eight years, a great deal of mischief and it crossed her mind as she gave Stillman, the handyman, the letter to post, that she had earned this little indulgence in the twelve hours that had elapsed since Denzil Fawcett had appeared at the kitchen door.

5

Swann Priorities

No prosperous farmer, riding his acres towards harvest time and contemplating his million stalks of wheat and barley could have derived more satisfaction from the survey than Adam Swann, making one of his periodical tours of what he sometimes called his 'snug parcels of British commerce'.

It was always a critical, self-congratulatory progress, as though he had been a master painter of vast, historical canvasses standing off a yard or two, adding a touch here, erasing a smudge there, and whilst there were times when a close inspection vexed him these moments of irritation were soon engulfed in a tide of complacency as he reminded himself that the entire enterprise had been conjured out of a single will in what was (if one thought in terms of history) no more than a moment of time.

Here, in the far-flung outposts of his personal empire, was all the evidence of his initiative and imagination, his flair for picking subordinates who shared (or so he would remind himself) his breadth of vision and power to adapt, methods and systems he devised and they put into effect, and the mere contemplation of his handiwork, as he moved from one corner of the land to another, increased his sense of identification with the ethos of Britain.

In this sense, if in no other, he was a Chauvinist. Music-hall patriotism made no appeal to him. He had no particular respect for the flag as a flag, or for the ageing queen and her tribe of royal descendants and puppet rulers now girdling the globe. He was not stirred, as were his contemporaries, by the multiplicity of the red sploshes on maps unrolled in Imperial schoolrooms, or by the saga of half-forgotten clashes between armed men that was (he could never say why) the thread on which Imperial history was strung. He saw those battles and campaigns for what they were, unimportant in themselves unless trade fell in behind the flag and pushed the popinjays aside to make way for the men with steel rails, loading bays, quays, cranes, acres of docks, and warehouses without number, to serve the potential yield of an island, a peninsula, a delta or a sub-continent over-run by professional brigands that most people still thought of as soldiers.

When this happened (and often, if his interpretation of Imperial despatches was correct, it did not) two prizes were there for the taking. A source of raw materials, and a ready-made market for man-ufactured goods. People were mistaken in imagining that soldiers were the pioneers of this endless game of catch-as-catch-can. The real founders of the enterprise never left these shores, and fought all their battles right here in mines, factories and foundries, in the makeshift workshops of men like Watt, Crompton, Stephenson, Brunel, Faraday and others, most of them long dead, and some who had died in want and obscurity. But Swann knew them and Swann acknowledged them, that small, self-dedicated band of adventurers, whose faith in themselves had transformed a nation of rustics into an army of expert usurers in a little over two generations, had made their clamour heard across the world, drowning all the Te Deums of all the victories on all the fields of honour, cutting a swathe a hundred miles wide in every direction, beginning right under his nose on the banks of the Thames and ending, who knew where? In Cathay? In Batavia? In Siberia or Timbuctu, with riches undreamed of for every man-jack under the flag? In satiety and decline after the manner of Rome? Or in stalemate as other tribes bestirred them-selves and demanded their share? It was a conundrum he was happy to leave to the social prophets and statisticians. For himself it was not the goal that absorbed him but the challenge it had offered in his early thirties, and would continue to offer until the day he died.

*   *   *

Where the brown, flotsam-fouled flood of the Thames split on the arches of London Bridge above Swann's convent belfry, the barges, wherries and lighters were boosted downstream as fast as a man could run over level ground. But when they drew abreast of him the current slowed, so that the river traffic faltered for a few seconds, giving a trained observer time to make a guess at the substance and value of the argosies. Then, as though recollecting the City's maxim that time was money, the water cavalcade swept on, booming downstream to its rendezvous with ocean-going steamers, clippers and coasters that would swallow its cargoes and spew them out into market-places at the ends of the earth. For this was the rhythm of the century, replacing the timeless, agricultural year, already, to Swann and his peers, as archaic as the sundial and the Julian calendar.

He would observe this flow for a spell but then, usually in spring and autumn, a restless mood would possess him, and he would button his topcoat and sally out into his regions, armed with his daybook and his campaign travelling kit, lunging off in one direction or another, so that the network hummed with messages that the Gaffer was on the rampage, that sluggards had better watch out, and the young and thrustful could start thinking about promotion.

The latest expedition had taken him as far as Dublin but he did not make much of his immediate prospects in Ireland. The Irish, to his way of thinking, were a noisy, rollicking lot, lighthearted enough in their overall concept of life, yet haunted by a sense of grievance that would not be exorcised by the Home Rule they were screaming for in Westminster. He had served alongside too many Irishmen in India and the Crimea to be deceived by men like Parnell and Redmond and the fiery speeches they were so fond of making to anyone who would listen. They were not equipped to mount a long, carefully-planned campaign for freedom or for anything else. They enjoyed the fight for its own sake and the devil take tomorrow, so that it followed that the growth of his Dublin branch was likely to be slower and less certain than that of territories he had opened up in England over the past twenty years, or, more particularly, those areas Fraser had recently exploited among the businesslike Scots. He spent no more than five days in Ireland, going down to Cork and then up to Galway, admiring the country but chewing his lips over the likelihood of profits to be made by expanding the odd outpost in these areas. As like as not his waggons would be waylaid and pilfered, or borrowed to transport guns and proclamations for the revolution they were always talking about, and he congratulated himself then in adhering to his principle of putting a native-born foreman in charge of localised territory. He told O'Dowd, his man in Dublin, "Continue to operate from here for the time being. Things are too unsettled in the west and south to encourage me to invest at the moment. It'll mean longer hauls, of course, but I'll give you all the waggons and teams you need. And I'll make damned sure of their springing. Your roads are atrocious."

Then he left, catching the steamer to Liverpool and feeling that here, on one of the most prosperous beats of the network, he was on safer ground, for he had a first-class man in Catesby who, as a child of eight, had stood to a loom for fourteen hours a day, and subsequently served time in gaol for his part in a riot.

Years of responsibility, and the complete trust reposed in him by the Gaffer, had sobered Catesby but the slow match of working-class pride still glowed in his belly at fifty-five. Adam knew all about his involvement with the Trades Union Congress, a federation Catesby had helped to launch twelve years before, an organisation that Sam, Adam's mill-owning father-in-law, regarded as a kind of Commune, with access to guillotines and infernal machines. Catesby's open enlistment with the militants, however, had never troubled his employer. He preferred to judge a man on his merits and he had always liked and trusted Catesby above any of his lieutenants except, possibly, Edith Wadsworth (he still thought of her by that name) in the Crescents on the east coast. The trust was mutual. Catesby always declared that if there were more gaffers like Swann there would be no need for working-men's federations. Yet, for all their accord over the years, Catesby still hesitated to accept this last position urged upon him after Sam Rawlinson's mill had passed under the Swann aegis.

The two men met by appointment in the Salford yard and as he picked his way between a clutter of vans, each bearing the Swann-on-Wheels insignia, Adam recalled a day when he called here six-teen years ago, a time when the whole of the north-west area, marked on his maps as the Polygon, had been palsied by the cotton famine, caused by the war between the States. Catesby, he remem-bered, had lost his only son in that dogfight, a boy about twenty, who had seen the Civil War as a crusade for human dignity, and because of this he had allowed the old radical to use idle teams and waggons to haul vegetables to city soup kitchens, and had later upheld Catesby's refusal to carry contraband cotton to local mills. It seemed no more than a storm in a teacup at this distance and he wondered a little at his manager's queer dedication, knowing, deep down, that the profit motive would always win the last battle and that the Catesbys of this world would die on crosses, like all the other torchbearers. Perhaps he had something like this in mind when he bought Sam's mill, for Catesby was surely the ideal man to run it, and see if he could put his high-flown principles into practice when occupying a seat of power. He made his way across to the office and Catesby rose to greet him, affably but without the bustling deference his regional managers displayed elsewhere.

He said, with a grin, "Yard looks busy enough, John. Are you still making money hereabouts?" But Catesby refused the bait, replying with a shrug, "That's a damfool question, coming from you! You know to a pennypiece how much the Polygon has made since we last met."

"Aye, I do that," said Adam, cheerfully, "and if I didn't Tybalt could tell me in less time than it takes to turn a ledger page. I'm here for your answer about that post before moving on into Fraser's territory. If you turn me down I daresay that canny old Borderer would regard mill-management as a sinecure when he retires and moves south, the way they all do when they've got enough put by." And he waited. Catesby was not a man to be hustled.

"See here," the manager said, desperately, "you're asking a hell of a lot of me, Gaffer. I've been fighting mill-owners all my life, and I'm fifty-five this month. Now you're asking me to join the opposition. How many years have I got left, granted I stick to my trade as a haulier? Ten? Five? It's too late to start all over again."

"Not for you it isn't," Swann said, "for you're not like most of them, dreaming of the day you put your feet up, or grow sweet peas in a cottage garden. It'll take half a dozen undertakers to box you. And as many master spinners to keep you planted." Then, suddenly, he became serious, saying, "Look at it this way, man. You've done all you can expect to do in this field. Whoever runs the Polygon after you can't help but make it pay, for we're that well entrenched up here. This is a chance to meet a new challenge before you're too stiff in the joints, or too cynical to back yourself to win. For good or bad I'm stuck with a mill that employs getting on for six hundred men and girls, and is reckoned to turn out the best quality cloth in Lancashire. I don't know a damned thing about spinning. What's odd in looking about for a man who does?"

"I haven't stood to a loom since I were a lad," Catesby said, still surly but now, Adam thought, less truculent than he had been when the proposal was first made more than a month ago. "I turned my back on cotton after that spell in gaol and were at sea until I ran into you, twenty years back. Where's the sense in retracing my steps now? Beyond knowing how to manage a work force what qualifications have I got for t'bloody job?"

"Managing men and girls of your own kind is the one qualification I need, John," Adam said. "My father-in-law will still keep an eye on the finances, and you'll have all the technical staff you need at your elbow." Then, seeing his man waver, he went off on another tack and thought himself a fool for not having tried it long since. "The truth is you'll be doing me a personal favour, John. That mill is one of the best in Lancashire. I've always been a man to stick to a trade I know, and leave dabbling to others, but that place has been willed to my wife, so I can't sell it, so long as Sam Rawlinson's above ground. There's no point in reminding you you'll earn twice the money you're getting as a transport boss, for I know well enough you've never been kept to a job by what it produced in pounds, shillings and pence. There's an aspect you've overlooked, however. All the years I've known you you've been bellyaching about how badly these sweat shops were run, and what a raw deal the owners gave the operatives from one end of the county to another. Well, here's a chance to put theory into practice and see if it works, to find out if it's possible to make concessions regarding pay, conditions and hours of labour without your output falling off. If you succeed you might convert some of the scabs about here. That would be a feather in the Trades Congress cap, wouldn't it?"

Catesby, all but won over, still hesitated, fighting the battle every Lancastrian has to fight before admitting that he might have made a misjudgement. "A thing like that would take time to prove," he said. "Granted I'd do my damnedest to step up wages and slash time at the machines, but I don't reckon I could do it and show a profit over the first year or so. I'm looking at it from your standpoint now.

You're the best Gaffer hereabouts and I've never made any secret o' that. But you're no man to keep white elephants in t'stable."

Adam said, quietly, "No, I'm not, John, for white elephants are as much a drag on those who tend them as to the man who owns them. However, you'll admit I've never been a man to put short-term profit before everything else. When this yard was stagnant, without one haul a day coming in or out, I gave you authority to use my waggons to help feed empty bellies and you'll recall how well it paid us when the looms were busy again. With you running the mill the way you wanted it run I wouldn't breathe down your neck until you'd had a fair crack of the whip. After that, I reckon, it'd be up to you to climb down, and admit your radical theories weren't good arithmetic. What do you say to that?"

The manager's expression remained clouded for a moment but then the lips parted in one of Catesby's rare, sardonic grins. "I'll tell you what I say. You'd gammon the devil into attending a prayer meeting on a promise to give him a free hand wi' bloody collection. Well then I'll do it and, by Gow, it won't be any fault if I don't show the scabs how they can treat men and lasses like human beings an' still look t'bloody bank manager in t'face! Here's my hand on it, and be damned to any lawyer's contract between us until this day twel'month."

"Safest way to do business," Adam said. "I use lawyers when I have to, but not with men I picked myself."

They shook hands and Swann declined an offer to join Catesby in a chop and a pint of ale at his favourite eating-house across the street. He was near enough to Fraser's beat to move north-east to the Scottish manager's headquarters at Edinburgh, reminding himself that Fraser would be retiring before he came north again in the autumn. He took a four-wheeler for London Road Station and within forty minutes of leaving the Salford yard had boarded a northbound express. His doctor, whom he consulted very rarely these days, had warned him that a sensible man should apply the brake when he had passed the fifty mark and was short of a limb, but here he was proving his private theory that most doctors were fools.

2

When he was launched on one of his tours Adam Swann cast more than his own balance sheets. He had always been fascinated by the slow tides of history, as they affected succeeding generations of Englishmen, Scotsmen, Welshmen and, to a lesser degree, the Irish. Continentals he discounted altogether, with the possible exception of the Prussians, whose efficiency had succeeded in astonishing him nine years back, when they had given the French such a drubbing. The Americans, he reasoned, were unlikely to prove serious competitors for another generation. It would take them that long to recover from their civil war, with close on a million dead. So mostly he thought in terms of his own countrymen, relating his passage to various parts of the realm with their insular struggle to shape themselves an identity.

When he was in what his maps labelled 'Bonus Country', based on the slow-moving rivers of the south-eastern plain, he would ponder the long struggle of the original inhabitants against Rome, and later, when the legions had packed up and gone, their absorption of land-hungry Balts and Saxons, who came plundering up the estuaries and slowly enlarged their grip on the eastern farmlands. When his work took him into the coastal areas of Lincolnshire, Yorkshire and Northumberland, he would remember the legacy of the Scandinavian invaders, that had equipped the islanders with a sound knowledge of ship-handling that had, in turn, enabled them to plant the English standard in every part of the world. When he moved west, chivvying his more leisurely managers in the pastoral areas of Devon, Cornwall and Wales, marked on his maps as 'The Western Wedge' and 'The Mountain Square', he would remind himself that the original Celt had shown remarkable staying powers down the centuries for here, in far less profitable lands, they were unchanged in habit of thought and seemed, almost, to have made a cult of survival.

From his schooldays he had been a diligent reader of history, so that the names of towns and villages that had grown up at river crossings and road junctions often meant something specific to him in terms of the island's story. He never crossed from Oxfordshire into Warwickshire, for instance, without thinking of the men who had fought and died in that first constitutional clash at Edgehill. He seldom passed the Severn at Tewkesbury without remembering the final defeat of feudalism at the hands of the first commercial king, the genial, womanising Edward IV. Battlegrounds, cromlechs, cathedrals, stone crosses marking martyrdoms of one sect or another, were memoranda to him in his unceasing assessment of the nation's purpose and potentialities, so that when his express roared across the border into Scotland he was able, by looking out across the un-dulating moor where Hadrian's Wall still divided the two realms, to recall Ian Fraser's real motives in battling away to enlarge Swann Territory at the expense of Scottish hauliers.

Fraser, himself a Borderer, had never acknowledged the Act of Union, had continued to regard all those north of his Berwick and Hexham bases as quiescent cattle-thieves, who would oust him the moment he lowered his guard. This was surely why, Adam reasoned, the man had proved such a thumping success up here, after a local collier wreck had presented him with a chance to get his foot inside the Lowland door. That had happened in the early days of the enter-prise but since then Fraser had gone from strength to strength and was now, he supposed, the best-known haulier between the Tweed and the Grampians, with bases at Edinburgh, Glasgow and Perth, and plans to break into the Highlands and skim the cream from the beef trade linking the breeding grounds and its meat market at Smithfield.

The entire enterprise, he reflected, had changed its character over the last ten years. When he first launched it, in the autumn of 'fifty-eight, he had been concerned with filling in the spaces between the main railways that bisected the country and left isolated country districts to wither. Now Swann-on-Wheels and the railways (that his ex-coachee waggoners had once reviled as 'the bliddy ole grid-iron', or 'the stinking tea-kettle') were in cahoots, having aban-doned attempts to cut one another's throats for the odd shilling to be earned in transportation of goods.

Swann-on-Wheels' sacks, carrying almost everything portable made in the country, now travelled vast distances by rail, to be off-

loaded for local distribution at specified points. It was a system originally devised by Edith Wickstead, then Edith Wadsworth, in an
attempt to justify her existence after she had come to terms with
spinsterhood, but since then it had been enlarged and perfected,
until it now carried nearly half the traffic in the Swann regions.
Latterly Adam assured himself that he had the better of the bargain.
The elimination of small, pettifogging hauls left his waggons free
to compete for heavier traffic, yet without sacrificing his bread-and-
butter runs.

With Fraser close to retirement the enterprise had now come to
maturity, with its teething troubles behind it, and an enormous
accumulation of experience to ensure its steady advancement. There
was now hardly a village or hamlet in the land where his insignia,
the swan with a wheel where the wing should have been, was not
accepted as a guarantee of safe and rapid transportation of goods,
and new aspects of its drive and expansion were seen every year,
like the establishment of Swann excursions to beauty spots in the
holiday season, and the scheme his lawyer Stock was working on for
a small fleet of coasters. Perhaps, one day, someone less insular than
he, his son George possibly, or George's son if he had one, would
convert the business into a global enterprise, opening depots at places
like Capetown, Sydney and Toronto. But gambler that he was he
would never adventure that far. His best years were already behind
him. A man could only do so much, before his memory and judgement began to play tricks with him, and in a trade like this memory
and judgement were everything.

*   *   *

Fraser was waiting for him at Waverley Station, tricked out in his
Sunday best and trying to pretend that the accolade of senior manager, bestowed upon him at the annual conference, had not gone
to his head and was no more than his due.

Driving to the hotel in Princes Street, where the vast bulk of the
castle was silhouetted against a herring-bone sky, and the city seemed
to crouch under its ramparts as though fearing a descent of claymore-
swinging clansmen, Adam recalled the day he had first met this man,
a defeated haulier, with a few battered carts and half a dozen knock-
kneed teams, a man on the point of throwing in the sponge because,

like so many others, that 'bliddy ole gridiron' was heading him to the poorhouse.

He said, gravely congratulating the Borderer on his fantastic turnover, "I remember when I came north to buy up your ramshackle business, Fraser. You told me then you were going back to peddling from a single van because railway competition had made you exchange the whip for pen. You've come a long road since then, longer than any of them. What kept you so interested all these years?"

And Fraser replied, with a tight smile, "The bad blood between me and the kilt I'd say, although it sounds fanciful. I'm Scots originally but my family crossed the border when they were still cattle-raiding thereabouts. For long enough we were looked on as renegades, who could expect no quarter if we were laid by the heels. I took it into my head to best them at their own game, and I have, for here I am, gaffer of all Scotland, with any number of Macdonalds and Campbells and Douglases using my waggons. Up here a grudge dies hard. Folk still talk of Glencoe and Culloden as if they were last week's news."

"You'll be wanting to retire now, I imagine," Adam said, "have you anyone in mind as a successor?" and Fraser said he had not, for there was no Scotsman he knew whom he would recommend to run a firm based on London. "It's not that he'd cheat you," he added, "but he couldn't help letting clan feuds come between him and a quotation for a haul. A Macdonald, for instance, would tend to overcharge a Campbell, and Macgregor or a Gordon would shortchange the pair of them. No, Mr. Swann, if you'll take my advice you'll put an Englishman in here."

"It's breaking my rule," Adam said, "but I had it in mind on the way up. Do you recall that time a chimney sweep choked to death in one of my flues, at 'Tryst'?"

Fraser said he did, for it got about at the time that the incident had rattled the Gaffer so badly that he was rumoured to be selling up and standing for Parliament. Was that a grapevine scare or true in substance, he asked and Adam admitted that it was true, smiling at further evidence of the grapevine's efficiency. He wondered how many other rumours had reached Fraser by this means, and whether one of them was that Edith Wadsworth was his kept woman before she met and married that chap Wickstead at the time of his accident. Fraser said, "Would there be some connection with that incident and the man ye have in mind to follow me up here?"

"A close one," Adam told him. "There were two boys in that flue and one got out alive. A tough little devil called Jake Higson. I took charge of the boy afterwards and put him to work as a van-lad in the yard. He's a man rising thirty now. Quick with his tongue, and just as quick with his fists, I'm told, but a rare hard worker and good with horses. If I send him up here for training would you coach him until you qualify for your pension in October?"

"Be glad to if you recommend him," Fraser said, "for you've never sent me a dud yet."

"Then it's done," Adam said, and they went on to talk of other things, of the establishment of a central clearing-house for the handicrafts that reached them in driblets from the west coast, of the need for more heavy vehicles in the east, where Fraser had captured a sizeable slice of the haulage between scattered factories and Leith, Dundee and Aberdeen but, above all, the rumour that Gladstone was to emerge from retirement in the autumn and wrest the Midlothian seat from Lord Dalkeith, the popular Tory member. Up here, Fraser assured him, people took their politics as seriously as their kirk. Gladstone was revered as a demigod. "If he fights it will set the whole of the North alight," he added, "and if he wins, why then all Scotland will be Radical for a generation."

"I take it you're one yourself," said Adam, and Fraser seemed slightly offended by the remark, but said, solemnly, "To be sure I am, Mr. Swann. Aren't you? You've behaved as one ever since I've known you."

"Less dedicated than I was," said Adam. "I've heard them all in my day and Gladstone is more convincing than most, but I sometimes wonder if he thinks he's down here deputising for God Almighty. I can't say I care for the political company Disraeli keeps but I've always seen him as a man with a clearer vision of the future than anyone else at Westminster."

He saw Fraser's mouth tighten and reminded himself that he was breaking another rule, discussing politics with senior staff. It didn't do to take sides in these matters. Half his working force of close on a thousand men were keen Radicals, but the other half hero-worshipped the Jew with the fervour Fraser and his like reserved for his rival. One could easily get oneself accused of favouritism when sharp differences between the regions flared at the annual conference, or someone was in line for promotion or a rap over the knuckles. He said, withdrawing from the subject, "If Gladstone fights up here he'll win but the man to watch among the Liberals they tell me is Joe Chamberlain."

"Aye, maybe he is," growled Fraser, "but he's Brummagem and that's just another word for counterfeit. For my part Chamberlain *needs* watching, Mr. Swann."

"They all need watching," Adam said, reflecting that one of the things that made Britain a rare place for sharpening the wits was the passionate regionalism of its sons and daughters. One had only to sit in at a conference to watch it work on tempers, like yeast on bread, the Celts siding with one another against the Easterners, the countrymen trying to convince the townsmen that city sophistry was no substitute for brains and that they were not necessarily half-witted because they lived a hundred miles from London.

The thought returned to him during his survey of the Lowlands under Fraser's chaperonage but they parted on genial terms, Fraser promising to send Headquarters monthly progress reports on the ex-chimney-sweep Jake Higson, his deputy elect. "Make sure it's marked 'Private'," warned Adam, "for I'm damned if I'll have Tybalt telling me my business about men I've got my eye on. That's one aspect of the business I won't share with anyone." And then, as they were standing beside the southbound express, "That pension scheme I started eight years ago . . . I was checking before I left, and I see you qualify for a mere fifteen shillings a week. You'll remember you were slow to join but you'll have something put by, I daresay." He went on, before Fraser could reply, "You don't have to tell me how much. You've more than justified the faith I had in you, so I told Tybalt to upgrade you to the 'A' class. You'll get the full rate. About a guinea a week, I believe."

The whistle sounded then and both men were grateful, Fraser because he had a Northerner's horror of expressing gratitude, Swann because he hated to have anyone think of him as a sentimentalist.

The long train gave a lurch and he settled back for the journey south to Peterborough and a brief reunion with his old flame, Edith Wickstead.

3

Long ago he had mastered the trick of entering up his day book in fast-moving trains but he did not spend more than half an hour or so of the southbound journey making notes on the regions he had visited. He felt far too complacent for that, luxuriating in the sense of achievement these journeys promoted in him, and although he did not sleep he looked as if he was dozing, as his mind ranged up and down the network like one of those grapevine rumours Fraser had mentioned. O'Dowd, given time and no civil upheaval, would enlarge his hold on Dublin; Catesby would make a great success of Sam's mill, so that the old rascal, who had been grinding the faces of operatives all his life, would have to admit that there were other ways of mining money from industry. Jake Higson would respond to authority under a man of Fraser's experience and perhaps prove another Rookwood, underlining Waggonmaster Keate's precept that, here and there, human beings could be salvaged from the rubbish heaps industrialisation had spewed about the land and converted into sober, useful citizens.

His thoughts probed Keate for a moment, returning to the night the huge, bumbling evangelist had conducted him on a tour of the Thameside Saturnalia, and first suggested his plan for sweeping some of the urchins from the streets and teaching them a trade. He thought, "By God, between us we must have saved the country a pretty penny over the years! I can think of a score of those lads who would have turned pickpocket and finished their lives in gaol, or maybe on the gallows. The professional Holy Joes, in and out of the pulpits, make a lot of noise about their rescue societies and good works, but Keate's charity proved the more practical in the long run . . . Rookwood, a boy I first saw dredging coal from Rotherhithe mud, sits on Salisbury Town Council now and has a pretty wife and five healthy children to work for. Jake Higson, who would have died like young Luke Dobbs before qualifying as a master sweep, could be a man of substance before he's half Fraser's age. We've had our failures, as Keate prophesied at the time, but our successes outnumber them. And here I am at fifty plus, with any number of trained men to hand whereas most gaffers in my line of business still rely on casual labour, with its sloppy-mindedness and high percentage of petty thieves. It all comes back to the same thing. Personal selection of deputies. It isn't the goods that matter so much as the men one finds to handle them. Tybalt did a complicated sum once, and came up with a remarkable answer. According to him the average wage I pay, higher than anyone in the trade, or so I'm told, is twenty-nine shillings a week, whereas the average weekly yield of each man in the network is three times that sum judged on annual turnover. Why can't more men understand that pinchpenny wages and brutish conditions defeat their own objects? Why the devil don't they face the fact that the first rule of any man who wants to convert a shilling into a sovereign should be to use men as allies instead of helots? Capital versus Labour, that's the bugbear of business today but it shouldn't be, not now we've had a century to work things out, not now there are so many jealous competitors just across the Channel . . . If we want to hold on to our lead we should change our tune and call it Capital-*plus*-Labour and get ahead as a team! Damned if I won't impress that on young George when he takes my place and if he heeds me Swann-on-Wheels will roll into the twentieth century lengths ahead of its nearest competitor . . . !"

The train had passed Darlington, and was rushing south to Northallerton, before he thought again of his immediate destination, Wickstead's prosperous sector, based on Peterborough. He glanced out of the window to his right and saw the rolling dale country over towards Middleham, and it reminded him sharply of the woman whom he had once hoped to make his mistress, but whose good sense had prevailed at the last moment, second thoughts for which they should both be grateful in middle age. For here he was, settled in his way of life, and on very amiable terms with a wife he wouldn't trade for a Sultan's harem. It might not have been so if, on that summer day nearly twenty years ago, Edith Wadsworth had not had the sense to discern his real motives in seeking her out, so that all that resulted in their encounter under Middleham Castle was a kiss and a clarification by her of his innermost desires that relied on a settled domestic background. It was then, he remembered, she had urged him to buy 'Tryst', and sack half the parasites who were making a lazy little trollop of Henrietta, and he had gone home and done just that, giving her young George in the process, and steering their marriage back on course again. He was glad now that Edith had found a consolation prize in that likeable chap Tom Wickstead, who always looked at him in a curious way, as if he was very well aware of the relationship that had existed between wife and employer before he bobbed up from nowhere. There was something a little wary about the chap when you came to think of it, or perhaps it was not Wickstead himself that suggested it so much as the interdependence between man and wife, who had been married thirteen years but could still be mistaken for a couple of starry-eyed lovers. Was it a residue of jealousy that made him notice this, marking the way they stood close together when he called on them last year, and the fact that, during a discussion on heavy haulage rates at the last conference, he had seen them holding hands during his summing-up from the chair? He smiled at the memory of this and realised that, married or not, he always looked forward to seeing her again. Somehow she was associated with the very earliest days of his struggle and also, to some extent, with the splendour of his youth. And at this, skimming through Northallerton, the insistent rhythm of the wheels lulled him to sleep.

* * *

He was amazed to see her awaiting him at the Peterborough barrier, for he had expected Wickstead to be there in response to his telegram from Edinburgh and was aware that she had surrendered an active role now that she had a home and young children to occupy her.

He said, taking her hand in both of his, "Where's Tom? Not sick, I hope?" and she said Tom had never been sick in his life, and was enjoying a day off at home, for they had guests, or rather *a* guest and this was the real reason why she had met him and saved him a fruitless journey. If he would take her advice he would travel straight on to London by the next train.

"There's another fast in just over the hour," she said, "but an hour is long enough. I brought you this telegram. It came with the early post. Don't read it here, let's go into the buffet and talk over a pot of tea."

She seemed, he thought, a little agitated but porters and passengers were pushing past them as they stood together just outside the barrier, so he led the way across to the buffet, finding a table furthest from the door and the hissing clamour of the station. While she was pouring tea he opened Tybalt's wire and his jaw dropped at the message that had originated, not from the head clerk, as he had assumed, but from Henrietta. *Come home wherever you are stop Alex safe stop Other matters requiring urgent attention stop Love Henrietta.*

He said, mystified, "Do you know what's behind this? Is that why you met me instead of Tom?" and she said, "I suppose it is, now that I think about it." And then, less definitely, "I'm involved—marginally that is—but don't ask me to go into details. That's Henrietta's job and she wouldn't thank me for interfering." She smiled at his puzzled frown. "Don't worry. It's not all that serious. Henrietta seems to have coped very efficiently up to now."

"I don't like guessing games," he growled, "and I'm damned if I'm going to play one all the way from Peterborough to Kent. Is Alex wounded? Is that what the fuss is about?"

"Alex came through without a scratch. I got a second letter from Henrietta yesterday, saying he was back at Durban. He was in that awful battle at that unpronounceable place in Zululand, and after that at Rorke's Drift. The urgent matter concerns your daughter. The married one."

"Stella?"

"She's with me now. She's the guest I mentioned."

"Stella is up here? With you and Tom?"

"Yes." She laid her gloved hand on his. "She's in bad trouble, Adam."

"Then damn it, I'll go to her . . ." and he half rose. But she stayed him with a gesture.

"No, Adam. Not now. Go on home, like I said. The fact is . . . well . . . she's in a state. A state of severe shock, I'd say. Henrietta will explain. She sent Stella to me for a purpose."

"Stella came alone? Right up here?"

"A neighbour brought her. A very nice young man, called Fawcett."

"Denzil Fawcett? The farmer's son?"

"I don't know, Adam. I didn't ask him. He gave me Henrietta's letter, handed over Stella and went back on the next train."

"You expect me to go home without asking any more questions? Damn it, Edith, that isn't reasonable . . ."

"It is, Adam." She paused. "I've given you good advice before, haven't I?"

"Many times, but if the girl's ill . . ."

"She isn't ill, not physically that is. She's had a bad shock but she'll get over it. She's on the mend right now, but if you blundered in on her, and began pestering her with a lot of questions, you'd set her right back, the way she was when that Fawcett boy brought her."

He thought for a moment and she glanced across at him sympathetically, a pretty, very composed woman, perhaps five or six years older than Henrietta but with the same youthful figure that had attracted him all those years ago when she drove his waggons to and from the Crescent Centre base near Boston Stump. She said, reluctantly, "Very well, against my better judgement I'll give you the gist of the matter. Stella's left her husband. For good, I understand. There now, that's as far as I'm prepared to go, for I'm putting myself in Henrietta's place and she'd have every right to feel slighted if I put my oar in deeper."

The balloon of complacency he had been inflating all the way from Edinburgh exploded, pricked by the certainty that here was a situation likely, indeed certain, to invite scorn and ridicule and amused incredulity among all the Johnny-Come-Lately customers whose goods he hauled from one end of the country to another. He had a reputation for prickly pride, as well as for speed and reliability, and a thing like this, mushrooming from county to national scandal, would be snapped up by the wits from one end of the City to the other. He could hear the coffee-house wags already—"That chap Swann, always in such a hurry, y'know. Always prattling about speed and punctuality. Well, here's a turnup for the book! Nothing equalled the turn of speed he showed marrying into the aristocracy— girl of his, nineteen they say—thousand a year settled on her—and she bolts back to mother faster than one of Moncton-Price's fil-

lies . . . !" Something like that. Or a variation of it. Or a conjugation of variants, all the way from the jocular to the obscene.

He picked up his hat and stick but she said, quietly, "Drink your
tea, Adam. There's no train for a while. I checked before you arrived."

And glumly he laid hat and stick aside, saying, "How much did
Henrietta admit in her letter?"

"No more than necessary. I understood that well enough."

"And since then? The girl herself . . . ?"

"She's only confirmed what I guessed. I encouraged her to talk.
She needed to talk to someone but whatever she said won't be passed
on, not even to Tom."

"You don't have to reassure me about that, Edith." Then, "Can
you keep her up here for a spell? Without putting yourself or Tom
to too much inconvenience?"

"For as long as she cares to stay. Nobody knows she's here except
you, her mother and that boy Fawcett."

He drained his cup and stood up. "Very well. Go back to her now.
Give her my love. Tell her I'm handling it. I'll look to myself, Edith."

"There's no hurry. Tom's at home, as I said."

"She'll need you, none the less." They walked out into the hazed
platform area. He said, "I was preening myself all the way down
here. The way I used to in the old days, when I'd opened up a new
sector or landed a new contract. Things have been going so well
lately. But it doesn't do to take a damned thing for granted, does
it?"

"You never took anything for granted, Adam. You were always
prepared to work for it."

He said, mildly, "I took you for granted for a good many years,
Edith."

"I was always there for the taking," she said, and paused at the
barrier of the down platform.

She noticed that, despite his impatience to get moving, typical of
his approach to every crisis in the past, he seemed unwilling to leave
her. The clock pointed to ten minutes to five. He had about twenty
minutes to wait for the London train.

Suddenly he said, "You and Tom, you're well suited and very

happy, I believe. I'm grateful for that, Edith. I should have told you
long since."

"There's something I should have told you long since, Adam,
but never did. I'll tell you now, however. It'll take your mind off
your own troubles, and maybe give you something else to think about
on the way home. This business with Stella, and it getting talked
about among your staff and customers. It isn't all that important,
providing you and Henrietta hang on to a sense of proportion. Tom
and I faced worse and came through with our chins up. You never
heard how we met, I suppose?"

He looked at her sharply. "He was a waggoner in your yard, wasn't
he? At the time I lost my leg in that train smash."

"He was a professional thief. He signed on with us for the sole
purpose of stealing a consignment of precious stones we were sending to Harwich by train parcel."

He stared hard at her and she realised then she had at least succeeded in diverting his mind from his daughter for a time, probably
the time it would take him to reach his wife and get the full story
from her.

"You married him? Knowing that?"

"Because of it. Or so I like to think. But not before pouncing on
him in the guard's van when he was making off with what he
thought was the package. I won't bother you with the details now
for there isn't time. The fact is I was able to stop him but in doing
it I learned just how and why he became a thief, and why he carried
a revolver strapped to his wrist. He had served two years in broad
arrows and had made up his mind not to be taken alive again. Well,
somehow I managed to change that, to help him along once he came
to me and asked for help. I didn't know then I was doing myself a
more useful service than I was doing him."

He was silent for a while. Finally he said, "I would have trusted
him above most of the managers. I think I still would."

"Yes, I know. And he knows it too. That's why I don't mind telling
you now. Left to himself he would have told you years ago. He was
always afraid of you finding out by chance."

It moved him very much that she was prepared to trust him with
such a secret and for no other reason he could discern than that of
switching his thoughts from a gloomy personal dilemma. He said,

after a brief pause, "The problem you faced then, and the one that confronts me now—they haven't much in common, have they?"

"I think they have."

"Then tell me."

"We solved ours by a mixture of patience and faith in each other. I've no doubt you and Henrietta can do the same."

"It sounds a pretty sordid story."

"About as sordid as I've ever heard. She'll need all the help you and Henrietta can give her. If I were you I wouldn't let yourself be influenced by sniggering tittle-tattle. That isn't in the least important. It's the girl who matters right now."

She thought it wise not to press the point and extended her hand again. "I'll go to her now and I'll keep in close touch by letter. She's among friends, Adam."

"Yes," he said, and then, with a touch of the old devil-may-care approach he had brought to so many crises in the past, "Take Tom into your confidence if it helps. I don't mind him knowing. In view of what you've just told me he's probably very familiar with people like the Moncton-Prices, and their propensity to ride roughshod over people like us, who have had to fight every inch of the way."

He nodded then and turned away and as she watched his tall frame thrusting itself along the platform, with that peculiar bobbing gait he had acquired along with his artificial leg, she was conscious of a great surge of tenderness for him, far more broadly based than the instinctive sympathy she felt for his wretched daughter. Stella's problem was personal and could be resolved, one way or the other, inside that arena of time that was the prerogative of the very young, but his involved not so much his family as the whole edifice of his life, erected after years of toil, thought and risk. Perhaps it was foolish to assume that an enterprise as sound as his could be threatened by what most people would see as a purely domestic crisis, albeit a very unsavoury one, but she knew Adam Swann well enough to understand that for him commercial probity and domestic background were inseparable and she did not think the worse of him for viewing it in this light. His entire being was absorbed in what he had created over the years with his own hand and brain and his first line of defence, in a situation such as this, was necessarily the health of the network rather than his daughter's personal happiness.

She turned away and passed out into the street, hailing a cab to take her back to the yard where her trap was waiting. She felt older and sadder than when she had stood watching his train slide into the platform.

4

It was nearly midnight when he turned his gig into the avenue that led up to the house under the outcrop, just visible as a cluster of winking lights on the first crest.

He had always seen the big, sprawling house as an unequivocal pledge of his powers to bluff and cozen, to scheme and hold on as though, in the first instance, it had been a citadel in enemy hands and he was the man charged with storming it and making it his, a vast, rambling, weather-beaten pile, set there three centuries ago by a man just such as he, who put an equally high price on himself. But tonight, in a curious way, the house seemed to mock him, as though those lights winking through interlacing branches were signalling a fresh challenge that had the power to frighten him a little, reminding him that challenges of this sort were for the young and hale, not for someone well advanced upon his fifties, with a truncated leg tormented by a March wind that probed among the raw nerves of the stump, much as it tormented the boughs overhead.

He said aloud, giving vent to his exasperation, "God damn that stupid girl for landing me in a mess like this!" but then he remembered that he had always claimed to be the arbiter of his own destiny and that he was far more to blame than Stella for failing to reconnoitre the situation before permitting her to rush into an alliance with people he hardly knew and was not much disposed to know.

Henrietta, as always, came down to the stableyard, having glimpsed the lights of his gig from the drawing-room windows. She called into the gloom, "Is that you, Adam . . . ?" and he called back, "Yes, it's me!" mumbling, "Who the devil would it likely be?" as Stillman emerged yawning to take charge of the gig, saying that the groom had waited up until eleven but had now gone to bed, assuming that he would stay overnight in London.

There was restraint in their greeting but this, he told himself, was partly due to a feeling of extreme exhaustion that had overtaken him during the long, cold drive from Croydon. What he needed more than anything, more than rest even, was a stiff brandy and water and she mixed him one while he was disposing of cape, hat and gloves. When, gratefully, he was rolling the spirit on his tongue, she said without looking at him, "You got my wire at Peterborough? Tybalt wrote saying you were due there today. Did you . . . stop off and see her?"

No, he told her, he hadn't. Edith Wickstead had urged him to press on home and hear the story from her lips. "She has some woman's prejudice that it wasn't her place to tell it," he added and she replied, "Yes, that would be Edith's way. You think I did right to send the girl to her?"

Her uncertainty touched him a little so that he set down his glass, crossed to the hearthrug and put his arm across her shoulders. "Of course. I suppose you anticipated a descent by the Moncton-Prices. Have they been over here demanding her return?"

"No," she said, "but I've been to them." And then, more assertively, "It's all more or less settled, providing you approve, of course."

He looked at her in astonishment. "*Settled?* How the devil do you mean, settled? She's still married to him, isn't she? And there's the matter of the thousand a year I made over to them. Edith told me practically nothing. I'll have to know precisely what led up to it and how that old roué Sir Gilbert views it."

She refilled his glass then and said, in an uncompromising tone, "Sit down, Adam. And just you let me have my say before you make one of your snap judgements. They serve well enough in your business, I daresay, but they won't help one little bit! That's why I asked Mr. Stock down."

"Stock, the lawyer? But good God, woman . . ."

"He's here now but he had a dreadful cold, poor man, so I sent him to bed with a hot toddy when I guessed you were likely to be home tonight. You can talk to him in the morning, when you have both had a good night's rest. Now then, will you listen? Without interrupting?"

He nodded, smiling in spite of himself. It always amused him to catch her in one of her bustling moods, when she tried so hard to treat him as one of the children.

"Say your piece. I won't interrupt, and I won't make a snap judgement."

"Very well. In the first place Stella can't possibly go back there. Nothing would make me agree to that, you understand? In the second place, and Stock can confirm this, it isn't nearly as bad as it might have been, for we have very good grounds for a divorce."

The word scared him, as she knew it would. He frowned. "Great God! On what grounds?"

"Stock had a lawyer's word for it. It was non-something or other!"

"Non-consummation?"

"That was it. She never has been a wife to that . . . that monster. What she must have gone through these last few months is more than I care to think about. I still can't begin to understand why she didn't come to me weeks ago, or at least say something that made sense when they were here at Father's funeral last January. It seems he's only half a man, and his father made no bones about it. But that's not the worst of it."

It didn't surprise him all that much, remembering Lester's woman's mouth and that fastidious, catlike walk of his, but he growled, "What the devil *could* be worse than having that kind of thing dragged through the courts and printed in the newspapers?"

"I'm not concerned with publicity and scandal. We'll cross that bridge when we come to it. I'm thinking of something you couldn't lay before any court." She took a deep breath and looked directly at him. "That dreadful old man made a . . . well . . . a certain proposal. It was that that sent the girl flying into the dark like a mad thing. What might have happened to her, if she hadn't been found and taken home by that Fawcett boy just doesn't bear thinking about. Denzil behaved splendidly but I'll come to that."

He was puzzled now. "The old man made a proposal? What kind of proposal?"

"He asked her to stay on and live out the lie for the rest of her life."

"Well, that's not surprising. He wouldn't want a scandal any more than we do. Or not a scandal of that kind, reflecting on him and his."

It amazed her then that a man who had roamed half across the world, and fought in wars and rubbed shoulders with men of every kind, should need such an explicit statement. For a moment she thought of fobbing him off with a half-truth, but then she realised it could never be sustained, or not for long, between two people as close as they had been since they married more than twenty years before.

She said, "You'll have to know. Otherwise you'll never understand. That scoundrel suggested he should . . . well . . . take the place of his wretched son. It seems he's anxious to get an heir . . ."

She broke off, watching him closely, her eyes never leaving his, so that she was able to gauge the impact of her words, watch his senses recoil and then, like a prize-fighter absorbing the shock of a tremendous buffet, fight back to secure a firm grip on himself. He was a man, as she well knew, capable of exerting tremendous self-control and his training, as a soldier and a commercial freebooter, helped him now. Slowly he unclenched one fist and reached out for his brandy, lifting the glass and draining it at a gulp.

He said, between clenched teeth, "So that was it. Edith hinted . . . she used the word 'unsavoury' . . . But it isn't that, is it? It's an outrage!"

It was time then to run in under his guard. "You promised to listen, you promised you wouldn't interrupt . . ."

She could hear the whistle of his breath. A vein in his temple pulsed and he seemed aware of it, reaching up and slowly massaging that side of his face where a crooked seam of flesh marked the passage of a splinter lodged there at the time of the Staplehurst crash. She had grown so accustomed to the scar that she rarely noticed it but now, in the soft glow of the lamp, it looked livid and half-healed. He said, at length, "Go on. Finish it."

"Stella did the best she could under the circumstances. It was late at night and she was in her nightclothes. She got rid of him on some pretext, pulled on some clothes and ran out through the French windows."

"Ran where, for God's sake?"

"She was on her way here but luckily she met young Fawcett at Carter's Copse, out seeing to his lambs. He took her to the farm and Mrs. Fawcett fed her and put her to bed. Then he came straight here to fetch me."

"So as well as the Fawcetts the whole damned household knows what happened!"

"No, we were very lucky. I came downstairs, after the paddock oak crashed down in the gale and I was the only one about when Denzil arrived. I went with him as soon as it was light."

"What was she like, after an experience of that kind?"

"Physically she was well enough. She slept through until afternoon and then I coaxed it out of her, bit by bit."

"She told you everything?"

"Not quite everything, I imagine. But all that mattered. It seemed the right thing was to get her clear away from here, so I asked Denzil to take her to Edith's."

"But before that you went over to Courtlands?"

"Denzil drove me there. I only saw the old man. I was glad of that. I don't think I could have stood a meeting with his son."

"Well?"

"I told him Stella was never going back and I took her clothes away there and then."

He stared at her, wondering anew at her hardihood and how, time and again, it continued to astonish him, as though she was some kind of phenomenon, a small, innocuous-looking mountain that continually erupted after one had come to terms with its quiescence and permanence. He remembered how she had taken his breath away when he returned here after a year's absence spent learning to walk again, to find her not only running his business as capably as he had run it but the mother of a child he had not even known existed. And now, while he had been gallivanting about his network, telling himself how clever he was, she had coped single-handed with a situation that would have reduced most women he knew to hysterics. Pride in her submerged every other emotion in him, even the rage and disgust he felt for Moncton-Price and that son of his, and to some extent this moderated his self-reproach, for at least she, as his deputy, had done something positive to atone for his stupidity and indifference.

He said, at last, "Did you accuse him to his face, on his own hearth?"

"Yes, I did. It seemed to me the only way I could make him agree to a divorce."

"You're telling me he actually admitted trying to seduce his own daughter-in-law?"

"Not really, although he didn't deny it."

With one part of his brain he continued to assess her strength and courage, but at a much deeper level he was already at work assembling the factors, risks, stresses and counter-stresses of this extraordinary situation. The habit, formed over the years, of standing well clear of a crisis, and forcing himself to take an objective view of its complexities and likely developments, enabled him to do just this with something as personal as his daughter's involvement with a lecherous old ruin and a homosexual. Already, as she recounted her story word for word, he began to see the vague outlines of his strategy. Stock, the lawyer, was almost certainly correct in his surmise that his daughter could extricate herself from the mess on a plea of non-consummation but to do this, he supposed, evidence of her virginity would have to be submitted to a court and any compromise they reached would be bound to depend on the co-operation of the Moncton-Prices, father and son. However one approached it there was certain to be publicity, and most of it would be highly sensational, of a kind likely to put a tremendous strain upon any family, especially one bearing a name as well known as his. Yet there were elements in Henrietta's story that encouraged him to hope. Moncton-Price was not going to risk a public airing of his approach to Stella, however difficult that might prove to establish in a court of law, and in the end, he imagined, it would come down to money, as most things did, so that he began to weigh the probable cost of a Moncton-Price stand-off in terms of hard cash. They were known to be in difficulties. Nothing short of near-bankruptcy would have persuaded a man like Lester Moncton-Price to marry in the first place, much less to marry into trade, and it occurred to him then that the wily old rascal who had promoted the match had had something like this in mind from the very beginning, banking, no doubt, on Stella's reluctance to become the storm centre of a case like that of Ruskin's wife, still the subject of bar-parlour jokes. He would probably be advised to leave the settlement undisturbed and although the prospect of this nettled him, he had never been a man to put money before peace of mind. If he got Stella clear of them the money could go hang.

He was dragged from his reverie by awareness of a change in the tone of Henrietta's voice as she said, with a hint of reproach, "You haven't asked about Alex."

"Edith told me he was safe."

"That's so, and no thanks to you, I might add."

He blinked at her. "You're not holding me responsible for War Office blunders in Zululand, are you? I accept responsibility for Stella's marriage. I was a damned fool from start to finish."

She said, earnestly, "Just listen, Adam . . . no, perhaps now isn't the time. You're tired, and very much upset. But soon . . . well . . . we'll have to have it out, and come to some kind of understanding."

He gathered from this that she did blame him for Stella's plight, as much as she blamed the Moncton-Prices possibly, but her broadening of the issue, to include Alex, puzzled him.

"Listen here, Hetty," he said, affably, "I'm completely at fault as regards the girl. I should have known it couldn't possibly work and that something rotten would emerge from it. But she ought to have been warned to some extent. She has instinct, presumably, and we didn't keep her blinkered, as most parents do in this so-called enlightened age. She's had far more freedom than most girls of her age. Damn it, I'd have credited her with as much common sense as a milkmaid but I was wrong apparently."

"It isn't just Stella," she replied, stubbornly. "It's all of us. I thought . . . well . . . never mind now, we'll discuss it tomorrow, once we've made up our minds how to go about getting Stella's freedom."

He poured himself another brandy, his third, and a small one for her. "We won't," he said, "we'll get it over and done with now. I've had enough of drifting for one evening . . ."

"That's the point," she exclaimed, vehemently. "In matters of business, anything remotely connected with those waggons of yours, you never once followed a policy of drift! You made plans and stuck to them. Or you took expert advice from one person or another. Or you sat down and worked everything out, down to the last detail. But you've never paid your children the compliment you pay those teams, those routes, or even the men who look to you for a livelihood."

He heard her without irritation or displeasure. He was thinking again of the crisis in their own relationship, dating back to a time when he walked in here and found a dead chimney-sweep on his hearthrug. He countered, gravely, "I always paid you that compliment, Hetty."

"Yes," she said, eagerly, "you did, Adam. And I've always loved you for it, but I'm not talking of *me*, but of your children, from Alex and Stella down to the little ones. You've left them to me, or to Phoebe Fraser, or to their schoolmasters, and that isn't fair and it isn't wise either so it has to change, don't you see?"

"Not really," he said, with a touch of humour. "Why don't you explain precisely what you're driving at in your own words? And don't say you can't for I know very well that you can. I'll listen, I promise you."

"Well, then," she said, taking a deep breath, "there's Stella, of course. I was worried about her from the start, but I'm not excusing myself on that account, for I didn't act on it, or try and talk you into acting. What surprised me at the time was you giving in to Stella so easily and I think I know now why you did. Years ago you never had much time for the airs most people in your position put on, grasping at every opportunity to climb the social ladder, and hoping everyone forgets just how they came by their money, but I can't help thinking some nonsense of that kind played a part in letting Stella have her way and marry into that awful family. Am I right or wrong about that?"

"Only half-right," he said, "but I was indulging Stella more than myself. You once had delusions of grandeur, I recall. Perhaps Stella inherited some of them. You've outgrown yours, and I daresay she's shed most of hers by now. Where you come far closer to the truth is when you say I'm obsessed with the network. The fact is a man can only carry so much in his head at any one time, and I didn't give that marriage nearly as much thought as it merited. But if you had made a stand I should have listened. So we'll split the blame fifty-fifty."

"But not as regards Alex," she said, obstinately. "Alex, or Giles for that matter."

"Where the devil do they come into it?"

"You oughtn't to need me to point that out to you."

"Well I do."

"Very well. You've fought in two wars and spent years as a soldier, but you let that boy scamper off to Africa just as if he was catching a train to London Bridge. I was all for him taking up a military career, and when you read his letter you'll see it wasn't so fanciful as you've always thought, but you could have stirred yourself, used your influence, and got him into a good regiment where he would have had the benefit of basic training. As it was he was extremely lucky not to get himself killed."

"Where does that leave Alex?"

"I want him home now, and properly prepared for his work, the way you would train the least of your employees earmarked for a special job of work."

He thought briefly of his words to Fraser about Jake Higson, selected for the Scottish post, and at once conceded her point. "That makes good sense, Hetty, and I'll act on it. Now, what about Giles?"

"He's unhappy at Mellingham."

"He *is*?"

"Yes. It isn't the right school for a boy of his kind. For one thing he's not as strong as the others and that cough of his is beginning to worry me. He needs upland air and a smaller, less anonymous school, an environment where he isn't poured into a mould, like his brothers."

"Has he complained?"

"Good heavens, no, of course he hasn't! And if you knew him well you'd know he never would. But I can read between the lines of his letters, and you could if and when you take a moment to read them."

"How about the others? Are they in such dire need of a father's guidance? No, Hetty . . . I'm not teasing, there's something in what you say, and on the whole I plead guilty. There must be more to raising a family than providing a good home, three square meals a day, and an education. But remember one thing in extenuation. All day and every day I'm involved with youngsters who haven't had that, not even in small measure. Most of those van-boys of Keate's slept under sacks on wharves and when we found them not one in five could lay claim to a mother, much less a father."

"That's all very well," she said, impatiently, "but I'm concerned with the children under this particular roof. I'm a wife and a mother, not a missionary!"

For all her vehemence she still had the power to make him laugh aloud. His mind returned to Edith's Tom, an ex-convict, who once walked the streets with a revolver strapped to his wrist, and then again to all those derelicts Keate was always sweeping into the yard, and suddenly it occurred to him that perhaps the social reformers of the nation were all on a wrong tack, that extreme deprivation was more likely to foster hardihood and self-reliance than vice. How else did one explain poxed out failures like the Moncton-Prices or, for that matter, his own daughter's utter lack of instinct and common sense?

He said, "George. You haven't mentioned George," and she replied, sharply, "George will always be able to look after himself."

"Maybe," he said, "but it occurs to me, in view of the family post mortem we're having, that even George might need a push to head him in the direction I want him headed. I'll make sure Alex gets into a good regiment. I'll write to my old friend Roberts—*General* Roberts now, if you please—and I'll see Giles within the week, and talk his future over with him. But unless I'm mistaken my business stands or falls with George so I'm taking no chances there. No damn sense in wasting time making a gentleman of George. He'll get his education on the network, and start as soon as maybe. As to the others, I'll promise you one thing, my dear. From here on they'll be spied on from afar, the way I spy on my managers and foremen waggoners. So I daresay this wretched business might show us a profit in the end."

She was not surprised that her directness had had this effect on him but it warmed her nonetheless, clearing away the fog of uncertainty and apprehension that had clouded her life over the last few days. For possibly the thousandth time since she had met him on that rain-soaked moor half a lifetime ago she thanked God he was a man open to reason, a man who, despite his dominance and towering success in business, was yet able to get along without the insufferable arrogance one took for granted in the male animal. She said, yawning, "Well, that's surely enough for one night. Let's go to bed," and without waiting for his assent crossed over to extinguish the lamp and set the guard before the fire.

He followed her to the door stumbling a little with fatigue, but not too fatigued to catch her by the shoulders as she stepped into the hall and hold her close against him for a moment, lowering his head to kiss her neck where the fastening of a thin, gold chain she wore showed above the collar.

"I've struck a lot of bargains in my time," he said, absently, "but taken all round you were the best of 'em, Hetty."

She warmed her hands at that all the way upstairs and the time it took her to undress, brush her hair and climb into bed, by which time he was asleep and snoring heavily.

Settling, she indulged herself in one of her suppressed, school-girl giggles, for it occurred to her to wonder if he would endorse the testimonial when he learned that she was pregnant again.

6

The Gladstonisation of Giles

ONE of the unlooked-for consolations of being uprooted, at the age of twelve and a half, whisked across south-east England and set down among three hundred Philistines (the fate of Giles Swann, in September, 1878) was his casual introduction to lyrical verse by one James Horace Talbot, M.A., tutor in English in the Junior School according to page two of the Mellingham brochure, 'Prodder' according to the boys who dozed under him five times a week in the narrow desks of the Second Form.

Nobody minded Prodder's periods. Prodder was old, frayed, wispy, shuffling, snuffling, defeated and very round-shouldered, not given to demanding the earnest attention of classes demanded by younger, more ambitious masters, but content, as his nickname suggested, to resort to the absentminded prod rather than more defined correctives, so that those unable to share his love of cadences and dreamy communions with Wordsworth, Blake, Goldsmith, Alfred Lord Tennyson, Shelley, Hood and poor mad Cowper, could use his periods any way they chose, catching up on neglected prep, perhaps, or reading coarse-print sagas of Turpin, Dan Daring, and Robin Hood, or even sitting back, closing their eyes and sucking durable caramels, so long as they observed the basic conventions and rotated the confection unostentatiously between all but motionless jaws. For Prodder had long since shed any illusions concerning his ability to lure boys into the garden of English prose and poetry. He was satisfied, for the most part, to wander there alone, mouthing familiar couplets and sometimes whole extracts, with a kind of bemused ecstasy that fascinated Giles, sitting immediately below Prodder's rostrum.

Here, oblivious of the subdued hum of a class at his back, he would sit entranced, staring fixedly upwards while Prodder Talbot paced and intoned back and forth along his platform, only rarely glancing up from his book to point a finger, ask a question, or descend the two steps to floor level to administer one of his gentle, absentminded prods.

In this way, by the end of his second term of banishment from the well-loved woods and pastures of 'Tryst', Giles Swann unconsciously memorised great chunks of *The Deserted Village, Summer Images, Ode to a Nightingale,* and *Song of the Lotus-Eaters,* together with innumerable fragments from shorter poems, like Wordsworth's *Daffodils,* Tennyson's *Brook,* the opening stanzas of Gray's *Elegy,* and Blake's heartcry, *London,* imbibing the stanzas like great draughts of wine, so that he was often half tipsy when the bell clanged from the quad, and Prodder pottered away, trailing his shredded, chalk-dusted gown, to intoxicate others along the corridor.

Giles, loving them all, had his favourites, usually those of Prodder because they were the most overworked, but there were fragments here and there that he had heard only once and later traced in his text-book to learn for himself. These fell into two categories that he thought of as the Pastoral and the Pitiful, the one inducing a sensation of infinite peace and transportation back to his beloved woods and meadows, the other a sense of confused indignation sometimes amounting to fury that so many could contrive to make so vast a desert of so much colour, scent and melody, available to all who turned their backs on a town.

He would contemplate this baffling paradox, wondering how it was that—with torchbearers like Blake and Burns and Gray so vocal and so plentiful—a majority elected to immerse themselves in commerce (a religion to his father), military panoply, that had obsessed his brother Alex from childhood, and extravagant practical jokes alternating with competitive games, that regulated everything George did from rising bell to lights out. As for Giles, he had already mastered the art of personal withdrawal, so that his life was now lived on two levels. The one, practised within the limits of his actual being, was concerned with responses to bells, orders and rituals, whereas his real life, fed and watered by Prodder Talbot's excerpts, and underwritten by remembered images of 'Tryst', its people and its surroundings, was private but intensely compelling, presenting him with an ever-expanding world of tremendous diversity, and setting him innumerable problems that he could never hope to solve but offsetting the boredom and predictability of life within a regimented society.

In this way, moving effortlessly between a waking state and a dream state, he adjusted to the two extremes of the human spectrum, each implicit in the moods of the poets, that offered alternates of despair and ecstasy. The former mood, Giles thought, was to be found in Blake, who had once written:

> I wander thro' each charter'd street
> Near where the charter'd Thames does flow
> And mark in every face I meet
> Marks of weakness, marks of woe.
>
> In every cry of every Man,
> In every Infant's cry of fear,
> In every voice in every ban,
> The mind-forged manacles I hear . . .

And then, for Giles, came the four lines that exactly expressed the poet's despair, as Blake added:

> How the Chimney-sweeper's cry
> Every black'ning Church appals;
> And the hapless Soldier's sigh
> Runs in blood down Palace walls . . .

The words, as he weighed each of them separately, came to have a frightening relevance for him, for he had often visited his father's Thameside yard and noted, among the many wayfarers in streets surrounding it, unmistakable 'marks of weakness, marks of woe'. The chimney-sweeper's cry was often heard in that neighbourhood. The blood of soldiers on palace walls could be seen quite clearly in any illustration of his brother Alex's favourite book, *Deeds That Won the Empire*.

Happily, however, Blake's prophetic gloom was offset by the tranquillity of more sanguine poets, whom Prodder thought of as the arbiters of the Universe. One could always climb with relief on to the alternative plank of the seesaw and join Tennyson's brook in chattering descent to the plain 'through brambly wilderness' and past banks of forget-me-nots that, or so the poet assured him, 'grew for happy lovers'. Or one could also dip haphazardly into one's own experience, identifying John Clare's rapturous summer images with remembered vistas of Kentish ploughland rising, furrow by furrow, to the crown of elms where Denzil Fawcett, the local farmer's son, had a hut to shelter him during the lambing season. For whenever he repeated to himself:

> . . . I see the wild flowers in their summer morn
> Of beauty, feeding on joy's luscious hours:
> The gay convolvulus, wreathing round the thorn,
> Agape for honey showers
> And slender kingcup, burnished with the dew
> Of morning's early hours . . .

Giles rose up from bench or cot, seated himself on his magic carpet, and took the path that followed the circumference of Plover Wood across the river from the islet below 'Tryst' to the rim of the downs that offered a view of half Kent. Here, times enough during his early morning wanderings, he had seen a thousand convolvulus wreathing the thorn, and as many kingcups, along with hundreds of other wild flowers that grew there.

Then, for a time, he would luxuriate in the sense of well-being that accompanied him everywhere he went within a five-mile radius of 'Tryst', cocking an ear for the sound of Mr. Gray's 'drowsy tinkling' lulling distant folds and congratulating himself, a little smugly perhaps, on his keen perception, on being so splendidly equipped to share Wordsworth's 'inward eye that is the bliss of solitude'.

Yet these periods of serenity were of short duration. He had what his father would have recognised as the split mind of the Celt, capable of taking the keenest pleasure in its own company but prone, at any moment, to tip him headfirst into an abyss of gloomy introspection, so that it was not so much a matter of where he was, or what he was doing, but what he was not doing and where he would go when, like Alex, he attained the unimaginable age of eighteen and was required to translate hoarded moments of conscious pleasure into positivity of the kind the poets seemed to demand of one of their number. He wondered sometimes if Blake had ever gone out and wrestled with those mind-forged manacles of which he wrote so bitterly, or whether, in fact, Alfred Lord Tennyson, the revered

Poet Laureate, ever gave a serious thought to chimney-sweeps and soldiers spilling blood on palace walls.

The gap between sermon and action troubled him. One day he made so bold as to buttonhole Prodder in the quad and ask about it, but it was clear that the old chap was at a loss for a satisfactory answer. He promised to think about it, however, and evidently did, for a day or so later he called Giles over and gave him four lines of Shelley written on a sheet torn from an exercise book that was covered, on its reverse side, with geometrical figures, proving that Prodder had salvaged it from the mathematics master's wastepaper basket. Giles could not make very much of the lines that read:

> As I lay asleep in Italy
> There came a voice from over the sea
> And with great power it forth led me
> To walk in the visions of Poesy.

"It's some kind of answer, boy," Prodder said, apologetically. "Shelley wrote it as the opening lines of a poem called *The Mask of Anarchy*. How far are you forward in history?"

Giles told him as far as the first Tudor, whereupon Prodder shook his head. "Not far enough to help you make something of the full poem," he said. "It was written on the occasion of the Peterloo Massacre. Ever hear of the Peterloo Massacre, boy?"

"No, sir, I never did. When was it, sir?"

"In your grandfather's time, before even I was born and that's a long time ago. However, as I said, it's part of an answer. A few poets see it as their duty to go out and actually man the barricades. Byron was one of 'em, and you can't but admire the man for that alone. But most of 'em see their duty end as a prophet and preacher. They point the path and it's up to men of power and influence to follow it. They never do, of course." He blinked down at Giles with mild affection, an expression he did not often use in the classroom. "Glad to know some of it stuck. Who is your favourite?"

"Blake, I think, sir," and the old man's eye kindled.

He said, "Ah, Blake! He had a conscience if any of 'em did. You're Swann, aren't you? Second term here?" And when Giles confirmed this, "Swann . . . 'Swann-on-Wheels' . . . Your father's in transport, isn't he? Never met him. Like to. There now. Introduce me when he's up here?"

"I will indeed, sir," Giles replied, though wondering what a busy, bustling man like his father would make of a dry old stick like Prodder, a school joke, even among the masters.

From then on, however, Prodder took the keenest interest in him, and sometimes appeared to be addressing him exclusively when quoting a poem, or explaining a piece of prose. The introduction to Swann père was formally carried out about a month later, when Adam appeared to collect George and himself for the Easter break. Against all probability they seemed to get along very well indeed, standing apart for a long time and apparently sharing a succession of jokes.

A day or so later, when his father saw him in the paddock bridling his pony for an early morning ride up to the downs, he emerged from the French windows, asking if he would like company, and when Giles said that he would be glad of it Adam threw a saddle over his mare and they rode out together, taking the path their side of the river and cutting into the woods opposite the islet to pick up the winding track that led to the escarpment overlooking the house under the hill.

They reined in here, kicking their feet free of the stirrups, sniffing the clear, April-scented air and watching the sun shooing the mists from the valley below.

Adam said, suddenly, "I took to that old geezer Talbot. He seems to think you've got more brains than either of your brothers. Went so far as to have a word with him concerning your future. Don't think I've told you George won't be returning to Mellingham."

The boy's crestfallen expression disarmed him so that it occurred to him that, although the brothers were not particularly close, Giles did not relish the notion of returning to school even more vulnerable than he had been during his first two terms. He said, "Your mother seems to think Mellingham may not be the best place for you but you'll have to go somewhere. You're too big for Phoebe to handle and anyway, to judge from the chat I had with Talbot, I daresay you could teach her a thing or two by now. I've a smaller place in mind, down in Devon. It's on the fringe of Exmoor, and has the air your mother thinks you need after that cough you had last winter. It's up to you, however. Wouldn't want you to start all over again against your will. It's a newish school, deep in the country, country rather like this. Caters mostly for farmers' sons, so they tell me. Would you like to see the prospectus my Devon manager sent me and give it a thought during the next day or so?"

"Yes, I would, sir," Giles said, a little alarmed to discover his mother had read more into his duty letters than he had put there. It wouldn't do, he reflected, to let anyone know that he was scared of returning to Mellingham without George, or that he had made no real friend in the Lower School. Indeed, he sometimes felt as much of a misfit among all those empire builders as old Prodder himself.

They turned away then, cantering up to the downs, Giles riding a length or so behind his father and marvelling at his firm seat, despite a left leg that was metal and cork from the knee down. He had always respected his father without, however, getting to know him in the way the younger children did and, to a degree, Alex and George as they grew up. He had always seen himself as a kind of halfway-house between the three older children and the four younger ones, still in the nursery. Yet sometimes he felt almost as old as his father, and a great deal older than his mother who was inclined to coddle him and yet accord him an adult status that she did not display towards Stella, Alex or George.

He said, when they reined in to give the horses a breather, "Will George be going into the business, sir?" and his father said he would, for his academic progress had been unspectacular and he was far too independent to make a success of soldiering. "I'm sending him on a tour of the network," he added, "with a month's stay in each region. That's the only way to learn my business. From stables, invoice trays and warehouse upwards. If he shapes well I'll fit him in at the yard in a year or so." He gave Giles a sidelong glance. "I don't suppose you've got the least idea what you'd like to do when you leave school?" and half-expected Giles would say he wanted to be a poet.

Instead, to Adam's secret bewilderment, he said, thoughtfully, "Do you happen to know about Peterloo, sir?"

"Peterloo? You mean Waterloo, don't you?"

"No, sir, Peterloo. Shelley wrote a poem about it. It was a massacre in Manchester, I think."

"Indeed it was, but not such a massacre as all that. It was more of a riot. The yeomanry and hussars cleared the streets, and knocked over some people attending a meeting. The Chartists made a great fuss about it but you'll forgive someone like me, who was at Cawnpore and Sebastopol, for not regarding it as a milestone."

"What was the meeting about, sir?"

"Overdue Parliamentary reforms, I think. But what the devil has that to do with thoughts you might have on a career? You don't fancy yourself as a street orator, do you? You've always had less to say than any of 'em to my way of thinking."

"I suppose it's to do with the *difference*, sir."

"Difference between what?"

"The kind of lives people lead, the rich and poor. It's hard to explain, sir, but . . . well, there was that old couple over at Twyforde Green last Christmas. It seemed so wrong, putting them out of their cottage, and not letting them stay together. I wanted to ask you about it at the time but you weren't there when I got home. And after that it was Christmas, with so much going on, and then the Colonel died so I couldn't ask him."

"Ask me now then."

"They were a very old couple called Farthing. Someone said Mr. Farthing couldn't work any more on account of arthritis, and his cottage was wanted for a younger man coming in. So it was the workhouse and workhouses don't cater for married people, so one went to Tonbridge and the other to Sevenoaks."

Suddenly Adam recalled the case, one of many hereabouts he supposed, privately thanking his stars he didn't own any tied cottages. It shocked him a little that Giles should have witnessed the eviction, and even more that he should have brooded over it. He said, "Damn it, you sound just like our Deborah! She's bitten with the reforming bug they tell me, and whilst I wouldn't have you think I'm not in favour of a square deal for the less fortunate, I'm bound to tell you there's no livelihood in fighting campaigns on their behalf."

"No, I suppose not," Giles said, but added, improbably, "Phoebe Fraser says you're a good man to work for, sir. That you pay good wages and give people the chance to get ahead if they want to."

"Phoebe Fraser is prejudiced," he said, with a grin. "Her father happens to have won the Swann accolade for turnover last year. However, I'll let you into a secret. When I started the network, back in 'fifty-eight, I made up my mind that the only way to muster a reliable work force is to pay a fair rate, and promote every man who shows initiative. I've lived by that rule ever since and it's paid me handsomely."

"How many men do you employ, sir?"

"Nearly two thousand. Why?"

"Well, sir, what I mean is . . . I don't want to sound impertinent but . . . there are thirty millions living here, and I've read that half that number don't have enough to eat, and have to live in awful places like those houses near your yard. Would you say that was true, sir?"

"Yes, it's quite true. But deduct the percentage that will never make much of their lives, no matter what kind of start or helping hand they get." He paused, wondering how to expound the popular doctrine of self-help without seeming pompous. "What a man makes of his time here is largely his concern, son. My waggon-master Keate sends me a stream of street arabs he finds sleeping out on the wharves and under arches. He's done it for years. Well, two of them have got ahead famously. One, name of Rookwood, is manager of my Southern Square. Of the rest, about half moved up so far and then stuck and the other half dropped straight back to the gutter. That's my notion of charity. Give a man a push and let him forge ahead or run clean out of steam, whichever he chooses." He glanced at Giles trying to decide whether or not he had made any impression. When the boy made no reply he said, "Have you a fancy to be a parson?" and at once saw Giles colour, not with embarrassment but more, he would say, from the effort of concentration.

"No, sir, I don't think so. Most parsons—well—they seem to do what most poets do. Preach, and leave the rest to the congregation. Your idea sounds a lot better than that, sir."

"Well, I'm obliged to you," Adam said, turning his head to hide one of his tight grins.

They moved off then and went jogging down the dust road that ran under the hedge bounding the estate from the north. On their left was a larch coppice, relieved by a few Scots firs and where the leaves were sparse Adam could just see the ruin of a pheasant hide some ten yards back from the road. A queer thought occurred to him as they passed it and swung in the main gate. That hide was the place where this solemn, rather likeable boy had been conceived one hot June afternoon some thirteen years ago. It seemed a curious yield to an unconventional tumble on a pile of bracken. And yet, now that he came to think about it, there was a kind of design about it for his presence as an embryo had played a vital part in helping Henrietta ride out that frightful period that began the very next day, with the crash at Staplehurst. Perhaps this had something to do with the boy's addiction to poetry, his serious approach to life, his concern for the world's troubles. It was possible, he mused, to guess the course of all the other children but no one could predict much about Giles save that he would suffer, and learn something important on that account. He thought, "Henrietta already senses something about the boy. That's why she talked me into changing his school . . ." and it occurred to him then that Giles was the most interesting of his brood. Perhaps, who knew, he would prove the most rewarding.

He said, urging the mare into a trot as they tackled the drive, "Well now, after all that I could do with bacon and eggs. How about you?" and Giles said, with a smile, "I can almost smell them from here!"

And they rode into the stable yard, a little closer, to Adam's way of thinking, than they had set out an hour before.

2

The morning ride had immediate consequences. Giles took up the option of changing schools that same day, after leafing through the prospectus of a foundation called West Buckland, pictured in the illustration as a rather gaunt, neo-Gothic building, standing on the crest of a long ridge and looking, he thought, a little incongruous in its rural setting. It seemed an unpretentious place, nothing like as splendid as the Mellingham foundation and had apparently developed from a school set up in a North Devon farmhouse by a local parson called Brereton, himself a pupil of the famous Arnold of

Rugby. Had Giles known it, the prospectus had caught Adam's eye on account of its modesty. It did not pretend to compete with the well-to-do schools that were springing up all over the country, to cater for businessmen whose sons were still not welcome at top-flight schools, but seemed to aim at providing a sound education within the limits of a far smaller income than he possessed. He had glanced at many school prospectuses in his time (he had hauled building materials for many new schools) but this was the only one entirely innocent of attempting to promote in pupils a sense of privilege, that seemed the badge of the newly-rich who patronised these places.

A day or so after Giles had made his decision Adam drove him and his mother into London to stay overnight, and do some shopping on his behalf and hers in and around Oxford Street. An hour or so of this, however, was as much as Adam could stand and by mid-afternoon he announced that he would rejoin them for high tea at the Norfolk Street hotel and proposed taking himself off in a hansom. Henrietta then remembered she had a fitting at a costumier's in Haymarket and said, "Take the boy off my hands, then. It'll embarrass him to sit about in one of those places. Drop him off at the hotel on your way down to the City."

They hailed a cab and went on down towards Trafalgar Square where Giles said suddenly, "I've never seen the Houses of Parliament, sir. Could we go there tomorrow?"

"You can go there now if you've a mind to," Adam told him. "I'll drop you off at the corner of Whitehall and it's not ten minutes' walk. Here's half a crown. Walk around a bit on your own, and get a cab to run you back to the hotel at around five. You're not scared of getting lost, are you?"

"No, sir," said Giles, seriously, "I've got a map. I bought it at the station for twopence and I've already ringed the hotel," and he produced a folded street map and held it up for Adam to see, a circumstance that Adam welcomed, for it concealed the smile Giles' solemnity encouraged.

"That's capital," he said, and watched Giles step down and merge into the crowd outside the National Gallery, thinking, "Damned if I get the hang of him, somehow. He's more like a little old man than a boy. A gentlemanly old man, with the innocence of a six-year-old . . ." But then, because he was on home ground, he dismissed his family in favour of a complicated contract Tybalt had sent to the hotel by messenger that morning.

Giles set off in high spirits, never having previously been given the freedom of London and was tempted to look in at the National Gallery but decided instead to cross the Square and walk on down past the Horse Guards Parade to Inigo Jones' banqueting hall where, he recalled, King Charles had been beheaded one bitterly cold January morning, in 1649.

He found the plaque marking the spot and studied it with interest, wondering if it was true that Charles (whom he always considered a dignified and rather ill-used monarch) really had worn two vests that day, in case he shivered and gave witnesses the impression that he was afraid to die. It was not difficult, providing one could ignore the steady stream of landaus, four-wheelers, hansoms and gaily-painted tradesmen's vans, to imagine this same street thronged with buff-coated soldiers and thousands of Londoners, each straining to catch a glimpse of the tremendous drama being enacted up there. As he had admitted to Prodder he had not yet embarked upon the Stuarts, but the story of King versus Parliament was well known to him, for it was graphically illustrated in one of Alexander's books, so that he was able to put himself in Charles' place as he stepped from the window to play the leading role in the tragedy. Beheading, he thought, must be a clumsy, bludgeoning kind of death but somehow, he could not have said why, far more dignified than hanging. Today, of course, they were more civilised about these things. Not so long ago, or so the old Colonel had told him, the brother of the reigning Emperor of Austro-Hungary had been executed by his Mexican subjects, but he had been tidily shot. Giles decided that if called upon to die, he would prefer this method, for at least it enabled a man to face death unbound and stand erect while he was about it.

Pondering these matters academically, he drifted into Parliament Square where he overheard a red-bearded policeman tell a group of sightseers that the House was not in session but they were permitted to enter so long as they did not venture beyond the door of the Commons. Giles tagged along behind the group, getting the benefit of a rather hectoring guide who joined them a few steps beyond, learning that the hall they were in was called St. Stephen's Hall, and that the present debating chamber was designed along the same lines as the church that had stood there and that this was why, on entering the House, members were required to bow towards the Speaker's Chair where the altar had stood.

It was while he was standing there, gazing reverently at the tiers of benches and the wide strip of carpet that separated them, that he noticed a young man who had disobeyed the policeman's instructions and actually crossed the threshold. He was obviously not a member of the guide's group for they had disappeared but remained standing there, a slim, rather good-looking young man aged about eighteen, wearing what struck Giles as homespun clothes that marked him down as a countryman. His expression, Giles thought, was absorbed, but slightly contemptuous, as though he rather doubted what he saw, and would presently go away to tell the first person he met that the chamber ran a poor third to the Tower of London and Westminster Abbey.

Giles could not have said what it was that caused him to concentrate on the young man's expression rather than on the various features of the empty chamber. He stood so still that he might have been one of the wax figures Giles had seen on a visit to Madame Tussaud's, and in the next minute he had leisure to study every detail of the alert, determined and rather aggressive face, crowned by a mop of dark brown hair and lit by a pair of lively and intelligent eyes. He was still staring when the young man spoke, as to himself, saying, in accents that were unmistakably Welsh, "Much smaller than one is led to believe. Disappointingly so. Fine buildings, yes, but here—why, man, it's suffocating. It's *crabbed*." Yet he went on looking.

Giles, although a very solitary boy, was amiable enough and could not but assume that the young man regarded him as his audience. He therefore coughed politely and said, "I thought it would be bigger. I mean . . . considering the tremendous things that happen here . . ."

And then the young man turned his head and studied him, his eyes lighting up in a lively, mischievous manner, as he said, in that pleasantly sing-song accent of his, "Tremendous? I wouldn't say that, or not of most of the men who come here. The great majority spout a lot of old nonsense, concerning things of which they know very little at first-hand and can't be bothered to find out. *I* could tell them. I mean to if I ever get the chance."

Giles could not have said why the young man impressed him so much more than any of the prefects, cricket-colours and 'bloods' of approximately the same age, who could be observed any day of the term swaggering about the quad and corridors of Mellingham, but he did, for all his patched boots, and a suit that seemed to be homesewn from pieces of tweed.

He said, respectfully, "Do you come here often and listen to them, sir?" and the young man's eyes twinkled in a way that suddenly made him seem very friendly and approachable.

"No, I haven't that pleasure," he said. "To be truthful, this is my first visit to London. But if I did come here and listen I wager I should find it difficult not to interrupt them sometimes." And then, as the twinkle died, "You, lad, do you live in London?"

"Not really," Giles told him, "I live in Kent but my father is in business here."

The young man looked interested.

"*Here?* In the House of Commons?"

"Oh no, sir . . . in the City. He has a transport service. It's called Swann-on-Wheels. It takes goods all about the country."

The young Welshman did not seem as impressed by this as Giles hoped he would be. " 'Swann-on-Wheels'," he said, thoughtfully. "I remember. I've seen your vans, as far north as Llanberis. They haul slate from there. The best slate in the world comes from Llanberis. And the worst wages paid to the men who risk their lives and health quarrying."

At that Giles identified him, at least to some extent. He was obviously 'Radical', a term he had heard applied to his father from time to time, although he was not at all certain what it meant, except that it implied a sustained protest against something or someone. He was going to ask, politely, if the young man was a Radical but the Welshman anticipated the question by asking another. "Why do you address me as 'sir'?" he said, and Giles was so dismayed that he stuttered a little, replying, "I . . . I suppose because you're older. Isn't it the polite thing to do to someone a lot older?"

"Not where I come from," the young man said, grimly, but suddenly he twinkled again and asked if 'Mr. Swann' had taken the opportunity to cross the road and look at Westminster Abbey. Giles said no, for he was due to meet his father and mother very shortly and had better start back at once in case he kept them waiting. Instead of using this as a means to shake him off, however, the young Welshman grew more expansive and said, gaily, "You can't be more than thirteen. Why did you come here by yourself to look at this place?" and Giles said he supposed it was because it was famous all over the world and because his grandfather, who had died a few months back, had told him every other parliament was a copy of it.

"Well, that's so," the Welshman conceded, grudgingly, "but it's very far from perfect for all that. One would have thought, after six hundred years' practice, it would have found ways of doing more to help the people it represents, particularly folk in my part of the world. Wales," he added, quite unnecessarily, so that it occurred to Giles he must be unaware of his warbling accent.

"Are things so bad there?" Giles asked, more from politeness than a desire to prolong the discussion, and the Welshman said warmly that they were very bad indeed. Most Welsh folk, he said, lived on pittances and were made to pay for a Church and a system of education that was alien to them. They were also, he added in passing, forbidden to kill so much as a rabbit on their own hillsides to make a Sunday dinner. He sounded so resentful about this that Giles said, "It sounds rather like the feudal system, sir. We've been revising that at school, you see. We've got to that bit about William Rufus turning everybody out of doors to make the New Forest into a hunting ground and cutting off peasants' hands for poaching."

The young man, he noticed, was now looking at him speculatively and at the mention of the New Forest his extraordinarily expressive eyes, that seemed even more volatile than his tongue, blazed up like two bonfires. But then, unpredictably, they veiled themselves in a friendly, almost conspiratorial glance as he said, "That's precisely *it*! The feudal system. You ask my Uncle Lloyd. He could tell you all about it. But I'll tell you something else, lad, and you can pass it on to your Dadda with my compliments. You've got a good head on your shoulders for a lad of your age so don't let anyone addle it at that fine gentleman's school I dare say you attend. Keep at your history. That's the only way to learn anything worth learning. Aye, and don't forget what happened to that chap Rufus when he got his hunting ground. Someone who knew what he was about shot an arrow through him and they carted him home on a wood-chopper's chariot like a carcase. Now then, before you go, let's shake hands on it, Mr. Swann. My name is George, and I live and work near those quarries where your Dadda hauls slate. A place you won't have heard about. Portmadoc, it's called."

"But you can't be a quarryman, sir," said Giles and Mr. George replied, chuckling, "No, indeed. But I'm a quarryman's advocate. A solicitor."

They shook hands very cordially as Big Ben struck the half-hour, and Giles recollected that it would take all the time left to him to find his way back along Whitehall and the Strand to Norfolk Street. He touched his cap as he turned and sped away and the young Welshman watched him go, his eyes alight with yet another expression, one that Giles would have identified, had he seen it, with the kind of glance Prodder and his father directed at him when he asked one of his complicated questions.

3

That was the beginning of what he later came to think of as the learning time, a phase in his boyhood when he began to make a conscious effort to organise the confused thoughts and fancies that buzzed about in his head, when he began to seek answers to some of his questions in the library of his new school, and in the comprehensive but sadly neglected library at 'Tryst'.

He took the young Welshman's advice literally, concentrating exclusively on history, and discovering that it was far more absorbing than the fiction prescribed by Phoebe Fraser, or his housemaster, or even his father, whose tastes were wide and who was known to be a great admirer of the late Mr. Dickens, who had also been involved in that terrible Staplehurst crash. He read his way steadily through the works of Macaulay, Froude, Green and Clarendon, pecked industriously at Lecky and Gibbon, and dipped into some of the heavier biographies. He set himself to make a kind of ground plan of social development within the British Isles, from the mid-sixteenth century, the point he had arrived at on leaving Mellingham, to the famous Peterloo Massacre, that he came to regard as a starter's tape for a marathon on the part of reformers to promote legislation enabling more or less everyone to participate in government.

Certain points of crisis fascinated him. The reign of Henry VII, for instance, recognisable as a time when power passed from feudal barons to London, with the king as the real head of the State. Or a century and a half later, when Pym and Hampden challenged the monarch's right to govern without parliament. He read at tremendous speed, skipping pages and pages devoted to interminable wars with France and Spain. What interested him much more was the tide of popular opinion that advanced, year by year, to swamp tyrants of one sort or another and wash them down the years, together with their privileges.

By the time the year ended and Christmas festivities were upon them again, with his brother Alex home from his adventures in Zululand and his sister Stella (who, unaccountably to Giles, was engaged in becoming unmarried) living at 'Tryst' again, he was entrenched in a world of his own and had become a dedicated if secretive Radical, so that he would have liked very much to have run against that friendly young Welshman again and discussed matters like the Declaration of Rights, the revolt of the American colonies, and the wave of reform bills that dominated the first half of the present century.

Many questions, of course, remained unanswered. Others were partially resolved by his father, for whom he formed a different kind of respect after their first real communication had been established during that early morning ride in the Easter holidays. From time to time, diffidently at first but later with confidence, he would approach him with some passage that needed simplification and although he suspected Adam was amused by his earnestness, he was always ready to attempt the translation of a flattish piece of prose into something within the scope of Giles' day-to-day experience, and would sometimes answer a query with a kind of parable. For this reason, if no other, Giles began to invest his father with an infallibility and profundity that had been absent from earlier assessments.

What puzzled Giles most was the dragging slowness of justice.

He would have thought that any man of sense could introduce the precepts of, say, the beatitudes into the everyday life of a nation that never ceased to boast of its regard for freedom and fair play, particularly the kind of fair play prescribed on the football field. The full implications of the word 'franchise' eluded him for a long time, and this was one of the topics he brought to Adam towards the end of the Christmas holidays.

They met one afternoon in the library, whither his father had gone in search of an atlas. Giles, glancing up from a heavy tome dealing with the Chartist agitation, found his father gazing down at him with that expression of affectionate bewilderment that had become the common currency of their relationship over the last few months. Adam said, banteringly, "You've become a regular bookworm, haven't you? Never see you when you haven't got your nose in a book. What are you reading now?" And Giles showed him, but Adam's expression only became more quizzical as he returned the book, saying, "Odd kind of book for a lad your age," but then, more seriously, "Tell me honestly, son, what do you make of it so far?"

"Well, it's not as exciting as the one I was reading yesterday about the machine-wreckers. It's interesting, though, to find out we nearly had a French Revolution."

Adam said, balancing himself on a leather armchair and shooting out his artificial leg in a half-petulant, lunging movement Giles had associated with his father all his life, "Aye, we came near enough. I remember thinking that when I came home after seven years abroad and rode the full length of England, to run smack into a regular riot in a mill town up north. Matter o' fact, they were burning your grandfather's mill at the time. I was lucky to fight clear of it and wouldn't have done if I hadn't had a damned good horse under me."

It staggered Giles to learn that his father had actually witnessed street riots, of the kind described in the book. Somehow it made him frightfully old, almost as old as the Colonel.

"How long ago was that, sir?" he asked and Adam, reckoning up, said it would be the summer of 'fifty-eight, the year he started the business and met and married his mother.

"But that was only eight years before I was born! Everyone had been given a vote by then, hadn't they?"

"Everyone? No, by George. Only those with the necessary property qualifications."

"But doesn't everybody get to vote as soon as they're grown up, sir?"

"They will, if Gladstone wins the next election. Except the women, of course. Can't see Parliament entertaining nonsense of that kind. But see here, don't imagine the vote is the beginning and end of it all, boy. The major reform bills concerning the franchise were law when that riot I saw took place but they didn't stop children being worked to death in mines and factories, or one man in every eleven dying a pauper. Can't hurry these things that way. Once you start hurrying there's no knowing where it will all stop. Main reason we've got ahead of everyone else is because we believe in taking our time. Bend rather than break, that is, as we did when the Chartists put their spoke in." He considered the boy gravely a moment. "Ever hear of a doctrine called 'the inevitability of gradualness'?"

"No, sir. What is it?"

"You could say it's the system we've adopted over here. Without acknowledging it officially, that is. The country's wealth improves and with it, bit by bit, the privileges of the people who contribute to it. It's a kind of tug-of-war. The lower class pushing upwards, the class above them pushes the people above them and the chaps on top have to make room or be shown the door. Been happening one way or another ever since the Reformation. Slow? Yes, it is, and a bit of a muddle sometimes, but a damned sight better than the iron fist and then a mob loose in the streets. Read a bit of Russian, French and German history and judge for yourself."

He paused, still regarding the boy with an expression that reminded Giles, improbably, of his last glimpse of the talkative young Welshman he had met at the door of the House of Commons. "You're an odd one and no mistake. Do you think we'll make a schoolteacher out of you?" He leaned forward, and Giles saw now that he was addressing him man to man for the first time, almost as though he had been discussing a choice of regiments with Alex. "Seriously, what would you *like* to work towards? Anything in my line of country?"

And the boy replied carefully, "I don't think so, sir. Not unless you wish it, that is. I think I'd like . . ." and he stopped.

"Speak up," Adam said, sharply. "I won't erupt. Most fathers in trade take it for granted their sons will pick up where they leave off, but I'll tell you something I wouldn't tell your brothers. Not yet any road. Nobody who isn't dedicated to commerce the way I am can make a success of it. What would you *like* to do with your life, allowing for the certainty you'll change your mind in a year or so?"

"I think I should like to help speed things up a bit, sir. That . . . what was it . . . 'inevitable' something . . . ?"

"Inevitability of gradualness."

"Yes, sir, I see what you mean, of course, about revolutions and riots, but we really ought to get on with it a bit faster, didn't we? I mean, make laws against throwing those Farthings out, and sending them to separate workhouses, and giving those Welsh quarrymen Mr. George told me about a big enough wage to stop them risking being sent to prison for poaching local rabbits."

His father must have looked quite blank at this so he went on, hurriedly, to explain the gist of the conversation he had with the young Welshman when he visited Westminster. As he spoke, however, he saw the twinkle return to his father's eye, so that he faltered, concluding, "Oh, I daresay it sounds vague, sir . . ."

But Adam exclaimed, thumping his leg, "Not a bit vague for a lad your age! It's more than your sister Stella or your brother Alex could have put into words at eighteen, much less thirteen. That new school of yours seems to suit you. Well, now, here's my advice for what it's worth. Follow that Welshman's advice and read everything that interests you and when you've read it think about it, and try and put your thoughts on paper some time. I'd be interested to read 'em, and so would your mother. Looks to me as if we've got a real radical in our family after all, and maybe it's time for, as I told you, I'm only half one. Here, what the devil am I doing gossiping to you by the hour? I've got a county schedule to work out by lunch time," and he stood up and lunged off with the atlas under his arm, leaving Giles to reflect that the Governor wasn't half bad compared with most, for at least he didn't talk down to a fellow as most governors did.

*   *   *

For all his passionate love affair with constitutional history, he did not consign Prodder Talbot's poets to the attic. From time to time he still read poetry, finding he had acquired, somewhere along the line, the trick of memorising lines that caught his fancy in a way that he could never remember a method of solving sums, or a conjugation of French verbs.

His new surroundings on the edge of Exmoor helped him in this respect, for here he inhabited a countryside that seemed to him much closer to the England of Goldsmith, Wordsworth and Gray than his native Kent, where the ancient townships were within hailing distance of one another and the fields, woods and rivers were, for the most part, tamed, and at a cultivator's disposal. Only a mile or so from the grey Gothic pile on the ridge the river Bray ran between steeply-angled pastures, covered with heath and sown with granite spurs, and tangled thickets of ash and sycamore crowded into the folds and river bottoms forming dark islands in a sea of green and purple moorland. In spring and summer it was a gay, companionable region, a pretty patchwork of primrose, violet, celandine, hawkweed and foxglove, and by late summer, if the season had been dry, the moor lay parched under a sky that seemed twice as tall as the skies over Kent and Berkshire. Shy, unfamiliar birds hovered there, and you could sometimes run three miles between the widely-scattered farms without seeing another human being, for the homesteads about here were old and crumbling, and most of the young men and women had moved away to the west, where the land was relatively level and the soil richer.

With the coming of autumn the woods slipping down the steep hillsides turned guinea yellow, plum purple and, here and there, russet, as though stained with old blood, and the school buildings put on their evening mantle of violet vapour even before the tea bell brought the boys trooping into the covered playground from the football field and the entire establishment, that smelled of boiled greens in high summer and damp cloth under the spring drizzle, seemed to smell of chrysanthemums and dead-leaf bonfires.

Full winter he had yet to experience up here but he judged it would be a time of tearing winds and flurries of sleet hurling showers of Exmoor-tempered darts against the windows of Big School, where the boys gathered between tea and prep around a fireplace burning a mixture of logs and pungent peat. For all its austerity and remoteness, it had a magic of its own that could absorb you if you let it, and didn't hanker after the creature comforts of more civilised places.

The school itself was barely twenty years old but the locale was as old as time, the tiny East Buckland churchyard coming closer to Gray's Stoke Poges than any churchyard about 'Tryst', whereas the hills and valleys they crossed in the bi-weekly runs might not have been traversed since the day the earth cooled, leaving the country-side as seamed and flawed and crinkled as a twice-baked apple. He felt at home here, as he had never felt at Mellingham, or even at 'Tryst', where the surrounding countryside was trim and settled, worked over by fifty generations of gardeners, every one an advocate of the regimented bloom and the trim half-moon bed. It was a place to work, a place to think and, above all, a place to put a keen edge on one's appetite. By the end of his second term Giles had put on almost a stone and grown, or so his mother told him, an inch and a quarter in eight months.

He had developed in other ways but Henrietta, who could spare him little enough time now that yet another baby had arrived in the last week of October, took no heed of this, whereas Adam kept his observations to himself. He made time, however, to write a jocular fortnightly letter about the hubbub surrounding the political issues of the day, notably his old friend General Roberts' march to Cabul, and Gladstone's Midlothian campaign that was setting a new style, so Adam said, in Parliamentary elections and would doubtless have Giles' approval, for "it was likely to speed things up a bit".

It was on account of this last exchange that Adam felt obliged, in the first days of the New Year, to grant Giles' request to stay over-night in London in order to attend one of Gladstone's monster rallies at Exeter Hall.

Adam, although interested in overall Imperial trends, had never wasted time attending political meetings, having decided long since that one was more likely to come at the heart of an issue by reading and reflecting on newspaper accounts rather than by subjecting oneself to blasts of platform oratory. Thus he had gone through life without ever hearing Gladstone or Disraeli address a public meeting. Having been beguiled into attending one by his son, he found himself enjoying it more than he had anticipated, largely because the boy's enthusiasm was as infectious as measles.

*   *   *

It began quietly enough, with twelve hundred people, jammed shoulder to shoulder, listening attentively to a succession of preliminary speakers—'warm-up men' as Adam informed his son, adding that this was a type the political and boxing fraternities had in common, providing they could coax a Titan into the ring. Having satisfied himself, however, that Giles was impressed by what they had to say about Irish Home Rule, the disastrous errors and injustices of the Zulu War, the extending franchise bill, and various other inflammable topics, he surrendered himself to the atmosphere of moral self-righteousness that hovered above the meeting like a cloud of incense. By the time the last warm-up man had said his piece he actually caught himself murmuring "Hear, hear" when the speaker described the battle of Isandlwana, and the vindication of Lord Chelmsford at Ulundi, as "a needless blood-letting, an outrage against the noble savage by a Christian nation turned pirate". He wondered, privately, what Giles would make of that now that his brother had returned from the piratical affray, with heady tales of the defence of Rorke's Drift, but his reflections were cut short by a sustained rumbling sound, like a ship-load of cabin trunks being trundled down a long flight of stone steps, and the distant roar soon enlarged itself into a storm that became, within seconds, a tempest, so that it was with some surprise he identified the cause of the uproar with a movement of the platform curtains as they parted to allow the great man to advance to the centre of the dais and bask, for some five minutes, in the hysterical adulation of his supporters.

All traces of cynicism deserted him then for there was absolutely no denying that he was confronted, not by a professional politician but A Presence, likely to regard a moment's inattention as blasphemy. Great, thunderous cadences emerged from the lips and the bright, unwinking eye held him rigid in its beam, a beam that had the power to isolate every one of those upturned faces and convey a curious impression of nakedness, as though Gladstone was addressing not one meeting but twelve hundred meetings held in as many sound-proofed cubicles.

It was extraordinary, Adam thought, how defenceless one was against the compelling logic and booming oratory of the spellbinder for somehow, despite an acute awareness of personal vulnerability, one knew it was a spell, but a spell capable of suspending reason and checking any attempt to weigh the content of successive declarations, words and phrases, each of which hit the audience like a jet of scalding water, so that one might as well have challenged the tablets of Sinai as the edicts flung the length of Exeter Hall.

His theme, Adam had noted, had been advertised as "the power and potentiality of a fully-enfranchised electorate" and had promised, he thought, to be insufferably dull to a boy not yet fourteen. A swift glance at Giles, however, told him how wrong he had been to take this for granted and make no allowance for the impact of an orator buttressed by an unshakable conviction that every word he uttered was put into his mouth by Jehovah, whose vessel he was.

If Adam and everyone else in the great hall were spellbound then Giles was hypnotised as effectively as an African primitive at the feet of a paramount witchdoctor. He sat with his small body thrust forward, hands gripping chair-arms, elbows slightly outthrust and shoulders braced, as though crouched at the starting line of a race upon which his life depended. The deluge of words from the platform seemed to sweep over the boy like Atlantic rollers but it was manifestly clear that, far from being stunned by them, he welcomed the drenching as the most enriching experience of his life.

". . . We cannot reckon upon the clergy of the established Church either in England or Scotland . . . We cannot reckon upon the wealth of the shires, nor upon the wealth of the country . . ." The rhetoric belched from the man like a succession of crashing broadsides, overturning everything between cannon-mouth and target. ". . . In the main these powers are *against us* . . . we must set them down as our most determined foes! But, gentlemen . . . *gentlemen* . . . above *all* these things, *behind* all these things, THERE IS THE NATION ITSELF, and this great trial of strength with justice and true, unsullied pride as the inheritors of the great democratic tradition as its prize, is proceeding *before* the nation! The nation is a hard power to rouse but when roused harder still and more hopeless to resist!"

It occurred to Adam then, a mere fleeting thought skimming

over the surface of the flood, that this man was not really speaking of the nation at all. He spoke for no one but himself but this was more than enough. No party, no coalition of parties, not Crown, nor Lords, nor consortium of privilege could hope to resist such a force for long and must, inevitably, be engulfed and sent flying, so that at length all England, all Britain and, ultimately, he supposed, all parts of the world where British interests prevailed, must be Gladstonised, even as Giles was Gladstonised where he sat straining forward in his seat resolved not to miss a syllable of the oration, or a single gesture that accompanied them.

Even the tempest of applause that followed Gladstone's withdrawal to the semi-circle of seats where sat the stupefied officials and warm-up men, could not top the majesty of the speech itself. As they rose, and knots of fussy, rosetted stewards began to dart up and down the aisles, ushering the bemused audience into the street, the rolling echoes of Gladstone's broadsides continued to reverberate, so that Adam, one arm on his son's elbow, had to make a conscious effort to manoeuvre his artificial leg round the angle of the bench-end, as though awakened from a trance and not sure where he was or which direction he should take.

In the street it seemed banal to make a comment so they walked briskly along the gas-lit pavements, each coming to terms with the tremendous experience, each preoccupied with striking a bargain between the reality and the fantasy of the splendid occasion. It was only when, somewhere around the Haymarket, Adam hailed a hansom, and they had hoisted themselves into the snug interior, that Adam was able to say, "Well, Giles . . . ?"

And Giles replied in the voice of someone who had been a witness to some astounding natural convulsion, "It's . . . like . . . like *Moses* . . . That bit where he comes down from Sinai with the tablets . . . What I mean is, you *have* to listen . . . You *have* to obey!"

And Adam thought it strange and rather comforting that at least one of his sons should have inherited his own reflective powers, for it had been of Moses, descending from Sinai with the dictates of God Almighty tucked under his arm, that he had thought at the very beginning of the peroration.

For himself already the numbing effects of the bombardment were beginning to wear off, the long rumbling echoes of those measured cadences merging into the steady roar and rattle of London traffic, but then, he thought, he was fifty-three, and had seen and experienced pretty well everything, whereas the boy at his side was open to everything new and strange and compelling. Giles' Gladstonisation, no doubt, would take like a smallpox injection, and stand him in good stead in a world that could do with any amount of moral uplift, even if some of it was misdirected and took no account of the frailty of men, Englishmen along with everyone else.

7

George Orders Oysters

GILES he was getting to know. Alexander, having made his decision, presented few problems. His daughter, Stella, in her present situation, needed a mother's help, whereas the five younger children were primarily Phoebe Fraser's concern. There remained George, Crown Prince designate of the Swann empire.

Most people, including his mother, brothers and sisters, and especially the staff at 'Tryst' and families within calling distance, took George for what he seemed—a happy, hearty, excessively amiable extrovert, with a propensity for getting into scrapes but enough guile to talk himself out of most of them. George had always been the most popular of the Swann children. School-fellows found him amusing, inventive and companionable, whereas even schoolmasters who wrote "Will not apply himself . . . could do better . . . a disappointing term", or an uncompromising 'Idle' on his school reports, referred to him jocularly as "that young rascal Swann" when his name came up, as it frequently did, in common rooms.

Taken all round the word most frequently applied to him, particularly by the ladies, was 'engaging' and this he indubitably was, for, although irrepressible, and resentful of all disciplines, his amiability rarely deserted him, not even when he was carpeted and flogged. He was one of those fortunate males whose grace, good looks and sense of humour enabled him to escape the full consequences of irresponsibility at all levels, so that he was usually dismissed as 'a real boy', whatever that might mean in scholastic parlance. It was a generalisation that fooled everybody but his father, who had been assessing him ever since he could toddle as far as the cistern loft and find out what happened when the outfall pipe was blocked with one of his sister's dolls. Latterly Adam had come to certain conclusions regarding George's potentialities and failings.

In their last confrontation Henrietta had accused Adam of paying strict attention to the merits and demerits of the men he employed but maintaining a benevolent neutrality in respect of his family. On the occasion of Stella's present trouble she spelled this out but long before that, and on many less serious occasions, she had charged him with parental neglect, even going so far as to declare that, in some respects, he resembled a dog fox who trotted across country overnight, sired a sizeable litter, and then trotted back again to his earth over the county border. This, a vulgar thought no doubt, was nonetheless an accurate summing-up if one excepted George, his second son. For George, alone among them, had not been sired absentmindedly but purposefully, almost deliberately one might have said, as part of an openly arrived at bargain between man and wife.

Sometimes, when she was in one of her maternal moods, Henrietta would reflect upon the occasions when each of her nine children had been conceived. She could isolate three such occasions specifically, the remainder being guesses. Giles was easy to isolate. She had come by him less than twenty-four hours before the Staplehurst crash, whereas the last of them, the baby born but a few weeks ago, owed his existence to his parents' endeavour to dispel the gloom that descended on 'Tryst' after they had laid the old Colonel to rest. George was a similar case, except that here she recalled in detail the circumstances of his conception, as marking a reconciliation between man and wife after the one serious quarrel of their married life. George had resulted from an industrious night they shared at the old George inn, in Southwark, ending the sour period that succeeded the death of one Luke Dobbs, chimney-sweep, in a 'Tryst' chimney.

It was a time she did not like to dwell upon, even at this distance, for it had seemed to her, after a month of domestic turmoil, that she had lost Adam to Edith Wadsworth, to whom he had gone seeking balm for a bad conscience. But Edith, God bless the woman, had not pressed her advantage. Instead she sent him south again with some good advice and the upshot of it had been that almost ritualistic reconciliation, with herself installed as mistress of a house to which they could lay title, and a new understanding between them concerning their individual responsibilities. George—laughing even then according to his father—had appeared on Valentine's Day in the following February, a day that marked a spectacular advance in the fortunes of Swann-on-Wheels, and perhaps it was on this account that Adam had always seen George and no other as his commercial heir, with a significance that had not attracted itself to any of his other children. He knew, for instance, that George used charm and good looks as an insulator, disguising a natural indolence that, in turn, concealed a lively intelligence. It was Adam's intention to peel away his son's protective layers of bluff and enable the brain beneath an opportunity to expand. Not only for George's sake but for the ultimate glory of Swann-on-Wheels.

Adam Swann had not been selecting deputies for twenty years without learning how to sift wheat from chaff and something told him unequivocally that here was his natural heir, whose high spirits and ingenuity might be turned to good account in the next two decades. George, of course, was still at the stage when he pretended to make light of money but he would get over that once he had taken the fever of competitive commercial enterprise, once his curiosity had been aroused by the infinitely subtle manifestations of mer- chandising that was the national substitute for poetry in a race mainly composed of traders of one sort or another. The important thing, as he saw it, was to make an early start on the boy, to fire his imagination and foster in him the pride of personal achievement, of the kind his father enjoyed every time he totted up a sheaf of monthly returns. Plenty of people seemed to think that there was something ignoble in money-making, and even those who had dedi- cated their lives to it often went to extraordinary lengths to apologise for their obsession. Adam Swann had never subscribed to this social fiction and neither would his son George if he could help it.

These were among the reasons that prompted him to cut short his son's formal education and introduce him, at the earliest pos- sible age, to the source of all the good things in life he had enjoyed so far. He was not looking for a gentleman to replace him when, if ever, he retired and took to fox-hunting three days a week. What he needed, what he was absolutely determined to salvage from his family, was at least one person, bearing his name, who was a com- bination of a realist and a romantic. For at the hub of a concern like Swann-on-Wheels there was need for both.

*   *   *

George was not sorry to be released from the strictures of school, although he had a few misgivings when he learned that he was to

169

sacrifice the prospect of an idle year or two at 'Varsity where, so the seniors told him, life was tailor-made for someone lucky enough to possess a father who sneered at examinations and degrees and had a city niche awaiting him when (as must inevitably happen in George's case) he was sent down in disgrace. There were, George reflected, during his initial apprenticeship period at the yard, certain compensations in being regarded as a man after passing one's seventeenth birthday. One was having one's own rooms five days a week, and the privacy that went with them. Another was a sufficiency of pocket-money. But best of all, of course, was the prospect of having London as his first oyster, with any number of replacements awaiting him as soon as he began his travelling scholarship in the provinces.

His first independent act was to cultivate a moustache, very modest as yet but destined in time to become one of the most luxuriant in the network, where fierce moustaches had long been accepted as the badge of manhood. At seventeen he already looked like a man, being five feet eleven with shoulders to match, so that the progress of his moustache (after an anxious week or two) pleased him without surprising him. George, in fact, rarely was surprised. He was not precocious exactly, and few thought of him as cocky, but he had a way of winning the trust of almost everyone he encountered, not merely those who might have been expected to show respect for an amiable youngster with certain expectations in the City. Indeed, most of the people he met during that first six months began by patronising him on this account but soon they succumbed to his charm and good humour, so that instead of referring to him behind his back as 'Swann's cygnet', they sometimes spoke of him among themselves as "That nice young chap with all his wits about him, the one the Gaffer's schooling for the succession".

He had, of course, certain basic advantages and could take for granted deference from the old hands like Tybalt, the chief clerk, and Keate, the waggonmaster. But this did not explain how he won over the semi-independent men of the network, shrewd characters like Stock, the lawyer, and Godsall, a former army lieutenant, who had exchanged a commission in a crack regiment for a regional post under Swann and was currently managing the Kentish Triangle.

It was Godsall, under whom George worked that first summer, who initiated him into the mysteries of the Swann System, explaining the kind of decisions regional managers were expected to make twenty times a day, and the hundred and one processes, all insignificant in themselves, that contributed to the overall pattern of an enterprise that kept a thousand waggons moving along the roads of Britain and hauling everything from a flatbed printing machine to a barrel of herrings. By the time the introductory period was over, and George was ready to embark on his travelling scholarship, one of Adam's initial hopes concerning the boy's indoctrination had been fulfilled. He no longer took the network for granted, as something that had absorbed his father ever since he could first remember him. Instead, he came to regard it as a complicated, extremely efficient piece of apparatus, that seemed to have evolved from nothing and was nurtured through the years by his father's highly-charged imagination, plus the devotion of a handful of men he had selected to project a policy of nonstop expansion.

It was the unctuous, bald-headed Tybalt, possibly, who was responsible for this indoctrination. For Tybalt, chaperoning him during his week in the estimates section, was inclined to talk nostalgically of the earliest days of the concern and how, at times, it had seemed they must go to the wall when his father (whom the clerk clearly worshipped) reinvested every penny that came in from the regions in order to follow the drumbeat of expansion. He spoke of many other things, of which George had been dimly aware—Adam's desperate situation when his partner, Avery, had become involved in a scandal and fled the country, after squandering the firm's reserve capital on a Spanish dancer. Of days and nights when Adam, with no guidelines apart from his intuition, and deep-rooted faith in himself, had remained closeted in that belfry overlooking the Thames, wrestling with the kind of problems that beset a besieged general. Of the invention, during one of these all-night sessions, of the firm's ready reckoner known as Frankenstein. And of Adam Swann's hardihood after he had lost a leg and returned to work a year later, having learned to walk again in Switzerland. Tybalt seemed shocked when George cheerfully admitted that most of this was new to him, that he had always been inclined to regard the

Governor as someone far too set in his ways to be interesting to one of the rising generation. After a week in Tybalt's company, however, another in the company of Keate, the waggonmaster, and the pursuit of one or two private lines of enquiry touched off by their confidences, George Swann was able to see his father in a new light. He was not, as most fellows' fathers seemed, a conservative old buffer, self-harnessed to a juggernaut, and incapable of leading a gentleman's life with the money he had made. In his own way he was an artist, almost as much an artist as that chap Michelangelo, who had spent years (or so they said) lying on his back in a hammock painting a ceiling. Or perhaps someone like Christopher Wren, who had raised St. Paul's out of the ashes of the Great Fire of London. However one looked at it, it was undeniable that Adam Swann had done something useful with his life when he might so easily have frittered it away like the old Colonel, for whom George had had affection but certainly no awe, of the kind he was beginning to have for his father.

He pondered this for some time without making a direct reference to it. At last, however, his curiosity got the better of him when they were on their way home in a thick pea-souper one Saturday afternoon and he said, suddenly, "Why *haulage*, sir? I mean, when you threw up the army after the Mutiny, and decided to go into business on your own account, why not banking? Or anything a bit less strenuous?"

Adam said, with one of his tight grins, "Now what touched off that, I wonder?" and said it in a way that implied he knew very well the source was Tybalt or Keate.

George was not a boy to beat about the bush. He said, promptly, "A man can't spend a week at the yard without hearing the old hands talk about you and the early days. There must have *been* a reason for the choice."

"Oh, there was," said Adam, chuckling. "I knew absolutely nothing about anything else that went on in the City. From your age, until I was turned thirty, I was trained in two skills. How to stay alive, and how to blow the head off the chap the far side of the breastworks. Apart from that nothing save how to care for horses. I took someone's advice about it. I do that from time to time and it saved my bacon in this instance." He paused a moment, cocking his head, as though listening to the hiss of the halted train, now enveloped in thick, yellow fog. Then, "You ever remark on your mother's ring? That fine ruby, with the Swann crest on the shank?"

"Often. Has that anything to do with it?"

"Everything to do with it. That's the sole survivor of a string of thirty Burmese rubies I lifted from the field at Jhansi, in January, 'fifty-eight, the last action I was in. I smuggled it home in my sabretache and raised money on it. I was going to invest in railway stock but a railwayman I met had a better idea. He advised putting it all on the horses, but not in the usual way. He gave me a railway map of the period and told me to fill in the empty spaces. That was the start of it. Whole damned outfit emerged from that."

"Did you never have second thoughts."

"No," said Adam, "I never did. Not even in the worst times. I believed in what was happening around me. Most people didn't. Most people, particularly the well-educated, regarded the industrial wave of those days as a flash in the pan. I knew it wasn't. I knew Watt and Stephenson and Brunel and all the pioneers had changed the face of the world, not just the face of the country. I kept a hold on the horse, that was beginning to go out of fashion just then, with everybody around me going mad about railways. But horse or rail I like to think I kept ahead of the best of 'em. Does that answer your question, George?"

"Very fully, thank you, sir," said George, with his usual politeness, but Adam noticed that he remained thoughtful all the way home to Croydon where they picked up their gig. The fog was thinner out here, although visibility was still bad and they were moving under dripping trees a mile or so short of 'Tryst' before Adam broke the long silence, saying, "As to questions, lad, never mind asking 'em of me or anyone else. You learn that way. As to decisions, make 'em yourself, right down the line. Good, bad or indifferent they're the better for being your own. Do you follow me?"

"Yes, sir," said George, reflecting yet again that the Governor, however formidable he might look and sound, was a bit of a card when you really got to know him.

2

That was in the final weeks of the preliminary canter as he came to recognise it. After that it was a life of movement and bustle the full length of the country, in order to learn at first hand the local difficulties and advantages of every region in the network, together with what they hauled, what equipment and teams they rated, how high or low their managers were on the Headquarters' table and why, how far their territories extended, where it merged into a sister territory, what the local roads and railway services were like, what the rate of growth was in their cities and market towns. There was so much to learn. Who was hauling what, and why, and in what quantities? Why were hauls geared to certain factors—overall weight, roads, weather, and availability of teams? How did Swann's service compare with that of other hauliers? Who was on the way up and on the way down, a vast proliferation of agencies and special circumstances that sometimes caused a newcomer like himself to wonder how men like Tybalt had stayed sane all these years. And also how Adam Swann had forged ahead on two legs, much less one.

Sometimes he was tired and very occasionally he was bored, but usually he was absorbed in what he was doing, in the men he met and the country he travelled over. Just occasionally, as when he came up with an idea that looked like saving money, or tapping an unexploited field, he was exuberant, and prepared to work half the night putting his ideas on paper.

By the end of summer he was fairly familiar with the Kentish Triangle, the Southern Square, the Western Wedge and the Mountain Square of Wales. He had taken a liking to the ageing, cherry-faced Hamlet Ratcliffe, and his adoring wife, Augusta, with whom he lodged in their seaside house at Exmouth, in Devon. On the other hand instinct warned him that the manager of the Southern Square, an ex-vanboy (whom everyone at H.Q. continued to refer to as 'Young Rookwood', although Young Rookwood was nearly forty) regarded him as an interloper, so that he was relieved when he moved into the far West.

174

He got along well with Bryn Lovell, in the Mountain Square, based on Abergavenny, discovering that Lovell was as much a legend in these parts as was his employer on the banks of the Thames, for they told him that Lovell had once been instrumental in saving the lives of fifty-seven entombed miners and had thus put the name Swann on the map in these parts.

Towards autumn he moved up into a region marked on the office maps as 'Southern Pickings', a triangle of territory angled on Worcester, and concerned, in the main, with the transport of high-grade china. Still later, as winter drew on, he had worked his way north into 'Northern Pickings', hinged on Derby and Buxton, and after the Christmas break he began the New Year in one of the largest and most profitable of the regions, named on the maps as 'The Polygon', a five-sided square embracing the whole of Lancashire and parts of Cumberland and Westmorland.

By then, of course, as Adam noted but did not comment upon, he was converted. He ate, thought and slept haulage. Adam was content. The Crown Prince Designate looked like settling to the collar as comfortably as a well-broken Cleveland Bay.

*   *   *

George arrived in The Polygon at a time of transition.

Less than a year before John Catesby, who had ruled the region since its inception, and was known as one of his father's closest friends notwithstanding his militant Radicalism, had resigned to manage Grandfather Rawlinson's cotton mill, a few miles north of the Salford base, where he was experimenting with co-operative production, a process that involved sharing the duties of management with senior hands through a consultative committee. Sam Rawlinson, who now spent most of his time 'on 'Change' as he called it, shook his head over this when he met his favourite grandson at Manchester's London Road Station, in the first week of January.

"Eee, lad," he said, in the fruity North-country brogue that had fascinated George from childhood, "tak' no bloody heed of anything *that* chap tells you about handling men an' lasses! Time was when I thowt he was one o' them anarchists, ready to blow us all to kingdom come, but Ah've since come to reckon him soft in t'bloody noddle. When a chap in t'charge o' mill has to run to hands for ad-

vice on how to reckon profits, it's time he put his feet up to my way
o' thinking. Will tha' be staying along o' me and my Hilda while
you're getting the hang o' things hereabouts?"

George said, regretfully, that he would not. His father had thought
it more practical for him to lodge with Broadbent, the man who had
replaced Catesby as manager of The Polygon, and was reputedly
making a success of his stewardship. Sam, it seemed, had met Broadbent, and had reservations about him. "He's sharp," he said, "but
then he's Liverpudlian and they're all sharp out there. They have
to be, living cheek by jowl wi' twenty thousand blacks, and any
number o' Paddies, not to mention a sprinkling o' Greeks, Turks and
heathen Chinese. But there's summat Ah can't put a name to about
yon Broadbent. He's not lah-di-dah, for he come up t'same way as I
did, but he's got what we call a downy look. He's been twice married,
like me. They tell me his second wife were barmaid at the old Cock
and Hen, in t'Shambles, and free with her favours before she took
up with him. But maybe that's rumour, on account of him getting
John Catesby's job over everyone else's head. However, his turnover's good and that father o' yours is a rare picker when it comes
to finding men to make brass for him." He looked at George shrewdly
and added, "Your mother's well, I hope?"

"Blooming, grandfather, and sent her regards," George said. But
Sam commented, with a grin, "That's blarney. Our Henrietta
woulden tell me t'time o' day left to herself. I don't hold it against
her, mind. She's done well for herself and no thanks to me, for
you'll ha' heard she married dead agin me, when she was nowt but
a bit of a lass. Ah've owned Ah were wrong about your father mind,
but women don't forget easy and that's a fact. Well, now, you'll be
wanting to get out to Bowdon, where that chap Broadbent has a
snug house Ah'm told, wi' two servants and a carriage and pair. And
him nobbut a wharf-rat one time. That's the way of it up here. Rags
to riches if a man looks out for hissane, as me and your father did
when we were young an' spry like you."

George would have liked to have asked him a great deal more
about the family story concerning Henrietta's runaway match but
decided it could wait. Curiosity concerning his family background
was continually enlarging itself during his drift around the regions.
Every manager and every foreman had something to say regarding

the amazing career of Adam Swann, one-time mercenary soldier, who had built a transport empire on the proceeds of a necklace picked up on a battlefield. Already, in George's imagination, a romantic picture of the enterprise was assembling having about it the elements of a regular fairy story, complete with runaway brides, irate fathers, burning mills, train crashes and a hotch-potch of other exciting ingredients.

Sam piloted him to a suburban railway station and he was in the pleasant village of Bowdon within thirty minutes, finding it occupied a steep hill overlooking the Cheshire plain, its church standing out like a citadel against the grey, smoke-tinged sky. A sense of adventure stirred in him that had not accompanied his entry into other regions and he wondered if this was due, in part, to the fact that he was now standing on the heart of industrial England, where the helter-skelter began about a century ago, to spill down over the shires, catch its breath beside the Thames and then sweep halfway across the world.

Broadbent, and his wife Laura, were on the doorstep to greet him, together with Broadbent's two sallow daughters, Lizzie and Hester, one a year or so his senior, the other a sly-looking girl about sixteen. The atmosphere was one of nervous expectancy, as though he was a lodger of some consequence, and after being shown his comfortable, over-furnished room at the front of the house, he sat down to a dinner that was served with claret and port wine, luxuries that appeared at 'Tryst' on gala occasions only.

During the meal he was able to study Broadbent and his wife, looking for clues to the man's obvious success, evidenced by his relatively high style of living and the furnishings of a home that would not have disgraced a mill-owner. Broadbent was a well-muscled, hard-faced man about forty. His wife was a pretty woman more than ten years younger, with auburn hair and little to say for herself, for she seemed subdued in the presence of her fast-talking husband. Broadbent's daughters contributed nothing to the occasion but sat primly at board, gazing at him as though he had been a duke's son who brought unimaginable prestige to the house by consenting to sit at table.

Like Sam he did not quite know what to make of Broadbent, who seemed enterprising and well on top of his job, with any number of ideas for expansion, so that George could make a guess at the reason why he had been promoted over the heads of senior men. He seemed anxious to ingratiate himself with a son of his employer, treating George more like a Headquarters' delegate than a raw apprentice. As the meal proceeded George got the impression that he was unsure of himself, despite his bombast and was also, to some extent, sounding him out on how Headquarters had reacted to his spectacular progress up here.

"I've had to cut away a lot of dead wood, Mr. Swann," he said, using an ironed-out accent in which traces of his native Liverpool lingered. "Catesby, of course, was a first-rate man at his job but . . . well, at the risk of sounding superior, I'd say he was too provincial, too inclined to go after the minnows outside the hub of the beat, which is right here, in Manchester. We get little enough profit from cross-country hauls in the hill country to the north. Time was, of course, when we depended on 'em. The railways had it all their own way in the Cotton Belt then but nowadays we're landing more of the big fish, who look for time saved on a haul and to the devil with freight costs. I've just signed up Barlow's, the biggest packing warehouse between here and Liverpool. I've got a two-year contract out of them and it'll mean taking waggons off the rural runs. There's talk now, however, of cutting a deep-water canal between Trafford Park and Eastham, on the Mersey. It's my belief a haulier should get his foot in the door of every warehouse in the area before that happens. When it does carriers working on small budgets are going to the wall."

He rose, abruptly, before George could comment on the prospect of a canal linking Manchester with the coast and ordered Lizzie to play the piano, an upright, silk-fronted instrument in the parlour. "Lizzie has a good touch," he said, "or so I'm given to understand and Hester is having singing lessons. No damn sense in a man getting ahead if he doesn't put a bit of polish on his family, eh, Mr. Swann?"

George wondered how he would adapt to six weeks' domesticity in these surroundings, but followed his host into the parlour, seating himself dutifully in the brocaded armchair while Lizzie entertained with 'The Battle of Prague' and Hester, who had a high-pitched, rather warbling voice, sang some of Moore's Irish lyrics to her sister's accompaniment.

Mrs. Broadbent still said nothing but sat with folded hands in a high chair beside the huge coal fire looking, George thought, as if she was insufferably bored with her step-daughters' clumsy attempts to entertain. She was, he noted, a very attractive woman, with soft, brown eyes and a high complexion that might or might not be the result of merciless corsetting that made a cottage loaf of her youthful figure. He had thought of her as around thirty but now he realised she could be no more than twenty-five, and prettier than she had looked under the flaring gas-jets of the dining-room. She had soft features and a generous, slightly crumpled mouth, as if, at any moment, she would begin to cry, so that he wondered whether the assertive Broadbent bullied her and lavished all his affection on his plain, rather marionettish daughters.

In spite of the efforts they made to please, an atmosphere of strain remained present in the group and he was relieved when the clock on the mantelpiece struck ten and he could excuse himself on the grounds of being fatigued by the long journey north. Mrs. Broadbent had put a hot-water-bottle between his stiffly starched sheets and when he thanked her she said that Mr. Broadbent had instructed her to do all she could to make his stay up here a pleasant one and she was glad to do it, for he was young to be so far from home and at the mercy of the climate that prevailed up here in winter.

"I'm Welsh, myself," she said, "from Denbighshire and although it isn't so far from here it seems a long way sometimes."

She left then, presumably to see her daughters to bed in a room they shared along a corridor, and later, as he drifted off to sleep, George could hear them talking and giggling and concluded they were speculating about him. The thought led him on to the improbable subject of marriage, and how it affected people as they approached middle age. His travels were teaching him other things besides how to run a haulier's business. Down in the Southern Square Young Rookwood's home ran on patriarchal lines, his wife deferring to him on everything. In the Western Wedge the true if unacknowledged gaffer of the household was Augusta, Hamlet Ratcliffe's ageing wife, who treated her little husband like a pet bantam. Up here there was obvious tension between man and wife and half-consciously he compared it with the balance of power that existed between his mother and father at home, the one mistress of the home, the other absorbed in his role of provider, and using 'Tryst' as a hotel at weekends. Marriage of one sort or the other, he decided, was not for him. Whatever else it did it anchored a man, and the last year or so had given him a taste for movement and personal freedom. He went to sleep, lulled by the prospect of indefinite bachelorhood.

3

As the weeks passed, and he came to know the hub of the Polygon with its slippery setts, its winter sleet and fog, and its traffic problems that rivalled those of London, the character of Broadbent and Broadbent's real attitude towards him remained elusive, as did certain aspects of Swann's new rush of business in the area, almost all of it based on Manchester and its environs.

In all the other regions he had visited business was far more broadly based, no one town having a virtual monopoly of teams and waggons. Here it looked as if the new manager had decided to let the country traffic wither, placing all his resources at the disposal of half a dozen large concerns, like the huge packing warehouse of Barlow, at Old Trafford, and a new engineering works a mile or so nearer Manchester.

Every day, George noted, teams of waggons, most of them three-horse flats that his father always referred to as men-o'-war, went off to haul Barlow's bolts of cloth, the greater part consigned for Liverpool, and thence to the Near East and India. It puzzled him that a firm as large as Barlow's should not use its own transport or, alternatively, and seeing its premises were astride a railway, send its goods to the docks by rail, but when he put this to Broadbent the manager had an explanation. He could quote cheaper rates than the railway, he said, and all Barlow's waggons were used for home market distribution.

It was difficult, George found, to gather much basic Swann data from Broadbent, who continued to treat him as a guest rather than an apprentice learning the trade. Once he came near to admitting this, saying, "Of course, there's no harm at all in you seeing things first-hand in the regions. But when you settle in you'll surely be based at Headquarters along with your father. Meantime, make the most of it, Mr. Swann, for I should, given your opportunities. You're under no obligation to stay around this yard all day and are quite welcome to make free of my home. And my carriage and pair for that matter."

No such invitation had been offered him in more southerly and westerly regions, where it was taken for granted that he was there to work and not amuse himself, so he took occasional advantage of Broadbent's invitation and sometimes drove out with Mrs. Broadbent and her two step-daughters. Once, joined by Broadbent after dinner, they all went into town to see the new Gilbert and Sullivan opera, *H.M.S. Pinafore*, at the beginning of its first provincial tour.

He also accepted Broadbent's invitation to join him in a glass of whisky at one or other of the local taverns, making himself very drowsy in the afternoon after endeavouring to match his host drink for drink. He was given no chance to study the paper work, for Shawe, the chief clerk, a crony of the manager, watched over his ledgers and day books like a miser guarding his coffers.

Time passed pleasantly enough, however, and he came to enjoy Mrs. Broadbent's company, especially when her step-daughters were out visiting, or at one of their singing or piano lessons in nearby Altrincham. Someone far less perceptive than George would have concluded that Laura Broadbent was not a happy woman, for Broadbent was absent all day and when he returned, usually pretty well oiled George would say, he lavished his attention on Lizzie, who seemed to be his favourite. His inspired geniality towards George, however, never wavered, and the latter found it difficult to decide why he found the man repellent. Privately Mrs. Broadbent admitted that he was a hard case, driving others as ruthlessly as he drove himself, and added that his first marriage had not been a success, the first Mrs. Broadbent having left him on two occasions before dying of an illness brought on, it was whispered, by her overfondness for port.

"I don't know why I should tell you that, Mr. Swann," she said, colouring, "it just slipped out. That comes of having no one to talk to, I imagine, and I was always one for a bit of company before I married Harry." She paused a moment, whilst George, anxious to hear more, made sympathetic noises. She went on, "He or the girls will have held their tongues about something else, for they're on the way to becoming regular lah-di-dahs since he was made manager. But I was never ashamed of it. It's honest work, and you soon learn how to keep the men at arm's length, so long as you don't mind them thinking you're gormless. I'm talking about when I was a barmaid, at a place in the Shambles. They had a concert hall there, and first-class turns, try-outs for the big musical halls. I waited on the tables sing-song nights, and it paid well, what with the tips. I didn't come to Harry empty-handed."

He said, unguardedly, "Why did you marry, then, Mrs. Broad-bent?" She did not seem offended but smiled, so that her rather crumpled mouth curved upward instead of down and he saw her as her chorus-bawling customers must have seen her on a Saturday night at the Cock and Hen, a pretty, vivacious woman, who enjoyed her bit of fun and would likely extend a helping hand to anyone who needed it, drunk or sober.

"Why do any of us get married?" she asked. "It's a man's world, there's no denying that. We're brought up to look for it above all else, I suppose. He was a good-looking chap, and you've heard how he can talk when he's out to please. That wasn't all either. He played his cards well, did Harry Broadbent, not forgetting the trump. A widower, wi' two daughters, sore in need of a mother. Well, it didn't take long to spot that as a misdeal. Those two girls of his don't need a mother so much as a bottle of castor oil to improve their complexions and a switch to their backsides to teach them manners. They'd get that, the pair of them, if I had any say in bringing them up."

It seemed to him then, interested as he was in Laura Broadbent's troubles, that she was a little vindictive. "They aren't so much to write home about, Mrs. Broadbent," he said, "but they've been civil enough to me," whereupon she looked at him very steadily and seemed inclined to elaborate her point but then dropped her gaze, saying, with a shrug, "Aye, they have, so let it pass. They've had their orders, same as me. Especially that Lizzie."

She moved off then, on the excuse of attending to her baking and did not seem disposed to renew the conversation later but from then on she went out of her way to mother him and in a way that made a direct appeal to his chivalry, so that he found himself beginning to dislike Harry Broadbent against all reason, and look forward to the time when he moved over the border to the Edinburgh base, his next port of call.

It was February by then and he inadvertently let it be known that St. Valentine's Day marked his eighteenth birthday, regretting it instantly when Lizzie exclaimed, "St. Valentine's Day! Why, then we must celebrate!" and Mrs. Broadbent promised to bake a cake and set it with eighteen candles. But the day prior to his birthday he stumbled on a partial answer to one of the imponderables surrounding Broadbent and his change of policy in the Polygon.

The manager had gone off early, taking Shawe, the clerk with him, and during the breakfast break George wandered into the clerk's office to warm himself by the coke fire. Lying on the desk, apparently overlooked by Shawe, was the big ledger, with its alphabetically-listed sections, each devoted to a Swann customer in the region. Without looking for anything specific he opened it at 'B', running his eye down the quarterly returns for Barlow, the packer, but then he noticed a loose slip of paper, pencilled with two short columns of figures that he identified at once as percentages of the daily yield of hauls credited to the warehouse. He looked at the ledger again and made a rough cast of the total since the first day of the year. The figure astonished him. It was far larger than that of any two other customers combined and this caused him to check the slip of paper again, noting that each column was headed by an initial letter. One, the longer column, was equivalent to exactly five per cent of the total and was headed 'B'. The other, representing three per cent, ran under the letter 'S'. It did not take much intelligence to deduce that the 'B' stood for Broadbent and the 'S' for Shawe, the clerk, or that the percentages represented personal commissions.

He knew the system of rewarding regional managers on turnover, Tybalt having explained it in London. Swann's senior representatives in the provinces were paid a quarterly percentage on their gross, reckoned by Tybalt himself. There was no provision made for managers deducting their own commissions and, in any case, it was fixed at two-and-a-half per cent, not five, whereas clerks received a wage and did not qualify for commission. It all seemed to indicate that Broadbent, with Shawe as the jackal, was systematically helping himself to a substantial private commission and this explained a good deal, notably the manager's eagerness to keep him at arm's-length during office hours, Shawe's jealous hold on the paper work of the yard and, above all, Broadbent's prosperity, that could not be accounted for by his official income, however successful he had been in increasing turnover.

He looked again at the paper before folding it and putting it in his pocket book. At the bottom of the slip was the single word 'Drayton', and George recalled that Drayton was the name of the man who supplied the yard with forage. He turned to a page in the day book devoted to Drayton and found there the monthly sum expended for first-grade hay, making a note of the total and the price per bale. He then turned back to Barlow's entry and jotted down the daily totals on a pad, after which he went across the yard to locate Steedman, the head stableman.

Steedman was in the tack room, making an inventory of harness and in reply to George's query concerning forage he said the price of hay had come high this winter, owing to a wet summer, and all the teams used for short hauls were fed on second-class bales, delivered in bulk the first of every month. "It's poor stuff," he added, "and I've complained to the Gaffer about it. It's well enough for a short period, but the teams will drop back if it continues indefinitely. Seeing you're a privileged man up here, Mr. Swann, I'd take it kindly if you backed me in the matter. If the teams are under strength by early spring it'll be me who gets the rap over the knuckles, not Mr. Broadbent."

George said he would discuss the matter with the manager and left him, wondering whether to double check on his suspicions by making a call on Barlow but decided against it. The slip of paper in Shawe's handwriting, plus the information concerning the hay, converted his suspicions to near-certainties, warranting a report to Tybalt, or his father. But then, reflecting on what might happen as a result of disclosures, he began to feel uncomfortable about his detective work, reasoning that not only Broadbent would be dismissed, and possibly prosecuted, but that the penalty would extend to Laura Broadbent and Broadbent's daughters, none of whom could have been aware of what was going on at the yard or how Broadbent could afford a detached house, two servants, a carriage and pair, and regular pianoforte and singing lessons for the girls. Disclosures, so far as he could determine, would rebound upon the entire family, and whilst he had no special regard for the Misses Broadbent, he had a real affection for their stepmother, who had gone out of her way to make him welcome at Bowdon.

The thought caused him to examine his attitude to Laura Broadbent closely. Was it, he wondered, more than affection he felt for the lonely, hard-pressed woman? She had stirred something in him that had not been there a few weeks ago. He could not say what exactly except that it amounted to an awareness of women that had nothing in common with the feelings he had for his sisters, or the girls of the West Kent Hunt, with whom he had skylarked during school holidays. Laura had charm and a prettiness that grew on a man, together with other things that were new to him, an appreciation of her figure, of the way she moved, of the way she sometimes looked at him with a half-smile during one of Hester's warbling Irish songs and, above all, that towering pile of Titian hair, fastened by a row of combs. It occurred to him then how exciting it would be to see Laura with her hair down and the fancy excited him in a way that made him feel restless and at odds with himself. He thought, with a spurt of exasperation, "What the devil's happening to me up here? What is she to me anyway? A married woman getting on for thirty and married to a thief milking something like three hundred a year from the firm . . ." But he knew he lacked the inclination to sit down and write the report that, sooner or later, would have to be posted to Tybalt.

Then he had another idea, that at least had the advantage of postponing a decision for a day or so. On the following Saturday, only three days from now, he had arranged a visit to his grandfather, Sam Rawlinson. In view of what old Sam had said concerning Broadbent he might look for guidance in this quarter, stressing the fact that the Broadbents, one and all, had been at pains to make him welcome during his stay. The decision relieved him of the pressure his discoveries had laid upon him, so that he spent the rest of the day helping to load waggons and unharness returning teams. It was heavy work and gave him something else to think about so that he was able, with no more than a qualm or two, to get through his dinner in the company of the Broadbents and take a soda bath and retire to bed early, pleading stiffness after all that heaving in the yard.

The next morning brought him a huge Valentine card, obviously from Lizzie, for it bore a local postmark and a verse that ran,

> I love but you
> Pray love me too.

More to the point was a money order for two pounds from his father, a morocco leather cigar case from his mother, and an assortment of cravats, shirt studs and other gifts from the younger children. Opening his parcels he missed his train for the yard so that Broadbent went off in advance and while the girls were upstairs he showed his gifts to Laura, who admired the cigar case but frowned when she saw the gaudy Valentine card.

"I think that's right vulgar," she said. "Harry must have put Lizzie up to it, for she hasn't the brains to think of it herself. However, since it's your birthday, I've bought you a little something myself," and she gave him a cardboard box containing a small gold seal in the shape of a wedge, inscribed with his initials and the Swann insignia. "It's for your watchchain," she said, "all the fashionable young gentlemen are sporting fobs. Here, let me fasten it for you," and she faced him, lowering her head to clip the shank of the seal on to his chain.

It might have been her nearness, and the heady perfume she used, or perhaps the need of a gesture to express his appreciation. It might even have had something to do with his feelings of guilt that he was likely to be the agent responsible for boosting her out of this comfortable home and setting her adrift with a jobless husband. Whatever it was he surrendered to it. Holding her by the shoulders he kissed the top of her head, instantly regretting it and expecting, if not a slap across the face, at least a rebuke for taking such a liberty with her.

Nothing like this happened. All she did was to tuck the thin gold chain back into his waistcoat pocket, straighten herself and say, with a smile, "That's not much of a birthday kiss, lad. Here, let me show you how," and she threw both arms about his neck, inclined her full weight towards him and kissed him full on the mouth.

He had kissed girls before, perhaps a dozen or so at Christmas parties and hunt balls but he had neither given nor received a kiss of this sort. It made his senses reel. Her mouth, soft as a petal, touched off a succession of sensations that were at once alarming and extremely pleasurable, so that he was at a loss how to proceed from this point on and was immensely relieved when, standing back, she looked at him with complete unconcern and said, gaily, "Why, lad, don't look so sad about it! What's a kiss between friends on the day you come of age? Royalty don't wait upon twenty-first birthdays, and you're royalty up here, seeing whose son you are. Besides it's time some woman kissed you as if she meant it. You've got to start some time and what better day than this?"

That was the rub, he thought, dismally. What day was it, apart from the one marking his eighteenth birthday? The day he would have to start thinking how much or how little he put into that report he would have to send to Headquarters concerning the secret commissions her husband was milking from Swann hauls. The day when he had it in his power to make paupers of all four of them. He said, hoarsely, "Listen, Mrs. Broadbent . . . Laura . . . I . . . I'd like to say something, something I want you to remember. I'll be leaving soon. I'm moving to Scotland at the end of the month and maybe I won't see you again. But whatever happens . . . whatever comes of my stay up here, I'd like you to know how much I appreciated your kindness. If it hadn't been for that I would have cut this stint short and moved on almost at once. But you, well . . . you're one of the nicest persons I've ever met. And one of the prettiest into the bargain!"

He was astonished to see her blush, to watch the colour surge into her cheeks and then, swiftly it seemed to him, ebb as she said, with a rather pitiful attempt to sound gay, "Well, thank *you*, George! That was a lot more than a watchchain seal merits. And far more than I deserve in the circumstances," and without commenting on his hint she walked quickly through into the kitchen quarters where he heard her call sharply to one of the maids.

4

He had been dreading the birthday dinner all day but when it was well launched, and he had swallowed three glasses of Madeira, the wine worked on him in a way that kept harassment at a safe distance. Broadbent was excessively jovial, and even Lizzie seemed worth looking at after her father had given her permission to drink a glass of the wine on top of the sherry she had used to drink his health. When he blew out the eighteen cake candles there was another toast, after which Broadbent, saying briefly he had a call to make, rose and filled George's glass with port, urging him not to hurry over his coffee for he would be gone some time and the ladies would entertain him. He then left, Lizzie accompanying him to the door and Hester helping to clear the table. For a moment or so he and Laura were alone in the room.

He noticed then that she looked particularly drained and listless, so that he said, jocularly, "Here, take a glass of port. It's very good," and poured it, ignoring her gesture as she said, in what seemed a very urgent voice, "Listen, George . . . I really must talk . . ." But then the front door slammed and Lizzie came bouncing back into the room, pretending to be tipsy on her one glass of sherry and one glass of Madeira, and Laura Broadbent, addressing her sharply, said, "For heaven's sake grow up, Lizzie! Drink a cup of coffee. A big cup."

He was getting the slightest bit muddle-headed then with all that food and wine, and the heat of the room, with its banked-up fire and windows closed against the cheerless night outside, but not too tipsy to miss the swift exchange of glances between Lizzie and Laura, so that he wondered if the day had seen yet another of their tiffs. Nothing more was said, however, and they all carried their coffee into the parlour, where the atmosphere was even more oppressive and presently, after she had tinkled the piano for a spell, and Laura had left to carry the coffee tray into the kitchen, Lizzie poured him a generous brandy from a new bottle on the sideboard, saying that her father said he was to sample it for it was a brand he had laid in on the advice of his vintner, Mr. Gossage.

George sipped the brandy and it seemed to settle very comfortably on top of the port and Madeira so that a haze of geniality surrounded him like a gauze curtain, enabling him to see Lizzie, lolling on the arm of his chair, in a role that was new to him. He had always thought of her as a sallow, rather angular girl, with very little that was prepossessing about her but now, cheerfully admitting to himself that he was well on the way to being drunk, he reached out and pinched her thigh so that she giggled and told him to behave and finish his brandy before Laura came back, for she wouldn't approve of him drinking brandy after all he had taken at table. He thought this likely and tossed it back, whereupon Lizzie exclaimed, shrilly, "Why, I do declare you're bottled, George!" and when, unconvincingly, he denied it, "All right. Walk a straight line as far as the piano!" and he did but not as straight as all that, and when Mrs. Broadbent returned they were both walking lines to and fro across the patterned carpet so that she said, sharply, "That's enough, both of you! George, upstairs to bed and sleep it off! You too, Lizzie, before you make a complete fool of yourself! I'll see to the fires and gas," but Lizzie replied, calmly, "Don't forget father is out. If you draw the bolt at the front he'll bring us all down with his knocking, the way he did last time!"

"It was you who drew the bolt on that occasion," Mrs. Broadbent snapped and Lizzie, turning sulky, said, "I was only telling you . . ." and left, George following her after a carefully articulated goodnight to Laura.

On the way upstairs he banged against the banister and ricocheted, so that he suddenly felt very irritated with himself, thinking, "Great God, I couldn't have shipped that much! If I can't hold my liquor better than this . . ." But then Lizzie was there to help him, giggling like a schoolgirl, and saying she had to be sure he knew his own room, for gentlemen in his condition were often not too particular where they laid themselves down.

She piloted him across the landing and would have followed him over the threshold but suddenly, inexplicably it seemed to George, Laura was there again, saying in a voice with a keen edge to it, "Leave him be, Lizzie! What are you thinking of, following him to bed? Next thing you'll be undressing the boy!" to which Lizzie replied, "I'll leave that to you. You're well used to it, I daresay!"

George, now sitting on the bed, had not been fully aware of the exchange but suddenly he saw Laura's hand fly out, and heard the sharp smack and the yelp of dismay it produced from Lizzie. Then, without really comprehending what had occurred, he leaned back and the ceiling descended to blend with the counterpane and there was a roaring in his ears as if he was standing beside a waterfall.

* * *

He had no idea what time it was when he awakened, dry-mouthed but more clear-headed than he would have expected and well aware that the door of his room had opened and closed and that someone was standing there, over by the window.

He was still wearing his clothes, with the exception of jacket, waistcoat and boots, so that he had no immediate access to his watch and lay still trying to count the slow chimes of Bowdon Church clock. It told him nothing, save that it was striking a half-hour. He called, presently, "Who is it? Who's there?" and Laura's voice answered pitched low and charged with anxiety.

"Me. Laura . . . Get up and find the rest of your clothes, but quietly . . . You must go now, before Harry gets back . . ."

He sat up then, running his hand through his hair and trying to make out her outline over by the curtained window.

"Go where? What time is it? Light the gas . . ." but she said, urgently, "No! If I do he'll see it when he comes up the path and he's due any minute. It's half past midnight but you sound sober enough. *Are* you?"

"I'm quite sober. It was the heat of the room as much as the wine and all that food . . . What on earth's the matter? Why do you want me to go?"

"Because they're up to something."

"Mr. Broadbent's up to something?"

"Him and Lizzie. Don't ask me how I know. I just sense it . . . He had no plans to go out again tonight, but Lizzie went to the front door with him, and they were whispering. She's not been in here, has she?"

"Lizzie? Not as far as I know. Why should she? She's asleep, isn't she?"

"She's in her room but she isn't asleep. She's waiting until she hears her father's key in the lock in order to time it properly. I almost decided to slap it out of her but then I realised this way is better. You can just leave. Go to a hotel, then home first thing in the morning."

His bewilderment increased. She sounded so tense and fearful, almost as though she was here to warn him Broadbent and his daughter were plotting against his life. He said, spiritedly, "Look here, Laura, I can't do that. I can't just walk out, in the middle of the night, without saying why or even knowing why. What's happened that concerns me?"

"You won't take my word for it and go?"

"No, I won't, and I've got reasons, apart from it being idiotic."

"What reasons?"

"Private reasons. Concerning the yard."

She was silent a moment. Then she said, with resignation, "You're on to him, aren't you?" and he absorbed this, disturbed that she was obviously aware of Harry Broadbent's practices and feeling very deflated on that account. For he had wanted very much to believe she had no knowledge of what was going on down there.

"*You* knew about it?"

"I know that Harry and that man Shawe are up to monkeytricks involving your father's equipment and money. He's told me nothing and I wouldn't expect him to. But it's always been plain to me we couldn't live in this style on what he earns in salary and commission. Is that why you came here? Did your father send you up here to watch him?"

"*No*, Laura."

He swung his legs down on the floor. "I found out accidentally . . . It was his manner more than anything. He went out of his way to be affable but tried his damnedest to keep me away from the yard and the paper work. I haven't found anything very important. Just that he's taking a percentage of Barlow's hauls and charging the firm for first-class hay when the horses get seconds. It's the kind of pilfering that goes on in lots of places."

"You've said nothing to him?"

"Not yet. I only found out yesterday."

"What had you got in mind?"

"I shall have to tell Headquarters. In a few days perhaps, when I've had time to think."

"Why do you need time to think? It's robbery, isn't it?"

"There's you and the girls to consider. He'll get discharged and Tybalt, the head clerk, would try and persuade my father to prosecute. But that doesn't mean he would."

"Why not?"

"With him it usually depends on circumstances. There was a case rather like it six months ago. The foreman was just sacked."

"Then it depends on what kind of report you make?"

"I imagine so. That's why I needed time. As I say, there was you to consider."

"You don't think I had anything to do with it?"

"Good Lord, of course not! But you've been jolly decent to me. What sort of return would it be to see you turned out of house and home?"

About a minute ticked by. He could hear her controlled breathing, as she remained in the window bay. Finally she said, "He knows you've stumbled on something. He sent Hester to Shawe with a message before dinner. That's where he must have gone, to concoct some story I suppose. But there's far more to it than that. Lizzie's involved in it now."

"In what's going on at the yard? But that's nonsense . . ."

"Not in what happens there but what's meant to happen here. It's beginning to make sense. I knew I was right. Did Lizzie give you something more to drink when I went out with the coffee cups?"

"Yes. She gave me a brandy from a new bottle. It must have been a stiff one. I seemed to pass right out when I moved from a hot room to a cold one."

"Well, there you are. I understand it now. He intends to use Lizzie as his first line of defence."

"But how can Lizzie help him?"

"You'll find that out soon enough if you stay here. Do I have to spell it out, word for word? Haven't you noticed what she's had in mind all along, even if he's only just given a thought to it? You lads who go to expensive schools . . . they don't teach you a damned thing worth knowing! How to watch out for yourselves, for a start. The moment Lizzie hears his step on the path she'll skip in here stark naked and climb into bed with you, hoping you're still dead drunk or, even if you aren't, would want to make the most of the opportunity, as lads would, you included, I wouldn't wonder. I'll ask you something, and risk outraging your modesty. Have you ever had a woman? Properly, I mean?"

"No, never."

"My God, lads like you take their time growing up, don't they. No wonder I scared you with that kiss this morning. I did, didn't I?"

"A little. No one ever kissed me that way before. But . . ." and he stopped, feeling himself flushing, and very thankful now that she had not put a match to the gas-jet.

"But you liked it. Well, that proves they knew their man. I'll light the gas now and you can pack a few things. Then I'll let you out the back and that'll make nonsense of their little game. Wait . . . I'll make sure of the curtains, the least chink of light would put him on his guard."

He heard her fumble with the curtains, pulling them so that the join overlapped. He understood then precisely what she was driving at, why she was here and why she was urging him to leave. Shawe, or Broadbent, or both of them had discovered something amiss after he had left the yard. Probably they had searched for the paper he still had in his pocketbook and after failing to find it had made enquiries that led them to the stableman, and the questions he had asked about the hay. They would know then that the game was up, unless he could be silenced in some way. And what better way to make him forget the whole incident than to discover him in bed with Lizzie? Some kind of bargain would have to be struck and contemplation of the various alternatives made him feel sick. He stood up, belching, and then she was beside him, and the gas mantle was glowing, and he realised that she was in her nightdress with a robe over her shoulders, and her hair flowing free. He said, "I'll get my things . . ." But then stopped, looking across at her distractedly. "How about you, Laura? What will happen when he finds out you took a hand?"

"He won't if you hurry. Don't make a sound."

Together they padded around the room, collecting some of his clothes and stuffing them into the larger of his grips. It occupied no more than a minute and then they were out on the landing, listening. No sound came from the hall or the girls' room so they crept downstairs, leaving the landing gas burning, passing through into the kitchen and thence to the scullery, where she slipped the bolt of the back door.

"I'll want to know what happens to you. I'll go to the yard now and send myself a telegram as soon as an office opens. I'll say I've had orders to go to Edinburgh earlier than I planned. He'll swallow that, won't he?"

She smiled. "After you having decamped in the middle of the night? I think not, my dear."

"I'll find some way . . ." He stared at her, feeling cornered but fearful of what might happen to her when he left and Broadbent returned to discover his bargaining counter gone.

"I've never met anyone like you, Laura. There *isn't* anyone like you . . ."

And suddenly thanks seemed utterly inadequate and he dropped his bag and threw his arms around her, kissing her cheeks and then her mouth, holding her so closely that they lurched against the door.

His back was to the kitchen so that he did not see Lizzie's approach but felt Laura's body contract and whipped round to see her with candle held high, like a figure in a melodrama—Lizzie Broadbent, mouth agape, nightdress hitched in one hand and neck ribbons trailing, so that he could glimpse her small, flattish breasts. He felt Laura stiffen and then heard Lizzie's shriek, expressing the wildest indignation but also a sound that somehow epitomised the terrible tensions that had existed between these two women all the time he had lived in the house.

"*Bitch! Filthy bitch!* It was you! All the time it was *you* . . . !"

And then the scene resolved itself into a nightmare, from which all sense and predictability departed, so that he felt caught up in their hatred like a cork swirling between two crashing waves. Laura darted past him as Lizzie slammed down the candle on the kitchen table, raising both hands to ward off the blows Laura rained on her but the older woman's onrush carried Lizzie as far as the kitchen door where Laura followed her, pulling her down and screaming, over her shoulder, "Get *out! Go!*"

And he went, having no stomach to watch two women rolling the width of the kitchen floor, clawing and spitting at one another like a couple of frenzied cats.

He had a final glimpse of the mêlée as he swung round to slam the door on them. Laura, her nightdress ripped as far as the waist, was on top. Lizzie, her bare legs spreadeagled, had seized a double handful of her opponent's hair and both women's mouths were wide open in screams of fury and pain.

Their outcry followed him as far as the yard where he groped his way down the path to the back gate giving on to a parallel road behind the house. He had reached the end of the passage before he was sick, leaning against the roughcast wall of the adjoining house and standing there for what seemed a long time until his stomach was empty and a spate of dry retching had subsided, leaving his mouth parched but full of the sour taste of bile. Then, pulling himself together, he picked up his bag and went on down the road towards the orange blur of the station lights, telling himself that, however the situation resolved itself, nothing would induce him to return to that place.

By the time he reached the booking office he had some kind of control over himself and was able to ask the sleepy clerk if there was a train on to Salford. There was not but the man said a goods train was moving off in a few minutes and he was welcome to ride with the guard for a shilling. Having said this he winked very solemnly and pocketed the coin, so that George thought, "God damn everybody in the whole world! All anyone cares about is money!" but he climbed aboard gratefully and travelled the short distance to Salford, where the train slowed to a crawl and he jumped off and made his way through empty streets to the Swann yard.

The night-watchman and a couple of stable lads were on duty and seemed not to find anything odd about his demand to be let into the office on the excuse that he had lost his key to his lodgings and meant to spend the rest of the night beside the stove. It was warm in here, so he settled himself in Shawe's swivel chair, with his feet on a crate. And soon, without having resolved anything but to keep clear of Broadbent and revert to his original idea of consulting Sam Rawlinson, he was asleep, the office cat on his lap.

*   *   *

He jumped up like a man shot in the backside when somebody nudged his foot and there, his back to the door, and looking across at him with a sardonic grin, was Harry Broadbent, and beside him, looking less sure of himself, the clerk Shawe, a pudgy little man of indeterminate age. It occurred to him then, if briefly, that he was not cut out to be a thief-taker, or even a watchman, for here he was, once more robbed of the initiative. All he could do for the moment was blink foolishly and flex a numbed right arm.

Broadbent said, easily, "Well, now, why should a gentleman like you prefer a night over a coke stove to a comfortable bed, with ladies to wait on him? Aye, and keep him warm if need be," but as Shawe made a furtive move to slip away his hand shot out like a boxer's and he grabbed the clerk by the shoulder, spinning him round and saying, in a grating voice, "Stay put man, and face the bloody music! You're in this as deep as me but neither one of us so deep as Lord Tom Noddy over there!"

The complacency of the man had the effect of rallying George somewhat. He said, looking steadily across at them, "Bluff won't help, Broadbent. I've got a good idea what you two have been about and if I were in your shoes I'd own up to it. You may even come off with a flea in your ear. My father has overlooked worse, or so they tell me at Headquarters."

"Ah, I don't doubt it," Broadbent said, thoughtfully, "and I'm obliged to you for the hint. Maybe you'd even speak up for me, seeing you wouldn't care to have me tell Headquarters of the commissions you've been collecting as my star boarder ever since New Year."

Shawe said, indecisively, "Listen here, Harry, why don't we . . ." but Broadbent snarled, "Shut your gob and leave the talking to me. As one man of the world to another, eh, George?"

"I don't know what the devil you have in mind, Broadbent," George said, slowly, "but whatever it is it won't wash. I've nothing to apologise for. I daresay Mrs. Broadbent will have told you I left your place and came over here before Lizzie had a chance to play the part you wrote for her."

196

Broadbent pursed his lips but his genial expression remained unchanged. He said, in the same bantering tone, "Mrs. Broadbent didn't have all that to say for herself, George. She was too busy applying a beefsteak to her eye and lard to her backside. Not the way gentlemen like you handle women, maybe. But then, gentlemen's wives don't hop into bed with star boarders as soon as their old man is out of the road, do they?"

It was as if Broadbent had struck him hard an inch or so below the navel. He said, in a voice that did not seem to be his, "If you've laid a finger on that woman you're really for it! I'll make it my business to see it's not just the sack. I'll make my father press charges and you could do up to three years for cooking those books and pocketing money on Barlow's hauls. You know it and Shawe knows it. And from the look of him right now it won't take much to make him turn State's evidence!"

For the first time Broadbent lost some of his poise but he was a hard man to outface. In a matter of seconds he regained control of himself, saying, "Now who's bluffing? My wife has been your doxy ever since you unpacked, and talking of witnesses Lizzie will swear to that in court if necessary. Damn it, Swann, you were cuddling her in my scullery a few hours since, weren't you. Why don't we call quits? I'll forget my gripe, you forget yours. I'll go one better. If you fancy Laura that much you're welcome to her. She was always a bad bargain . . ."

He seemed to have made inadequate allowance for George's youth and fitness, raising his guard no higher than his chest as George cleared the crate at a bound and brought his fist crashing into the manager's mouth, dislodging a front tooth and hurling him against the flimsy door so that its panels splintered under the impact. Shawe, bawling an oath, tried to dodge behind the desk but George caught him by the collar, jerking him sideways so that he reeled against the stove in the centre of the room. As his hands came into contact with the red-hot lid he screamed like an animal, but by then Broadbent was up again and charging forward, head lowered like a bull, so that it was easy for George to land a second blow on his ear as he skipped to one side and when the manager's rush carried him as far as the window aim a flying kick at his buttocks. The kick hit Broadbent behind the knees, so that he pitched on his face among a pile of cartons. He was on his feet again in an instant and glaring wildly round for a weapon, finding one in a heavy ebony ruler that lay on Shawe's desk but as he pranced forward, blood streaming from his lip, the frantic bookkeeper impeded him and George had time to slip round the end of the desk and grab him by the throat. Shawe, still screaming with pain, somehow became entangled with the pair of them so that they lurched, all together, against the window frame that burst outwards with a shattering crash. Broadbent landed a glancing blow on the temple with the ruler but the pain only increased George's fury and he exerted every ounce of his strength to force Broadbent backwards over the wrecked frame, half his body projecting into the yard. Men came running then from two or three directions but it took the combined efforts of watchman and stable staff to wrest the manager free from George's grip, yanking him clean through the window and ripping his coat to shreds on the jagged glass. The room was a shambles. Everything in it was overturned and Shawe, sitting against the wall with his blistered palms tucked under his armpits, continued to yell and yell at the top of his voice.

It was Shawe's nonstop racket that recalled George to his senses so that he retreated to the centre of the room and was still standing there, dazedly surveying the damage, when the watchman ran in, shouting, "Gor' dammit, Mr. Swann, what's to do? What the hell's goin' on . . . ?"

George said, "Broadbent's not hurt. See to Shawe. He burned his hands on the stove-lid," and Shawe was led away, still yelling, and George picked up his bag and went out into the yard where two stable lads were dousing Broadbent's head under the pump.

The manager did not look up when he paused in front of the group. He seemed fully occupied in an attempt to check the bleeding of his tongue, lacerated by the dislodged tooth.

George said, to no one in particular, "He could do with a wash. Particularly about the mouth. When the deputy comes on duty tell him I've gone south but no one is to take any more orders from Broadbent. I'm suspending him on my own responsibility. Headquarters will confirm that by telegram tomorrow."

The watchman followed him out, saying, "You're cut over the ear yourself, Mr. Swann," and George, lifting his hand, saw a streak of blood on it but said, "It's nothing. I've a train to catch," and went out to the cab rank opposite the station, telling the cabby to drive straight to London Road.

He was well on his way before it occurred to him that it might have been wiser to go to his grandfather, or more chivalrous, possibly, to check on Broadbent's statement that he had given his wife a hiding. For a few moments he pondered the alternatives but then made his decision. Nothing much would be gained by involving Sam at this stage, whereas he thought it more than likely that Laura would have cut her losses and walked out on Broadbent to seek re-employment at the Cock and Hen, in the Shambles. As for himself there seemed no real alternative now but to make a clean breast of it to Tybalt, the head clerk, if his father happened to be absent from the yard, or to Adam himself if he was lucky enough to find him alone in his tower. He stopped off at the post office in Market Street and cashed his two pound money order. Ten minutes later he caught the eight forty-five for Euston. The journey gave him five hours to convince himself that life as a Swann travelling scholar was not simply a matter of opening one oyster after another.

5

The thing that astonished him was his father's calmness, as though it was commonplace to learn that his son had been involved in a fist fight before witnesses with one of the regional managers, that the same manager had been milking the firm's till for almost a year, that, tucked away in a south Manchester suburb, was a woman whose body was laced with welts on his account, or that Broadbent would almost certainly charge the Gaffer's son with seducing his wife and probably his daughter into the bargain.

Now that he had told his tale, and submitted his one insignificant-looking piece of evidence to back it, the entire episode appeared to him as indescribably muddled, a chain of sordid blunders culminating in him giving Broadbent the undoubted advantage by striking the first blow and being the agent of Shawe's burns. Now that he considered it there were so many things he might have done, so many more rational courses open to him after he had proof of the manager's dishonesty. Surely a man as experienced as his father would fasten on this and look on him as a hysterical fool, with less initiative than one of the vanboys swinging from the tailboard rope of a frigate in the yard.

He said, dismally, "Well, that's about it, sir. I'm sorry I made such a howling mess of it but the fact is I lost my head when that swine took it for granted I was involved with his wife. I wasn't, upon my honour, and that's the truth, although I see now that Lizzie might have grounds for believing I was. There was something odd about that place from the start and I should have made it my business to look for facts, instead of relying on luck and guesses."

Adam said, turning the slip of paper over and staring at the back of it that was quite blank, "This isn't a guess, George. As regards ferreting out what was amiss up there you did better than a man has a right to expect of someone a year out of school." He laid the paper aside. "Tybalt can look into this and do a back-check on the Polygon returns since Broadbent replaced Catesby. He'll enjoy that, especially as I promoted the man against his advice. How does one go about solving a problem of this kind? Don't ask me that, son. I've been at the game all my life and experience doesn't insure you against a blunder, although it's a long time since I made one as big as installing Broadbent up there. It happened once before in the Southern Square but that was a different kind of mistake. That time I put in a manager with a penchant for pretty stable lads."

He got up, seemingly preoccupied with his own mistakes rather than his son's and lounged over to the window, looking across the range of angled roofs to the sluggish river. "The important thing is to learn from one's mistakes. Did you learn anything useful up there?" And George saw his mouth twitch, as though he was finding it hard to restrain a smile.

"Only to take no one on trust," but at that the smile broke through as Adam said, "Well, that's worth the price of a fleet of waggons. Or would be to most men of business. Two let-downs in a hundred isn't a bad average, and at least your experience was offset by this woman . . . what was her name again?"

"Laura. She'd been a barmaid before she married Broadbent."

"Care to tell me about her?" And when the boy flushed, "Oh, you don't have to. It's only that it might help to get the whole silly business in focus. She seems to have been a good sort. I know women who would have gone to work on you in quite another way. If that had happened we should have been stuck with Broadbent, like it or not."

George said, slowly, "I can't forgive myself for what happened to her on my account. She was, well . . . different somehow." He hesitated a moment and Adam made no attempt to prompt him. Finally he went on, "Look sir, you've been far more decent about this than I've any right to expect. I've let you and H.Q. down badly, haven't I? I mean, as soon as it gets around that I pitched into Broadbent on account of his wife, everyone in the network will read more into it than a scuffle in the office, or a manager and clerk turning a guinea or two on the side. But you ought to know the real facts. The truth is there *was* something between me and Mrs. Broadbent. Nothing like he implied. Just a bit of flirting you could say. Well, no, more than that. She wasn't the kind of woman one flirted with."

"Was it because you felt sorry for her?"

"No, it wasn't. She gave me this seal for my watchchain yesterday and until that moment I'd never thought of her as anyone but a woman who was . . . well, a good sport, and pretty with it. I kissed her then. His daughter Lizzie might have seen me and told her father. And then, when Laura let me out through the back door last night, I kissed her again but in a dif . . . well, as if I meant it. That was all, but it was enough to give a swine like Broadbent a hold over me. So in that sense I suppose I asked for it."

Adam said, "Well, you might have asked for it but he seems to have got it. And don't think I fail to appreciate the epilogue, boy. Tell the truth and shame the devil, they say, but there's more to the truth than that if you're dealing with people one's obliged to take on trust. You're right about the network's construction, however. There never was a concern like this for silly gossip. I sometimes think of it as an internal telegraph system, so God knows what they'll make of Broadbent being beaten up and shown the door. However, there are ways to anticipate that, thank God. I'll sack him, of course, but I'll keep Shawe on. That way I'll be insured against anything Broadbent spreads around. It shouldn't be much, or not so long as we hold the threat of a prosecution over him. That takes care of that, but it still leaves you in the air. You can't complete what I had in mind, a stop-off at all the regions. Did that occur to you on your way to confessional?"

"Yes, it did, sir. Perhaps you'd prefer me to back out and find something else. The army, maybe . . ."

"I damned well would *not*," Adam said, emphatically, "for although you can't be expected to see it from where you stand, I can assure you that you'll do very well, once you learn to keep your temper in a crisis. Aye, and stay clear of disconsolate wives. No, don't take that seriously. You'll laugh at it yourself in a month or so. Listen here then, and tell me what you think of a change of plan. Suppose you spend a year or so abroad, somewhere in Europe, where they're catching up on us in many ways and improving on every idea we originate but are too lazy to market? Would that appeal to you? Somewhere new, where you were obliged to learn the language and stand on your own feet?"

"I'm not sure, sir. Granted that I'm to work here eventually, would it help? Apart from giving gossip time to die down?"

"It might. I've done all the travelling I intend doing outside this country, but I learned from what I saw overseas when I was your age. You've had a close look at five regions, and the other ten won't run away. After all, there's a technical side to our business, and somewhere among this desk litter are coach-building and packing warehouse catalogues from Paris, Munich, Berlin, Vienna and other centres. I'll sift through them but in the meantime don't mope. It isn't the end of the world. Care to go on home now?"

"No, sir. I'd sooner wait and go back with you."

It warmed him to hear George say that. He got along well enough with all his children but although some of the older ones were, he suspected, beginning to have second thoughts about him as a man dedicated to something outside their comprehension, he had never looked for real affection from any one of them. George had always been the most extrovert of the bunch, making friends easily wherever he went and, until this moment, had seemed entirely self-sufficient. He did not need a more explicit statement of the boy's involvement with this Broadbent woman. Somewhere along the line his emotions had been stirred and that, he supposed, signified growth. It was hopeful, to say the least, and suddenly he felt grateful to a woman he had never seen and never would see.

He said, "Suit yourself then and go down and tell Tybalt precisely what you discovered concerning our friend's sidelines. Stick to figures. There's no call to make a personal statement, of the kind you made up here," and, to spare George further embarrassment, he at once readdressed himself to a mountain of correspondence on the desk.

He waited until he could hear George's footsteps on the stairs before he looked up and permitted himself the luxury of a chuckle that had been waiting to surface for twenty minutes. He thought, having tried and failed to project himself back to the age of eighteen, "We start out thinking we know the lot . . . how the cards fall . . . how all the tricks are ours in advance. But maybe it's as well we do, or we should throw the hand in before we were thirty . . ." He frowned down at his desk, finding it difficult to concentrate and after a moment or two rose and went over to his look-out post. The inevitable string of barges drifted down on the tide and the mastheads of shipping down river were barely visible under a low canopy of ochre-tinged murk. For once, however, he was not thinking of Thames traffic and Thames argosies but of his own flesh and blood, the clutch of isolated entities owing their existence to his chance meeting with a runaway girl of eighteen in the parched summer of 1858. One took it for granted that sons and daughters would inherit all manner of characteristics from parents and grandparents but they rarely did, or not to any great extent. One could look in vain among the new generation of Swanns for unmistakable traces of Sam Rawlinson, the Colonel, himself or Henrietta. Mostly it was a business of finding one's own way, without benefit of anything more than instinct, with the real sources and guidelines as far away in time as the Pyramids and Babylon. Environment, that the social prophets were always prattling about, played little or no part in determining the end product that resulted from the drift from childhood to adolescence, adolescence to maturity, maturity to dotage. Stella, Alexander, and now George had all in turn bitten off far more than they could chew before they were twenty, and each was now occupied in spitting some of it out and digesting what remained. In their own way and in their own time. It would be the same, he imagined, with Giles, and with all the others once they emerged from the nursery and were launched on a life unregulated by bells. The only way one could help was to show each of them a little patience, a little tolerance, a gleam or two of humour. He was not given to regretting his lost youth, as Henrietta was inclined to do when she peeled off her corsets at night and postured in front of her mirror, not knowing that he was sometimes watching and laughing at her through the chink of his dressing-room door. Today, more than ever, he was sure he was right in preferring the present to past or future. "Damned if I envy any one of them," he muttered. "What man in his senses would want to start out all over again?" He turned away from the window and settled to his papers again. In five minutes he had forgotten Broadbent and George.

8

Stella as Hod-Holder

HENRIETTA SWANN recalled little of her childhood and adolescence. Her life had not seemed to begin until the day Adam rode over the crest of the moor, scooped her into the saddle and carried her off like a mercenary looting a city. The years preceding this stupendous event were humdrum, when she was growing up in the neo-Gothic monstrosity that her father had tortured from an erstwhile hunting lodge a few miles south of the Manchester to Liverpool railway. The countryside about her home had been pleasant but rather featureless. Company was rare and a succession of amateur governesses came and went, so that it was only the odd moment of passing seasons she recalled at this distance, insignificant cameos that had no special significance at the time but had, for one reason or another, taken root in the memory of a woman now breast-feeding her ninth child.

One such cameo she thought of as the advance of the reapers, the slow, purposeful march of September scythesmen, spaced the full width of a long, upsloping cornfield on the westerly edge of her father's land, men advancing under a flaming noonday sun, slashing their way across the forest of stalks like a small, disciplined army operating in extended order; shoulders braced, blades flashing, unswerving in their progress to the tree-clad crest so that it had seemed to her at that time no routine chore, of the kind men must have been performing on fifty thousand farms at that season, but something splendid and inexorable, something hatched by a professional and executed by minions, whose several destinies he ordained from afar. It was, she told herself in retrospect, a childish fancy but when her older children were grown and beginning to scatter, it acquired a curious relevance. She began to identify her sons and her daughters as the reapers and herself as the unseen mastermind who directed their advance on the horizon.

She was not an introspective person. Mostly she lived her life, and exerted her influence on other lives, casually and intuitively. Because her vocabulary was limited (despite the improving books Adam read aloud to her of an evening) she would have been puzzled if someone had told her that all her sources of energy and most of her random thoughts led back to a single, subconscious compulsion, an unrelenting quest for permanency that governed everything she did as a wife and mother. For she looked on her children and the rambling house in which all nine of them had been born, as guarantees against rootlessness and obscurity, spectres that had dogged innumerable ancestors on both sides of her family. Something less identifiable than the land and money-hunger, transmitted to her by generations of Irish and Lancastrian cottagers; something less tangible than soil, less time-serving than gold and silver.

Adam, who had always been aware of the half-hidden secret would have called it by different names, depending upon his mood. Generally he saw it as the female equivalent of getting-on-in-the-world, a twin sister of his own thrust and power lust, and so it was but not wholly so. It was deeper rooted and more broadly based than it appeared to his wholly practical mind and it was also more generous, inasmuch as it embraced not merely Henrietta's family but her race. For she was Celt all through and Celts have been on the defensive for forty generations.

Her mainspring was thus deeply personal and unconsciously tribal, an unremitting, undaunted, unwearied, implacable, ineradicable determination to found a dynasty and see it advance in her lifetime, as a flood seeps across a passive countryside.

It was this resolve, that she could never have put into words, that had been the strongest link forged by her relationship with Adam Swann. For the Swanns had insinuated themselves into the fabric of the nation centuries before she met and married one of them. The grafting of her stock upon his had thus been no more than a first step towards fulfilment. She saw each of her children as adding, one might say, to her stockpile, a further guarantee of the course the dynasty would take into the future. That she would live to witness this she did not doubt and the certainty of this made child-bearing a privilege. She had always taken pleasure in physical communion with a demigod but the act of receiving and bringing forth his seed was more than physical. It was a mystical and devotional experience, a benison granted to very few.

*   *   *

A man as perceptive as Adam Swann might have read something very significant in all this and perhaps he did when Henrietta speculated aloud on the various possibilities available to the generation of Swanns hatched under a Kentish spur between 1860, when they first settled here, and 1880, when the two eldest of them returned after clumsy trial flights. He would have seen his chubby, indomitable wife as an unmistakable product of their times, a living symbol of all that preoccupied the tribal unit to which both of them belonged. For it sometimes seemed to him, as he clumped about his business up and down the country, that every Jack and Jill between Land's End and Cape Wrath was driving towards the goal that had been Henrietta's from the moment he first saw her a mile or so from Sam Rawlinson's gaudy perch. One and all they were obsessed, to the exclusion of all else, with getting on, making their mark and founding, if not a dynasty, then a unit of one kind or another capable of staking a claim in the spoils that were going to the swift and the sharp-witted. In a tribe bedevilled by class this was one area where every class barrier was down and had been for a generation.

In the England into which he had been born blood and breeding were still paramount and continued to call the national tune. Ancient wealth was still the legislator and determiner of the national destiny. But all this had changed when he was still a lad. By then the man of brass and the man of iron had come into their own, elbowing their way forward and demanding, at the top of their voices to be heard and heeded. The newcomer was no longer content to be patronised and used as a pawn in the game of diplomatic chess played across the board of the Western world. He rated, he said, the rank of knight or bishop, and by the time Adam was launched this claim had been all but written into the statute books. By the early 'seventies the real men of brass and iron were not only on equal terms with the blue-blooded. In some areas, notably the north-west, the midlands and the metropolis, they were dominating every field of affairs if one excluded the cricket-pitch and the race-track. In every one of Swann's regions they were the men who had to be deferred to and consulted in all matters concerning the public weal, so that as the century advanced, creating the maximum noise and fume, ruling families of earlier generations were edged aside, obliged to be satisfied with local lip-service and seek refuge in a kind of archaic withdrawal that was quickly recognised and caricatured by the editor of *Punch*.

Adam, who sometimes conjured with these abstracts, saw the process as a second Reformation, a phase of history repeating itself, with inventors, engineers and their sponsors matching the hard-faced adventurers of Tudor times, who had appropriated to themselves the temporal powers and spiritual leadership of the Church, as well as that section of the nation's acres owned and farmed by monks. For his part he welcomed the transformation. To him it was a cleansing tide, notwithstanding the mountains of muck and rubble it left behind, and he did not quarrel with it until, to his amused disgust, it seemed to be doubling in its tracks, not only across the spectrum of the nation but under his nose where the Henriettas of the era, consciously or unconsciously, were striving to reproduce the very pattern of society their fathers and husbands had cast aside.

He never did succeed in coming to terms with this enigma and ultimately dismissed it as yet another indication of the astonishing capacity of the British for self-delusion. For it seemed to him that the wives and daughters of the men of brass took no pride in their menfolk's astounding victory. All they wanted, it appeared, was to replace their former masters without deviating by as much as a single inch from their ways of life, or discarding a single one of their prejudices. They counted their pile, nagged their providers into finding a place in the shires clear of the muckheaps they had raised, sent their sons to gentlemen's schools, cultivated the manners and speech idioms of the grandees, and then sat back to watch promoted foremen and industrious apprentices repeat the metamorphosis all over again.

Adam Swann, practical above all else, could not or would not see this game of swings and roundabouts as something giving expression to the deepest yearnings of the English who remained, despite all, agriculturalists at heart. This was one reason why he had not opposed his daughter's alliance with what he thought of as a poxed-out family of patricians. People like the Moncton-Prices were irrelevant and to him, notwithstanding his essential liberality, daughters were expendable, there being no place for them in the present scheme of things. Thus, although tolerant with Henrietta's fanciful theories, he gave her no credit for the ability to take a more embracing and long-term view than himself.

As it happened it did not matter, or not all that much. By now Henrietta had his measure to the thousandth part of an inch. A business as large and involved as his was likely to occupy him for the rest of his days. When her final attempt to involve him, more than marginally, in her scheme to promote a Swann offensive on all fronts had failed at the time of Stella's flight, she decided to make the best of what could not be altered and went about her self-appointed task alone. By now, of course, her ambition, once restricted to breeding scarlet-coated warriors, of the kind that had decorated the toffee tins and scrapbooks of her nursery days, had evolved into something more practical. She still retained her reverence for scarlet and gold but one, or at the most two, inheritors of the Swann military tradition would suffice. The Swanns, she decided, could be trained and trusted to do far more than add lustre to the flag in faraway places. They could take their places beside her as future master-minders of the advance of the reapers. By the summer of 1880 she was fully engaged, savouring her limited triumphs and surmounting, sometimes by storm sometimes by guile, all the incidental hurdles.

*   *   *

Alexander, the eldest boy, was spoken for. Seasoned by his hair-raising experiences in Zululand, he was now enrolled at Sandhurst, a cadet whose personal association with the epic at Rorke's Drift had already singled him out. Alexander, Henrietta decided, could be left to himself for a spell. Not only had he been mentioned in despatches for killing Zulu snipers overlooking the embattled compound, he also had the unique advantage of a father on friendly terms with Roberts of Khandahar.

George was clearly destined to be a merchant and could, therefore, be left to Adam. The prospect did not dismay her. Her prejudice against merchants had moderated since the time when she had felt called upon to apologise for a husband in trade.

Giles, the next in line, had baffled her for a time, but she had come to accept his separateness, and what seemed to her his astonishing precocity. He was, she felt, tailor-made for the role of a masterminder, but she was not yet sure which of three fields he should be encouraged to till, that of statesman, scholar or priest. He might even write a book and the prospect of seeing the words 'By Giles Swann' on the title page of one of Mr. Mudie's weekly offerings, was as alluring as that of seeing him in bishop's gaiters, or rising to speak at Westminster. Meanwhile he was doing well at his new school and seemed so much happier, healthier and better adjusted than during his first period away from home. She did not know whether that new college he attended had produced any statesmen or divines as yet but was confident that Giles, with her sponsorship and his father's capital, would do it proud before long.

Hugo and Edward, the two younger boys, qualified as reserves. She might encourage Hugo to follow Alexander's footsteps, and take a commission in a smart regiment. But equally well, considering the boy's glibness in manufacturing watertight excuses for bad behaviour, he might provide excellent material for the law. Edward was only just beginning to talk, although he had walked upright at the age of fifteen months and promised to be the liveliest of the flock, so that it was possible he could be encouraged to shine in the field of athletics. The English seemed increasingly preoccupied with activities of that kind nowadays, although Henrietta belonged to a generation that still thought of them as the outdoor equivalents of forfeits and blind man's buff.

As to the younger girls, she had noted, with satisfaction, that each of them gave promise of being even prettier than Stella. Helen was already a prize-winner at local gymkhanas, whereas Joanna, a creature of extreme grace, showed a more-than-average aptitude for ballroom dancing.

There was, of course, the family's one lame duck, Stella, concerning whom they had all made such a hideous mistake, and secretly Henrietta was beginning to fret about Stella. With her usual optimism she had assumed that the scandal of an annulled marriage, whilst having an inevitable effect upon the girl's future prospects, would not have crushed her to the degree that it had, and this despite the fact that the wretched business had been effectively hushed up and piloted through the courts in under a year with the minimum of publicity.

People enquired about it, naturally, but Henrietta had anticipated that and fobbed them off with a volley of incomprehensible medical terms, all rehearsed in private and all aimed, as a matter of course, at the groom, so that local nosey-parkers went away with a vague impression poor Lester was a chronic invalid and the victim of a nameless disease or possible diseases.

Taken all round, therefore, she had been gratified by the smallness of the stir in the locality but Stella's low state of mind remained unaltered. Indeed, it sometimes seemed to her mother that the girl's experience could hardly have had a more lowering effect on her had the matter been fully aired in all the newspapers and picked over at every fête and soirée from here to Maidstone. She would go nowhere and take no interest in anything. Indeed, she rarely spoke unless spoken to so that sometimes it seemed to Henrietta that she had not yet emerged from the trance-like state in which she had found her the morning Denzil Fawcett came tapping on the kitchen door.

The doctors were no help at all. Privately they assured her there was nothing much amiss with the girl and prescribed iron tonics, exercise, good food and the company of people her own age. They did not tell her how this could be achieved so long as the girl flatly refused to reintegrate herself into the life of the county and spent her days mooning about like a wraith, listlessly helping Phoebe Fraser in the care and education of her younger brothers and sisters. When she was not in demand in the nursery, she would efface herself, riding alone across the downs or taking a solitary walk along the banks of the river in a direction she was unlikely to meet neighbours or villagers.

Adam, confound him, did not seem to see anything sinister in this prolonged withdrawal, and sometimes appeared to approve of it. "Damn it, woman," he told her irritably when she returned yet again to the subject, "she's had a bad shock and a frightful disappointment. Naturally she doesn't want to discuss it with every old trout who attends those gabby functions of yours! And that's what she'd be obliged to do if she made herself available. We were lucky to get off as cheaply as we did, implying that young waster sought annulment on medical grounds. I daresay the gossips find plenty in that to keep them happy. Believe me, in six months it'll all be forgotten, in favour of some other scandal, so my advice is to leave well alone, and let her ride it out as best she can."

It was thoroughly typical, Henrietta told herself, of masculine logic in matters of this kind. How could any male appreciate the need of a personal triumph of some kind, something to offset the dreadful humiliation of being bandied about between two men, one who had bought her for the price of a dowry, the other who heaped one outrage on another by doing his best to use her as a brood mare? For Henrietta, although she had no difficulty in viewing the dismal business through a woman's eyes, had no idea how to set about restoring pride and self-respect to someone from whom it had been gouged with a butcher's knife, and a blunt knife at that. That, she reasoned, was a task for someone with more knowledge of the world than she possessed, someone trained in finding their way among the shoals and reefs of the human soul and that, she supposed, implied a priest of some kind. Neither did this line of reasoning help, all priests being male.

The problem of rehabilitating her eldest daughter, and launching her on a second trip to the matrimonial market, occupied Henrietta Swann's thoughts right through the winter of 1879–1880, and into the succeeding spring and summer, until they were approaching the first anniversary of the annulment. By then she had begun to think about it almost exclusively, to the neglect of plans concerning her other reapers, and as the weeks passed she became more and more edgy with everyone about her, including Stella, for it maddened her that the girl's apathy remained, that she still drew back from any attempt to be reabsorbed into the happy-go-lucky scene of which she had been a part before Lester Moncton-Price had appeared as suitor.

The weather was hot and sultry for mid-September and the impending return of Giles to school had the effect of increasing her preoccupation, for Giles, throughout the holidays, had devoted a great deal of time to Stella, even accompanying her on disconsolate wanderings about the local countryside. If she had communicated anything of importance to him, however, Giles kept it to himself. Indeed, Henrietta got the impression that Stella's gloom was rubbing off on the boy, who became increasingly preoccupied as the summer holiday drew to its close. "Drat that boy," she told herself one day, as she saw them pacing the forecourt together, "it looks as if I shall soon have a pair of professional mutes about the place! This house used to quake with laughter . . ." and she thought how cheerfully she would have gone about the task of tying a stone to Lester's neck and heaving him into the river for playing such havoc with her peace of mind.

It was about then that she decided to attack, descending on Giles as he was packing his school trunk, determined, if necessary, to shake information from him as she had once upended him and relieved him of a halfpenny he had swallowed. It was not a task she found congenial. He had studiously avoided her during the last few days, as if half-suspecting a grilling, and it was humiliating to have to beg help in a situation of this kind from a fourteen-year-old schoolboy but there seemed no alternative. Something told her that what she was seeking, what could help her formulate a practical plan concerning Stella's future, was a clue, or a hint of a clue, as to whether or not Stella herself was pondering what life still had to offer her. This, she reasoned, would at least give her a lever to open a discussion that would not be terminated (as all previous conversations had been) by disconsolate negatives and, if pressed, a storm of tears. There was no time to beat about the bush. Staking everything on a single direct question, she said, "You'll be off tomorrow, about your own affairs. Before you go I just *have* to know something and I don't care how many promises you've made that girl since you've been hobnobbing with her. Has Stella discussed her recent trouble with you? For if she has, then you'll oblige me by repeating exactly what was said, for the fact is I'm very concerned about her and she refuses to confide in any one of us. There now, it's out! Have you anything to say to me? Anything at all?" and when he betrayed himself by looking away, she had the greatest difficulty in preventing herself from boxing his ears. But then she noticed something that deflected her mind from Stella for a moment. He had suddenly turned pale and his hands, clutching a neatly-laundered football jersey, were shaking, so that Henrietta at once regretted her sharp tone and took the jersey, placing it in the trunk and saying, gently, "There, now, Giles, I don't mean to bully you. I came to you because . . . well

. . . there was no one else to go to. I want so much to help Stella but apart from yourself she goes out of her way to avoid us all, almost as though we wanted to pry."

He said, rising from his knees, "Wait," and crossed to the door, looking out across the landing to the stairhead before closing the door and rejoining her.

"It means breaking my word of honour," he said, at last, "but the fact is I think she's wrong. Wrong not to tell you, that is, before she finally makes up her mind. Would you promise to say you stumbled across it some other way? Or maybe just *guessed* it? She trusted me, you see."

"I promise, of course I promise!" She would have promised him anything, so alarmed was she by his expression and the implication that Stella was on the verge of making another disastrous decision. "There, I've promised. Before she makes up her mind about *what?*"

"About becoming a nun."

He said it without emphasis, as though he had been relaying some trivial piece of family memoranda—the time Stella would be home from a party, or where he had left his cricket bat, or how many kittens the cat had had in the cistern loft. She wondered whether he could be aware of the impact his words made upon her and heard herself echoing his words of doom in the voice of a terrified child, utterly rejecting their fearful portent.

"Becoming a *nun?* A *nun*, you said?"

"That's what she's thinking about. She's almost decided. She's made up her mind to go to Father Gregory, over at Copley Priory."

The pieces of the puzzle representing Stella's enigma began to fall into place and each seemed to press cruelly on her chest, so that she seemed to stagger under their weight. He was beside her then, his face full of solicitude but, behind solicitude, a harassed expression she remembered seeing on his face when he was going through that difficult period at his first school. She knew all about Father Gregory and where Stella had conceived the notion of entering a convent. As a child she had been very devoted to Deborah Avery, Joshua Avery's daughter, who had been absorbed into the family after her father fled abroad and whom they all regarded as sister. Deborah, herself a Roman Catholic, had been brought up in a Folkestone convent, and there had even been talk of her taking the veil when she was passing through a religious phase about the time she was sixteen or seventeen. But Adam, thank God, had talked her out of that, and entered her at that smart ladies' college over at Cheltenham, and once there Deborah had been absorbed in a variety of interests, some of which seemed very eccentric to Henrietta. But whatever they were they all fell short of turning one's back on life and burying oneself behind the grey walls of a place Henrietta could only think of as a prison.

It would not have caused her so much concern had Stella been younger, at a time of life when growing girls were struck with all kinds of fancy notions. Or, for that matter, had she not undergone such a shattering experience at that ratty old barn of a place across the county border. As it was, with the girl turned twenty, and isolated by her own wretchedness, a need to make a final break with life seemed not only logical but understandable.

She subsided slowly on Giles' bagged-out basket chair, hands on lap, staring across at him with a kind of desperate appeal. She said, at last, "Why . . . why did she confide in *you*? Why not *me*?" And he replied, "She knew very well you would stop her seeing Father Gregory, or even discussing it with him. But she had to talk to someone."

"What did you say to her?"

"That she couldn't do it without consulting you. She wouldn't be allowed to anyway, until she's twenty-one, would she?"

"What's that to do with it? She'll be twenty-one in April. Did she . . . did she tell you *why*, exactly? Did she tell you anything about . . . about what happened to her with those awful people?"

"Not really. Except that she was dreadfully unhappy there. But I can guess, I think."

She looked at him very sharply, impressed yet again by his maturity, his prescience, by everything about him that made him seem so adult when each of the others, even someone like Alex, who had fought for his life on a battlefield, seemed a child by comparison.

"I don't think you could guess, Giles."

"Yes, I could. It's the kind of thing you would expect from people like that. What I mean is they *think* differently from people of our kind. They see everybody who isn't born into their set as . . . well

. . . as peasants. People of that kind treat animals more kindly than human beings, particularly animals that have cost them a lot of money. It's always been so."

For some reason his positivity comforted her, bringing him appreciably closer, so that he was as deeply involved in the problem as herself.

She said, "Go on, Giles. Say just what you think about it. For I have to talk to someone too and it won't help at all to talk to your father at this stage. He'll only storm and rage, and that won't do, will it?"

"No," he said, very definitely, "it would make things worse." Then, cautiously, "I did *think* of something. It might sound silly. You'll think it's silly, no doubt. But well . . . as I say . . . it occurred to me when she told me what happened to her that night. After she'd run off, I mean."

"Well?"

"She ought to talk it over with someone outside the family and I don't mean a priest. Someone who . . . well . . . who remembers her as she was, before it happened, someone likely to understand . . ."

He stopped there but she knew at once of whom he was thinking. Denzil Fawcett not only remembered Stella as she was when she had dashed about the local coverts shouting and laughing and getting into mischief. He had also been deeply in love with her, was surely still in love with her, and suddenly she thought herself an absolute fool to have to be reminded of him by a child. For Giles had clearly grasped what she had failed to grasp. The need to find someone who could approach a thing like this objectively, someone who wasn't prejudiced by family ties and family loyalties but represented a world utterly opposed to that of the Moncton-Prices who yet knew something of their background.

"You think that's silly?"

"I don't think it's the least bit silly, Giles. I think it's the only possible way of going about things, and one day you'll realise just how much you've helped me to understand all kinds of things. In the meantime, thank you for helping me," and to his surprise and, she suspected, his embarrassment, she embraced him and kissed him on both cheeks, after which she marched down the stairs, through the kitchen, and out into the stableyard, calling imperiously to Stillman to harness up the gig and tell Phoebe Fraser she wouldn't be present at nursery tea.

2

She identified the acrid stink before she had topped the long, tree-sown ridge that was the watershed between their own river and its little tributary, the Linney, beyond which, in a cutaway beside the stream, lay Dewponds, the Fawcett place, a neat if sprawling farmhouse, as old as 'Tryst' but hedged around with a gimcrack assortment of barns, sheds and huts, enclosing the midden yard on three sides.

The smell was that of burning timber, distinct from the autumn bonfire smell that hung over most hollows at this time of year but tinged with something else, a smell that called to mind burning fat or overcooked meat, the smell of a joint a careless cook had popped in the oven and forgotten.

She thought it curious but her mind was far too occupied to do more than record it until, as she crested the rise, she could look down into the horseshoe curve of the Linney and see the great cloud of smoke that hung over the dell, a cloud drifting her way, so that it made her nostrils twitch and her eyes smart. She understood then that something was sadly amiss down there, possibly a rick fire, for the summer had been a dry one and already several local ricks had gone up, one as near as Button's Farm, between 'Tryst' and Twyforde Green. She gave the cob a flick with her crop and trotted on down the hill, heading straight into the dense, grey-blue smoke and as she neared the first of the barns she was aware of a harsh, crackling sound and a confused scurrying to and fro near the farmhouse, together with a continuous hum of voices broken by sharp, isolated shouts and the clank of a pump-handle screaming for a drop of oil.

She pulled up fifty yards short of the place, hitching the cob to a gate and hurrying forward into the smoke-cloud. What she saw there drove all thoughts of Stella out of her mind.

Dewponds farmhouse, and its adjoining cow byres, were ablaze from end to end, blue and crimson flames licking the full length of the thatched and gabled roof, with a shower of blazing straw drifting down on to the thatched roof of an adjoining building, part stable, part hay loft. Even as she watched the byre roof took fire with a soft, sustained puff and people about her began to shout and run across one another's paths with clanking buckets and ladders and firebrooms that were obviously inadequate to deal with an outbreak of this extent.

Then, milling about outside the byre, she saw another group, including two women whom she recognised as the wife and elder daughter of Fawcett, and this party were surrounding a hurdle supporting something shrouded in folds of sacking.

The outcry around her was continuous now, swelled by the scream of horses, and the bellow of cows, with here a farm dog yapping and scampering, and there a terrified hen fluttering madly about the feet of a queue of men prancing around the pump.

She ran across to Mrs. Fawcett and reached out to touch her shoulder but then she saw the woman was hysterical, and being forcibly held back by her daughter Ruth, a girl about a year younger than Denzil, who seemed determined to prevent her mother from approaching the hurdle. At one end of the litter was Denzil, his heavy features drawn and in his eyes an expression of despair. At the other was a farmhand, crying, "Get her clear! Tak' her out o' here, for Christ's sake!" and the desperate appeal in his voice caused Henrietta to glance down at the stretcher and recognise Stephen Fawcett, the skin on his face oddly bleached and taut where the beard and whiskers had been and every hair gone from his head. Denzil saw her then, just as Ruth succeeded in heaving her mother clear, and called, "You got your gig, Mrs. Swann? The doctor! We got to get him to the doctor . . ."

She pointed down the road to the spot where she had tethered the cob and he nodded, shouting something to the farmhand who shifted his grasp on the hurdle and fell in behind him, with Henrietta following until they were clear of the smoke, although they could still hear the frightful clamour of the firefighters and the steady creak of the pump handle.

She said, as they lifted the shrivelled thing into the gig, "He's dead, Denzil . . . you must realise he's dead," and the boy said, "Yes, ma'am, I know. It was mother who didden. I tried me best to stop him but he would go into the byre. His herd was tethered there and he's bin half a lifetime raisin' 'em. But what's the good of it now, with him burned to a cinder in front o' my eyes and hers?"

The farmhand took charge then, settling the dead man on his back and making shift to straighten the limbs. Fawcett's heavy boots protruded from the open door of the little vehicle, so the man took a horse-blanket from the seat and covered the face and the upper part of the body. He said, with a curse, "Happened in a flash. One minnit I see a trailer o' smoke, nex' the whole bliddy roof's ablaze. Will you bide with him lad, while I go after the animals, if there's more to be got out?" The young man nodded and then shook his head violently, as though to deny the finality of death. Slowly and absently he rubbed the back of his hand where a wisp of blazing thatch had settled, inflicting a small, wedge-shaped burn.

He said, woodenly, "You think of this happening. You know it does happen from time to time. But then it happens to you an' some-how you can't . . . can't think what to do first, where to run, who to look to! I better get back. Dick's right. Maybe there's time to get the rest o' the herd clear. That well's so low on account o' the drought . . ." Then, looking at her with a kind of baffled anger, "He *is* dead, isn't he? I mean, it'd be no use rushing him over to Doctor Birtles?"

"I'm sure he's dead, Denzil. But you'd best check. Or I will . . . if you wish it."

"God, no, ma'am, I'll do it!" He was himself again and she had time to appraise his strength, and the tremendous effort he brought to controlling himself, as he turned the blanket down, peeled away the charred remains of the flannel shirt and laid a hand on his father's heart. He said, replacing the blanket, "I'll fetch Ruth then . . ."

"No, Denzil. Your mother needs Ruth. Where will they go, to-night? Would they like to come to 'Tryst'? They'd be very welcome and she'll need looking after."

"Maisie's here," he said, "and Art Wilkins, her husband, who's got the place over at Nine Oaks. It's nearer and I reckon she'd feel better among her own folks."

He hesitated a moment longer, torn between staying with his

father and making the attempt to save more of his stock. Filial obligations won. He said, slowly, "Lookit, Mrs. Swann . . . would you go back and tell mother and Ruth, and ask her to tell Art to take charge. I can't leave him. Someone has to bide with him and I reckon it should be me, seeing I'm eldest. Will you do that, while I find a place to lay him? Somewhere well clear of it?"

She nodded, walking back towards the yard and thinking how trivial her own troubles were compared with the desolation that had engulfed the Fawcetts in a moment of time. She had another thought then, as she hurried past the string of firefighters, and heard that Mrs. Fawcett and her daughter Ruth had gone into the copse behind the farm. It was how Denzil Fawcett had looked as he had made his decision and how much, in some ways, he reminded her of Adam. Especially Adam in a moment of peril.

She did what she had to do and came down into the yard again. Other people had gathered now and two groups were using the water in the horse trough and the duckpond to fight the flames. The roof beams of the farmhouse had crashed down, thousands of sparks shooting into the pall of smoke that overhung the entire dell. Some of the horses must have been saved for she saw men blinding them with sacks and trying to quieten them over by the hen house.

The extent of the desolation staggered her, with two sides of the group of buildings in smouldering ruins and the animals setting up an unceasing din. There was nothing more she could do, however, so she went out through the gate and down the path beside the river, looking for Denzil and the gig but not seeing him anywhere. She thought, briefly, "I'll walk back. He'll need the gig and the cob for his mother . . ." and tackled the ascent that led up to the chestnut wood where she paused, looking down into the clearing now completely obscured by two great columns of smoke, but lit on the underside by the pulsing glow of flames.

*　　*　　*

She found Stella in the hall, listlessly tidying some of the litter the children had left there and said, shortly, "Come into the sewing-room, Stella. I've something to tell you. Something very important!" and the girl looked at her wide-eyed, her glance travelling from smutted face to her ash-stained skirt and dust-coated boots. She said nothing, however, but followed her mother into the room that gave on to the hall, one hand lifting the folds of her grey skirt, the other raised distractedly to her mass of coppery hair. Henrietta said, "I was over at Dewponds. They've had a dreadful disaster there. A fire has destroyed the house and killed poor Mr. Fawcett," and she saw the girl catch her breath, thinking "She's not so far gone that she can't be shocked by someone else's troubles . . ." and waited.

Stella said, after a pause, "*Dead*, you say?" and then, "Just . . . just *Mr.* Fawcett?" And the query told Henrietta what she wanted to know, that Denzil's grief would be hers and that this, in a way, was important.

"Just Mr. Fawcett. I left the gig and cob with Denzil. His mother and sisters are going to the son-in-law's place at Nine Oaks. But he'll be staying on to see what he can do with all that's left of the place. I'm exhausted and had to come away. Tell Stillman to harness up the waggonette and then drive on over there, with blankets, food and some of Alexander's clothes. Denzil's clothes are in tatters."

"You mean me? Me go to Dewponds?"

"Why not? He was kind to you once. I don't know how you would have managed without him. Besides, we're neighbours, and what are neighbours for?"

She watched the girl narrowly, trying to assess the impact the news had made on her and it looked as though something in Stella's mind had surfaced and was floundering about seeking an anchorage. She said, at length, "I'll see to the waggonette. You and Phoebe sort out some things. Shall I take Stillman with me?"

"No, go by yourself. Denzil won't want all and sundry intruding on his grief. I know I wouldn't. Stay there as long as he wants you. I'll wait up until midnight, and the rest of us will go over and give a hand in the morning. I don't want to alarm the children."

She went out then before Stella could change her mind and ten minutes later she was helping Phoebe to load the waggonette with things he might need, a kettle and a tureen full of cold stew, a jacket and trousers that Alex had left behind, and a pile of blankets. Stella climbed on the box and drove off without a word and she watched the vehicle jolt down the drive and turn right in the direction of the wood. Seeing it disappearing behind the fir coppice she thought, "Who knows? It might work. Something wholesome might come out of that stinking ruin over the hill . . ." and turned back into the house, too tired and shocked to eat the cold supper the girl laid for her.

3

She saw him crossing the deserted, rubble-strewn yard with big, ponderous strides, his smudged and scorched shirt sticking to his shoulder, chin lowered, eyes on the cobbles under his feet. She called, "Denzil!" and he looked up sharply, staring at her as though he doubted her presence but then changing direction and looking from her to the back of the waggonette piled with replacements, then back again.

"You! Is your mother back, Miss Stella?"

"No, I'm alone. Mother said I was to bring things you might need. Where is everyone? Surely they didn't leave you . . .?"

"Mother and the girls have gone to Nine Oaks. The hands are seeing to the animals, those we managed to save. We've put them all in the big pound behind the wood. There's water an' feed there, enough until morning."

"Your father . . .?"

"He's in the saw-mill down the road. He'll bide there until they come for him," and suddenly his face crumpled like a child's, tears began to course down his filthy cheeks and his body slumped so that he had to steady himself against the shafts. She was beside him in seconds and her arm went round his shoulders. She said, passionately, "Don't mind, Denzil! Don't mind me! Who wouldn't weep for it all . . . your father—everything you've worked for burned and spoiled and ruined!"

He braced himself then and looked down at her with a kind of wonder, his hand uplifted to his cheek where the tears had driven two furrows in a thick film of ash. He looked, she thought, no older than young Hugo, her brother, after a storm of tears and temper following a rebuke or disappointment.

"Listen," she said, "listen to me, just a moment, Denzil. You'll build it up again, all of it, and you'll restock too, sooner than you think. Everyone about here will help, the way your people always helped others when they needed it. And I'll help too if you want me, in any way I can. You can't do anything more tonight. Let me get the stove going in the piggery. That's not burned, is it? You need to wash and change and by the time you've done that I'll have the stew ready. No . . . no, don't argue! I came here to help and God knows you need help, don't you? Just as I did, the night I found you in the lambing hut."

She led the horse through the gate and round behind the only wing of the farm left standing, a long, slate-roofed building, housing pig-pens and nesting-boxes, with a little store at the far end fitted with a copper they used for boiling pig-feed and hen-mash in winter. He followed her wordlessly, watching her gather scraps of paper and sticks to light the fire, after putting the stewpot inside the copper that was well scoured and hadn't been used since the spring. She noted how clean everything was, even in here, an old shed adjoining a piggery and thought, bitterly, "It would have to happen to him. He and his father tended this holding like a couple of fussy old maids," but then, seeing the fire blaze up, she told him to fetch Alexander's clothes and throw away his half-burned shirt and corduroys and wash himself under the pump while she foraged around at the back of the caved-in scullery and rescued an enamel dish, a tin bowl and one pewter spoon.

He was sitting on a pile of folded sacks when she returned, knees clasped in his hands as he stared morosely at the glow under the copper. Shock was having its effect, even on a big, phlegmatic ox like Denzil Fawcett, for every now and again he yawned and shivered, so she went out and got the blankets from the waggonette and brought them in, draping one of them over his shoulders and then looking to the stew that was beginning to bubble.

He said, watching her ladle the savoury mess into the bowl, "Why are you doing this? It isn't right for someone like you to be here, with the prospect o' riding home in the dark," and she replied, handing him bowl and spoon, "I'm not going home. Not until it's light and you've had some hot food and rest. Then I'll get things organised over there and send more help. A lot of your stuff could be salvaged at the back and when it is we must find somewhere with a roof on to store it until you need it again. Here, eat man. Eat it all. There's plenty here," and roused by her gentle bullying he took the bowl and began to sup.

The moon had risen by the time he had finished, so she told him to unharness the mare and turn her loose. "She won't stray," she said, "she never does if I'm about," and while he was gone she made a bed of the sacks, stuffing one of them with clean straw for a pillow and using the blankets she had brought as coverings.

He looked down at it with amazement when he came stumbling back but when he began yawning again she said, authoritatively, "Lie down and stretch out. Try and sleep, for you'll have a lot to attend to in the morning," and he began to obey her but moved like a big, clumsy automaton, so that she knelt and unlaced his boots, pulling them off, pushing his stockinged feet under the blankets and tucking the end under the improvised mattress.

He said, sleepily, "You can't stay, Miss Stella. Woulden be proper to. Why don't you ride bareback over to Nine Oaks. It's not much above a mile and the moon's bright."

"Stop worrying about me and go to sleep. Mother knows where I am and approves of me being here," and when he wrinkled his brow she gave a little gurgle of laughter, the first time she had laughed in what seemed like years so that the sound, and the sense of relief that accompanied it, surprised and puzzled her.

"Who would have thought of me tucking you up in bed in your own piggery?" she said and then, moved by impulse to express the utterly irrelevant sense of fun that was pushing through the crust of her isolation, she bent forward and kissed his unshaven cheek, blushing the moment she straightened herself, but it did not matter. Shock had finally caught up with him and he was asleep.

*   *   *

'Tryst' saw little of Stella Swann that autumn and winter. All through what remained of September, through the months of October and November, she was at Dewponds every day, often from round about nine in the morning until it was dusk when they would see her toiling up the drive in the waggonette, her muddied skirts gathered about her knees, her hands holding the reins slackly, her copper hair, as like as not, free of pins so that she looked as if she had been romping in the hedgerow.

Henrietta watched her with a kind of awe. She was a complete stranger to the girl she had packed off to the ruined farm with a load of blankets on the night of the fire but neither did she bear the least resemblance to the shallow, feckless girl who had romped about the house, horse-crazy and chock-full of impudence, before she married Lester Moncton-Price. She seemed, in some ways, to have aged ten years in less than two, yet, in another way, she looked not only young but radiantly healthy, her face glowing under a film of brickdust and flecks of spent ash when she heaved herself down from the box, went up to wash and was back again, clean but tousled, in five minutes to eat a farmhand's supper.

They knew, of course, what she was about over there. She was acting as builder's mate to Denzil Fawcett, who had elected to restore the farm almost singlehanded and seemed to be doing it. Curious passers-by, wandering along the banks of the river of a morning, would sometimes see him perched on a roof beam, hammering and sawing, with the girl half-way up the ladder, her mouth full of nails and perhaps a short length of planking or a sheet of zinc under her arm or held between her breast and the stone wall he was raising to replace the charred cob. It was astonishing, observers told one another, how much two people seemed to achieve working upwards of ten hours a day on such a daunting task. By late October all the litter had been carted away and burned. By early November the six survivors of Stephen Fawcett's herd were back in a rebuilt byre. Towards the end of November, when dusk stole into the dell before five o'clock, new roof beams and rafters had been slotted in and Denzil had begun thatching, moving inch by inch up the steep pitch of the roof to the blackened chimneys, then inwards towards the right-angle of the building where it abutted the byre.

Sometimes the girl would be handing him things but more often, as the thatching progressed, she was in the stable, temporarily roofed by a tarpaulin, where such furniture as had been saved had been stacked, together with a huge washtub full of blankets and linen. Christmas came and went and they were still at it. Then the day came, around mid-February, when they spent all morning resetting the lintel and rehanging the great studded door on its hinges.

It was bright and frosty that particular morning and towards noon, when the door was in place, and Denzil was oiling the lock, she went around to their temporary kitchen quarters in the store-shed and boiled two great mugs of cocoa, carrying them back to where he stood, surveying his handiwork.

He said, with schoolboy exuberance, "It fits, Miss Stella! It opens and closes a treat. Look at that now!" and he swung it to and fro for her benefit.

"Well, why wouldn't it fit?" she replied. "You measured it times enough. And something else I've been meaning to tell you. Do stop calling me 'Miss' Stella. It sounds terribly stuffy, and anyway it isn't the kind of title due to a bricklayer's mate, plumber's mate, carpenter's mate, reed-cutter and charwoman about here. I don't call you 'Mr. Denzil', do I?"

He had to think about this. He gave considerable thought to most things. "No," he said, at length, "but then you wouldn't, would you? Coming from the big house, I mean?"

"You've got a big house of your own," she said. "I should know, for I helped build it. Just look at my hands, Denzil Fawcett."

He looked at them and pursed his lips, in the way she had noticed so often during their partnership. What he saw seemed to displease him for he frowned, saying, "Ah, they'm fair ruined! But I kep' tell-ing you to wear gloves, didden I?"

"You get nothing done with gloves on," she said, and then fell to examining his work more closely, noting the new floorboards just over the threshold, and the new banister rail he had fashioned from a discarded ladder they found in one of the undamaged haylofts.

"It's marvellous," she said, "absolutely marvellous when you think hardly anyone has had a part in it except you, Denzil."

"I woulden ha' cared to tackle it on my own. You've been around since the first, haven't you?"

"Yes," she said, with modest pride, "I have that, but I've only handed you nails, and bundles of reeds, and run errands of one sort and another. My mare and mother's cob have done more than I have."

He seemed to be considering something and the effort creased his brow so that his expression reminded her of that first night, when she ordered him to bed on a pile of sacks.

"What's bothering you now?"

"How to say thank you, I reckon," and she flashed back, with a laugh, "I'll show you how. Pick me up and carry me over the threshold!"

He regarded her so solemnly that she laughed again, "Well, why not?"

"You know very well why not, Miss Stella," he said, carefully, "because o' what that means." He stood fidgeting with his enormous hands looking, for all the world like a yokel at a fair who had just been the victim of the three card trick.

She was sorry then, sorry that he should take it for granted that she was teasing him and said, hurriedly, "Suppose that's what I want it to mean? Would you do it then? If no one was watching?"

He surprised her then, moving with remarkable speed for some-one so big and clumsy, and scooping her up as though she had weighed no more than a bag of feathers, marched through the door as far as the foot of the stairs. But here, where she expected to be set down, he did no more than readjust his grip, spinning on his heel and rocking her, as she had seen him cradle one of his lambs.

Crushed hard against his massive chest, she was physically aware of his strength, of the kind that had enabled him to perform so many herculean tasks in the last few months, at the same time solving as many problems as Crusoe when he found himself alone on the island. A kind of joyous recklessness swept over her, so that she threw both her arms round his neck, pulling his face down to hers.

His kiss did not match his strength. It was not really a kiss at all but more of a salutation, short and infinitely restrained, so that even if anyone had observed it they would have been entitled to regard it as brotherly, she supposed. She realised then that he still needed a great deal of prompting but there was no sense in neglecting a opportunity unlikely to come again.

She said, boldly, "That's it then, Denzil! Assuming you mean what I mean, and I sincerely hope you do."

But at that he looked terrified and set her down hastily so that she had a horrid fear that she had taken far too much for granted. She remembered also something she had forgotten all the time they had worked here, that this was not merely his home but his mother's, and his sister's, and that possibly he too was remembering this but had no words to explain his dilemma.

Then she decided she was wrong again. There was a glazed look in his eye, as if he was seeing something, and experiencing something, that was incomprehensible to him and was so far out of his depth that he doubted if he would ever find bottom again. His helplessness touched her, so that she thought, "We can't leave it here . . . if he's too shy and too tongue-tied to take the initiative, I shall have to finish what I started, with only myself to blame if I make a fool of myself!" She said, desperately, "Listen, Denzil, say what . . . whatever's in your mind! Perhaps I *was* jumping to conclusions. I mean, there's your mother and sister Ruth. You have to finish rebuilding here and you have to restock but I'm not afraid to say right out that I love you, and that until I came here, the night of the fire, I hadn't the least idea what love was or could be. I'll wait, for as long as you like. Or I'll go away, and leave you to settle in and take your time. It's for you to say. I've said enough. Too much I wouldn't wonder."

He had continued to stare at her with that bemused expression but when she said the words 'go away' he suddenly came to life, making a wild and fiercely negative gesture with his right hand, as his look of bewilderment changed to one of alarm and he caught up her hands, pressing them both to his mouth and blurting out, "Leave? . . . Go away . . . ? Don't talk o' such things. Don't say it nor think it!" It was as though the broken protests were a cipher, releasing the key to his pent-up thoughts, so that he rushed on, "All this time . . . long before you showed up that night . . . years and years, ever since I picked you out o' that ditch, under Short Wood, wi' mud all over you . . . ! By God, but you can't *blame* me for bein' slow, for not understanding . . . ! You an' *me?* Man and wife on our own land? Can you think for one minute I'd ever want anything else, or ask anything better, so long as there was breath in me body?"

It was a declaration unlike any she had heard about or read about so that it seemed not to qualify as a proposal, even allowing for her efforts to bring it about. Yet, when she measured him in her mind against all the other men she had flirted with, or who had flirted with her, or someone like Lester Moncton-Price, whose proposal had been phrased like an attorney's letter, he seemed to her the only man in the world who qualified as a suitor, and ten times as impressive as all the heroes in the romances that had come her way through her mother or Phoebe Fraser. Intense pride possessed her, that she could be in receipt of so much steadfastness. This was like rebirth into a world where the sun shone every day and the memory of the last two years was so blurred as to be all but banished from mind and memory.

She said, raising a hand and stroking his cheek, rough with the day's bristles, "I'll make you a good wife, Denzil. A far better one than I would have made you before. I think we could be very happy here, the two of us, providing I could get it through your head that I'm finished with all that foolishness about us coming from different worlds. I daresay you'll think I treated you badly when I was younger but since then I've been treated very badly myself and it teaches you something. I didn't in the least understand the kind of person you were until this awful thing happened to you and instead of whining and moping, the way I did, you at once set about putting all the pieces together again, without so much as a call on anyone to help. Well, there it is, and I daresay most people would think me very forward. But I don't care about that either. The truth is I only care about you, and what becomes of you now that you've made up your mind to start all over again."

She wondered then if he had been listening, or whether what she was trying to say had got through to him for his brain moved as ponderously as his body, step by step, studying the landscape with a countryman's eye for pitfalls and possibilities. He said, triumphantly, "There's one thing you don't know. Mother won't never come back here to live. She says she couldn't, on account o' what happened to father. As to Ruth, she's courtin' a chap over at Twyforde Green, and like to be married before the year's out. Wait on, you said. Well, I've done wi' waiting. Seems like I been waiting all my life and there's on'y one thing that'd come between you and me right now."

"What's that, Denzil?"

"Your folks. Your Mam especially, for she's a rare trier when she's up against it, as she showed that time I drove her over to Moncton-Price's place. I got a lot o' respect for Mrs. Swann and if she set her face against a girl of hers being a farmer's wife, and that within shouting distance of her own place, I wouldn't run against her. It wouldn't make for harmony, so you'd best think on that and sound her out."

It was strange, she thought, that he should fear her mother and discount her father altogether. But then she saw that this was how he was made, someone who went right to the heart of things, judging people by standards he set himself, that had nothing whatever to do with money and power but everything to do with the qualities of self-reliance and human dignity.

"Mother won't stand in our way," she said. "I know that well enough. I believe she had something like this in mind when she ordered me over here, the night your place burned down. In many ways she's got far more horsesense than father."

"Aye, but it won't do to run against him either. He's a big man, the biggest round here, I'd say."

She said, calmly, "We'll jump that ditch when we come to it. I'll be twenty-one in April, and could please myself. That's the day I'd like us to marry if you're willing."

"April? Two months from now?"

"Why not? The place will be ready enough to live in, and you've just said yourself you're tired of waiting."

She would like to have added something to this. She would have liked to have burned every bridge that linked her to the old life and done it here and now. So many things that had been obscure to her were suddenly startlingly clear, and one of them, that made her tremble with delight, was the prospect of assuring him beyond all doubt that she was his for the taking. She sensed, somehow, that only the closest physical contact with him could obliterate the last traces of the shame and degradation attending that last night over at Courtlands, where that pomaded old roué had looked her over as if she was a horse at a fair. To lie under him, to absorb him completely, translating his worship into workaday terms—that would equalise them, as they could never be equalised by words, and it seemed to her something that ought not to wait upon the empty rituals of marriage. But she knew him well enough to understand that this was something that he could not be expected to view in her terms, that to him the rituals represented something not merely specific but highly desirable. That did not mean, however, that she was prepared to forgo all the pleasures of courtship denied her in the past, so she said, briskly. "You can leave my family to me, Denzil. You won't have to come asking in the usual way. I think a man like you would find that intolerable. Is it to be on my birthday, as I said?"

"By God, yes!" he said, joyfully. "Nothing c'n come between us from here on!" and then she realised that she had, after all, misjudged him to a degree, for he seized her in an embrace that drove the breath from her body and covered her face with kisses so that when, reluctantly, he released her, she was not merely breathless but limp. She learned something else about him in those few moments and it added, if that was possible, to her sense of fulfilment. He was not, it seemed, so shy in his handling of a woman as she had supposed.

Part Two

ADVANCE OF THE REAPERS

1

A Swann Levee

BRAZEN it out. Let the county snobs stay home and clack but let the village folk, who wished them well, have another Swann spectacle for their money, especially as it was spring and the altar was loaded with churchyard-grown daffodils and narcissi.

That had been Henrietta's advice and he took it. It made good sense to him and he applauded, as always, her audacity. For she made no effort at all to conceal her utmost satisfaction concerning the match. Or, for that matter, the fact that it was she who had accomplished it.

It was a happier if less spectacular demonstration of Swann solidarity than the old Colonel's funeral, more than two years ago. No one outside the family and firm was invited yet people came, more than two hundred of them, filing into the little church to witness the Swann filly's second try over a dramatically lowered jump. Marrying a rustic, no less. Some said with indecent haste but others, a majority, were more charitable. For the Swanns, to give them their due, had never been noted for putting on side.

There they were then, almost a dozen of them, absorbed in the bridal group, or wedged hugger-mugger into the front pew, for this time there was no protocol to observe on behalf of the military.

A Swann rally and a Swann occasion. A whole boiling of them arrayed in their Sunday best. Adam Swann (whose jaw, the wits would tell you, had set a thousand waggons rolling), his handsome, unapologetic wife, Lieutenant Alexander Swann, in scarlet bumfreezer and braid, and all the lesser Swanns, from Giles down to pageboy Edward, rising four. As impressive a spread as you would be likely to find anywhere in Kent on a fine April morning, with a brisk south-easterly herding a flock of laggard clouds across the Sussex border.

Two only were absent. George, learning coach-building (why

coach-building, when his father was said to buy waggons by the gross?) and away in foreign parts, and baby Margaret at home in the nursery, but all the others made such a fine showing that everyone was prepared to forget that this was Stella Swann's second time round in thirty-two months, fast going by anyone's reckoning for a filly who came of age that very day.

The villagers turned as upon a single spinal cord when Mr. Gibbs, the organist, received his signal and began to play, and in she marched with her blushes (if she had any left after all those months as Denzil Fawcett's journeyman) concealed under a veil that was, they supposed, a compromise between virginity and widowhood. They were not exactly clear what had happened but whatever it was it must have been blessed and it must have been legal or she wouldn't have been here at all and looking so pleased with herself. Down the aisle she swept on her father's arm, while Denzil, poor wight, was the only one present unable to turn his head and mark her bearing on account of a three-inch collar, that had his neck in a splint and obliged him to continue to stare fixedly at the altar candlesticks and listen to heartbeats that seemed to him loud enough to drown the organ.

It was all very pastoral and cosy, all very much in keeping with the end of a sharp spell of frost that had stopped hunting but enabled amateur skaters to acquire a spread of bruised buttocks and scabbed kneecaps on the river below the islet. Twyforde Green, settling back, could gaze its fill, familiar, of course, with the two younger bridesmaids, Joanna and Helen, in their blue satin frocks, their Kate Greenaway bonnets, elbow-length mittens and posies of hot-house anemones, but wondering at the rows of strange attentive faces in pews further back, representing, so they were told, Swann hirelings from all over England. It occurred to the more prescient then that this was not so much a wedding as a Swann muster, a carriers' convention that stamped Adam Swann's seal upon the locality, but nobody guessed that this public unfurling of the Swann banner was a deliberate act, the outcome of a compromise between man and wife when the latter informed the former that his daughter's hibernation was over, and that he was likely, God willing, to prove the grandfather of a string of Kentish yeomen once the new thatch had weathered over at Dewponds Farm.

Adam remembered it, however, smiling one of his sardonic grins as he stood beside his daughter and it occurred to him again that Henrietta did well to indulge a passion for soldiers, for she was temperamentally equipped to conjure with tactics and stratagems. Little by little, he told himself, the balance of power was shifting at 'Tryst', but then, he had never subscribed to the Victorian cult of the patriarch. Patriarchs sported beards whereas he remained obstinately cleanshaven. Besides, this was her victory. The match, it seemed, had been engineered by her. But that, he would say, had not been the beginning of it, recalling now the part that lumping great bridegroom had played in the first act of the tragic farce. Since then, he imagined, it must have been a devious story, and very much a woman's story, concerning which he had no real curiosity. He was content to accept their presence here as a traditional happy ending, although it did occur to him that he and others might have been spared a pack of trouble if that stupid girl of his had made a grab at her rustic years ago, before leading everybody such a cheerless, cross-country dance.

He glanced sideways over his daughter's shoulder and what he saw reassured him. Denzil Fawcett was undeniably a chawbacon by a city man's standards but it needed little imagination to identify his unique qualifications for groom at this particular ceremony. He was not even listening to the words that invested him with the Swann-on-Wheels insignia but was gazing at the bride as if vouchsafed a vision of Thetis, the silver-footed sea-goddess. And there was relevance here unless his classical memory was at fault. Thetis had been condemned to marry a mortal and this mortal, judged by his expression of stupefied reverence, had no quarrel with the judgement of Zeus.

He would have liked very much to have looked over his shoulder at Henrietta, if only to assure himself that the smug expression he had noticed when she set out for the church was still there but he did not dare. He had been enjoined, given the special circumstances surrounding this remarkable event, to be on his very best behaviour and on no account to let his attention stray, as he usually did when he accompanied the family to church.

*   *   *

237

The expression was there, the look of a merchant who, against all probability, had recouped heavy losses by investing in a venture that promised a steady trickle over the years. For she did not care a curse what the croquet-lawn gossips said (and she knew them well enough to realise they were saying a great deal) for this was not a match in the conventional sense of the word. It was more of an adjustment from a state of bankruptcy to the status quo, and what woman in her senses would not prefer a rustic son-in-law to a daughter mumbling prayers behind a convent wall? God knows, she had reason enough to congratulate herself. The game had been as good as lost when she took it in hand but here they all were, confronted with a healthy, beaming bridegroom and an almost embarrassingly felicitous bride, and all in a matter of eight months, and no one save Giles a penny the wiser concerning the horrible scare that had set it in train.

She looked across at Giles, noting that he was absorbing every word of the ceremony and it occurred to her that he would be likely to see this not as the direct result of his troubled confession but as a triumph of true love. For Giles, alone among them, was a romantic.

It was a pity, she reflected, that Alexander was not, remembering his bleak stare when told the news. He was bearing up, however, and this no doubt was due as much to his kind heart as to her cautionary lecture, for he had said, on being asked for loyalty, "Very well. I suppose a fellow can't really be held responsible for the chaps his sister takes up with, and from what you say there's no denying the gel went through a beastly time while I was away." The transposition of the word 'girl' to 'gel' did not pass unnoticed. That would be Sandhurst rubbing off on him, she supposed, but he had clearly taken her point. A beastly time, forsooth! Thank God he was unlikely to discover just how beastly and she assumed, her eye reverting to the groom, that poor Denzil was likely to remain equally ignorant if Stella had her wits about her. And even that, when you came to think of it, was something to be grateful for. She wasn't coming to him second-hand but as a bride should, and it might not have been so had Stella shown less fleetness of foot the night the Conyer oak came down in the paddock.

Henrietta usually enjoyed a wedding but this one gave her more than the customary flutter. It produced a warm, pleasurable glow under her heart and this on account of its shape and rightness, for surely, all things being equal, nothing frightening would ever happen to Stella again. Denzil Fawcett would make sure of that and watching them, in the act of giving and receiving the ring, she did what she always did at a wedding, that is to say, compared the immediate prospects of the bride with her own experience at eighteen. There was a difference, of course. One only had to glance at the boy to know he was also virgin, so that at least they would start level. He was sure to be gentle too, and far more patient than most men, having already waited so long and so hopelessly. Well, the very best of luck to them, tonight and every night. All in all, mother and daughter had every right to exult. One had exchanged a bad husband for a good. The other had completed a smart exercise in salvage.

2

The precise significance of his substitution of Swann's viceroys for bonafide wedding guests had escaped her until the return from church where the entire muster, suitably awed she noted, reassembled in the hall before passing, two by two, into the drawing-room where bride and groom stood beside the table supporting the three-tiered cake that was crowned—God forgive him—with a sugar-icing Swann waggon instead of the usual assortment of cherubs and angels. Then she understood that it was not, as she had imagined, a piece of buffoonery and that like her, he did not see this wedding as a conventional match. It was not and could not be, with the best will in the world. For him it had another and distinct function that was characteristic of him and had impelled him to make it a private family occasion; *his* family, not Stella's or Denzil's. It was at once a sneer and a challenge, underlining his creed that commercial undertakings, in this day and age, had far more relevance than dynastic alliances of one kind or another and here was his fanfare played in public and be damned to what the local quality thought about it.

She stood slightly apart, observing their advance and remembering to smile but her smiles were really for him. Most fathers would exhibit paternal pride in a pretty daughter on an occasion like this but his was reserved for the guests. She noticed something else that escaped the bridal pair. As they advanced for the presentation they made no more than token obeisances to the sweating groom and the composed and radiant bride. Their fealty was for him, standing there on his gammy leg, dispensing a mixture of patronage and geniality, so that she thought, as she kissed Edith Wickstead, and shook hands with Edith's Tom, "There's really no curing the man! And no making a real father out of him either! Here we are, celebrating the miraculous reprieve of our eldest daughter from a nunnery, and what will he and this mob of free-booters talk about the moment the toasts are behind us, and poor Denzil has retired to Dewponds with his glittering prize? Not the wedding, certainly. More likely the cost of a haul of bacon from a Wiltshire curing factory to the nearest siding, or the wastage of horseflesh on roads half-ruined by the spring thaw!"

It was Edith, who knew him almost as well as she did, who put this into words when she whispered, slyly, "Don't mind him, Henrietta. Or us either for that matter! We wish *her* well *because* of him, don't you see?"

And she did see, and had to laugh in spite of it all, reasoning that there were many more than nine to his family.

3

To Edith Wickstead who, as Edith Wadsworth, was the only woman present to have held an independent command in the regions, it was like visiting her home town after an absence of half a lifetime.

Moving among the clamorous males and their fashion-conscious wives from every corner of the Swann empire, the past came alive to her in a way that it never had after she had turned her back on the Crescents and become, at thirty plus, a wife and mother, as well as tutor to the husband who succeeded her.

For Edith, nibbling wedding cake and isolating the burr of a dozen provincial accents, the enterprise was invested with a kind

of magic, conjuring up, at one and the same moment, fanfares of
trumpets and the laughter of circus clowns. For they were all, she
told herself, compounds of swashbuckler and mountebank, pedlar
and packman, freebooting mercenary and commercial pace-setter,
and there was both poetry and logic in this. Adam Swann, who
had been and still was all of these things, had fashioned each of
them in his own image, singling them out one by one as his dreams
expanded, imbuing them with his distinctive sense of vocation, almost as though he had been recruiting missionaries to go out into
the highways and byways and proclaim the gospel of first-come-first-
served on the assurance that God (whom he probably saw as an
English wholesaler) would help those who helped themselves.

Every face and every voice recalled some milestone on the road
they had travelled together, and many of those present had travelled
it all the way in his company and hers. The Welsh lilt of Bryn
Lovell, introducing his half-caste wife to Henrietta, recalled how
Lovell had achieved fame for Swann-on-Wheels and himself by
stepping forward like a Pied Piper and plucking fifty-seven entombed
miners from a flooded pit. The buzz-saw vowels of Hamlet Ratcliffe,
introducing his wife, Augusta, called to mind the story of Hamlet's
recapture of a toothless lion allegedly terrorising a Devon plateau,
to the glory of Swann-on-Wheels and himself. Everyone here had a
story to swap or a reminiscence to contribute, so that it seemed to
her that each volley of small talk began with the words, "Do you
mind the time . . ." or "That was around the time . . ." or simply,
"Time was . . ." an inevitable preamble for a jeremiad denouncing
the present in favour of the past.

John Catesby, who always reminded her of the phrase "Such
men are dangerous", had mellowed more than most, for there he
was engaged in amiable discussion with that old rascal Sam Rawlinson, the bride's grandfather, on the rival merits of Georgian and
Egyptian cotton, when she had no trouble at all remembering a
time when Catesby would have gladly hung Sam from a Salford
lamppost, whereas Sam, for his part, would have had Catesby trans-
ported as an industrial wrecker. Their fusion, she supposed, was
another achievement of Adam's. He had never had much difficulty
in persuading lions to consort with lambs given, of course, that the
consorting occurred in a waggon that bore the Swann insignia.

It was possible, standing here in this room, to pinpoint a dozen examples of this rare talent of his for deputising and this, she supposed, was a trick that all successful men had in common. Over by the window was 'Young' Rookwood, of Southern Square, talking to Godsall, of the Kentish Triangle. Both were relaxed and each was using the other's Christian name without affectation. Who would believe, at this range, that Rookwood had begun life as a Thameside waif, whereas Godsall, at the same age, had been a lieutenant in one of the oldest regiments in the British army?

The same, in a sense, was true of Morris, the manager of Southern Pickings, and Jake Higson, another of Keate's vanboys, for when Morris had joined them, an acknowledged expert on highgrade porcelain, he had thought himself a cut above men like Higson, Rookwood and Ratcliffe. He had soon learned otherwise. Beneath the banner of Adam Swann every regional manager was equal, irrespective of birth, background and even annual turnover. And so they would remain, until the day it came to his notice (as everything did sooner or later) that one or other of them had run out of steam.

*   *   *

She carried her cake and glass of champagne out into the hall, finding an unoccupied bench near the foot of the staircase and sitting there contentedly enough, basking in satisfied memories. She remembered the day she had first crossed this threshold, a woman without hope, for Adam Swann, whom she had once loved (and still did in a way) was said to be dying, and the future of everyone in that throng across the hall was at stake.

That was the day she had first met Henrietta and discovered, to her dismay, that she was not the spoiled doll of her imagining but a woman with wits and courage equal to the best of them and superior to most. It seemed to her, looking back, that she had taken a prodigious gamble to have admitted, there and then, that she was Swann's woman. Soul certainly, aye, and body too if it could have been accomplished with dignity. But Henrietta had not been outraged, or even astonished. It must have seemed to her then (it probably still did) that every woman in the world could be forgiven for falling in love with Adam. Looking back on that extraordinary interview Edith saw it as the real turning point in her own life, for she had no alternative then but to stop dreaming and begin the laborious process of rebuilding her life.

It was odd how Swann touched and changed the lives of so many others, and she wondered whether he impinged to this extent on his children. It seemed unlikely. Why else would he have allowed Stella to run herself into such a corner.

A step on the stairs made her glance up and see Henrietta in her blue and silver finery looking as if she too would appreciate a momentary withdrawal from the babel. She said, descending the last few stairs to the hall, "Come into the sewing-room, Edith, and take a dish of tea while Stella changes. I really don't know why people make such a fuss about champagne. My throat is parched with the stuff and tea is what I need. Besides, I've never thanked you properly for all you did for Stella that time."

Edith said, as they shut the door behind them, "It didn't seem to do any good at the time. Stella left much as she arrived, walking in her sleep."

"Ah, yes," said Henrietta, merrily, "but she's wide awake now I assure you. I expected a little panic now the public part of it is behind her but there she is, getting her things together as offhandedly as a French maid. It's Denzil who has his heart in his mouth."

"How did it happen, Henrietta? If you don't mind telling me."

"I don't mind telling you anything. They say two women can't enjoy real friendship, of the kind men boast about, but that's only bluff on their part. Underneath they've got far more capacity for rivalry than women. Especially women who have faced trouble together, as you and I have. How did it happen? By a mixture of luck and guile, I suppose," and she told Edith the story of the last few months. "Do you think I did right? To settle for what most folk would regard as a poor second-best?"

"Most folk haven't your ability to cut the cackle and concentrate on essentials," Edith said, and meant it. That farmboy might be all he looked, a ponderously-put-together peasant, but he was clearly what Stella Swann needed at this juncture, someone who worshipped her and Henrietta must have appreciated this, notwithstanding her well-known determination to put down social roots.

"How did Adam take it?"

"How I intended he should. In matters of this kind he gives me my head. And why not? It's the least he can do, seeing that the family he's concerned with is in there, converting this wedding into a board meeting. But I don't have to tell you that, do I?"

"No," said Edith, smiling, "you don't, but I've often wondered whether you resent it. Do you?"

"Not really, seeing the person he is, can't help being, and will always be to the day he dies. I read somewhere—I forget where—that Napoleon's last words were 'head of the army . . .' and thought of Adam at once. His last words will be 'Did Tybalt double-check that forage bill from the Crescents?' "

Edith laughed and Henrietta, after a moment, joined in. The conspiracy that had existed between them since the day the one had bullied the other into taking the Swann helm and piloting the enterprise through a bad winter against the spring of his return, persisted to an extent. In a way they were still plotters, conspiring together for his own good and for their own peace of mind.

Henrietta said, by way of an epilogue, "A man like him could never devote that much nervous energy to anything as small as a family. That's why I take upon myself the job of directing everything that happens here. I make mistakes from time to time but who doesn't? He does and Stella was the worst of them. It was that, I imagine, that finally decided me. He accepts it gracefully. At his time of life a man wants something more of a woman than a bedmate, and that's all I was for long enough."

"I don't think so," Edith said, "but maybe, looking back, it seems that way to you. It's a problem I never had to face with Tom, seeing that I was . . ." but she stopped, remembering Adam would choose his own time for telling her about Tom Wickstead's past.

Henrietta did not press her, as most women would have done, and this encouraged Edith to add, "When you've got rid of us all, and peace descends on the place once more, remind Adam that he has my permission to tell you something remarkable about Tom and me. I think it will interest you because . . ." But then, to their mild embarrassment, Adam popped his head in the door. His flushed face indicated that he had had more than his share of the champagne.

"What the devil are you two gossiping about in here?" he demanded, jovially. "Am I expected to entertain a hundred guests singlehanded while my wife and her crony sip tea in seclusion?"

"We've been discussing men and what happens to their wretched wives when they drink too much," said Henrietta, but a ragged cheer from the hall cut short any further exchange.

Adam said, "They're leaving now. I told Alexander to make sure that send-off nonsense is confined to a shower of rice. That poor devil Fawcett couldn't be bullied into taking more than a sip or two of champagne."

"He'll not need champagne," Henrietta said, rising and giving a touch to her hair and earrings. "Your daughter's his substitute for liquor and has been, ever since she put her hair up. Not that *you* could be expected to notice it. Come, Edith, let's see them off and afterwards we'll offer tea to all the wives in the dining-room and leave the men to talk haulage alone. After all, that's what they came for, the wedding was just an excuse."

They followed him out, through the hall and into the forecourt, where Giles (in a way the touchstone of the occasion) was holding the bridles of the team hitched to a rosetted waggonette. The April sun flooded the front of the house and over towards the downs there was half a rainbow, arched across a sea of brown, green-tinted woods. Edith thought, amid the storm of cheers and jokes directed at the couple, "By God, Henrietta knows her business. As well or better than he knows his, and that's saying a good deal!"

4

She brought up the subject that same night, when most of the guests had departed, and the few remaining were scattered about a house that seemed silent and deserted after such a sustained commotion.

She asked him less out of curiosity than as a means of sidetracking his thoughts and his misgivings concerning Stella, for she believed he was troubled by guilt regarding his share in the Moncton-Price debacle. In fact, he had more or less admitted as much, saying, the moment he climbed into bed, and laid himself down with a grunt,

"Couldn't get near the girl when she drove off but she looked happy enough from the glimpse I got. Was that your impression?"

She said it most certainly was, smiling at her reflection in the mirror but he added, with a rather pathetic attempt at raillery, "You gave her a second helping of mother's advice, I hope," to which she replied, laying aside her hairbrush, "Indeed, I did not. I started to, a week ago, but she laughed in my face. She'll be giving me advice soon, I wouldn't wonder."

He sat up at that, saying, "Great God, you're not hinting that our first grandchild will come across the fields, are you?" and then she laughed, for the conclusion was typical of a male, so ill-equipped to deal with subtleties of this kind.

"The difference between this marriage and the last is that the girl was courted and that taught her far more than I could. She's head over heels in love with that humping great farmer's lad, and not simply concerned with rescuing her pride, as you seem to think."

He said, settling back, "Rubbish. What the devil can she know of love, except the kind she found in those trashy romances you and Phoebe Fraser leave lying about the house?"

She came round to the bedside then, turning the lamp low and saying, "Simply that working alongside him has sharpened her instincts. That's what I meant by 'love'. She caught him at the right time, when he was crushed under his own troubles, and that gave her an advantage, rare enough in a woman's case. Don't worry your head over Stella any more. She's off your hands, and for good this time. Instead, tell me about Edith and that Tom Wickstead. It's all right, Edith told me to ask you. It can't be so dreadful, can it? Was he married to someone else when she threw her cap at him?"

"Not to my knowledge," he said. "He was a convict on licence."

His revenge was in the look of dismay on her face and he was glad then that she had not quite extinguished the bedside lamp.

"He was *what?*"

"A ticket-of-leave man. She first met him when he was pilfering one of our Harwich-bound packages. Later she managed to talk him out of his profession on the promise of a job with us. I don't usually put much faith in these road-to-Damascus reformations but it worked with him. He's one of the best men I ever had. The Crescent staff think the world of him."

"But that's crazy," she said, "Edith marrying someone like that . . . did you know all the time?"

"No. She told me to cheer me up, that time I met her in Peterborough, after you had sent Stella to her. I always thought there was something a bit odd about the chap. Not that odd, however." He looked at her anxiously. "Look here, Hetty, if you let it make any difference to your approach to him or her I'll be damned sorry I told you. I wouldn't have done, without her leave. Why did she make a point of asking you to ask me?"

"That would need a lot of thinking about!" said Henrietta, but she at once began to think about it, weighing the enormous reserve of faith and courage that would be needed to take a gamble of that size. Or perhaps faith and courage hadn't played such a spectacular part in it, for she remembered now how glum and at odds with herself Edith had been when they had parted after all that patient coaching at the Thameside Headquarters. Adam was away learning to walk. Edith had been nearly thirty then, and might have seen Tom Wickstead as a final chance to make something of her life.

She said, wonderingly, "What made her do it? She's always had nerve but it seems a terrible chance to have taken. Besides, Edith never struck me as being my type of woman as regards a man."

"What kind of woman is that?"

"You know very well what I mean. She's a woman who would be attracted to a man mentally more than physically, someone who could do without one if she had to. Oh, I know very well that you think every woman in the world prefers a man of her own to the inside of Aladdin's cave, but that's only male vanity. It isn't necessarily so at all. Your own Aunt Charlotte was one. I remember when I went to her seeking advice, of the kind I needed so badly at that time, she was absolutely scandalised. Not at my asking but at the notion of my thinking she could provide any of the answers."

He said, chuckling, "If you plied my Aunt Charlotte with those kind of questions you deserved a Victoria Cross at least. The wonder is she didn't upend you and lace your backside with a raspberry cane, the way she used to handle some of the saucy little madams who went to her school when I was a boy."

"She probably would have done if she hadn't been so embarrassed.

But don't sidetrack me. You should know Edith. She was madly in love with you for years. Did she ever strike you as the saucy type?"

It was his turn to think back on Edith Wickstead. "No," he said, thoughtfully, "she was always out looking for something more lasting than a tumble in the bracken. She wanted to insure against lonely old age. She wanted children, too, and I'm glad she had the good sense to make the leap before it was too late. She's a good wife and a good mother, I'm told, but the source of my information is prejudiced. Tom still looks at her like . . . well, damn me, that's odd!"

"Like what? What were you going to say?"

"I was going to say 'Like Denzil was looking at Stella when he put the ring on today.' Did you notice it? Some would call it the Prince-in-the-Sleeping-Beauty look but he reminded me more of a newly-landed salmon!"

"You're insufferable," she said, and reached out to turn the lamp screw, reducing the wick to a red glow. But then, as the glow faded, and her eyes adjusted to the moonlight penetrating the curtain joint, "Yes, I noticed it, and any little difficulty that does arise while those two are getting used to one another is in that look. He's a good, sturdy boy but it must be an odd feeling to be worshipped like a goddess by someone twice your size and weight. I daresay Stella can cope with it but I confess it would make me uncomfortable."

She heard his sleepy chuckle and then, after a moment or two, his snore. The old feeling of escaping from everybody and everything stole over her, as it never failed to do when they were alone in this room in the dark and she thought, sleepily, "The first family wedding behind us . . . the first real wedding that is. And in two years Adam and I will be celebrating our silver wedding. With luck I'll be a grandmother by then. I've earned my luck . . ." She turned, stealthily enlarging her sleeping space already invaded by him and as she settled, one arm across him, the other tucked under her cheek, she had another pleasant thought, "I don't envy the young, as I once did . . . this is the best stretch of all . . . the middle stretch, when you know where you are going and why."

5

Dusk had fallen before they had turned the horses loose in the pasture, still scarred with half-burned rubble. She was too excited to eat but she stirred the log smouldering in the open grate so as to boil water for their cocoa. It was very pleasant, she reflected, to be able to do a simple, humdrum task of this kind, to work in one's own kitchen, instead of someone else's, or in the outhouse that had served as a kitchen for the last six months. Already Dewponds seemed more familiar than 'Tryst'. Parts of its structure dated from the fifteenth century but most of it was his creation and hers, so that the strangeness, and the feeling of desolation she had experienced on her arrival at Courtlands as a bride, did not trouble her now. Instead she pottered about happily, reminding herself every few minutes that she was mistress of the place in fact as well as name.

She understood, of course, that one hurdle lay ahead. Somehow, she was not clear how, his veneration of her would have to be moderated. Somehow she would have to teach him to take the initiative as master of the household and not defer, as he had been inclined to do ever since she had proposed to him, on everything pertaining to the establishment, even the purchase of new stock concerning which he knew more than she would ever know. There was so much to learn and he would have to teach her but how did one convey this to a man stunned by the swift rush of events, from the moment he had picked her up and carried her over his threshold as far as the stairs?

Adoration, of the kind that stemmed from his every glance, was well enough during courtship, but she had no wish to reign here as a goddess or a fairy queen, waited upon by a chosen mortal, who moved and spoke as if he was under some kind of spell and had reverted, in the last few days, to the gentle, dutiful boy who had plucked her out of that ditch all those years ago.

She thought about this seriously whilst she went about her unpacking and he was pottering about downstairs, doing some job that had been overlooked in the final stage of renovation. She accepted the fact that any significant advance in their relationship would have to be prompted by her and she had a feeling that it had best be begun at once, before his shyness hardened into an attitude that could easily reverse the pattern of marriage. Her mother's hints concerning physical submission were irrelevant in a situation of this kind. Ordinarily, she supposed, all that was required of a bride was passivity but theirs was not an ordinary marriage, not by any standards. Denzil Fawcett, indeed, all the Fawcetts had lived in the shadow of 'Tryst' all their lives and this was sure to inhibit him, apart from his evident difficulty in acknowledging the reality of his dream. In a way, she felt, she was like the Queen on the eve of the Prince Consort's arrival at Windsor as bridegroom-elect. He might see any approach on his part as lese-majesty and this simply would not do as a basis of marriage between master and mistress of a run-down farm. Before she knew it she would be acting out a parody of her life at Courtlands, this time with herself as the patron and Denzil as the hanger-on. The thought, whilst making her wince, hardened her determination to resolve the situation without delay. She went down to the kitchen, made the cocoa and called his name so that he emerged from the dairy in his shirt sleeves, a saw in one hand, a square of plywood in the other, looking, she thought, more like a workman interrupted in a task than a groom whose word, from here on, was manorial writ.

She said, gently, "I've made the cocoa. I'm sure you won't want any supper after all that food. I couldn't manage a mouthful. I was too busy and excited to eat anything except cake. What on earth are you doing with that saw and piece of wood?"

He said, abstractedly, "I didn't have time to put the dairy window in. I thought I'd board her up for the night and set about it in the morning."

She could have laughed at this and told him that she did not propose spending the first night of her married life in the dairy, but she was learning something new about him every moment, and assumed that he had only begun the task as an excuse to absent himself whilst she was unpacking a trunkful of feminine garments. Then it occurred to her, with relief, that he must be familiar with feminine garments, for he was a boy brought up in the company of a string of girls, whose small clothes must have fluttered from the clothes-line every Monday since he was a child, and this thought led her on to an acknowledgement that he must be equally familiar with mating, for he had never spent a day of his life out of sight of a byre or barnyard. She understood then that all that was really required on her part was some positive encouragement, of the kind she had given him the day they hung the door, a final but necessarily spirited attack on the class barrier that stood between them as two people reared in circumstances so widely separated by money, manners, education. That and heaven only knew what else prescribed by the rigid county class structure that she had accepted as complacently as she accepted the passage of the seasons.

She said, drawing a deep breath, "Put that stuff away, Denzil. This is your wedding night. *My* wedding night. We've been working on this house for months and heaven knows, there's still plenty to do. But not now and not for a day or so, seeing there's no hope of a farmer's wife having a honeymoon."

He smiled, a little nervously, she thought, but laid aside the saw and the piece of wood and took up his cocoa, sipping it as though it was a love potion she had prepared for him, avoiding her eye over the rim of the mug. She waited patiently for him to set down the mug before rising, crossing to him, and taking both his hands in hers.

She said, encouragingly, "Well, now, tell me what you thought of it all? Were you nervous waiting for me to appear at the church? Did all those people back at the house scare you?"

He replied, "Scare me? No, they didn't. Not like I thought they might, for they weren't grand folk, of the kind I expected. As to waiting at the church, by God I was scared an' don't mind admitting it." He grinned and she accepted the grin as a slight thaw. "I kep' thinking— 'She'll like as not change her mind las' minute, for it can't be true, none of it!'"

It elated her that he should admit to this for it gave her the opening she was seeking. She said, "Then let *me* tell *you* something. *Two* things! First, Papa must have had it in mind that you would feel easier with his work people than the kind of guests he would likely invite to my wedding. He's like you in that respect. I never did see him put on airs in all my life and those people he brought in from the network don't either, for he wouldn't keep them five minutes if they did. As to you acting as though I've conferred the greatest favour on you by marrying you, it's very important you put that right out of mind, Denzil Fawcett! I love you very much. I'm happier now, at this moment, than I've ever been, in the whole of my life. Will you please keep that very much in mind and something else along with it? It's natural for you to feel the Swann family is still, well . . . looming over you, in the same old way, but it isn't, not any longer. For now you belong to it, just as I belong in your family, and for my part I think I've got the better of the exchange. I really do, Denzil. I've never been involved in Papa's business. None of us have, except perhaps my brother George. It's always been 'The Network'—something Papa concerned himself with, quite apart from our lives down here, but with Dewponds it's different. I was about the place all the time you were rebuilding, so that already I *feel* a farmer's wife. I feel a Fawcett too, more than a Swann, for the first day I came here, when it was all in ruins, was like being born all over again but with a new name and a different place in life. I'll never cease to be grateful for that, or to you for letting me help and grow into the place, as if there had never been a time when I belonged anywhere else, but now it's more than the kind of game I played with myself all autumn and winter. It's real, and I'm part of it. I *am* Mrs. Fawcett, Mrs. *Denzil* Fawcett, of Dewponds, Leatford, in Kent, and it makes me very proud and very happy to be so! But I shan't enjoy it if you go on treating me as if I was somebody in a dream and you were likely to wake up in a minute. Can you understand that, Denzil? It's very important that you should, from the very beginning."

He had been listening to her like a schoolboy having a lesson explained to him and it seemed to her that she was making very little impression upon him. She was wrong, however, as she so often was about his power to reason. It was so easy to mistake his ponderous deliberation for stupidity, the way some of the wedding guests had done. He was very far from stupid. All he needed was time to mull over everything he saw and heard and sensed, and then evaluate it, in the way he would consider the potential of a stubble field, a cart horse, or a crossbred cow.

He proved as much by saying, "I can't understand it right off. Or not like that. It's too much in one helping, I reckon. But I'll get around to understanding in time, though I don't see myself as ever thinking of it as anything but the best slice of luck anyone like me could expect. Why wouldn't I do that, seeing I never give a thought to another maid from the time I was fourteen? I reckon we all have our fancies, and like to think on how it would be if they come true. But you know all along they *are* fancies, and in my case, making you Mrs. Fawcett, and bringing you here to bide as my wife, well, it's like one of them miracles you hear about in the Bible. You read 'em but you can't really believe 'em!"

He paused and frowned, as though the effort of putting such complex thoughts into words taxed him to the limit of his capacity but then, quite suddenly, his expression cleared and he beamed down at her, almost indulgently. "However that may be, there's things a grown man don't *have* to think on and one of them is how it feels and what it does to have his arms round someone as pretty as you, the way I did back in February, the day we hung that door over there. And that goes back longer than I can tell you, to the day you rode up bold as brass under Shortwood, and put your arms round my neck and kissed me, just that once. I daresay you've forgotten that, but I never did and in a way it kept me hoping. Not much mind, but enough. Enough to make any other maid not worth a look."

He had surprised her a little. It was common knowledge at 'Tryst' that he had always mooned after her but she had taken it for granted that, notwithstanding this, he had done his share of larking with village girls and the young women about his father's farm.

"You mean there never was any other girl? Not even at harvest supper or the goose fair when you were growing up?"

"Never the one. Oh, they tormented me about it times enough, mother and the girls that is, but there it was. It always seemed to me a man ought to *know* what he wants, even if what he wants is away out o' reach, and likely to stay so. Then you come up across that field in the rain and wind, and I took you back here, and since then I was content to wait around, never dreaming it would come to this, mind you, but just to be on hand in case you were in trouble again, for it seemed likely you would be soon as they got word where you was. I'll add something to that, too. I'd have wrung that Moncton-Price's neck like a fowl's if he'd shown up. Do you believe that?"

"I believe it," she said and the admission enlarged him, for she now saw him not so much as an infatuated swain, waiting hopefully in the wings for a word or a glance but as a positive champion, of the kind she had read about in *Ivanhoe* and this invested him with an aura of romance very much at odds with his manner and appearance.

She was beginning to wonder, however, how this conversation could be turned to advantage, thinking that it had begun and developed promisingly enough, but still seemed to skirt the edges of the central dilemma. But then, in a barnstorming rush, most of her doubts were resolved, for suddenly he moved round the end of the table so that they faced one another and she saw that all traces of the bemused look he had worn throughout the day had vanished, and that he was regarding her objectively for the first time in the association, as though he had been selecting a partner for a dance and had finally made up his mind.

He said, fervently, "By God, but you're a fine woman, Stella Fawcett! You been worth waiting for and that's a fact!" And he made a bearlike grab at her, crushing her to him until it seemed to her that all her ribs would crack like a row of trodden sticks and there was nothing particularly sacramental about the way he kissed her either. It crossed her mind then, as she struggled to catch her breath, that she must have been a regular ninny to sit here wondering how to coax him and encourage him to accord her her rightful place in his life. She had very little share in his dispositions then or a moment later, when he plumped her down, exclaiming jubilantly, "Wait on, don't stir! Something I'd clean forgotten . . ." and he strode back into the dairy, re-emerging almost at once with a bottle of champagne, one of eight dozen her father and brothers had opened for the guests as they were presented after the wedding. She remembered then a remark her mother had made the night before her marriage to Lester, something about father filling her so full of claret the night she was married that she might have been walking on cushions. It enabled her to guess at the source of the bottle and she exclaimed, "Mama slipped that into your bag, didn't she?" And he chuckled, the first real chuckle she had ever drawn from him, and nodded as he placed the bottle between his knees and drew the cork.

There were glasses to hand, two of a set Giles had given them for a wedding present, and as he poured he said, "Never tasted the stuff before today. My old Dad used to say it were no diff'rent from cider, but he must have tried the wrong sort. A glass o' this is headier than a pint o' scrumpy on an empty stomach."

"Did you try it up at the house?"

"Aye, I did. One more'n I would ha' got up and made a speech. It gives a man a diff'rent look on things, as though, well, as though he was up a tree and looking down on the fields after an April shower. You'll take some, won't you, me love?"

"Half a glass, no more."

"Well, I don't reckon it's a proper drink for a woman. But I'd wager you all used to drink it wi' your dinner up at the Big House."

"You'd lose your wager," she said, letting a drop lay on her tongue and trying to decide if his rather poetic simile had substance. "We were never allowed anything but claret and only a thimbleful of that if Phoebe Fraser was around. Well, here's luck to us, Denzil!" and deciding she liked it she raised her glass and emptied it at a draught. She heard him say, "Go along up then, my love. I'll run the tap on these things and put the bar across . . ." just as if he had addressed her in those identical terms every night of her life and a comforting sense of familiarity bore her up like a cloud, so that she floated up the stairs and surveyed the half-furnished bedroom with heady proprietorship.

The bed was a gift from his family and the blankets and sheets were from 'Tryst'. Two wool rugs were from Phoebe Fraser and the red velvet curtains she had made herself. A terror of fire was still with them, reinforced perhaps by the ineradicable smell of charred beams and thatch, so that the light up here was confined to a couple of small, hooded candles in pretty fluted sticks, a gift from Deborah Avery.

Presently, humming to herself, she tumbled out of her clothes and put on her nightgown, removing all the pins and ribbons from her hair so that it fell not far short of her waist and then he was there, moving about the room with the same ponderous certainty he displayed when heaving a roofing beam into position or stripping the harness from Henrietta's cob, or saddling the mare for her ride home in the twilight of a winter's afternoon.

Sitting up in bed, hugging her knees, she watched everything he did, wordlessly but attentively, seeing him strip down to his cotton drawers, that gave him the look of an eighteenth-century prizefighter in a print that hung for years in her father's study, Mendoza or one of his opponents. He had the same build, solid and muscular but taut and a great deal more graceful than he appeared in his rough working clothes and great clod-hopping boots. He moved like a boxer too, placing his weight on the ball of the foot, so that whereas she had always thought of him as an ox or a bull, she now identified the source of those calculated movements he made when he was reaching down for a bundle of reeds from his perch on a gable-end, or when, with a kind of effortless precision, he lifted the twenty-rung ladder and planted it against a wall.

She said, suddenly, "You said I was beautiful but I'm not, Denzil, or no more so than most women my age. But you're beautiful. Like no one else in the world," and he first looked absolutely astonished and then blushed to the roots of his straw-coloured hair, saying, in an aggrieved tone, "Good Lord, love, you can't say *that* of a man . . ."

But she replied, obstinately, "*I* say it, and most women would agree with me if they could see you now."

He stood still then, stripped of his equanimity, something of the old baffled bewilderment lurking in his eyes and at the corners of his mouth. But then, magically, the incongruity of her compliment must have fused with the champagne, so that he smiled, a little sheepishly, and said, "Now there's a turnip-head you've married! That bag o' mine is still in the waggonette, wi' all that new stuff Mother would have me go out and buy. I'll slip my breeches on an' fetch it, for my nightshirt's in it."

But she exclaimed, impatiently, "Oh, to the devil with the nightshirt, Denzil Fawcett! You suit me well enough as you are, and it's very snug in here, seeing your mother had the goodness to air the bed with her own bottles. Blow out the candles and put your arms around me, for I'm beginning to see what you mean about doubting this is as real as we want it to be!"

He did as she directed but slowly, having snuffed the candles and pulled the curtain aside to take a final sniff of the night air through the half-raised window. Then he padded back to the bed and very carefully climbed into it. For a moment she could have cried out against his maddening deliberation but then his hand touched her hair, caressing it lightly, and she could hear his breathing as his hand passed over her shoulder and lightly cupped her breast in a way that made her shiver. It was too dark to see his face but she realised somehow that he had misread the tremor for he said, "Don't you be afraid of me, my love! Not now, not ever! We're right for each other, and this was meant to be, I reckon. Maybe I knew that, back o' my mind, but couldn't face up to it until we closed that door behind us an hour since." And then, after a brief pause, "Not until now, I reckon."

"Nobody would ever be afraid of you, Denzil," and she made her point by reaching up, plucking the ribbons of her nightgown loose and guiding his hand to her bare breasts. He said, mildly, "It don't have to be so, my dear, not until you've got used to me being here. We waited a long time and a day or so . . ."

"I don't want to wait, Denzil. I love you and need you, even more than you need me."

He hurt her a little but not so much as she had anticipated and not, she was sure, enough to make him conscious of the fact. She was proud then that no other man had laid a hand on her. There would be, she supposed, all kinds of difficulties ahead but at least one thing was certain. Neither of them, so long as they both lived, could ever be lonely again.

2

Swann Migrations

THAT was a time when it seemed to Adam, in his belfry overlooking the wide curve of the Thames, that his sons and daughters were reproducing the rootlessness of long-dead Swanns and wandering the face of the world in search of pay, promotion and pickings.

For himself, he was done with foreign travel. He did not regard a round-the-network jaunt as anything more adventurous than a brisk reconnaissance, designed to keep his viceroys up to their work but he had not crossed the Channel now for close on twenty years. Why should he, when he thought of Britain, and particularly England, as the pivot of the world, and of Englishmen as the chosen pace-setters in planetary affairs? Some of his friends and many of his business associates thought him a Chauvinist, with his roots too deeply imbedded in an industrial past but they were mistaken in one respect. He could extract everything he needed from the many newspapers, periodicals and bluebooks he devoured, and his memory, far from failing him as he entered his mid-fifties, seemed instead to improve and operate like a well-devised filing system, selecting all that was likely to be useful, discarding everything else as fashionable chaff.

By August, 1882, two of his sons were lost to him, or so it seemed. Alexander, gazetted to a Highland Regiment, was stationed in Malta, and daily expecting a move further east with Sir Garnet Wolseley's Nile expeditionary force. George, supposedly prowling the Continent to widen his technological education, had drifted through France and Germany and finally down the Danube to a waggon yard south of Vienna, whence he wrote at rare intervals, giving Adam the impression that he found the raggle-taggle empire of the Habsburgs very much to his taste but was learning, so far as his father could determine, little that would contribute to the future prosperity of a British transport undertaking.

For the time being, however, he bore with him, reasoning that George was a lively, likeable, adaptable fellow, who might as well sow his wild oats at a safe distance before settling to the collar in a slum overlooking a river with far fewer distractions than the Danube.

Both Giles and Hugo, the one sixteen, the latter fourteen, were still at school in Devon, but both, during the Easter break, had paid their first visit to foreign parts, forming part of an athletic team that travelled to Milan to compete in some kind of schoolboy jamboree concerned with track events. Adam let them go, thinking the experience might teach them something, but taking no pride in their selection as athletes. The fashionable cult of games-worship made small appeal to a man born within a dozen years of Waterloo, and sometimes, in one of his tetchy moods, he would point to it as a sign of national decadence, telling Tybalt that obsession with gladiators was an indication that the British would ultimately go the way of Rome. He was out of step here. Even sober men of business were beginning to talk of cricketers like that chap Grace as if they added more lustre to the country than merchant princes and the emphasis placed on games and pastimes in the new gentlemen's schools had, in Adam's view, already reached the point of absurdity. They were even telling one another that Waterloo had been won on the playing fields of Eton when his own father, who had actually fought in the battle, had never played an organised game in his life. It went along, Adam assumed, with the cock-a-hoop mood of a tribe that, in his lifetime, had launched a revolution far more germinal than that street riot the French were still talking about, but had yet to learn, it seemed, which side their industrial bread was buttered. For real education—technological education that is—was at a discount. A man who could hit a boundary and kick a ball the length of a pitch was esteemed far above one who invented a safety device to save miners' lives, or patented a machine that would double the output of a rolling mill. Meanwhile, the drift from the land was accelerating every year. Dedicated farmers like his son-in-law, young Fawcett, told him it was becoming increasingly difficult to tempt lads leaving the new state schools into agriculture, notwithstanding the fact that British farmers were far and away the most progressive in the world. More and more factories were springing up from the southern rim of Rookwood's beat, where it touched the Channel, to the northern limits of Jake Higson's territory beyond the Tay, and while Adam did not quarrel with this he could see no sense whatever in the wild scramble among their owners and sponsors to turn themselves into country squires before they were forty, or in their eagerness to launch sons in professions that were rapidly becoming outdated, like those of the army and the church. A man's life was where he made his money and there, in Adam Swann's view, he should remain, hard at work until they carried him away in a box. It continued to irritate him when coffee-house acquaintances, all men of substance, declared his an old-fashioned, stick-in-the-mud outlook.

Equally irritating, to Adam's way of thinking, was the proliferation of public busybodies, men and women, who spent their lives poking their long noses into everybody else's concerns, launching one crusade after another, few of their doctrines based on the principle of twenty shillings in the pound, of the kind practical reformers like John Catesby had put forward when building the Trades Union Congress.

But here again Adam Swann was at odds with most of his contemporaries, for he had always held that a country's prosperity depended on a friendly alliance between master and man. It maddened him to see a prosperous merchant, known to work his hands like field slaves, contribute a large sum of money towards the cause of Temperance, or a new church, or some other short cut to Paradise, when they were ready to see their foundries close, or their ships left unladen, before they could be talked into paying their furnacemen or dockers an extra penny an hour.

The besetting sin of the nation, as he saw it, was hypocrisy, sometimes so blatant that it could be mistaken for insanity. In the old days, when he had been founding the network, men like Shaftesbury and others had battled ceaselessly against exploitation of the underprivileged, but the generation that followed them seemed to think that the existence of extreme poverty and affluence side by side in the same society was ordained by their night-shirted God. They were busy fashioning a new feudalism to replace the old.

Even this made sense to those with tougher hides and tougher bowels than he possessed but how the devil did one explain the earnest preoccupation of commercial bandits with missionary and religious tract societies, with teetotalism, with campaigns to stop the honest prostitute from making a living at street corners and on the promenades of the music halls? Everybody wanted to be something as well as a merchant: a sociologist, an amateur priest, a public benefactor or an educationalist. He was sometimes amazed at their collective conceits and inconsistencies. He knew men who had amassed fortunes in their twenties and thirties but at fifty had not yet discovered that it demanded fourteen hours a day to make a success of one job, much less three. He knew a shipper in Liverpool, whose boast it was that he employed only teenage boys and shambling old men—the one because he could sack them the day they finished their apprenticeship, the other because he could pay them starvation wages—yet this same man, when he died, left a fortune to found a library, and a further sum to pay for a golden angel on his grave. God, in His mercy, saw to it that the angel took flight within weeks, but Liverpudlians still regarded the shipper as a public benefactor. He knew a haberdasher in Rye Lane, who sacked his girl assistants if he caught them sitting down, who sent them to bed in dismal top-floor barracks on tepid cocoa and a slice of bread and dripping. Yet on Sundays this same rascal compelled them, one and all, to attend a chapel where he had just paid out a hundred pounds for new hassocks and hymn books!

Where would self-deception on this scale lead the nation? Men like these were not qualified to inherit the revolution of Brunel, Watt and Stephenson. Historians were already comparing the British Empire with Rome but it had taken Rome five centuries to reach the ramp of complacency that launched it into oblivion. To his way of thinking this kind of leadership would achieve the same result in Britain in forty years.

He did not know the answers to these questions. He did not really seek to know them. He could applaud the severely practical rescue work of men like his waggonmaster Keate, or the efforts of a man like Barnardo to find refuges for children who slept out in winter, but this passionate involvement with other people's souls baffled him, as did the fashionable vanities of everyone he met who pocketed more than a sovereign on a Saturday.

He did not, by any means, dismiss the shortcomings of his own family as regards planlessness, or preoccupation with what he thought of as fads.

Alexander, something of a coxcomb after his spell at a military academy, was already costing him more in the way of a quarterly allowance than he earned as a lieutenant in the field. George, who seemed in no hurry to return home and hitch himself to a waggon wheel, had not earned his beer and baccy money since leaving school. Hugo, at fourteen, seemed to think that fleetness of foot was all that was needed to justify one's attendance at school, as though his ambition was to qualify as the fastest pickpocket operating between Aldgate Pump and the Law Courts. Giles, although intelligent and well-read, was no more than a dreamer, who had yet to make up his mind how, if ever, he would put dreams to work on something more practical than Gladstone's diatribes concerning Armenians in Asia Minor, a place that was not even under the flag. Stella, to some extent, had made amends, and sometimes he saw her as the pick of the litter. At least she was proving a good wife to that husband of hers and had recently presented him with a nine-pound boy, the first Swann grandchild, and secretly his grandfather's pride and joy, although he grumbled at Henrietta's inclination to spoil the child, and denied her claim that little Robert favoured the Rawlinsons rather than the Swanns.

As to the younger girls, Joanna and Helen, all they seemed to think about was horses, dancing lessons and piano-tinkling, Phoebe Fraser having reported that neither showed any aptitude for cooking or needlework. How had it come about that an industrious father and an eye-to-the-main-chance mother had produced such a feckless tribe? He asked this question of her more than once but she seemed to find it no more than amusing, telling him, when she had had her laugh, that he was getting stale and frayed down there at the stinking yard of his, and failed to make allowance for youthful high spirits. And after that, half-seriously, she added a rider. "Give them time," she said, "and they'll do you proud, every man jack of them! And the girls too, I wouldn't wonder. How old were you before you made a serious decision? I can tell you exactly. Thirty-one, whereas Stella, your eldest, is still only twenty-three!"

There was, he had to admit, something in what she said. He had made a very late start but was none the worse for it. It was unfair, however, to compare him with a generation that had begun life with so many advantages. At eighteen, like it or not, he had been pitch-forked into the army, and it sometimes seemed to him that he would have been well-advised to repeat the process with his sons, whilst making sure that his daughters equipped themselves for something a little more useful than a steeplechase or a set of lancers.

2

He was in such a mood as this one airless summer morning when Tybalt appeared telling him that his adopted daughter, Deborah Avery, wanted an audience. The prospect of seeing Deborah, and fighting one of their time-honoured, amiable duels concerning the ultimate meaning of the universe, promised a welcome diversion from desk-work, so he told Tybalt to send the lady up and be sure to bring counting-house coffee at eleven sharp.

Deborah appeared a moment later, a graceful, slender woman of twenty-eight but looking, he decided, much younger despite her dowdy clothes, perhaps on account of small bones and a healthy complexion, although he did wish she would spend her allowance on boots that made the best of pretty ankles, instead of squandering it on drunks or fallen women or whatever flotsam she collected these days.

The relationship between them had always been that of two people who agreed to differ but it still pained him to see a hand-some, intelligent woman like Josh Avery's girl spend herself on an assortment of waifs and strays, most of whom, to his mind, were professional beggars.

There had been some silly talk, Adam remembered, of Deborah taking the veil when she was about seventeen but he had come down very heavily against that. Instead he had seen to it that the girl re-ceived the very best education that was available to her, a spell at Cheltenham, and afterwards as one of the first girl undergraduates at Girton College, so that he could now regard her as the one really educated woman of his acquaintance. Nothing could shake his belief that one day, given the right opening, she would surprise not only the Swanns but her generation.

She kissed him affectionately and he noticed that, unlike most of his visitors up here, she did not wrinkle her nose at the stink of the tannery and soap factory but began, gaily, "I want you to be the first to know, Uncle Adam. I've got what I wanted at last, a real job of work that could lead somewhere if I'm lucky. I wonder if it will have your blessing?"

"I doubt it," he said, gloomily, "for I don't regard anything you've done so far as a job. It's been mostly curate's work, but even curates, poor devils, get some kind of stipend. No one has ever paid you wages for all that poking about you do among the city layabouts. Indeed, it wouldn't surprise me to learn that six out of every seven shillings you've ever had from me hadn't found its way down the gullets of plausible scoundrels. Are you telling me you've got a billet that actually earns you money?"

She said, with a merry smile, "Come now, Uncle Adam, that Gradgrind attitude never did fool me, not even when I was a child. I wonder that you still trouble to use it in my presence. Underneath it you're as soft as a tub of butter and always have been, ever since you appeared at the convent that morning with a Dutch doll under your arm, swearing my father had sent it. Just ask me how much I expect to be paid."

"Very well, how much?"

"Thirty shillings a week, rising to two pounds in six months if I succeed in getting evidence."

"Evidence of what? How many families in London use a communal privy?"

She laughed. He had always liked her laughter. There was no ruffling Deborah. She had a quality that was rare in men and almost extinct in women, an ability to laugh at herself, heartily and often.

"That's not all that wide of the mark," she said, and her glance shifted to his desk, where a pile of newspapers were stacked beside trays spilling over with invoices. "Do you read the *Pall Mall Gazette* regularly?"

He was impressed. "Has that firebrand Stead had the brains to publish something you've submitted?"

"Not yet," she said, "but I think he will. Tell me, uncle, what is your personal opinion of 'that firebrand Stead'?"

"That he's a good journalist, one of the best in the country, but that he could sometimes do with editing himself," and she laughed again, saying, "Well, that's one thing we might agree on, but I won't oblige you by passing it on. He can be very irascible when challenged, particularly on his home ground. Now tell me something else. What do you know of the Contagious Diseases Acts?"

"That they were passed in the sixties to combat the spread of venereal diseases among troops in garrison towns. Is Willie Stead still riding that hobby-horse?"

"Indeed he is, and will be until we get the Acts repealed. You do believe in repealing them, don't you?"

"Never made up my mind," he admitted. "They serve some kind of purpose, I imagine, but it's always struck me that Stead, and that volcano of a woman, Josephine Butler, have good grounds for asking why compulsory examination is confined to women when their customers can pass on infection to their wives without so much as a smack on the back of the hand."

"Then I can see you're well on the way to being converted," she said but suddenly she read in his expression a repugnance for the turn of conversation and he at once proved as much, saying, "It defeats me why a personable young woman like you, with an education that equips her for anything, should be encouraged by chaps like Stead to lift the lid on that kind of stew. Damn it, I'm not a prude and never have been. If I was I wouldn't be sitting here discussing soldiers' pox with a woman your age. Are you writing a piece for the *Pall Mall Gazette* about the prospects of repeal?"

"No," she said, "but it was a letter I sent on the subject that got me an interview and a trial with Mr. Stead."

"What could you possibly know about it that you hadn't dug out of Hansard and medical studies?"

She looked at him coolly, her head on one side and for once he caught a rare glimpse of her father, the man who had launched him and later swindled him. She said, mildly, "I know more than most people. More than Stead, for that matter. And much more than those Westminster windbags whose speeches are printed in Hansard. I was arrested by the Morals Police in Portsmouth one night last autumn, and spent the night in a cell while they found someone who could vouch for my story that I was on my way to pay a call on a naval chaplain stationed there. Well, he turned up and claimed me and efforts were made to hush it up when they found out who I was. But supposing I had been someone else, or they hadn't been able to locate that chaplain? Do you realise what could have happened to me?"

He was shocked but not in the way she had hoped.

"It's absolutely monstrous," he burst out, "that the cranks you consort with expose you to that kind of risk! What the devil were you doing in Portsmouth? At night? And alone on the streets? And how did it happen that the Morals Police didn't apologise and turn you loose the moment they saw you in a good light?"

"You ask them that," she said, tight lipped, "just as Mr. Stead did when he published my letter. What happened to me isn't uncommon. It happens to respectable women every night of the week in Portsmouth, Plymouth, Colchester, Chatham—anywhere members of the armed forces congregate. I wouldn't like to tell you how many women's reputations have been ruined in that way, and that's only one reason why this monstrous insult to all women, including outcasts, has to be removed from the statute book. Every woman abroad in a garrison town after dusk is assumed to be a harlot, and liable to arrest and medical examination. She has the right to refuse, of course, but God help her if she does if she's poor and friendless. If the chaplain hadn't let slip I was entitled to call myself 'Swann', and was a close friend of Mrs. Butler, I know very well what might have occurred. The worst thing about the whole incident was their grovelling attitude when I was shown the door. It was that more than the filthy blankets and the unemptied slops in the cell that made me vomit on the way out!"

He said, unable to keep the depression from his voice, "Very well, you've made your point. I'm glad you got to Stead through it, for once you make allowance for that chap's fire and brimstone he's a force for fair play and social progress, and there aren't so many around that we can afford to sneer at him. What kind of work does he want you to do? Isn't he running a series on slum housing south of the river?"

"He has other campaigns in mind. One is an investigation into the export of British girls to Continental brothels. That's what I shall be doing. A preliminary survey on the spot."

"He'll send you to Brussels? To meddle in that kind of undertaking?"

"Oh, not alone, I assure you. My inclusion is more for training than anything else. Mrs. Josephine Butler is going over and a young Free Church minister, by the name of Gordon."

"It's mad, none the less. Mad and dangerous."

"It might be dangerous, if all they say about the Belgian police is correct, but it isn't mad, Uncle Adam. Someone has to do it and the government won't lift a finger to help us. Do you realise how those girls are recruited?"

"By their own folly mostly, I'd say."

"You'd be wrong. Not one in twenty go there willingly, or go knowing what is expected of them. The houses don't want that kind of girl. The more innocent they are on arrival the higher the price the madams can get from a client. Those girls are nearly always country girls, drawn to London by an advertisement offering a good situation and appearing in journals that are Sunday reading in British homes."

"But in God's name, girl, they must know the purpose behind transportation to the Continent."

"They don't. They're met and told some plausible story about their new employers being abroad. After that they are fitted out, escorted across the Channel, and tricked into signing some document that absolves the procurer. Even if they make their escape the police can charge them with stealing the brothel-keeper's clothes, the only clothes they have since their own have been taken away. How many get home again? Or would care to come home after an experience of that kind?"

He looked at her steadily, reluctantly admiring her involvement with the underdog and her courage and ability to put a case, but convinced, for all that, that people like Mrs. Butler, and Stead, and especially novices like her, had no real knowledge of the kind of opposition they were facing in a theatre of this kind. Her father, Josh Avery, could have told her plenty about organised vice. Himself a virtuoso, he would, no doubt, have been outraged to learn that a child he left behind to be reared by nuns should be venturing into the kind of stews she described, with only theoretical knowledge to guide her. As a mercenary who had spent years in the Orient he himself could have told her stories that would make her hair stand on end, but he held his tongue. She was really no different from any of his children. She would have to discover for herself that it takes more than a band of dedicated reformers and a newspaper, even such a newspaper as Stead's, to make more than a dent in the social conscience of a society with money in its pocket, and its vices driven underground to fester.

He said, resignedly, "You're twenty-eight. Any guardianship I exercised over you lapsed years ago. Neither would anything I could say turn you aside, for in your own way you're just as pigheaded as your father, and see where pigheadedness landed him in the end. I'll wish you luck but don't ask for my blessing. An investigation here, perhaps, into any evil you can name, but not one conducted outside the jurisdiction of a British court. That's to sit up and beg for trouble and I believe you're intelligent enough to know it."

"Yes, I know it. And it was to ask your help in guarding against trouble that I came here and risked a quarrel. We never have quarrelled, have we, Uncle Adam?"

"We're close to quarrelling now."

"I don't think so. I think you'll help if you can. You haven't earned the reputation you have among your work-people by turning your back on them. Half those boys down in that yard would have ended as pickpockets and pimps if it hadn't been for men like you and Saul Keate."

"That's neither here nor there," he said, gruffly, hating to be identified with any cause but his own. "I don't sign on those urchins from motives of charity, I can assure you. They earn their bread and salt once they get their names on my tally book and I see to it that they do. But how the devil can I help you spy on Brussels whorehouses?"

"By giving me letters of introduction and an excuse for being in Belgium," she said. "You don't think we shall proclaim the purpose of our visit, do you?"

"Was that Stead's idea?"

She flushed and stood her ground. "No, it wasn't. I put it to Stead and he fell in with it. Very readily."

"I'll warrant he did," said Adam, with a grin, and it struck him again that this was precisely the kind of deviousness for which Josh Avery had been famous, as soldier, financier and rake. "They always said of your father that he could charm a fakir from his bed of nails. That's one thing you do have in common. Am I to understand that you and Mrs. Butler and that parson want to pose as representing my interests in Belgium while you've got your eyes to the keyholes?"

"That would be as good a way of going about it as I can think of. We could be doing a survey into the prospects of Swann-on-Wheels opening a Continental branch. That would give us the entrée into some of the big warehouses and I don't doubt that we should make contacts with any number of gallants who might talk. That's what Ned thinks, at all events."

"Ned?"

"Ned Gordon, the minister I mentioned."

"So you're on Christian name terms? I take it this crusade is inter-denominational?"

"All of Mrs. Butler's campaigns are. The fact that Ned is a Free Churchman and I'm a Roman is a strength not a weakness."

"But that woman Butler is known to half the whore-masters in Europe! She's been stirring up dung heaps for years. The word will be passed around the moment she steps ashore from the packet boat."

"Of course it will but who's to know we're with her? We're a couple of English visitors and she's our decoy. People watching her won't be watching us."

He said, sourly, "So be it. I'll do what I can, but against my better judgement. I admire your spirit but the whole damned lot of you are short on horse sense. Well, you've robbed me of a morning's work already and it's coming up to midday. Am I to have the pleasure of lunching a busybody at the George down the road? You only come here when you want something, like all the rest of them."

"Stella doesn't."

"Stella did. She's since had the good sense to settle for hearth and home. It would give me the greatest pleasure to see you follow her example."

"Ah, that's not for me, uncle," she said, cheerfully. "I'm already in the bargain basement among all the other unclaimed blessings."

"Nonsense," he said, meaning it, "you're as eligible as any other girl, despite that old maid's get-up. I'll give you a tip for what it's worth. Buy yourself some fashionable clothes before you call on Continental businessmen. They notice such things. When do you propose starting, anyhow?"

"Tomorrow. We leave from Victoria, on the afternoon boat-train."

He said, "You were pretty sure of me to leave it this late. I'll get the letters copied this afternoon and you can call in for them tomorrow."

"No, uncle," she said, "I'd take it as a great compliment if you came to Victoria to see me off. Will you do that."

"On one condition. That we part at the barrier, for I wouldn't care to be identified with tub-thumpers like Josephine Butler and that fellow Stead. Unlike them I can't afford to play gadfly to men with big bank balances."

"The train leaves at two," she said and he growled, "You don't have to tell me the time trains leave for anywhere. I know. That's what comes of minding my own business."

*　　*　　*

It cheered him a little to see that she had taken his advice concerning her travelling clothes. She was wearing what he knew they were calling a sheath tie-back, a skirt stretched tautly over a bustle and held there by elastic, with a high-necked jacket frogged with astrakhan and a highwayman's hat, trimmed with fleur-de-lys in blue velvet.

He said, greeting her, "You'd best look out for your own virtue in that get-up," but she was ready for this.

"If I'm representing Swann-on-Wheels I should want it known that you were a man of taste and discrimination. Are your sure you wouldn't like to be introduced to Mrs. Butler and Ned Gordon? Mr. Stead is here too, to wish us good luck," and she nodded towards the ticket-window where the little group was standing.

"No," he said, "and it isn't because I'm unsociable. Or, for that matter, because I disapprove of the business. If you're purporting to be on a commercial mission it wouldn't do for me to be seen talking to Stead or Mrs. Butler. I like the cut of your partner. He seems more qualified to look out for himself than you."

He did at that, Adam thought, letting his eye run over the broad-shouldered young man in mufti, who looked more like a burly lieutenant embarking for a foreign station than a parson getting marching orders from a London editor. Stead he already knew by sight, a bearded, strong-jawed man, with fanatical eyes and any number of swift, nervous gestures that marked him down as a man of action. He had seen magazine photographs of the famous Mrs. Butler too, a handsome, fashionably-dressed woman, who carried herself like a Celtic queen. They were untypical, he decided, of the swarm of busybodies infesting London at present. At least they had money and a powerful press organ behind them, and it struck him that the victory of Daemon Lust might not prove the walkover he had assumed.

They passed into the buffet where he bought two cups of tea and Deborah said, "Did you ever hear how Mrs. Butler became associated with this kind of work?" and he said he supposed it to be a cure for boredom, common enough among wealthy women who were well educated and then turned loose in a world where intelligent women were regarded with suspicion.

"Wrong again, Uncle Adam," she said, "it was one of those Road-to-Damascus conversions that you never believe in. She is happily married to a cultured and very charming man. He was Vice-Chancellor of Cheltenham College some twenty years ago, when they lost one of their children under tragic circumstances. They had been out for the evening and on their return their little boy ran on the landing to greet them. The banister gave way and he crashed to his death on the stone floor in front of her eyes. From that day on she and her husband have devoted their lives to people less fortunate than themselves."

"She would have done something of that kind anyway," said Adam. "One only has to look at her chin. I still don't put much trust in instant conversions. It's a slow and very laborious process. Like Stella's," he added, with a touch of malice.

"Stella is over that dreadful business now?"

"Never gives it a thought. She looks at that lumping great farmer's son as if he was young Shelley, writing a sonnet. That's the way it should be with all you women, notwithstanding your involvement in all manner of fashionable causes."

"That's a very old-fashioned point of view."

"It may be. I'm fifty-six and getting old-fashioned. Your Aunt's father, old Sam Rawlinson, once put it to me neatly. 'Tuck t'lass in bed an' give her plenty o' children,' he used to say. Taking the long view I'm inclined to think he was right."

She said, slyly, "Yet I can recall a time when you had to take a more generous view. It was when you came home with one leg and found Aunt Henrietta had taken over your business, and was running it as well as you ever did." But he refused to withdraw.

"Your Aunt Henrietta is a very extraordinary woman," he said. "I came to that conclusion long since and get confirmation of it every day. I'm no longer gaffer in my own house but I daresay you noticed that."

"You never were to my recollection," she said, mischievously, "you just pretended to be."

Passengers were picking up their baggage and leaving. They went out on to the platform approach and watched the trio of missionaries passing through the barrier. He said, kissing her, "Watch out for yourself, Debbie. You mean as much to me as any one of them," and she replied, "Do you think I haven't known that, from the day you walked into that convent with the Dutch doll under your arm?"

She kissed him and hurried away towards the barrier and he watched her until she caught up with her friends. The complexity of human affairs came with the realisation that he was witnessing a kind of moral somersault. Josh Avery, a sensualist if ever there was one, had spent the whole of his life popping in and out of whore-houses, but here was his daughter, the fruit of a brief liaison between Josh and that silly woman who had been the wife of Avery's colonel, staking her entire future, her life possibly, on an attempt to deny whorehouses their raw material. He turned away and stumped through the arcade to the cab-rank, thinking briefly of all his children, and the courses they were charting for themselves, each a course that he would never have chosen for them, but why not? Training, parental influence, even education didn't amount to a damn when everything was totted up. The only thing that mattered was what was there to begin with, what you might call a man's starting-out capital.

3

Far away to the south-east Lieutenant Alexander Swann watched the white façade of Valetta harbour melt into the morning heat haze as the ship bore him due east to the Nile delta. He was glad to be going at last, a trained blade in the company of other trained blades, few of whom, he reflected with a certain smugness, had ever seen a shot fired in anger.

He was able to think of his life now on two distinct levels, professional and individual. Professionally he identified, perhaps too glibly, with the rituals and affectations of the regiment, interspersing his sentences with the obligatory 'haw-haw', the fashionable hallmark of a professional officer, taking care to dress well and spend freely, to drink with gusto but moderation, to cultivate the regard of seniors who could be useful to a man with his way to make in his chosen profession. At the deeper level he had more confidence. The brief campaign in Zululand had taught him many things, not least among them that no man could lay automatic claim to courage, even a man who lived by the sword and came from a long line of professional swordsmen. Courage, real courage and not bravado that is, had to be buttressed by training, as he had learned during the scramble from the lost field of Isandlwana and afterwards, staring down on the embattled mission station at Rorke's Drift. Men like those four V.C.s, Cogshill, Melville, Chard and Bromhead, were not heroes because they wore scarlet coats and thought of themselves as warriors but because they had been trained to order their reflexes in any given situation. He was very glad now that he had had the supreme advantage of witnessing the deeds that had won all four recognition. Without their example he would have continued to identify the outward panoply of war with reality and its reality, even now, still had the power to make his stomach contract when he contemplated the prospect of facing fire again. He was sure of one thing, however. He would not, under any circumstances, take part in a rout again and flee blindly and hysterically from involvement, as had almost every white man under that sandstone peak in South Africa. Death was preferable to that, for it still made him squirm with self-disgust when professionals congratulated him on his escape, and behaved towards him as someone who had shown initiative and carried himself gallantly. He knew the reason for this, of course. He was identified not with Isandlwana, that had brought shame on the flag, but with Rorke's Drift, an incident that politicians, publicists and military men alike had seized upon to obscure the real upshot of that terrible day. He was one of the very few men alive who understood that, man for man and weapon for weapon, they would never have beaten the Zulus in the field, and that burning a royal kraal and wiping out the last of Cetywayo's impis with Gatling guns and controlled volley fire, reflected no credit at all on the nation that had achieved it, much as it was needed to make South Africa safe for whites. One other thing he had learned during that short, murderous campaign, and it was to stand him in good stead for the rest of his life. Never, on any account, would he underestimate an enemy.

4

A few hundred miles north of Alexander's shipping lane, as the transport ploughed into the eastern Mediterranean, another Swann was poised on the threshold of a career but was, as yet, only dimly aware of it.

The shame and confusion of mind brought about by his ridiculous involvement with Broadbent and Broadbent's wife had soon cleared in the head of George Swann, leaving him very much the man he was when he had taken lodgings with the Polygon manager.

George Swann's natural ebullience was boosted by the glorious sense of personal freedom he enjoyed now that the Channel was between him and his father's concerns. At eighteen it was difficult to take anything seriously, especially in new surroundings where, at every turn of the road, he came upon something amusing, or interesting or both.

He went to Paris first, where he was at once aware of a mood of feverish gaiety and irrelevance that was beginning to succeed the terrible humiliation of France at the hands of the Prussians ten years before. Here, within a week of latching on to a firm of hauliers supplying the wholesalers of the Paris vegetable market at Les Halles, it seemed to George that nobody was concerned with anything save sharp dressing, loose change, frolic, food and girls. In the company of a group of lively young executives he spent that first heady spring as a boulevardier, a role that suited him exactly. He visited all the music-halls and some of the more notorious cafés, where he witnessed things that taught him more in ten minutes than he could have learned in a year travelling the British provinces.

Parisians, as a species, intrigued him. Like all young Englishmen he had been reared in the belief that Paris was the modern Gomorrah, and that its recent tribulations at the hands of Bismarck, the Communards, and the reactionaries had been an expression of Divine displeasure. The theory, he soon discovered, did not fit the facts. The bourgeoisie were very respectable folk, stuffier, if that was possible, than their counterparts across the Channel, and such vice as he witnessed in the Montmartre and Montparnasse districts, was staged for the benefit of English and German tourists and regarded by the French as a kind of extension of the Louvre, or a visit to the Palace of Versailles.

Over here, he discovered, existed a class system that made its English counterpart relatively fluid, and that despite everything he had read of murdered aristocrats and anarchy stalking the streets. The working men at the depots were simple, amiable chaps, generally half-bottled by the quantities of cheap local wine they drank, and devoted, in the main, to pleasures of the table, schoolboy practical jokes and noisy but indeterminate political discussion. The middle-class families, of which his host's ménage was a fair example, were very straitlaced, devout and parsimonious. The wealthy people, represented by the directors of the firm to which he had been attached as a student, kept very much to themselves, communicating their orders through a long string of underlings. Two things, he decided, all Frenchmen had in common, a repellent preoccupation with food that converted the simplest meal into a ritual, and an unremitting hatred of Prussians, which incubated the idea of *la revanche*. They held to this, he thought, in the way the British pursued the concept of empire. *La revanche* was the national Holy Grail that would one day redeem their tribal honour.

These observations, however, were acquired subconsciously, like the language that he found easy to learn by ear, so easy, in fact, that he began to have a poor opinion of the methods employed to teach it in English schools. For the most part he lived, as he would have said, the life of Old Reilly. Nobody expected industry from a student and he spent most of his time in the company of genial cicerones exploring the city, watching the crowds go by, and drinking, but modestly, at boulevard cafés, while savouring the delights of freedom in warm, spring sunshine and among folk who accepted him for what he seemed to be, a convivial English boy sent abroad by indulgent parents to pick up a smattering of their language.

He took to Paris and Paris took to him so that he might have stayed on indefinitely had not his sense of self-preservation been whetted by his unhappy involvement with the Broadbents, particularly Broadbent's daughter, Lizzie, who had marked him down as such a good catch. He owed his escape from a somewhat similar situation to his quick ear for the French idiom, his hostess having no fewer than four unmarried daughters on her hands, whom she was prone to push forward one by one, unaware, it seemed, that her pink-cheeked, courteous lodger had learned to conjure with more than a couple of dozen conventional phrase-book gambits.

Thus it was that George, at first to his amusement, but later to his dismay, heard himself described by Madame Drouet in terms that made him feel like a prize bull due to be awarded to the most diligent of the Drouet daughters and a change of lodgings, to a pension nearer the warehouse, did nothing to secure his retreat. Showered by invitations to soirées, Sunday picnics and 'improving' expeditions, the object of Madame Drouet's unrelenting social pressures and felicitations (and inhibited, on this account, from making the most of his opportunities with Clothilde, the prettiest of the Drouet girls) he began to realise that his name, the cut of his English tweeds, and the sufficiency of spending money that reached him by banker's draft from across the Channel, could be fatal disadvantages to a young man who valued his freedom. After Clothilde, whom he had regarded as a somewhat prim girl, had hinted that the only real place to learn French was in bed, he began to see the Broadbent pattern repeating itself in tricolore, and decided that it was time to cross the Rhine. Without communicating his plans to anyone at home or abroad he slipped out of the city on a bright June morning and boarded an express for Munich, where he presented a letter of introduction to a firm engaged in manufacturing sewing-machines, with whom his father had a distribution contract in that part of the network known as 'The Border Triangle'.

Within a week he was absorbed effortlessly into the life of the old city and found it even more to his taste than Paris. The Bavarians, wholly untroubled by thoughts of tomorrow's demands upon their national honour, seemed to George content to live each day as a separate existence. The only noticeable link they had with the French was a common hatred of Prussians.

Here, within days of settling into Frau Ledermann's guesthouse five minutes' walk from the factory and ten from the famous Münchner Hofbräuhaus, the city's most celebrated beer house, George soon discarded his preconceived notions of the Germans, much as he had shed those concerning the traditional depravity of the French. Munich was a city where the clamour of the machine age had been assimilated into a much older, less insistent rhythm imposed by the jolly Wittelsbachs, who had made Munich a Mecca for all kinds of craftsmen, silversmiths, glass-stainers, bronze-founders and wood-carvers. It was a city where the mediaeval peasant culture was a living, active force among jovial mechanics, their statuesque wives and flocks of blond, blue-eyed children, where people moved slowly but purposefully, without the jostle and bustle of French and British industrial cities swept along by the pace of the century, where sunshine reflected from the white walls of baroque buildings like the Nymphenburg Palace and the citizens, women as well as men, seemed to consume a barrel of beer apiece every day of the week without becoming either somnolent, aggressive, or even excessively talkative.

He could hardly have picked a more congenial base than Rosa Ledermann's establishment. The hostess had a penchant for lively young boarders, and every communal meal was a social occasion, presided over by Rosa herself, whose broad jests George soon realised —once he had acquired a smattering of German—would have emptied any British boarding-house in minutes.

From the day of arrival George was fascinated by Frau Ledermann, a widow in her mid-thirties, on excessively familiar terms not merely with her boarders but every caller at the house, including the wall-eyed postman, Gustav, and the local policeman, Kurt, a giant of a man who seemed to spend half his working day in her kitchen and never varied his unwinking gaze at her whilst spooning his way through one of her succulent fruit pies. So much laughter, feasting, and bucolic flirtation was conducted in Rosa Ledermann's house that it was almost impossible to believe the landlady had been widowed a little over a year ago, when her husband, whose tinted oval portrait in the parlour still wore its mourning bow, had been decapitated by a broken fan-belt at the factory. George formed a private belief that Rosa, whose animal vitality arched over the house like one of the fountain jets in the old square outside, would not remain inconsolable for long but was, in fact, already engaged in the task of choosing a successor to the father of the three pretty children who helped her about the house.

She seemed to take an immediate fancy to her pink-cheeked, broad-shouldered English 'student', one of so many students at large in the city, but this neither surprised nor dismayed George. He was beginning to admit to himself that he had a flair with the ladies, particularly mature ladies, who clearly enjoyed mothering him, and was soon enlisted in the stalwart band of Rosa's admirers, telling himself that when at length he married he would look out for a girl of Rosa's build and complexion. It was clear that a high colour and generous curves went with good cooking and a tolerance of male weaknesses, of the kind exposed by the discovery of her sixteen-year-old son closeted with one of the maids in the linen cupboard, or the appearance on her doorstep, at two in the morning, of three of her Württemberg boarders, so hilariously drunk that the entire household had to be roused to convey them up four flights of stairs to their rooms.

'Tryst' had never been a particularly circumspect household. In contrast to most English parents of the sixties and seventies, Adam and Henrietta demanded no more of their children than good manners, and Phoebe Fraser's efforts to raise them in the image of good Scots Calvinists had been regarded as a family joke by everyone from Adam downwards. The general atmosphere prevailing at Rosa Ledermann's boarding-house, however, was of the kind that was likely to startle an English youth less urbane than George Swann and all that summer he let himself be carried along on a tide of bawdy laughter, noisy good-fellowship and Munich spring beer, daily enlarging his vocabulary by virtue of Rosa's broad jests, any number of undemanding flirtations, and the repertoire of Bavarian folk songs that were the invariable accompaniment of an evening spent at one or other of the city's beer-gardens. He never drank to excess, however, and never suffered from a hangover in the morning, for the beer was lighter than the English brews he had sampled in the West Country or in the North. It sharpened rather than dulled the senses so that, of a fine summer evening, he could survey the old city through a colourful and convivial haze, sometimes in the company of a group of strapping factory apprentices, sometimes accompanied by fellow boarders and occasionally in the congenial company of Rosa and one of her kitchen-haunting admirers.

His life in Munich, however, was not completely confined to pleasure. The modern techniques of the engineers and distributors of the sewing-machine factory surprised and interested him, so that at last he was able to write home giving an impression that he was profiting by his study of Continental business practices. Armed with letters of introduction he paid courtesy visits to a number of neighbouring factories and workshops, including the local brass foundry and a big transportation concern situated on the banks of the Iser, a mile or so below the Wittelsbach bridge.

It was during these explorations that he began to discern underlying reasons for Germany's rapid emergence as the likeliest challenger to Britain in industrial fields. Outwardly ponderous in their approach to a commercial possibility, lacking the sustained competitive thrust of the British, or the Frenchman's rather slapdash efforts to convert a pastoral into an industrial society, the Germans were none the less making noticeable headway in almost every sphere of industry. Their splendid railway network, for instance, seemed to George more prolific and predictable than that of Britain, hitherto regarded as pace-setter in railways, and there was none of the grinding poverty commonplace in London and the big provincial cities at home. Here in Bavaria he saw no evidence of the hunger of the German for an overseas empire on the British style but there was, he noted, a profound and general interest in urban mechanisation on every level, even among the traditional craftsmen for which the city was famous. Electricity was beginning to be adopted as the principal means of power and electrically-operated trams were already replacing horse-drawn public vehicles.

An interesting factor of this modernisation was the surprising ability of the Bavarian to adapt to industrialisation without the smut and clamorous squalor that had converted ancient English boroughs into industrial slums almost overnight. Mentally he compared Munich, a city still abundantly rich in mediaeval culture, with Manchester, much to the latter's disadvantage, for here, somehow or other, the Municher was taking what he needed of the new without entirely discarding the old and certainly without tearing up the roots of his pastoral and cultural heritage and covering the raw wounds with grime and rubble. The survey absorbed him so deeply that he would spend hours reducing his observations to notes, a practice, he thought, that his father would have applauded, for Adam was reckoned the most compulsive jotter-down of memoranda in London. George, however, was not endowed with his father's obsession for work and was always ready to exchange notebook for stein mug and join one of Rosa's evening expeditions to the Hofbräuhaus. Thus it came about that he was a delighted participant in the *Oktoberfest*, the liveliest feature in the Municher's carnival calendar.

The noise and gaiety of the occasion was responsible for his consuming rather more beer than usual so that on his way up the last short flight of stairs to his room he stumbled and fell head over heels to the first landing, where his fall was broken by the muscular Rosa who happened to be there, unmarked by the evening's hilarity, directing the dispersal of her reeling lodgers to their various quarters.

"*Gott oh Gott!*" cried Rosa, "*das ist ja fatal!*"

But it was not fatal. George came off with a few bruises and a jarred shoulder and Rosa insisted on conveying him to his room under the steeply-sloping roof and applying arnica to the injured shoulder, repairs that necessitated George stripping to the buff and lying flat while the majestic landlady ministered to him.

He had never seen her from this angle and although bemused by beer fumes, and still dazed by his fall, he was struck by the splendid symmetry of her curves and the radiant good nature expressed in her broad, beaming face, as though all the distilled jollity in the world had taken residence in this one statuesque woman, whose mission it was to dispense good cheer to exiles. The clamour of the *Oktoberfest* rose unabated from the street and while he was recovering his breath, and reflecting how pleasant it was to be handled so masterfully but gently by such a splendidly proportioned woman almost (although not quite) old enough to be his mother, Rosa strode across the room and moderated the uproar by closing the wooden shutters, returning to stand looking down at him, her expression softened by affectionate amusement at his plight. His intense appreciation of her as a person, as a synthesis of ripe femininity, demanded something more than he could express in his limited German. Responding to some deeply-rooted instinct of male appreciation he extended his sound arm and reached under her skirt, caressing the muscular edifice of her nearest buttock and expecting, perhaps, a saucy rebuke but no more, for familiarities of this sort were commonplace in Rosa's kitchen, particularly after an uproarious homecoming from the beer garden. She made no move, however, but remained quite still, smiling down at him as she said, with the utmost mildness, "So! You are what we Munichers call a *Popokneifer*, Herr Swann?"

The remark, uttered with childlike innocence, none the less had the effect of belittling him in his own eyes so that he said, converting the caress into an assertive pinch "Damn it, Rosa, I'm no kind of man yet, though I wouldn't admit it to anyone but you."

He was quite unprepared for the change of expression the admission produced on her broad, good-natured face.

She said, standing back a pace, "So! You are how old, Herr Swann?"

"Nineteen. Almost, that is," and hoisted himself into a sitting position. The fall, the beer fumes, or Rosa's overpowering presence were beginning to have a curious effect on him. He felt stimulated and excited but, at the same time, curiously young and inadequate, and a sustained stomach rumble produced by all the beer he had shipped at the Hofbräuhaus added to his sense of confusion. He noticed then that she was still gazing at him and with a curious intentness, as though she found it hard to believe in his admitted innocence.

"Nineteen," she echoed, giving tongue to what could only, he assumed, be incredulity. "Ach, but it is shameful!" and then, hurriedly, "No, no, Herr Swann, that is not the word! I do not know the word but I know the reason, yes? It is the way rich young men are trained in England. You were sent to an *Internat* as a child, away from the women, to live like the *Mönche!*"

He could smile at this, and at her emphatic nods as though expressing her profound disapproval of such a debilitating and unnatural educational system.

"It is much the same with the Junkers' sons," she went on, sadly, "they are taught nothing but war games, but even they are permitted to *sich amüsieren* with the servants. Perhaps it is good you should come to München. If it were not for your hurts . . ." and she sighed gustily, turning aside to lift the coverlet she had folded back when she applied the arnica.

He heard himself saying, with a kind of desperate urgency, "I'm not hurt, Rosa! Just a shaking . . ." And then, swinging his feet round and planting them on the floor, "Everyone is asleep, Rosa, and drunk into the bargain . . ." But a brief spasm of vertigo assailed him so that he could not finish what he had hoped to say but sat hunched on the side of the bed, watching the customary expression of affability return to her broad, florid features. Then she replaced the coverlet in its folded position and stood so close to him that she was touching his knees. With both hands she reached forward and patted his flushed cheeks and then, with steady pressure, inclined his head to her bosom. "As you wish, Herr Swann," she murmured, "I will make a man of you. Please to lie back and unfasten your belt."

It astounded him that she could go about it in such a brisk and unemotional fashion, that she could issue that singular command in the voice he had heard her use when compiling a shopping-list, or giving some trivial instruction to one or other of the women about the house. In other circumstances, with his head clear of the beer fumes he might well have reacted in quite a different way. He might have panicked and begun to protest or, being George, with humour never far from the surface, he might have laughed and passed it off as one of her broad jests. But the sheer magnanimity of her offer and the matter-of-fact way in which it was put, had the effect of hypnotising him so that he hesitated no more than a moment before obeying her and with his return to a recumbent position the fumes clouded his brain again but richly and pleasantly, as though he was hovering on the edge of sleep.

She saw to it, however, that he did not drop off. With a single, expertly judged jerk as if stripping a bed, she divested him of his trousers, with another his underpants and then she was regarding his naked body with sober interest and saying, speculatively, "*Ach, wie schon stramm,* Herr Swann. You are man enough for any woman. Please to lie still.*"

With an adroit heave and a twirl or two that George saw as a brief exercise in Swedish drill, she undressed herself, folded her clothes methodically, laid them aside, and drew herself slowly erect as if for inspection, flexing her arms and pivoting slowly, as though upon a revolving pedestal.

He had a vision then, not of a naked woman getting on for twice his age, but of a perfectly formed and immensely impressive Teutonic goddess who had materialised for his specific gratification. His senses, groping wildly for some link between mortality and the elect, between Rosa, his statuesque Munich landlady, and Rosa, the essence of every adolescent fantasy he had ever had concerning women, telescoped in a memory that plunged him momentarily back into his childhood and a coloured illustration in a nursery edition of a book called *Myths and Legends of the North*. He recalled it in the greatest detail, a picture of a huge, flaxen-haired Brunhild, poised to hurl her spear in the celebrated contest with King Gunther, and here was Brunhild herself, stripped of her winged helmet and quilted armour, confirming what he had always suspected concerning Brunhild and Rosa alike, that their splendid strength and symmetry was all but subdued by draperies that blurred the majestic rotundity of their breasts and the sublimity of their powerful thighs that swept past dimpled knees to shapely calves and surprisingly neat ankles. Strength and vitality were there in abundance, revealed in every line of her body, but the impact remained essentially soft and feminine, perhaps because everything about her was so perfectly proportioned.

He cried, involuntarily, "Why, Rosa, you're beautiful! You're perfect . . . !" but she seemed unimpressed by his veneration, seemed, in a way, to be looking past him, for her expression was thoughtful and it came to him that her mind was already engaged with the mechanics of his initiation.

She said, contemplatively, "There is a little difficulty. On account of your shoulder," and then, "Ja! It would be best if you were to stand, Herr Swann. So . . ." and she took his sound arm in a firm grip, levering him upright and then, with a movement that seemed to him as deft and sinuous as a wrestler's, took his place on the edge of the bed and enfolded him as though he was a warm and welcome garment.

His share in the encounter was purely passive, an instrument or appliance of some kind that she was using to demonstrate a trick that she had decided he must learn without fuss and without delay. It was accomplished in the same subdued key, without a flicker of urgency on his part or hers, so that any sensual delight he might have derived from her swift and effortless absorption of him was submerged in the great tide of deference she inspired inasmuch as he did not see himself as possessing her, as a woman is possessed by a man, but making obeisance, as a pilgrim before a shrine. And yet her own impassivity, distinct from his, was an integral part of her bestowal, for while a goddess might unbend to a mortal, she could not be expected to be moved by one, physically or otherwise. In the moment immediately preceding the climax he saw himself as having been advancing towards this specific point in time throughout the whole of his life, not to spend himself in the complacent body of a German woman but to attain a status and dignity hitherto denied him. It was this that he acknowledged as her intention. It was for this purpose and no other that she had made herself available and sprawled on the edge of his bed, enveloping him, body and soul, with her great, muscular limbs while drenching him in her vitality that she might promote him, in the instant, from child to man.

Perhaps less than a minute elapsed before she elected to break the spell, stepping out of her Olympian role to reappear, miraculously, as humdrum Rosa Ledermann, a genial hausfrau, who had taken it upon herself, from motives hidden in the timeless history of personal relationships, to drag him over a threshold of the human family. She said, with shattering finality, "*Gelt!* It is very simple, Herr Swann. There is no mystery here, as the poets tell you. You are a man now and will begin to think as one."

He said, hoarsely, "For God's sake, Rosa . . . after this . . . how can you address me as 'Herr Swann' in that way? George! I'm *George* . . . !" and he cautiously withdrew from her, standing mute, confused and utterly undecided how one was supposed to conclude such an apocalyptic experience.

To his enormous relief she smiled, her broad, beaming features composing themselves into their homely, familiar cast as she heaved herself up, took his face between her hands again, and kissed him lightly but tenderly on the lips, saying, "*Georg.* A very English name. It suits you, I think. You will sleep now and lie upon this side. There will be bruises in the morning. A little stiffness also perhaps. But for you it was a rewarding tumble downstairs, *gelt?*"

Her forthrightness, her terrible directness, was the most awesome aspect of her. But perhaps this was true of all women, the young, old, plain, handsome, prim and sensual, down the corridors of time as far as Eden. For here she was no longer in the least concerned with his attainment of maturity. That had been briskly accomplished. What occupied her mind now was that painful jar he had given his shoulder on the newel post of her staircase. Swiftly but methodically she drew on her skirt and blouse, making a neat roll of the rest of her clothes and tucking them under her arm. He watched her every move, not knowing what to say in the way of thanks or even acknowledgement but she did not seem to expect a comment. When she had buttoned her blouse and smoothed her skirt she said, as though addressing herself, "George," nodded rather absently and moved towards the door.

He called, "Rosa—don't go! Stay with me all night, Rosa," but she replied with mild reproof, "Ach, that would be foolish. With that hurt how could we expect to have rest in that little bed? Besides, there is work to be done. For me if not for you. *Gute Nacht, Herr Georg.*"

The door closed on her. The single candle threw long shadows on the raftered ceiling. The subdued roar of the *Oktoberfest* seemed to reach him from another city. His shoulder ached but not unbearably and he lifted a hand to the swelling, massaging it slowly and thoughtfully. His brain was sharp and clear for the first time since he had come rolling home from the festival, climbed the stairs, stumbled and fallen from what now seemed to him the summit of a mountain, so distant was the experience in relation to all that had happened since. Carefully he retraced his steps, move by move, from the moment when he had sportively fondled her behind, to the moment when she had gone her careless way. Something eluded him and he searched hard for it, lowering himself carefully on to the rumpled bed and holding himself rigid with the effort of concentration. Then he understood what was missing. It was guilt. That was the strangest thing of all. He felt no wisp of guilt or regret. If it had been there at all it was lost in a long groundswell of uncomplicated affection for Rosa Ledermann.

5

Far away to the north-west, where the serried wrinkles of Exmoor channel a dozen rivers from purple heath and brushwood wilderness to seas north and south of the Atlantic-facing tip of England, two other Swanns might be said to have been migrating but they moved in tight circles, temporarily haltered to base. At that particular moment they might also be said to have been celebrating their own *Oktoberfest*, the opening of the autumn term cross-country season, for here, in at least one respect, the occasion bore some slight resemblance to the Bavarian festival. It was launched with sustained and discordant clamour.

It does not take a British schoolboy long to establish distinctive rituals. The influence of the late Arnold of Rugby upon the British educational system was admittedly profound but it was not confined to concepts involved with culture and character-formation. Pride of place in all these new, stylish and singularly Anglo-Saxon foundations, was accorded to ritual and West Buckland, although no more than a quarter-century in being, had already acquired traditions that would, in time, become fossilised. One such tradition was the series of cross-country runs over set courses of moorland pasture and river bottom, and each began with a ritualistic cacophony of Dervish-like yells flung at the indifferent hills as competitors swarmed through the narrow quadrangle arch and streamed east across the playing-fields towards the larch and conifer plantations marking the limit of the school enclosure. Among them, yelling as loud as anyone, went Giles and his brother Hugo, the one completing his third year on the moor, the other entering upon his second term.

For Giles especially this was one of the most stimulating moments of the school year. The opening of the cross-country season marked the renewal of his licence to roam far beyond school bounds and this meant the granting of a personal freedom that he found essential to his peace of mind within a closed community. It also marked the last yellowish glimmer of the upland summer and the onset of winds and sleet showers that would, in a matter of days, turn every leaf of every tree in the twin drives a different shade of rust red, soldier scarlet, guinea gold and apple russet. Soon, from the high window of the Brereton dormitory where he was splashing himself after rising-bell, he could contemplate the forced march of autumn across the hills that rose behind the plantation to the spot where, years and years ago, one of his father's managers had stamped the name 'Swann' on the local map by recapturing a toothless circus lion and hauling him the length of the Exe Valley to Exeter and for the boy this event had significance. It had already passed into legend, so that as soon as the smallholders learned one of Swann's boys was up at 'skuel' (the local blanket word for the straggle of neo-Gothic buildings crowning the ridge) they made the story public. Giles, answering their questions as to whether or not it was true his father had paid the captor a shilling a mile for the haul, found himself saddled with the nickname 'Chaser' in honour of the half-forgotten feat.

From October onwards Giles, Chaser Swann would take full advantage of the lifting of school bounds and set off on any number of officially sanctioned training runs across the slab-sided fields, through blue-black coppices bordering rushing streams, over miles of purple heather and spiky yellow gorse, as far as the very summit of the moor where a line of barrows marked the burial places of Iron Age kings. And once here, blessedly alone under a wide sky of drifting cloud, he could identify with a landscape in a way that brought him an inward tranquillity he prized above anything in his experience. For up here there were no time, no bells and no people. Nothing at all to come between a man and his search for the meaning of existence, pursued all day long between the covers of books, and at the feet of men further advanced upon the journey than he but not, seemingly, so concerned with the all-important questions of when, in what manner and, above all, *why*?

All this, of course, was before Giles Swann found a disciple in his younger brother Hugo. A very unlikely one to most observers for it was difficult to imagine two brothers less alike, physically or temperamentally. Giles, though stocky, was below average height, whereas Hugo, at thirteen and a half, was already five feet ten and a half inches in his knitted socks. Giles was recognised by masters and boys alike as being exceptionally bright. Hugo, everyone soon discovered, was an amiable peasant, possessed of astonishing strength and agility certainly, but without the ability to recall where he had left his football boots much less tangle with Euclid and Pythagoras. Thus it soon became accepted that Giles carried Hugo, nursing him as he had been seen to nurse a succession of other new boys now able to fend for themselves, and if Giles resented this intrusion into his rare moments of privacy he did not show it. When he set off for the Barrows Hugo usually tagged along, a great bumbling bear in the wake of its trainer, capable, if called upon, to cover ten miles of track in just over the hour without intruding once on his brother's train of thought so that, little by little, the relationship between them strengthened and deepened. People watched them and people wondered about them. But nobody ever knew what they talked about on these excursions. How could they know that Giles was already charting Hugo's destiny. Or that Hugo saw Giles as an old, old soul, a celestial guide invested with the distilled wisdom of the ages who happened, for reasons of his own, to be masquerading as a schoolboy?

*　　　*　　　*

They had made a great, right-handed sweep striking out across the hill pastures in a north-easterly direction that would have carried them beyond Bratton Fleming had they held to it. But then they swung south and south-west, so that by four o'clock they were breasting the great wooded escarpment that rose behind Lord Fortescue's seat and could see, in the near distance, the grey and purple blur of the school and the straight lines of the angled plantation enclosing it in the east. They paused here for a breather, for the escarpment was a rough, steep climb, resting their elbows on the palings faced with wire mesh that the estate workers had put there to keep the rabbits out of the park.

Giles said, "This is the best place of all, kid. The best place to see it as it *was*," and Hugo took this to be a rare admission on his brother's part that Giles had indeed been here before, perhaps several times, and was remembering what this stretch of empty moorland had looked like when they buried those kings in the Barrows thousands of years ago.

He said, incuriously, "What was it *like*, Giles? I mean, were there farms then? And a big house, like Castle Hill on the Barum Road?" and Giles said, "Not farms as you think of them. Hut circles, and long-horned sheep out on the hillsides, and as for that house, why it's newer than 'Tryst'. The lie of the land was the same. That hasn't changed in a million years. Not since the earth cooled."

He looked up at the great crimson ball suspended over Barnstaple Bay in the west, as though judging the distance it had yet to fall. "Come now, we can make it back in twenty minutes and change before tea bell. Take it slowly to the level and I'll pace you over the last mile."

They set off one behind the other, picking their way unerringly over tussocks of coarse grass, heather clumps and outcrops of stone that studded the reverse slope. Nothing more was said about how the western edge of Exmoor had looked to Giles four thousand years before Caesar landed in Kent or, indeed, about anything more important than a pot of apricot jam enclosed in a recent parcel from home. After tea, of course, they had to separate, Hugo to sit at prep in lower school, Giles, as a prefect, to take his turn supervising middle school prep. It was not until several hours later, when everybody else in the Brereton dormitory was asleep, that they resumed communication.

It was after silence bell then but down at this end of the long room, where a shaft of moonlight fell across the line of washstands touching the upper half of Giles' bed, their discussions were never overheard and they had come to regard their bedspace as another area of privacy.

Hugo had noticed long ago that Giles never seemed to need sleep. Perhaps old souls didn't. Perhaps they took their rest in long hibernations between spells on earth. He could see him now, flat on his back, fingers interlocked behind his head, gazing up at the ceiling, as though it guarded all the secrets of the Universe and was feeding them, one by one, into the head of the only person Hugo regarded as fully qualified to absorb them. Presently he said, "What will you *do*, Giles? After you leave here, I mean. Will you go to Cambridge like they say? And then into the business?"

"No. I won't do that. I'm not sure what I shall do. But whatever it is it won't be that."

"Why not? Fulbrooke Major told his brother he heard Tommy tell Mr. Shaw you could pass any examination they set if you wanted to."

'Tommy', the Reverend J. H. Thompson, M.A., had been headmaster of West Buckland more than twenty-five years now, and enjoyed Giles Swann's respect and affection. Nevertheless, he replied, "Tommy's a schoolmaster. He has to think in terms of examinations. But they aren't any guide at all to a man's capabilities and never will be. Don't forget that. It's very important that you shouldn't, because you'll never pass any."

Hugo, reflecting that this was almost certainly true, asked, "If that's so then what should I go for when I move up next year. I'll be nearly as old as you then and they'll be sure to write home and ask."

"What you can do better than anyone else."

"But no one can make a living running and playing games," Hugo said but then wished he hadn't. It was only rarely that he questioned Giles' pronouncements and what was surprising about that? It was ridiculous to argue with someone who knew what the Bray valley had looked like thousands of years ago.

Giles said, without taking his gaze off the ceiling, "Some people can. If they're as fast and beefy as you are."

"How, Giles?"

"People are beginning to think very highly of athletes. Nobody expects an athlete to be clever, or to cram for examinations and degrees. George will be home by then and I daresay Father will put you in his charge. You won't work all that much but your being there will make it worth their while."

"Why, Giles? How will it?"

"In the way Hamlet Ratcliffe boosted the firm by catching that lion. They've never forgotten that. But the boost was local and yours could be national; international, if you're as good as I think you are. That's why I intend to keep you hard at it so long as I'm here."

He paused, waiting for the obligatory hiss of indrawn breath that passed for Hugo's assent to almost everything he said. When it did not come he went on, "Maybe you're too young to understand it yet but it is so. Someone who can break track records, and get his name in all the papers, would be the best advertisement Swann-on-Wheels ever had. You'll enjoy doing it, too." The boy's silence puzzled him so that he raised himself, propping chin with hand. "It's *all* you think about, isn't it? Ever since you staggered everybody walking off with the under-sixteen mile your first term here. And you a kid of thirteen."

"Not 'thought' exactly. Dreamed tho'; the same dream over and over again."

"Tell me. Tell me about the dream."

"I don't think I can."

"You try. It's important that I know."

"It's just a sound."

"What kind of sound?"

"A sound like a waterfall. Or a gale, like the one we had the first week of term that brought all the trees down."

"How do you and that sound come together?"

"I don't know. It sounds so silly."

"It won't sound silly to me."

"You wouldn't tell anyone? Ever?"

"Of course I wouldn't."

"God's honour?"

"God's honour."

"Well then, I'm running you see, running hard, much harder than anyone runs here, and I've got a clear lead, half a lap maybe. I don't even have to look over my shoulder, you see?"

"Go on."

"That sound is all round me. It's *for* me and *because* of me, and it's . . . well, wonderful, the most wonderful thing you could imagine. It gets louder and louder, until it seems like everyone in the world is shouting. But then it stops and everything goes quiet and I'm by myself but glad, you see? Glad and comfortable and . . . well, satisfied. The way you feel when you've finished a Christmas dinner. Is that just a dream, Giles? One of those dreams you keep on having and not always when you're asleep? Sometimes I think . . ." but here, conscious of his brother's unwinking gaze across the narrow strip of moonlight separating their cots, he stopped, feeling himself blushing.

Giles said, "You don't have to be ashamed of dreams of that sort. Everyone dreams of doing something splendid, of being someone important, but mostly they accept the fact that they *are* dreams and go on doing something ordinary. And you don't, do you?"

"No. That sound is more real than real sounds. More real than bells, for instance. Sometimes I don't even hear the bell at the end of a period. Sometimes I think that's the reason I don't remember anything much and why everyone here thinks I'm bone from the neck up."

"Don't let that bother you," Giles said, grimly, "they'll all be glad enough to have known you when they hear that sound, kid."

"You think it'll come true, then?"

"Certainly it will. I'm glad you told me. I wasn't sure I was right about you but now I know I am."

He lay back, lifted the blanket level with his chin and clasped his hands behind his head in what Hugo always thought of as his secret-probing posture. "It's after eleven now. Go to sleep, kid."

"Yes. Goodnight, Giles."

"Goodnight, kid."

Streamers of blue-black cloud moved to obscure the moon and Giles watched them fight a losing battle. Finally they gave up, slipping past in wisps and tatters as the moon rode out high and full into a clear sky. He saw it as a kind of object lesson in purpose. In the pursuit of purpose. In the end it was all that mattered. Everybody had to have purpose. Almost everybody he knew had. His father had the business. Alex had glory. His mother had the family. His sister Stella, now that she was married again, had a husband, a baby and a farm. If George's letters home were anything to go by George's purpose was to wander the earth, watching and learning, but even this was not profitless, or not to Giles' way of thinking. Neither was young Hugo's obsession with a sound that he had not yet identified as applause from a crowd at a sports stadium. The really difficult thing was to find the purpose, identify with it, train for it and then hold fast to it, the way his father had when he founded Swann-on-Wheels all those years ago, the way Phoebe Fraser did when she rose at six-thirty in winter and summer and tackled the endlessly repetitive task of teaching children to mind their manners. The headmaster's purpose here was to mould a young school into the pattern of older, more famous schools. The purpose of Gladstone was to build a new society so universal that it might even make sense of his father's jovial boast that God was an Englishman. They all had a purpose and it piqued him that here he was, turned seventeen and still without one.

He had hints. That old couple being turned out of their cottage, and Gladstone's thunderous proclamation of the power of the common people meant something but as signposts they were not explicit. Perhaps they would be, for purposes did not always define themselves as clearly as his father's, Alexander's and Hugo's. Tomorrow, mulling over Swift, or Shakespeare, or Bacon, he would give it more thought. It was impossible to hurry these things. You waited and thought and read. Sooner or later a phrase jumped at you out of a page and there was another signpost you hadn't seen before. He lay back and looked up at the high-riding moon. A dead planet they said. But it knew its purpose in the scheme of things.

3

Reapers Reaping

His daily mail, reaching him in two streams, one as a steady flood at the yard, the other as a slow trickle at 'Tryst', were in great contrast judged by the relative pressures they applied to him, the concentration they demanded, the effort needed, here and there, to read between the lines.

The yard mail arrived by the sack but was winnowed by Tybalt and his industrious clerks. Only regional reports and letters demanding urgent decisions were passed directly to him and most of these were annotated and clipped into relevant files. Heavy as it was his office mail never occupied him more than an hour or so. He worked at it like one of those new sorting machines, recently installed at the General Post Office, papers flying this way and that, with a dash of a pen here, a marginal note there and, just occasionally, a well-aimed flourish in the direction of the gluttonous wastepaper basket that stood between the window and Frankenstein.

It was very different with his private mail, laid on his study desk against his return home in the evening, or sometimes handed to him opened by Henrietta. These letters could not be dealt with quickly for they were not overt communications, involving waggons, teams, infringements of territorial frontiers, bad debts, new customers, new contracts, the fabric of regional premises, tiresome changes in railway timetables, complaints concerning dilatory employees, pleas of extenuation involving bad roads and dishonoured promises —all the small change that came cascading from the tailboards of twelve hundred waggons and two thousand hired hands dotted about Britain, from the Grampians to the Kentish Weald, from the Cornish tin mines up through the Mountain Square to the Polygon and the Cumberland fells that knew him as a boy.

The letters he pondered in the great study at 'Tryst' were about people and herein lay the difference. Whereas one could base a decision concerning, say, the gross weight of a haul of Llanberis slate, on past experience, experience was of little use to a man on the look-out for unspoken thoughts in the artful phrase or the telltale post-script.

* * *

Usually the despatches arrived singly but one raw evening in November of that year he found four such letters on his desk, three with broken seals, proclaiming that Henrietta had passed a pleasant (and almost surely an idle) forenoon, and one more bearing a Brussels postmark that was sealed and marked 'personal'. He recognised the handwriting as that of Deborah Avery.

He scooped them up, crossed to the open fireplace, kicked a smouldering log into flame, lit one of his Burmese cheroots and made a random grab at the sheaf, coming up with the envelope postmarked 'Cairo' and addressed in Alexander's schoolboyish block capitals.

The first paragraph told him the boy had been in action again, at a place called Tel-el-Kebir in the Nile Delta, and the realisation of this stirred in Adam a near-extinct ember of his military past. He had never fought in Africa, had no more than glimpsed the Continent as a troopship passenger en route for India, but he had taken note of newspaper reports concerning Sir Garnet Wolseley's expedition to bring Ahmed Arabi's firebrands into line with Imperial policy in that part of the world. The tone of the letter was jubilant. Official despatches, it seemed, had not exaggerated the importance of the victory out there. Egypt had passed into the sphere of British influence. Cairo was occupied. The Arabi revolt was crushed. And all in less than a month from the day of disembarkation.

Alexander's regiment, Adam learned, had played a vital part in the one decisive engagement and Alexander himself had taken part in the night march across the desert and the dawn attack on a strongly-fortified position. He had come off unscathed, thank God, although regimental casualties had been high. What elated him, however, was not the victory itself so much as the fact that the infantry had stolen a march over the cavalrymen, leaving them nothing to do in the way of pursuit.

Adam found he could still smile at this, one of those gambits as old as war, the rivalry between mounted men and the footsloggers, and the footnote told him something he was anxious to know. Alexander had lived down his initial disappointment, very bitter at the time, caused by his failure to get a place in the dragoon guards or the lancers. It told him something else; to some extent the boy had vindicated himself in his own eyes and exorcised, possibly for good, the secret shame of having shown a clean pair of heels at Isandlwana.

He read George's letter next, posted in Munich three days earlier, and hinting that George might soon be on the move again, this time across the frontier into Austria, where he hoped to make contact with the Viennese waggon-maker, whose products had prompted Adam to send him abroad eighteen months ago. The letter puzzled him a little. It had, he would say, a rather wistful note, as though the boy was finding it difficult to up stumps and turn his back on Munich, and mentally he compared it with the racy letters George had written since his arrival in Bavaria. There was camouflage here. He had never had a doubt but that George found Munich very much to his taste and could hazard a guess why. There was a woman in it somewhere.

Giles' letter absorbed him more deeply than those of his brothers. It was not about Giles, as he had learned to expect from a boy compulsively attracted to lame ducks, but young Hugo, for whom Giles seemed to have formed a particularly close attachment now that Stella was off his conscience. Hugo's athletic prowess was developing rapidly and clearly the boys had been conferring on where it could lead, for here was Giles, confound him, soliciting parental sanctions of a fourteen-year-old's determination to make a career of athletics, with the ultimate idea, if you please, of adding it to the Swann assets!

Always open to a new idea Adam toyed with this one, projecting his mind forward to coffee-house conversations six, seven and eight years from now, and to sportswriters' comments of the kind that were beginning to appear on the back pages of all the national journals, even such journals as Stead's crusading rag, the *Pall Mall Gazette*.

Adam had been an early convert to the cash value of publicity. The triple exploits of Hamlet Ratcliffe, lion-catcher, Bryn Lovell, rescuer of entombed miners, and Tim Blubb, executioner of marauding Fenians, had convinced him, long ago, that a man's success in business did not necessarily rest upon the excellence of his service. Something else was needed in these days of cut-throat competition, a flair for keeping the name of one's firm in the national consciousness, so that coffee-house gossips, and even croquet-lawn tittle-tattlers, came to associate name and product with high adventure and romance, of the kind people looked for in war correspondents' despatches. And here, in his hand, was proof that Giles understood and appreciated as much at the age of seventeen!

It gave Giles, if not Hugo, a new dimension in Adam's eyes. If a boy could come up with a suggestion as sophisticated as that before he left school, what might be his potential at the age of thirty? What a hopelessly unmanageable team they were to drive! A man could plan a business down to the last detail, but how, in the name of God, did he go about organising a string of youngsters with the blood of Irish peasants, Anglo-Saxon mercenaries and Lancastrian factory-hands in their veins? He gave it up and opened Deborah Avery's letter.

There was the greatest difficulty in reading between the lines here. Deborah Avery had inherited her father's trick of hoarding secret thoughts, so that her letter told him very little concerning her approach to the chancy work she was about. They had done this. They intended doing that. They had gone here. They hoped to go there. The Belgian police were outwardly co-operative. The police were secretly hostile, so that he formed the opinion that she was laughing at him a little, just enough to convey to him that she was old enough, and certainly intelligent enough, to take good care of herself and he would be well advised to stop assuming she would be drugged, whisked into a pander's cab and sold to a Turkish satyr in Asia Minor. Yet the fears were real enough. He loved her and his sense of responsibility concerning her was that much keener because he was all she had in the way of a refuge. He thought, sourly, "Damn that rascal, Avery, for saddling me with a responsibility of this kind at my time of life! It was well enough when she was a child, and a biddable one at that, but she's now thinking of me as a man set in a money-making mould and only marginally interested in anything outside the counting-house; and she's wrong at that! The trouble with people like her and Stead, and that sainted Mrs.

Butler, is that they deal in abstracts, like their nightshirted Jehovah. They'd do better to take an objective look at humanity and see things for what they are, neither good nor bad but a matter of maintaining the struggle from nursery to funeral parlour. And yet, if anything happened to her I'd never forgive myself for sanctioning the silly caper in the first place."

He stuffed the letter in his desk drawer but the self-questioning it had provoked remained with him for the rest of the evening, so that he contributed little to Henrietta's supper chatter, concerning the avalanche of news from the family outposts. He said, in response to her query as to what he thought of the day's mail, "No more than I always think. They're young bears, as the saying goes, with all their troubles before them. There's hope, though. Alex is settling in, I'd say, and even George seems to be maturing a little."

"And Giles' silly notion concerning Hugo?"

He said, to her surprise, "It isn't so silly. The idea behind it is sound enough."

He was slow to rise to the bait, and when, baulked by his taciturnity, she asked a direct question concerning Deborah, he replied, guardedly, "She's working on a social survey for that Holy Joe, Stead."

"In Brussels? Not alone, I hope?"

"Certainly not. Don't you know missionaries hunt for lost souls shoulder to shoulder, like a shooting party on a grouse moor?"

He left it at that, not relishing the prospect of spending half the night reassuring her that Debbie was in no kind of danger but he should have known better. She had been living with him and his concerns a very long time, and could read his prejudices and apprehensions as easily as Tybalt, the clerk. He was a long time getting off to sleep and this, if nothing else, confirmed her in her private opinion that he still worried about Avery's child. "It's like him," she told herself, as soon as he began to snore. "I might have known Debbie would bother him more than the prospect of Alex getting a bullet, or George getting himself into another scrape, or Giles trying to get our sanction for Hugo's idleness . . ."

She told herself then she had been a fool not to steam Deborah's letter open and reseal it. He had always thought of Avery's child as the most vulnerable of the flock. The others were Swanns and capable, in his mind, of making their own way in the world. And yet he was wrong, for Debbie had something better than brains to sustain her. She had her deeply-rooted faith in God, and that was something neither she nor Adam had been able to instil into the others, despite regular churchgoing and any amount of encouragement from Phoebe Fraser. As for herself, she believed God was around somewhere, but he had always taken second place to Adam. Whenever they sang 'Rock of Ages' at morning service, it was not God in his heaven she visualised but Adam Swann, riding out of the morning mists on Seddon Moor when she was a slip of a girl.

* * *

For all his doubts Adam's reading between the lines had been reasonably accurate in every case. Deborah Avery, her mission all but complete, was cock-a-hoop over the pile of damning evidence they had accumulated without directing attention to themselves, whereas her feelings for her co-worker, Ned Gordon, were approaching those of a hero-worshipper. She was beginning to see him as a Launcelot of the Bordellos, a man of endless resource and matchless courage, prepared to risk life, limb and reputation in order to lay hands on a witness they could smuggle back across the Channel and use to confound the bigots in Westminster, who had declared over and over again that girls found in Continental brothels would have got there without the help of agents working on commission in London.

As for George, Adam was nearer the mark than he suspected. George was now entering upon the most bewildering period of his life, alternatively uplifted and downcast, in the way of all young men who fancy themselves enslaved. He sometimes half-believed Rosa Ledermann when she told him it was preposterous to imagine himself in love with a woman old enough to be his mother, but he wanted time to satisfy himself on this account. He still found it puzzling when she welcomed him into her bed after the merest pretence at reluctance, and then spent the precious moments urging him to move on to Vienna where, she assured him, he would forget her and Munich in less than a week.

Giles, preoccupied with someone else's problems, was the only one among them who received a return-of-post reply to his letter. His father promised to call upon the headmaster the next time he was in the Western Wedge, and hear at first hand why Hugo seemed unable to hoist himself out of a class where his age was more than a year above the average. As to the boy's athletic prowess, that was another thing Adam preferred to judge for himself. It might well be that Giles was as prejudiced in favour of Hugo's promise as he was in respect of Mr. Gladstone's oratory.

2

He had no idea what the quarrel was about, or how they came to be here, twelve thousand strong, crossing the desert to bring a dissident chieftain to battle and replace him with someone who would welcome inclusion in what the newspapers called 'the British sphere of influence'. He was not in the least clear what a 'sphere of influence' was. To Alexander Swann this was a personal adventure, offering him an opportunity to reassess himself as man and professional soldier.

The African adventure was a long way behind him now but similarities between the two campaigns returned to him after the sun had gone down and the advance continued by starlight.

Then, as now, they had marched seeking a confrontation, supremely confident in their strength, firepower, discipline and overall superiority. But in an hour they had been reduced to a fleeing mob. Was there any guarantee that the same thing would not happen again here in more open ground, with savages herding them back to their ships and every man among them concerned with saving his miserable hide? He wondered, uncomfortably, if his Rorke's Drift dedication would survive that kind of test and whether, after a rout, he would be sought among the heroes or the terrified fugitives on the path to the Blood River. There was no way of knowing short of ordeal by fire and that, so they said, was awaiting them out there under the stars, at a place marked on his field map as *Tel-el-Kebir*, and ringed in red pencil *'Arabi's entrenchment. Sixty Krupp guns? Strength est. 25,000'*.

The march from base to Nine Gun Hill and onward, under cloak of darkness, towards the Arabi camp, offered him an unlooked-for opportunity to rummage among his hopes and fears in this land that he had once thought of as a place of mystery and awesome antiquity but was now seen as a grey, featureless desert, populated by swarms of gigantic flies, scuttling scorpions and droves of beggars and, as the Delta advance got under way, clouds of hostile Bedouin horsemen who went through an impressive display far out on the flanks of the column but dispersed at the gallop after a few long-range shots had been fired in their direction.

At Nine Gun Hill the column halted for a double rum ration and orders were passed, mouth to mouth, down a chain of command that was thus seen to exist, even in this velvet blackness and upswirl of dust. No firearm to be loaded; bayonets to remain unfixed until the order to charge; no pipes; no conversing; no hurry. Just a creeping advance across the sand towards an entrenchment lit by the North Star, that was said to be the compass of a naval lieutenant almost as young as himself and introduced to him, at the last halt, as Lieutenant Rawson. They were about to move off when a shape appeared out of the gloom and he heard his name called, twice and rather testily, so that he recognised the voice as that of his Colonel, Sir Archibald Allison.

"*Swann? Lieutenant Swann?*" and he answered up promptly, "Here, sir, next the guide!" and Sir Archibald said, more genially, "Are you the young shaver Hargreaves was telling me about? Present at Rorke's Drift?"

"Yes, sir."

"Serving under who? Eh? Eh?"

"I was with the N.N.C."

"The what, boy?"

"The . . . er . . . Natal Native Contingent, sir."

"Good God!" the Colonel said, and it struck Alexander that he almost certainly thought of the N.N.C. as a mob of locally recruited headhunters. He went on, however, with the air of conferring a great favour, "Well, you're damned lucky, boy! Special assignment from the C-in-C. One subaltern to march with the guide —told me to find someone who had smelled powder. Well, then, listen hard. Elbow to elbow with Lieutenant Rawson here. Pair of you a hundred paces ahead and not a squeak from either of you until you're challenged, or run up against the first enemy ditch. Any questions?"

"Do I fire or holler back, sir?"

"You holler back. Top of your lungs, boy, then go forward without waiting for the rest of us. You, too, Rawson, providing you're not leading the whole damned column on a wild goose chase. You sure you can keep direction by the stars?"

"By one star, sir. The North Star."

"Aye, and suppose it clouds over?"

"It won't cloud, sir. Not until peep o' dawn."

"I'll hold you to that, by God. Let us down and the Navy and Sir Garnet'll fall out and you'll find yourself in a rare scrape, young feller-me-lad. Well, well, off you go. We'll give you a clear minute by my watch. Your nearest contact will be Sergeant Mackenzie, who'll follow on within hail. Good luck. You, too, Swann."

"Thank you, sir."

Rawson brought his chin down and there was light enough to see that he had been staring up at his star, so that Alex wondered how the devil he could tell one from the other and would dearly liked to have asked him, but sensed that the young man, outwardly so debonair, needed all the concentration he could bring to his task of steering an army across a desert to a fixed point somewhere out ahead and bringing it there not a moment too late or too soon.

From where they marched, some eighty yards ahead of Sergeant Mackenzie and the vanguard, the small, inconsequential sounds of the advance reached them as a long uninterrupted sigh, punctuated by the half-heard scrape of a hobnailed boot on a sliver of shale, or the occasional rasp of a buckle on a rifle butt; tiny, insignificant sounds, that could not have been identified in a less rarefied silence, so that he thought, "It's too much to hope that so many can move so far without an accident of one kind or another—a stumble, a curse, a cough, a sneeze . . . *something* over and above the rustle of twenty thousand boots planted on twenty thousand patches of sand. His confidence ebbed and flowed, his body a paper bag filled by a boy's breath, squashed, emptied, refilled again, waiting to be popped. Rawson continued to advance very steadily, lifting and placing each foot with care, but not as any man would cross broken ground in the dark, for every now and again he lifted his nose high, as though smelling the way, and whenever he did this

Alex, glancing sideways, saw starlight reflected in his upturned eye. A man consulting his compass and on the correct interpretation the fate of every man present.

The experience was surely unique, more singular in every way than its forerunner thousands of miles south of this sandy wilderness, and as they groped their way forward, moving at no more than two miles an hour, he found that its very singularity enabled him to temper his fear.

*   *   *

The sentry's challenge, reaching him as a string of yammering, incomprehensible sounds, acted like a lit fuse on an arc of combustibles to the rear and flanks, so that the sustained murmur that had orchestrated the night-long march became a gust and then, erupting as a long roll of thunder, snapped the tension like a severed hawser and brought him, on the instant, a sensation of ecstatic release. The roaring tempest of sound boosted him forward into a matching tempest as the darkness about him was lit by myriad yellow flashes so that for a few seconds it seemed that he and Rawson were lifted by two giant waves of sound before they could add their trifling quota to the uproar and begin to run, aware of a sharp rise in the ground that ended in a hillock of tightly packed sand.

The exhilaration of being here, of being the first of the first, was almost tangible, so that he heard himself bawling his triumph aloud as he clawed his way upward and found himself on level ground again. He lost touch with Rawson who fell away into the thinning darkness but was replaced, as by a conjuring trick, by Sergeant Mackenzie, howling like a banshee as he lost his footing and plunged down an almost vertical slope into a ditch packed with still, greyish-white bundles that suddenly became mobile and hideously vocal and darted this way and that, colliding one with the other and bouncing off on a fresh tack as a following torrent of yelling kilted men spilled over and through them, driving a compact course up the reverse slope of the breastwork.

It was almost light then, with the sky streaked with coral and heliotrope over the Delta but blue-black darkness immediately ahead where the half-seen sand seemed to boil, spewing men in twos and threes and dozens the full width of the ditch and along the level ground beyond the parados. It was Isandlwana all over again but shorn of its terrors, the same series of swiftly changing cameos, each with a different shape and texture but all heliographing an identical message of personal triumph and majestic infallibility. Everything happening around him was extraordinarily vivid yet his own part in it seemed automatic. He did not remember at what point in the rush he drew his sword or stopped to load his revolver. Neither was he more than vaguely aware of scaling the parados, crossing level ground, clearing a second ditch and mounting to the plateau where the last Arabi defences were carried at a rush. Later, when the sky was flooded with pinkish light, and the battle, resolving itself into hundreds of little eddies, had surged down the far side of the plateau and through the enemy's tent lines and horse lines, he saw that there was blood on his sword, that its lower edge was turned, and that three of his revolver chambers contained empty, unejected shells, but he had no memory of the encounters these things implied. The first real awareness of what had happened and how it had happened, came when he heard the bugler blowing the recall and watched the breathless Highlanders driving their prisoners into a marked-out square at the foot of the plateau. Some of them were laughing and soon he saw why, for there to receive them was Sir Archibald himself, demonstrating his exuberance in a pot-bellied, hat-waving prance and looking more like a successful punter at Epsom than an elderly field-officer commanding a brigade in action.

He called out, in his fruitiest voice, "Well *done*, boys! Well *done*, by God!" and then, seeing Alexander, whirled on him, shouting, "Well done, Swann! Heard your holler! Couldn't be better! Couldn't be better! Eh? Eh?" and Alex flushed like a schoolboy complimented on a faultless construe in front of his class, and pretended to be occupied with the business of cleaning his sword-blade as two squadrons of the 4th Dragoons cantered down from the ridge and the leading horseman, a black-moustached captain, reined in, shouting over his shoulder, "Here's a how-de-do! Damned Jocks have left us nothing to do!"

It was true. From the edge of the plateau Alex saw that the attack had been a text-book success. The wings of the British column were on the point of meeting less than a mile beyond the tent lines and inside the ring, tossing down their arms and equipment, was what

looked like the greater part of Ahmed Arabi's force. Only on the
plain beyond were small groups of horse and foot, widely scattered
and soon lost to view in swirls of dust. A few hundred others lay
scattered about between the camp and the twelve-foot ditch on the
far side of the plateau, and suddenly recollecting his duty Alex called
Sergeant Mackenzie and gathered a party to make a circuit of the
dry moat.

Here, at the point where they had broken in, the dead lay thick-
est, perhaps ten Arabi to every Highlander. Three of his own pla-
toon lay there, two wounded and one, Private Campbell, with a
hole through his temple. He remembered Campbell, a hard case,
with a long service record, and the reputation of a heavy drinker
and inveterate card player. Not the kind of man likely to get half
his head blown off in a hit-and-miss fight of this kind. Looking down
at his narrow, sunburned features he remembered the dead Zulu
sniper on the Oscarberg Terraces, the first man he had killed and
there was a link between them. Both had greying hair and small,
well-muscled bodies. Both looked indifferent to death in someone
else's cause. He asked, of Sergeant Mackenzie, who was applying
first aid to Private McCabe's bubbling thigh wound, "Did Campbell
have any family, Sergeant?"

"Och, no sir," Mackenzie said, carelessly, "he's a string of half-
caste children here, there and everywhere but he was no' a marrying man." He stood up, wiping bloodstained hands on a turban.
"He was a bonny blade in a fight!"

"I take it we'll bury him here, with military honours?"

"Aye, sir," Mackenzie said, "I'll detail a burial and firing party."

They gathered them up, carrying them over the plateau to one
of the larger tents, miraculously still standing, and just as they
arrived the Surgeon-Major and his orderlies bustled up with their
pack-horses and set about improvising an operating table from a
pile of abandoned ammunition boxes.

He hung about listlessly, not knowing what to do until orders
were issued to move on to Cairo, but the sense of elation remained
with him all through that day and through the succeeding night
when they were occupying the conquered city and finding themselves quarters for a stay that promised to be short.

He saw Sir Garnet Wolseley and his staff clatter by and thought,

idly, "They're right about his ability, by George! Tel-el-Kebir was a
tougher nut to crack than Cetywayo and his impis, with scarcely
a modern firearm among them. It's a question of mapping out a plan,
sticking to it, using trained men instead of lumbering yourself with
a swarm of amateurs . . . Training is everything, given a cool head
at G.H.Q. . . . You won't catch me playing blind man's buff with
the opposition, as Chelmsford and Durnford did away to the south,"
and he turned into his quarters and took up his note pad to write
home saying he was safe and well. The telegraph system would
have conveyed news of the victory to London by now, and there
would be headlines in *The Times,* the *Westminster Gazette* and
the *Pall Mall Gazette.* His father, a cynic concerning all official
bulletins, would require confirmation of this one, and he was going
to get it, together with an undertaking that his eldest son, from here
on, was a text-book soldier, of the kind Adam Swann, who had
exchanged shako for city topper, made the subject of so many jests.

3

Deborah Avery, putting the finishing touches on a master report
to Mr. Stead, her editor, was not a text-book fighter. Her new profession did not rely on text-books, preferring, indeed demanding,
individual initiative. For all that it had rules and she was learning
them. Rule One was to discard the orthodox in favour of the un-
orthodox. Rule Two to take nothing on trust. Rule Three was to
be devious when assembling material but direct when reducing that
material to words. For W. T. Stead, crusader extraordinary, was not,
as one might have assumed, a romantic. Stead dealt in facts and had
a notorious impatience with theories unsupported by facts. "I did not
send you to Brussels as an evangelist," he had written testily, when
Deborah added a page or two of reflections to one of her weekly
despatches. "Think of yourself—if you are tempted to self-dramatise
—as a professional spy. *Use any girl you interview* as a source of
information that might, conceivably, give us a back-door key into the
enemy's camp. *DO NOT WASTE YOUR STRENGTH ON PITY.*
Laws are not changed for compassionate reasons but by the pres-

entation of facts used to mobilise public opinion. Eyes we can always use, Miss Avery. But never eyes blurred by tears."

The snub had upset her at the time but she got over it. He was right, of course. It simply did not do to identify too closely with the individual on an assignment of this kind.

She had been prepared, during her briefing, and her trial investigations in British garrison towns and dockyard ports, for a sorry picture, but nothing as cynically evil as she found here among Continental businessmen who were sometimes ready to hint of their experiences, or in the horrific stories Ned Gordon told her from his closer look at the brothels and, above all, from her gentle but relentless questioning of Katie Doherty, a fifteen-year-old Irish waif, whom they had succeeded in smuggling out of a Lille brothel across the border, passing her off as a travelling maid, and sending home.

Katie's story was typical of several hundred British girls domiciled in Dutch, French and Belgian licensed houses. Born in a Dublin slum she had crossed to Liverpool about a year before and applied for a post of living-in housemaid advertised in *The Sunday Companion*. Her fare to London had been sent north, and, in high glee at having found a billet within days of leaving home she had reported to a Mr. Eversley, who introduced himself as the steward of a wealthy English family at present on holiday at Spa.

At that time Katie did not even know Spa was in a foreign country but she had no reason to suspect the gentlemanly Mr. Eversley when he proposed a shopping expedition in order to fit her out with what he called travelling clothes, suitable to her situation with a fashionable family who spent much of their time abroad. It had, she admitted, struck her as curious that housemaids in foreign parts were expected to dress like music-hall artistes, and she also questioned the appearance of a doctor, whom Mr. Eversley had called in to examine her before she travelled on to Dover and caught the Calais packet. But Eversley explained that the medical examination was a formality, concerned with her entry into a foreign country, and was usually carried out this side of the Channel to avoid fuss on arrival in Belgium. She was met at Calais and escorted on to Brussels by a woman who spoke no English, so that it was not possible to ask further questions until she found herself at a *pension* in charge of yet another courier, who must have been an agent for domestic servants, for he had eight awaiting despatch to identical British families living abroad.

That same night her suspicions were aroused by a second medical examination but her protests were brushed aside and she was told she would be returned to London immediately unless she submitted and signed a paper stating that the inspection had been carried out with her consent. The paper, she told Deborah, was printed in French. Katie, who could not even write English, was told to make her mark at the foot of the page.

From that moment what had been a puzzling adventure became a nightmare. With two other bewildered girls from Ipswich she was taken by cab to another establishment, where all her belongings, save the new clothes bought in London, were confiscated and she was made to drink two glasses of wine with her supper, so that her memory of what occurred that same night was blurred although, despite the fumes of the wine, she soon realised that she was now caught in a net from which escape was all but impossible. She remembered a perfumed, middle-aged man coming to her room and endeavouring to get into bed with her, but she was a strong, spirited girl and put up such a fight that he eventually left without violating her. Almost at once, however, one of the women couriers appeared and read her a severe lecture in broken English, saying that her purpose here was to entertain any gentleman who presented himself, even if he was sufficiently playful to want to share her bed. After that she was locked in and left without food or drink for twenty-four hours, until one of the Ipswich girls brought her some food and wine and told her she had no alternative but to co-operate with the people who kept the house. The other girl, it seemed, had succeeded in escaping down a drainpipe, and had sought the protection of the police but her enterprise did not appear to have helped her much. She was now back in the house, with a suspended gaol sentence over her head, having been charged at a night court with attempting to run off with clothes and trinkets that did not belong to her. She had been told, by the magistrate, that she had signed a contract to work in the establishment for six months, in exchange for bed, board and tips, and that her situation there was regarded as legal by the Belgian authorities.

After that Katie and both the Ipswich girls made the best of what could not be altered and after a month or so began to adjust to the life. Eventually Clara, the girl who had escaped, fell ill and was taken away, and they had heard nothing of her since. The tips were generous and Katie had accumulated several hundred francs during her four months' stay at the place. She estimated that during that period she had 'entertained', as she put it, about two hundred gentlemen.

"It was scary at first, miss," she told Deborah cheerfully, "but most of 'em use you kindly, and soon you get to thinking of nothing except how much they're going to leave, over an' above what they pay the Missus downstairs. They didn't hurt me, not after the first of 'em that is, and some was so drunk that you could have gone through their pockets while they was at it but I never did. I got used to it quicker than most, until that Swede happened along, that is."

The Swede, it seemed, had decided Katie to try and regain her liberty. He was a big, grey-haired commercial traveller in haberdashery, who thrashed her unmercifully when she refused to submit to practices that revolted her. This brought her into opposition with the hostess, who said that it was her duty to accommodate all clients, whatever their demands, and it was on this account that Katie enlisted the help of a young, English-speaking regular who, for the sum of one hundred and thirty-five francs representing half of her savings, put her in touch with the British consul, who at once passed her on to Mrs. Butler, without making a single comment on her adventures.

Katie Doherty, Deborah learned, was extremely lucky. Other case histories had less tidy endings. Letty Burrows, for instance, a girl from Bristol, was enlisted by the same Mr. Eversley as a governess. Letty could read and write, and came from a respectable family. When she understood what was expected of her she jumped from a three-storey window and broke her neck. Nothing concerning the tragedy appeared in the Brussels newspapers. Jill Hardcastle, a Yorkshire girl, who was only fourteen on arrival, became pregnant and was taken away, to disappear as completely as the Ipswich girl. A Scots girl, whom Katie knew as Flora, took to the bottle and one night went berserk, wrecking one of the salons before being frog-marched to gaol by two gendarmes, summoned by the management.

Currently, Katie believed, Flora was serving a six months' sentence in Malines.

Deborah sifted most of these stories and sent the bare bones of them to Stead in her weekly despatches, but all the detailed information she gleaned from the Irish girl, from contacts among men whose names and addresses she had obtained in her role as Swann's Continental representative and, above all, information supplied by a certain Father Ambrose at the church she attended, went into a bulky master file that she kept hidden in the lining of a travelling bag. Only Ned Gordon and Mrs. Butler knew of its existence, for it was deemed too dangerously comprehensive to be sent through the Belgian mails.

The file represented her achievements over here and in a modest way she was proud of it. She knew Stead well enough to realise that it was her diploma into his good graces and that its appearance on his desk would ensure her a permanent engagement on the staff of the *Pall Mall Gazette*.

As the file grew so did her confidence and she took to making decisions of her own, without consulting Ned Gordon or Mrs. Butler, who were often out of touch when information came her way. Thus it was that she established contact, through an address given her by Katie Doherty, with a minor police official, who turned out to be surprisingly helpful, and said that he could introduce her to one of his seniors, anxious to put a stop to the introduction into his country of foreign whores. There was a condition, however. The English lady would understand that both he and his superior would be compromised unless their names were kept a close secret. Any information forthcoming would be passed to her in her own rooms, and if the lady cared to make an appointment for ten o'clock that same evening, a Monsieur Sicard, the senior officer concerned, would call on her and make a significant contribution to her dossier.

Ideally a lead that promised to be as helpful as this demanded the presence of a reliable witness, but Ned Gordon was not expected back from Malines until after midnight, whereas Mrs. Butler was keeping a Paris appointment with the Salvationist, Mrs. Booth, and would not be available for forty-eight hours. She said, "You can depend absolutely on secrecy, m'sieur. If we compromised people who helped us our information would be limited to gossip. Am I to assume you would name officials, police officials?"

"At least one, and very highly placed," the man said, and then, with a smile that she thought condescending, "To be honest, mademoiselle, the information is of a personal nature, and is almost certainly being divulged for personal and political reasons. We Belgians are not attracted to moral crusades. Would that make a difference?"

"No difference at all. The information is all that we are interested in. Why should we protect men of that kind? At the moment, however, my colleagues are not in Brussels. Could your source call at my lodging two nights from now?"

"No," the man said, "that is quite impossible. M. Sicard's duties take him to Louvain tomorrow and after that he has appointments in The Hague. It is tonight or not at all."

"He would be prepared to talk to me personally?"

"Why not? It was you who came seeking information. Might I ask who gave you this address, mademoiselle?"

"I told you we never disclose our sources of information."

He smiled and nodded. "I am glad you gave me that answer, mademoiselle. Had it been otherwise the appointment would not have been kept."

4

She told the aged concierge she was expecting a male visitor at ten o'clock. He did not seem to find it strange that she, an unmarried woman, should entertain a man at that hour but merely shrugged and took a pull at the bottle he kept on the floor of his cubby-hole. She reflected then how lucky they had been to find an apartment with such a phlegmatic custodian. A younger, more alert man, and any woman, old or young, would have been interested by the mysterious comings and goings at all hours of the day and night in the Englishwoman's apartment, but this old ruin had never shown the slightest interest in his tenants, not even when he was pocketing their tips.

She had her meal, built up the fire and entered up her diary and

file, returning them both to their hiding-place inside the lining of
her bag and re-stitching the canvas, as she did on every occasion.
When a knock sounded on her door, however, she realised that M.
Sicard had not used the lift but the back stairs and cautiously at that,
for she had been watching at the window and had not seen anyone
turn into the alley leading to the rear of the premises.

She was surprised at his elegance and comparative youth. He was
wearing a well-fitting swallow-tail coat of dark blue, tight strap-
under trousers of a lighter shade of blue, suede gloves and a bowler
with a curved brim. He was handsome, too, in a suave, aquiline way,
with a well-trimmed moustache, an Imperial tuft and unusually light
blue eyes that were disconcerting, for there was patronage in the
glance he gave her as they shook hands, an action he performed without removing his glove. He laid his hat and silver-handled rattan
stick on a chair just inside the door and advanced to the fire, spreading his hands as though glad to see the blaze. He then glanced at
the curtains, nodding approval at the fact that they were closely
drawn, but as she was shutting the door he said, over his shoulder,
"Please, mademoiselle. I would prefer it left ajar. You appear to be
alone. I would not like to compromise a lady."

"No one else lives on this floor," she said, but he flashed her a
smile, saying, "Servants use the stairs and corridor and servants
gossip, mademoiselle. What we have to say will be said discreetly, I
hope. It should not take long."

She left the door ajar. His courtesy reassured her. She said, "I
shall not take notes, m'sieur. That way you are not likely to be compromised either. You know the purpose of my presence here. Mine
and Mrs. Butler's?"

"Indeed I do," he said, smiling. "We have had our eye on you ever
since you arrived, Mademoiselle Avery. We were puzzled at first. It
is not usual for a woman to represent commercial interests in Brussels. Particularly a firm of British hauliers, however reputable that
firm might be!"

She could not have said why but his words and manner worried
her. Behind his polite badinage there was a sneer and his eyes played
over her in a way that robbed her of initiative. Then, before she
had a chance to ponder this, he was speaking again, softly, politely
and in faultless English.

"You have had your eye on *us*, of course. Three pairs of eyes. You spoke of writing down, mademoiselle. I take that to mean keeping records of your diligent enquiries in a specific trade. A profession, some would call it, but there is no point in mincing matters. Let me be equally frank. I should be obliged if you would hand me any records you have in your possession. It would save us both a great deal of time and inconvenience," and he held out his gloved hand.

She glanced instinctively at the door and he followed the glance. "You said yourself no one else is lodged on this floor, Miss Avery. The concierge is below, of course, but he is drunk by now. One of my men will have seen to that, as well as a small commission for minding his own business. Now, mademoiselle, you're not a fool, although I admit to finding you very gullible. A common fault with missionaries, I believe. You have records here, of your visits, your contacts, your interviews with certain young ladies, all but one of whom still lie within our legal jurisdiction. It would be wise, I think, to surrender them at once."

His insolent directness, and his obvious estimate of her fallibility braced her. To gain a moment or two she attempted a bluff.

"You have a search warrant, M'sieur Sicard?"

"No, mademoiselle, no warrant. Why should I bring a warrant? I was invited here. Whatever I found in the way of disorder, or evidence that the place had been searched and its tenant maltreated, would go into my report as having happened at nine o'clock, an hour before I arrived. Who could challenge that? The concierge, who has difficulty in reading his watch when he is sober?"

She said, bitterly, "You'll find no records here. Mr. Gordon keeps them. There is one thing that might be worth reflection on your part, however. I'm not a missionary, in the sense you use the word. I represent W. T. Stead, one of the most influential journalists in Britain, and if I was molested in any way your superiors would be likely to ask you some very awkward questions within an hour of copies of the *Pall Mall Gazette* reaching Ostend."

He was not paying the slightest attention to her. His eyes darted about the room, a brace of rapiers in the hands of an expert duelist, and she knew he was considering possible hiding places for the papers he sought. Then he walked to the door and whistled, and in a matter of seconds two other men trotted into the room, approaching him like a couple of well-trained mastiffs.

"Search the place," he said, in French. "Take the bedroom, Tallien."

The man addressed as Tallien, the smaller of the two, sidled off into the bedroom and she could hear him turning things over, pulling out drawers and hauling the bed clear of the wall. The other man, a moonfaced, lumpish fellow, with heavy shoulders and blue-rimmed fingernails, poked diligently in the desk, throwing down papers, including her half-finished letter, and probing the back of the compartments as though expecting to find a hidden drawer or a sliding panel. Sicard, still ignoring her, ran his hand down the crevices of the sofa and armchair, then stooped to tug the corner of the carpet free of its floor tacks. Presently the man called Tallien reappeared, carrying both her travelling bags which he handed, wordlessly, to his superior. Sicard emptied the contents on to the table, examined each garment separately and then upended her workbox, scattering pins, needles and reels of cotton on the floor.

"What time do you expect your colleague back, Miss Avery?"

"You think we share the apartment, monsieur?"

He made a gesture of impatience, the first since he had entered the room. "His lodgings are on the floor above. Do you suppose we fail to keep dossiers on people who come to Brussels to stir up trouble? We know he has been to Malines today. A train gets in from there shortly before eleven. The cab ride here will occupy him ten minutes."

"If your information is so complete what point can there be in cross-examining me?"

"There is a point, Miss Avery."

He picked up hat and cane and drifted back towards the table. "I am sure the young priest's pockets will yield additional data but the main record is here. In this room, mademoiselle. I could find it, of course, if I had the patience. But I am not a patient man, Miss Avery."

He moved across to the fireplace. The two other men went on searching unhurriedly but with thoroughness. He said, at length, "See here, Miss Avery, we are not only wasting time, we are embarrassing one another. I am a trained police official and I do not intend leaving here without those papers. Points I would wish to

make are these. My name is not Sicard, and I am not here in an official capacity. You and your people have made enemies in Brussels,
and across the frontier in Lille also. If I go away emptyhanded you
can be sure they will pay you a visit and as I am not renowned for
my patience they are not distinguished for their scruples. They could
be—almost certainly would be—crude in their methods. A good deal
more crude than I, for instance. They feel their livelihood threatened, and if they were to take steps to guard against that threat—at
your expense let us say—then no doubt that editor of yours would
stir up a considerable fuss in London, and my people over here
would be moved to make diligent enquiries concerning the culprits.
But not so diligent as to find and punish them. Important people are
involved, you see. Some of whose names appear in your records."

"I've told you I keep no records here."

"I have other information, mademoiselle. You have a buff file with
leather corners. Loose-leafed, I believe. You have also a personal
diary in the form of a pocket book, small enough to be carried in a
reticule. The pocket book is red. With gold edges. Does that refresh
your memory?"

She understood then the source of his information. Monique, the
chambermaid, had often passed in and out of the apartment when
she had been entering up the master file and diary, and the certainty
that the girl had been bribed, or even planted here as a spy, made
her fully aware of her own amateurism. Stead had warned her that
these people had allies among the police and judiciary but she had
thought of corruption as small and localised.

They were standing facing one another as his two henchmen continued to prowl about in the background. Late traffic was passing
up and down the Rue de la Loi and, at any minute, she supposed,
Gordon would knock on her door to report any progress he had made
in Malines. They would almost surely arrest and search him and it
was up to her to warn him if she could by creating some kind of
diversion.

She did the first thing that came into her head, grabbing a heavy
vase that stood on the mantelshelf and hurling it over his shoulder
in the hope of smashing the window and attracting the attention of
passers-by in the street below. He would easily bluff his way out of
any ensuing scene, of course, but the action would attract attention
to the search and he would surely wish to avoid this at all costs.

She had no luck. The vase struck the window frame and bounded back into the room, smashing at the feet of the probing Tallien, who was in the act of stripping the cover from a cushion. She saw Sicard's brows contract but she did not see the hand holding the cane go up. The movement was too quick for the eye to follow and the horrid pain caused by the vicious slash across her shoulders was the very first indication she had that he had struck at her with the full strength of his arm.

She let out an involuntary yelp and turned instinctively towards the bedroom, with some idea of rushing there, slamming the door, and locking herself in, but again he was far too quick for her. His foot shot out, tripping her neatly, so that she fell face-foremost among the broken shards of the vase where he pinned her with his foot. Then the cane was flailing down on her, striking her neck and back and buttocks and thighs, a shower of blows that left her sick and dizzy with pain and a kind of paralysing anger. Somehow she got to her knees and dragged herself round facing him. He was standing looking down at her smiling. Behind him, grinning, was the smaller of his creatures, Tallien, and over by the door, was the other man, head cocked on one side as though listening.

It was quite silent in the room then, so that the sound of the clanking lift reached them clearly and unmistakably. He made a sign to his men who stood on either side of the door and she was in the act of dragging herself upright when the first tap came and Gordon's voice called, "Deborah? You're not in bed are you?"

It all happened with the same fatality, like a scene from a familiar play. She opened her mouth to warn him but no sound came beyond a choking sob. Pain surged through every area of her body but more crushing than pain was a desperate sense of failure. It was all she could do to check herself vomiting at the feet of her bland, smiling tormentor.

They took him as he entered, moving with expert nonchalance, as though they did this kind of thing every night of their lives. In a matter of seconds she was sitting in a chair, held by Sicard, and Ned Gordon was gaping across at her, arms handcuffed behind his back, with Tallien on his right and the other man on his left.

Sicard said, almost apologetically, "We have had a little difficulty here, m'sieur. The lady has forgotten where she put her records. Perhaps you could help us?"

He said, thickly, "Who . . . who are you? What are you doing here?"

"Does that matter? Let us say the opposition. Be so good as to give us the papers, m'sieur, and we shall not detain you or Miss Avery another moment."

He still seemed quite incapable of taking it in but continued to gape, first at her and Sicard, then at the disordered room, a big, flustered man, passive and helpless, with his hands secured behind his back.

She said, jerkily, "Police . . . searching . . . made an appointment . . . silly of me . . . silly of . . ." And then, as Sicard raised his arm again, and Gordon cried out in protest, she fainted, crumpling forward so that she slid from the chair, her cheek coming into contact with a jagged piece of pottery lying there.

5

They were gone when she opened her eyes to find herself lying on the sofa. The room seemed insufferably hot and when she tried to sit up ripples of pain ran the length of her body, seeming almost to reach her ankles and the tips of her fingers. She was aware of something wet and sticky on her cheek and when she raised her hand there was blood on her knuckles. Then Gordon was bending over her holding a cloth and an enamel basin and gently bathing her cheek and as she winced in response to the smart, she saw her bag lying open on the armchair, its lining showing as ragged folds.

"You gave them the papers?"

"I had to. Could I stand by and watch you tortured by that fiend? He was about to apply his cigar butt to your feet to bring you round."

She sniffed and smelled tobacco, then lay back, so tired and painracked that she wished she was dead. He said, eagerly, "We'll prosecute . . . he's a man with something to hide. Most of the police are honest and when they hear what happened . . ."

But she cut him short with a tired gesture. Even that caused her renewed pain.

"We can't do any such thing, Ned. Not from here, not after this. We'll go home and make a clean breast of it to Mr. Stead. We just aren't equipped to fight them on their home ground. The only really useful thing I've done here is to find that out."

"We can remember some of the people and their addresses. And there's that girl, Doherty. She will have been interviewed by Stead by now."

She was too tired and far too battered to argue with him. He was a kind, simple man, who assumed, as indeed she had until tonight, that the Belgian authorities were as anxious to clear up this dirty business as were the people Mrs. Butler had enlisted at Westminster. It was understandable that he should continue to believe this. He had not been thrashed from head to foot with a rattan cane, tipped with a metal ferrule.

She said, "The cut on the cheek is nothing. I tried to warn you by throwing a vase at the window but missed. I've missed in so many ways."

He said, eagerly, "Don't keep blaming yourself. Do you think Stead won't appreciate the lengths you went to to keep those papers out of their hands? Let me call a doctor before I go to police head-quarters and report what happened here."

It amazed her now that anyone could be so naïve. He seemed incapable of absorbing the fact that this raid had been mounted by the police, almost certainly planned before she had played directly into their hands by making the appointment with Sicard. They had known precisely what kind of data was being assembled here. Every move that he or she or Mrs. Butler had made, every contact they had established, had been checked and re-checked. Bribes had been paid out. Threats had been issued. Dossiers had been built up word by word, and all the information about them had been classified and expertly evaluated. Her approach to the police clerk earlier in the day had been the final piece in the jigsaw, an excuse to get in here without fuss and blow the entire operation sky-high. Whatever charges were laid now, here or in London, would be written down and quietly filed away, to gather dust in some depository of police dossiers. Printed accusations from Stead would be met with counter accusations, involving his reputation and hers. Witnesses like the chambermaid Monique, and that police clerk, would be primed. The beating she had received would be attributed to some enraged brothel-keeper, who had taken steps to protect his business in his

own way, with a couple of hired roughs. There was absolutely nothing to do but to go home and advise Stead to make what he could of
Katie Doherty's statement. Katie, almost certainly, would be dis-
credited in advance, a young harlot who had picked her clients'
pockets and fled across the Channel before she could be arrested.
All an exposé would do, she supposed, would be to warn other girls
to take elementary precautions against accepting employment with
'rich English families living abroad'. It was something but it was not
nearly enough. Nobody would understand that better than Stead.
Already a majority in Parliament was seeing his campaign as an attempt to whitewash wantons and sell more of his newspapers into
the bargain.

She said, carefully, "No doctor, and certainly no report to the police. Nothing whatever would be gained by going down there and
something might be lost. As it is they will have to wait a day or so to
learn how Mr. Stead handles the story. Believe me, Ned, I know
what I am about. For the first time since I began this business. Sicard
was a good teacher. I'll run him down in the end but it may take
years. A new start will have to be made. My uncle was right after
all."

"Swann? What can he know about it?"

"He knows the way of the world, Ned. Better than we do, and
better than Stead. He told me something like this could happen.
From here on I'll listen to him, rather than my conscience. If you
want to be useful start making arrangements for us to travel back
and make sure you meet Mrs. Butler's train when she gets back from
Paris tomorrow."

"She'll know what to do, Deborah. She's still in charge, isn't she?"

"Not of me she isn't."

She left him then, moving stiffly into the bedroom and closing the
door. It was curious how finally she could turn her back on people
like him and Mrs. Butler, on the fervent and vociferous, who clamoured for reforms and spouted scripture in support of their crusades.
She understood now that Stead was more right than he knew when
he said that compassion played little part in work of this kind. She
took a jar of cold cream from a drawer left open by the searchers,
applying it gingerly as best she could. Very gradually the heat went
out of her wounds and she lowered herself gently on the edge of the
bed.

4

The Transmogrification of Jake Higson

IN the early days, whenever Adam Swann looked covetously on an unexploited piece of territory and decided, sooner or later, to make it his own, his method was to cast about for a lieutenant born and raised in that area, someone familiar with the local quirks of character and the local speech idioms, someone with friends and relatives within close call, who would hold the door ajar, wide enough for a Swann waggon to move through on to new ground.

By and large the method had served him well. Hamlet Ratcliffe, who had ruled the Western Wedge for more than twenty years now, was Devon born, and had won the west in a single day by recapturing the Bamfylde lion and returning him to Exeter in a Swann two-horse frigate. Bryn Lovell, who had spoken nothing but Welsh until he taught himself English by reading Tom Paine's *Rights of Man*, had done the same for the Mountain Square, a great tract of land almost innocent of railways north-west of his base at Abergavenny. John Catesby, who had opened up the Polygon, north of the cotton belt, was Lancashire born, had stood beside a loom as a child and served a term in a Lancashire gaol for rioting in the 'forties. Edith Wadsworth, and her father before her, who had made the Swann-on-Wheels insignia familiar in the east coast crescents, were natives of the North Riding of Yorkshire, and had later moved down into Lincolnshire. Godsall, a Kentishman, had been picked to replace coachman Blubb in the Kentish Triangle. Morris, a Worcestershire man, was in charge of Southern Pickings, based on Worcester. Vicary, of The Bonus, north of the Thames estuary, was a native of Southend.

When it was not possible to apply this golden rule Adam saw to it that his managers were started young in the territories they were to command, as in the case of Rookwood, the Thameside waif who had taken over the Southern Square at the age of twenty-one and

320

was now well-established at Salisbury. In only one case was an exception made to this method of pre-selection and this was in the far north where Fraser, once a pedlar, had watched and waited for years before mounting his successful foray into the country of his Scots ancestors and had finally established himself in Edinburgh, with the whole of the Midlothian and Border Counties under his hand and a footing north of the Tay. But even so Fraser had known his beat and the canny customers who inhabited it, so that eyebrows were raised at Headquarters when Adam sent a raw young cockney to replace Fraser, who reached the age of retirement in the autumn of 1880. Conservatives like Tybalt, the chief clerk, and Saul Keate, the waggonmaster of the network, regarded this selection as a mistake, although Jake Higson, who had begun life as a chimney-sweep and been lucky to escape with his life in one of Swann's flues back in the 'sixties, was a forceful character, with good leadership potential, who might, in Keate's view, have done well as a depot manager in the south-east. They did not question the Gaffer's judgement openly, however, suspecting that he knew what he was about and remembering his uncanny knack of picking deputies. Thus it was that no one at Headquarters was much surprised when Fraser's beat held its lead after the transfer, and returns from the Edinburgh depot began to forge even further ahead. Only Godsall, in the Kentish Triangle, ground his teeth with rage every time the quarterly circular came in showing sectional turnovers.

There was a reason for this, a reason of which Swann himself was unaware. He had noted the glowing health of the Scottish section, of course, had even commented upon it to Tybalt when the returns came in but he put it down to the cordial relationship that grew up between Fraser, a man of sound judgement and enormous experience, and his heir apparent, young Jake Higson, supplemented, perhaps, by Fraser's decision to stay on for a period, in order to play Higson in.

This was indeed a factor in the prosperity that obtained up here but it was not the main reason for it. The underlying cause was at once more subtle and more unlikely. It concerned what might have been called the Transmogrification of Jake Higson.

*　　　*　　　*

Higson, who did not know his correct age but judged it to be somewhere around thirty, had carried his cockney prejudice north of the Tweed, although he had been careful not to let that prejudice show when selected as a possible successor to Fraser, the Scottish viceroy.

There was a Napoleonic tradition in the Thameside yard that every Swann vanboy carried a managerial baton in his lunch box. The founder of that tradition, of course, was 'Young' Rookwood, of the Southern Square, whose name dangled like a carrot in front of every urchin who swung from the tailboard rope of a Swann waggon.

Rookwood had been one of Waggonmaster Keate's successes, scraped from the Rotherhithe foreshore, scrubbed, taught to read and write, set to work, and ultimately installed as stableman in a provincial capital, where he had attracted the notice of Abbott, the slave-driving gaffer of the depot. Abbott had later left the network under a cloud but his recommendation—surprising in the circumstances—had won Rookwood a trial as manager. By the time he was twenty-three Rookwood had established himself as one of Swann's most thrustful lieutenants and had gone on to astonish everybody, including Keate, his original sponsor. He had married his landlady's daughter, come into a modest income when her father died, attended church regularly, behaved circumspectly in every conceivable way, and was now, believe it or not, a city councillor, a member of the Board of Guardians, a sidesman and the father of three clever children, one of whom was up at Oxford reading Greats.

Rookwood was thus the central figure of a Swann cautionary tale and his name was mentioned whenever promotion was discussed, but those who knew Jake Higson did not expect to see Rookwood's career duplicated in the north, for Higson was not that kind of chap at all. Indeed, to those who knew him well, nothing seemed less likely than that Higson should marry, settle down and become a sidesman or a guardian. Unlike Rookwood, he had never made an attempt to discard the shell of the cockney waif, that armour of impudence and derisive humour that accounted for his survival in his chimney-sweeping days. Neither had he shown any desire to improve his education but continued to glory in backslang and use the thin, nasal vowels of the London guttersnipe. He had the cockney's rooted contempt for every other city, town and village in the four nations. To him every settlement outside the southern rim of Essex, and the northern boundaries of Kent and Surrey, was a kind of wasteland where the pickings for the artful might be lucrative, but where no sane man would choose to live, unless it paid him handsomely to do so.

It would have been useless to tell Higson that, from time to time, the provinces threw up a giant, a Shakespeare, or a Brunel, or men of unquestioned commercial importance for whom Swann-on-Wheels shifted goods. He would have replied that none of these men would have amounted to—in his quaint phrase—'a bleedin' pennorth o' cold gin' had they not shown sufficient enterprise to move south-east in their formative years. For Higson did not acknowledge Britain or the British Empire as such. To him both were no more than convenient terms, applied to a loose federation of tribes, each looking to London for everything from pence to puddings. If he thought of Scotsmen at all before his translation among them he would have seen them as music-hall turns, attired in kilt and tam-o'-shanter, blowing bagpipes and proclaiming their obscure origins by prefacing every sentence with the phrase 'Och, aye!' He had never heard of Doctor Johnson but would have confirmed his doctrine that the best sight a Scotsman could hope for was the road to England.

*   *   *

It was in this frame of mind, or something like it, that Jake Higson boarded the express out of Euston about the time Gladstone was making his conquest of Midlothian. The coincidental arrival in Edinburgh of Higson and Gladstone confirmed Higson's estimate that he was now among savages, for he passed out of Waverley Station straight into an overflow meeting of Edinburgh Liberals so that it seemed to him he had arrived in time to witness a native fertility celebration, or some other rite whipped up by kilted witch-doctors.

The streets were thronged with men and women, each wearing the same rapturous expression, each given to making identical outbursts of spiritual ecstasy, the like of which Jake had never heard, not even in the Old Kent Road during a weekend Saturnalia. The uproar was stunning and the press of people so great that it seemed useless to wait about for Fraser, scheduled to meet him, so he made his own way to his temporary lodgings in the Cowgate, arriving there battered, breathless and not sure how one would begin to set about the process of taming such people.

Fraser, equally battered, appeared an hour later, apologising for having missed him, and explaining that the Scots took their politics very seriously and that he would doubtless adjust to this. He gave Jake directions to the Grassmarket close by, where Swann's stables and yard were situated, and promised to take him on a tour of the city the following morning.

Jake lay awake half the night, listening to reverberations attendant upon Gladstone's visit, and the very fervour of the occasion sapped his confidence in himself so that he thought, with uncharacteristic humility as he drifted off to sleep, "Dunno what I'll make o' this bunch . . . if they put as much 'eart inter 'aggling as they put inter pollerticks they'll be flamin' 'ard to best an' bang goes my chance to show the Gaffer wot I'm made of . . ."

But then, in the morning, a curious thing happened, something that he could never have foreseen when he emerged from Waverley Station, with the air of a man conferring a favour upon the Scots by being here. Dramatically and emphatically, so that the experience was almost physical, the spirit of Auld Reekie descended from the frosty sky above the looming bulk of Castle Rock, and staked a claim on him so that he began to sense the permanence and antiquity of a place and a race that he had thought of, up to that time, as being good for nothing beyond a quick profit and a chortle.

He could never have said what caused this manifestation. He was very far from being a romantic, susceptible to atmosphere, and yet, as he made his way through crowds of solemn-faced Scotsmen, and overheard snatches of their solemn conversation, a conviction grew upon him that he had been whisked from a city of frivolity and inconsequence to the heart of a civilisation where the meanest-looking rascal carried himself like an exiled king, where the small change of barter acquired the status of ceremonial, and the business of the day, conducted in and around the stalls, was entered upon with a gravity and punctilio that made London marketing seem trivial and digressive.

It had to do with buildings as much as people, for the towering rock, topped by the castle and rising starkly out of a cleft filled by violet mist, appeared to him as a kind of symbol of the terrible earnestness and sobriety of Scotland, and this impression was deepened hour by hour as Fraser showed him the sights and introduced him to the heart of his new kingdom.

For a time—it was not more than an hour or so—he took refuge in the gamin's irreverence but he soon dropped this defence. Quips concerning John Knox and Jenny Geddes (whose place in Scots history, Fraser said, had been gained by throwing a stool at a parson in St. Giles' Cathedral) sounded childish and facile among all this granite and gravity, so he let himself be carried along on the tide of the centuries, so meekly that the perceptive Fraser was instantly aware of the sobering effect the city was having upon him and even praised him for it, saying, "It's the right approach up here, Higson, and you'll do well to stick to it. Your cue, as I soon found, is to forget the Act of Union. Let 'em see you think of 'em as a separate nation, allied to England for purposes of trade but nowt else, if you follow me."

Jake, who did not follow him because he had never heard of the Act of Union, said, "You mean the Jocks was *seprit* once? With a king an' parlyment diff'rent from ours?"

And Fraser, himself ancestrally Scottish, took a deep breath and said, "Good God, man, of course they were! Until around about your great-great-great-grandfather's time."

It was this casual exchange that set the tone of the relationship between the two men on the first day of their association, for Fraser had always regarded himself as an infiltrator up here and it seemed important that he should coach his successor in the essentials of his own technique. He said, "Heed me, lad, and you won't go far wrong. Up here are the canniest people in the world, not excluding the Jews, so start off on the right foot. Forget all the jokes you've heard about a Scot's stinginess. He has his failings, and mulishness is the worst of 'em, but make friends of a Scotsman and he'll never turn his back on you, not even if he sees a profit in it, and that's a damned sight more than you can say of most people! They'll strike a hard bargain but when it's struck they'll stand by it, even when it goes against them. As to education, why man, that shoeless bairn over there could tell you more of his country's past than many a fine gentleman in London could tell you concerning what happened on his doorstep the day before yesterday! Learn something of Scots history. Never joke about business. Never get into an argument with them about religion or politics, not because they're intolerant, like the Irish, but because theology and economics is in their blood-stream and if you open the door to them they'll hold you in argument half the day when you've business elsewhere. Take them and their traditions seriously. Don't look to be short-changed but don't try and steal a march over them, either. Drift about a bit while I'm at your elbow, and get the *feel* of the country. Above all, stand by your word and handshake, for they mean more up here than south of the Border. If so much as one of them decides you're not to be trusted then word of it will run across the city like a heath fire and we'll be slipping down the Swann ladder to sixth or seventh place in the regions, instead o' pride of place that we occupy right now! There, that's enough advice for one day. Come on down the hill and I'll show you the very spot where a Queen's husband and his lickspittles put fifty-six dagger wounds into a foreigner they distrusted."

They moved on to Holyrood Palace, then up to the Castle, then down again into Princes Street and the Georgian squares behind it. They visited museums, art galleries, the site of the gallows where Burke the body-snatcher was hanged (he and Hare were the only Edinburgh worthies of whom Jake had heard tell), and on to Greyfriars, Surgeon's Hall, and other places of antiquity. But perhaps the edifice that most impressed Jake was the Scott Memorial, with its three score statues of celebrated figures in Scottish history, for he had always thought of authors as long-haired starvelings who lived in garrets and it came as a shock to him that so much money and effort had been expended on a monument to a man who wrote stories.

He said, wonderingly, "Gawd luv us, Mr. Fraser, they muster thought a rare lot o' that chap!"

And Fraser replied, "They think a rare lot of any man who pulls himself up by his bootstraps, Higson."

They set out, in bleak winter weather, on a sweep of the territory that took them the length and breadth of the Lothians and down into the Border counties, where they paid homage to Scott, Burns, and a man called Carlyle, another of whom Jake had never heard but whose fame, he was amazed to learn, rested on a book about the French Revolution.

326

Little by little, as they drove about the towns, villages and mist-shrouded moors of the beat, meeting prominent customers and dining in homely inns, a feeling grew in Jake Higson that he was an exile and outcast, separated from these people not so much by race and language (he could understand less than half the conversation between Fraser and his customers) but by a kind of mental inferiority.

Full awareness of this was not as definite as all that, or not at first, but it was there from the first day and steadily enlarged itself as he listened to Fraser's stories of Wallace, Bruce, the Covenanters, the Porteous riots, the 'Forty-five, and all manner of legends that had been retold by that indefatigable chap Scott, to whose memory they had raised that expensive-looking memorial. But it was not merely his own ignorance that teased him. It had to do, in a way he was at a loss to define, with the ability of the ordinary men and women up here to absorb book-learning, an accomplishment that Jake had always regarded as one reserved for the rich and high-born. Yet Burns, they told him in Ayrshire, had been the son of a ploughman, and Carlyle, they told him in Dumfries, the son of a mason and in these humble cottages and granite cities they were both measured with the London great, like the Duke of Wellington, and that chap who built St. Paul's, and the only yardstick Jake could use as a comparison was Dick Whittington who, like everyone else, had been obliged to trudge Londonwards before making his mark. Here in Scotland, however, one found a Whittington in every hamlet, and as many as three in some villages, as was the case at a little place called Denholm, on the road from Jedburgh to Hawick. It was here, of all places, that Jake's feelings about the Scots suddenly crystallised, so that Denholm became for him the crossroads that gave his life a shape and purpose that it had not had up to that time.

2

He was settling in by then, and had driven in his smart waggonette, drawn by two high-stepping bays, to call on a new customer in the Kelso area. Because the spring morning was sharp and clear, and the road ran beside the pretty river Teviot, he was at peace with himself, and conscious of slowly coming to terms with the country-side and its people. He stopped off at Denholm for a bite to eat, and crossed the village green to read the inscription on an obelisk set there, finding it was erected to the memory of one John Leyden, born in a cottage that still stood on the north side of the village.

Leyden, it seemed, who had died at the age of thirty-six, had been a very famous scholar indeed, having educated himself to a point where he could confound the learned on every conceivable subject. He had even managed to pass examinations in medicine in six months in order to equip himself for a post in India, where he went on to become a brilliant orientalist.

It seemed to Jake, spelling out the inscription, that Leyden some-how epitomised the Scots. A man who could do what Leyden did in a mere thirty-six years might have gone on to rival King Solomon, of whom Jake had heard during enforced sessions in Mr. Keate's van-boys' Sunday School, and a furious, impotent envy stirred in him as he stood pondering John Leyden's astonishing career in the warm April sunshine.

What little remained of his urchin pride, imported from London, ebbed away, leaving him naked and pitiful, so that his extreme dis-satisfaction with himself rose to his lips in a kind of involuntary protest and he growled aloud, "It ain't *right*! It ain't *fair*! Gawd knows, I tried me best . . ." But then he stopped, flushing, for he saw that he was not alone, and that a young woman was standing close by and a very fetching young woman she was, with soft brown eyes, dark, looped-back hair and the pink and white complexion all the girls up here seemed to have in contrast to the pallor of the London girls.

She was smiling, he noticed, but in the friendliest possible way, as she said, obviously with the intention of helping him out, "Oh, don't mind, I'm always talking to myself. Why not? It's the only way to learn anything about yourself," and his heart warmed to-wards her as he grinned, sheepishly, saying, "Down home it's reckoned a sure sign o' goin' barmy, miss. It's just that . . . well . . . this bloke Leyden . . . it set me thinking and it come out, before I could stop it!"

She said, drawing her fine dark brows together, "*What* came out?" and he noticed then that she had little trace of the brogue but spoke like a person difficult to place. Not 'ladylike' exactly, but easily and naturally, with effortless enunciation.

"I suppose I was thinkin' o' brains," he said, slowly. "Brains, like this chap had an' muster bin born with. I mean, some are and some ain't, and if you ain't you c'n on'y get so far and then, bang goes the door, smack in yer faice, if you see wot I mean."

"Oh, I see what you mean," she replied gaily, "but it isn't in the least true. Leyden started from nothing, right here in this village, and so did John Scott, the famous botanist, and Sir James Murray, the man who made the dictionary. It's no more than a matter of making up your mind to do whatever you want to do."

"*Three* of 'em! From a place this size?"

She smiled. She had, he decided, a bewitching smile. "Up here it's the only way to a better life and it's always been so. Education gives a man something to set his sights on, for money is hard to come by this far north. Is that your waggonette over there?" and when he nodded, "Then you don't have to worry, do you? To run a team like that, and wear broadcloth of the kind you're wearing, you must be comfortable to say the least."

The statement amazed him. He had never once thought of himself as being 'comfortable' as she put it, although Swann paid his provincial managers very well and he had been putting money aside for some time now.

He said, carefully, "Well, the waggonette an' cattle ain't mine, exactly. I'm Scottish manager fer Swann-on-Wheels, the carriers. At least, I will be, soon as Mr. Fraser packs in. Mr. Swann—our Gaffer that is—he likes us to drive a good rig. Says it's good fer business."

"And so it is," she said, but then, to his amazement, "Why don't you step across to the Manse and take a dish of tea with myself and my father? We don't get much company and someone from London is a rarity about here. It's well enough for father. He has his work to occupy him, but I'm on holiday and I miss Edinburgh, I must confess."

"You live in Edinburgh, Miss . . . ?"

"McKenzie. Mary McKenzie. I'm a teacher there in a school near the Infirmary. I know your yard. It's the one in the Grassmarket, isn't it?"

"Yes," he said, eagerly, "and I'd like very much to take tea with your father, Miss McKenzie. I'd . . . I'd like it fine!" and with that, a gamin's trick to identify with the locality by using a local idiom, she laughed, showing two enormous dimples and he thought that never, in the whole of his life, had he seen a prettier or more engaging face.

He walked beside her across the green to the Manse and was introduced to a gnomish little minister, who gave him the welcome he was learning to expect up here, and they all drank tea together and exchanged mild courtesies, Miss McKenzie telling him she lodged with an aunt in George Square, and he telling her and her father the nature of his work as Swann's manager in Edinburgh.

It was past three o'clock before Mary McKenzie walked him to the inn where his team had been fed and watered, and as they shook hands he said, falteringly, "Everyone I met up 'ere 'as bin . . . well . . . so friendly like. But it's all give an' no take. Mr. Fraser says no one expects tit-fer-tat, like they do dahn south, but seein' you work right alongside our headquarters coulden I, coulden we . . ." And he stopped, for somehow, although well accustomed to making assignments with young women, ordinary techniques failed him in the presence of the daughter of a minister, clearly a respectable girl, of the kind he rarely met outside business hours.

She said, to his gratification, "Couldn't we meet? Why, of course we could. It would be a pleasure, Mr. Higson. You shall pay a call on me at my aunt's, and then show me your stables if you wish, for I love horses and your firm is famous, isn't it? I remember that trademark on vans when I was a girl about here. Well, then, goodbye for now, and we'll meet again after Easter, I hope. You can reach me at this address," and she whipped out a pocket book and wrote the address, her pencil flying over the paper in a way that made him as envious of her as he had been of John Leyden, for he found any kind of writing very laborious.

*   *   *

It was difficult to accept that a chance encounter in a remote Teviotside village could have wrought such a devastating change in his life.

She seemed, on the instant, to bring him luck, for he landed a lucrative haulage contract in Kelso that same night, and later, as the evenings began to draw out, he paid several uneventful but pleasurable social calls on Mary McKenzie and her widowed aunt, Mrs. McFie, in the latter's home in the city. Mrs. McFie had been housekeeper here when her late husband had been a coachman to a rich old bachelor. He had left her house and furniture when he died without heirs a year or so before.

He got along very well with Aunt Flora, a bustling, cheerful woman, who seemed to think of him as someone very important in the commercial life of Edinburgh, but although his admiration for Mary McKenzie's face, figure and accomplishments grew and grew, so that soon he found it difficult to give his full attention to anything else, he made little progress with her save as a source of information concerning the history of a city that he was already beginning to think of as his own.

He once called for her at her school near the Infirmary finding it daunting to watch her queening it over some three score neatly dressed children, who paid her the kind of respect accorded to royalty. In a way it removed her still further, if that was possible, from the orbit of his daily life, for he now began to regard her as a female equivalent of John Leyden, who must assuredly think of him as a gauche, coarse-grained creature, forever hanging about in the background of her well-ordered life, with nothing much to say for himself unless it was about horses.

Their relationship remained on this one-sided level until one day, out of the blue as it were, she said to him, over the ruins of a supper cooked for them by Mrs. McFie, "You're hazed about something, Jamie Higson, apart from the responsibilities you'll be called upon to face when Mr. Fraser retires. It's to do with that first conversation we had by John Leyden's obelisk, isn't it? Come now, we're friends, aren't we? If I can help I'd be glad to."

Her prescience, in being able to go directly to the heart of the matter in this way, amazed him, so that he blurted out, "You'll think me daft, no doubt, but the fact is . . . well . . . sometimes I wonder why you bother wi' me at all. Wot I mean is, you're a scholar. You mus' be, to teach in school, but me—well, I'm ignoranter than any one o' them bairns o' yours. You're right tho', it does get me down in the mouth sometimes. Oh, I c'n manage the job all right, but that ain't the point, is it? Not if a man wants to *make* something of 'imself! He's got to have book learnin' and 'ow does he go abaht gettin' it at my age?"

She said, "How old would that be, lad?" and he said, glumly, "I dunno, reely. About thirty, I reckon. I don't remember no mum or dad. I was a chimney-sweep as a nipper, straight aht o' the Guardians. That's 'ow I come be the one piece o' luck I ever 'ad."

"Tell me, Jamie."

"My mate Luke choked ter death in one o' Mrs. Swann's flues. Twenty years ago, that was, an' Mr. Swann bashed the livin' day-lights out o' that gaffer of ours, took me away from 'im, and set me to work as a vanboy, then a waggoner, then head stableman and 'ere I am. 'Ere, why am I tellin' you all this?"

She said, gently, "It's time you told somebody and I really can't see why you have to feel so humble. You've already come a long way by your own efforts."

"Ah, yes," he said, "abaht as far as I c'n 'ope to go, an' that's the rub when I meet people like you. Money don't come into it. I thought money was everythink once but it ain't. I found that out soon as I got 'ere. It's . . . it's, well, *torkin'*, knowing things, bein' able to put 'em dahn on paper. It's being able to *think* abaht things outside o' work, and readin' books, like that chap Scott wrote, besides the latest murder in the *Police Gazette*." He stood up, driven to a point of desperation by his own sense of inadequacy. "You know something else, Miss Mary? I can't even read the bits in the paper about poller-ticks, for I don't know 'arf the words. Now how could I begin to go abaht putting that straight?"

She said, smiling, "You could begin by ceasing to address me as 'Miss Mary'. Then you could get it into that head of yours that you can go just as far as you want to go, if you've got the patience. If you really want to educate yourself it's a perfectly straightforward process. You can do that by reading, once you've spent a little time on the spadework, and I could help there. Suppose you spend an hour or so at my school in the evenings. We have primers there, and a blackboard, and copybooks, and everything you need, and I'm sure I could get permission from the authorities to coach you from seven to eight, three evenings a week. They've started evening classes for adults, of course, but I don't think you would make much progress there because you're shy with people outside your business. Besides, no pupil could expect a teacher all to himself as you could have if you wished it."

Her practicability, her patent understanding of his plight elevated her to a niche in his mind almost as high as that occupied by Adam Swann. He said, fervently, "You mean you'd do that? You'd take that much trouble?"

"If it's so important to you, of course I would, Jamie."

"It'd be the most important thing that ever 'appened to me, Miss Mary."

"*Mary*," she said, and looked at him in a way she had never looked at him before, as though she was already assessing his ability as a student.

Then began for Jake Higson a sojourn in a kind of euphoric purgatory, where his senses, sharpened in one way to a degree where he became aware of all manner of irrelevant detail, were dulled in another way. For while his wits responded to the instruction he was receiving, with his long legs cramped under one of the small schoolroom desks in front of her blackboard, the rest of him was half-anaesthetised by the presence of Mary McKenzie, who moved to and fro before his ecstatic gaze and sometimes (moments that he came to anticipate as a foretaste of Paradise) stepped down from the rostrum and bent over him, correcting his exercises and addressing him as though he was not a future manager of Swann-on-Wheels but a chimney-sweep again, albeit a privileged one.

She went about the process with great practicality, dividing their three hours a week, hours when the caretaker was cleaning up after the children and attending to the stove, into six periods, four devoted to improving his word power and handwriting, the remaining two to what she called 'free periods', in which she strove to bring his knowledge of geography and history up to what she called 'Standard Six level'.

He found each period equally absorbing, imbibing the rudiments of grammar (he had not realised until then that the English language was something that could be taken apart and examined piecemeal) and labouring away at what the children called 'pot-hooks and hangers', copied from a book compiled for someone just such as he, who had the greatest difficulty in shaping letters and getting them to run together legibly, so that his scrawl began to take on a monkish aspect, uniformly sloping and, to him at least, as stylish as the writing of Tybalt, the chief clerk.

Sometimes she would hang a large, shiny map on the blackboard and take a pointer, moving about the world in a way that implied she was as familiar with, say, the upper reaches of the Congo and the foothills of the Andes, as the Royal Mile and Castle Rock. At other times she would read passages describing Wallace's struggle against King Edward, or the Young Pretender's foray in 1745, but there was a handicap here, for it meant a tedious session at his lodgings after they had parted, when he was under orders to summarise a passage of Scott's *Tales of a Grandfather*, or some other book, in what she called 'a composition'. The next time they met she would turn the pages he had written and strike out words with her blue pencil, and sometimes made a disparaging comment on the work. He made progress, however. Even he was not oblivious of that, and she was just as ready with praise, when he earned it, as with reproof concerning his spelling, or the use of a phrase borrowed from the *Police Gazette*.

All the time, however, part of him was observing irrelevancies attendant upon their sessions, some relating directly to her but others to aspects of the room in which they worked, with its rustling stove and ineradicable smell of chalk, dust, ink, paper and apple-cores, so that ever afterwards he associated the smell of school with snugness and serenity, in a way that must have been unique among those who had occupied those desks all the years the building stood there.

He had, of course, other, sharper impressions. The way the evening sun filtered through the tall, Gothic windows, lingering for a moment or two in her hair, and it astonished him sometimes that he could be aware of such things whilst bending the whole of his attention to the loop of a pothook, or Bruce's order of battle at Bannockburn, a word, incidentally, that he loved to hear her speak aloud, for it was one of the few that proclaimed her race, emerging as a long, rolling, rattle—'Bannockburrrrrrne'.

So they continued, in the role of tutor and pupil, right through the summer and autumn, never missing a single session, for he adjusted his business trips to fit into the schedule until Christmas loomed, and word arrived from Headquarters that there was to be a gathering of Swann's viceroys in London on the first day of the new year.

Ordinarily, he would have been delighted to attend his first conference (and what promised to be an important one according to the circular) as trainee gaffer of the Scottish territory, but he realised that this would mean missing at least three evenings in her company. He was only slightly comforted by the way she frowned when he announced the fact, for to him the grimace proved she took his lessons as seriously as he did.

She said, pouting, "Eight days? Ten, allowing for travelling time? Now there's a nuisance! It'll mean you missing Hogmanay, and Aunt Flora was looking forward to it so much."

"Me too," he said, "but it can't be helped. The Gaffer's keen on all of us meeting round that table once a year. He must have something special lined up or he wouldn't have risked leaving the branch without someone to keep an eye on things."

She stepped off the rostrum and stood close to him as she made a pretence of correcting his latest exercise. Her neat grey dress, or the little tartan cape about her shoulders, held the scent of lavender. He had never seen her in that high-waisted dress before, that fastened to the neck with a long row of jet buttons and a brooch shaped like an Irish harp. Probably, it had been laid away in a drawer and that explained the scent of lavender, and now that he looked closely at it he thought how smart and trim it was, emphasising the gentle swell of her breasts and the long, graceful sweep of her thighs as she half-sat on the adjoining desk looking, for once, as if she was impatient with his work. Then, laying aside the pencil, she leaned back on her hands and smiled down at him.

"It's odd," she said, "but I'd almost forgotten you worked for Swann-on-Wheels. All the time we've been here, ever since I heard you talking to yourself about John Leyden, I've thought of you as a bairn learning his lessons in front of a blackboard."

"You mean . . . as a kid? Never as someone older'n you?"

"I mean just that," she said, and there was a hint of teasing in her voice. "After all, Jamie, that's what you've been to me for nearly a year now, a boy who came here to learn how to spell and write and parse. Why, we've hardly ever talked of anything else, have we?"

"No," he said, "we've not that, but sometimes it wasn't so easy not to."

She reacted to this. "No? Well, that *is* a surprise! Tell me, Jamie, or are you too shy?"

"I dunno," he said, guardedly, "I reckon that depends on you, Mary."

"Why, Jamie?"

"Well, see here, I've put me mind to the work, you'll own to that. But I'm not a kid, am I. Why sometimes . . ." but he stopped, biting his thumb nail.

"Sometimes what, Jamie?"

"Aw, let it go."

"But I don't want to let it go. Just you say what you had in mind to say."

"Well, then . . . sometimes, wi' me down here, and you up there, moving about before that blackboard, you seemed a lot more'n a teacher and that's a fact!"

"Just what did I seem, Jamie?"

"Why, a woman, and a mighty pretty woman at that."

She did not blush or look bleak and disapproving. About half a minute ticked by, the schoolroom clock regulating the pace of his thoughts but doing nothing to regulate his heartbeats. Then she said, slowly, "Do you know that's the first compliment you've ever paid me, Jamie. And so long as you mean it, it's very welcome, tho' long overdue!"

"*If I mean it!*" He sounded outraged. It seemed inconceivable that she could have failed to detect the worship he had directed towards her all these months, that she could have mistaken all the unwavering looks he had aimed at that rostrum for dutiful attention. "Why, Gorlumme," he complained bitterly, "I sat here . . . every word you said . . . every time you moved," but, notwithstanding his lessons in word power, he had no phrase that was adequate to this occasion and fell back on instinct, catching up the hand nearest to him and crushing it against his lips and holding it there for what seemed to him a long time before he realised what she would take such a gesture to mean, whereupon he dropped it like a hot coal and stood up, looking, she thought, like a bull calf awaiting

336

the slaughterer. "I'm sorry," he growled, at length, "that's spoiled things for us, 'asn't it?"

It was her turn to be amazed. "*Spoiled* things? The Lord give me patience, why should it? Why would it alter things in any way, except for the better? Do you imagine I haven't been hoping and praying you'd do something like that for months and months, instead of just . . . just *sitting* in that silly little desk, with your tongue peeping out as you copied those dreadful pothooks into your books? I told you once to stop being humble and you heeded it so far as your work went. But in all other ways—why, you think less of yourself than the day I met you, and for the life of me I've never known what to do about it, without seeming forward! Well, that's done with, thank goodness, for now I don't care a hoot how forward you think I am. I love you, Jamie, and I've been waiting and waiting for you to tell me you loved me. And now you have, or *I* think you have, at least enough to get things moving. So here's how I feel about it and if I'm wrong I don't care if you run out of here and never come back!"

She jumped off the desk and threw her arms about his neck, showering his face with kisses and finally, having tugged him round so that they were face to face, finding his mouth, and straining herself to him so that he had to brace himself against the angle of the desk lid. Having done this, however, he was able, to some extent to lift her clear of the dusty floor and crush her in an embrace that drove the breath from her body, so that neither of them saw the grey head of the caretaker through the half-open door, or his grin as he bobbed out of sight and rattled a warning with his dustpan and brush. At the sound they leaped apart but when they heard his shuffling steps moving into the adjoining classroom, he said, breathlessly, "I never dreamed anything like this could 'appen, never once! I thought . . . I bin thinking . . . well, put yourself in my place, Mary. You're educated, and a parson's daughter inter the bargain. A girl like you could hook just about anyone, anyone at all . . ."

"I don't want anyone. I want you, Jamie Higson."

"Then by God, you got me," he said, fervently, "and we'll marry soon as you give the word. And what's more I'll tell the Gaffer to make my managership final and let Fraser go. How soon could we get married? I don't mean the daft way some of 'em do up here, plighting their troth an' what not, but properly married. In your Dad's church. Wi' bridesmaids and hymns and all the trimmings?"

And at that she laughed and said, "Oh, Jamie, Jamie, you are a bairn in spite of it all. But I wouldn't have you a whit different, and as to us getting married, 'with all the trimmings' as you say, that *will* take a little time. I shall have to discuss it with Aunt Flora tonight, or perhaps you could, after supper, for I'm sure she'll be surprised as I am! Now strap your books and kiss me again and we'll talk about dates on the way home. April, perhaps. Why not the first Saturday in April?"

"I can't wait that long," he said. "Just you and Aunt Flora hustle it up and make it early in the new year. My birthday—the one the Guardians give me that is—is the 29th o' January and I can't think of a present I'd like more. Will that be too soon?"

"Not a minute too soon," she said, gaily. "I wish it could be tonight!"

And then, to the surprise of both of them, a sudden shyness took possession of them, and they avoided one another's eyes as they pottered about rolling up the map of the world, and packing his books away, but afterwards, when they stepped out into the frosty night, turning their backs on the great bulk of the Castle to cut through narrow streets to George Square, the wonder of the occasion demanded some physical expression and they slowed down and walked with arms about one another's waists and Jake, transmogrified not merely as a man but also as an honorary Scotsman, had the feeling that he not only owned Edinburgh but was on his way to claim it.

5

Through the Floodgates

EDITH WICKSTEAD—'Edith-Wadsworth-that-was' as she was still thought of in the network—derived considerable amusement from these occasions.

As one woman among so many men she could sit back and watch them ride their hobby-horses into the ground, for she no longer had a region to defend and only bothered to attend a conference in case Tom, a very amiable man, allowed himself to be put upon by the more aggressive of Swann's viceroys.

She always saw them, in her mind's eye, as an assembly of privateer captains, reporting to the Admiral-in-Chief and hoping to gather praise or evade blame for personal triumphs or errors of judgement over the past twelve months. As for Adam, he fitted the role exactly and over the last few years had even begun to look like a pirate, with his narrow, dark-browed face, mahogany tan, and that way of sitting with his artificial leg extended as he listened, without seeming to listen, to their interminable wrangles and debates, to their judgements, extenuations and excuses, almost as though his handicap was the result of a broadside in some half-forgotten venture of his splendid, predatory youth.

The fancy returned to her now as they sat grouped around the long trestle table, puffing vigorously at their pipes and cigars, until the atmosphere of the warehouse smelled like a taproom and an ill-favoured taproom at that. Privateers, the whole damned lot of them! Owing no loyalty to anyone save to themselves and to him, each concerned with his own private venture and profits that would result from it, spilling from his pockets to theirs.

She had known most of them for a quarter of a century now and a few, she told herself, were past their prime, but Adam never pressed for retirement so long as a manager was up to his work, like that little cider-apple of a man, Hamlet Ratcliffe of the Western Wedge, still living on credit reaped from two incidents early in his Swann career, the recapture of a circus lion and his initiation of the now famous holiday-brake service that operated throughout the midland and southern regions but had never caught on in the northern sectors of the Swann Empire.

Then there was Catesby, reinstated as manager of the Polygon after a brief spell as gaffer of Sam Rawlinson's cotton mill. She always thought of him as Caius Cassius, of the lean and hungry look, and the temperamental affinity between him and Adam accounted, she supposed, for the success of their partnership. Both were idealists, although their idealism was no more than a kind of furious obstinacy and dedication to a job of work. Catesby was now an important man in his own right, having been a founder of the Trades Union Congress in days when it was regarded by most employers as a nest of Jacobins, plotting bloody revolution. Never by Swann, however, who had always held eccentric views in the field of capital-versus-labour and was rumoured by some to have encouraged John Catesby in his efforts to form a trades alliance strong enough to strike bargains with bosses.

There were others round the table who had little in common with bumpkins like Ratcliffe and fanatics like Catesby, or nothing beyond a steady devotion to the firm, and she remembered Adam had once commented on this, saying that a Swann-on-Wheels conference was as good a cross-section of England and Englishmen as one would be likely to find anywhere on earth, even in a regiment. It was true, too, as she could judge for herself, letting her glance move down both sides of the table and half-listening to the free-for-all that invariably attended these occasions.

There was the patrician Godsall, known among them as 'The Grandee', who had once held the Queen's commission but now ruled in the Kentish Triangle; the dapper Morris, from Southern Pickings, shrewd enough to have made a fortune on his own account but who had clung to Swann's coat-tails ever since the two had met by chance at a Worcestershire inn. There was the Welshman, Lovell, who always sounded as if he was preaching a sermon when submitting views on insurance rates, or the useful life-span of a Clydesdale pulling a frigate or a man-o'-war. There was the shock-headed Dockett, of Tom Tiddler's Ground, another Swann original, who had been the first to speak at the first conference held in this room twenty years ago, proposing the introduction of box-waggons for house-removals, and later that saucy slogan painted on each of them—*From Drawer to Drawer*, a boast, she recalled, that had irritated the clerk Tybalt, who disapproved of all forms of commercial levity.

Keate, the missionary-waggoner, was still in his place, urging the claims of one or other of his waifs, who passed through the yard in an endless stream and were represented here by the primfaced Rookwood, of Southern Square, and that new broom Higson, who had made, so they told her, a very promising start up in Scotland under Fraser, formerly of the Border Triangle.

In a way she shared his regard for every one of them and why not, since she was married to the best of them, Tom Wickstead, who did not shine at conferences.

The line of talk they were taking surprised her today. They were planning, with the collective enthusiasm of a gang of schoolboys about to swoop on an orchard, a breakout from the accepted policy of the network up to this time, and she wondered who had set it in train. Not Adam, she was sure, for he had grown conservative over the years and inclined to shy away from innovations, of the kind they were now discussing. Perhaps that thrustful youngster, Jake Higson, or perhaps Dockett, who had always been something of a maverick. Or possibly Morris, or the ambitious Godsall, or even Young Rookwood, who had once confounded them all by digesting a large slice of England when he still grew down on his upper lip.

Rookwood's spectacular spurt, she remembered, had been encouraged by early marriage, and the responsibilities of fatherhood, and her mind shifted a little, contemplating the effect their several womenfolk had had upon the careers of these men. A considerable one she would say, taken all round. Hamlet Ratcliffe had been rescued time and again by his great, motherly spouse, Augusta, whereas Bryn Lovell had moved from triumph to triumph after marrying that half-caste woman, and saddling himself with her brood of coffee-coloured children. Godsall, she knew, was well-married to a handsome, happy-go-lucky woman, whereas Morris, to buttress an independence he had always flaunted, had married money years ago. And on top of this was the part she had played in

341

the making of Tom Wickstead, who had graduated, under her tutelage, from professional thief to third place on the managerial graph that Adam kept locked away in his tower.

It was a matter of making some kind of pattern of one's life, she supposed, and Adam himself had done that by marrying Henrietta Rawlinson a month or two before he recruited this colourful army. It was strange, in view of that, that he should have fathered five sons and still wanted for one to follow him. Then, having caught the word 'diversify', uttered in ringing tones by Godsall, she began to pay closer attention to what they were discussing and the theme of the conference began to emerge, with the usual factions lining up beside one another, the 'Diehards', like Fraser, Ratcliffe and Vicary of The Bonus, and the 'Thrusters', represented by Morris, Rookwood, Godsall and the Irishman O'Dowd.

It took her no more than a moment to realise that the day would go to the venturesome. She could read as much in the tolerant eye of Adam Swann, as he sat rolling a cheroot round his lips at the head of the table, and she thought, smiling, "They've won him over, that's for sure! There'll be a right about turn before we're through today's agenda . . ." And she understood precisely how eager all of them were to play the parts she had sketched for them—privateers, each with a proud ship of his own and an individual way of sniffing out a prize and boarding her.

A verse or two of Longfellow came to mind, illustrating the thought, a poem entitled *A Dutch Picture* concerning an old corsair called Simon Danz, who had retired from piracy to live a bourgeois life by the river Maas but had thought better of it. How did it go . . . ?

> . . . but when the winter rains come on
> He sits and smokes by the burning brands,
> And old seafaring men come in,
> Goat-bearded, gray, with double chin,
> And rings upon their hands . . .
>
> And they talk of ventures lost and won,
> And their talk is ever and ever the same,
> While they drink the red wine of Tarragon

From the cellar of some Spanish don,
Or convent set to flame . . .

That was it exactly! A score of ageing men, with a few younger ones eager to take their places, made permanently restless by success and prosperity, so that they came here to sit under a Thameside Simon Danz and plan ventures that would make them feel young again. He should hear about that when the time came, and it would probably flatter him. In the meantime, however, she owed it to Tom to listen, for wherever these new ventures led one thing was certain. Her Tom would be involved in them and so, God willing, would her sons, both earmarked for the Swann network.

2

There was a rhythm to Swann-on-Wheels, a rhythm and tempo that insinuated itself subtly and secretively as a theme that was not of his making, nor of the making of any one individual, or grouping of individuals, but stemming, in some way, from the rhythm of the tribe as a whole as it went briskly about the business of building the new Rome in the long afterglow of Waterloo.

He was aware of the inner rhythm but had no power to regulate it. It was governed by all manner of quirks and circumstances that arose out of his personal life and the lives of his associates, so that he was sometimes slow to isolate it and adjust to it. Once he did, however, he adapted swiftly, letting himself be caught up in the swirl of the concert, telling himself that it had been and still was his destiny to conduct the orchestra, to get it firmly under his hand, and encourage it to make its contribution to the deafening cacophony of the tribe at large. Once he had succeeded in doing this he was in his element. Once that happened he would not have been anywhere else but here, wielding a baton of his own choice and design.

It was always easy, looking back, to isolate the phases of the saga, beginning with the faltering overture of the years 1858–1862, when they had been no more than a bunch of amateur fumblers, with little but his faith to sustain them, and this was followed by a flattish patch when they had been occupied getting their second wind and groping for national recognition. But then something went wrong. By the autumn of that same year they were floundering, and in such awful disarray that it seemed to every one of them, to Adam Swann most of all, that the entire enterprise had been an exercise in personal vanity and was likely to take its place among all the other failures in Carey Street, that national repository of failed challengers of the century.

That this did not happen was due to a string of factors, including luck, a small injection of capital and legal expertise from an unexpected source, the personal reputation he had established among customers and creditors but, above all, to his obstinate belief in his own qualities of leadership, that had been proved beyond all doubt at that first managerial conference, a week or two before Christmas, 1862.

It was then, within hours of his putting Danton's audacious dictum into practice, that the rhythm and tempo had changed and changed very dramatically. By St. Valentine's Day, 1863, the day his second son George was born, they were forging ahead under a full head of steam, set fair for permanence and stability and imprinting themselves, week by week, on the national consciousness. The year 1864, and the first six months of 1865 had been a perfectly splendid period, with expansion in every quarter of the network, and more work than they could handle but then, because of a trivial error on the part of a foreman ganger on a fast stretch of rail between Ashford and Tonbridge, the entire enterprise had been brought to the brink of disaster and would almost surely have collapsed had it not been for the foresight of one woman, Edith Wadsworth, and the hardihood of another, Henrietta Swann, both of whom loved him for his courage.

There had been a break in the tempo then and the rhythm had faltered but it picked up again and was more insistent than ever when he returned, healed of his terrible wounds. After that, through the remainder of the 'sixties and the whole of the 'seventies, the beat had been strong and steady, with the whole island under his hand, and lodgements made as far north as the Grampians, as far west as the Dublin Pale.

But then a curious thing happened, something that those who

knew him well could never have predicted. A stale and repetitious theme began to emerge that first baffled and then exasperated the more discerning instrumentalists.

No one could put his or her finger on the precise cause of the loss of momentum. They only sensed that it stemmed from staleness and self-sufficiency, from too much assurance based on too many customers, from too big a turnover and too solid a reputation. All they could be sure of was that zest and crackle had deserted it, that from being a nonstop adventure, it had become just another solidly-grounded business, rolling cumbrously from quarter-day to quarter-day, sticking closely to a charted course and distrusting diversions, even those that did not classify as innovations but were no more than adjustments to the faster, more clamorous beat of the nation.

They told themselves and each other that the Gaffer was feeling his age, that he had too much money, that his old wounds were beginning to ache and sap his patience, that the disclination of any one of his sons to take the baton from his hand had, to some extent, robbed him of his initiative and would end in his putting on a paunch and spending more and more of his time in that place he maintained on the edge of the Weald. At sixty, they said, he would be growing prize turnips and patronising local charities like all the other city men who had made their mark before reaching middle age.

They were wrong, of course. Adam Swann was not cast in that mould, and in their hearts those whose associations with him went back to the earliest days knew it. But it did not check the swell of discontent in the regions, or close the widening gap between the Diehards and the Thrusters, the men older than Swann, and those who were younger or of the new generation.

He knew what they were saying, of course. It did not need an overheard conversation between two of his younger pashas, to the effect that 'the Gaffer's arteries were hardening', to tell him what some of them were thinking or what the more ambitious among them were talking about. He knew, and in the privacy of his turret would sometimes grin at Frankenstein, assuring that silent monster that he had still a trick or two up his sleeve. But it needed thinking about. It needed more thought than he had ever given any problem, for what he had in mind amounted to abdication and with his sons scattered, and the problem of succession still confused, he needed time to weigh one factor against another before arriving at a decision from which there could be no turning back.

There came a time, however, as the annual conference date approached in the weeks leading up to the twenty-fifth anniversary of the enterprise, when he had done his thinking, and was about the task of translating conjecture into project, sometimes spending entire nights at work in his eyrie, so that the watchmen, seeing a light at the Gothic window at four and five in the morning, were troubled, reasoning that only senility would induce a man with a wife, a comfortable country home, and credit at the bank, to work an eighteen hour stint in a tower overlooking a slum.

Before the first day of the assembly, however, he was ready for them. Checking and cross-checking were done, and concentrated in the form of a few pages of notes. All that remained now was to decide on the manner it would be put to them and that was a decision that provided him with a good deal of amusement. For, sharp as most of them were, they were not so sharp as he, and it would be a source of enormous satisfaction to demonstrate this once he had them all under his eye at the long trestle table set up in the warehouse where conferences were held.

*   *   *

He watched them gather from his unique vantage point, looking directly down on the yard, observing how they tended to coalesce into threesomes and foursomes, exchanging chaff, no doubt, but already sounding one another out on the agenda. It seemed to him then that he had been alone up here a long time, an ageing god on a mountain peak, surveying his handiwork and no more than moderately pleased with it. This year's conference was a crossroad. It could lead onward, across a limitless stretch of serene, untroubled country, or shoot off at a tangent into a future as strange and fearsome as they had faced when he called the first managerial conference twenty years ago and told them that they were facing bankruptcy and must sink or swim in convoy.

To diversify or to vegetate? To dig in, husband accumulated capital and let the enterprise coast along under its considerable momentum? Or to recast the entire structure of the network, dislodging it from its essentially provincial socket and letting it find its own level among the gigantic enterprises on which it had fed and fattened all these years?

Well, he had made his decision, the most difficult and complex of a lifetime, and now it would be up to them and he wondered what they would make of it and whether they had the wit, the hardihood and the nerve to play chuck-farthing with their money instead of his and discover, painfully for sure, that it was one thing to chivvy a man who had made the decisions but another to formulate a policy, disperse to their beats, and put that policy to work.

So many suggestions and so much advice. So many whys and why-nots. So much couldn't-we and why-can't-we. But in the end it all blew through that little Gothic door in the form of pieces of paper and settled on his desk. And after all the clamour came silence, awaiting *his* gamble, *his* directive. Over the years most of them had called him reckless. Now a majority was beginning to think him stodgy, as if he hadn't always known of the enormous potential that awaited them out there, providing they were spry enough to make the leap and wager, as he had always been ready to wager, on the destiny of the tribe to which all of them belonged.

For this, in essence, was how he had always seen it since the country had turned its back on its past and reached out across the world for bigger and better markets. In a contest of this kind, with one generation leap-frogging the other, there could be no individual destinies. Cohesion was what really counted and the nub of the problem was this; would the British hold on to their lead and if so for how long? In the answer to that lay the answer to everything, notwithstanding the pow-wow that would ensue at this conference or at any other conference. Did *they* know that? And if they didn't would they understand it when he spelled it out for them? For if they didn't then it was back on course for every man-jack of them, with no more whining importunities to expand, to innovate, to diversify! He was done with leading from centre, with younger men, the Godsalls and Rookwoods, tugging him forward, and older ones, the Ratcliffes and Lovells, dragging their feet and muttering that enough was enough.

* * *

They heard his preamble in silence, an uncomfortable silence, he would say, for on all previous occasions he had opened with generalities, spiced with a few jokes, a few grudging compliments, an ironic comment or two concerning the shortcomings of the government or the weather.

Today he was unequivocal. He said, in effect, that this year all customary procedures would be waived, that the ball was now at their feet, to kick or let lie, and that when every one had said what he had to say he had a single proposal to put to them and that this would do duty for the summing-up, of the kind usually made by Tybalt in the last hour of assembly.

It was interesting, he thought, to watch their reactions to that. In a curious way they seemed to draw closer together, as for mutual support, as though he was threatening them instead of liberating them from the restraints of protocol. It reminded him sharply of a grey December day twenty years ago, when he had done the same thing from the standpoint of a suppliant and seen them falter and then rally on him. Would the same thing happen again? He sat down, relit his cheroot and waited, already laying bets with himself as to who would be the first to speak.

He lost his wager. The Thrusters, Godsall, Young Rookwood, held their fire, making room for a comparatively trivial issue, as Markby, of Crescent North, aired his annual demand for 'ice-boxes', a term that had already passed into network slang to define waggons fitted with refrigerated crates for inland fish haulage. Markby put his case well, Adam thought, particularly as the Crescents were now under the overall command of Tom Wickstead, based on Peterborough.

Markby wanted ice-boxes and Markby meant to have them. Fish, he declared, constituted his bread-and-butter runs, and no one who had ever operated in Crescent North had solved the problem of converting a standard pinnace or frigate into a vehicle capable of making a scheduled delivery to inland markets. He was sorry to harp on this point. He knew it was of small concern to anyone here but himself. But nothing had been done to implement a request made around this table last year and the year before that. That was why he had come prepared. That was why he had gone to the trouble of providing his own design for the kind of vehicle he had in mind.

He produced his plan with a conjuror's flourish and passed it the length of the table until it stopped short at Tybalt and would have foundered there for Tybalt, having glanced at the estimated cost of a prototype, cried out as though stung by a wasp. Adam leaned forward and took the sketch, saying, mildly, "Markby seems to have got the general idea but accidentally. This is what I want and this is what I'm looking for this year. *Your* grudges. *Your* remedies. *Your* ideas. Not mine, or Keate's or Tybalt's, but *yours*, however revolutionary. Think of it this way if you like. For years now suggestions like Markby's have been reaching Headquarters through the post, but now, as you'll see, these decisions must be taken collectively." He addressed the flustered Markby directly, "It's a good design, Markby. I'll vote for it for one. Who's next, gentlemen?"

It was the phrase 'vote for it' that rattled them. Already, as he glanced the length of the table, he could see the sharper minds sheering out of line, as if anxious to commune with themselves. What did the Gaffer mean, exactly? He would vote for it! It wasn't his business to 'vote' for anything. He listened and decided. That was how it had always been in the past and if something fresh was afoot, some startling deviation from protocol, why the devil did he keep hinting instead of getting up on his wooden leg and spitting it out like a man?

Rookwood was on his feet now, asking this question outright. Not bluntly, as Godsall or Fraser might have done, but deviously, in the manner acquired, no doubt, among the city fathers of Salisbury, of which he was said to be one.

"On a point of order, sir . . . Wouldn't it help if the air was cleared at the outset . . . ? If the chairman has a proposition that is to govern all other propositions . . ." and so on, until Adam cut him short, harshly but unrepentantly, for Rookwood had touched on the very heart of the problem. His proposition did indeed govern all other propositions, but what validity would those decisions have if every man present could walk out of here his own master, providing he had sufficient nerve?

He said, gruffly, "I rule from the chair, Rookwood. At this stage we're concerned with regions and regions only. I tried hard to make that clear. Follow Markby if you like, but stay on his line. Keep to the particular, not the general."

Rookwood sat down, glowering, and Lawyer Stock took the cue, coming to everyone's rescue and not before time, Adam thought.

"I think I can help," he began, mildly, "and with the Chairman's permission I will. Do I have that permission, sir?"

"You do indeed," said Adam. "It seems I've lost the knack of expressing myself clearly."

"Very good," said Stock, as if this admission merited general congratulation. "Then, here it is, and there's no call for anyone to get ruffled over it. Mr. Swann's intention is that everyone here should speak his mind on the future of the firm *as he sees it within his area.* Not as you imagine Mr. Swann sees it, but as *you* see it. In terms of expansion, innovation and capital investment. Why put the cart before the horse in that way? Gentlemen, I confess I don't know why, for Mr. Swann hasn't taken me into his confidence. It was he who drew up the terms of reference for this year's conference, so we can assume he knows what he's about. Speak your mind, all of you, and let us get it down on paper. Then, I imagine, Mr. Swann will take it from there. Is that what you had in mind, sir?"

"Precisely," said Adam, with a curt nod and at that Stock sat down and Godsall, Rookwood and Morris rose in unison, each hoping to catch the Chairman's eye.

"One at a time, gentlemen," Adam said. "I'll take you, Godsall."

It was a lucky choice. Godsall, a volatile man but a forceful speaker, had advantages over every other manager in the network, a first-class education and a term at University before joining the army. In a few crisp sentences he set the tone of the conference and did a good deal more than Stock to clear the air.

"As to the particular—my patch—I'll come to that in sixty seconds. I crave that much grace from the chair. Do I get it, sir?" And when Adam nodded, "Here, then, as I see it, is what we want to decide once and for all at this year's conference. Do we diversify or don't we? Do we stand still, when every other concern about us is moving forward, or do we make a clean breakthrough into fields we've been too timid or too muddle-headed to prospect and exploit these ten years or more? I don't have to tell you where I stand in that respect. My views on diversification were laid on the table last year, and the year before that, and since, praise God, I've made converts around this table. But it won't do, to my mind, to make the advances I have in mind in odd sectors up and down the network. If we advance at all we must do it on a broad, united front and there's an end to it!"

From his seat at the end of the long table Adam could sense a clear-cut division in the nods of Godsall's allies and the grunts of Hamlet Ratcliffe and Tybalt, the latter already wearing his 'don't-ask-me-for-money' look.

Godsall went straight on to restate his policy of buying up defunct public transport companies, of moving out into the short-haul passenger field to gather in the pennies and twopences that were there for the taking if Swann-on-Wheels showed the enterprise of earlier sorties into the world of wheels. He spoke for forty-five minutes and when he sat down, amidst a scatter of applause from his allies, Adam thought, "By God, if I was out looking for a successor there he is. Nobody here, least of all me, could convince him he'll bite off more than he can chew at that counter! The omnibus field is already strewn with bankruptcies . . ."

But then Morris was on his feet, pressing home the attack, and after Morris, Rookwood, and after Rookwood, Jake Higson, who was not even qualified to speak as an independent manager, although it was clear he had Fraser's backing, so that Adam thought, "I would have wagered a pound to a penny Fraser would stand with the Diehards . . . Time was when all the man craved was to go back to peddling from his cart . . ." But then he reflected that that was twenty years ago, before Fraser had stormed into the Lowlands and captured Edinburgh. Success changed a man. Sometimes it made him canny and cautious but occasionally, as in Fraser's case, it made him reckless, and he wondered at the source of the accord between his Scottish viceroys, one in his early sixties, the other thirty years his junior . . .

That was Monday, the first day of the conference, and the talk continued through two long sessions, with a break for beer and hot meat pies at the George, where Adam went out of his way to avoid becoming embroiled in conversation with any one of them.

Tuesday was Tom Wickstead's day and Tom emerged as a progressive who had thought his theories through in a way that made some kind of appeal to men who opposed all change except changes proposed by themselves.

Like Markby of the Crescents, Wickstead was pleading for special purpose vehicles, this time for cattle transport. It was not only inconvenient to adapt men-o'-war and frigates for moving cows, horses, pigs and sheep over limited distances but wasteful of time, money and materials. A small fleet of waggons, specially built for this traffic, could be made to pay for itself in a single season in an agricultural region. And how many of Swann's regions did not look to farmers for their bread and salt the whole year round?

Wickstead's proposals interested Adam but not so much, perhaps, as the look in Edith's face while her husband was putting his case. Towards the end of Tom's speech he found his attention wandering a little as he reflected on the relationship between two people he numbered as friends as well as employees. Working partnerships between a man and woman had always intrigued him but none more so than that of Edith Wadsworth and Tom Wickstead, sometime highwayman and footpad. He wondered, as he watched her, what had touched it off and then he knew. It was Wickstead's animal magnetism and Edith's desperate physical hunger at the time, for she had never, as he well knew, resigned herself to spinsterhood. He thought, with an inward chuckle, "By George, I was lucky as well as Wickstead when she made her grab. If he had let her down, and it had come to a straight choice between the network and Tom Wickstead's neck I know damned well what would have happened to my interests! Once he had got her to bed she would have held up a train for him . . . !"

*   *   *

Wednesday, and the ding-dong battle continued. Markby and Wickstead won majorities on their proposals and Godsall, with more difficulty, forced through a pilot scheme for a short-haul passenger service. The network already sported men-o'-war, frigates, pinnaces, box-waggons and holiday brakes. Now they were lumbered with ice-boxes and cattle-transport vans for which Wickstead had already coined a slang phrase, 'four-footers'. Nor was that all. On Thursday Catesby declared himself for diversification, proposing, and getting accepted, a six-horse dray with a central shaft as thick as a cottage beam designed for transporting heavy machinery in the Polygon where, he declared, railway companies were still short-changing one another to the profit of the road haulier. No Swann waggon could take the road without a slang christening. By the time the lunch break was announced they were already referring to Catesby's six-horse drays as 'Goliaths'.

By then it was time for the Diehards' counter-attack but when it came it was little more than a disgruntled sally. A spirit of resurgent optimism had invaded the warehouse and only a rump of veterans were prepared to advocate a policy of letting well alone. Hamlet Ratcliffe was one of them and brought a welcome whiff of humour into proceedings when he declared, in his buzz-saw brogue, that most of the previous speakers were 'bliddy well mazed'. Undaunted by the roar of laughter this produced he went on to state as his opinion that "they talked as though the Gaffer had vallen arse over tip into a goldmine". The summing up was received with renewed laughter but Tybalt tut-tutted, partly because he was one of the few present who agreed with Hamlet but also, Adam suspected, because he disapproved of that kind of talk in front of a lady. He need not have bothered. Edith, catching Adam's eye, chirped up, "Don't mind me! I once drove waggons and I'm well used to it," and everybody laughed, even the solemn Keate, who had maintained a basilisk expression throughout the four-day discussion.

Vicary of The Bonus, reckoned the laziest of the managers, and Bryn Lovell, of Mountain Square, had their say in support of Ratcliffe. Vicary took a restrained line, saying the network was doing well enough without meddling in passenger transport, but Lovell was more emphatic. "Down on my patch," he muttered, "folk are used to walking to and from work on the feet God gave 'em. I see no call to meddle with omnibuses, when we've a good living out o' freight haulage these twenty years. As for this avalanche of special purpose vehicles, what are the carpenters for? We've been hauling high-grade china in waggons my men adapted inside twenty-four hours once I sketched out what was needed in the way o' racks and springing!"

It was getting dusk then and Adam suggested putting off his own statement until Friday, the final day of the conference, but at this there was a growl of protest and Stock said, spiritedly, "Take a vote,

Mr. Chairman: Do we prolong this session until dinner-time, or do we adjourn until tomorrow and try and cram everything into the final day?" Adam took the vote. Unanimously the conference decided to sit.

3

He was slow getting to his feet. For four days now he had sat with his gammy leg thrust alongside the centreboard of the table, where it got some protection from the draught from the warehouse double doors. The twinge in his stump caused him to curse under his breath but for all that he was glad he had held his peace until now, for there was not a man among them who had not, to a greater or lesser degree, committed himself.

He gave them a minute or two to relight their pipes, clear their throats, and generally settle down. He had then a sense of crossing a threshold that was as final and unconditional as that he had crossed twice before in their presence, once when he sent out his first waggons in the autumn of 'fifty-eight, and again, five years later, when he had thrown himself on their mercy after Josh Avery had squandered all his reserve capital on a Spanish whore.

He said, grimly, "I'll not keep you here until dinner-time. What I've got to say won't take long, although its repercussions may keep you at it for the rest of your lives. Here it is then, short and sweet. I've sat here four days listening to talk of expansion and diversification, with precious little said for sitting tight and playing safe, as I admit to doing these ten years or more, but let me get one thing clear. Broadly speaking, I'm with you, individually that is, but I'll add something to that. I've never been in a position to think and act individually, or not since the very earliest days, when neither you nor I had anything much to lose. Since then, by God, I've had to think and act for you all, especially those among you with families, and I've had that in mind all the time, even when some of you sitting round this table thought me a reckless idiot. A man in my position, starting from scratch, was dependent on the goodwill and loyalty of every one of you, and I've had both in generous measure. Times

354

change, however, and not one of us among the originals is the man
we were, when we set out, and whilst, as I say, I'm in agreement
with the most enterprising speaker who has had his say, I'm man
enough to tell you to your faces I'd sooner step down or sell up before I shouldered that kind of responsibility at my age. Risks of that
kind are for the young, gentlemen, but they can be faced and accepted by someone my age providing they're shared. For twenty-five
years now I've taken all the big decisions, and left you to make what
you can of them, and in the main we've had a smooth passage. But
I'm not here to harp on the past, so put it this way: we'll take a crack
at everyone of the projects aired here since Monday but we'll do it
in partnership if we do it at all, and by partnership I mean full and
equal partnership, as directors of a limited company, with every one
of you who cares to come in backing himself with his own stake, up
to the limit he can afford. A minimum of, say, five hundred apiece."

He had a fleeting impression of shock moving from face to face
like a travelling beam of light. There was no audible reaction, dis-
counting Tybalt's wheeze and Catesby's muttered oath heard from
the far end of the table but the shock was present in their several
expressions and in their silence, so after a brief pause he went on,
"There'll be conditions, of course, although not so many of them.
I'm no great shakes at finance and never was, as Tybalt will tell you,
but I've worked out a draft scheme for Stock's approval, and when
he's studied it, and given you advice and guidance if you want it,
then we'll convene an emergency conference, not in four months'
time but in four weeks or less. I'll hold on to fifty-one per cent of the
stock until we settle down. After that, dependent upon how my
family view it, I'll throw more into the pool, with a proviso that may
sound stupid to some of you but strikes me as being the only way to
maintain the policy we've held fast to until this moment—equity
among all managers in the eyes of H.O., irrespective of the size of
their territory or length of service. That means that no one of you
will have the edge over another for that, as I see it, would be the way
to ruin. One man one vote, as they say, whether he has a small stake
or a big one, up to a limit that could be adjusted year by year. And
instead of a conference each December we'll have board meetings
once a quarter. And one other thing, as vital as anything I've said
so far. No one will be penalised for not coming in. A manager who

stays out is still a manager, up to the moment of retirement. That's about it, then. There'll be questions, I daresay, and it's up to you whether we have them now, with a clear day ahead of us to sort out detail, or save them until tomorrow." And he sat down, just a shade embarrassed, but conscious none the less of having said all he had meant to say in far less time than he had anticipated.

Catesby's voice emerged from the continuous buzz as Adam's gammy leg again sought the limited protection of the centreboard. Catesby, his fanatical eyes softened by an almost missionary gleam as he said, in a voice pitched above his usual gravelly key. "Before questions . . . Before *anything*! . . . There's something called for now and I'm calling it! Three cheers for the Gaffer, and let 'em hear you in Rotherhithe!" and then, to be sure, Adam Swann was deeply embarrassed, more embarrassed than he had ever been in his life and flushed, lifting a protesting hand but it failed to stay them. By then they were all out of their seats and clustering round him, and there could be no question of himself or Stock or Tybalt or anyone else calling the conference to order and resuming discussion, for somehow, without knowing it, he had touched a common chord in everyone round that table and the spontaneity of their goodwill was something that moved him as he had never been moved in his public or private life. At last, above the general uproar, Tybalt managed to make himself heard, and convened the final sitting for ten o'clock the next morning. After that, in a convoy of cabs and waggonettes, they repaired in a body to the George where, in the hour before dinner, they swam in a tide of ale and even Keate and Tybalt, sworn teetotallers both, broke the rules of a lifetime by drinking the Gaffer's health in brown sherry.

4

It was late on the last day of conference before he addressed them again. By then a framework for the co-operative had been hammered out by Stock and given the finishing touches by Tybalt, so that they had something to work upon for their next general meeting, scheduled for the last week of January. All twenty of them took advantage of his offer, the better off among them buying in to the limit, the two sub-managers present, Markby, of Crescent North, and Jake Higson, who would soon be a manager in his own right, buying themselves a token stake. The less ambitious projects, Markby's ice-boxes and Tom Wickstead's four-footers were approved, Tybalt undertaking to make a careful survey of all the data sent to him in the next six months concerning the possible purchase of public transport concerns in four of the territories, none of them likely to be expensive at this stage, for each involved no more than two or three vehicles. Notwithstanding this, however, expansion and diversification on this scale promised to absorb a great deal more money than the new capital subscribed and Tybalt, making a hasty cast, estimated it would need upwards of ten thousand pounds to get a footing in public transport, commission the building of a fleet of special purpose waggons and provide the teams to pull them, especially if they went ahead with Catesby's project to compete with the railways for heavy haulage in the cotton belt.

Towards evening, when the gas had been lit in the reeking warehouse, Adam summed up and his talk took an unexpected turn, surprising most of them by its note of caution.

He had had time then to adjust to his new role as leader of a team rather than a one man band and found that the changed situation gave him a freedom previously denied him. He spoke of wider aspects of the haulage trade, and its relation to the economics of a trading nation, projecting himself into the next decade in a way that left the more slow-witted baffled. They could not see how industrial competitors across the Channel and the Atlantic could concern them, although they were impressed by his grasp of affairs when he expressed doubts concerning Britain's ability to hold on to the clear commercial lead she had enjoyed throughout the lifetime of every man present.

He said, as a kind of valediction, "Well, now, since you're all in it up to your necks I can say what has been in my mind for some time. From here on, to my way of thinking, pickings won't be what they were in the past and nothing like so easily come by. I shouldn't have to harp on our dependence on national prosperity. Catesby can tell you what happens in a region when there's a local blight, as there was in the Polygon through the war in the States when the cotton stopped arriving in Liverpool. It could happen again on a larger scale this time. We've grown up, every man jack of us, having it all our own way, with Britain carrying three parts of the world's trade, and having a clear lead over every industrial nation, but the gap is narrowing every week and that's why I'm in favour of diversification and more reliance on the home market. Years after we began here, back in 'fifty-eight, Germany was a hotchpotch of petty states, mostly agricultural. Now she's a full nation, with more up-to-date notions of what's demanded of an industrialised society than Britain, and a damned sight more energy judging by the letters my boy sends me. France and Italy are in the running too, and across the Atlantic the Yankees have only just begun to realise their potential. In ten years, in five maybe, we'll all be squabbling for markets, and it won't do for any one of us to go on living off our own fat, the way most big concerns have over the last twenty years. Don't be deceived by all the yammering you've heard about the Empire. I was once, and I'll own to it, but not any longer. In the years up to the turn of the century and probably beyond it, the Empire is likely to cost us a damned sight more than it earns. Right here is where the real money is minted and don't ever forget it. For the rest, it's a matter of building on the reputation we already have and don't doubt that we can do it, and give our competitors, including the railways, a good run for their money, but it can't be done without improving on the teamwork of the past. The first thing we've got to heave overboard is parochialism. From now on you don't haul to suit me and Headquarters but each other, particularly where territories adjoin one another. And keep in mind your pockets are concerned as much as mine in every decision you make. I'll add a tailpiece to that. I hope to God most of those decisions are taken independently for, to tell the truth, I'm getting too old and too testy to relish the role of peacemaker, a job I've been saddled with times enough in the past."

They said their goodbyes then, hurrying away to Euston, King's Cross, Waterloo and Paddington to catch their trains but Edith lingered, as she usually did, to say a private farewell, catching him in his turret as he was packing his grip to spend his first night at home in a week.

He looked very tired, she thought, and her heart went out to him as she saw his left hand massaging the muscles above the joint in his leg. She said, looking round his Spartan quarters, "You really did catch us on the hop, Adam, but you had that in mind, I imagine?"

And he said, with a chuckle, "You don't begrudge me some light relief, I hope. If I'm to spend the rest of my days in this slum I need compensations of some sort," and then, straightening himself, "It's my life. The role of country gentleman never did suit me. Henrietta decided that long ago, if that's what you're hinting at."

"It wasn't," she said, "or not altogether. I was thinking of your boys more than Henrietta. You've four of them well-grown, another in reserve. That's more than most men can boast of. Isn't it time one of them lent a hand?"

"They'll come when they're ready," he said, carelessly. "Until then I'd as lief they stayed away. A man has to have heart and soul in this to make a go of it. That's why I took the whole boiling of you into partnership."

"Your lads won't resent that?"

"I don't give a damn if they do. The family is Henrietta's concern. Mine is that quarrelsome bunch, scurrying back to their patches." He paused. "Does that seem unnatural to you?"

"No," she said, "not really. Not having watched Swann waving his banner-with-the-strange-device for a quarter-century. It's you, and I wouldn't have it otherwise. Neither would Henrietta from what I know of her."

And then, opening her reticule, she took out a small, well-worn book and opened it at a marked page. "I've only a few minutes," she said. "Tom is getting a cab from the rank. But I couldn't leave without giving you this. There's a poem by my favourite, Longfellow, and I think it's relevant to you and that bunch down there. Halfway through your talking marathon I saw you for what you were, a bunch of hard-boiled privateers. Read it in the train on the way back to Croydon."

He took the little book saying, "Longfellow, eh? I wouldn't have thought he was your taste. Tennyson or Wordsworth, perhaps . . . You carry this about with you?"

"No," she replied, "I've another copy at home. I popped across to that secondhand bookshop near the station in the luncheon break.

Keep it as a souvenir of our twenty-first conference. I've written in it."

He turned to the flyleaf and read her inscription. *For Adam, alias Simon Danz. In loving friendship and appreciation. Edith, Dec. 14th, 1883.*

"You always were one for the little touches," he said and kissed her, remembering another time when she had stood here in the dusk, and asked him to make her manager of the Crescents at a time of crisis in her own life.

"We've come through a good many crises in the past, Edith, and been a great help to one another from time to time."

"Yes," she said, "and we've a way to travel yet, I hope. I must go now. We're after catching the six-five. Otherwise it's a longish wait."

Then she was gone and he carried her gift over to the table lamp, screwing up his eyes to read the small print of the marked poem, *A Dutch Picture*.

He saw the relevance at once and, as she had anticipated, it flattered him. The three final verses made an immediate impact and he read them twice, adjusting to the rhythm as well as the congeniality of the lines.

> Restless at times with heavy strides
> He paces his parlour to and fro;
> He is like a ship that at anchor rides,
> And swings with the rising and falling tides,
> And tugs at her anchor-tow.
>
> Voices mysterious far and near,
> Sound of the wind and sound of the sea,
> Are calling and whispering in his ear,
> "Simon Danz: Why stayest thou here?
> Come forth and follow me!"
>
> So he thinks he shall take to the sea again,
> For one more cruise with his buccaneers,
> To singe the beard of the King of Spain,
> And capture another Dean of Jaen,
> And sell him in Algiers.

He closed the book and drifted over to the window just in time to see the yellow lights of her cab as it passed through the double gates.

They were all gone now, a staunch bunch in the main, but she by far the staunchest of them. Henrietta would own to that and maybe tease him about her when he showed her the Longfellow that night.

He picked up his papers and glanced at Tybalt's trial cast as he stuffed them into his bag. Up here, with all of them gone, he often addressed himself aloud. "Simon Danz," he said. "I hope to God you were well-found on that new voyage. Your namesake isn't, despite the fact that his crew have chipped in. He'll be scratching around for another ten thousand by the time spring is on the doorstep!"

He took a final look around the cluttered, friendly room and went stumping down the spiral stair to the yard.

6

Resurrection

ALWAYS, on Christmas Eve, he worked late, not merely to avoid involvement in the bustle and clutter of 'Tryst', with the house spilling
over with noise, laughter and wrapping rituals, but because he derived a deep, personal pleasure from despatching the end of year
bonuses to the networks, appending to each a brief note or a joke
that linked Headquarters and outpost in a way that would not have
been possible if the annual chore had been left to Tybalt and his
clerks.

He had promised to be home in time for late supper, for this year,
for the first time since the old Colonel's death, they would all be
present, Alexander having sailed in a day or two ago to be fêted as
one of Sir Garnet Wolseley's promising young men, and George having returned a day or two earlier from Vienna, where he seemed to
have based himself more or less permanently since dragging himself
away from Munich. But for Adam Christmas had always been less
of a family occasion than a time for reassessment of the year's progress, and in the days following the twenty-first annual conference,
and all that emerged from it, there had been so much to do if the co-
operative plan was to be launched in the new year.

About six-thirty, when everyone but the overnight staff had left
the yard, the Southwark Cathedral carollers came to serenade him,
singing 'Once in Royal David's City' and 'Oh, Come All Ye Faithful'
under his tower, their choirmaster hailing him when they had finished and directing one of his Cockney choirboys to catch the traditional sovereign Adam aimed at his cap.

After the choir's departure he stood for a moment at the little
Gothic window, looking out on the murky, yellowish glow surrounding the bridgehead, and across the river to the lights on Tower Hill.
The never-ending rumble of London came up to him, a background
noise you never heard unless you listened for it, and tonight it

seemed clearer and sharper in the frosty air, that went some way to moderate the sourness of the all-pervading stink of the yard, a blend of horse droppings, acrid smoke and tidal mud, not noticeably sweetened by the shut-down of the soap factory on his left and the tannery on his right.

Then, telling himself he must hurry if he was to catch the seventhirty from London Bridge, he returned to his desk and made out a score of bonus drafts, reflecting that this was likely to be the last time he performed this office. Directors could hardly expect private bonuses as well as a share of the profits.

He was sealing the last letter when the watchman, Hadlow, put his head round the door, saying, "There's a cocky little cove down in the yard, sir. Demands to be shown up. I kep' telling him we was closed for the 'oliday, but he took a sharpish line wi' me. Says he's an old friend o' yours an' won't detain you a minnit. Says he's got something you'll want."

"Let him come up," Adam said, carelessly, "but I mean to catch the seven-thirty so hold a cab, Hadlow."

"Yessir!" and Hadlow left, saluting, as they all did, although it was now more than twenty-five years since Adam had worn epaulettes.

People were always popping in and out of the tower at this hour, when the counting-house was closed, the weigh-bridge clerk gone and he was the only one in authority about the premises, so that he did not look up from his desk when he heard the scrape of a boot on the stair and the creak of the door.

He said, briefly, "Well, what is it?" expecting, no doubt, a complaint about an overdue haul from Vicary's territory across the river, or some optimist who was still awaiting a Christmas delivery.

The visitor said, in a voice that reminded him of someone attempting to imitate the quaver of a music-hall tramp, "Sorry to butt in, Guv'nor, seein' it's Christmas an' all, but I got a present for yer . . ." And he looked up very swiftly for, notwithstanding the disguise, there was something chillingly familiar about the voice and the stunted, round-shouldered figure swathed in a topcoat, scarf and jauntily-angled topper that stood in the doorway.

He said, rising, "What the devil *is* this . . . ?" and the visitor laughed. There was no disguising the derision in the sound. It was the laughter of a man dead to him for more than twenty years.

He said, jaw agape, *"Avery! Josh Avery, by God!* It *can't* be . . . !"* And he stumped round the end of the desk to confront the stocky figure, who raised his chin so that Adam could see the pointed features of a man who had first befriended him and ultimately betrayed him, leaving his nine-year-old daughter in his care as a hostage.

It was only then that he remembered the fearful risks Avery was running by coming here, a man with a double murder charge hanging over him and no means, at this distance, to establish his innocence, for who would be likely to believe that a rake like Avery had shot a man in self-defence after a whore had squeezed him dry, and afterwards fled into the night in the back of one of Swann's frigates as far as Harwich, where he had bribed a Dutch skipper to carry him to the Continent.

He would have expected Josh to have aged after all this time, and particularly after the kind of life the man had led up to the time of his flight, and probably since. He had not, or not all that much. The hair under the brim of the hat was grey but it was still plentiful and the pale, clean-shaven face, with its curiously sharp chin, high cheekbones, and restless green eyes, was that of an Avery he remembered long before their parting near Harwich all those years ago, a man who had scandalised the regiment in India by seducing his colonel's wife, and been drummed out once that silly, pretty Kitty Sullivan had been packed off home, with Avery's child in her belly.

The characteristic impudence was there too, in the man's jauntiness that nothing, it seemed, could eradicate, so that Adam thought, not for the first time, "How the devil did he manage to sire a child like Deborah, who crusades for outcasts and gets herself cut to ribbons for her pains?"

He said, carefully, "You know what you're about, I suppose, but I shouldn't have to remind you that you're taking a high risk coming here. Damn it, you haven't even gone to the trouble of disguising yourself. I would have recognised you anywhere, given a good look. You're still a brandy man, I imagine?" He went to his cupboard beside Frankenstein, and took out a bottle and glasses and poured a couple of stiff measures, giving one to Avery and disposing of his own in a gulp.

"As to anyone recognising me, that's nonsense," Avery said, cheerfully. "How often did I show up here when you were hardly more than a horse and cart man? You've come a long way, Adam, but that's no surprise, is it? I always said you would."

"We'll not talk about me," Adam said. "You'll have followed the career of Swann-on-Wheels, no doubt, for you always knew what was going on in city counting-houses, as well as city brothels." But then he relented, for he had never borne Josh any malice and added, "I don't mean to sound unfriendly, Josh, but a lapse of time, even twenty years or more, doesn't scotch a murder charge. Unless you've come back to face up to it, that is, and I don't think you have. It wouldn't be in character, would it?"

"Not in the least," Josh said, "but I had a purpose for all that. However, don't concern yourself about the possibility of my arrest and trial for that business at the Chanticleer. Even if they laid me by the heels I daresay I'd wriggle out of it, with my connections one place and another. Until they begin to suspect the author of these notes, that is," and he drew from his pocket a wallet containing a bulky envelope and laid it on the desk. "I dropped in to give you this. It was something I didn't care to entrust to the mails."

It was curious how quickly he could adapt to Josh Avery, who had always enjoyed making a prodigious mystery of everything he was about. The years between slipped away as though they had been weeks. They might have been sipping a brandy together in a regimental canteen, or in Avery's Guildford Street lodgings in the earliest days of the partnership.

Adam said, picking up the envelope and glancing at the addressee, "What can you and a chap like Stead have in common? He's the Holiest Joe in Fleet Street, and your daughter, as fine a young person as anyone could hope to meet by the way, works for him. Did you know that?" and when Avery smiled, "Damn it, of course you did. There's nothing you don't know, except how to lead a civilised life. I said once that I was done with your commissions, Josh. I'm damned if I deliver this unless you tell me what it concerns."

"No harm in that," said Avery. "A list of people in the pay of Brussels whoremasters. I settle my debts unconventionally, Adam. But I do settle them, as you'll find out when your bank statement comes in after Christmas."

"You don't owe me anything," Adam growled, not liking the turn

365

of the conversation. "What the devil do you mean, I'll find out via the bank?"

"A matter of nine thousand, plus interest. Paid into your account from a bank at The Hague. It was posted three days ago and will have been credited by now, so there's not a damned thing you can do about it. I've added the interest at eight per cent to cover the cost of raising my girl and giving her an education that leads her into the kind of scrape she was in a while back. I forget the exact sum. It was around the fifteen thousand mark."

"You've paid fifteen thousand into my bank?"

"Indeed I have and don't think I can't afford it."

"But Great God, man, you landed in Holland almost penniless, unless you were lying to me that night I took you to Harwich."

"That was one time I didn't lie," said Avery, "not to you at all events. I was down to one ruby and the odd guinea or two, but I had friends. Since then I've married money, a great deal of money. At a price, of course. My wife is a Hohenzollern. Hellishly plain but amiable in her own way, the way Prussians are when they want something and Lisa wanted me. Not that you could call me a remittance man. I earn my oats. I had something to do with promoting Government loans needed to build the fortifications systems round Liège and Namur, and after that one thing led to another. However, that isn't what I came to see you about. The repayment to you was an incidental and don't pretend you can't do with it. Is it true you've formed a company, and taken your managers into the firm?"

"It's true, but I'm damned if I understand how you knew it. My bank doesn't know yet."

"Ah, bankers," said Avery, "they only know what's sent to them in large print and misunderstand most of that. They won't understand your motives, for instance, as I did, the moment I heard about it."

"You should. The very last thing you said to me was take the staff into my confidence and I did just that. I had to. You'd squandered all my capital on that woman Esmeralda."

"That's so," Avery mused, unabashed, "but it was to your ultimate advantage. And my daughter's advantage too. That way she came by a respectable upbringing."

"We gave her more than that, Josh. She got all the love she needed."

That did disconcert him a little. He said, "Yes. I'll concede that, Adam. For all that, I think I would have had more sense than to let her stick her nose into a foreign hornet's nest at the nod of a rabble rouser like Stead. How did that come about?"

"It wasn't my doing. I did my best to stop her. After all, she's of age and as pigheaded as a daughter of yours is likely to be."

"Aye, I gathered that," he said, "when I read what happened to her in Brussels. How is she now?"

"Sadder and wiser, like most of us when we've had the stardust beaten out of us."

"Is she still hitched to Stead and that woman Butler?"

"She's still with Stead."

"Damn it, that's an odd line for a lass to take," he said, grumpily. "Is she so plain?"

"On the contrary, she's extremely attractive."

"Then why didn't you and that plump little pigeon of yours find a husband for her?"

"Because she didn't want a husband. Not everybody who has made his pile puts his daughters up to auction, Josh."

"You think of her as your daughter then?"

"God damn it!" he burst out, "of course I do! And so does Henrietta. We've had her since she was nine, and she's been our daughter from the moment I winkled her out of that seedy convent where you left her."

He remained unruffled, saying, mildly, "You've told her about me?"

"As much as I think she should know. If you're that interested why the devil didn't you write? The last word I had of you was from the Mother Superior, who died soon after I lost my leg in that crash at Staplehurst."

"I didn't have to write," Avery said. "You were always in the news. I would have got in touch with Henrietta if you had died in that shambles. You believe that, I hope."

"I don't know what the devil I believe about you," Adam said. "You turn up here, asking all these questions after twenty years . . .

Why are you here? It isn't to tell me about money you banked, and it can't be that you're associated with Stead in any way."

"I'm a man who likes to pay his score, and that letter will pay it. With interest. How much did Deborah tell you about what happened to her in Brussels?"

"No more than was in the papers on her return. I gather she was beaten up by some scoundrel in the pay of the brothel-keepers. It was no more than I expected. Stead carried an extensive report of it and you obviously subscribe to the *Pall Mall Gazette*."

He said, moving to the window, "They would have killed her if they hadn't got what they were after. She had a list of names. Big names. It was far more vital to them than she realised. Several high-ranking police officers were involved, as well as a couple of industrialists and a judge. She had all the pieces, and Stead, no doubt, would have put them together. Naturally they were scared. Well, they aren't likely to meddle in that traffic again, not this side of the Channel. So long as Stead has the nerve to publish, of course."

"Why don't you deliver it yourself and make sure that he does?"

"That wouldn't do at all, my friend. I should be sure to run into her and I wouldn't like that to happen."

"Listen here," said Adam, "you've taken this much risk so why not a little more? I'm catching the seven-thirty to Croydon. I could arrange for you to see Deborah privately. She won't reject you. She isn't that kind of person. She's a special kind of person. We found that out at the time of the train wreck. She saved Henrietta's sanity for one thing. A child of eleven or twelve, with more courage than anyone about us. Why won't you do that, Josh?"

"Mostly out of regard for you. She'd try and reclaim me and that would involve split loyalties. I'm past reclamation, anyway."

"You always thought of yourself as being," Adam said, "but it's mostly a pose."

"You know I'm talking sense, Adam."

He knew it and was surprised, now that it came to the point, to feel jealousy concerning their relationship. For him, for so many years now, Avery had been dead and buried, whereas he had always taken more pride in Deborah than in any of his own blood, seeing her, possibly, as something he had created, much as he had created the network.

He said, gruffly, "I wouldn't want her harmed, or even embarrassed by your arrest. She remembers enough of you to be deeply concerned if that occurred, so have it your way. I'll deliver your letter and say nothing about your coming here if you prefer it that way."

"I prefer it," Josh said, with a smile, "and so do you."

He walked slowly round the tower, cluttered with the apparatus of Swann's life. "This place hasn't changed," he said, "and neither, for that matter, have you. I hadn't looked for change, of course. Getting mauled in the train accident gave you a new lease of life. If you had come this far without a setback you would have been a Justice of the Peace by now, with any number of high-toned notions about letting a man like me walk loose. The possibility of standing trial as an accessory wouldn't have stopped you. However, as I say, that amputation presented a fresh challenge and a man like you can't exist without challenges. Will you shake hands, Adam?"

"Good God, why not? Do you suppose I'm that much of a prig?"

"I'm not calling you a prig," Avery said, "just a good old British Puritan and there's a difference. Prigs have secret doubts about themselves but Puritans don't, not even when the world falls about them. You have sons of your own, they tell me. Why aren't they here learning their trade?"

"I drive myself," Adam said, "but I've never made a practice of driving others. Unless they happened to share my objectives."

"And your boys don't?"

"I wouldn't say that. They're individuals. Alex has taken a commission, George is getting to know himself, drifting about Europe, Giles and Hugo are still at school. And the youngest is still a baby. There's time enough. Henrietta's proud of them, and I'm damned if I feel like wet-nursing a crowd of amateurs."

"And your daughters?"

"The eldest is married to a farmer's boy. Happily, I might add, to head off your sneer."

Avery said, with his woman's smile, "You're the last person on earth I'd sneer at. The only Puritan I know who is still a respecter of persons. A very *private* Puritan, Adam."

"I've always done what I wanted to do, Josh."

"Me too. And that's one definition of success they say. Give me

369

ten minutes to get clear of the yard. I would leave you a forwarding address but if I did the first thing you'd do would be to mail that money back."

They shook hands, much as they had done outside Harwich twenty years before. Then Avery pulled on his gloves, smoothed them very carefully and went out and down the stairs without a backward glance. Adam found that he was sweating, despite the nip in the air and the dead stove. He thought, "I suppose I'm closer to him than anyone has ever been but how close is that? A million miles?"

He picked up the letter, carried it to his wall-safe and locked it away. Stead had already devoted a year to his self-appointed task of stemming the flow of harlots across the Channel. He could wait another few days.

2

He was familiar with the offices of the *Pall Mall Gazette*, and his card was enough to get him an audience with Stead, who received him cordially, although there was apprehension in his manner when, after a formal handshake, Adam went straight to the subject of the beating Deborah had received in Brussels.

"You got my letter promising redress, Mr. Swann?"

"I did indeed," Adam said, "and I should apologise for not replying but the truth is I felt too damned outraged. Let's admit it, Mr. Stead, that wasn't an assignment for an inexperienced young woman, and a professional like you must have been aware of that. Why did you take such a risk?"

"Against my better judgement. The fact is, Mr. Swann, Miss Avery is an extremely rare find, a young person with an active social conscience who has the ability to write 'parlour-window' prose. Not easy to find, I assure you."

He must have noted Adam's baffled eyes, for he went on, "I think of writing in terms of glass. A dirty pane for obscurity, stained glass for literature, 'parlour-window' for words you can look through at the meaning behind."

Adam had come prepared to dislike the man, as he found himself disliking most of the over-earnest, over-shrill social campaigners he had met about the City in the last two decades. Stead, he discovered, had both charm and honesty, of a kind not easy to detect in his columns, that usually read like sermons by a latter-day Calvin, or at least a Luther, notwithstanding the validity of the wrongs they sought to right. He decided to hold Avery's letter in reserve while he explored the man. It was not often one had an opportunity of studying a Titan at point-blank range.

He said, "I won't pretend I like her being exposed to this kind of hazard. No responsible guardian would. Frankly, I'd sooner see her married, and settled in a suburb, with a husband and a couple of children to coddle. It's always been my belief that any young man would be lucky to have Deborah, apart from the fact that she is likely to inherit money in due course."

"I wasn't aware of that," Stead said. And then, "Would I be presuming if I asked you to tell me a little more concerning her background? She's been reticent concerning that, apart from yourself, of course."

"I can't tell you one thing about her background, Mr. Stead. Not because I wouldn't, and certainly not because I don't trust your discretion, but for reasons outside my control. All I can say is that her father was once a very good friend of mine. When he ran into difficulties and moved abroad, he made me her guardian. That was when she was nine. Since then I've always regarded her as my own daughter. I'm sorry I can't be more helpful."

"You need not be. Social backgrounds count for nothing here, Mr. Swann. Miss Avery has courage and she can write. That's all that is important to me. And now, I imagine, you'll use your influence to persuade her to leave me and dabble in journalism during spells between kitchen, sewing-room and nursery?"

"That's not the reason I asked for an interview," replied Adam, "but it's not such a bad notion at that. Fleet Street is hardly the place one expects to look for a well-educated, personable young woman, is it?"

"Not as yet," said Stead, "but it will be, hopefully in our lifetime. British women won't always be content to stay in the seraglio."

Adam made a guess at his age. It could not be much beyond the mid-thirties, yet he already looked ten years older. The face was lined and the eyes jaded. Only the set of the jaw, and his swift, nervous gestures indicated the man's lunging, restless character.

He said, "I don't deny that a great deal needs doing here and everywhere but squalor, lust, greed and injustice can be found in any big city. You see your duty as attacking it and most of us who care for the country's health applaud you, more often than not, but then . . ." And he stopped, reflecting how irritated he would be if a stranger walked into his tower and began telling him how to conduct his business.

Stead said quietly, "I'll heed advice from a man of your reputation, Swann. What did you intend saying before you thought better of it?"

"I've no reputation, save as a haulier."

"You are too modest. It's my business to know the good and bad among City businessmen." He opened a folder on his desk and glanced at it so that Adam, swearing under his breath, thought, "Damn his impudence! He must have a dossier on every one of us operating within the square mile," but then Stead smiled, shedding his extra years for a moment and looking almost boyish.

"You've been in business twenty-five years. I was a lad of ten when you set up but I remember your waggons when I played in the streets up north. Since then you've swept a thousand urchins off the streets and given them a chance to learn a trade. That's a contribution to the national spring clean, isn't it, Mr. Swann?"

"It's my waggonmaster's doing, not mine," Adam growled. "They make good vanboys as a rule."

"The case of Jake Higson, chimney-sweep, wasn't Mr. Keate's doing. It was a personal venture, according to my record."

It astonished Adam to realise that Stead knew chapter and verse of the Higson saga and he wondered, a little uneasily, what else reposed in that file. He said, "I was going to say that I've always fought shy of sensationalism. I was interested in Shaftesbury's early campaigns after I saw one lad die in a street riot and another choke to death in my chimney, but Shaftesbury's stage was Parliament."

"Ah, yes," Stead said, "but that was before a majority could read and write. The Education Acts of the first Liberal Government offered us a short cut, so why not use it? Offer me a choice between a newspaper and the House of Commons for getting something done in a hurry and I'll take the newspaper every time. If I didn't believe that I wouldn't be here. I'd get myself elected as an unaligned Radical and make my stand in Westminster. But it's the long way round. General Gordon is off to the Soudan in a day or so, and the Turks have stopped slaughtering Bulgarians. My achievements, both, Mr. Swann, not Parliament's. Not even Mr. Gladstone's."

Adam Swann had not been in business for a quarter-century without acquiring the ability to spot the chink in a man's armour when he saw it and here, he told himself, was Stead's. He might be sincerely dedicated to his work as a social reformer, and he was very far from being a hypocrite, but his dynamo was an unconscious lust for power. To some extent the discovery brought them on level terms.

He said, coolly, "That doesn't answer my point, Mr. Stead. Or not entirely. We don't have to pursue the argument, however. I had a reason for coming here and that reason only marginally concerns my ward."

"But I should like to pursue it," said Stead, smiling, "providing you're not in the usual city man's hurry to get back to your till."

"I'm in no hurry."

"Well then, in answer to that point you raised about the inescapable misery and squalor of any large centre of civilisation, it's true, of course. There's more misery, more hunger, more degradation and certainly more tyranny in Calcutta, Baghdad, Constantinople, Madrid, and even some of the cities in the New World, Chicago for instance. But in a way that proves my point. London claims to be the social, financial and democratic capital of the world. London is therefore under an obligation to swill out its pigsties from time to time. But I see our duty as something more positive than that. I see ours as a civilising mission, imposed upon us by God Almighty. Why else should we have amassed so much power over so great a slice of the globe? What we need here is a Christian approach to the use of wealth and the responsibilities money imposes on the wealthy. Yet we're as rotten at heart as the capital of any Eastern despot once national and imperial sentiment is peeled away. I'm dedicated to that peeling process, Mr. Swann. You can't look for a healthy society, much less a Christian one, if you cover festering wounds with Union Jacks, and that's what we've been doing for a generation. Does that

373

go some way towards convincing you that Miss Avery has a right to make her contribution?"

"It helps," Adam said, grudgingly, and then, recollecting that he had a trump card in his pocket, produced Avery's letter and laid it on Stead's desk.

"I'm only vaguely aware what that letter contains," he said, "but I've no doubt at all that you'll find it useful as a disinfectant."

Stead slit the envelope very methodically, the way he did most things Adam noticed, and then settled himself to study the contents of two sheets of closely-written writing inside. His expression did not change but Adam noticed the slim fingers tightened their grip on the pages. Stead said, without curiosity, "Where did this come from, Mr. Swann? I'm sorry, but I must know that if I am to use it."

"From Deborah Avery's father. It seems he read your account of what happened when she was in Brussels. I think he sees it as his way of hitting back."

"He's obviously a man of parts," said Stead, and now Adam noticed that he was excited and doubtless itching to put pen to paper. "I must say I'm uncommonly obliged to you. You would vouch for the authenticity of this?"

"I haven't seen it and I would prefer not to. Deborah went over there with a list of business contacts I gave her. However, if it's any help, I'll say this. The man who sent you that information is exceptionally well-informed, particularly as regards organised vice. He has carried out investigations for me in the past, in commercial fields that is, and I've never found him wrong in the smallest particular."

"I see," said Stead, thoughtfully. "Well, I've been taking chances all my life and I'll take one as regards this. I assume you would prefer Miss Avery to remain in ignorance as to the source?"

"I'm sure my former partner would. Otherwise he would have given it to her himself."

He stood up, reaching for his hat and gloves. "I won't detain you any longer, Mr. Stead. And as to Deborah, with reservations I'm prepared to leave her in your charge. We've all got something to contribute. How we do it is up to the individual."

"Mr. Swann . . ."

"Well?"

"Essentially you're with us. Why not admit it, man?"

374

"Concerning the traffic in domestics, the repeal of the Contagious Diseases Acts, things of that kind? I'm more with you than against you. But that doesn't make me a crusader. I'm an apostle of a different creed."

"What creed, Mr. Swann?"

"A man does what he can on his own patch, preferably a patch he's cleared for himself. But he stops short of trying to reform mankind as a whole. As to where we're going as a nation, I can only guess at that."

"Could you define that guess, in general terms?"

"Yes, I could do that," said Adam, genially. "It's my belief we're going to go on inflating the red, white and blue balloon for a long time. And then, one day, there'll be an almighty big bang. But when that happens I'll be gone, Mr. Stead. And so, most probably, will you."

They shook hands across the desk and Adam went out into the teeming street. On the whole he was pleased with the encounter. It was not often, he thought, that a city gent left the presence of W. T. Stead with honours even.

Part Three

SWANN OUTPOSTS

1

Swann Roundabout

IT was getting on for thirty years since he had thought in military terms but devolution enabled him to see the network in the context of a never-ending campaign fought on a score of fronts.

The territories, west to the Cornish peninsula and the Dublin Pale, north to the Grampians, were his furthermost outposts, with settled country between them and his base of operations beside the Thames, and the long lines of communication spread like a giant web across every shire in the four nations, wherever his polyglot army laid siege to factory, mine, warehouse, foundry, quarry, kiln and emporium.

The shift of power made itself felt almost at once. Invested with the status of partners men like Catesby and Bryn Lovell began to make vital local decisions without so much as formal recourse to Headquarters, and even relative juniors, like Markby of Crescent North, enjoyed flexing their muscles in the stream of reports that flowed south and east to where Tybalt and his clerks struggled to adjust to the fact that the latest conference had converted every regional capital into a miniature headquarters, with its own policy and its own overlord.

But if he saw himself as an ageing strategist so, in a different sense, did Henrietta, also engaged in a nonstop campaign and with outposts that were more remote than his. Headquarters, for her, was 'Tryst' where her reserves were mustered in the four younger children, temporarily held in check by her sergeant-major, the redoubtable Phoebe Fraser, but unlike Adam she had no well-established communications system, so that she was obliged to rely for up-to-date information on scrappy, infrequent letters and, in the last resort, guesses based on what she remembered of the quality of her troops plus occasional contemplation of the enormous family photograph album she kept handy on a shelf under her sewing table.

379

Of the nine of them, four were still under her hand. She could catch fleeting glimpses of the two elder girls, Joanna and Helen, as they scampered about the paddocks and stableyard on their forays into the Kentish countryside and when they were about the house she could usually hear them, together with young Edward, who was learning to hold his own with them. Baby Margaret, a quiet, contemplative little thing, reminded her a little of Deborah when she was a child but there was nothing contemplative about Joanna and Helen, who were both emerging from the hoydenish stage and developing into as pert and pretty a pair as one was likely to find, squabbling over trinkets or teasing one another over some fancied beau, or trying on dresses that gave them excuses to admire themselves in a mirror. She remembered doing this herself when she was shedding puppy fat and becoming aware of sly glances at dancing classes or garden-fêtes, and would sometimes compare her own lonely girlhood with their gloriously untrammelled life in this great, whispering house that had adapted itself to successive generations of children growing up in conditions of warmth and security. Nobody had ever lived here who was not buttressed by money and social position and Joanna and Helen would take these things for granted. They had never had to fight for them as she had when she made her grab at Adam Swann's coat-tails on that Cheshire moor so long ago.

Well, let them enjoy it while they could. Soon enough, she supposed, both would be spoken for and whisked away and then there would be only two where there had been nine and she would begin worrying about them at a distance as she worried, in varying degrees, about the four absent boys.

Alex, of course, claimed pride of place in her conjectures, for he was off and away again, this time to the cataracts of the Nile in the wake of that saintly General Gordon, the one the newspapers had so much to say about lately. It was weeks now since they had heard from him but she did not worry overmuch, despite scrappy reports of incomprehensible squabbles at places with incomprehensible names. A boy who could survive that awful shambles in Zululand could survive anything and at least, through her insistence, he was now a real soldier and an Imperial investment, and not a kind of hybrid likely to be considered expendable by fierce-looking generals like Garnet Wolseley and Roberts, or even saintly-looking ones like Gordon.

George was primarily his father's worry. Home at Christmas after nearly two years' absence, George had struck her as being a very suave and mature young man, able to talk fluently in French and German and obviously, if Adam was to be believed, benefiting from his Continental apprenticeship, although she could not imagine what he learned in foreign parts that he could not learn better over here where it was universally admitted that everything of the slightest use to anybody, be they black, white, yellow or coffee coloured, was invented, perfected, patented, manufactured and exported for profit.

As for Giles and Hugo, down at that remote school of theirs that she had heard so much about but never visited, they were off her hands too for the most of the year, and she sometimes forgot them for days at a stretch until she suddenly saw them looking at her out of the stiff pages of the photograph album, two children, caught at various stages between nudity on a rug and selfconscious circumspection in a studio portrait, outwardly and inwardly dissimilar in every way and yet, seen together, obvious brothers. They too, in a sense, were marking time like Joanna and Helen, and she had not yet made up her mind how and when to apply pressure to them, in the way she had applied it to Alex. Hugo, she sometimes thought, would make a perfectly splendid Life Guard, and put his four pretty sisters to shame in crested helmet and breastplate, but Giles was obviously not cut out for soldiering or business and it seemed unfair to expect Adam to be content with one son out of five, so that perhaps she would have to wait a year or two and see how Edward shaped before heading Hugo into the army and Giles, as his brain clearly merited, into one or other of the learned professions.

There remained Stella, near enough to be regarded as a kind of family adjutant but a somewhat disinterested one these days, for Stella already had two fat babies of her own and was inclined to give precedence to her affairs and Denzil's, so that Henrietta sometimes saw her as a friendly neutral who had made a separate peace and decided to put on flesh and complacency in that four-hundred acre farm of hers over the hill.

Such a lot of flesh and so much complacency, Henrietta told herself, without being able to resign herself to either, for the girl she visited once a week did not seem to need her now and Henrietta liked to be needed, so that her resentment, ranging about for a focus, settled on her daughter's weight, increasing shapelessness and—she had to say it if only to herself—the happy-go-lucky sluttishness that pervaded in the big kitchen at Dewponds whenever a well-turned-out Henrietta popped in for a gossip.

If Henrietta Swann could have been said to have had an overriding preoccupation these days it was probably centred in the deteriorating figure of her eldest child. To a woman of her experience and disposition it was courting an unnecessary risk to let oneself go in that way and, by implication, to take a man, even such a moon-struck man as Denzil Fawcett, for granted.

For her part—and she made no secret of it when dispensing motherly advice—she had gone to tremendous pains to keep herself trim and elegant down the years. A man coming home from a toilsome day's work needed a mistress as well as a wife but when (tactfully for her) she brought the conversation round to this delicate point during one of her duty visits to Dewponds, Stella laughed aloud and then compounded the ridicule by saying, through her laughter, "Corsets? And a Sunday-go-to-meeting get-up at this time of day? Good gracious, mother, however do you suppose I could pull my weight dressed in the kind of clothes I wore as a girl? And as for my figure, I'll tell you something that might amuse you. Denzil was deeply concerned with the way I looked when we married. He kept telling me I needed fattening up, and urging me to take second helpings of pudding, especially when I was carrying Robert. You'll never believe it, but I've put on nearly two stones since then!"

Henrietta did believe it but thought it nothing to boast about and it pained her a little that a son-in-law should presume to regard one of her daughters as a heifer who needed fattening. "Well, it's none of my business," she murmured, "but just look at me, after nine children! I'm small-boned, I admit, but do you want to grow like the side of one of his barns? You, who once had the neatest waist in the county!"

"I did indeed," said Stella, smiling, "and what did it get me?"

There was clearly no kind of answer to this so Henrietta let the subject drop, hoping, perhaps, that Stella would tell her more about the miracle of her rehabilitation after Dewponds had burned down and she had helped Denzil to rebuild it. She never did, however, and Henrietta, reasoning that Stella would see her life as beginning with her second marriage, was thrown back upon guesswork, based largely on the exchange of glances between husband and wife whenever he came clumping into the kitchen in huge, mud-encrusted boots and Stella hastened to serve him and his men the kind of meal that a feudal baron might have given hungry retainers after a battle. And this communal eating at Dewponds, where master, mistress and hired hands lived as a family, was something else Henrietta worried about.

At local social gatherings, At Homes, croquet tournaments and the like, she found herself very much on the defensive concerning her daughter's remarriage and did not need to be reminded that it was still the subject of tittle-tattle about here, sometimes wondering if Stella was aware of this and, if she was, whether it bothered her at all. But she need not have worried. If Stella Fawcett did reflect upon the world she had abandoned, a succession of soirées, hunter trials, hunt balls and croquet parties, she would have almost certainly considered it well lost. As for the gossips, she had no time for them these days, for she was on the trot sixteen hours a day and revelled in all the demands made upon her. In private as well as public for, in this respect, had Henrietta but known it, she was very much her mother's daughter. If possible, indeed, she was more smug than Henrietta had ever been, even when Adam returned home to find his wife not only in charge of his business but the mother of a child he had not known existed.

The relationship that had matured between man and wife since they had set up house in the rebuilt farmhouse afforded Stella the greatest satisfaction as well as the greatest possible pride. It was something, she reasoned, they had built together on sure foundations, and now that Denzil was back on his feet, and had a little more time and energy for more playful aspects of their association, she sometimes counted herself the luckiest woman in Kent. For who could have hoped to have salvaged so much from the wreck of her life at the time of her flight from the Moncton-Prices. As for Denzil's continuing adoration, she had no doubts at all regarding this. The plain fact was he worshipped her, had never really come to terms with his capture of her and probably never would, so that Stella, on the rare occasions she had a moment or two for reflection, contemplated this rather than her figure and decided that it had nothing whatever to do with the Swanns' local ascendancy and money but concerned herself alone. Of this she had evidence every time they pulled the curtains after a long day's grind in field, pasture and kitchen.

It was as though, every so often, he would look across at her to reassess the plenitude of his good fortune, so that there were times when she imagined he was almost grateful to Lester Moncton-Price for rejecting her. Whenever Denzil came to her as a lover he did it with the same masculine gentleness he had shown on the very first occasion. It was even difficult, under these circumstances, to initiate a renewed approach on his part, for she became pregnant within a couple of months of their spring wedding and the moment he learned of it he began to treat her as though she was made of spun glass. There were limits to complacency, however. She had no wish to be elevated to a pedestal that put her clear out of touch and in the end she was obliged to tell him so.

In the event, however, even this excess of gallantry proved an investment, for it helped, if obliquely, to moderate his shyness, and introduce a gleam or two of humour into their relationship, so that he would sometimes tease her about her swelling figure when they were preparing for bed and the pride he took in it was really quite comic. Or would have been if she hadn't found it so touching.

It was also enriching, she discovered, to be worshipped in this fashion and it sobered her sometimes to look back to a time when she had found his adoration ridiculous and embarrassing once it had become a family joke. Now she was ready to take shameless advantage of it, especially when she wanted her own way about something for the house.

There were tender moments, however, plenty of them as their first harvest was gathered in, and the raw buildings began to assume a permanent, weatherbeaten look. Sometimes, in the early autumn, after the livestock that claimed so much of his time had been tended, and his men and boys had trudged off home, they would sit for an hour or so beside the blazing apple logs that he had sawn from wind-blown trees down by the river, saying little but savouring a sense of permanence that neither could have put into words. It was then, after he had stirred himself to throw another log on, that he would sit on his hams regarding her with a proprietary air, or rest his back against her knees where she could run her fingers through his hair, talking idly of this and that, with the placidity of a couple who had been married years instead of months. Only occasionally did his steady adoration find expression in words, as when he said, taking her in his arms one gusty October night, "Most farmers'd look for a son first off, I reckon, but I'd as lief it was a maid, my beauty. For then there'll be a matched pair of 'ee around the house and that'll suit me fine, d'ye hear?"

She had read many passionate declarations on the part of swains who minced their way across the pages of Henrietta's novelettes but not one of them could have coined a statement as warm or as reassuring as that. No wonder Stella gained in weight and complacency.

2

Henrietta's occasional worries concerning Alexander were equally unjustified. A thousand miles or more to the east he was, in fact, adjusting the overall balance somewhat by losing weight, growing lean and taut and as brown as a Bedouin under the white glare of the sun somewhere between the third and fourth of the Nile's cataracts, where he guarded one of the last links with the Khartoum garrison that General Gordon was supposed to have evacuated long since but had not and was now himself invested and all but cut off.

It was strange, in the circumstances, that Alex's complacency equated with that of his sister Stella. He was quite untroubled by flies, scorpions, a merciless heat from dawn to dusk and sudden chills at night, to say nothing of the Mahdi's tribesmen now in possession of most of the towns higher up the river and the impossibility of saving Gordon from what the newspapers were already calling an Imperial martyrdom. Yet it was so, for Alexander, the least complicated of the Swann brood, had adapted comfortably and almost effortlessly to the strait-jacket of his profession.

It was just as well. Out here nobody, from Chief of Staff to corporal's guard, seemed to know where anyone else was, or what they were achieving, or what the British Government at home wanted them to achieve, or how this extraordinary tangle would be unravelled. There was Gordon and his forty thousand squatting in Khartoum, hemmed in by heaven knew how many dervishes. There was Wolseley and his staff, mounting a ponderous rescue operation in Cairo. And in between, strung along hundreds of miles of river and desert track, were forlorn little parties of Europeans, poor-quality Egyptian infantry, roving gunboats, allegedly loyal Ababda tribesmen, heavily bribed and less reliable troops who gloried in the Arabian Nights' name of 'bashibozouks' and were led by a scoundrel called the Mudir of Dongola and, always, disappearing and reappearing like Sinbad's Genie, the astonishing Major Kitchener, who had promoted himself Colonel and acquired the disconcerting habit of staring inferiors down with hypnotic eyes and a moustache that reminded Alexander of a squire in a melodrama.

It was very fortunate, he kept reminding himself, that he had never meddled in politics, not even Service politics, for a man might have lost his wits trying to make sense out of all this to-ing and fro-ing. As a subaltern, thank God, he was only required to obey the last order and he did this punctiliously, even when they despatched him across miles of desert to a place called Gadkul.

It was situated, according to his map, in the middle of a tract call the Bayuda Desert on a loop of the Nile well above Khartoum and with him marched a Bulgarian interpreter called Boris, a Highland corporal called McTavish, a score of jabbering Kababish tribesmen and—the object of the exercise—a string of fifty-seven camels, purchased by Kitchener in Dongola with a sack of silver sent up-river by the Sirdar.

For Alex it was a welcome change from fly-pestered garrison duty in one or other of the river posts. He had never held an independent command and had never, up to that time, sat a camel, whose gently swaying gait gave him the impression of riding a small boat across a whipped-up sheet of water.

For directions he was entirely dependent upon the Kababish

guide. Left to himself he would have wandered in circles for out here camel tracks seemed to lead in every direction and there were no land marks, nothing but sand and stone and sky. Their route, he gathered, was governed by desert wells and when night came they encamped by one, Boris the interpreter telling him that the guide said they could probably make Gadkul, and the advance post said to be established there, before the temperature soared to the hundred and twenties in the morning.

On that he turned into his bivouac tent and slept, to be awakened well before dawn by the corporal shaking his foot and saying, in the laconic voice of a swaddy who had long since adjusted to the Orient, "We'd best be aboot moving, sir. They've gone, the whole bunch of 'em."

They had indeed. Outside there was no Boris, no camels and no bashibozouks, nothing but miles of empty sand under the stars, and nothing to be done, it seemed, but to ask the corporal how they should set about retracing their steps to Korti, all of a day's journey on foot through the scorching heat of the day.

The corporal, a forty-year-old veteran, seemed to find nothing very surprising or even alarming in their situation. Neither, for that matter, did he see any necessity to seek orders from a young and obviously inexperienced officer. He was polite, of course, but he did not tender his advice in the form of questions, as was customary, but said, bluntly, "Hae ye the compass aboot ye—sirr?", and when Alexander handed it to him consulted it casually, as he might a watch and added "We'll aim for higher up river. We'd ne'er make Korti nor Gadkul on foot. It's my belief those heathen led us a goose chase north o' the route. I'm thinking we're no mair than three hours' march o' the big bend, at Abu Hamed."

The name Abu Hamed had some significance for Alexander. He said, "That's in the hands of the Mahdi, isn't it? Our advance posts were at Merowe, nearly a hundred miles down-river, or so I was told when I was given my route."

"Aye," said the corporal, patiently, "but you c'n tak' your choice—sirr. A brush wi' the Fuzzies, or slow death from thirst and heatstroke an hour or so after sun-up. If you'll tak' my advice it'll be the river at its nearest point."

There was no gainsaying a man as sure of himself as that, so they abandoned all but essential kit, filled their water bottles and struck off across the desert in a north-easterly direction, trudging on until the sun rose and every step became a penance. He soon had reason to be thankful that he had put himself in the corporal's hands. Not only did they find the river before the heat became unbearable but struck it opposite a grounded paddle streamer that McTavish recognised as one of the fleet of streamers General Gordon had sent out of Khartoum a week before under the command of Colonel Stewart of the 11th Hussars. Stewart, he said, had been lured ashore and cut to pieces, together with nearly all his party.

"It'll be the saving of us, nonetheless," said the Highlander, but added, with the pessimism of his race and calling, "for the time being, that is."

They waded out and climbed aboard. It had been systematically looted, of course, and there was nothing of any value aboard. The ten-pounder gun was still on its mountings, having proved too much trouble to break loose and haul away but there was no ammunition for it and every cabin and locker had been ransacked by the dervishes. Below decks it was relatively cool, however, and Alex gratefully accepted the corporal's offer to take first watch, stretching himself on the planks of a stripped bunk and falling asleep in seconds.

This time he was awakened by sustained and distant gunfire, that seemed to come from downstream so he went in search of the corporal, at first nowhere to be found but ultimately located flat on his back under one of the boilers in the engine-room astern. He said, in response to Alexander's query, "It'll be the Fuzzies, probing the flank guard above Merowe. They'll have come downstream from Abu Hamed as soon as they heard we were establishing base at Gadkul and were aiming for Shendi or Mentemma." It struck Alex then that there was a Gilbertian flavour about the chain of command out here. The lower you probed the more positive and coherent was the analysis of any given situation. This man, for instance, could make sense out of an assortment of sounds and produce a rational answer in a matter of seconds, whereas officers of Major and above would have made any number of guesses and lost themselves in fantasy. The Highlander talked and behaved as though he had been born and raised out here in the desert. The names of the squalid little river towns dropped from his tongue as though they were as familiar as Aberdeen, Kelso, Inverness and Glasgow. Everything he said had authenticity so that when he suggested the steamer could, with a little attention, be started up and refloated, Alex was positive that this was so and that he would do it. He had experience, it seemed, with marine engines, having worked for a spell on a paddle steamer that cruised the Inner Hebrides in the short Highland summers, and learning this Alex had a curious certainty that this adventure would end like all his previous adventures, in survival. It was as though he had inherited a talisman passed to him by his father, like the shape of his nose or the colour of his eyes. A certain amount of doubt, however, was expected of him as a bystander and an officer, so he said, "*How* could she be refloated? Even if you get the engine started she's still stuck on a sandbank," and the corporal replied, in that tone of mild exasperation the veterans reserved for boys in authority over them, "Aye, she is that, sirr. But there's more water come down since she struck a week since. Ye can see that if ye look at the paint on her hull. Full power and hard over and she'll float off easy enough, providing she isn't holed, and if we're lucky she'll drift down on the current and fetch up beyond Merowe." And then, most improbably, he made the kind of joke a friendly uncle might make at the expense of a venturesome nephew, saying, "Ye might even get a medal, sirr, for salvagin' Queen's property written off by the quartermaster," and smiled, showing discoloured front teeth under a red, ragged moustache and the wide cleft in them that Phoebe Fraser always said meant that the owner would die a wealthy man.

Alex left him to his work, after an offer to help had been declined and made a thorough search of the derelict, discovering, under a trap in the bows, a box of Martini-Henry rifle ammunition that had been overlooked by the looters because it was buried in oily rags and cordage. Alex was armed only with a revolver but the corporal carried a Martini-Henry, so Alex took the box down to him, thinking it might be useful if they were challenged from the banks on the voyage downstream. By this time the corporal, stripped to his underclothes and covered in grease, had made repairs to pistons and steampipe and was lighting the fire. His situation aboard ship seemed to have invested him with the gruff authority of a seagoing captain, for he waved the ammunition aside and ordered Alex aft, with orders to put the steering wheel hard over against the moment when the starboard wheel began to revolve.

It happened within minutes, the wheel seeming to heave and flutter a little, its metal-sheathed blades flailing the sand as it dragged the head of the little vessel around, pointing her mid-stream. After a moment or two of horrid uncertainty she edged herself clear of the bank into shoulder-deep water, where she at once began to spin in slow, ever widening circles, apparently not answering to the helm and Alex, craning his neck over the stern, saw that the rudder bar was bent to an angle of about fifteen degrees.

He shouted the news to the corporal who came up, took a look, and went below again without a word. A moment later he managed to start the port wheel going and thereafter the steamer pursued a crazy course into mid-channel and would have soon crossed the river and buried her nose in the eastern bank had not she chanced to strike a submerged bank or some other obstruction that diverted her into midstream current where the corporal was able to keep her clear of the banks for a zig-zag mile or so by starting and stopping the paddle wheels alternatively.

It could not last, however, for he was unable to hear the sailing directions Alex shouted above the grind of the ancient pistons, the hiss of steam escaping from a hole he had been unable to repair and the clank of churning wheels. Shutting off both engines he came on deck again dragging a long sweep he had unearthed from somewhere and having lashed it to the stern rail directed Alex to steer as best he could while he got a real head of steam on the patched up boiler. He seemed, Alex thought, completely absorbed in his work, with no concern at all for the possible presence of dervishes on either bank, or the heavy firing downstream.

It was a bizarre experience, sailing zig-zag down the wide and muddy Nile under a high, brassy sun and through a depopulated land, but all the time, Alex noticed, the firing became heavier, the crump of artillery punctuating a long rattle of musketry, so that it seemed to him they were drifting into a major engagement of some kind and he took the opportunity to clean and oil his revolver, freeing each chamber of sand and reloading with six fresh bullets taken from his ammunition pouch. Presently, during one of their involuntary lurches towards the eastern side of the channel, he saw dervishes, about a hundred of them, who began shouting as soon as the steamer came in view and tried a few long-range shots that fell short or dropped well astern. Alex, sweating freely over his unmanageable sweep, caught the silvery glitter of their impact on the reddish-brown surface of the flood.

It was all rather jolly, he decided, or would have been had the sweep not assumed a capricious personality of its own and jumped and bucked independently of his heaves and pressures. Where the river narrowed he saw more dervishes, mounted and unmounted, thronging downstream so far as he could make out, and every now and again a random shot struck the plates or superstructure of the steamer, ricocheting with a musical whine but doing them no harm, for the little tub continued to thresh her way downstream all the late afternoon and Alex reflected that, warm as it was up here under the canopy, it must be hellishly hot in that little boiler-room below. Then, as dusk fell, they came within sight of Merowe, perhaps five miles downstream and in the fading light he could see a continuous line of flashes on both banks but a heavier concentration where the British flank guard was posted to defend the Korti bridgehead.

The river was narrower here so that the rate of the current increased and he was obliged to give his full attention to keeping a reasonably straight course. It was on this account, perhaps, that he did not connect the source of a sudden glare of light with anything close at hand until a strong backdraught of smoke and flame shot from the stern companionway, blotting out everything about him as the vessel began to veer hard to port. Then as the smoke momentarily cleared, he saw a tongue of flame shoot vertically from the engine room and take a hold on the deck and the base of the deckhouse.

His only thought then was for that poor devil of a corporal trapped below, so that he abandoned the kicking sweep to run forward, but before he had taken three strides he was assailed, seemingly from every point of the compass, by a murderous cross-fire of small arms and as he dropped flat on his face the prow of the vessel came into violent collision with something more solid than a sandbank, the impact bringing it up short and tossing Alexander back into the stern.

Miraculously, or so it seemed to him, he was not hit but the firing continued unchecked, as though a whole battalion was aiming at the ship, the hundreds of isolated explosions merging into a metallic fusillade as the bullets smacked against plates, super-structure, funnel and paddle hoods. By then the ship was on fire from the engine room to bows and a number of other collisions ensued as it threshed about in the fading light. Distractedly he heard about him a chorus of howls and screams and behind them a long, grinding splintering sound, as of rending timbers and it at once occurred to him, staggering drunkenly about in the confined space astern of the engine room hatchway, that they had collided with another vessel and tossed its occupants into the water. Then, without being conscious of more than a tap on the side of his head, the whole crazy scene dissolved.

*   *   *

He came to in a tent lit by a single swinging lamp, aware of a sharp smarting in his right temple and was lifting his hand up to touch bandages when a man with the badges of a captain on his tunic grinned down at him, saying, "No more than a scratch, lad. Just a graze that put you out for a spell. Was there anyone else aboard the tub of yours?"

"My corporal, . . . in the engine room, he was . . ." But he saw from the man's expression that it was futile to make enquiries concerning the luckless McTavish, who had probably been suffocated before the fire took hold of the deck.

The man said, with a shrug. "Then he's gone. Are you from Khartoum?"

"No . . . we found the steamer, a derelict. Corporal McTavish got her working and eased her into mid-stream. The steering was gone . . . we made do with a sweep. I was taking camels to Gadkul . . ."

But then the Captain said something quite incomprehensible for him, something about 'showing commendable initiative, creating a timely diversion, and resorting to Drake's fireship tactics', so that he gathered the flaming hulk had butted into Fuzzy's reinforcements as they made the crossing from east bank to west, interrupting a renewed attack just when the post was running low on ammunition.

"You probably did for a score or more of them, either by drowning, or that cracking rifle practice you gave us on the way in. I would have sworn there were a score of you aboard. Take it quietly now. You'll have a sore head for a day or so but nothing worse!" And he drifted away, leaving Alex to lie still under the lamp, trying to make sense of a jumble of recollections since he had first noticed that curl of smoke from the engine-room hatchway.

In the event it was several days before he made a coherent pattern of the sequence of events between McTavish shaking his foot, and telling him that camels and drivers had melted into the night, and those final moments of uproar and enveloping flames. McTavish, poor devil, must have burst the ancient boilers in his efforts to put on steam when they were running through the dervishes and the comment of the Captain, concerning his 'cracking rifle practice', supplied another clue. The flames in the boiler room had touched off that box of rifle ammunition he had carried down there, giving the impression of the arrival of a company of riverborne riflemen during a lull in the dervish attack on the bridgehead guard.

When he was satisfied that this was so he made out his report but glumly, reasoning that his superiors were not likely to regard the exchange of fifty odd camels for one burned-out hulk as a bargain that would appeal to the Quartermaster. To his relief, however, he heard no more about the incident for weeks when, as one of the lightly wounded, he was detached to guard stores during the abortive advance to Metemna and Khartoum and the fighting withdrawal that followed it, a campaign that reflected little credit on anyone concerned.

It was much later, in the midst of what the enraged press was already calling 'The Scuttle' (of which the dead Gordon was the hero and Mr. Gladstone the arch villain), that Alex received a summons from his immediate superior, Colonel Kitchener, and answered it with some trepidation. A man who had reconnoitred in the desert for seventeen days at a stretch disguised as an Arab, and escorted by no more than twenty Bedouins, was unlikely to look kindly on a subaltern who slept whilst fifty-seven of Her Majesty's camels vanished into the night.

The hypnotic stare over the enormous black moustache was blank when he presented himself and saluted, but the tone of voice seemed conciliatory when Kitchener glanced up from a study of what Alexander recognised as his report, saying, "This statement, concerning the incident at Merowe six weeks ago. It represents the facts as you recall them, Lieutenant?"

Alexander said respectfully that it did, whereupon Kitchener scowled and said, brusquely, "You received a wound in the head, Lieutenant. In the circumstances let me make a suggestion. Take it away and rewrite it. As far as I am concerned one of my junior officers, finding himself separated from his company in enemy-held territory, refloated a derelict steamer, sailed downstream and halted an enemy attack on the flank of the British army. I am recommending you for a decoration, and I have to inform you you will be gazetted to the rank of captain, back-dated to the first day of January. Let me have the amended report by sundown, Captain Swann. That is all, except to congratulate you on your initiative."

Alexander returned to his quarters in a daze but slowly the extent of his unbelievably good luck established itself in his mind, so that he took a pen and set to work on a report that read rather differently to the original. He did not lie, exactly, but merely let certain factors be inferred, so that anyone reading the statement (from which all mention of the missing camels was omitted) could have been forgiven for supposing that Lieutenant Swann had himself repaired the engines and had, moreover, set deliberate course for the embattled flank, fired the vessel en route, and discharged over a hundred aimed rounds at such boats as he failed to ram in midstream.

It did not cause him much surprise, therefore, when a war correspondent sought him out on his return to Cairo in February, and pumped him dry of the facts for a story in *The Times,* or that, in due course, an account of the incident appeared under the arresting headline *Subaltern's Charge in Blazing Steamer,* with a sub-title, almost equally arresting, reading, *Two Men Rout an Army on Upper Nile.*

To the end of his life Alexander Swann never did discover the underlying reasons for his superior's deliberate distortion of the facts. How was he to know that, searching the wreck as it lay piled up among the debris of the Merowe encounter, Intelligence officers had found and pieced together fragments of final despatches from Khartoum that went some way towards exculpating the army, and fastening the blame firmly upon Mr. Gladstone's shoulders. Indeed, it might almost be said that Swann, a tiny cog in an extremely complex piece of machinery, had brought about the fall of the Liberal Government and ensured years of Conservative rule in Westminster. But of this also he remained permanently unaware.

Something to his advantage he did learn, however, and that was, in times of stress, the army could be relied upon to look after its own. That, in the light of his subsequent career, was almost worth the singlehanded capture of Khartoum.

3

Alexander, having donned the military strait-jacket, had most of his problems solved for him. The same did not apply to Giles, spending his final term at the school on the moor.

News of his scholarship to university had come through in the first week of the Lent term but it did no more than confuse issues that were already confused enough. He did not see himself spending three years in the rarefied atmosphere of Oxford, sensing somehow that there came a point in one's life where books should be laid aside in favour of the experience.

He had been very happy at West Buckland, and was to look back upon the five years he had spent there as among the most fulfilled of his life. He got along very well with Thompson, the headmaster, and most of the staff, and he grew to love this high, windswept corner of the land more than any place on earth, finding here time to absorb all he wanted to absorb, plus a physical stimulus that seemed lacking elsewhere. The persistent cough of his earlier years had ceased to trouble him and although he stopped growing when he had reached a height of five feet eight inches (four inches short of his young brother, Hugo) there was never a day when he did not feel fit and toned up and ready, if necessary, for a five-mile lope across the moor, or down through the woods that clothed the twisting valley of the Bray.

He read deeply and widely, reimbibing all his favourite poets, from Spenser and Marlowe, to Herrick, Waller, Gray, Hood and

Cowper, from Wordsworth, Tennyson and Shelley, to contemporaries like Matthew Arnold, and moved on to John Stuart Mill, Kingsley, Dickens, the Brontës and George Eliot, reading their books at the rate of about two a week. Perhaps his favourite book, however, was Carlyle's *French Revolution*, that some found difficult to read but Giles read and reread with a sense of actually participating in the event and finding there the answers to some of the questions he had been asking himself ever since political science attracted his attention at the meeting in Exeter Hall when he was a boy.

For a lad passing through his teens, however, he was well-informed on current affairs, reading many of the political debates in the headmaster's copy of *The Times*, supplemented by a radical master's *Pall Mall Gazette*. Thus he found himself absorbed in the topics of the day, only ripples of which reached this far west. As a privileged senior, during his last two years, he had stayed up late and discussed matters like Home Rule, the extension of the franchise, the disestablishment of the Irish Church and, above all, the Soudan Scuttle, with some of the younger masters, and always he found himself siding with Gladstone, who seemed to Giles justified in assuming himself to be the chosen instrument of God, destined to bring true democracy to a society now exercising dominion over vast areas of the earth.

One would have thought, in these circumstances, that he would have welcomed translation to the most famous University in the world, but his instincts were against it, and as the weeks passed, and his long stay up here drew to a close, he made his decision, discussing it with his father when Adam paid a call on the school during one of his visits to the West Country to find someone to replace the failing Hamlet Ratcliffe.

*　　　*　　　*

They had gone out one bright forenoon in early spring and taken the easterly road, turning north at the East Buckland crossroads and climbing up towards Forty Beeches, where they paused and leaned on a gate giving a distant view of the school a mile or so to the west.

Adam had always been puzzled by his son's identification with a place that seemed to him little more than a gaunt, rather tumble-down collection of stone and brick, set down somewhat haphazardly in what he thought of as heartbreaking farmland. To his mind the hills lacked the grandeur of Lakeland, where he had spent his own youth, and also the softness and sophistication of the landscape adjoining the Weald of Kent. It was a prehistoric land, from which little could be milked in the way of trade but he had not come up here to discuss the countryside, having more than an inkling that the most promising of his children was engaged in some inward struggle that had to do, in some way, with Giles' future. He said, bluntly, as was his way, "Spit it out, lad. You've won yourself a free place at Oxford but you're not disposed to go there. That's about it, isn't it?" And Giles, smiling at his father's lack of finesse, admitted that it was.

"It's a matter of value for money, sir, and you'll understand that better than most people. On the face of it it looks dazzling. Three years, maybe four, at the fountain of all wisdom. But I've read a lot about Oxford, and talked to several chaps who were up there, and it strikes me as a bit of a lotus-eater's land."

"Surely it's what a man makes of it, isn't it?"

"No, not entirely. There are so many pressures, you see—religious, social, athletic and intellectual. You get caught up in one coterie or another, and frankly I've never been much good at that kind of thing. I like to look at things, think about them in private, and then form independent conclusions. Does that sound frightfully smug?"

"About as smug as your sister Stella, when she rattles on about her farm and family, but go on, I get the drift of what you're trying to say."

"Well, how I look at it is this. The object of education isn't to stuff yourself with facts. That makes a chap a bore and a pedant. The real purpose, surely, is to learn how to *live*, evaluate the people you live with and the civilisation that surrounds them."

"You're away above my head," said Adam, "but then, you always are. Wouldn't a place like Oxford, where you would mix with the best brains in the country, help you in that process?"

"I don't think it would. I can't be sure, of course, having nothing in the way of experience to go on, but I've got a feeling the *atmosphere* at Oxford would be too rarefied. It wouldn't relate to the lives of ordinary people, like your managers and your waggoners, or even most of your customers come to that."

"Are you saying you want to come into the business, after all?"

"Yes, I am, pater, but . . . well . . . it sounds infernal cheek on my part . . . given a certain condition. Two conditions really."

"Well?"

"First, I'd like to spend the next six months exploring. I don't mean like George, who's getting technical knowledge, but exploring our country. Didn't you do something just like that before you founded the network?"

"Yes, I did, but it didn't occupy me six months. I rode horseback all the way from Plymouth, where I landed after seven years abroad, to Derwentwater."

"Did it show a profit?"

"Yes, it did. Are your suggesting you do a Cobbett Rural Ride?"

"Good Lord no, sir, I'd walk."

"*Walk?*"

"Why not? I can do upwards of twenty miles a day and I'd see a lot in six months, given good weather."

"I see. And what was the other condition?"

"That I could make another and final choice when I was—say—twenty-one. To stay on, and give you a hand wherever you thought I'd be useful, or take up a profession. The law, maybe, or the F.O., or journalism like Debbie, or even . . . well . . . politics if I saw an opening. Is that asking too much?"

In a way it was. The prospect of having Giles with him was a pleasant one for Adam, but not if his approach to the network was half-hearted, as sounded likely. On the other hand he saw the boy's point. There was no better way of getting to know one's own country than to walk over it, stopping off here and there, and with time to absorb encounters and experiences en route.

He said, "Listen here, Giles. There's no one who could prove more useful to me than you and that includes George, who is coming in anyway. George, however, is a technical man and the human aspects of the network won't interest him. They've always interested me, however, and that's why your conditions make sense. I'll accept them, providing you make me a pledge in return. When it comes to the point be absolutely honest with me. I'll be sixty then, and slacking off I daresay, so you might be inclined to stay on out of consideration for my feelings. The others wouldn't, but you would. Is that understood?"

"That's understood, sir," said Giles, seriously. And then, with a gleam in his eye, "I'll start mapping out a route. Will you do one other favour for me? Tell Tommy—the Head, that is—what I've decided, and why? He's annoyed that I don't share his enthusiasm for Oxford. I'm sure he thinks I'm dotty but . . . well . . . you don't, do you?"

"No," said Adam, "I never did. You just happen to have a bump of curiosity that wouldn't find room in the Crystal Palace. I doubt whether it'll ever be satisfied, but there comes a time when one has to compromise between living life and dreaming it. I shouldn't be too pontifical. I was thirty before I put dreams to work. Is that a bell they're ringing down there?"

"Yes, the lunch bell. You live by that sound up here. No matter where you are it carries in this clear atmosphere."

He took a long final look at the downsweep of field and coppice, one of the many views hereabouts that would remain imprinted on his mind until the day he died. Then, talking of Hugo, they started down the hill, the faint clamour of the bell reaching them on a south-westerly blowing in from the Atlantic.

2

George Hears Music

GEORGE SWANN never did things in a hurry.

The gentle pressures that finally prised him from the muscular arms of Rosa Ledermann, and extended his odyssey south and east to the curve of the Danube below Vienna, were such that he needed time to reflect and on this account took a meandering route that led him through the Tyrol to Gratz, a journey occupying him the better part of a week. The time was not wasted. Not only was he thus able to approach the Habsburg capital from the south, a route that gave him chance to absorb the beauty and tranquillity of the countryside sunning itself under the black pines of the Parapluiberg, he also had an opportunity to cast off the mood of gentle melancholy that had accompanied him this far. The city approaches made such an impact upon him that his spirit lifted at once, as though soaring on the bars of a Strauss waltz and whirling over the vineyards, the Kahlenberg and, finally, the imposing silver-grey needle of St. Stephen's tower. It was as though Vienna, having no room for the glum and careworn, spied him from afar and singled him out for a civic benediction.

He was a young man who was rarely downcast and almost never troubled, yet his obligatory move had disturbed him. By then, his involvement with Rosa was deeply emotional and how could it be otherwise? For George, packing his bags for Vienna, had a suspicion amounting to a certainty that frolic was on the point of exchanging its carnival mask for fatherhood.

He could not, despite his persistent search for an honest answer, be absolutely certain of this for neither, it seemed, could Rosa, who was somewhat careless with her favours. Yet to George it seemed probable and probability was enough to rouse his conscience, hitherto quiescent.

Judged on the standards of his day and generation George Swann

400

had received a very liberal upbringing but, although basically selfish, he was very far from being a callous young man, and would, at a pinch, have faced the music. Rosa, however, would have none of this having, it appeared, her own long-term plans. She saw him now as she had always seen him, a young and personable English gentleman, who had been sent out into the world ignorant, naked and vulnerable, who was likely, indeed certain, to fall victim to the first enterprising trollop he met. It had been thoughts like this that had encouraged her to make a man of him on the night of the *Oktoberfest* and she might well have left it there had not Herr Swann proved such a diligent pupil, making what she could only regard as spectacular progress throughout the winter and on into the spring. But there came a time, in the first weeks of April, when facts had to be faced and she faced them resolutely but genially, like the good Municher she was.

* * *

Their relationship had not undergone any dramatic change since his initiation. She continued to address him as 'Herr Swann', and behave towards him in the same manner as she behaved towards all the other lodgers who came and went, and all her regular callers who dropped in from time to time, men like the beaming, broad shouldered policeman, Kurt, and Ebert, the wall-eyed postman, whom George thought of as Kurt's most dangerous rival, for he was said to have money in State bonds.

To George, weekly and sometimes bi-weekly access to Rosa was an unlooked-for privilege but Rosa did not regard it as such. Her ability to divorce body and soul would have been unflattering to a man more experienced in these matters but George did not quarrel with it. In some way it absolved him from responsibility.

He found, after that first occasion, that he could look upon Rosa with a surprising degree of objectivity, as though a close study of her charms was part of his curriculum as a footloose student, and in this way, for a matter of seven blissful months, he contrived to have the best of both worlds, up to the night she told him, with a nonchalance that he found almost shocking, that she was pregnant and expected her child in August.

Up to that moment it had been a rewarding occasion for, although he had grown accustomed to Rosa indulging him as she might a venturesome, likeable schoolboy, on this particular evening she had shown signs that he was able to rouse her to some extent, and Rosa Ledermann, even half-roused, was capable of invoking a sense of considerable gratification in a man. She was so big, so powerful, so direct and possessed of so much positive energy, that her body seemed equipped to solace every man in the world. Her limbs had a way of enveloping a lover to the point of all but extinguishing him.

It was in the still moment that followed this shattering experience that she said, in a tone that he recognised as valedictory, "So, *mein süsses Kind* . . . You are a man now any woman would wish to please and it is time you went in search of her, *gelt*? It is not part of your father's plans, I think, that you should remain in München for one year more."

It made him uneasy to hear her say that, and in such a matter-offact tone, particularly at a moment like this, when he was savouring a sense of profound fulfilment. He said, raising himself on his elbow and looking down at her broad, placid features, "You wish me to stop coming here unless I am invited?"

"Ach, no," she said, impatiently, "it has been a pleasure, *mein Schatz*. You do not need to be told that, I think. But it would not do for you to live here when I marry."

He had completely forgotten until then that she might wish to remarry and for a moment he was too amazed to comment. Then he said, "Marry? Marry who, Rosa?"

"Kurt," she said, thoughtfully, as if not finally decided. "Yes, I will take Kurt. He is not so thrifty as Ebert but he is younger. Besides, I am with child, and Kurt is fond of children."

If the announcement that she was contemplating remarriage astonished him the fact that she was pregnant threw him into such a turmoil that he leaped from bed with a cry of dismay.

"A child? . . . You're expecting a child? And you can talk of it in that way?" But then the full significance of her announcement caught up with him. "A child! Why it might . . . *Is* it . . . ? I never thought! Oh, my God, Rosa!"

She looked up at him mildly. It seemed to her that he was making very heavy weather of so small a storm but then, she reflected, he was young and, until she had taken him in hand, touchingly innocent, like most Englishmen who had passed this way.

She said, "Ach, put it from your mind, *Hertzliebchen*. I should not have told you. It is likely that the child is Kurt's. But if it were not then there is no occasion to fuss. I too am fond of children, and it is time I had another. I am thirty-six. The years are flying."

Despite the numerous occasions he had surrendered to those white, muscular arms he had not yet adjusted to her philosophy that enabled her to regard the birth of a child, of whose father she was unsure, as a day's work that had been neglected and should be attended to before the light failed. He said, with a kind of despair, "But good God, Rosa! It might . . . it almost surely *is* mine."

"Ja, *es mag sein*—it is possible," she conceded, equably. "But I think not. It is likely to be Kurt's and that is why I told him I will marry him and that he may live here if he continues with the police until he has his pension. He has nine years to serve," she added, smiling.

He said, pulling on his clothes as though she had despatched him for the midwife, "What . . . what do you think I should *do*, Rosa? I'm sorry, God knows. If it *is* me, that is, but I never thought . . . well, it always seemed to me that you . . . what I mean is, you've *been* married and had children . . . I took it for granted you . . ."

She took pity on his frightful confusion at that point and hoisted herself up, smiling at him indulgently.

"Ach, I did not bother. Cease to blame yourself. The thing is done and it does not distress me. Why should it? I have a good home and money in the bank. I have good health and Kurt has been anxious to be the father of my children since two years. One more will not concern him. He will be made happy by the news."

He continued to gape at her as she swung her legs to the floor and then, heaving herself across to the mirror, began to pin up her abundant blonde hair.

On previous occasions he had enjoyed watching her perform this office, stark naked and with a mouthful of hairpins. It gave him a cosy, proprietary feeling, and a sense of being one up on all the gentlemen abed in England. But now there was no particle of complacency left in him. He said, dismally, "You've been so decent . . . such a sport, Rosa!" and she turned her head sharply but only, it appeared, to add to her proud collection of English idioms. " 'Sport'?

That is a word we do not associate with love. But the English, perhaps, yes?"

It was just too much for George's damped-down but resilient sense of humour. He chuckled, then tried to stifle the chuckle and began to cough and splutter so violently that his eyes misted as he said, "In a sense I suppose. Certainly as applied to you, *Liebling*. What I meant was you're such a . . . well . . . generous person, someone who gives and gives and never seems to expect anything in return," and he buttoned his shirt collar and went over to her, bending to kiss her neck and her shoulders.

For her, however, his dilemma needed immediate attention. Ignoring the gesture she removed six pins from her mouth and laid them in a row, like six grenadiers.

"You asked me what you should do, Herr Swann. It is clear what you must do. You are twenty-one, yes? You have a rich and indulgent papa, yes? You came here, on a letter of credit. Is that the correct phrase?"

"Introduction."

"*Ja*, introduction. And you have others, yes?"

"Three, and I could always get more. I have one for Stockholm, one for Berlin, and one for a big coach-building firm near Vienna."

"Then I will decide for you. Stockholm is grey and cold most of the year. And its people, I am told, do not laugh much. Berlin is full of Prussians. You would not like it there. Vienna, that is the place for a young man with money in his pocket. The wine is good. The women are very pretty. The waltz is a foolish dance but you cannot have everything. My advice, *Engelchen*, is go to Vienna. Go at once. Time does not wait upon the young, although they think it does." She lapsed into German, smiling her broad, maternal smile; "*Du bist ein Bienchen das am Sommertag Honig suchen sollte.*"

"What does that mean, Rosa?"

"It is difficult." She thought for a moment, hand on hip, looking like a muscular nymph in a painting he had seen somewhere on his travels, a nymph painted by an artist who liked his models round, ripe and full of promise. "You are a little bee who should be seeking honey on a summer's day. For you, *Hertzliebchen*, there will always be plenty of honey."

2

He thought of that when he left her at the station a week or two later and for some reason it reminded him of the poem *Venus and Adonis*, favourite reading among the more sophisticated of the Fifth at school and easier to memorise, he recalled, than excerpts from *The Merchant of Venice* or *Macbeth*. The lines returned to him now, doing service, possibly, as a requiem for Rosa, whom he sensed he would never see again but would never forget:

> I'll be a park, and thou shalt be my deer;
> Feed where thou wilt, on mountain or on dale.
> Graze on my lips; and if those hills be dry,
> Stray lower, where the pleasant fountains lie.

It seemed extraordinarily apt, although he had never seen himself as a candidate for anyone so churlish as Shakespeare's Adonis. It made the poem live for a moment, giving it a relevance that it must have had for many adolescents down the centuries. Rosa had indeed performed the office of a park, and a very verdant park at that, and now that it came to the moment of parting he was choked by the strength of his affection for her. He made a gesture then that had the power to touch her, crossing to an aged flower-seller sitting at the station entrance, dropping a handful of loose change into the woman's lap and gathering up an armful of flowers, daffodils, freesias and narcissi. Their scent and colour were redolent of all the gaiety he had experienced in her company and her city.

He thrust them towards her and hurried away, blushing, to catch his train, and she watched him go, her arms full of flowers, a rare expression of indecision on her broad, pink face. Then she sighed, so gustily that the flower-seller stared at her curiously, watching her stride away, carrying her flowers and her regrets, if she had any, into the swirl of traffic.

3

The firm of Hoffman and Sina, renowned for the quality of their heavy goods waggons and excellence of the river-boats they built in a recent extension to their premises opposite the wooded island of Lobau, was a much larger concern than he had anticipated.

All told it covered about twenty acres, stretching eastward from the left bank of the river and the setting, like so many semi-industrial patches on the outskirts of Vienna, had remained rural, so that it could have been mistaken at a distance for a huge farm composed of innumerable barns, sheds and outbuildings. The clamour that prevailed there, however, reminded George of a factory.

His letter of introduction seemed to carry more weight here than in any of the industrial centres he had visited so far, perhaps because it had been underwritten by Blunderstone, the famous London coachbuilder, from whom his father bought all his vehicles. Blunderstone was apparently well-known here as a craftsman who employed coachbuilders able to hold their own with the best engaged by Hoffman, the founder, or Sina, his son-in-law and successor, names synonymous with high quality products throughout the empire.

At his previous ports of call he had presented himself as a courtesy student, content to hang around watching and occasionally contributing to the output but without a salary. Here he soon found himself on a very different footing and regarded as the emissary of a well-known British haulier travelling under the patronage of an internationally-respected coachbuilder, so that he was accorded, from the very first day, a status he had not enjoyed in Paris and Munich.

After the inevitable tour, accompanied by an English-speaking director, he was placed in the charge of one, Maximilien Körner, a tall, spare, rather forthright man in his late sixties, who was not only his guide but also his landlord. George took an instant liking to Max, whom he thought of as the equivalent of a senior foreman in an English waggon yard, and as a craftsman of great repute, who had worked for a number of important German coachbuilders before returning to Vienna on the death of his son and accepting responsibility for his widow and children.

Max was a man of moderate means. The house he and his family occupied, in the neighbouring village of Essling, had once been a granary, a large stone building that had been used, so Körner said, as a strongpoint by Napoleon's troops during the Danubian campaign of 1809. It was commodious and well-appointed, and besides Frau Körner, sheltered seven children, whose ages ranged from the fifteen-year-old apprentice Rudi, born after his father's death at the battle of Sadowa against the Prussians, to twenty-three-year-old Gisela, eldest of four pretty daughters of Körner Junior.

There was something inevitable, George told himself, about his gravitation to lodgings spilling over with women. There had been the Broadbent family in the Polygon. There had been the household of Madame Drouet and her daughters, in Paris. And more recently, the delectable Rosa Ledermann, who had headed him this way, to be lodged alongside four grand-daughters of the patriarchal Maximilien Körner, who lost no time in instructing the family to accord him the honours due to a distinguished stranger.

Perhaps George was still excessively naïve in at least one respect. It never occurred to him that, on the strength of his spending habits alone, he would be likely to be regarded a good catch by any observant mamma. He had been taken unawares by Broadbent's efforts to embroil him with Lizzie, and slow to awaken to Madame Drouet's efforts to secure him as a son-in-law in Paris, but he could be forgiven for taking the welcome given him by the Körners at face value, for the Viennese seemed to him exceptionally happy-go-lucky people disinclined to take anything seriously unless it was their cuisine and the beauty of the lovely Wienerwald, a sacrosanct girdle of woodland and meadow where they spent their Sundays and holidays.

The area, George thought, remembering the urban sprawl of Lancashire and London, was like a garland, reaching from the river and the Nussdorf vineyards, to the forested slopes of the Kahlenberg. On one of the first of the Körner picnics he was taken here and on to the adjacent Leopoldsberg, where there were any number of enchanting little taverns selling the local wine and he could look down, from flower-decked gardens, on a magnificent view of the Danube, with smoke-plumed steamers chugging upstream and down and spring sunshine flooding the baroque splendours of the old city. The tempo of life here was very different from that of Britain, France, or even Bavaria, inasmuch as the Viennese were the first people he had ever lived among who could laugh at themselves as well as their social betters, represented by the fusty aristocracy of the top-heavy empire, already, so Körner told him, well-advanced on the road to dissolution and decay. Everyone seemed to live for the moment and the Körner household was fully representative of the prevailing Viennese mood. To George it seemed to sparkle and crackle in a way that was unique in his experience, although 'Tryst' had been a lively, outward-looking home in his childhood and boyhood. Even at 'Tryst', however, an awareness of belonging to a master race, dedicated to commerce and high moral values, was inescapable, and George never recalled his brothers, sisters or associates making light of their tribal destiny in a way that happened here whenever the conversation broke from the magic circle of food, wine, music, dancing, family outings and dressmaking, the one art, perhaps, that the Körner girls pursued with any degree of diligence.

From the moment he was introduced to them by the ageing Max (the one serious-minded member of the family) he told himself he had never met so many handsome, congenial people under a single roof, and his arrival seemed to begin a nonstop firework display of teasing mischief on the part of the girls, who were given free rein by the placid, ever-smiling Frau Körner. Once home, George noticed, Maximilien the dedicated craftsman, tended to efface himself completely, generally disappearing into one of the old granary buildings where, so the girls told him, he had a private workshop dedicated to a mysterious 'engine' he was inventing. The one prohibition existing in the Körner household concerned this patch of privacy. Everyone was enjoined not to enter, not because Grandfather Max would resent intrusion but because what he had there was said to be dangerous to anyone but an expert.

George's extreme curiosity concerning the nature of Max's invention remained unsatisfied for several months, the old man ignoring his veiled questions regarding what he was inventing. He was free with other information, however, notably the history of the locality and the various projects in train at the yard of Hoffman and Sina. George had always been interested in the mechanics of the haulier's trade and spent long periods in the coachbuilders' yard, the boatshed and wheelwrights' sheds, where it seemed to him they used old-fashioned tools and very traditional apparatus, but he had to admit they produced magnificent vehicles, capable of bearing heavy loads over all the unpaved roads of the empire, where gradients, particularly south and west, would have presented insoluble problems to men like Blunderstone.

Everything that emerged from the yards of Hoffman and Sina was built for strength and durability and looked as if it was, and when George commented on this Maximilien told him that the Austrian railways had been slow to adapt to the local terrain, particularly in the dependent states of the Dual Monarchy. Habsburg industrialisation, he said, was decades behind that of Britain, Germany and even America.

"We left it too late," he explained, "and now, with only Russia at our heels, we are last but one in the queue. Our economy is still predominantly agricultural. Sometimes I think we are all waiting for something of great significance that will change the lives of all of us. By that I mean not solely we Austrians, and those arrogant devils over in Hungary, but all our subject races—Czechs, Slovenes, Croats, Ruthenians and other minorities. One day they will all go their own way, and thumb their noses at the Hofburg and that dry old stick of an Emperor, who sits there working his fourteen-hour stint on a diet of cabbage soup so they tell me. He will be the last Emperor. No one expects much of Rudolph, his son, who devotes himself to debauchery, like his cousins. As to the Empress, she is not often here but roving about Europe, trying to stay beautiful and find a horse she cannot master. One day she will, no doubt, and it will break her back. That is where our trouble lies, to my way of thinking. Old Franz should never have married a Wittelsbach. All the Wittelsbachs are mad and since that rascal Bismarck hitched us to the Prussian war-chariot we have given up trying and live, as you see, for the moment only."

"It seems an extraordinarily jolly way to live," George commented, remembering the terrible moral earnestness, social posturing and unabashed greed he had seen in the north of England, and the thirst for revenge that obsessed the French, but the old man shook his head.

"I am nearly seventy. I can remember a time when the Habsburgs

amounted to something. But that was before Sadowa, and the humiliations in Italy, and the industrialisation of your country and
Prussia. In those days, in my youth that is, it was a fine thing to be
an Austrian. Culture and civilisation lived here beside the Danube.
We should have moved forward into the century of invention then,
as your countrymen did, instead of trying to preserve the past. You
will understand I am not typically Austrian. I began as a craftsman
but I have allowed my mind to conjure with new ideas, new
thoughts, new ways of developing trade. But that is a private dream,
of which I prefer not to speak. My son, Albrecht, shared it, but those
rascals the Prussians shot off his head, and I was obliged to return to
see that his wife and children did not starve."

George would have liked to have asked him more about his private
dream and how it was linked to the technological progress of engineering craftsmen in Britain, France and Germany, but Maximilien
abruptly changed the subject, and conducted him on a tour of the
Marchfield, where Napoleon fought the great battle of Wagram,
and after that showed him landmarks of the battle of Aspern-Essling,
that was fought about here and drove the first nail in the coffin of the
Grande Armée.

He was an excellent guide, both here and in Vienna, but he rarely
accompanied George and the family on their picnics, preferring to
shut himself up in the old granary with his invention and staying
out of sight until they returned sun-tired and wine-merry at dusk,
when he would emerge smelling of an engine-oil that George could
not identify, for it was more pungent than any of the oils they used
at the yard.

*   *   *

There was a timelessness about those first sunlit months beside the
Danube and sometimes, absorbed in everything he did and saw, and
carried along on the current of the younger Körners' ebullience,
George not only ceased to yearn for the charms of Rosa Ledermann
but lost his identity to some degree, giving hardly a thought to home
and family, and none to his immediate future.

The main reason for this, of course, was his preoccupation with
the Körner girls, all but the eldest of them, who was more withdrawn
than her sisters and was moving towards a maturity that put her on

410

a level with Frau Körner. It was easy to see why this had happened. Although pretty and, if possible, even more amiable than her three sisters, Gisela had begun to share with her mother and grandfather the work of rearing the family when she was scarcely more than a child herself and had since been unable, or possibly unwilling, to match their high spirits. She would smile tolerantly at the endless junketings and mock quarrels of her brothers and sisters but rarely participated, preferring to busy herself preparing the picnic hamper, or set about cutting, stitching and embroidering one of the traditional blouses the girls wore on holiday occasions.

This blouse was a confection of billowing georgette, muslin, lace or silk, richly embroidered and much approved of by George, who thought all the Körner girls looked stunning in their frills, Mozart ruffs, jabots, plastron-fronted bodices, hip-bags and intricately pleated skirts. They were not given, he noticed, to wasting materials on garments not for public display. Indeed, judged on standards of modesty, they were a great contrast to the girls at home and the bourgeois Drouet girls in Paris. Once, when two of them tumbled upside down on a punt after a head-on collision in the shallows, they displayed a glorious profusion of white thighs and pink buttocks but without the least loss of composure, either on their part, or that of other male witnesses save George, who, notwithstanding his six-months' apprenticeship under Frau Ledermann, found it difficult to equate horseplay of this kind with the ladylike qualities Phoebe Fraser had been at pains to instil into his sisters at home.

He got used to it, however, and was soon on kissing terms with all three, although he could never decide which of them exerted the greatest fascination over his senses.

There was Sophie, who followed the more restrained Gisela; Valerie, a year younger, and Gilda, the seventeen-year-old, so that like Butes, fairest of all mortal men, he was always poised to dive overboard and swim towards the Sirens, careless of any risk he ran of being gobbled up by one or all of them, for that, he thought cheerfully, was a fate some of the high-collared young men at home might envy.

Sophie was tall and slender and wore her light chestnut hair in finely-plaited coils over her small, pink ears. She had a spellbinding, swaying walk, as though, wherever she went, she carried a saucer of cream on her head, and her soft, tinkling laugh was the most musical sound George had ever heard. Valerie, nearly nineteen, wore her corn-coloured hair in a bang, with a bewitching fringe low on her broad forehead, and her eyes were as blue as iris petals. She was an inch shorter than Sophie but charmingly proportioned, her waist taking precedence over the daily measurements of her sisters, hovering around the seventeen-inch ideal. How she achieved this in view of her lust for confections of every kind, George never discovered. Gilda, the seventeen-year-old, was the most forward of the trio, and reckoned a prodigious flirt by all the young men in the village and it was perhaps George's gentlemanly inclination to give the local boys a clear field that caused Gilda to take the lead in a spirited but amiable contest for his favours.

He remained uncommitted, however, flattering himself that he had learned something useful during his sojourn in Munich, but to some extent his attitude was governed by his deep respect for Maximilien and Frau Körner, who had used him so kindly from the moment of his arrival on their doorstep. Nevertheless, he was able to indulge himself in a galaxy of perfectly splendid fantasies involving all three girls, individually and even collectively, for he had a conviction that, had he presented himself in their communal bedroom when the coast was clear (as it almost invariably was in the Körner household) they would either draw lots for him or agree to share and share alike.

As time went on, and he became familiar with the local dialect, the strain of living up to his obligations as a trusted guest in the house became the one arduous aspect of life spent in such enchanting company. Charming little idiosyncrasies of one or other of the girls tormented him and sometimes filled his mind, to the exclusion of all the technical information he was daily imbibing down at the yard. For who the devil could concentrate on subjects like axle stress and cubic capacity in the presence of Valerie's tantalising wiggle retreating in the near distance, or Sophie's pretended pout at some fancied frustration, or Gilda's taut blouse outlining her firm young breasts when she was working the pump handle in the yard? His profound restlessness could be traced, or so he assured himself, to his recent experiences in Munich, for he reasoned that he had never been bothered in this way before Rosa Ledermann's brawny arms had enclosed him and it would have been wiser, no doubt, to have sought lodgings with a couple of spinsters, or pensioners rather than settle here where, sooner or later, he would surely be tempted to commit an indiscretion that would leave him no option but to plump for one or other of the girls as a wife.

The prospect of marriage, certainly marriage to a foreigner, would have been unthinkable a few months ago. Until then George had seen no reason why, with shrewd planning on his part, this richly rewarding travelling scholarship could not be prolonged for years. But the regular embraces of Rosa Ledermann, and the possibility that he had fathered a child on her, had wrought subtle changes in George Swann. Women were becoming absolutely necessary, he discovered, to his peace of mind, and wherever he was, and whatever he was doing, he was sharply aware of all women had to offer, not merely physically, but as dispensers of comfort, gaiety and solace in a world organised and dominated by men dedicated to the pursuit of wealth and ambition.

His abrupt removal from young people of his own generation when he left school and plunged into the network may have helped to promote this state of mind. In England and, to a degree, over here, he moved, for the most part, among the staid and the middle-aged, where his natural high spirits found no sounding board and were necessarily bottled up during working hours, but there was more to it than that. George had discovered that he possessed great reserves of natural affection that needed some kind of regular outlet and, over and above all this, there was a vague and largely undefined yearning to be petted, cossetted and fussed over, perhaps to compensate him for growing up in a large family where the attentions of mother and governess had to be shared among so many. Further than that he had always sensed that Henrietta's affections had been centred on his father, whereas Phoebe Fraser had invariably put duty before sentiment and had, moreover, a strict North Country upbringing that made a display of affection a sure indication of Sassenach sentimentality. Between the ages of twelve and seventeen he had lived in an exclusively male community, so that he had a compulsion to catch up on lost time and where better than here, cheek by jowl with three pretty and vivacious girls?

All the same, it wasn't as easy as all that, or not if one did not wish to act like a cad. He wished, sometimes, that someone had taught the Körner girls (and Rosa Ledermann, for that matter) the trick of restraining natural impulses, in the way that was obligatory among the English. They were all good Catholics, of course, but religion seemed to sit so much more lightly upon them than upon the Protestant girls at home or, for that matter, the Drouet girls in Paris, and the daughters of a number of Lutherans he had met in his travels about Germany. Instead they had a propensity to display their charms and Frau Körner seemed almost to encourage them with warm, placid smiles and fond maternal gestures, as though she took it for granted that one or other of them would be certain, given time, to capture the gentlemanly English boy, who had appeared out of the west with a pocket full of crowns and the signal advantage of a father who was a famous English merchant.

In the circumstances it was as well, perhaps, that charm, pertness, red lips, nubility, gently undulating bottoms and tautly-stretched blouses, were shared so equitably among the sisters, for the gentlemanly English boy was permanently occupied in the delightful business of making up his mind which of the three exerted the stronger claim on his susceptibilities. It was a decision that would have taxed the wits of a more experienced man than George, whose yardstick in these matters was limited to his brief encounter with Laura Broadbent and a thirty-six-year-old widow who had taken pity on his innocence.

George, however, was by nature an experimenter, and made the most of his numerous opportunities during that gay if slightly troubled spring and summer in this enchanting land. At a picnic on Lobau one sultry afternoon, he isolated Sophie for a rewarding half-hour and later, during an expedition to the pinewoods on the Kahlenberg slopes, he ensured that he and Valerie took a wrong turning at a junction of forest rides. A week or so later, in the course of an evening punt ride down the river, he arranged it so that he was left ashore two miles downstream and obliged to walk home in the company of Gilda. Sophie's lips, he discovered in the course of these tentative experiments, were every bit as warm and inviting as they looked when they parted to emit one of her low-pitched musical laughs. Valerie, on the other hand, was even more forthcoming and engaged him in a prolonged wrestling match among the ferns that might have resolved matters there and then had the ferns grown under the pines instead of in a clearing where they were soon located by fellow-picnickers. But it was the more enterprising Gilda who might well have captured him on the moonlight walk home across the water-meadows, if he had been better acquainted with the local dialect, enabling him to follow more than the drift of her conversation between sighs as they stood together under a chestnut tree within sight of the lights of the village. As it was he could not be absolutely sure he understood what she was proposing but close and sustained contact with her deprived him of at least two hours' sleep and it was probably on her account that he paid a visit to a high-class brothel off the Ringstrasse, recommended by one of the directors of Hoffman and Sina on his arrival, rather in the way a thoughtful host might give a guest directions to the water-closet.

It was a chastening experience. Regretfully George decided that this was not what he sought and that the impersonality of these establishments, together with the mechanical performance of a thorough but unsmiling partner, was disappointing and depressing.

It was borne upon him then, regretfully but with a degree of certainty, that he was ripe for marriage, notwithstanding his footloose status and lack of independent means, and the act of pulling up stakes and going home, far from solving his personal dilemma would gain him nothing, for he did not see his father or his mother taking kindly to such a step until he was absorbed into the business. He could, of course, look around more cynically in search of a wife, perhaps someone who could bring him a dowry, but girls with sizeable *dots*, he reasoned, would be unlikely to possess the charms of the Körner sisters.

He wondered, forlornly, if most young men were as subject to these distractions as he was. All the same, there was some consolation in finally coming to terms with himself. With marriage half in mind, he could afford to be bolder in his experiments and this, in turn, communicated itself to all three girls, although it did nothing, at that stage, to advance the claims of one over the other.

What might have happened had not his attention been sharply diverted is difficult to say. He might have committed himself on impulse. Or he might have established a kind of ménage à quatre, in the heart of the Körner household, had not Herr Körner, at this juncture, introduced a fourth mistress, no other in fact than his mysterious invention, housed in the former grain store across the yard, where no female was permitted to penetrate on pain of the patriarch's displeasure.

3

It happened one wet Sunday when an outing of any kind was out of the question. Maximilien, who had been looking very thoughtful of late, suddenly issued an invitation amounting to an order that George should accompany him to the grain store and here, as the barn doors swung open, he had one of the most salutary surprises of his life.

He had made many guesses concerning the nature of Maximilien's invention but his wildest surmises did not prepare him for what he saw when the old man stripped away capacious canvas wrappings to reveal what George could only think of in terms of Wellington's funeral carriage, seen in the crypt of St. Paul's.

There it stood, a huge, unwieldy juggernaut built of iron, tin, brass, copper and baulks of timber, looking so powerful, so vastly complicated, that the imagination boggled at its purpose, providing of course that it had a purpose, and was not some kind of god assembled by a tribe of Baal-worshipping heathens.

It was as large or larger than a hay-wain, and looked second-cousin to one as far as its basic structure was concerned. It had four immense wheels, rimmed with iron like cart wheels, but padded with what looked like endless strings of sausages, each string having a diameter of about eight inches. The upper rear half, a sort of over-all casing, was a container of some sort, with a hinged backboard of the kind seen on a brewer's dray, but what he at once thought of as the brain of the machine, housed in the lower forepart of the works, defied description. It seemed to consist of an intricate network of brass rods and steel couplings, interspersed, here and there, with any number of ponderous levers and belts of cross-stitched canvas. Towards the front, where there was a sort of brass honeycomb, was a much broader, stronger belt, linking two cogs of different sizes, one being about twice the diameter of the other. It was clearly a vehicle of some kind, for it had steering apparatus, consisting of rigid rods branching from a central rod and meeting in another pair of inter-locking cogs below the front axle.

George gaped at it for a full minute whilst Max dragged the cov-erings into a corner. Then, without taking his eyes from the mon-ster, he said, "What . . . what *is* it? What does it *do*?" and Max replied, gravely, "It has no name but you can think of it as a me-chanical waggon. You will have heard, no doubt, of your country-man Trevithick's horseless carriage, the one that was warned off the roads a century ago?"

George said that he had, adding that he had seen an illustration of Trevithick's invention, but it had not resembled this in the least, save for the fact that it had wheels.

"Does it . . . is it meant to . . . to *go*?" he asked, and Max said that it was not only meant to but almost certainly would, and that, indeed, was why he had invited George to inspect it, for he had reached the stage where it needed a road trial but he hesitated to make the experiment alone.

"I need not only help but a witness, Herr Swann," he said. "I have been secretive about it all this time for fear of ridicule. Four years of my life have gone into assembling this carriage, and there are very many adjustments to be made before I can consider applying for a patent. In the meantime, however, it has proceeded as far as possible in here and the time has come to put it to a practical test, first on level ground, then on a gentle incline."

He then became impatient with George's expression of incredu-lity and added, testily, "Come, my young friend, the theory of horse-less carriages, of automatically propelled vehicles, cannot be strange to the son of one of England's greatest carters. Experiments of one kind or another are being made in all the capitals of Europe but machinists, in the main, have been concentrating on what I think of as ingenious toys, capable of conveying one, or at most two, persons from one point to another. This is not designed for that purpose. I have in mind a vehicle capable of doing the work of a team of ten draught horses, and in less than half the time. It is possible that Karl Benz, with whom I have worked in the past, and Gottlieb Daimler, whom I once heard lecture on the possibilities of steam propulsion have conceived something similar, and if they have I honour them. The time will come when carriages of this kind will cease to be diversions and become the apparatus of merchants in all industrialised cities. You will have heard of Benz and Daimler, I trust?"

George had, now that he came to think of it. In Munich he had read an article in a technical transport magazine, describing the experiments of Benz, who had claimed that he could, given time and capital, produce an oil-driven carriage capable of travelling at the speed of fifteen road miles an hour. Either in that journal or some other he had read of Daimler, at work on a similar project. Someone called Barnett had built an engine that ran on coal-gas, another called Brayton had done the same for a contrivance that used engine oil, and a third, whose name he had forgotten, had invented a form of transport that ran on a specially refined oil of some kind.

The sudden recollection of all this, particularly of oil as a source of propulsion, reminded him of the pervading smell in the grain store, that he now identified as the smell that clung to Maximilien's clothes whenever he returned to the house after working here.

He said, "I know engineers have been trying to make horseless carriages of one kind and another for years but I never thought of them as anything but substitutes for passenger vehicles, little coaches if you like. What I mean is, the cost and size of a machine like that for transporting goods overland, and not running over a track, would be very high, wouldn't it?" Maximilien cut him short with an impatient gesture.

"Benz and Daimler, and Marcus here in Vienna, they were all ridiculed," he snorted. "And before them were others, dismissed as tinkers by men who make a cult of horse-worship. Two centuries ago a Dutchman called Huyhens discovered a process of combustion that drove an engine and I have used his idea in this very machine, as you will see when I generate enough power to spin those rear wheels. I have also used Mackenzie's variable speed device, patented close on a score of years ago. Yet another of your countrymen has suggested the use of those inflated wheel cushions, that I hope might go some way towards reducing the risk of dislodging components when the machine crosses rough surfaces and road ruts." But by now George's astonishment as regards the machine had transferred itself to the inventor. He said, thoughtfully, "I always had the greatest respect for your scholarship, Herr Körner, but to invent something like that . . . even if . . . well, even if it needs any number of modifications before it goes, why, that's something stupendous. Almost like . . . like being God!"

Max accepted this compliment with a shrug. "My young friend, no one man invents anything. Many men, dead and living, contribute to every machine that passes into practical use. All one can do, the best that one can do, is to study the results of the processes piecemeal and then, after years at the drawing board and work bench, build something one hopes might result in further progress of one kind or another. That is all I have done. As regards locomotion itself, Karl Benz is already far ahead of me, and so, doubtless, are many others, both here and in your country and America. But we inventors do not hoard conclusions when we are sure of them. We are a brotherhood, yes? We correspond and confer with one another. All these diagrams have been back and forth to Herr Benz and Herr Daimler several times."

He pointed in the direction of the window, where an angled drawing board supported a large sheet of cartridge paper, scored with what looked like a chart of the anatomy of this monster, and possibly its predecessors. A stack of discarded drawings spilled from a tray below the board and a glance at them suggested that years of dedicated work had gone into the assembly of this prototype. But Max was done with preliminaries and held up his hand. "I will generate," he said, somehow reminding George of Moses descending from the mountain with the decalogue under his arm. "Stand away from the gas pipe, my friend, or you will be poisoned by waste vapour. That is a difficulty I have yet to overcome."

George watched him stalk round to the front of the brass honeycomb and crouch, as though paying obeisance to his creation. Then, using a metal crank of some kind, he jumped up and down with amazing agility for a man of his years, and before George's astonished eyes the machine suddenly came to life, belching a plume of bluish vapour from its waste pipe and filling the store with a hideous clatter made up of a dozen different rattles and hisses emerging from various parts of the machine. He noticed then, for the first time, that the huge rear wheels had been jacked up clear of the floor and saw that they now were revolving at a steady speed and generating a low humming sound, like the approach of a swarm of bees. In spite of his intense curiosity he moved back, as though the machine might jerk free of its moorings and run amok inside the barn, crushing everything that stood in its way. But then Max reappeared holding his crank. Beaming at George like a playful five-year-old, he circled the machine warily, adjusting a screw here and a lever there, and somehow managing to reduce the clamour so that his voice could be heard above the steady, pulsating roar.

The demonstration went on for about five minutes before Max climbed on to the step of the machine, threw a switch and spun a little brass wheel, situated about a foot above the front axle. Falteringly and after a few snarling coughs, the machine fell silent, but the rear wheels continued to spin for more than a minute.

Obviously the thing worked, inasmuch as it generated sufficient power to turn the wheels, but George's imagination shied from the prospect of turning such a monster loose on the roads. It would certainly terrify most people and all horses, and quite possibly create a riot. In addition, he could not help wondering if the drive was powerful enough to propel such a cumbersome vehicle along anything but smooth, level ground.

Diffidently he mentioned these doubts to Max who seemed to have anticipated them. "It will frighten some, yes," he admitted, "but so did cannon and the early steam locomotives. Is that a reason for a man like me to cease experimenting with a new means of progression? The noise is a drawback but I shall moderate that in time, partly by casings but also by filtering the waste gases in some way. Come, my young friend, let me introduce you properly," and he proceeded to conduct George on what amounted to a tour of the machine, beginning with the steering apparatus, which, he explained, was really no more than a variation of coach steering, based on a cog mechanism copied from apparatus at a local flour mill.

The central idea seemed to reside in the big brass cylinder, set midway between the steersman's seat and the box where, presumably, goods would be packed. A network of brass tubes connected this cylinder with the fuel or oil chamber, a copper drum built into the structure under the driving perch, and Max went on to explain how an electric spark ignited a mixture of fuel and air, supplying the impetus for the powerful central piston connected to the rear axle, where a heavier cogwheel device had been installed.

He was very modest, George thought, for he gave credit to a whole company of other machinists, some still living and experimenting, others long dead, whose ideas had made his experiments possible. A man called Magnus, it seemed, had been the very first man to harness a cylindrical explosion in this way and had used benzine as his fuel, and Max was proud to announce that Siegfried Magnus was an Austrian. It was the German, Benz, however, who had greatly improved the idea and made it practical as regards transportation, refining not only the layout but the fuel itself.

Pipe by pipe, lever by lever, Max's tour of introduction continued, as though he was conducting George round a ballroom filled with important guests and equally important ghosts. Flywheels, crank-shafts, all kinds of rods and their component parts were lucidly explained, and there was even a brake lever for bringing the machine to a halt. Excessive vibration, it seemed, had been one of Maximilien's principal difficulties and he had yet to overcome it, for when the machine was started up again every part strained and quivered as though attempting to shake itself loose. Max paid tribute to one Robert Hooke, an English inventor of whom George had never heard, who had lived in the time of Charles I and Manufactured a joint by means of which power could, so to speak, be made to turn corners. Without it, Max said, any engine capable of producing sufficient power to turn wheels of that size would shake itself to pieces in minutes.

It was dark when they emerged for supper, to be greeted by smirks on the part of the girls, Gilda the irrepressible remarking, as George took his seat beside her. *"Git-i-git,* you smell! Just like grandfather! I will not eat near you. May I sit beside you, Mamma?" And ostentatiously she changed her seat.

It was to take more than ribaldry, however, to deflect George from his new and absorbing interest. From that day on, through the wet months of January and February, he spent most of his spare time in the granary store, tinkering, at first fearfully but later with growing confidence, with the various components of the machine, until he was as familiar with its mechanism as was its creator. He even suggested certain modifications, including the introduction of a puncture plate in the exhaust pipe to help disperse escaping gases, and a means of strengthening the iron clamps that held the wheel-cushions in place on the rims.

By the time the spring came round, and the ground hardened on a level stretch of river bank south of Essling, Maximilien pronounced himself ready for the trial run but here, to George's surprise, the old man's fear of ridicule forbade him to make the experiment public. Although it was not possible to bring the monster into the open without attracting a certain amount of publicity, Max insisted on reducing it to an absolute minimum by arbitrarily confining the women to the house and towing the machine to the selected stretch of road by a pair of horses borrowed from the firm.

This was carried out under cover of night and the machine was housed in a derelict barn against a dawn start, when it was unlikely that anyone save a few labourers would be abroad. Having got it there unobserved Maximilien and George decided to sleep in the barn, partly as sentinels but also to be on hand for a start at peep of dawn.

The old man, George noticed, was feverish with excitement and inclined, at this stage, to be very pessimistic. As soon as it was light he fussed and fumed like an inexperienced housewife at her baking, leaving George to harness up the team and drag the engine to the appointed spot. The previous afternoon they had carefully surveyed the ground, marking it out with flags over a distance of about a kilometre. For accurate timing Max would have liked to have measured it but unfortunately, at each end of the level stretch, there was a slight hill. George thus calculated that the test run would be made over a course a fraction over half a mile by British standards and he had a stop-watch, borrowed from one of the directors at the waggon works.

River mist masked the operation while they were getting into position and unharnessing the team, which was then led away and haltered at a safe distance, and perhaps because of the mist there were no observers, for which Max thanked his beloved Danube.

When everything was ready he climbed slowly into his seat and then, as though about to sail halfway across the globe, stretched out his hand to George to shake, so that for the first time in their acquaintance he looked old and frail and drained of most of the enthusiasm he had exhibited so often in the store.

George thought, "The old boy would have liked to have put off this moment and damned if I blame him. It must need an iron nerve to trust oneself to that monster but that isn't what's bothering him. He's more afraid of failure than being pitched into the river, or cut to pieces in that mass of belts and wheels . . ." But he said, cheerfully, "It'll be all right, Herr Körner. I know it and feel it. We've checked and double-checked everything and now there's nothing left to do but to try it. Shall I start her? Are you quite ready?" And Max nodded, too moved to speak as George took the crank and went round to the front of the machine to set the ungainly apparatus in motion.

The noise, out here in the open, seemed much subdued when cogs and wheels were flying, and as he stepped back, leaving Max a clear field, it struck him that the old fellow looked positively unearthly perched on the steering seat, tense and grimly expectant, as though about to drive his juggernaut across the Styx. The sky in the east was lightening but river mist still veiled the lower half of the machine, so that its inventor, shrouded in vapour seemed almost to be riding the clouds. About two minutes elapsed as the requisite warm-up period, and then, with terrible deliberation, Maximilien's right hand released the brake lever and slowly, moving it seemed by inches or even centimetres, the vast equipage crept forward.

For George it was one of the most electrifying moments of his life, for by now he was as closely involved with the machine as its creator. It trundled forward, its heavy wheels grinding the gritty surface, its iron drainpipe belching blue, vaporous clouds, its pace so fearfully laboured that George was able to keep up with it, remembering, at the very last moment, to start the stopwatch he held in his hand.

So they moved south, two men and a machine, linked in what George now accepted as an inseparable bond, but the pace was so painfully slow that he shouted, above the clatter, "Faster, Herr Körner! Faster!" and Max's right hand moved to the valve whereupon the machine's progress quickened appreciably, its racket increasing in volume but its speed doubling over the next twenty metres, so that George was obliged to break into a trot to keep pace.

When he saw the terminus flag loom out of the midst directly ahead he overtook it at a run, darting across to the riverside and standing poised with his stopwatch, like a steward at an athletic meeting. The full distance, he noted, had been covered in a fraction over eight minutes and a rough calculation told him that this represented an average speed of about four miles per hour. In a way, a very modest way perhaps, it was triumph.

In spite of the chill of the morning Max was sweating freely when he brought the machine to an uncertain halt a few yards beyond the flag. He sat still for upwards of a minute, looking quite exhausted and when George ran across to him, shouting his congratulations, he switched off, carefully adjusted the brake and said, "A walking pace, eh? And a moderate one at that. It might have been worse, Herr Swann, but it should have been better, much better. What is your reading?" And when George said, by British reckoning, something over four miles an hour, "So! We must improve on that, but how to do it without boiling over or shedding parts?" so that George had a sudden insight into the mind of an inventor. For such a man, he told himself, there was really no such thing as achievement. Always he would be looking ahead, over the next range of hills.

"Try it again, Herr Körner. Give it a second run," but Max shook his head. "We have learned all we are likely to learn," he said, "I shall spend the next few weeks at the drawing board and then, perhaps, we will try again. You see, my friend, you have overlooked the main conclusion. Four miles an hour, and unladen at that, is ridiculous. A horse could do better, could it not?"

"Not with that weight behind it," George said, but the old man waved his hand. "A team of your father's horses, hauling on a metalled road, could average nearly twice that speed. It is a promising beginning but no more. Come, harness up, and let us get the machine behind locked doors before the rumour-mongers begin to swarm."

"You can't possibly keep a thing like this a secret for long, Herr Körner, and why should you try? You're entitled to credit for making it go at all, aren't you?"

"I look for none," the old man said, "until I can haul the equivalent of a loaded four-horse waggon from one point to another in half the time. Besides," and here he smiled, "what artist wants the world to see a half-finished painting? Many would destroy it rather than have judgement pronounced before it was completed and this, I feel, will not be accomplished in my lifetime. Come, my friend, get the horses and let us go home."

4

The trial was another crossroad in the life of George Swann, star boarder of the Körner family at Essling, beside the Danube. Its first effect was to deepen the relationship between master and apprentice, converting it into that of grandfather and favourite grandson based on mutual involvement with a great variety of technical problems resulting from repairs and modifications rendered imperative by the road test. All manner of unsuspected weaknesses in design and structure had been exposed but Maximilien's main concern was to develop twice or thrice the thrust of the engine whilst, at the same time, halving its overall weight and reducing the danger of overheating.

At first they tinkered, replacing a part here, enlarging and strengthening another there, but soon it became obvious that a complete redesign was necessary if the machine was ever to emerge as a serious competitor to anything more than a one-horse van in speed or carrying capacity.

By now George was so deeply involved in the project that he began to spend most of his spare time in the grain store but this was not solely on account of his genuine interest in Max's invention, or his faith that, ultimately, a marketable prototype would emerge. In another way he used Maximus, as he came to think of the ungainly monster, as a safety valve from emotional pressures building up within him on account of the continued presence and apparent availability of the Körner girls, pressures that sometimes seemed so intolerable that he began to think seriously of returning home or moving on, and this despite his intense interest in Max's experiments.

It was as though the three younger Körner girls had entered into friendly competition with one another to corner him in the way

Lizzie Broadbent had come near to doing in the Polygon, and Madame Drouet had tried to achieve in Paris, but there was a difference. Half of him delighted in the prospect of being trapped. Half of him (he liked to think of it as the baser half) yearned for some cosy arrangement, of the kind he had enjoyed in Munich, but common sense told him that this time there would be no easily obtained reprieve, of the sort made available to him by the accommodating Rosa Ledermann. Once committed to Sophie, Gilda or Valerie, his obligation under existing circumstances, would be clear. One way or another the close-knit family would absorb him and although, in so many ways, he longed to be so absorbed, instinct warned him that committal on his part would be folly, for he was clearly not in love with any one of them. Had he been, he assured himself, he would have stopped vacillating and established a serious relationship, even if it was no more than a trial relationship, with one sister to the exclusion of the other two.

Perhaps his hesitation prompted the seige. Using diabolical initiative they would isolate him in one or other part of the house, or at some unexpected moment during a family outing, parading their undeniable charms, and their several armouries of artifice, so that week by week, almost day by day, they began to deflect him from his work at the yard or his absorbing involvement with Max Körner's experiments and even, on occasion, to invade his sleep in a way that troubled him and left him at odds with himself. His brief encounters with them, from being light and inconsequential, began to take on a measure of exciting and deliberately-contrived experimentation, that would almost surely have been resolved one way or another had the field been less open, or the competition less keen and watchful. Once, in an alcove on the landing, he was embracing Sophie when Gilda swooped on them from the back staircase, shouting with glee at his embarrassment. Another time Valerie succeeded in enticing him into the bedroom and she might have won the contest there and then had not Marta, the maid-of-all-work in the Körner household, appeared unexpectedly on the landing with clanking bucket and mop, so that George slipped away while Valerie was sending her about her business. It could not last, however, and he was all too aware of this, for he was honest enough to see himself as a willing victim to the spirited, three-pronged attack and at times like

this would take refuge in the grain-shed where the girls could not
follow him. Here, with a kind of sullen resignation, he would go to
work on a set of cogs, or a wheel-clamp, telling himself yet again,
that if he had the sense he was born with he would make a choice
between turning his back on the Körners or paying regular visits
to the city joy-house, recommended by the director at the yard.

He was in just such a mood one mild spring evening when Max
found him banging away at one of the new springs they had designed, glowering at the strip of steel held in the bench vise as though
it was the embodiment of all his physical and spiritual frustrations.
The old man watched him for a while in silence, puffing away at
his heavy, drooping pipe, so that George, laying aside the hammer,
was glad to put Gilda out of mind in favour of the less demanding
subject of under-springing the metal container they had bolted to
the chassis, in preference to the clumsy wooden structure of the
original model.

He said, "Three thicknesses will absorb a good deal of shock,
Max. Is that what you had in mind?" and Max, smiling, said it was
not and that what he had in mind at that moment was his young
friend's abstractions and what, if anything, was to be done about
them.

"Come, my boy," he said, genially, when George growled that
he had no idea what the old man was referring to, "you are a long
way from home and I would be flattered if you regarded me in loco
parentis, as they say. It is a woman, is it not? You are in love,
perhaps?"

"If I was in love," George muttered, disarmed by the old man's
affability, "I could at least isolate the girl."

"Ach, so! My grand-daughters continue to plague you, no doubt?"

"Who else?"

"I have long been of the opinion," said Max, with a sigh, "that
there are far too many petticoats about this house. It is a pity that
my son Albrecht did not leave six boys instead of four girls and two
boys, both of whom, I regret to say, will live and die as peasants,
like their good mother. However, I understand your problem better
than you think. I may devote most of my thoughts to that," and he
nodded briefly at Maximus, "but I am not blind, and I was young
myself half a century ago. I assure you, my young friend, you have

few secrets from me, or from those artful hussies either. At your time of life distractions from the serious business of life are inevitable. How long is it since you paid a visit to the city?"

"I went there once," George admitted, "but it didn't help much, Herr Körner. Some men are made one way, some another, I imagine."

"That is a simplification," Max replied, thoughtfully. "I had forgotten that the Puritan instinct is inbred in most Englishmen. It has a way of denying them the easy solution to the problem of the young."

He sat down on a bench, relit his pipe and puffed away meditatively, as though his assistant's preoccupation was at one with those arising out of modifications and adjustments to the big, silent machine that all but filled the store. It occurred to George then that this might be an opportunity to warn Herr Körner, in a tactful way of course, that he was in danger of either losing his apprentice or having his hospitality abused, and he was wondering how he could put this into suitable words when Max said, calmly, "The girls will surely seek to exploit the situation, and their mother also, no doubt. But that does not mean you have to accommodate them, or encourage them in their conceits. It has not escaped my attention that they have beset you, to the exclusion of the other young men in the district."

"The fact is," George blurted out, seeing a fancied opening, "I've come to the conclusion it would be best for all concerned to cut my visit short and head for home," and was dismayed to see the old man's features assume a frown of extreme displeasure.

"Leave me? Before we have made a second test run? I won't hear of it, Herr Swann, not merely for my sake but for your own."

"It's you I'm thinking of," George said, "you and Frau Körner. You've both gone out of your way to show me kindness and hospitality and well . . ." He shrugged, not liking to spell out the situation as it was resolving itself from the daily skirmishes on the stairs, landings, and in the outbuildings of the old house. But then his sense of chivalry reminded him that it wouldn't do to implicate the girls specifically and added, "It's mostly my own fault. I've encouraged them, no doubt, and they're gay and lively, far more so than girls of their age in my country. Maybe it's the climate," he concluded,

lamely, and realised then how fatuous his excuses must sound, for
Max was smiling now, and it was clear that he regarded the whole
thing as a rich joke.

"Ja, they are young and high-spirited, my friend, and winsome,
too, no doubt. But so are you, are you not? And you are a man, with
a man's capacity to give his mind to matters of real importance. So
let me give you an old man's advice. If you have need of them, and
they are as venturesome and impudent as I suspect, with their frills,
flounces and saucy looks, then use them. Take your pleasure in them,
and be damned to their tears or squabbles."

"You give me that kind of advice? You, their grandfather?"

"Why not? Your presence here is more important to me than the
virtue of those hussies. For one I would happily sacrifice the other,
my friend. Besides, youth is a short run. One day it is there and the
next it is gone, leaving nothing but responsibilities."

"But look here, Max . . . I mean to say, I couldn't behave in that
way, or not under your roof. I can't swear that I won't sooner or
later, and as to responsibilities, one or other of them might find
herself saddled with more responsibilities than she bargained for!
You wouldn't give advice of that kind in their mother's hearing,
would you?"

"*Gott in Himmel,*" Max said, explosively, "of course I would not,
for women are not equipped to reason like men. For all that, Frau
Körner would not stand in the way of the girls, having regard who
you are, and the likelihood of a settlement."

"Settlement? You mean marriage, if it became obligatory?"

The old man's jaw dropped. "*Marriage,* you say? Marriage to
one of my grand-daughters? *Ach, du meine Güthe!* Herr Swann,
that is not to be thought of! Your father will find a wife with a sizeable *dot*, no doubt, and among your own people. These girls of mine
have no patrimony. Their mother has Albrecht's pension, and I have
nothing to leave them, nothing but that machine over there and a
handful of crowns saved over the years. Marriage? The idea is preposterous!" And he sucked his long teeth and beat a rapid tattoo
on his upturned heel with his pipe, so that a shower of sparks scurried before the draught from the door.

"But what you suggest . . ."

"Is unworthy? Base? Ach, perhaps, to a gentleman reared in a hot-house among Puritans. But to me—? It is no more than practical and of small importance. I am not a religious man, Herr Swann. I have not been seen at mass since they brought me news of my son's death in that stupid quarrel with the Prussians. Neither am I concerned with the virtue of a flock of peasant girls, even women of my blood. My virtue, such as it is, stands there, under those coverings and so, perhaps, does yours, for a man cannot hope to perfect more than one thing in his time on earth. For the rest, praise or blame, he must take his chance. That is why I say to you make free with them if that is the price you ask for your service to me over the next few months!"

For George, notwithstanding the initial shock, it was not as cynical as it sounded. He was learning about life and one of the things he had learned down here, in the company of Maximilien Körner, was that there were variants of the word 'dedication'. Dedicated men, epitomised by enthusiasts like his father or Max Körner, arranged their priorities according to their own set of values. Adam Swann had never made a secret of putting the network before wife and family all these years, so was it so odd that this gaunt old Austrian, who had laboured at one idea all his adult life, should do the same concerning his pretty grand-daughters?

And yet he knew well enough that he could not strike that kind of bargain, not in cold blood, and with a total disregard for the consequences. Neither, for that matter, did Max's cynical proposal have much relevance to his own immediate needs. Had they done, a weekly jaunt to the joy-house district of the city would have served and in this context the old man seemed to have misunderstood him, was probably incapable of understanding him. He saw then that he could not hope to communicate to such an obsessive mind the stresses and subtleties of the deep personal loneliness he had experienced so often during his wanderings, all the way from the Polygon, in Lancashire, to this stone house beside the Danube, or that such stresses and longings were unlikely to be eased for more than an hour or so by spending himself in the body of an immature girl, or exercising a transitory physical dominance over one or all four of Herr Körner's pretty grand-daughters. For all that he still felt drawn to the man and involved, more deeply than ever, in his dream. He said, briefly, "Leave it then. I'll stay and see it through, Herr

Körner, at least until we can make another road test, for the truth
is that contraption is as much mine as yours now and I think I've
more faith in its future. As to the girls, forget I was fool enough
to mention them."

The old man, however, seemed indisposed to dismiss the topic
so arbitrarily. He said, mildly, "It's true, then? You have no special
preference? They are as one to you?"

"Any one of them will make someone a good wife when the time
comes." He looked carefully at the old man, now occupied with
filling his pipe. "Perhaps I should start giving you advice, Herr
Körner. Perhaps you should spend less time in here and more out
looking for husbands."

"Ach, that is their own and their mother's concern," he replied,
impatiently, "but since you have lumped them together, and speak
of their marriage prospects, I take issue with you on one account. If
I were a young man about here, with his way to make, I would not
give the younger trollops a second glance. I would make myself
agreeable to Gisela, who is worth more than her brothers and sisters
combined. As a wife, surely, but also as a mistress if I know women
and I should, set down here among so many of them. Gisela has
brains and you are too young to understand that a woman takes
her brains to bed with her and they are still there in the morning.
She could have married more than once. Did you know that?"

"No, I didn't," admitted George and his mind conjured, for the
first time, with the sacrifices the years must have demanded of
Gisela, who seemed older than any of them and yet, when one
thought about it was just as pretty and only a year or two older
than Sophie, of the swaying walk.

"There's no need for Gisela to become an old maid on the family's
account," he said. "They're old enough to look for themselves now,
aren't they?"

"She will stay for all that," Max said, "until the others are married,
and the two boys done with their apprenticeship."

He stood up, knocking his half-smoked pipe on a piece of cowl-
ing that he used as an ashtray. "So too will you, Herr Swann. A
little longer, perhaps, until we get that monster on the road again.
But let me say this. If you are restive, and this time-wasting beast
does not dominate you entirely when the picnic season is upon us

once more, give a thought to Gisela. You would, perhaps, find her more rewarding than those other minxes."

He shuffled out on this, leaving George to lock the storehouse door. It was an improbable conclusion to what George thought of as a curious discussion between two people of widely separated generations, linked by a common obsession with an array of nuts, bolts, cogs, cranks and levers that added up to Maximus.

5

The discussion had one decisive result. In the light of what the old man had said George became increasingly aware of the self-effacing Gisela, as she went about her work in the house. He had assumed, up to that time, that she was already on the way to becoming a facsimile of the placid Frau Körner, always busy, often perspiring gently over the stove, but never occupied with anything not directly associated with running what amounted to a youth hostel. But he was learning about women and came to the conclusion that Gisela's abstraction was due to something less definitive than the preparation of endless meals and garments, that she had access to a world of her own behind the habitually amiable expression in her china-blue eyes, gentle mouth and high white brow, that had a way of wrinkling in a manner that suggested a restrained impatience with the sustained clamour of the family. Little by little he came to see her as the central but unobtrusive prop of the household, without which there might be no high spirits, no shameless shirking of domestic chores and certainly no skilful catering for the picnics and outings along the Danube, across to Labau, into the Wienerwald and on the wooded slopes of the Kahlenberg.

Their relationship was friendly but more of a brother and sister than that existing between George and the other girls. There was no tension here. He never flirted with her, she was too dignified for that, and he never teased her, as her sisters often did, but without in any way disturbing her equanimity. All the same he found himself watching her closely and it came to him that maybe the old man was right, and that she had a well-stocked, well-ordered mind, sealed off by what she accepted as her duty to a widowed mother, an ageing, eccentric grandfather, and five younger brothers and sisters, all of whom appeared to take her very much for granted.

She, for her part, did not unbend towards him, as all the others had by this time. To her he was still a gentlemanly English student, who brought distinction on the house by staying here and taking such an interest in grandfather's invention, so that it was difficult to establish the free and easy access he had won so effortlessly in the case of Sophie, Valerie and Gilda. When this did happen he discovered that the old man's guess had been shrewd. Gisela was rewarding in a way that the other girls were not, for all their gaiety and accessibility.

It came about by chance, when the family, including for once Max, had made a Sunday crossing of the short arm of the Danube to Lobau. They were playing some childish game (the Viennese adults, he had discovered, were much addicted to what he thought of as childish games) akin to hide-and-seek, among the oaks and chestnuts of the island.

He had just 'caught' Gisela, who had been hiding in a hollow tree some five feet from the ground, and as she clambered down to surrender he took advantage of her landing to embrace her, a little objectively, as though to decide how she would react.

Her response surprised him very much. Instead of simulating protest, as Valerie or Sophie would have done, or subsiding gleefully, as he had come to expect of Gilda, she took control of the embrace, as though resolved to make the very most of it, and as they were screened by a cluster of oaks and waist-high bracken she was able to bring so much enthusiasm to the contact that he found himself being kissed in a way he had never been kissed by her sisters, not even the venturesome Gilda. She kissed him with parted lips, using her tongue and she used her body too, exerting so much pressure with her thighs that they parted and enfolded his braced leg so that he was reminded instantly of Max's dictum concerning women who took their brains to bed with them. But the disturbing result of this was that it reawakened in him all the bittersweet longings of his first weeks away from Rosa Ledermann, making his impersonal hankerings after Sophie, Valerie and Gilda seem relatively adolescent. The scent of her hair, the flickering movement of her tongue and, above all, the sustained pressure of her thighs drove him wild and he thought, savagely, "If I don't get a woman of my own I'll go berserk . . ." But then her abandon touched some spring of tenderness in him and he spoke her name, three times, four times, and raised the hand that was beginning to caress her body to her hair, stroking it gently at the back of her head where it parted to divide into two thick, swinging plaits. They heard the family hallooing for them from the adjacent glade and presently they separated and walked back wordlessly and a little shyly, keeping their distance, but the sharp-eyed Max, puffing away at his pipe where he sat on a log, looked up smiling as he saw them emerge from the thicket and conveyed what he had seen by winking at George over the shoulders of Frau Körner, who was kneeling before the picnic hamper that always accompanied the Körners on these occasions. There was no immediate sequel to this encounter although sometimes, when Gisela was coming and going about her work, they would exchange a level glance, as though each knew something the others did not but then, like a summer storm that blew up out of the sky over the looming Alps, the pleasant rhythm of the Körner household was shattered.

They returned home from an evening boat trip one summer dusk to hear the engine rattling away across the yard and saw, what was unique in these circumstances, the barn door swinging free in the evening breeze that had ruffled the surface of the river all the way from the Kai.

George realised at once that something was wrong. Shouting to Gisela to keep the others back he ran across the grain store to find Maximus running at full power, its rear wheels spinning above their blocks and the place full of acrid exhaust. For a moment, bemused by the fumes and stunned by the roar of the machine, he could not see the old man but then he noticed his red slippers protruding beyond the front wheels and beyond them a hand, clutching the heavy crank that they used to start the engine.

He guessed then what had happened. The engine had a fierce kick and the old man, having clearly ignored George's plea that only he should use the crank when they were testing, had either collapsed over the task or had been flung clear by the recoil, perhaps strinking his head on a bulkhead or the stone floor.

He switched off, lifted Max and carried him across to the house, leaving one of the girls to bolt the doors and telling another to despatch Rudi, fleetest of the boys, for Doctor Dahn, who attended the Körners for minor ailments. He tried to give Max a sip of brandy but his lips were blue and unresponsive so that it was obvious to George, aware of the danger of those fumes, that the old man was half-suffocated, as well as suffering from shock. With the womenfolk fussing around him, he carried him up to his room and laid him on the bed, whereupon, to George's relief, he vomited, and became half-aware of his surroundings, gesturing feebly with his left hand, as though to shoo them away from his bedside.

George interpreted this as a command to clear the room of women and ordered them all outside, for it seemed to him important to learn precisely what had occurred inside the store, so that he could brief the doctor on arrival.

As soon as they were gone, Max made a great effort to pull himself together, continuing to gesture feebly with his left hand, then speaking in a slurred, hesitant voice, as though having difficulty with his breathing. George understood then, with a sinking heart, the reality of the situation. Max had not necessarily been flung backwards by the kick of the crank, and there were no external injuries to his head or any other part of his body. It was clear, however, from the thickness of his speech, and the strange inertness of his right arm, that he had suffered a stroke. He said, detaining George with a surprisingly fierce grasp, "Doctor?" and when George nodded, "Cylinder flooded . . . slow to start . . . should have waited . . .", and then, "Switched off?"

"Yes, yes," George said, "forget the damned machine. I warned you to leave heavy work to me, and I mean to see that you do in future!"

But the old man smiled feebly and said, carefully enunciating his words. "No future, boy . . . only for you, and that engine in there. Finished . . . Dahn will tell you . . . here," and he lifted his sound hand to the cage of his ribs.

"Damned nonsense!" said George, explosively, "and don't let Frau Körner and the girls hear you talk like that! Rest will put you right, and I'll see you get it. As soon as the doctor comes . . ." But then he stopped, for the old man was looking at him pleadingly, his lips moving as though he had something further to say. When George

435

was silent he took a long, rasping breath and went on, "Listen . . . haven't long . . . damned doctor will dose me . . . know him . . . sleep for a week . . . mightn't wake . . . another pillow behind me . . . mustn't . . . lie . . . flat . . ." so that George eased him into a sitting position, supporting his back with cushions taken from the chair under the window.

"What is it you want to say, Max?"

"This is the end for me. Don't waste time, clucking like those women . . . known about this for years. Dahn warned me times enough, but what is a man to do? Went on with what I started. Like Benz, like all of them. Now that engine passes to you . . . don't argue . . . put it in writing, diagrams and records too. Witnessed. Saw to it months ago. Dismantle. Get it crated and carried to London."

He could say no more. The effort seemed to bring on a second seizure for he writhed and groaned but was just able to swallow a sip or two of brandy George held to his mouth. Then he lay still, breathing very heavily and George stole away, dismayed and angry that a man as tough and resolute as Maximilien Körner could be demolished so quickly and so finally and knowing, somehow, that whether or not the old man survived this attack, he would never do more than shuffle round the inside of that shed of his, watching someone else at work on his creation.

Gisela sought him out after the doctor had left, giving instructions that Max was to be kept in bed, free from worry and on a light diet for at least a month, and thereafter was on no account to tackle the staircase leading to the ground floor. Gisela was not profoundly upset, as all the others seemed to be, but it was clear that she had guessed the truth, and saw this as evidence of a heart condition the old man had somehow succeeded in concealing from all save the doctor. She said, quietly, "You were alone with him. I heard him talking. Was he speaking of that engine of his?"

George admitted that he was, telling her that Max seemed insistent he should take it with him when he returned home, and had even instructed his lawyer to this effect. He said this with embarrassment, as though they were already discussing the terms of the old man's will. "No matter what he wants I wouldn't deprive his family of any of his property. You know that, don't you, Gisela?" and she said, calmly, that she did, but that no one else was likely to want it, for none of them understood it and all but himself went in fear of it.

"Would it be worth money in your country, Herr Swann?"

"No," he said, "not in its present form. It might ultimately but it needs a great deal of modification before it could be patented. I could arrange that for your mother. If it ever did produce money I could make sure she got it."

"We'll discuss it later," she said, and went away to comfort her mother.

From that day on Max never left his bed, although, as the summer drew to a close, he progressed to some extent and could sit up and talk more or less coherently. His right arm, and to some degree his leg too, was paralysed, and when George went in to talk with him he realised the old man was resigned to the fact that he would never work again. He gave George messages for the firm, among them his resignation.

He was a tiresome invalid, however, and insisted on smoking his pipe, so that the pungent smell of his tobacco hung over the upper floor night and day, and Frau Körner was forever voicing fears that he would set the house on fire when they were all asleep. Then he had another slight seizure, and the family took turns to watch with him, George, Gisela, and Frau Körner sitting by his bedside in two-hour spells throughout the night. He slept fitfully and when he awoke to find George there he would mutter endlessly about things he should have done, or ought not to have done, concerning recent adaptations to Maximus. George had not the heart to discourage him, even though he seemed to get excited when he saw, or thought he saw, a way of improving the steering, the braking power, the transmission, or the variable speed mechanism. He asked George to duplicate a full report on their progress to date, to be sent to Benz and Daimler, including scale diagrams of all their recent modifications. Grumbling to Gisela that this kind of activity was only reducing his chance of recovery, George was puzzled by her defence of the old man's whims. "Let him have his way. That engine was always more important to him than we after my father died. It is his dream. You cannot prevent a dying man from dreaming, Herr Swann."

After that he made no further protest but let the old man run on, and carried out all his commissions concerning the engine, on which he worked from time to time through the sultry weeks of September, when an unnatural stillness had settled on the once-riotous household.

He had gone to bed tired and depressed after a spell of watching one night to find the brilliant moonlight prevented sleep and the room very stuffy, despite the breeze from the river. He was restless now, and hopelessly at odds with himself, and stood a long time at the window, looking out across the moonlit countryside until he heard the whirring notes of the Essling church clock strike two, that meant Gisela would be relieved by the family help, Marta, who had been fitted into the schedule in order to give the exhausted Frau Körner some rest.

He was turning away from the window when he heard the door latch click and suddenly there was Gisela in bedgown, her hair unplaited and her feet bare. He said, urgently, "Max? Another spell!" but she laid a finger to her lips and came in, closing the door and standing with her back to it in such a way that it seemed perfectly natural for him to cross to her, saying nothing, and take her in his arms, as though her appearance here had been prearranged.

When he kissed her lips, however, she shivered, so that he would have released her but she clung to him fiercely, as in the grove on Lobau, and he said, gently, "Why then, Gisela? Why did you come?" and she replied, with an improbable catch of laughter in her voice, "Because I love my grandfather, Herr Swann. He knows I am here." And then, still with a suggestion of laughter, "No, no, perhaps not. But he would approve, I am sure, for he talks of no one but you."

"He said you should come? At night. Like this?" and when she nodded eagerly, "Ah, but *you*, Gisela, that's a matter for you, not him! You must understand that?"

"Yes," she said, in her familiar level tone, "I understand it. I am not quite a fool. Neither am I a wanton, like Gilda, who sets out to tease every man who looks at her. I would not be here if I had not wished it myself more than anything in the world. I would have pretended I did not understand grandfather's talk concerning you. I would have dismissed it as an old man's nonsense." Then, calmly, "You wish for me to leave, Herr Swann?"

"No, by God!" he blurted out and threw his arms about her again, but she said, taking control of the situation, as she had on Lobau, "Wait, then. And do not talk. My mother is asleep but perhaps one of my sisters is not. You would not wish my presence here discussed by them, I think."

"Of course I wouldn't, but . . ."

"Then be silent."

She slipped out of her flannel gown and he saw she was not wearing a nightdress, or a shift of the kind the Körner girls wore in bed, and gazed at her rapturously. He had only seen one other woman without clothes and this one was in great contrast to Rosa, who had conveyed to him an impression of strength and majestic symmetry. Gisela was well-formed, with full breasts and well-covered thighs, but her small waist and stature added a daintiness to her figure that he found at one with her essential stillness and femininity. In the bright moonlight he could see her quite clearly, and said, as she made a move towards the bed, "No, Gisela, over there by the window . . . I want to look at you. You're beautiful, Gisela. You're so much more beautiful than I imagined!"

She took a step towards the window and stood quite still in the broad beam of moonlight, her chin high, her hands at her sides in a pose that was somehow submissive but she looked, he thought, like some lovely vision who had materialised out of Danube watermeadows. In that soft light her form appeared quite perfect so that it amazed him that he had ever thought of her as less graceful than her sister Sophie, or less prepossessing than Valerie or Gilda. Then he remembered that she, alone among the Körner girls, wore corsets that gave her a bulkiness, for the corsets the Viennese wore were ridged with heavy wire, of the kind Max used to bind joints on his machine.

When he embraced her again she was warm and very supple but seemed, in some way, to have herself in hand. Perhaps she was only here because Max had all but proposed it to her, or perhaps, most of her life, she had been at the disposal of others and it was therefore natural that she should do him this small service.

He said, breathlessly, "You must be sure, Gisela. Quite sure," and she said briskly, "Please to go to bed," and gave him a push in that direction.

Once there and holding her, he had no further misgivings concerning the motives that had brought her there. Pleasing grandfather must have been incidental.

*   *   *

439

It was possible, when he opened his eyes soon after dawn, to look at her and think about her as though he was seeing her for the first time.

For perhaps ten minutes he lay very still, his face turned towards her, studying the clear, unblemished skin of her cheek framed in a skein of golden hair that had always been severely disciplined in carefully-arranged plaits but now spread itself clear across his pillow in the wildest disorder. He found that he could relish every part of her individually, a man who has stumbled upon a treasure and has yet to count it and come to terms with his luck. A single finespun hair, venturing from somewhere behind the rounded lobe of her ear, caught the first gleam of morning sun so that light seemed to travel down it, over the heavy-lidded eye, down the length of the short, straight nose to the upper lip. It caught the shoulder of a tooth and stayed a moment before passing on over the little chin to the neck and losing itself in the cleavage of her fine young breasts over which the coverlet was drawn taut, pinned by his weight.

She was quite perfect. Fairy-tale perfect. An amalgam of every quality he had ever looked for in women for, as he watched the slow rise and fall of her breathing and the tiny flutter of the errant hair where it cut the corner of her mouth, he saw her as all the women who had touched his life and his dreams, so that it was as though he had conjured her out of his conscious and subconscious mind and breathed life into her for his own exclusive comfort. She was Laura Broadbent, infinitely caring, infinitely maternal, Rosa Ledermann, joyous and positive in the act of loving a man, herself, whom he had watched unknowingly all this time, pouring her concern into the affairs of everyone about this house. But, in addition to all this, which had reality and substance, she was something else, the princess-waif of nursery days, the fragile, stoic heroine, a little figure symbolising everything that was wholesome, challenging the dark forces of the fairy-tale world and triumphing after many dangers and hardships. She was Gisela Körner and now, God be praised, she was his and there came to him a triumphant awareness of what it meant to be unequivocally in love and to know that love was returned in full measure.

Physically, in retrospect that is, it was profitless to compare her to Rosa, the only other woman he had held in his arms for more than a

440

few breathless seconds. Rosa's responses, if they could be called that and not regarded as storming advances, had been calculated, conditioned by her experience and her assertive energy. With Gisela, everything had to be reversed, he supposed, and yet, thinking back, this was not the whole truth. Her very lack of experience, expressed in her expectancy and desire to please, had communicated itself to every nerve in his body, convincing him that he was the bestower. And some strange alchemy of emotions, stemming from this, made it implicit, that this single act of love had integrated her into his life and that, by possessing her body, he had possessed himself of her entire being. And this, following some strange logic, was the essence of everything he had experienced in this stone house by the river.

Outside, in the windblown lilac trees, finches squabbled, a sound that had often awakened him as it now awakened her, but slowly, so that he could watch awareness stir in her as she turned her head from the light and opened her eyes, acknowledging him with a small, shy smile. An incongruous smile he might have said, given the circumstances, and yet it was not, for it had within it a distillation of her personality. Restraint, infinite patience, infinite courtesy.

He said, as though it had been in his mind months rather than minutes, "We must be married, Gisela. Soon, you understand? We must marry before Max is too sick and confused to understand what has happened. Would that be possible, since I am not a Catholic?"

She said nothing for a moment and continued to smile but then, the smile slipping away, she turned her head back to its sleeping position and seemed to be contemplating the high, arched ceiling.

He said, "Would it? Would your priest marry us very soon?" and she replied, without looking at him, "I did not seek that when I came to you. You should understand that."

He raised himself on his elbow and stared at her. "Listen, Gisela, I don't care what brought you here or what you or Max had in mind. I'm in love with you, very much in love with you. I want you and I need you and I mean to have you as soon as it can be managed. Is it that you couldn't bear to leave Austria and your family and come away as my wife to England? Because if so I wouldn't expect that right away, not so long as we were married. We could stay . . . where are you going?" for suddenly and effortlessly she had slipped away and was standing by the window, shrugging herself into her flannel bedgown, her hands tugging the girdle into a knot.

"I shall go now," she said, very quietly, "before anyone stirs. I will not have you made the subject of jokes in this house, you understand?"

He said, in a hoarse and urgent whisper, "Don't go, Gisela. Not until you've promised, not until I'm sure . . ."

"Ach, I will come to you again. Or we can talk of it at a distance from the house. But not here and at this moment, for I will not be judged as one of my sisters . . ." He was alarmed and confused now and lunged the length of the bed, catching her round the waist before she could reach the door. "Listen, Gisela . . . yes, yes, I'll keep my voice down, but you must tell me. I must know before you leave here. I love you, Gisela. Understand that, please. I love you and I want very much to marry you. You love me, don't you?"

She said, gravely, "I do not think you need to ask that question."

"But of course I do. Any man would, wouldn't he?"

She seemed to consider this, standing looking down at him gravely and fidgeting with the knot of her girdle. He had the advantage now, holding her tightly by the waist, and was in no mood to surrender it, saying, "If necessary I'll rouse everybody in the house and make it public this instant. I love you, Gisela, and I mean to marry you. All I want from you is yes or no."

She smiled at that and this was all the answer he needed, that and the note of laughter in her voice as she said, judiciously, "I will consider it. Very carefully. I will consult my grandfather and follow his advice. But now I must go and nothing is to be said of this without my consent, you hear me?" and she bent swiftly from the waist and kissed him on the forehead.

He released her then and she left the room as silently as she had entered. He crossed to the window, sniffing the dawn and watching the pinkish light spread across the river, as though the grey sky in the west had been punctured and day came as a transfusion to the woods and meadows on the far bank. The sense of peace and certainty that possessed him was almost tangible but he plumbed it guardedly, wondering at the strength of the hold it had upon him and thinking, "All this time and distance . . . and she was here,

right under my nose . . ." And in a curious way she fused with the
recollection of Laura Broadbent, who had embraced him swiftly on
his last night in Bowdon, and Rosa Ledermann, who, he supposed,
had done more to mature him than all his travels and experiences.

*   *   *

They were married in mid-November, when the first snow was driving in from the Tyrol. The trees along the river, and over on the
island of Lobau, were hung in sheets of beaten gold that gleamed
dully in shafts of sunshine that came between half-hearted snow
showers.

It seemed to him a very short, incomprehensible service, and afterwards they all trooped back to the house, and he and Gisela presented themselves to Maximilien, who beamed at them from his bed
and said that, apart from his 'handful of crowns', he had no patrimony other than Maximus, already dismantled and packed into
crates in the grain store where it had stood on blocks for so long.

There was a great deal of feasting and jollity after that, Gisela's
sisters, somewhat to George's surprise, extracting what seemed to
him an inordinate amount of fun out of the situation, and showing
no indication at all that they resented Gisela's swooping capture of
the English milord. For that, it appeared, was how the village had
come to regard him. They drank each other's healths in rivers of local
wine and he managed to evade the traditional local custom of seeing
bride and groom to bed, by whisking Gisela away to the city by late
afternoon for a brief stay at the most luxurious hotel on Baedeker's
list. By then, however, arrangements were well advanced for his return home, and he had written a series of cunningly worded letters
hinting that he might in the near future be marrying and bringing
his Austrian wife back to 'Tryst' for family approval.

His first letters in this vein made little impression on Henrietta,
who found it impossible to take them seriously, but Adam was not
fooled and when, on the day of the wedding, a telegram arrived announcing that he was married, and would be returning home in
early December, he set to work to moderate Henrietta's extreme indignation by saying, "Might even be a damned good idea. Steady
the boy, and by God he needs steadying! Anyway, it's brought him
back, hasn't it? And with the intention of going in for some steady

work, I hope. That's something to rejoice over, for I'd half come to believe we should never see him again."

"But an Austrian girl," Henrietta wailed, "it's . . . it's so *silly*, when there are plenty of pretty English girls about here who would regard any one of the boys a splendid match. She obviously hasn't a penny or he would have said so, if only to soften the blow!" But Adam said, mildly, "Good God, woman, do you suppose any one of our children ever gave a thought to money? They've lived soft for the whole of their lives and that's your fault and mine more than theirs. However, I'll wager one thing, knowing George. She'll be very fetching, and it's time we had more grandchildren. Perhaps the second generation will prove a sober, predictable lot, to comfort our old age."

"You seem to take it all as a great joke," she grumbled. "As for me, I simply can't imagine why he was in such a tearing hurry. He could have invited us, couldn't he?"

"If he had you wouldn't have got me as far as the Danube in winter," he said. "I've done my globe-trotting. Movement within the network keeps me sufficiently exercised." But he did not see fit to voice thoughts that occurred to him as he reread George's telegram in the train between Croydon and London Bridge that same morning. The hurry, he suspected, might indicate that a fresh source of grandchildren had already been tapped. He had always suspected that women were more important to George than to any of his other boys but that, on the whole, was nothing to wring one's hands over. He himself had never got started in life until he found a mate.

As to the boy's mother's misgivings, he could understand them well enough, although he intended to keep his own counsel concerning them. Their source was probably threefold and there was nothing to be done about them, beyond hoping that the young Mrs. George Swann was amiable and possessed plenty of tact. Henrietta and George had never really hit it off and one did not have to probe deeply to decide why. In one respect they were too much alike, both having predominantly sensual natures, but sensuality in a man and a woman meant different things, he supposed, and she would be very unlikely to make allowances for George on that account. Then there was George's strong sense of humour and Henrietta's lack of one, but the absence of any channel of communication between them went back to the day of George's birth, almost, one might say, to the night of his conception, at the old George in Southwark. For George had been a pledge on her part, and she had never ceased to regard him as such, a son intended from the very beginning to follow his father, that she might have a free rein with the others who preceded him and followed him. For the rest there was nothing to do but wait and hope that this girl, the first of their daughters-in-law, would do something to bridge the gap.

So it was that George Swann landed at Folkestone a week or two later accompanied not merely by a wife, whose undeniable modesty, lisping English, daintiness and general air of malleability conditioned her mother-in-law's approach from the first embrace, but by twelve immensely heavy crates that required a small waggon train to convey them from the nearest off-loading point to the old stables the gardeners had been using as potting sheds since the new stable block was added at 'Tryst' four years before. When Adam queried this avalanche of heavy luggage, wondering what on earth the boy had brought back with him, George said, with a grin, "That can wait, sir. It's a very long story and likely to give you more to think about than a routine event like a wedding in a family of nine!" So he forgot the crates for the time being and let his fancy play on George's other acquisition, deciding at once that he was going to like her, that she would be a sobering influence on the boy, and also, as Henrietta cheerfully admitted when they went to bed that night, that George was what the younger generation would call a rare picker when it came to girls.

3

The Seasons at 'Tryst'

It would be extravagant to say that Henrietta Swann equated the timespan of her existence with the rhythm of a solar system, but that, in a sense, was how it communicated itself to her senses in the years succeeding her fortieth birthday. It was, in fact, an interlocking series of rhythms, centred on a dominant theme that was Adam; and about Adam the Swann network.

Beyond that, an immeasurable distance beyond it, was the wider orbit of the family, with its little clusters of planets and its lonelier, more distant star, Alexander, looming largest among them. Beyond that again was the rhythm of the tribe to which they all belonged, that cohort of swashbuckling, purse-proud argonauts, ranging the five continents and co-ordinating everything and everybody under a symbol that was the Union Jack, and the remote, disgruntled little figure who had achieved, in Henrietta's lifetime, the status of legend.

Victoria. *Victoria Regina et Imperiatrix*. Pudgy and rather drab. Imperious, arch, mulish and rabbit-toothed. Surely the most unlikely symbol of splendour and permanence in the history of kings, courts and federations of tribes.

To Henrietta, however, the more general aspect of the planetary system was of small significance and she was able to consider it with a certain detachment, the way one thought of mountains, seas and islands. Her base and her being were here, in the heart of the Weald, midway between the North and South Downs, and her focal point was, and always had been, the tall, far-ranging black-browed figure, who rode and drove and stumped between his base and hers, dominating both and issuing his edicts off the cuff, so that all manner of men serving him scurried to obey, but cheerfully, sometimes almost gaily. For under the bark, and the gruff certainty of command, was a broad strain of geniality and boyishness that sometimes reminded her vividly of the young, erect horseman who had come riding out of nowhere at crack of dawn one summer morning and pounced on her when she was halfway through her nineteenth year.

It seemed so long ago now, that improbable (and, still to Henrietta) intensely romantic incident. So distant that it was as though she had lived all of half a dozen lives, the first spent in waiting and wondering in rural Cheshire, the rest as his consort, bearing him children and queening it here in a house that was already more than three centuries old; deferring to him, arguing the toss with him, sometimes digging in her heels against him but, on the whole, sharing his life and hopes and attainments as a near-equal partner and sometimes, even now, romping with him in that great canopied bed the Conyers had used to perpetrate their tribe, the one place where he seemed to her able to relive his youth at will and then stow it away again in order to shoulder the monstrous burden he seemed to enjoy lugging the length of the country.

Whenever he was absent, however, she was able, without much difficulty, to readjust to a wider orbit where the house itself, and its rural environs, replaced him as pace-setter and generator. Over the years she had, perforce, to learn the trick of making this adjustment a hundred times a year, if only to fill the vacuum he created the moment he rattled off to that slum of his beside the Thames. Now, to a degree at least, abrupt substitution of Home for Husband had become an easy habit of mind. After the birth of Margaret, the last of her children, the importance of background had increased year by year, season by season, so that she was able to separate, study and evaluate each successive spring, summer, autumn and winter, thinking of them in terms of daily rotas, with their individual demands upon her time and patience.

*   *   *

She enjoyed them all in their several ways and was never able to decide which season exerted the most compelling demands, or brought with it the most delight, disappointment and dismay. They were four mettlesome, highly unpredictable steeds, ruled by caprices that encouraged them to behave well or ill, according to mood or perhaps the contents of their nosebags. For this was England, where one could never be absolutely sure whether it was January or June, April or October, and it was weather, above all else (given Adam's absence) that governed Henrietta's spirits and ordered Henrietta's schedule from time of rising to time of going to bed.

In the spring, that began for her any time between early March and late April, she was always aware of a personal renewal that kept step with her surroundings. She would ignore the snowdrops, that rightly belonged to winter, and concentrate on the humped up verges of the long, winding drive down to the stone gate pillars where Dancer, the homing carriage-horse, had flung her one April evening half an hour before the birth of Stella, her eldest daughter. She always regarded these pillars with the greatest respect, for she had come to think of them as the most prominent mileposts of her life. Had it not been for them, perhaps, she would never have spent her life here under the wooded spur, so that the pillars acquired, over the years, a mystical significance, a couple of cromlechs that held all the secrets of past, present and future.

To approach them, however, one had to half-circle the rhododendron clump at the head of the drive and move down between the double avenue of copper beeches where, in spring, the daffodils and narcissi showed in great, sprawling clusters, a double wave of yellow and white that was never still, not even on a windless day, but danced and joggled and shifted under mottled patterns of sunlight formed by the branches overhead, so that Henrietta would see them as Wordsworth had, a million children full of glee and ripe for mischief.

In spring she rarely went far afield on foot or on horseback. Her tours of inspection were usually limited to the paddocks, where the children's ponies were out to grass, or the walled kitchen garden west of the house, where the gardener and his two adjutants were to be found at this time of year. For by then, of course, she had had a surfeit of the house and spent a great deal of the day outside, sometimes climbing the zig-zag path to the summit of the spur above the house and pausing for a moment at the worm-eaten shelter made of half a whaler, that the old Colonel had used as a painting perch all the years he had lived with them.

Up here the old man never seemed dead. His gentle, jovial ghost pottered about among the fronds of pea-green bracken fighting for living space among the rusty spurs of last year's growth. The tenuous cord that had linked her to the dear old fellow had never really been severed by his death and burial and here, in his favourite spot, it seemed to strengthen a little so that she could, if she wished, commune with him and perhaps enjoy one of his sly, gentlemanly jokes.

Then she would move on to the level stretch that directly overlooked the house and stare down on the weathered pantiles and crazy cluster of crooked chimneys that looked like drunkards helping one another home, wondering at all that had gone on down there since the first Conyer had chosen this very spot to set the seal on his conquest of the handsome, long-nosed Cecil girl, whom he had wooed and at last won, buying her, as it were, with the profits of a privateering foray along the Dutch coasts in the years preceding the sailing of the Armada.

It was pleasant up here so long as you didn't mind the strong gusts of wind that coasted down from the higher ground to the east. Wild flowers grew here in great profusion beneath the squat oaks and tall, bosomed beeches, under the odd, self-seeded sycamore or mountain ash, primroses and peep-shy dog violets, crimson campion and hawkweed, sunspray dandelion, daisy, herb robert, stitchwort and bugloss, and always, of course, huge lacy umbrellas of cow-parsley that were, when one came to acknowledge them, the most splendidly fashioned of all.

Then Phoebe Fraser's lunch gong would begin to throb and she would retrace her steps, remembering the myriad of things she had to do, and within minutes she would be reabsorbed into the rhythm of the house but refreshed, somehow, by that pottering interval of solitude on the perimeter of her realm.

2

Summer, full summer that is, was a very different time, more demanding in every way for then, though there was no hunting, the young children spent almost all their time out of doors, where they soon grew berry-brown and even more vociferous and high-spirited than at Christmas, when the place erupted like a violated hive.

Sometimes, around and beyond midsummer day, it could be baking hot beyond the shade of the chestnuts, and whenever she walked south from the terrace she hugged the crown of the drive until she reached a gap in the fence that led through the little pine wood to another of her favourite spots, the pheasant hide alongside the road to Twyforde Green where, one sultry June day in 1865, Giles had been conceived, minutes after she had ambushed Adam on the way home.

She could never pass here without chuckling, and sometimes the place seemed to chuckle back at her, reminding her of that ridiculous tumble, performed almost in public, that neither of them had ever forgotten or ever could forget, for it was another milestone, and almost a year was to pass before she held him in her arms again and then he was not the same man and she was not the same woman, one being shorn of a limb, the other having matured in a way she found incomprehensible in retrospect. Yet the seed of that riotous encounter had remained in her, surviving a terrible season of stress and despair, and the result was young Giles, somehow, perhaps by reason of this very circumstance, apart from them all in some way, half child and half man and, so far as she was concerned, as symbolic as the pillars the far side of the hedge.

She would sit here deliberately recreating the scene, reminding herself of what they had said to one another on that occasion, and even recalling what she had worn, a sprigged muslin dress that afterwards had to be discarded, although it was almost new. She could recall, even at this distance, every trivial circumstance of that hourlong idyll, her mingled shame and defiance, her underlying sense of triumph at her ability to slip from role of wife to mistress at the first touch of his hand on her breast, and of a curious awareness of having, at long last, anchored the man who later sped her on her furtive return to the house with a jovial slap on the bottom.

God knows how young and zestful they had been in those days! And how long, how improbably long, this relationship had endured, for even now, with him fifty-seven, and herself nearly thirteen years younger, they were still lovers, as inseparably bound to one another as they had been when he hustled her into that hide and rumpled her to such an extent that she had to sneak back to the house like a village wanton, terrified of being spotted by one of the children or maids.

But the summer, for the most part, was not really a time for ruminating. There was always a round of fêtes and garden parties and birthday celebrations, with any number of visitors to entertain and gossip with, and croquet matches on the lawn over by the solitary cedar, and, more recently, lively games of tennis that were too strenuous for her but served to demonstrate the astonishing agility of the Inseparables, Joanna and Helen.

Alex, home to take up a special appointment—something to do with a new quick-firing gun somebody clever had invented—watching them whirl their long-handled rackets and leap this way and that in a flurry of skirts and petticoats, had called them dervishes and Henrietta, who had never seen a dervish, took his word for it. For her part she thought of them as tomboys, reflecting a little glumly that, when she was their age, such a pastime would have been out of the question for young ladies, who were taught instead to glide like ghosts in their bell-crinolines, and acquire poise by parading round the schoolroom with books balanced on their ringlets. Adam had always been extremely liberal in his attitude towards the girls but she supposed freedom was in the air nowadays, for when she repeated that silly story, about having to refuse a chair offered by a gentleman because it was warm from his bottom, the Inseparables had almost split their sides and Adam, recalling how he too had laughed when she recounted it the first day they met, admitted that some of the stuffiness was being beaten from society by the rising generation. "Not before time, either," he had added. "I remember I was appalled when I got back here, after seven years out east, and found the British were raising their women under glass."

"I didn't do much to steady your gallop," she had reminded him but he replied, gaily, "You were already running from your hothouse when I met you," and she had laughed with him, remembering that this was true.

She had always enjoyed solitary rides along the river bank on her gelding, Patch, pretending she needed the exercise, but actually using the outing to escape from the ceaseless clamour of the children. Round about June or early July she would alternate between riding upstream to Dewponds, and passing the time of day with Stella and that enslaved husband of hers, or downstream to the tail of the islet, that she had always thought of as Shallott, a triangle of wooded shingle where the stream formed an ox-bow a mile below 'Tryst' bridge.

This place too had its memories. It was here that that insolent puppy of a gunner (his name she had conveniently forgotten) had tried, rather clumsily, to seduce her a year or so after they settled at 'Tryst'. Her way of paying forfeit for that liberty, however, more than exorcised any fears she had of the place now, and she would smile a self-congratulatory smile as she reined in to let Patch drink his fill in the shallows, remembering how she had plucked a sharp stone from a drystone wall and drawn blood from her assailant's scalp, and afterwards—as the old Colonel had so aptly put it—landed a second blow in that part of his anatomy where his conceit lived. She had never seen him since and had never wished to, but she sometimes wondered if she had done him a permanent injury and rather hoped she had not. She could see now that he had reason to suppose she was genuinely flattered by his attentions, instead of using him to mitigate her boredom while Adam was off on one of his trips.

Summer was a time of splendour for their Scots gardener but Henrietta had never cared for cultivated flowers. The old Colonel had prejudiced her in favour of the flowers that ran riot down here about this time, huge, multi-belled foxgloves, yellow iris, purple orchis and toadflax that he had loved to reproduce in old-maidish watercolours, many of which were still about the house.

September and October brought its own round of activities, the fruit-gathering and bottling, the nutting and, of course, the harvest home, her favourite church service, when churchgoing had a meaning for people who spent most of their days in the country. She loved the autumn smells, particularly the acrid whiff of burning leaves and weeds, that seemed to hang over 'Tryst' for weeks and help her come to terms with shortening days and remind her of the compensations of winter.

Not least among these was the opening of the hunting season on the first Saturday of November, and although Henrietta had never ridden to hounds she took the greatest pride in seeing her little clutch of equestrians and equestriennes set off booted and spurred for Long Copse where, by tradition, they always held the opening meet. On these occasions, particularly when there was a meet at 'Tryst', she followed the hunt in the dogcart, expertly driven by old Stillman, the old Colonel's batman, who had been a hunt servant for the 16th Light Dragoons in Ireland during his youth and was a great favourite among all the young bloods within riding distance of 'Tryst'.

Stella was still the most accomplished horsewoman of the family and Denzil, bless the boy, encouraged her to hunt, even though she was now the mother of two boys. Joanna and Helen, however, could hold their own with the thrusters of the local hunt, and if Alex was home, and a local meet coincided with school holidays, Hugo went out, but never Giles. Giles had renounced hunting on principle, something to do with organised bullying, he said, although how one set about bullying an artful rascal like the fox was more than Henrietta could say.

She would sit on the grass hillock opposite Long Copse, absorbing the rich panoply of the scene, excitement charging the crisp autumn air and all the neighbours coming and going on their glossy mounts as the hounds trotted in about the oaks and chestnuts and beeches of the wood until the warbling blare of the horn echoed across the valley and the field resolved itself into a thunderous, hallooing, shouting, stamping, jingling, leather-squeaking storm-column of pink and black and white and grey, every rider jostling for a place as the pack broke for open country. Then Henrietta, wildly exhilarated, would risk a broken neck by standing up in the jolting dogcart, in an effort to pick out Alex or Hugo or Stella or one of the Insepa-rables stampeding into the east, the line the fox always took early in the season.

At times like this, pride would stir in her for it seemed to her a very remarkable thing that she was the mother of four or five of these spirited young things, spattering mud in all direction, and she had a sense of having done something quite splendid by pro-ducing them and endowing them all with such health and high spirits, something as impressive as Wren had done by raising St. Paul's, or the original Conyer by founding a dynasty and building this house where every one of them had been born and reared.

She never had any credit left over for Adam on these occasions. Somehow it seemed to her that his share in creating them had been so casual, and so relatively trivial, that it could be discounted al-together. After all, she had not only conceived them but had carried them in her belly for months on end, and now here they were, dashing across the Kentish countryside like a race of warriors, of the kind she had always promised herself when she and her friend Sarah Hebditch whispered of husbands and babies, at a time when such talk, had it been overheard, would have earned her a scolding and Sarah (whose mother was very frumpish) a sore backside for a week.

Although Henrietta did not hunt she enjoyed a hack, particularly a solitary hack. Sometimes, of an autumn afternoon, she would urge Patch up the eastern escarpment and through the straggling timber to the open country beyond where she had a rich choice of views. She could look north to the pastures of Dewponds, that she had come to think of as acres belonging to the Swanns rather than the Fawcetts; or west, where the Sussex Weald melted into the blue-grey distance; or east, over the Kentish Weald, dotted with patchwork fields, farms, half-timbered manor houses and oast houses; or south, across uncultivated country to the Channel. Then, whichever way she had looked, her imagination would quicken in the rush of wind, so that she could think herself into an extravagantly fanciful role, the scion of a family that had dominated this corner of civilised England for generations, someone like the Cecil girl, who had been the original mistress of 'Tryst' and rode, not a bottle-nosed cob like poor old Patch, but a mettlesome bay of sixteen hands or more. Often the illusion was so sharp and sparkling that Henrietta would shout into the wind and canter back along the leaf-sodden path to the clearing where the chimneys of 'Tryst' gulped the down-draught of the hollow and here, on the instant, she would become herself again, remembering there were muffins for tea and a little sewing to be finished before supper was laid against Adam's escape from that stationary sulphurous cloud on the far horizon.

*   *   *

Then, almost before she knew it, Christmas was upon them and the old house would erupt with chatter and laughter, its rooms strewn with festive litter and a twelve-foot tree, tubbed by the head gardener and trimmed by Phoebe Fraser, herself and the children, would glow and glitter in the hall, and everybody would eat too much, and have too much to say, so that the house might have been prised from its bed under the spur, trundled across the county, and set down within shouting distance of London Bridge Station.

It was at Christmas time that she cherished another illusion, seeing herself as a cosier miniature of the queen at Windsor, surrounded by gay (but respectful) relatives, each a prince or princess of the blood, and some, like George or Stella, having a consort, summoned to the presence to perform Yuletide homage.

It was then too that she would note the inevitable cliques and alliances that existed within a family of this size and speculate on the sympathies that had resolved them and the rivalries that kept them in being. Alex and George, so dissimilar in temperament, had always been close, and so had Deborah and Stella, another ill-matched pair. Then there was the alliance between the two younger girls, Joanna and Helen, that dated almost from babyhood, and the later partnership, again curiously unbalanced, that was developing between Giles and Hugo, the bonehead of the family. By reason of age alone the two youngest, Edward now six, and Margaret, less than a year behind him, were easily paired, and within these groupings they all seemed to move freely, with the possible exception of Giles, who, despite his patronage of Hugo, walked alone, would always walk alone, holding himself in readiness for what? As referee, perhaps?

Watching them, listening to their banter and amiable bickering on these festive occasions, Henrietta would smile her complacent smile. For a quarter-century now Adam had been making prodigious hauls about the country but could his network look back on a haul as long and as triumphant as hers? For here she was, the queen of 'Tryst', and who was she, now that she thought about it? The sole issue of an exiled Irish peasant and a coarse old rascal who had started out as a bale-breaker in a small-town mill and made his pile by clubbing his way to the front. Not that she held that against herself. Indeed, it went some way to sustain her pride, for how, she would proceed to ask herself, had she achieved such a peak? Well, partly by exercising nerve and common sense at the time of his injury, and partly by having the courage to reject a safe background and trust to luck when she was a chit of a girl. But more, she would say, by learning how to please a lusty, independent male animal and keep him interested over the years. And that was a trick nobody could teach anybody. You either learned how or you didn't and lost out.

The weeks that followed Christmas were always something of an anticlimax but they too had their compensations. When snow was falling, the children took to tobogganning, or, if snow held off, and New Year downpours converted all the country roads between here and Croydon into a chain of little morasses, Adam would ease off a little, sometimes spending days together at home, where he would seek a cure for restlessness by shifting the furniture around, 'to make a change' he would say, although that wasn't the real reason. She never stopped him, however. Aside from giving him something to do, it afforded him an opportunity to congratulate himself on the astonishing changes he had wrought in the original spartan country seat of the Conyers, and Henrietta secretly marvelled at all he had achieved, for many of the items of furniture he had bought during his jaunts up and down the country were regarded by local connoisseurs as masterpieces of English craftsmanship. There were pictures and porcelain too, and pieces of old silver worn smooth by use, so that gradually the house acquired a splendour that it had lacked in their pinchpenny days and it was not necessary to know about these things in order to appreciate them.

All in all she was more than content, but sometimes she did have a nagging doubt or two that a pleasant rhythm such as this could not be expected to last indefinitely and her misgivings were strong enough to prompt her to voice them from time to time, especially after they had shared a particularly satisfying day.

She did this a month or two after that rascal George had bounced back with his pretty Austrian wife, whom Henrietta had been prepared to dislike on sight but had discovered, within minutes, that she had little to fear from. Gisela, the silly girl was so besotted with the boy that she hardly took note of anybody else and was proving not only manageable but dutiful, something Henrietta had not expected of a foreign-born daughter-in-law. All the same, Gisela's presence about the house reminded her that all manner of changes and upheavals might lie ahead, and she said, as they were going to bed that night, "Do you ever get scared deep down inside, when there's no reason at all to feel anything of the kind?" and Adam said, without looking up from the task of removing a top-boot from his sound leg, "To be sure I do. Everyone does, if they've a ha'porth of sense. That's the time one should look out for squalls." And then, but incuriously, "Is it George turning up with a wife that's put you on that tack?"

"In a way," she said, marvelling at his intuitive powers so far as she was concerned, "for the truth is I expected to have to choose between a fortune-hunter and a frump, and Gisela is neither. She's just a pretty girl hopelessly in love with the boy, and still would be if he hadn't a penny to his name."

"That's so," he said, finally removing the boot and standing it beside the other, but then added, "I'll tell you something else about her if you're interested. She pays George a deal more deference than you ever paid me. Certainly in public and in private too, I shouldn't wonder. Keep your eye on her, you might learn a thing or two about handling men!"

But she answered, with a shrug, "Pooh! There's not a woman alive who could teach me one thing about handling *you*, Adam Swann! You know it, and I know it, so don't you dare to compare us as wives, not even mentally, d'you hear?"

"I'm not such a damned fool as to do that," he said, and she was glad to note seriousness in his voice. "Gisela? Well, she's pretty, she's graceful and submissive and most men look for that in a woman, I imagine."

"But you don't?"

"If I had I wouldn't have stayed a bachelor until I was thirty-one. John Company's India was chock-full of Giselas, and I daresay, penniless as I was at that time, I could have had my pick of 'em. However, I didn't, so turn down the lamp and let's get to bed. I intend to make an early start in the morning, rain or shine."

She did as he asked and neither of them spoke for a few minutes but then, as always when she found herself the subject of a discussion, vanity and curiosity joined forces to nag at her and she said, "*Why* didn't you? Having said so much tell me the rest. So long as it flatters me, that is."

She heard him chuckle and his arm went round her. The vague uncertainties released by the turn of conversation left her at his touch and he went on, "I'll tell you, my love, but briefly."

She heard him yawn and hoisted his hand to a breast, a trick she

457

had often employed when he was sleepy and she was not. "Go on, tell me."

"I suppose I was looking for promise. Your kind of promise. Good-night, my love."

The trick wasn't working tonight but no matter. He had said enough, or all that she wanted to hear. A moment later he was snoring gently and she thought about the word, one he had often used regarding women in the abstract but had never, so far as she recollected, applied to her. *Promise*. Promise of what, exactly? Free access to her body, whenever he expressed the merest flicker of desire? That was a part of it certainly. He was a sensual man and they had both been lucky in that respect, for she had decided long ago that she was a particularly sensual woman, and could match him any night of the week, but there was some other connotation and it continued to elude her until, as though someone had withdrawn a veil on his youth, she saw precisely what he meant, for there, in her mind's eye was a hill-station or garrison town, of the kind he had so often described and it was crowded with simpering husband-hunters, newly disembarked from the bride-boat, and she was able to stand off and study them all, as through a peephole.

There were blondes and brunettes and redpolls. There were women nudging thirty and girls halfway through their teens. There were blushers and girls who had forgotten how to blush. There were the dowered and undowered, the chaperoned and the unchaperoned, the tall and short, the tightly corsetted and the uncorsetable, the shy, the talkative, the earnestly informed and the twitterers who specialised in the vapours, all kinds of women on the *qui vive* for a glance, a stammering invitation, a chance word that could, with luck, persistence, skill, or all three, be coaxed into a proposal. For that, in her experience, was how women set out in search of security and the freedoms a hearth of one's own had to offer. They had always done it and they were about it still, but no one in that room of husband-hunters had been clever enough to spring a trap on him and she thought she knew why. Some of them must have had promise of a kind but it was not his kind. He was looking for something that no one there was equipped to provide. It wasn't money and it wasn't beauty. It wasn't charm, good breeding, fidelity, or even the most urgent of his needs at that time, simple physical gratification. It was something far less tangible and definitive than any of these things, and by the mercy of God, she had it in her bones and her blood. The spirit of adventure that was at once her patrimony and her matrimony, for Sam Rawlinson, with all his faults, had been a trier, whereas her mother, moved by who knew what primeval instinct, had gone in search of a destiny across the sea, turning her back on home and kin and sailing deck-passage to Liverpool, years in advance of those who followed her during the famine years.

That was the promise he had been looking for and he had recognised it in her. At a glance, possibly, certainly after a day or two in her company, when they were cooking rabbit stew over their first campfire under the Pennines and he had revealed to her not merely the necklace, the touchstone of his fortunes, but also his dreams.

Certitude, of the kind she looked for whenever he was here at night with what she still thought of as his sword-arm flung across her breast, settled on her like an extra quilt.

4

Scholar Gypsy

GILES SWANN, eighteen, and more curious about himself than those who had come to know him well, had no special favourites among the English lyrical poets. He loved them all, for one verse or couplet or another, deriving so much satisfaction from their work over three centuries that he sometimes wondered if poetry was not his true vocation. But then the practical streak, that showed in all Swanns sooner or later (and was, Adam said, the legacy of a string of greedy mercenaries reaching back beyond the French wars), would reassert itself, so that he would remind himself, severely, "No, no! That's not me, not really. Poets contribute certainly, but most of them point the way and leave it at that!"

It was in this kind of mood that he closed his well-worn copy of Matthew Arnold's poems in early April, 1884, unpacked and repacked his knapsack (discarding all but what he considered essentials to get the overall weight below the sixty pound maximum) and set off due north, over the first few miles of his private odyssey, with Arnold's lines from *The Scholar Gypsy* running through his head . . .

> But once, years after, in the country lanes,
> Two scholars, whom at college erst he knew
> Met him, and of his way of life inquired.
> Whereat he answer'd, that the Gipsy crew,
> His mates, had arts to rule as they desired,
> The workings of men's brains . . .

He saw himself, at that moment, as the gentle Arnold's prototype, putting theory into practice, turning his back deliberately, a little self-righteously even, on the temptations of a three-year intellectual spree at Oxford, in order to search more diligently for secrets where they were more likely to be found. In the lanes and hedgerows.

Along the high road. Through the old, close-set woods. On windy uplands and, more surely perhaps, among the fume and clatter of the industrial North and Midlands, where his father's waggons moved through complexes of railyards, back-to-back houses, and tall belching chimneys.

He had no clear idea what he was seeking but whatever it was he was sure, in his own mind, of one thing. He was more likely to find it here than in the pedant-haunted quadrangles of Arnold's city of spires that he had visited (and at once distrusted) when he went up there to sit for his scholarship the previous autumn.

Thompson, his earnest, monocled headmaster, thought him mad and told him so, more than once. "You've got more intellectual promise than any boy I've had under my hand," he said, a day or so after Adam gave Giles permission to bypass Oxford. "I'm not questioning your father's judgement. Unquestionably he made his way without the mental disciplines and friendships available at a good University. But you're both forgetting something. Your father travelled the world in his twenties, and fought in a number of wars. War and travel educates a man and sometimes enables him to recognise truth when he sees it. Truth about himself and truth in general. But you don't even intend crossing the Channel or looking down the barrel of a gun in the way your eldest brother has since he enlisted. What, apart from a bit of botany, are you likely to learn living the life of a tramp? That's what I'd like to know, lad."

Giles could be stubborn. "Stevenson learned something in the Cervennes, didn't he, sir? And so did Borrow and Cobden, by moving around." But 'Tommy', who had nourished the boy for five years now, made an impatient gesture, so that his monocle fell from his eye-socket.

"Stevenson is a sick man in search of health. And as for Borrow and Cobden, they were eccentrics, who didn't live in an industrial age. Like it or not, technology is taking over from here on. You would be far better advised to make an engineering pilgrimage, like your other brother. Poking about local hedgerows, as you propose to do, is no more than a fad and if you ask me your father is merely humouring you."

Was he? Giles was by no means sure, despite the amiable discussion they had had a month before up at Forty Beeches. The governor had done the same thing himself it was true, but with a specific purpose in mind and to survey a field in which he meant to operate. He had no such specific purpose, only a vague curiosity to discover for himself the underlying reasons why this country, alone among Western nations, had sloughed off its ancient traditions, turned its face from an agricultural past, and sprouted wings that had carried it to the ends of the earth and made it the new Rome.

The answer, diligently as he had searched, was not to be found in books, but it was there somewhere lying out among the broken shards of the old civilisation and the smoke-tainted manufactories of the new. The important thing to discover was how this convulsion, less than a century old but now pushing shock-waves across the world, governed the lives of ordinary people. People like that old couple, for instance, whom he had seen ejected from their cottage and separated by Bumbledom; people like those wharf rats his father recruited as vanboys; people like the sweep Luke Dobbs, who had choked to death in a 'Tryst' chimney only a few years before he was born.

He said, uneasily, "I don't know what I'm looking for, sir, but if I find it I'll make use of it one way or another and you'll be the first to hear about it. I've been very happy here. This is a wonderful place to spend one's formative years, and I'll always need to come back, again and again. Maybe I'll come back for good one day. I don't know. I'm not sure of anything save the need to learn more before I can teach."

Thompson did not miss the hint and regarded the boy thoughtfully. "I'll tell you one thing more, Swann, before you raise blisters on your feet. I always have thought teaching was your vocation. You've got something most professional teachers haven't got and rarely develop. Genuine intellectual curiosity, plus natural tolerance. They're your principal assets, so don't squander them on social indignation."

They shook hands on that and Giles went up to the Brereton dormitory to spend his final night at school. Hugo was asleep, his great limbs sprawled half in and half out of the narrow iron cot, and Giles, regarding his genial, slightly bovine features in a shaft of moonlight that clipped the line of wash basins and touched the bed, thought, a little enviously, "Good old Hugo! One of the lucky ones. Whatever he does, wherever he goes his physical apparatus will be his compass, for the needle doesn't swing above his neck," and outside, in the beeches of the east drive, an owl corroborated.

*   *   *

The route of his first stage differed from that of his father's ride of more than twenty-five years ago.

Adam had ridden north-east from Plymouth to Gloucester, before heading north to the cotton belt, so that his way had taken him through nearly two hundred miles of predominantly agricultural country as far as Warwickshire and then, a day or so later, to the Potteries. To an extent this had governed the entire nature of his enterprise, at least in the early years, for even now around half his hauls involved produce.

Giles, having come to manhood in a more sophisticated age, aimed at the heart of the new Britain, striking across familiar North Devon moorland to the Bristol Channel where he found a collier at Minehead. For half a crown the captain set him ashore in Wales, midway between Cardiff and Swansea.

His instinct, at this time, was to explore the mining districts, where newspapers said there was always industrial tension, where militant radicalism was gaining ground in the ruined valleys, where hundreds of thousands of Welshmen whose fathers had been farmers now clawed for coal, the staple commodity of the nation. Coal. That gritty, shining substance that looked worthless when you held a knob in your hand, wondering at its relationship to the primeval forests that had covered all England when England was a spread of green fingers thrust into the Atlantic, with the wrist somewhere about the delta of the Rhine. Coal, that black, yellow-seamed, rather brittle substance was really everything inasmuch as it made everything else work when you thought about it. For without it, without the men who risked their lives every day to get it, there would have been no industrial revolution, no factories and foundries, no ironclads and no ships to carry four-fifths of the world wealth from one coast to another. There would have been no Swann-on-Wheels either, and probably no Giles Swann to ask questions about it. Yet here it lay in abundance, enough, they said, to last for another century, or so long as Welshmen could be bribed or bullied to hack it from seams deep below the spoiled hills and valleys of their homeland.

He had never previously visited Wales and took an instant liking to the Welsh, with their tug-of-war between body and soul that was evident, even to a stranger, in the number of chapels in every township and village he visited, in their sad songs, in the soft lilt of their tongue and, above all, in the terrible squalor of their pits and crowded dwelling areas close by, every brick hutch seeming to lean on its neighbour, like stacks of very grubby, finely balanced playing cards laid in rows across the hillsides where no grass grew and the scrabble for coal had converted what had once been an enchanting land into a midden.

Even here his terms of reference remained vague but he had done what he could to prepare himself. In his knapsack was a sheaf of introductions and the first put him in touch with Bryn Lovell, manager of the Mountain Square, who met him at a small town in the Rhondda and obtained permission from a customer to take him down a coal mine.

Bryn, whom he had met briefly at Stella's wedding, refused the offer of a guide. He had himself been below on many occasions, he said, and knew this particular pit, having worked on top as a boy when his father had been in charge of the pumps. He said, as they made their way to the pithead, "You'll ask awkward questions, no doubt, and I might find it embarrassing to give you a straight answer in the presence of their outside men. After all, this mine is worth good money to your father, and it won't do to let them know my convictions concerning the industry as a whole." He looked at Giles shrewdly. "Just what do you expect to find in the Rhondda, Mr. Swann?"

"I haven't the least idea," Giles told him, cheerfully, "but I'm very curious about coal-mining, and I've heard all about the risks these men run down there. I suppose I want to see the conditions they work under and the compensations there are, if any. I've talked to miners on the way up, and spent a night with one family. There were seven of them sharing three little rooms. Two of the boys, both pitworkers, were under thirteen. I was amazed to learn they were working underground."

It seemed to Giles then that Lovell's face hardened, taut lines showing either side of his mouth. He had, Giles decided, a very ascetic face but his manner, even when you made allowance for the fact that he was entertaining one of his employer's sons, was uneasy. He said, briefly, "Nothing unusual about that. Within a mile of where we stand there must be two to three thousand lads under twelve on the lower levels. We've been agitating for legislation to stop it for years." He gave Giles one of his shrewd, impersonal looks. "Can you imagine this place as it was when I first remember it? And I'm only sixty."

Giles glanced up the valley, noting the rampart-like ridges of the mountains and, between them, a widespread smouldering furnace, spiked with skeletal pitheads and scarred in a hundred places by the steeply rising tiers of miners' houses. It was a fine day but the sun did not penetrate here, or only in fitful gleams, occasionally striking a slag heap or a patch of turgid water. "I can't imagine it was ever pastoral, Mr. Lovell."

"You'd be wrong," Bryn said. "There were open-cast workings, plenty of them, but no real blight, as you see now. Men grubbed coal from near the surface, with hardship, maybe, but not much danger. Read Roscoe, and discover for yourself what it was like to walk down the valley of the Rhondda, and other Glamorgan streams a generation ago. Roscoe talks of waterfalls, of the mountain current breaking clearly on rocks, of pools you could fish in and heavy timber on those hills. Look at it now and judge for yourself the price we Welsh have paid for the coal-owners' country estates, and the nation's industrial lead you read so much about in newspapers printed by men who have never drawn a breath of Welsh air, fair or foul. However, we'll go below as your father did once in my company."

"My father went down a coal mine?"

"He did that, for he's also a man who likes to see for himself. Maybe that's one reason why he's reckoned a good gaffer in the network."

Giles would liked to have asked him more but Lovell was obviously bent on an object lesson rather than a lecture. They borrowed miners' caps, lamps and leather jerkins from the pithead store and entered what seemed to Giles a very insecure cage that rushed them down into the mountain at a speed that made his senses reel.

"We'll start in from the lowest level," Bryn said, when, retching slightly, Giles staggered into a low-roofed underground chamber.

It was like yet another scene from the illustrated Dante's *Inferno*, seen in Mr. Thompson's library, a pall of velvet darkness shot through with indistinct points of yellowish light, where gnomelike men stumped to and fro across a maze of intersecting rails. Trolleys, pulled by ponies, rattled by and other trucks, recently emptied, were riding into one or other of the tunnels, or roads as Lovell called them, leading to the coal face.

He did not know what he had expected but it was not this, and neither was it the long, toilsome journey down a foot-wide track beside one of the railways. The darkness, a darkness you could almost grab by the handful, would have been absolute had it not been for the glimmer of Lovell's lamp, moving ahead, or the welcome break of a dimly-lit bay, scooped in the face of the road at rare intervals. Everywhere the roof was so low that Giles, despite his lack of inches, had to crouch, and it crossed his mind to wonder how his brother Hugo would have fared down here. Bryn said little, confining his occasional comments to a word or two flung over his shoulder, and Giles gathered that nobody wasted breath in conversation down here. One needed it all to adjust to the crouching stumble if one was to avoid tripping over the rails, or smashing one's head on the revetted roof that constantly scraped the leather hat he was wearing. He had thought of himself until then as very fit and agile, but movement, and survival too he would wager, demanded a different kind of fitness to that a man acquired on the Exmoor upland. One needed to be a dwarf, a contortionist and a tightrope walker, so that when, at a bay, Lovell stopped to permit the passage of an unseen oncomer, he gasped, "How much further to the face?"

"Two—three hundred yards. If you're that puffed . . ." But he did not complete the sentence, holding up his hand and cocking an ear in the direction of the approaching footfalls.

They were hurrying. Even Giles noticed that, and when a miner came level with the bay he at once linked his expression with a subdued but definite pattern of sounds that issued from the tunnel, a sustained murmur punctuated by a series of sharp, metallic clankings, and then an agonised cry from close at hand.

Lovell said, detaining the passing miner, "A derailment? Is the road blocked?" and the man, shaking himself free, replied, "Truck running free. And some of Owen Williams' toes along with it," and he jerked his head towards the opening.

"Badly hurt?"

The man shook his head. "They're bringing him outbye. Stay here, whoever you wass," and plunged onwards towards the shaft, moving very swiftly at a loping crouch that was like the passage of a hunted animal.

It struck Giles at once that Lovell did not seem so concerned as he should have been, and when he asked if this meant there had been a serious accident the manager said, unconcernedly, "Truck over a man's foot. It happens every day. It might be trivial, or it might mean amputation when they get him to the pithead." And then, with what Giles thought of as a tincture of malice, "There's far worse happens down here than the loss of a couple of toes or even a foot. At least that means Williams will be kept on, and work above ground, and that doesn't happen to most casualties. The ones that survive, that is. I've seen a dozen men carried out on stretchers from one shift and they were the lucky ones. Two dozen more were under a fall, or gassed and beyond human aid."

The clank of a string of trucks approached until its rattle made speech impossible. On the first of them lay Owen Williams, a young man about Giles' own age, or possibly a year or so older. In the light of a brace of lamps carried by the boy leading the pony, and an older miner riding the tub behind and supporting the injured man's shoulders, Giles caught a swift glimpse of the recumbent man's face. It was twisted with pain that the mask of coal dust could not conceal, and it seemed to Giles that he was having as much as he could do to keep from screaming. His left boot had been removed and his foot was swathed in roughly-applied bandages. Thick as they were blood was seeping through. The mournful little procession passed in a matter of seconds, so that it was as though it had been part of a confused dream. Bryn Lovell called after the last loaded tub, "Good luck, man . . ." but nobody answered and he moved forward again, Giles following, sweat striking cold in his armpits and under the browband of the hard leather hat he was wearing.

It was only the first of a series of revelations, nightmarish most of them, although here and there, particularly at the coal face, he found himself technically interested in the processes of removing

467

coal from a seam and transferring it, via the conveyor, to the waiting tubs.

He saw men stripped to the waist lying in crannies that were hardly more than eighteen inches high, clawing away at the seam with a speed and precision that he would not have thought a machine could accomplish in these cramped, claustrophobic galleries. He saw the place where the truck had left the rails and crushed Owen Williams' foot; he saw a shift of boys, none older than Third Form boys at school, eating their 'snap', as Lovell called it, before starting another four-hour spell at the conveyor, where they were charged with the work of tipping the loaded sections of the conveyor into tubs and easing the string down an incline to an open space at the hub of the galleries. He did not speak to them. It seemed to him that it would have been patronising on his part, but he stored in his mind the deep impression they made on him, a dozen bleary-eyed imps, gossiping gaily among themselves, as though they were taking part in a parody of a junior-school tuck-shop spree.

He saw many other things that he never afterwards forgot, for the hours spent down there, beginning with that backbreaking scramble to the bay where they waited to make way for Williams, and ending with the blessed relief of smelling daylight at the top of the shaft, were etched into his memory in a way that nothing he had previously experienced could rival in terms of truth and sobriety.

He said, as they walked down the narrow-gauge tracks that led to the sidings below, "How much do those men earn, Mr. Lovell?" and Lovell said, "It depends what they're doing. A boy stableman a few shillings. An experienced miner about the same as one of your father's waggoners."

"Why do they go on doing it, generation after generation?"

"What else could they do? They have no other skills to sell and there are compensations."

"I haven't noticed any."

"Ah, you would have to live here and work with them, shift for shift. Your father realised that but he's been under fire himself."

He stopped and seemed to consider for a moment. "See here, lad, you plagued me to show you a coal mine and I've done it. You seem shocked but, unless I'm mistaken, you're still very curious. That chap

Williams lives close. Suppose we go and enquire after his chances? Would that embarrass a young gentleman like you?"

"Not in the least. I should like it very much, Mr. Lovell. I came here to learn."

He may have been mistaken but it seemed to him that the grim-faced manager of the Mountain Square relented somewhat, and came some way to meet what he probably regarded as an inquisitive boy, who was proving a time-wasting nuisance. "Then we'll go," he said, "for I fancy I know that poor chap's father, although the name about here is as common as Evans and Jones."

*   *   *

It was one of those leaning slate-roofed hutches he had stayed in on his way from the coast, very cramped but spotlessly clean and oddly over-furnished. Owen's father was a used-up little man, himself a surface worker, with two other sons, both out working middle shift when they called. Mrs. Williams, a talkative, fresh-faced woman about fifty, made a great fuss of Lovell, who seemed to be on familiar terms with everyone about here, and Giles wondered if this was because he had been born in the area or because local men still remembered his almost legendary feat of twenty years back, when he had hauled a pump to a flooded mine in time to save the lives of entombed miners.

The house did not strike Giles as being the centre of domestic tragedy. Indeed, the reverse seemed to be true, for Williams Senior, having told them that Owen was at the infirmary and likely to have three toes amputated, added almost gleefully that this would result in the lad getting a job on top. It struck Giles as astonishing that a family could rejoice at such a gruesome slice of luck and he asked, diffidently, "Won't your son be lame, Mr. Williams?" and Williams said cheerfully that he might but that lameness, to that extent, was preferable to an injury that would stop a man doing a full day's work. He did not say what Giles judged to be in his mind, that a job on top meant Owen would be likely to live out his full span of life, and he thought that these men, every one of them, were like soldiers occupying an exposed redoubt, sniped at from all points of the compass and unlikely, in the very nature of things, to survive indefinitely.

Giles asked Mrs. Williams how many children she had and was told five, three boys, all down the pit, and two girls in domestic service at a big house in Breconshire, further north. "It's not often they come home," she said, "except Christmas and Mothering Sunday, but it's glad I am for them for they've a good place up there, and plenty to eat." She then brought him tea and a piece of home-baked cake and asked him, but not inquisitively, what he was about in the Rhondda. Luckily Lovell heard the question and answered for him. "Mr. Swann is going into his father's business. He's getting the hang of things in the regions before settling in London."

"Ah, London," Mrs. Williams said, as though Lovell had mentioned Pekin, "that's a racketty ole place, I'm told. I've never been, and not likely to go, although Trevor Jones' boy down the street, has gone to work there. Got a job as a clerk in a warehouse, he has. That's what comes of attending to his lessons at the new school. Owen and Huw would have likely gone there if it had been open in time but it wasn't, so they have to make do with evening class when they're on day shift." She addressed Lovell, directly, "It's making good progress they are, Mr. Lovell, or so the minister tells Gwyn." She turned to Giles again, smiling. "You'll have forgotten your schooldays by now, Mr. Swann."

It occurred to Giles then, more forcibly even than when he was clawing his way along those black galleries, that the contrast between sections of the British was so great that they might be inhabiting different planets. He was eighteen, and less than a month ago he had been a schoolboy. Those children he had seen eating their snap were six years his junior and had probably been at work for a year.

Lovell said, rising, "I'll look in next time I'm round, Williams, to enquire after Owen. He's a good strapping lad, and I've no doubt he'll be at work again in a month."

"I hope so indeed," Williams said, gravely, "for he's getting top rate and Mam'll miss the money."

Giles said, as soon as they were clear of the house, "Won't Owen get compensation for an injury like that?" and Lovell said that the miners did operate some sort of mutual provident scheme, that would possibly yield a temporary sickness benefit of three or four shillings a week, but there was no official provision for injuries.

"But that's monstrous! Can't the employers work out some kind of scheme for contingencies of this sort?" Lovell stopped and looked at him quizzically. "The owners? About here? Good God, no lad. That wouldn't occur to the best of them. A man is no good to them lying on his back, is he?" He smiled then, a wry and wintry smile, that seemed to hurt a little. "You're a budding radical, I perceive. I can see you and John Catesby getting along if you get so far as the Polygon. But let me give you a grain of comfort, concerning our business at least. Your father has the right ideas about the relationship between capital and labour. He's a good gaffer as I said, even though he's a hard man in some ways, or hard to those who don't attend to their business to his satisfaction. Catesby's ways and his ways are different, however. Catesby has been trying to turn the world upside down ever since I've known him, and can't understand why me and the other regional gaffers won't help him."

"Why won't you? You have to admit that life bears pretty heavily on people like the Williamses. I've seen very little so far but what I have makes me wonder if a thumping good revolution isn't needed here, as it was in France, in 1789."

"Ah, that's for the young to dream about," Lovell said, tolerantly. "Dreamed something like it myself when I was your age, but I've learned since. By reading and by observation. I believe in slow pressures, applied through Parliamentary processes, of the kind Gladstone applied in the early 'seventies. Change things too quickly and what happens? You invite reaction, of the kind that spread clear across Europe in 'forty-eight. A few months of freedom and then *snap*, the collar's notched a hole tighter. The art of government isn't to be found in a revolutionary tract but stodgier reading. It's a slow, toilsome process, take it from me. One Ewart Gladstone is worth twenty Dantons and any amount of Wat Tylers."

It was in Giles' mind to admit that he had heard Gladstone, and been spellbound by him, but he said, instead, "I'm greatly obliged to you wasting a whole day on me, Mr. Lovell. I'll write and tell my father how kind and helpful you were and that you may have thought me a great nuisance but didn't show it."

"Aye, I did think that, up to the moment you agreed to pay a call on the Williams, but I don't think it now. I'm thinking something different and I'll tell you what it is. I'd be right content to work un-

der a young gaffer like you, if your father ever took it into his head
to retire. Years at a gentlemen's school hasn't spoiled you the way it
does most young men o' good family. You could think like one of us
when you've seen more and read more and had time to digest it. If
ever you're this way again, I'd take it kindly if you called in at Abergavenny and met my missis an' boys. Will you do that?"

"To be sure I will, and gladly," Giles said, and they shook hands
again, this time less formally.

2

Over the battlemented tip-scarred hills enclosing the valley and north
into the green, unravished country of Brecknock, Radnor and Mont-
gomery, where hardly anyone he met spoke English, and the smell
of the sea reached him when the wind was in the west.

Mile after mile across sheep pasture and woodland valley, where
rivers dashed over boulder-strewn beds and the landscape, he would
say, had remained unchanged since Edward Longshanks' French-
speaking cavalry had ridden this far to kill Llewelyn and build their
ring of fortresses in the north. Into the higher, wilder country about
Dolgelley and through the frowning Llanberis Pass, where he spent
one day looking over the quarries and another climbing Snowdon,
but saw little for his pains on account of the dense trailers of mist.
Fifteen and twenty miles a day on average, sometimes sleeping in
remote little inns, where old stone bridges spanned rushing mountain torrents, more often, as a dry spell followed a week of clouded
skies, camping under the edge of a wood, and sleeping in his sack
until dawn put a razor edge on his appetite and he was glad to restore circulation by a tramp to the nearest village, where he would
wolf down bacon and eggs and a pint of the local ale that would
sustain him over the next stretch of rough walking. In this way he
progressed within a day's walk of Caernarvon, having half-decided
to visit the castle and then head for Chester through the lovely Conway Valley and afterwards perhaps, take a look at the engine sheds at
Crewe before moving into the Polygon to renew his acquaintance
with Catesby.

The rushing, frothing, chattering rivers fascinated him up here, especially in the early mornings, when the sky above the jagged mountains was coral, streaked with heliotrope and the soft rush of the water over the stones was like the chorus of an old Welsh battle-song. He would sometimes pause, resting his elbows on the stone parapet of such a stream, looking about him with satisfaction, but telling himself that he was unlikely to learn much about the state of the nation up here, for the purple hills and the wooded slopes clothing the lower parts of the valleys, did not look as if they had altered since the earth cooled. Yet curious and unpredictable things did happen, as he discovered for himself one sunny morning in mid-May, whilst taking a breather at Pont Aberglaslyn, a river-crossing a mile below Beddgelert, where the road to the Vale of Conway led through a ten-mile pass of incomparable splendour.

*   *   *

He saw her when she began her hop-skip across the river, two hundred yards upstream, but paid her no special attention. At that distance she looked no more than a leggy, overbold schoolgirl, trying her luck on stepping stones formed by random boulders. Then he heard her squeal and saw a splash, and after that the glimpse of a red bundle spinning slowly in the current, rapidly gathering momentum and moving towards him as fast as a man could run.

The river was no more than shoulder deep, save where it ran in pools under the bank, but a child could easily drown there and, suddenly alarmed, he darted across the bridge and jumped ten feet to the gravel, wading in up to his knees and trying to judge where she would pass as the current swirled her towards the arches.

There was a long forked branch wedged between two rocks and he tore it free, calling to her and holding it out, as she swept level with him. He saw then that the red bundle was not a child but a girl about his own age, and also that she had not completely lost her nerve, for she was making strenuous efforts to save herself, striking out for a smoother reach between the boulders but not, so far as he could judge, making enough progress to gain the bank.

He went in deeper, right up to his chest, waving the stick and shouting to her to grab it as she bobbed past but she did not seem to understand him and ignored the branch, kicking clear of a smooth rounded boulder and somehow getting into an eddy that carried her not only underwater but clean between his legs, so that he was able to grab a handful of her skirt as the impact caused him to lose his footing and they rolled together in the shallows.

He dragged himself ashore and the girl with him, but he was weighed down by the heavy knapsack on his back so that it was she rather than he who played the more active part in reaching the triangle of shingle below the bridge. Then, dashing the water from his eyes, he saw that she was laughing and instead of feeling a hero he felt a complete idiot, for it occurred to him then that the girl had been in no danger after all and probably knew the course of the river much better than he did.

She said, shaking her head like a spaniel, "There, now! Who rescued who?" and laughed again, so saucily that he was obliged to join in, saying, "I made sure you were a child . . . What possessed you to cross there? It isn't a ford, is it?"

No, she told him, it wasn't, but the river was fordable anywhere at this time of year, unless spring had been late and very wet.

He looked at her more closely then and saw why he had underestimated her age. She had the face of a child, a pretty and rather spoiled child he would say, with blue, slightly upslanting eyes, long, fair lashes, a retroussé nose and a red, petulant mouth that looked as if it could sulk as well as chuckle. Yet her figure, revealed by her wet clothes, was that of a woman, and even here, dripping wet on a river bank, she flaunted it like a favour at a fair, heaving herself up and resting her weight on the buttress of the bridge, so that she could wring the water from her skirt. Her boyishness, and complete lack of concern over the wetting, reminded him of his younger sisters at home, who would make nothing of a thing like this but would never, he thought, have lifted their skirts above their thighs in front of a strange woman, much less a young man.

He said, to cover his confusion, "Do you live about here?" and she said offhandedly that she did, a mile or so along the Caernarvon road, but did not explain what she was doing here by the river at six o'clock in the morning, or indeed, offer any explanation as to how she came to fall in the stream and half drown in front of his eyes.

Then, having dropped her sodden skirt, she peeled off the little hussar jacket she wore over a white silk blouse and began to wring that out, bending forward so that he had to avert his eyes, for the front of her blouse was open and as she was wearing neither corset nor petticoat he could look the length of the cleft between her breasts. She noticed his glance, swift as it was, and laughed again, throwing the jacket over her shoulder and fastening the blouse buttons, but so casually that he thought "She might be well grown but she's obviously weak in the head. Maybe she's an idiot but the bonniest I ever saw!" and he said, "Let me have the jacket," and took it, turning his back on her and wringing it almost free of water. When he turned she was still regarding him humorously, one finger pulling at her lip and one bare foot (she had lost her shoes) braced against the corner-stone of the bridge in a way that revealed a dimpled knee.

"I can go home and change," she said, "but *you* can't can you? And your knapsack is just as wet as my bolero, and probably has all your things in it."

He had forgotten his own plight and now had to make a new assessment of her. She obviously wasn't the village idiot but an extraordinarily self-possessed young lady, as he realised the moment she went on, "We'll go on home, and you can breakfast with us while Maggie is drying you out. It's not far if we cut across there!" and she pointed to a zig-zag track climbing the furze-covered hill on the far bank. Then, without waiting for his assent, she took hold of some stones protruding from the buttress and hauled herself up the ten-foot wall and back on to the road level, moving with the precision of a gymnast. He followed more slowly, having thrown his dripping knapsack up to her, and together they took the hill-track that wound over the shoulder of the hill, leaving the little town of Beddgelert on their right.

"What's your name and what were you doing here this early?" she demanded and he told her, adding that he had slept in the woods and had been making for the town to buy breakfast before tackling the pass to Capel Curig and Conway. For some reason this seemed to impress her and she stopped to take a long, unabashed look at him, saying, "Just how *far* have you walked, Mr. Swann?"

"About a hundred and fifty miles," he said. "From North Devon. I left a month ago," and she gasped, again looking like a child.

"Why, that's *marvellous*! Papa will be *most* interested to learn that! He doesn't walk much, of course, but he knows all the places you must have passed. All those dreadful coal-mining towns, in the south."

"Who is your father? Is he a farmer?"

"Good heavens, no!" she said, laughing again. "He's nothing really, but his hobby is geology when he's here. Usually he's in London, or at one or other of his factories. He's got lots of factories in the south."

"What kind of factories?" Giles asked, for it was very difficult to visualise a factory-owner who lived up here in the very heart of the mountains, had a daughter like this pretty, unchaperoned creature, and studied geology into the bargain.

"Oh, all kinds of factories," she said, carelessly. "A dye works, a processing plant for coal-tar, a tannery, I believe . . . oh yes, and a foundry for making chains. Anchor chains, you know, the kind they use on ironclads and liners."

"You mean his home up here is his country-seat where he comes for holidays?"

"Yes, you'd call it that, I suppose, but I live here most of the time. I can do what I like up here whereas in London I always have to keep finding ways of outwitting Prickle. Prickle is strict and has the stupidest notions about how young ladies should behave once they put their hair up. That's why I had mine cut short," she added, as though that was what she had been leading up to.

"What's your name?"

"Guess. It begins with 'R'."

"I might guess all morning. Is it Rachel?"

"No, that's Biblical, and Papa is an atheist, like Mr. Bradlaugh. Try again."

He would have liked to have asked her if she had met Bradlaugh, who had recently been ejected from the House of Commons by ten policemen but decided to humour her.

"Rhoda? Rosalind?"

"You're getting warm. Rhoda is nice and not at all common, is it? But you'll never guess, no one ever does." She sounded as if this was deplorable. "It's Romayne. Do you like it, Mr. Swann?"

He liked it very much, not only because it had a pleasant sound on her lips but because it suited her exactly. It had a gypsy flavour.

"Romayne what?"

476

"Rycroft-Mostyn. The Mostyn bit I never use unless I have to. There's a whole lot of Mostyns about here and over on the coast. Papa married one, and took the name but she's dead now. Years and years ago."

It was difficult to adjust to her lack of sentimentality, so that he had to assume the late Mrs. Rycroft-Mostyn was a step-mother. "That wasn't your mother?"

"Of course it was, but I can't remember her. She died having an operation when I was three. What's your Christian name, Mr. Swann?"

"Giles," he said, and to his embarrassment she repeated it twice as though tasting it and then added, "I like it. *Giles*. He was the patron saint of cripples, wasn't he?"

"Yes," he said, adapting to her somewhat, "and that's how I come to be called after him. I was born soon after my father lost his leg in a train crash. He didn't even know I existed when he came home with an artificial leg and as I hadn't been properly named, Giles seemed appropriate."

The information seemed to impress her even more than his mileage. She said, "But that's a *wonderful* story! The kind you might read in a book. Come to think of it, you jumping into the river after me was like a book. *Giles. Giles Swann!*" She rolled the name round her tongue in a way that made him smile. "It's the right name too, I mean, for someone who *would* jump into a river to save a young maiden in distress."

"That's about the last role I would give you to play, Romayne," he said, using her Christian name without shyness, for although he had no experience with girls other than his sisters, she was obviously a person who discouraged reticence of any kind and he was beginning to find communication with her very easy.

"Why do you say that?"

"Because you're clearly a person very well able to look out for herself. That's true, isn't it?"

"Yes," she said, thoughtfully, "I suppose it is. But it was nice *being* rescued, and I haven't thanked you for it, have I? There, now I have!" And she spun round, grasped him by the shoulders and kissed him on the mouth.

The embrace was so swift and so ingenuous that he had no time

477

to feel anything but charmed by her gaiety. Suddenly the sun shone even brighter, and the sky over the mountain ridge behind Beddgelert seemed cleaner and fresher, so that it was a privilege to be alive and exciting to be walking along beside this dashing, wayward girl, whose father owned dye works, iron foundries and processing plants, as well as the house that came in view just then as they topped a rise and began to descend towards the road.

It was a beautifully-sited building, about a century old he would say, with a way of conforming to the landscape as though it had grown there and was as much a part of the scene as the gorse-covered crags above and the flashing river below. It looked a very large house, with any number of tall windows and a well-tended lawn at the front enclosed on each side by great clumps of hydrangea and flowering cherry.

He said, somewhat startled, "You live there? That's a holiday home?"

"Oh, it's not very grand," she said. "We've only four servants, including the gardeners. In Eaton Place we have seven."

For the first time he hesitated, saying, "Look here, Romayne, I'm not in the least sure your father would like you inviting a complete stranger in for breakfast. After all, look at me. I've slept rough three nights in a row . . ."

But she squeezed his arm in the friendliest fashion and said, "Don't be so humble. You saved my life, didn't you? At least, that's what I shall say, and that's surely worth a plate of ham and eggs and some toast and honey. Besides, as to sleeping out, you've just had a bath, haven't you?"

There was really no resisting her, so they went on up the short drive and through the open door below an impressive portico, where Maggie, presumably the housekeeper, pounced on Romayne from a door leading to the rear of the house, screeching at her in unintelligible Welsh, so that Giles held back, almost inclined to run for it. But then Romayne answered her in Welsh and soon they were laughing together and he was hustled up the broad staircase to a dressing-room, and ordered to take off his wet clothes and give Maggie his knapsack to be emptied and dried on the kitchen range while they had breakfast.

His protests that he had nothing to wear were swept aside, Maggie producing some assorted garments from a huge press, saying they were clothes house-guests used when they came here to fish, but there were no guests here now and that he was not to worry, for "Sir Clive would be honoured to entertain an English aristocrat." This, it seemed, was how Romayne had introduced him in the torrent of Welsh she directed at Maggie. Romayne then disappeared to change her own clothes, saying she would not be ten minutes, and left to himself he stared at his reflection in the mirror, deciding that he looked like a stage parody of an English sporting gent in his pepper-and-salt knickerbockers, fisherman's jacket, a flannel shirt and a mustard-coloured cravat.

Romayne was back in eight minutes, wearing a crimson velvet gown, with embroidered gold facings and gold buttons on the sleeves and revers. It suited her admirably, giving her a vaguely mediaeval look, although it occurred to him as being highly unsuitable wear for breakfast in the Welsh hills and he said so, adding that her father would think they were all playing charades. "Papa won't be down for breakfast," she said. "He never is, for he doesn't go to bed until all hours. As to this, I wore it for you. It goes with knights and Camelot, you see."

She said this seriously, so he studied her carefully as she bobbed about in front of the mirror. Although it was cut so short (as short as the hair of a Camelot pageboy) her hair, he decided, was one of her most attractive features, for it was as gold and sleek and shining as her buttons and fitted her small, neat head like the husk on a hazel nut, reaching her prominent cheekbones in two balanced sweeps and in a way that framed her face, enhancing the depth and blueness of eyes that were full of mischievous sparkle. The only feature that was at odds with her ebullient nature was her mouth, full and heavy lipped but so spoiled, he thought, that at any moment it promised to tighten, expressing frustration, disapproval or perhaps hysterical rage. Her teeth, however, were quite perfect, very white and evenly set, and the little tongue that peeped between them, as she admired herself in the glass, was like a pink dart and reminded him of his initial impression of her when she emerged dripping from the river shaking her head, a highly-strung spaniel, likely, indeed almost certain, to dash off here, there and everywhere at a whistle from someone it loved.

Breakfast was a riotous affair. Watched over and encouraged by Maggie, they consumed what seemed to Giles vast quantities of porridge, eggs, bacon and sausages, pints of coffee, and toast spread with marmalade that Maggie told him she made herself. Romayne ate as much as or more than he but, notwithstanding this, kept up a flow of chatter about 'her adventure', as she described it, and the mountains, Maggie's marmalade, their home in Eaton Place, London, and her formidable-sounding governess, who went by the name of Prickle, a dragon from whom, it appeared, she spent her life escaping. It was half-an-hour before Giles discovered that Prickle was a nickname, the governess's real name being Thorne.

He enjoyed listening to her and the food was welcome indeed, for he was very sharp-set and the smell of bacon and coffee was delicious when he entered the heavily-furnished morning-room, with its gleaming silver, heavy mahogany furniture and oil-portraits of severe-looking men and disdainful-looking women, that Romayne said were Mostyn ancestors.

"Papa has always been secretly impressed by them," she said, "because his family aren't anything special, but I think they look terribly stuffy, don't you?"

He did, and thought also that they looked the kind of people who would be likely to set mantraps for poachers but the thing that interested him most about them was the similarity of their mouths to Romayne's, and this made him slightly apprehensive, particularly as, at any moment, the factory-owning geologist was liable to appear and ask him what the devil he thought he was doing breakfasting with his daughter and wearing clothes reserved for his guests.

He need not have worried. Towards the end of the meal Sir Clive Rycroft-Mostyn did appear, a slightly-built man about fifty, with sharp intelligent eyes, a fresh complexion, carefully-combed grey hair, and a rather distant manner moderated, to some extent, by the excessive mildness he displayed towards his uninvited guest, as though his daughter brought rescuers home to be dried out every day of the week.

One of the most definite impressions Giles got of the man was that he had long since come to terms with Romayne's eccentricities and his extreme tolerance was the result of self-restraint he seemed to practise. Everything Sir Clive said, and everything he did, was con-

sidered, as though he thought it fitting to bring the same deliberation
to spreading a pat of butter on a piece of toast, that he would to planning one of his industrial enterprises. He was the kind of man, Giles
assured himself, almost certain to be rich and powerful, and probably
ruthless into the bargain, incapable of being surprised in that he had
discovered how to maintain a quiet ascendancy over everyone, including Romayne, towards whom he was affectionate but patronising,
as though he was dealing with a lively ten-year-old instead of a handsome young woman. Towards Giles, however, he was gravely courteous, thanking him, a little ironically, for 'saving' his daughter from
being washed down river, but somehow implying that it was a service
no one in his senses could be expected to make a song and dance
about.

It was not until Giles' surname had registered, and his host had
time to ponder it, that his alert brown eyes showed a flicker of genuine interest, as he said, thoughtfully, " 'Swann'? With two 'n's? No
relation to *the* Swann, I suppose, the big transport concern?" and
when Giles admitted that Adam Swann was his father, he laid down
his triangle of toast and became very much aware, saying, with great
sincerity, "You must forgive my surprise, Mr. Swann. My daughter is
not usually so discriminating. Yours is a famous enterprise, isn't it?
As a matter of fact, your father hauls for me in several parts of the
provinces. He would know me well, I daresay, not so much in South
Wales, where we use our own transport, but up in Clydeside, where
we have shipping and mining interests. May I ask what brought
you up here? Are you on holiday?"

But Romayne interrupted, saying, "A man doesn't *walk* a hundred
and fifty miles for a holiday, Papa! He's footed it, all the way from
Devon! He's doing it for a wager, I believe."

Sir Clive elected to take this seriously, for a wager involved money
changing hands and this was a serious matter. "Is that true, Mr.
Swann?"

"No, sir, it isn't," said Giles, promptly, catching Romayne's twinkle in the corner of his eye, "the fact is I am on a sort of holiday. I
shall be joining my father shortly, but before I do I thought I should
like to see the land he operates over. He has a flourishing branch in
Wales. It's called The Mountain Square on our company maps and

right now I'm on my way into the cotton belt, and then north to Edinburgh, where we have our biggest branch."

"You intend to walk the whole of the way?"

"Yes, sir. It seems to me the best way to see things."

He said this defensively but Sir Clive nodded slowly, with approval Giles thought, so that he was not surprised when the industrialist said, "You are quite right, of course. I hope your father approves. I am sure he does, for what can a man learn about customers, real or potential, in the compartment of a train travelling at sixty miles an hour? My congratulations, Mr. Swann, on your perspicacity as well as your hardihood. Where did you attend school?"

"At West Buckland, on Exmoor," Giles told him, "but before that I was at Mellingham a short time."

"Mellingham? But that's primarily a military establishment, is it not?"

"Yes, sir, but I preferred West Buckland. Partly because I'm very much a countryman and the country about there is as rewarding as this, although not as spectacular."

"I don't think I've heard of the school," Sir Clive said, mildly, smiling as Giles said, "No sir, it's not famous, like older and larger schools. But it was founded by a pupil of Arnold of Rugby and I very much enjoyed my time there."

Sir Clive digested this half-rebuke, and Giles had the impression that Romayne was watching him approvingly, so that he thought, "He might have her well in hand but she doesn't miss a thing about him either; or anyone else for that matter. They're both as sharp as pins and the only difference between them is that he has the trick of hiding his thoughts . . ."

But then Sir Clive succeeded in surprising him, for he rose, extended his hand, and said, earnestly, "Thank you again for being of service to Romayne, Mr. Swann. There's really no curing her. She's always in some scrape or another, and perhaps it's my fault and her mother's. We very much wanted a boy, you see."

"I'm sure you're resigned to a daughter now, sir," said Giles, and Romayne cried "Bravo! Now isn't that gallant of him, Papa? I'm sure he's a reincarnation of Sir Galahad!" Then, turning back to Giles, "You just can't put those damp clothes of yours on your back and march out of here. I won't let you, you'd surely catch cold. He

could stay on, couldn't he, Papa? I could show him places about here
he'd never find by himself!" and before Giles could protest her father
said, very cordially, "Certainly he can stay if he wishes. I should be
delighted if he did, for it's time you met someone to teach you how to
behave in public and private. Will you do us the honour, Mr. Swann?
Be our guest for a few days, while the weather lasts? Romayne can
walk you off your feet if she cares to and we've a couple of good hacks
if you want to ride."

"It's extraordinarily kind of you, sir," Giles stammered, "but really,
I can't help feeling I'm imposing on you. You don't owe me anything
at all, sir. Miss Rycroft could have pulled herself out of that river
without any help from me."

"You don't have to tell me that," he said, and Romayne pouted,
saying, "There now, you've spoiled it all!"

"Indeed he has not," her father said, "for you should learn to take
the will for the deed. How was Mr. Swann to know you were fooling? I daresay he was persuaded you were in real danger."

"*Were* you, Giles?"

"Yes, I was. As I said, I thought you were a child."

"She is a child, Mr. Swann. And a very spoiled one at that, as
you've probably decided by now. She seems to have made a private
vow never to pass beyond the age of fifteen. That's so, isn't it, my
dear?"

"More or less," said Romayne, equably, "sixteen and a half perhaps," and they all laughed, at least Giles and the girl did, and Sir
Clive smiled indulgently, as at someone whom he regarded as in-
corrigible.

"So you'll stay, Giles?"

"Well . . . a short while . . . there is more I should like to see up
here, and your father has been so kind . . ."

Romayne gave a whoop of triumph and pranced from the room,
shouting something about getting the horses saddled for a jog into
Caernarvon to see the castle.

Sir Clive said, the moment the door closed on her, "You're probably thinking I'm ridiculously indulgent, Mr. Swann? Well, I daresay I am, but she's all I have, for I never cared to marry again and
it's true I was anxious to have a son to follow me. Your father would
understand that. He has several, or so I'm told."

"Five, sir," Giles told him, wondering at his source of information concerning the Swanns but remembering it would be the business of someone with manifold business interests to have made a study of prominent hauliers.

"Five, by God!" Sir Clive said, suddenly becoming enthusiastic. "That's the kind of investment every enterprising man should look for. Will you all go in to the business?"

"No, sir. Alex, my eldest brother, is already a captain in the army, and the youngest son, Edward, is only a toddler. My brothers George and Hugo may, George certainly. As for myself, I'm not fully committed. My father and I have . . . well, an arrangement. I am to try it until I'm twenty-one and then change horses if I wish."

"You hanker after some other career?"

"Not really. I've thought about literature, teaching, and even politics. But at eighteen it's hard to be sure." For the first time Sir Clive Rycroft-Mostyn dropped his half-bantering approach, saying, "I was. At the age of six. It was then I decided to make money and I didn't really care how. I still don't. Your father would probably confirm that."

It seemed, Giles thought, an odd thing to say to a stranger but then, Giles thought, they were a very odd pair, exceptionally sure of themselves and buttressed, no doubt, by enormous wealth. He was still reflecting on this when he heard Sir Clive say, "I'll find some more suitable clothes for you. Marcus Slessor, the flour man, was here with his son a month ago and I had some jodhpurs measured for the lad. A hacking jacket too, I seem to recall, and he was about your size. I do know they left a good deal of luggage that hasn't been sent on yet, for want of a forwarding address." He nodded and glided out, moving, Giles thought, like a woman wearing slippers a size too small for her.

3

Then began, for Giles, the most absorbing and exciting month of his life up to that time, when all day and every day was spent in the bewitching company of Romayne Rycroft, and part of the evenings with Sir Clive who possessed a billiards table and played an excellent game. Surprisingly he also played the piano, "A trick I picked up years ago to encourage relaxation," he explained, almost apologetically. After a day or so it seemed to Giles that he had been up here for years, had known Romayne since she was a child, and had himself been raised in this ruggedly beautiful part of the country, where everyone spoke Welsh, and life moved as slowly and predictably as it did on the Exmoor plateau.

It did not take him long to persuade himself that he was hopelessly in love with Romayne, who seemed in some way to personify the landscape, with its untamed beauty and swiftly changing moods, sometimes buoyant, sometimes subdued, but always holding off slightly as though it saw him as yet another English predator threatening Welsh independence.

At first he was confused and disturbed by her sudden plunges from reckless gaiety into what he could only regard as nursery petulance, but he soon adjusted to it, and learned the trick of teasing her out of what she called a 'fan-tod', a prickliness that appeared out of nowhere and encouraged her to take offence (manifestly counterfeit) at some trivial disappointment or something he said or did. But mostly she was gay and vivid, and always she was restless, whirling him north or south or across to the coast on horseback or on foot, or in the Rycroft waggonette, once as far as Llangefni in Anglesey, where Maggie, the housekeeper, had relatives she liked to visit. They explored the Portmeirion peninsula, with its tidal estuary, and what Romayne described as its 'Arthurian woods'. They visited the local castles, Harlech, Caernarvon, Conway and Beaumaris, and sometimes accomplished round trips of thirty miles a day, climbing some of the easier mountains, or tracing the sources of rivers that rushed between the folds of the lower hills.

For the truth was in her dashing company, he forgot the initial purpose of his journey, and the social curiosity that had brought him thus far and this did not surprise him. Who, he asked himself, could brood on the wretched condition of the miners and the lives of the poor, when the June sun reflected the glitter of a pretty girl's eyelashes, as well as the waterbreaks in the mountain rivers and the specks of quartz in the surface of rocks, where every cleft held a solitary harebell with petals as blue as her eyes?

He would gaze at her sometimes when she was in one of her momentarily abstracted moods, when she seemed not to be aware of anything at all as they rode and walked up a hill-track, or threw themselves down on a crest to eat a packed lunch prepared by Maggie, a woman dedicated to the task of doubling his weight, despite all this exercise.

She was, he decided, the most graceful and desirable creature in all creation, and he would say nothing to bring her back but poke among his memories of paintings by the masters, or the fashionable Academicians, for her equivalent, finding none save, perhaps, a hint or two in models of the kind the Pre-Raphaelite brotherhood favoured, girls touched by some brooding melancholy. But then, in a flash, she would make the comparison ridiculous by suddenly coming out of herself and darting an impish glance at him, as though willing him to pay her one of his grave compliments (many of them borrowed from Waller, Marvell and Herrick), or perhaps take her in his arms and kiss that sulky mouth, the key to all her swiftly changing moods.

He kissed her often but always lightly as though he might be called upon to defend the impulse as an expression of high spirits, and it was not until word came from the unseen but omnipresent Prickle that she was to return to London to prepare for her season that he decided they must arrive at some understanding before they parted, for he was convinced, to his own gloomy satisfaction, that he could not continue to exist without hope of seeing her again in the near future.

It was time, he thought, to make some tentative arrangement to meet in London, possibly in a month or two, when she was settled there and was approaching the tail-end of the round of balls and fêtes the diligent Miss Thorne was preparing for her, as the prerogative of all socially-ambitious young ladies with fathers able to afford a conventional launching.

Adam, he recalled, had little patience with this rigmarole. Stella, his sister, had not had a season, and neither Joanna nor Helen looked for one, but he supposed it was obligatory for the only daughter of a man as rich as Sir Clive, and even Romayne seemed to regard it as an inescapable part of growing-up, like wearing a corset.

He had a horrid fear, however, that she might meet someone far more eligible than he at one or other of these functions, the son of an earl, maybe, or even a duke, or at least someone whose family background was more splendid than his. It therefore seemed imperative that he should stake some sort of claim here and now, while he had the chance. Yet it was not easy for a bookish person like him, with no previous experience of being in love, or ever having contemplated love other than in the abstract, to say how he felt about her and how important she had become to him.

He thought about it a long time, until the days seemed to be flying by, but then, providentially, she herself brought it up, saying, as if it was a perfectly natural extension of their relationship, "You'll come back here, Giles? When I've done with London, I mean. The autumn up here is the best of all time. The streams fill up then and go rushing down like cataracts, and the air is so clear and sparkling that you can see the mountain tops for days at a time."

He said, suddenly alarmed, "Come back *here*? Why, no, that isn't possible, Romayne. I shall have to work, and spend most of the time in town. I thought you understood that. I'm sure your father does, even if he agreed to me coming back."

He was surprised then, and embarrassed too, by the blankness of the gaze she directed on him, saying, "If Papa approves? Do you imagine I haven't discussed it with him? Take it from me, you have his blessing to squire me indefinitely. For always, maybe!"

"For always . . . ?" But he realised then that she was only teasing him, as she so often did, and said, "Let's be sensible about this and arrange something practical. For a start, tell me when you would like me to call on you in London, for I don't want to feel embarrassed, and I don't want to embarrass anyone else, particularly after all the kindness and hospitality you and your father have shown me up here," but then he saw that she was looking at him with exasperated amazement.

"*Embarrass* anybody? What *can* you mean by that? Why should you embarrass anyone by calling on us? Sometimes I just don't understand you, Giles Swann. Why are you so . . . so *humble* about who you are and what you are? My father thinks you're one of the cleverest young men he's ever met and me, well, I should have thought it would have been obvious by now that I'm much fonder of you than anybody in the world. Including Prune!"

Her injection of Prune, her sleek and impossibly foolish black Labrador into the tail of this astounding declaration was a kind of lifeline. Somehow it lowered it to the level of comprehension, as well as inviting laughter. He was not completely taken in by her implication that she was in love with him. She was the kind of person very likely to say this on impulse and forget it an hour later, or qualify it in some way. What did astonish him, however, was that Sir Clive Rycroft-Mostyn, who he had decided was one of the most important magnates in the country, should regard him, even momentarily, as a potential son-in-law, and for the moment he preferred to test this apparent evidence of progress.

He said, "Listen Romayne, you're very much given to making facts fit private wishes. I've noticed that and well . . . I love you for it because it's an essential part of you. But it won't do at all at this stage to pretend that your father who, so far as I can make out, is almost a millionaire, could regard me as anything more than a half-grown schoolboy, with his way to make in the world. We get along very well. I don't deny that, and I won't deny that I like him . . . well, I admire him anyway. He's achieved so much, without anyone pushing him from behind and that's rare nowadays. But that doesn't mean he would encourage me to stay on here if he thought I was serious about you, and not just fooling around, if you see what I mean!"

"Oh, I see what you mean well enough," she said, gaily now, "and although it was very cleverly put—the way you always manage to put things—it isn't very flattering to me, is it? Not when you take the wrappings off and examine it closely."

"Just what can you mean by that?"

She said, smiling her rather absent-minded smile, "Well, all this hedging and dodging the real issue, like Prune chasing a rabbit he knows he can't catch. Why don't you speak plainly, and say exactly what you do have in mind? About me, of course," she added, as though he might likely miss the essential point.

He took a deep breath, the kind all lovers seemed required to take in poems by Herrick and company.

"Very well then, since you demand it, I will. I love you, Romayne. I can't think of anything more exciting than the prospect of marrying you. Now then, how do you suppose your father would react if he heard me say that?"

"He'd be very relieved, I should say."

He gasped, too surprised to exclaim, so that she went on, easily, "As a matter of fact, he's already hinted at it. 'Sooner have that young Swann feller around than any of the chinless fortune-hunters Miss Thorne is likely to steer your way'. He said just that only the other day, after you had beaten him in that boring argument you had about the importance of Austria-Hungary as a what-do-you-call-it?"

"A political counterweight?"

"Something like that. I don't understand the half of what you two say to one another, but it seems to impress him. How much you've got upstairs, I mean."

He remembered the discussion very well. He had politely challenged Sir Clive's claim that the sooner the Habsburg empire broke up the better it would be for the peace of Europe. He had argued that if this did happen Prussia was likely to become a serious menace and in the end Sir Clive had half agreed with him. It did not seem a relevant argument concerning his daughter's choice of a husband, however, so he said, "That's all very well, but let's be clear about this, Romayne. I haven't any great expectations. My father is well-established, of course, but in one field, not twenty like your father. And in any case, you're an only child and I'm the third eldest son, and my brother George is already earmarked for the chairmanship of the company. I'm no more than a kind of hanger-on."

"You won't always be," she said, "and in any case, it doesn't make a ha'porth of difference, to Papa or to me. For one thing, we've got all the money we're likely to need. For another, I'd want you if you worked on a farm, or in a factory. You don't plan these things, the way Prickle seems to imagine. They just happen, as they did to us. We're right for one another. I knew that the moment you pulled me out of that river and I kissed you on the way home and only a day or so later I told Maggie I'd never marry anyone else."

It made his head spin to hear her talk like this. It was not a particularly bright day. The skies were grey and low over the mountains, but suddenly the world was basking in sunshine and his future lay ahead of him like the path to the Celestial Mountains that the pilgrims sought in *Pilgrim's Progress*. He said, breathlessly, "Well then . . . let me say this . . . there's nothing I want more than to marry you, Romayne. Nothing at all, just as soon as I can stand on my own feet. But that will take years. You must understand that."

"Years?"

She made it sound as if he had proposed something preposterous but he held to his point.

"Yes, years. Do you suppose I'd marry you, and live on your father's money? I couldn't do that, not even for you. I've got plans. They aren't very well defined, and they probably aren't his kind of plans, but I mean to . . . well . . . to *be* somebody, to make some kind of mark before I'm middle-aged, and as set in my ways as my father, or yours."

To some extent he seemed to have satisfied her, for she said, carelessly, "Oh, *that?* Well, that's easy enough. You could take over one or other of his businesses. Or if you didn't like being beholden to Papa you could go into Parliament. Yes . . ." her imagination took fire, "that would be splendid! I mean, you already *talk* like a Member of Parliament! You'd be famous in no time at all. You might even be Prime Minister while you were still young, like Pitt," but at that he was obliged to laugh.

"There's a lot more to getting a seat in Parliament than that. This conversation is getting far too hypothetical for my liking. Now just listen to me, Romayne, and please don't interrupt with suggestions. I don't want you sounding your father on this. It isn't fair to him or us, because I only left school a few months ago. We're only eighteen, after all, and even the nobility don't get married until they're of age . . ." But suddenly he broke off and laughed at himself and her, possibly at the artless way they were discussing the subject, as though it was no more momentous than tomorrow's visit to Caernarvon. He went on, "Let's take first things first. When do people start leaving London again? After the season, I mean. For I know it isn't much use my calling round at Eaton Place until then . . ." But she wasn't looking at him, and the big, childish mouth was already formed in a prodigious pout, so that he moved closer to her, put his arm round her and kissed her cheek, saying, "Don't you *see*, Romayne, darling? You'll be caught up in a whirl of social 'musts' the minute you get within nagging range of that governess. Unless we make a plan now I can't guarantee the certainty of seeing you. Are you listening? Or don't you care to be tied down?" and he gave her a little shake that was really no more than a disguised caress.

"Oh, I'm listening," she said, "and it certainly isn't me who is scared of being tied down, Giles Swann!"

"What?"

"You know very well what I'm getting at!"

"But I don't! I say, look here . . ." and he floundered, miles out of his depth, but understanding dimly that the path of love had as many pitfalls as primroses. He understood, too, in that instant, that although they were much of an age, he was a rank amateur at the game and couldn't hope to disguise it. "You don't think I'm pretending, that I'm fooling myself for some silly reason . . ."

"Well, aren't you?" She faced him, squarely. "If you aren't why don't we go back and find Papa right now and let him decide how soon we can be married?"

He had no kind of answer to this frightening proposition. It was not that he had reservations concerning her, but common sense told him that a man as intelligent and down-to-earth as Sir Clive Rycroft-Mostyn would almost surely think him the greatest fool he had ever met if he marched blithely into his presence demanding his daughter in marriage, on the strength of a couple of weeks' skylarking in the Welsh hills. What puzzled him even more was her apparent inability to take this into consideration and her obstinate belief that her father (who must have given some thought to whom she might marry) would be likely to gratify her wish as casually as he had accepted her suggestion he should stay on as a guest, after the incident at the falls. He was beginning, slowly and rather painfully, to adjust to her immaturity and it struck him that any child of an extremely wealthy man would be likely to behave in this headstrong, purblind way. He realised too that he was singularly ill-equipped to deal with a situation of this kind, never having previously met a person his own age with whom he could compare her, for the girls his sisters had introduced into the house were all, to a greater or lesser degree, disciplined young women with conventional tastes and manners.

She seemed now to be watching him carefully, almost speculatively, and it gave him a feeling of inferiority to be cornered in this way, unable to show her that marriage, or even a progressive courtship of the kind he had in mind, was not something you rejected or accepted, like a second helping of dessert. For this was clearly how she regarded it, and it cost him a pang to face the fact that this very circumstance trivialised her. He said at length, "Somehow I've got to make you understand, Romayne. What I've said, what you've just said . . . what I mean is, you'll probably think differently about it in a week or two . . ."

"You wouldn't mind if I did?"

It was not often Giles showed irritability but he did now. "Good Lord, of course I'd mind! I've told you I love you, haven't I?"

"And I've told you I love you, so what on earth are we arguing about? We ought to be pleased and happy, didn't we? You ought to be holding me, instead of examining all the pros and cons, like Mr. Tilsley marking my theory book!"

It was too much. There was simply no reasoning with her, or not in her present mood. He knew all about Mr. Tilsley. Mr. Tilsley was her music-teacher, an inoffensive, myopic little man, to whom crotchets and quavers were the breath of life. He said, taking her hand and lifting her chin, "You're absolutely right. This isn't something we can map like a route, or solve like a sum on a blackboard. And anyway, we're wasting precious minutes," and he kissed her possessively on the mouth and then, liking it so much, repeated the kiss and stood off to watch his doubts swamped in a great wave of exultation as her arms went round him, and she pulled him down on her, kissing his cheeks and eyes and mouth, and murmuring his name over and over again. No more than that, just "Giles . . . Giles . . . Giles . . ." so that she invested it with a sort of glory and he heard it as music more enthralling than anything Herrick or Marvell had written on the subject of love. They lay there, saying nothing, for a long time, until the certainty of their need for one another seemed to him as defined and permanent as the hills and the silver thread of river where it wound between belts of timber a mile below. He had no idea now how matters would resolve themselves but was happy to postpone analysis, blessedly content that it had happened, that she was here in his arms willing him to kiss her and touch her hair, that he could feel her grip tighten on his shoulder when he made so much as a token attempt to release her.

4

They gave him a lift as far as Chester in the waggonette, dropping him off near the great red cathedral when he told them that he did not want to travel on by railway but preferred to head on down the road to Warrington, where Catesby, of the Polygon, had arranged to meet him in the heart of the beat.

She made no complaint about this. She had been very silent during the last forty-eight hours, so much so that her father went so far as to acknowledge the fact by a wink across the breakfast table, implying that he was under no misapprehension as to the meaning of this wholly uncharacteristic sobriety on her part. The wink made Giles very uneasy until, the moment she had gone about her packing, he said, casually, "I daresay she's bothered by the prospect of all that mumbo-jumbo awaiting her in town. Makes me damned glad I'm not a woman. Young shaver like you can't imagine what those old beldames get up to at a time like this. However, I suppose I should congratulate myself on having one daughter instead of a clutch, like your father." And at this Giles thought he might as well correct any impression Sir Clive had concerning the social position of the Swanns, and said, "The truth is, sir, my father won't subscribe to it. I once heard him tell my mother he thought a season was a huckster's way to go about getting daughters married off!" and to his relief Sir Clive laughed.

"And so it is, by God. I'm beginning to think your father and I would see eye to eye on any number of things. No doubt I shall have the pleasure of meeting him sooner or later."

"I certainly hope so, sir," replied Giles, fervently. But if the magnate noticed his elation, he gave no sign but said, rising, "Let me say this, in order to spare my girl's blushes. I'm uncommonly obliged to you for breaking your journey, and keeping her company the way you have. It's lonely for a lass of her age, stuck away up here, and you've succeeded in keeping her out of mischief, where everyone else has failed. Are we likely to see anything of you in London later in the year?"

"I'd be delighted to call, sir, when I get back from the north. Would some time in October be convenient?"

"Whenever you like, my boy. Glad to see you. Or any of your brothers and sisters for that matter. What are your immediate plans? Or don't you know?"

"I'm taking a look at the Polygon, sir . . . I'm sorry, that's what it's called on my father's maps. Broadly speaking it's the cotton belt, from Cheshire to the Lakes. Then I hope to visit Edinburgh and spend a month exploring our Scottish beat. After that it'll be no weather for walking, so I shall take a train south, and hope to study the business from our Headquarters near London Bridge."

"Good . . . good," said Sir Clive, but vaguely, Giles thought, as though he had only asked out of politeness.

After that, on the landing near her room, he had no more than a brief moment with Romayne who seemed preoccupied and barely responded to his kiss saying, in extenuation, "I'm sorry, dearest . . . I'm in a terrible tizzy. That Prickle wrote again this morning, with hundreds of last-minute instructions, and I'm sure I shall leave something important behind."

He said, with an air of modest triumph, "Your father has just invited me to call in the early autumn," and that had the effect of riveting her attention for a few seconds. "Around October," he added, "so if you feel inclined to fall in love with anyone else don't make it final, will you?"

"You don't need reassurance concerning that," she said, "you're just fishing for compliments," and then, looking him carefully up and down, "Don't ever throw away those walking clothes, Giles. It might sound silly but I'd rather you didn't, not even when they're worn out. You see they're *you* . . . the first 'you' I ever saw and several minutes before you saw me. Just a young tramp but a very handsome one, of course. That was why I pretended to drown," and before he could comment on this she gave him a peck on the tip of his nose and darted back into her room.

*   *   *

He stood and watched the waggonette weave through the traffic of the narrow street towards the station and then, whistling softly, turned his back on the city and began his dusty tramp along the flat Cheshire hedgerows, remembering when he saw a signpost for Daresbury that he was crossing the countryside Lewis Carroll had used as a background for Alice's adventures in Wonderland. From here on he moved in his own Wonderland and the miles passed unheeded as he thought and thought about her, and all she meant and would come to mean in the future, so that it was with some surprise, towards sunset, that he saw the chimneys of Warrington on the skyline, and recalled that it was about here that his father and mother had met, much in the way that he had met Romayne. The recollection, vague as it was, gave him a curious feeling of drawing level with Adam, who, until then, had seemed as far removed from him in terms of age and experience as Chiron, the centaur-tutor of the Argonauts, who was his favourite character in mythology. He was tired and dust-parched by then and glad to accept a lift from a passing milk-float, finding the run-down-looking inn near the goods yard and falling asleep over his game pie and porter.

He was up and about, however, when the landlady called him about eight, telling him that a Mr. Catesby was enquiring for him. It struck Giles, as he hurried downstairs, that his father's managers were a punctilious lot, for he had not expected him until mid-morning.

He had met Catesby at Stella's wedding and five minutes' exchange of conversation confirmed his opinion that Lovell had been right, and that 'he and that revolutionary chap would get along well'. Concerning his odyssey Catesby came straight to the point.

"It's not just transport you're interested in, is it? I hear you want to take a close look at working conditions in the Belt. Does that mean you'll be reading philosophy up at University?"

Giles told him that there was no question of his going up to University, and was surprised to discover Catesby's reaction was similar to Thompson's. "I'm not sure that's wise, lad," he said, gravely. "Education's a fine thing, and a man ought not to pass up on it lightly. You'll have heard plenty about me and my views I daresay, but what we need, if we're ever going to remake society, is leaders above factory level, youngsters like yourself, maybe, with no personal axe to grind, men who can take an impersonal look at pay, conditions of work, bad housing, sanitation and God knows what else that's amiss in places like this and the coalfields. Oh, I'm not denying it hasn't improved since I were a lad, standing thirteen hours a day beside unfenced machinery. But the working day is still far too long, the factories are neither safe nor sanitary, and we still have to fight for every penny an hour on piece rates. However, you shall see for yourself if you've a mind to, and don't be shy of asking questions. Your father never is, I'll say that for him."

"I'd like to ask one right now," Giles said, warming to the man, "and it concerns my father. I've never really understood his attitude to the social problems of an industrial society. I mean, is he with you or against you? Sometimes he seems progressive but other times, well, he's got a touch of the old-time gaffer about him. How do you rate him as a boss, or is it unfair to ask?"

"No, it isn't unfair," Catesby said, thoughtfully, "but difficult to answer. He's a progressive certainly, and you'll have heard in the Mountain Square that he's looked on as a good gaffer by the men, top and bottom grades. He's fair, generous, and won't look on his work force as cattle, the way most of 'em still do about here. But he's the most obstinate cuss I ever struck. If he gets a wrong-headed notion it takes blasting powder to shift it but if you succeed in changing his mind he's never too high and mighty to own he was wrong. We've had our ups and downs over the last twenty-five years, mostly ups I might add. He doesn't take kindly to sharing power with a trades federation, of the kind I've been working for all my life. I understand that, mind. He's the last word in individuality and it'll take another generation to hammer out a set of rules that'll stand four-square, without leaning one way or the other. The thing is, however, your Dad is one of the few big employers who recognises the right of hands to have a say on their pay and conditions, and that's why he and I get along, and why I've any amount of respect for him. If that answers your question let me put one to you. How does he rate as a father?" And Giles laughed, saying that this was even more difficult to answer, for Adam Swann's real family didn't live at 'Tryst' but were spread across the network. "According to my mother," he added, "he forgets our names sometimes, but I never knew him to forget one of yours."

"Aye, that's what I reckoned," said Catesby, "and there's a reason for it. After all, any damned fool can reproduce himself any number of times but it takes a rare spirit to create a business like Swann-on-Wheels out of a Johnny Raw's dream."

The conversation established the tone of their relationship and all that week, and part of the next, Giles travelled about Lancashire in Catesby's company, visiting half a dozen mills, from the model establishment, once owned by Sam Rawlinson, his grandfather, but now a co-operative, nominally owned by his mother, down to the ramshackle eighteenth-century concern in Rochdale, where Catesby had worked as a lad.

"That wasn't so long after they'd installed Cartwright's power-looms," he said, "those that were burned out time and again by hand-loom weavers, who saw their livelihood threatened. Not that I've ever had a dam' bit o' patience with Luddites, or any other give-us-the-old-days bleaters, although I understand well enough what scared 'em at the time. I never did see the sense of fighting machines when you can make 'em do the hard graft for you."

Giles looked at the line of clattering looms and expressionless men, women and girls tending them. Much earlier in the day he had seen a hundred or more turn out and clatter down the cobbled streets in their clogs, and he supposed they would stand here until shutdown, unable to communicate one with the other above the ceaseless roar and rattle of the looms, and the monotonous whine of the complex of belts above their heads. The fearful drabness of their existence compared to his, or that of someone like Romayne Rycroft-Mostyn, occurred to him, so that he recalled, for the first time in a month, those smutty-faced urchins in the gallery below the Welsh hills. He said, as they regained the airless yard, where the bale-breakers were hard at work, "Do the machines work for them? Are they ever going to squeeze anything out of them, beyond a pittance to keep them penned there in all that racket? What's gone wrong and when did it start going wrong? Surely people led richer and more interesting lives in mediaeval villages."

The manager grinned. "Aye, lad, you got it bad, haven't you? But there's nowt to be ashamed of on that score. Your father tells me you called in on Lovell, in the Rhondda. How does it compare?"

"If I had to choose I'd prefer the silence underground, for at least a man can think down there. From the safety angle the mill's better, or looked so."

"A damned sight safer than it were. In my young days every fourth man you passed in a mill town lacked a hand or an arm. We reckoned to lose about one lad a day from an accident. Keep your eyes open and you'll still see some of the old uns at their begging." He lit his short pipe, drew on it, and led the way out on to the railway sidings, where a Swann-on-Wheels pinnace stood with a sleek Cleveland Bay between the shafts. From the box-seat Giles could see clear across the landscape, a grey sea of tile and slate, broken here and there by a tall chimney and the looming bulk of a mill. High above the blue-black streamers of murk the July sun was fighting a losing battle with a pall of smoke that lay over the entire plain, dense where chimneys proliferated at a town, ragged above strips of green, featureless country between, almost solid over Manchester to the south-east.

Catesby said, "When did we start going wrong? You might say a century ago, when they moved the power-looms in, took the weavers out of their cottages, and herded them into brick and tile gaols of that kind. But don't run away with the idea it were all beer and skittles before that. I've known families work from dawn to dusk in their own hovels for less nor one skilled lass takes home today. It's not just a matter o' living in towns either. You're country-bred. I don't have to tell you what a farm-labourer living in a tied cottage picks up come Saturday. Or what happens to him when the damp in his bones slows him down. When did it all start? The day some fool invented the wheel and money, I reckon, but that's neither here nor there now for we're hitched to 'em both, for better nor worse, and it's up to all of us to make 'em work. That's what the Trades Union Congress is all about, some kind of attempt to strike a balance between master and man. I daresay Lovell let on I was for revolution. That's a cock-eyed notion on his part. They're always trying that on i' France, and take it from me, for all their bloody brickbats and barricades, working conditions aren't so good there as they are right here, i' Rochdale an' Burnley. Or in the Rhondda for that matter. Nay, lad, that's no way to change industry. You've got to have gaffers who know what they're about, and gaffers won't work for nowt any more than a mill-hand or a miner. The thing to do is to admit that right out and work at it together. I'm as loyal to t'bloody system as anyone, and don't let anyone tell you diff'rent. I'm hopeful too, at long range that is. All I've fought for since I came out o' gaol, after the rioting back in the 'fifties, is common sense. Common sense on both sides. I don't ask for more than that, and your Dad will tell you the same." He gathered up the reins and cracked his whip over the nag's head. "We'll move on then. You've a rare lot to see yet."

Slowly and inquisitively Giles picked his way over the Polygon, surprised to find, here and there, sizeable stretches of arable land and any number of prosperous farms. In this way it differed materially from the coalfields, for here industry had been concentrated in densely-populated pockets, with the spaces in between relatively sweet if one could ignore the all-pervading acrid whiff of smoke carried on the wind high above ploughland and pasture.

The towns, he noticed, had many things in common with the Welsh mining villages. The serried rows of tiny dwellings were almost identical, acres of brick and slate broken, here and there, by a red-brick chapel of one sect or another. But the men, women and urchins he encountered did not seem bowed down by the drabness of their surroundings or, for that matter, by the terrible demands made upon them in the slab-sided, smoke-belching factories where they spent upwards of seventy hours a week. On the contrary, they seemed as perky and easy-going as the miners, and there was often the sound of laughter in the steep cobbled streets, even from home-going shifts at twilight. When he drew Catesby's attention to this the manager's reply was similiar to Lovell's, in the Rhondda.

"Nay, an' why not? A Lancashire man in work is an optimist, no matter how much bloody muck he lives in. There are compensations, lad, that a Southerner like yourself can't be blamed for missing while he's wiping smuts from his eye. For one thing the folk hereabouts are proud o' what they produce, and so they should be. Best spun cotton i' t'world. For another, they've got their pastimes, pigeon-fancying and suchlike. But the main thing that keeps 'em going is one another, I reckon."

The Polygon tour stirred him deeply but it did not have the scarifying effect of the day spent below ground in Wales and this was not because the people up here had less to put up with or worked, in the main, under better conditions. It was a personal amelioration, his state of mind having mellowed in the interval. A very young man deeply in love is not the best kind of emissary for an expedition of this sort and instead of concentrating his mind on the glaring evidence of social injustice, Giles found himself making mental notes that would never find a place in a blue book or statistical survey. The girls, he noted, still ogled young men under the gas-lamps after dusk, and young men, pale but neatly turned out, still circled the gravel paths of the blighted little parks of a Sunday afternoon, sporting their buttonholes and twirling their canes. And once, when they were jogging back to Salford yard through a thunderstorm an hour after sundown, they happened to pass a junction where a flash of lightning revealed a lad and his girl locked in a passionate embrace under a tilted umbrella. Catesby, noticing his glance, grinned and said, with a perception Giles had learned to expect of him, "Aye, lad, that's still free. Even here, in t'bloody Polygon downpour." Then, in that aggressive tone they all seemed to use up here, "You can tour the regions from Tay to Channel but there's another product that gets pride o' place i' Lancashire, apart from cotton. Rare pretty lasses if you're looking for 'em, and I alwus was at your age!"

Giles said nothing to this. He liked and trusted Catesby but could not bring himself to speak Romayne's name to anyone as yet.

*　　　*　　　*

The day he was making ready to move one of the clerks came into the Salford warehouse and asked if he had a moment to spare for a lady enquiring after him. His heart missed a beat for the only woman who knew his whereabouts, with the exception of his mother, was Romayne, but it seemed very unlikely that she had followed him up here. He was so excited at the possibility, however, that he dashed across to the weigh-bridge without enquiring the visitor's name, stopping short when he saw a fashionably-dressed woman in her thirties standing beside the checker, who pointed to him, saying, "There's Mr. Swann, Mrs. Broadbent."

The woman looked confused but then smiled rather nervously and said, "You won't know me, Mr. Swann, but I heard you were here. I . . . er . . . just wondered if you could give me any news of your brother, Mr. George Swann."

There was something so hesitant in her approach that his chivalry was touched and he said, tipping his hat, "You're a friend of George, Mrs. Broadbent?" Then, seeing her glance at the checker, "Would you like to come into the office? The clerk there is having his lunch and Mr. Catesby is away today."

She murmured her thanks and followed him, saying, as he motioned her to a chair, "You'll think it frivolous, no doubt, but I was always anxious to hear about George, and it didn't seem . . . well . . . fitting to write to the firm. After all, the dear boy has probably forgotten all about me by now. Does the name 'Broadbent' mean anything to you?"

"I'm afraid not," he said, knitting his brows and trying to guess the relationship between this shy, pretty woman and George, but she went on, swiftly, "My husband was manager here for a time. He left. There was . . . well . . . trouble and I thought your father or brother might have told you. Obviously they didn't."

"You mean trouble involving you, Mrs. Broadbent?"

It seemed unlikely but one never did know what George might get up to and he remembered now that, prior to going abroad, he had lived in the Polygon.

"No, Mr. Swann," she said, firmly, "not in any way. I daresay my husband tried to imply as much but there was nothing . . . *nothing* you understand that Geo . . . Mr. Swann need regret in any way. The fact is he stayed with us out at Bowdon while he was up here, and I grew very fond of him. He's a very charming young man, Mr. Swann, and in the circumstances . . . well, naturally I've wondered about him. Is he well? Is he working in London with your father's firm?"

A few weeks ago Giles would have been completely mystified by Mrs. Broadbent but Romayne had taught him to distinguish between a polite enquiry and a concealed canvass, of the kind she was pursuing now. He said, "George has been abroad ever since he left here, Mrs. Broadbent. Paris, Munich and now Vienna. He's been learning the haulage business with Continental firms and I believe he's expected home around Christmas. We exchange letters occasionally. Could I give him any message from you?"

"Oh, no," she said, suddenly alarmed, "no message . . . it was just . . . well, I've wondered how he was getting along. He wasn't very happy here."

She broke off there, rather pointedly, but then, as though forcing herself to continue, "He . . . he wasn't *sent* abroad? Because of me, I mean?"

"Indeed no. My father thought it was a good idea to learn the languages and broaden his experience. We deal with many Continental wholesalers and he's to take over when my father retires. He and my father get along very well. They always have because . . . well, because, George is cut out for a business career, more than any of us." And then, because by now she was twisting her handkerchief into a knot, and seemed close to tears, he said, "Look, ma'am, it's none of my business, but if you would like to send a message or write it wouldn't go any further than these four walls. George and I have always been friends. Who could help liking George?"

She seemed to consider this for a long minute. When she looked up she had herself well under control and smiled. She was, he decided, a very handsome woman, with a curious combination of fragility and dignity. At the same time she somehow conveyed an impression that life had not used her kindly.

"Very well," she said, with a kind of forced brightness, "just give him my very best wishes, and say I'll always be interested in what he does when he becomes as important as your father. He was extremely kind and considerate to me when I badly needed a friend and because of that I won't ever forget him. Don't tell him that, of course. It wouldn't do, would it, although my husband and I parted company long ago, and perhaps he would like to know that. Tell him that I went back to my old job at the pub in the Shambles. There!"

She stood up, very relieved it seemed to bring the interview to a close. "Thank you for listening, Mr. Swann." She paused, regarding him intently with serious grey eyes. "You aren't much alike, are you? Temperamentally, maybe, but to look at I mean?"

"My mother always tells me I'm the odd man out," he said. "George is more like Alex, the eldest, and Hugo, the one after me. There are nine of us altogether, you know, and we're a mixed bunch. Are you sure you wouldn't like to write to him yourself, Mrs. Broadbent? I could enclose it in a letter."

"Quite sure," she said, and sounded as if she meant it.

He saw her out to a cab waiting on the far side of the weigh-bridge, handed her into it, and returned her surprised smile at the courtesy. "Nine!" she said, after a nod towards the cabby. "My word, but your mother must be right proud of you! Goodbye, Mr. Swann, and thank you so much."

He watched the cab move off and returned thoughtfully to the yard, wondering just what to make of Mrs. Broadbent and her emotional involvement with George. He had always envied his brother's high spirits, and the ease with which he established a personal relationship but perhaps he had taken too much for granted and now he found himself hoping that George would enlighten him when he passed the message on. The encounter, however, explained something that had puzzled not only him but all the family. That was the sudden termination of George's apprenticeship on home ground and the abruptness of his departure abroad. The key was obviously Mrs. Broadbent and he was glad he had made her acquaintance. In a roundabout way it enlarged George and brought him that much closer as a brother.

5

North along the western edge of the Pennines, round the elbow of the Ribble and seaward towards Kendal in dry, August heat. Then, having got his second wind, and adjusted to the demands of the rough hill tracks he chose in preference to roads, on to Windermere, Ambleside and the pass that ran under the western shoulder of Helvellyn, pausing hereabouts to visit Wordsworth's cottage and wonder what secret lay behind the self-imposed exile of a man who had blown such a lusty trumpet on behalf of the French Revolution and then hidden himself away in this lonely spot, where Sister Dorothy had written of gathering foxglove seeds, tying up scarlet beans, nailing honeysuckles and listening, long after William had retired to bed, to Coleridge reading part of *Christabel*. Fresh from his tours of the coalfields and the cotton belt Giles saw it as a kind of defeat, a rather shameful opting-out of the role of zealot, that had inspired the *Sonnet to Liberty*. Or maybe it had something to do with the springs of creativity. Having reached the age of thirty the man's genius had seemingly spent itself so that he turned his back on everything but the cycle of the year under these fells. He realised then that his journey had confirmed something important. Poetry was well enough but he could no longer think of a poet as a man marching with the vanguard. Poets had a job as standard-bearers but the real fighting was for more down-to-earth chaps, the Lovells and the Catesbys maybe, who would probably regard poor old Willie Wordsworth as a windbag.

He pushed on, leaving Wordsworth to his soul-searching and daffodils, passing along the margin of Thirlmere and over level ground to Keswick, visiting the church where his father and mother had been married twenty-six years before, and later viewed Derwentwater from Friar's Crag, remembering that the old Colonel had often sat here trying to capture a lakeland sunset but had never once succeeded if his water-colours at 'Tryst' were anything to judge by.

Twenty-four hours later he crossed the border at Stanwix and turned east for a mile or two to look at Hadrian's Wall where it began its wandering journey to Wallsend, on the shore of the North Sea. Then, welcoming cooler weather, he followed the course of the Esk into Selkirk and the Lothians, covering twenty miles a day until, on the first day of September, he saw the violet smoke haze over Edinburgh and dropped down into the crowded, bustling wynds of the old city to seek out Higson, youngest of the regional managers, who had charge of the largest slice of territory in the network.

He had heard rumours of Higson's zeal up here. Word had travelled south that he had set the seal on Swann enterprises in the far north by marrying a Scots teacher and was said to be so bemused by the Scots that Headquarters were expecting any day to hear he was wearing a kilt, calling himself MacHigson, and learning to play the bagpipes.

The Scottish viceroy showed him more deference than Lovell or Catesby and this, Giles realised, was not because they were more of an age but because Higson was unsure of himself in the presence of a son of the man who, almost literally, had plucked him out of a flue. Adam Swann, indeed, was a subject Higson was prepared to discuss without reserve. It was clear that he idolised the man.

Giles, knowing little of the circumstances of their association, gave him the opening he needed by saying, "Everywhere I've been so far, Mr. Higson, I've been living off my father's fat. Weren't you one of Mr. Keate's original trainees?" and Higson, indignant that Giles should remain in ignorance of the manner in which he became associated with Swann-on-Wheels, said, "You never heard the truth about me? Maybe you'd best ask your father. It ain't my place ter gab, except to out an' say I owe everything to 'im, an' no other. Bin more'n a father to me, he 'as, though I don't reckon he'd own to it. He's not one o' them Holy Joes, who do a good turn an' never stop slippin' it into their prayers to make sure Gawd A'mighty don't forget it!" and at this Giles laughed.

Higson asked him if he would be his guest during his stay in the region and when Giles protested that this would impose on a man who was newly married and hoping to become a father soon (Catesby had fed him this titbit) Higson blurted out, "It's not that way at all, Mr. Swann. Mary, my missus that is, told me I was to insist, for the 'otels this side o' the town ain't up to much, and the fact is we'd like a chance to pay yer Dad back a bit, if you see what I mean."

So Giles had no alternative but to hump his knapsack across to Higson's ground-floor flat in a little Georgian house in the Tollcross, a few minutes' walk from the yard, where Mary Higson, several months pregnant by the look of her, made a prodigious fuss of him, as though he had arrived in Edinburgh by royal train instead of on foot. He was at once given a tin bath-tub, four cans of boiling water and a plate of buttered scones to stay his hunger until supper.

He understood then why Higson had been so insistent about lodging him, for Mary, like any prudent Scots wife, had obviously decided that she must put herself out in any way likely to improve her husband's standing with the firm. Her eagerness to do this was touching, Giles thought, for it did not take him long to come to a number of interesting conclusions about this oddly-matched couple, the one sufficiently close to the gutter to congratulate himself on having escaped it, the other a self-contained, exceptionally intelligent young woman who, for a reason difficult to perceive at first, worshipped the ex-waif she had married a few months before.

Being in love himself Giles found he could look benevolently, (and sometimes enviously) at Jake and Mary Higson during the month he spent in the territory. Their delight in one another was so uninhibited that it was embarrassing to share a meal with them, or to be present, kicking one's heels in the hallway, when he and Jake were on the point of setting out on a trip to one of the more remote areas of the beat. It was often difficult to decide which of the two was the more besotted by the other, for while Jake dodged about her as though her 'pledge of affection' was liable to appear on the hearthrug any moment, Mary, for her part, insisted that Jake's needs took precedence over everything else, including the honours due to a house guest, who in Jake's view, happened to be the son of the most important man in the world.

Having grown up in a patriarchal household Giles was accustomed to male dominance but never, in the whole of her life, had Henrietta Swann shown his father this kind of deference, catching his tender solicitude in mid-air as it were, and feeding it back tenfold, showering him with soothing words and soft glances, and despatching him on a routine journey as though he was embarking on a trip to Cathay and facing untold hazards. It could have been cloying, but somehow, perhaps because he saw their reciprocal affection as utterly sincere, it was encouraging, so that he thought, "He's a lucky chap to be sure, tho' she is inclined to overdo it. I can't see Romayne fussing over me in that way, and I'm not sure I should welcome it if she did." But he wondered about it nevertheless. It made nonsense of the precept that, to ensure harmony, like should marry like.

It was Jake himself who went some way towards explaining the phenomenon once he had had an opportunity to demonstrate his talents as a regional gaffer and could begin patronising his guest as a lad fresh from the schoolroom. He said, as they were driving through a village near Jedburgh, "That's where it 'appened, Mr. Swann! Right over there, on that green!" and when Giles asked what had occurred there, supposing the spot to be hallowed in some way, the cockney said, solemnly, "A miracle, that's wot. You carn't call it less. Leastways, I carn't," and went on to describe how he had met Mary McKenzie whilst gazing at the memorial to the famous Denholm scholar, John Leyden, and how this encounter had reoriented his life, providing him, progressively, with an education and a wife.

"Sometimes," he mused, as they left the Rubicon behind, "sometimes I get the feelin' it really ain't 'appened, that I'll wake up sudden and find meself the man I was. What I mean is, you 'ear of things like it, and even see 'em sometimes, at one o' them Saturday night Come-to-Jesus kerbside meetings in the Old Kent Road, when a drunk gets to seein' blue monkeys an' swears orf it on the spot, but it was just like that an' no kiddin', Mr. Swann. I mean, there I was, feelin' right sorry for meself, telling meself I'd 'ad all the luck I deserved getting picked up by your Pa, and sent up 'ere on trial. God's truth, I didn't think I could 'old on to the job for long. Not for want o' tryin', mindjew, but lack of education, of not bein' able to write an' figger properly. And then, there she was, like a bloomin' fairy godmother, and nex' thing you know I was 'avin' lessons from 'er, and after that standin' beside her in the kirk—church that is—with her own father tellin' me we was man and wife. A miracle. That's what it was, and if ever anything like it 'appens to you—with a woman I mean, because you got education, why then, *grab* it. Grab it with both 'ands. Like *that!*" And to make his point clear Higson dropped the reins of the trap to the buckboard, clapped a double handful of nothing and scooped up the reins with a flourish in the manner of a veteran cabby negotiating London Bridge traffic.

It was a miracle, right enough, Giles decided, as he watched them greet one another on the doorstep of the little Georgian house on their return, and any doubts concerning this would have been erased by Mary Higson's lightning seizure of the opportunity she must have been awaiting.

Jake had darted across the street to a druggist with a prescription left by Mary's doctor, letting his supper go cold rather than risk the shop closing in the interval, scudding from the house as though charged with saving the lives of mother and child.

She watched him go, standing by the window and then, drawing the curtains on the gloaming, turned to Giles with an expression very different from the rapturous one she reserved for Jake whenever he had been absent from the house for ten minutes. Aware, no doubt, that her husband would come thundering back into the room within minutes, she came straight to the point, saying, "He'll ha' told ye how it came about, Mr. Swann. Jamie and me, that is?" and when Giles acknowledged that this was so, "Then I'll ask a favour if I may, Mr. Swann. One I couldnae ask in his presence, or not without shaming him, poor lamb. You'll own he's worth his salt to the firm?"

"Worth his salt, Mrs. Higson? As my father's gaffer, north of the Border?"

"Aye, aye," she said, impatience broadening her accent, "that's what I mean. Ye'll own it, will ye no'?"

"Why, of course I'll own to it," he said, a little startled by her vehemence, "he's reckoned a great success up here. What makes you think otherwise?"

"Did I say I thought otherwise? My Jamie can do anything he's a mind to do."

"He has doubts about himself?"

She regarded him so unwinkingly that he had a notion that, even when Jamie was absent, she was subconsciously addressing him, not being equipped to acknowledge the existence of other men.

"Aye," she said, "cruel doubts sometimes."

"How can you be sure?"

"Could a woman love a man as I love yon Jamie without being sure of a thing like that?"

"Well, then, he's young for a job of this size. Isn't it understandable that he should sometimes have second thoughts . . . ?"

"*No!*"

She almost shouted the word at him. "A gentleman like you, maybe. But not Jamie, not someone who was used so cruel as a bairn!"

He was not in the least sure that he followed her. From his own viewpoint, and within his limited experience, he saw Higson as a rather forceful man, but clearly something was amiss, and she was making some kind of appeal for help. Jake would be back any moment and there was no time to waste on reassuring her. He said, "If you think I can help, Mrs. Higson, tell me how. I'd like to, and I'm sure my father would. In spite of what you say, however, they think a deal of him in London. He's reckoned a trier and that's what counts, isn't it?"

"No," she said, again, "it's no' what counts. See here, he could hardly read nor write when I took him in hand, and I've done my best with him. But my best isn't good enough. With that load of work he can't spare me more than an odd hour or so, and only then when he's fair fagged out, and needs his sleep. I've a notion how it could be done, though, how I could work wonders with him. But it would have to have your father's blessing and Jamie mustn't know I brought it about, for that would hit him hard. His pride, do ye ken?"

"You're asking me to try and get him relieved of the job for a time?"

"Aye, for six months. Mr. Fraser, who taught him the ropes up here, is still active. At a word from your father he'd stand in for us, and I could go back to work on Jamie. It's the right thing to do, Mr. Swann, believe me! Up here, we set great store by education and if there's one thing a Scotswoman can't abide it's a botched job o' work. I had Jamie at his lessons for two hours a night, three nights a week. It's not enough. He needs to stick at it six days a week, from morn till night, with nothing else on his mind, with no interruptions!"

They heard his steps clattering up the short flight of steps to the front door and she looked across at him with desperate urgency, as though the completion of Jake Higson's education was the most important issue in the world.

"I'll see Fraser myself and arrange it if it can be arranged," he said, hastily. "Then I'll get my father to confirm from Headquarters . . ."

"You'll not regret it, none of you! I'll swear to that!" and as though changing a mask she wiped the expression of urgent concentration from her face and replaced it with the eager smile that he had come to recognise as Jamie's standard welcome over the threshold.

*   *   *

It made a kind of pattern, a theme for all his wanderings, all the signposts and stages he had passed in the years since he was first aware of people and their complex concerns. It was a thread that strung his experiences together, offering him a guideline that led on into the future. And whenever he stopped to wonder what awaited him out there he would go back, like a man restringing beads, to the very first of them, the glimpse of that broken old couple at Twyforde Green, dispossessed of their tied cottage and going their separate ways to paupers' graves.

There was that, and his talk with his father a day or so after he changed schools. And hard on its heels was another pointer, the finding of a frozen shepherd in an Exmoor hovel after a week of

snowstorms. There were all the social prophets he had read and pondered, from Kingsley to Carlyle, from Tom Paine to Cobden. Then,
like runaway railway trucks mounting one another, there was the
glimpse of Owen Williams rumbling past the bay with crushed toes
that would get him a job on top, the half-grown boys eating their
snap in the gallery, the permanent pall of smoke over the teeming
towns of the cotton belt, the expressionless men and girls standing
like rows of automata at chattering machines. But within all this
there were more explicit pointers, each involving a woman and a
woman's viewpoint, as distinct from a man's; Romayne, content to
buy a husband with the profits of dye works, mines and foundries;
Mrs. Broadbent's hesitant enquiries after George; and finally, the
desperate concern of Mary Higson for time to groom an ex-chimney-
sweep into a scholar. In some way it all had a place in his personal
destiny, but just how and why he had no way of knowing and
doubted if he would ever find out. All one could do was to follow
his nose and see where it led and it was time, he felt, that it pointed
him south, to the slum overlooking the Thames where he would be
based for the next three years but also, praise God, to Romayne, who
might one day do battle for him as Mary Higson battled for Jake.

He saw Fraser and got his agreement to stand in for a period, subject to Headquarters' approval, and said goodbye to the Higsons at
Waverley Station, rushing south at eighty miles an hour. His senses,
caught up in the beat of the iron wheels, isolated the theme that
had launched him on this odyssey half a year ago, Arnold's scholar
gypsy crying,

> O born in days when wits were fresh and clear,
> And life ran gaily as the sparkling Thames;
> Before this strange disease of modern life,
> With its sick hurry, its divided aims,
> Its head o'ertaxed . . .

There was more than a poet's lament here. ". . . This strange disease of modern life, with its sick hurry, its divided aims . . ." But
Arnold, like all the poets, had shirked the issue. He had made his
protest and then withdrawn himself, leaving the healing, if healing
could be achieved, to workaday people like Lovell, to Owen Williams who walked lame, to the hard-bitten Catesby, juggling with

the demands of capital and labour and to the Higsons, man and wife, looking for the answers in text-books. To himself also, perhaps, when he had time to digest all he had seen and experienced since he set out so hopefully in the spring.

5

Maiden Tribute

IT began as a rich, secret joke, the culmination, in a way, of all his secret jokes at the expense of the English, with their whorehouses and Bible Societies. But then, taking a twist, it became an embarrassment, a source of disquiet, an adventure and finally, in retrospect, a kind of conversion.

Those who knew him, of course, did not see it in this sequence. He was fifty-six then, and had learned how to keep a change of heart to himself. But Deborah Avery was aware of it and years later, when the steamy summer of the Maiden Tribute to Modern Babylon was forgotten, she remembered his part in it, summing it up, for Swann posterity, as 'the time of Adam's softening of the arteries'.

That was June-July 1885, when he was riding high, higher than he had ever hoped to ride. A period in his life when the sun shone for weeks at a time, when he and his affairs prospered, when it seemed to him and those about him that nothing could dent the armour of his self-sufficiency and when Henrietta began to see signs of his two families fusing and federalising.

And why not, indeed? The evidence was all around them, both at the yard and at 'Tryst', with family trends emerging and the diversification and expansion of his other children in the network. There was no room for doubt anywhere.

Late spring and early summer, 1885, a time approaching her forty-fifth birthday and change of life. A time she saw the more mature among her reapers harvesting a little on their own account. A time, like so many other times, that she would look back on with laughter, regret and thankfulness but also, as summer wore on, with a certain amount of dismay.

*   *   *

His policy of giving the viceroys their head, of letting them run free to their own profit or ruin, was proving as successful as his breakout in the winter of 'sixty-two, when, teetering into bankruptcy, he had taken them into his confidence at the first annual conference.

He had had his doubts about some of the more bizarre aspects of diversification but he was obliged to admit, some eighteen months later, that they had been unjustified. Young Markby, up in Crescent North, was showing a profit on his fleet of fish waggons (known, within a network renowned for its slang, as Ice-boxes) and Godsall's early ventures into the field of short-haul public transport were settling down after a shaky start with a few ramshackle vehicles acquired from failed companies in the Kentish Triangle. Tom Wickstead was trying his luck in the same field in the Peterborough area, but Wickstead's main efforts had been concerned with his Four-footers, the purpose-built cattle waggons he had urged on the company. Edith had written to say they now had contracts with more than fifty farmers specialising in fatstock, and that prospects in the new departure looked excellent. But then, he supposed, Edith would say that, for anything Tom did was right in her eyes. She might even be hopelessly out of touch with trends now that her family was growing up, and she spent all of her time at home.

Two of Catesby's Goliaths were on the road, crawling across the Polygon like gigantic, humped-back centipedes, and Tybalt, noting the profit margin on successive hauls of heavy machinery, had lost his head over this venture and talked Waggonmaster Keate into ordering one for the Border Triangle, the only other region where there was likely to be a demand for such a dinosaur.

All in all, as Adam was ready to admit, they had been right and he had been wrong. It made him wonder if he was getting too set in his ways and whether, as time went on, he should begin clearing the ground for retirement, say as soon as he slipped over the hill into his sixties. Not seriously, however, for he found it impossible to imagine what he would do with himself when someone else was sitting here, or in some more comfortable perch they had built themselves, sifting through contracts, estimates and breakdown costs, comparing one set of returns with another, and juggling, during spells of bad weather, with the movement of frigates, pinnaces, men-o'-war, Ice-boxes, Four-footers and Goliaths, on a thousand roads between the German Ocean and Dublin Bay.

The other area where he had had to climb down a rung or two lately was that of the family, for Henrietta was never slow to remind him of her prophecy that they would all do him proud if he had the patience to look for a long-term profit instead of a succession of overnight miracles.

He was mellowing, she noticed, just a little year by year, and she was the first to notice his improved relationship with the elder children. In this way, as in so many other ways, he seemed to differ from other patriarchs, who were given to sentimentalising over children when they were in the knee-climbing stage but frowned on their shortcomings the moment they were old enough to express an opinion of their own.

His favourite, she suspected, was still George, but he had warmed towards Stella now that he had adjusted to Denzil and evaluated his worth as a farmer. The prickliness apparent between father-in-law and son-in-law in the first years of the marriage had amused Henrietta but she had the sense to keep the joke to herself. Their lack of accord stemmed, she suspected, from the one's disapproval of watching a man defer to a woman (even when that woman was his own flesh and blood) and Denzil's obstinate belief that Stella had been hustled into marriage with a seedy aristocrat. By the time the second child arrived, however, mutual wariness had moderated. It only needed the news that Denzil had made a down payment on Underhill, an adjoining smallholding, for Adam to admit that he might have misjudged the boy by regarding him, up to that time, as a handy life-jacket for a daughter going down for the third time. He had no interest in agriculture, seeing it as a dying way of life, but he had to admit that the boy qualified as a trier, always a passport to Adam Swann's good graces.

As for Alex, he was coming to terms with him too, though he still thought of him as a little dull and what he dismissed as 'mess-pompous'. Mess-pompous or not, Alex was making steady progress in his profession, a captain at twenty-four, with three campaigns behind him and the possibility, she had heard, of marrying as soon as he got his next step.

It was George and Giles, however, who were showing the best pair of heels, and Adam made no bones at all about having been impressed by their recent showing. George may have racketed about during his long spell away from home but he had clearly benefited by his travels, for he and Adam could now baffle a croquet party with a laconic exchange of technical jargon. He was also, she gathered, a first-class salesman and had already hooked some lucrative fish into the Swann network. Indeed, the only complaint Adam voiced about him nowadays was his neglect of his pretty little bride, whom he often forsook in favour of a stinking mechanical contrivance he had found somewhere and shipped home in crates, each as heavy as a cannon.

Adam, she noted, had been mildly impressed by the machine when it was assembled but she soon realised he did not regard it as anything more than a toy and one night, when they were going to bed, and could hear the cough and splutter of the stinking thing from its new home in the old stable block, he growled, "Beats me how a boy his age, less than a year married, can stay tinkering with that contraption, when there's a girl like Gisela warming the bed for him!" She laughed, reminding him of a time when he was much older than George, with an equally dutiful wife at home warming the bed, but had preferred to spend nights on the road and had been absent for weeks at a stretch.

He rejected this argument, dismissing it as unrealistic. In those days he had had his way to make in the world for both of them, and in any case, he had more than made up for time lost the moment he returned and had a family of nine to prove it.

"Well, at least George is home *every* night," she argued, "and I haven't heard Gisela complaining, have you?" and he had to admit that he had not, adding that the one thing all their children seemed to have in common was an ability to bewitch members of the opposite sex.

"Damned if I don't go hot under the collar whenever I drop in at Dewponds to pass the time of day with young Fawcett," he went on. "He talks sense just so long as Stella stays out of the way, but the minute she comes into the room, looking like a sack tied round the middle if she's been out meddling with his concerns, you might as well expect a conversation from a mute under hypnosis. All the boy does is gape at her, as if he's married the Queen of Sheba. Then there's young George, confound him. Why, a girl as pretty and dainty and lissom as Gisela, could have married any man in her community I'd say, but no, she has to turn her back on home and family at a nod from him, and come trotting like a bitch to the whistle."

"I really don't know why you're quarrelling with such a happy state of affairs," she said. "In a way it's reflected glory, isn't it?" That made him grin and say he wasn't quarrelling with it, merely commenting on it as a phenomenon that young Giles had underlined by capturing the only child of a millionaire during a tramp across the Welsh mountains.

In fact, it had taken him a week to absorb the shock of Giles' conquest and what it was likely to mean in dynastic terms. Already Sir Clive Rycroft-Mostyn had steered a sizeable contract their way in the Mountain Square, and there was every likelihood that he would soon be backing Swann waggons against the loading bays of all manner of enterprises, if only to keep the money in the family. That George, or even Alex, should achieve something on this scale was conceivable, but that Giles, not yet twenty, had attracted the daughter of a man owning a coal-mine, a dye works, a cable factory, God only knew what else, and who lacked a male heir, was the kind of coup one read about in one of those trashy novels Henrietta used to borrow from Mr. Mudie before he weaned her on Dickens and the Brontës.

Henrietta found it less surprising. She had always seen Giles as the dark horse of the family, and no one could ever be sure what was going on behind that patient, anxious brow. She never had, and she was virtually certain nobody else had, unless it was that overpowering little minx he introduced into the house last Christmas, without paying anyone the compliment at the time of announcing they were engaged to be married.

She had eventually prised this tremendous secret from Sir Clive himself, who used Adam as a go-between when he dropped in at the yard to discuss, of all things, the transport of a twelve-ton anchor from his chainworks in Wales to Avonmouth, letting it be known that he not only approved of Giles but would consent to them marrying as soon as the boy came of age.

She had the greatest difficulty then in not making an immediate descent upon Giles, with a demand to be kept fully informed on the subject, but Adam had talked her out of it. Giles, he reminded her, had more sensibility than the rest of the brood lumped together and would doubtless tell them in his own time and probably had reasons for reticence. He had, in fact, half-guessed what they were but here it was he who kept his own counsel. A man as well-heeled as Rycroft-Mostyn would naturally assume he was buying a son-in-law, and Giles, if he knew the boy, wasn't for sale, not even at the price Rycroft-Mostyn was in a position to pay. As to the girl herself, he could not come to any definite conclusions about her, save that she was very fetching, and as unpredictable as a two-year-old filly whose training had been botched somewhere along the line. She did offer a clue, however, of Sir Clive's willingness to see her settled in the not-far-distant future, and to someone who was not an obvious fortune-hunter. A girl like that, he wouldn't wonder, had a trouble-record somewhere. It wouldn't have surprised him to learn that, not so long before Giles came drifting down the Aberglaslyn pass, she hadn't cost her father a pot of hush money one way or another, got herself involved with a married man, maybe, or headed for Gretna Green with some young scoundrel. Watching them, as they played charades at Christmas, however, he had no doubts concerning her feelings regarding Giles, and this made him remember again the inexhaustible stock of charm his sons and daughters seemed able to pool. There wasn't one of them, baby Margaret included, who hadn't mastered the trick of making themselves agreeable when they chose. They hadn't inherited it from *him*, and Henrietta in her younger days, had been as wild and hard-mouthed as that Rycroft-Mostyn filly. Maybe it was a legacy from much further back, from her saucy Irish ancestors possibly, blended with the geniality of the old Colonel, who could coax a mastiff out of the sulks with a smile and a couple of pats.

Henrietta was right, of course. One should not quarrel with one's luck, providing it was fair to middling, and they had all had their share over the last twenty years, notwithstanding that brush with bankruptcy, and the loss of a leg in that crash over at Staplehurst in 'sixty-five. The business was booming along under a full-spread of canvas; Stella, after that idiotic first marriage of hers, seemed as contented as a cow put out to permanent pasture; George, notwithstanding his eccentric interest in engineering, was more than proving his worth at the yard; Alex was staying alive and in line for promotion; and Giles had already succeeded in winning the friendship of at least three of the regional managers. As to the younger ones, they were as handsome and healthy a spread as one was likely to find anywhere in Kent. Taken all round, he supposed, he was much luckier than most men who had had to make their own way in the world and he meant things to stay that way, as he told Henrietta one stifling July night, when sleep evaded them and they passed the time counting their blessings.

He recalled afterwards how Deborah's name cropped up towards the end of a chat that had started with Henrietta expressing an opinion that Gisela was pregnant, and tailed off with him telling her that Giles, although no salesman, might be worth his keep as a peacemaker when the viceroys went to bickering again, as they surely would if the business struck a bad patch.

She had said, after a longish pause, "There's still Deborah, of course. Do you think we'll ever succeed in pushing her over the hump before it's too late?" and he said, chuckling, "If, by the hump, you mean a cheerless spinsterhood, no, I don't, Deborah has other fish to fry."

"Oh, stuff and nonsense," said Henrietta, kicking her legs free of the sheet and settling herself with her hands clasped behind her head. "All fish are tiddlers compared with getting a husband and the longer she leaves it the more limited her choice. It isn't as if she was a frump, like most unmarrieds her age. Why on earth don't you steer someone her way? He would have to talk like a college professor, but you must know plenty of men who would be attracted to her. She doesn't look a bluestocking and only gives herself away when she begins to talk."

Digesting this he told himself that, had a man been asked to select the extremes of womanhood, he could not have done better than to cite Henrietta Swann and Deborah Avery. How did one begin to explain to a sensual minx like Henrietta the social conscience and intellectual curiosity of a woman like Debbie? It was too hot to try anyway, so he said, "A man doesn't waste time parading possibles before a woman as sharp as Deborah. All one does is to wait and hope. She'll probably stumble on someone when she's in her forties."

"And what'll be the use of that, for heaven's sake?"

"It wouldn't be the slightest use to a wanton like you," he said, leaning on his elbows and looking out over the moonlit paddocks, "but all Debbie needs from a man is companionship. So long as her health and vitality hold out she's enough to occupy her, take it from me."

They forgot Debbie then, for she joined him at the window, lifting her face to the kiss of the south wind that drifted off the escarpment in tiny, teasing gusts, so leisurely in their approach that one had to listen for them in the foliage of the trees. But he remembered their exchange of views when he read the first of Mr. Stead's articles a day or so later, for then it was clear that he had made a very accurate guess concerning Avery's daughter, and what she was about just then. It was a long way short of husband-hunting.

2

He bought the paper at the foot of Ludgate Hill, a trader's instinct warning him that something sensational was being hawked, for the newsboy's stocks were diminishing as fast as he could distribute copies and the circle about him continued to widen as more and more top-hatted, frock-coated city gents moved in from Blackfriars, Fleet Street, or down the incline from St. Paul's.

It was, of course, Stead's broadsheet. He would have been surprised had it not been. The *Pall Mall Gazette*, God bless it, could always be relied upon to divide the nation into two warring camps, until the next broadside dissolved old alliances and formed new ones in British smoking-rooms, suburban trains, and basement kitchens too, where it was usually smuggled in with the milk or the muffins.

Today's issue qualified for that distinction. A single glance at the lead-story assured him that few British patriarchs, whilst they would themselves enjoy every word of Stead's latest sally into the stewpots, would leave the paper lying around the house for the edification of wives, daughters and domestic staff. The main feature, blazoned in headlines that other editors might use to announce a run on the banks, or the collapse of the government, screamed, *The Maiden Tribute to Modern Babylon*. Stead was astride his favourite hobby-horse again, mounting another attack on city vice that would send temperatures and circulation soaring wherever the journal went on sale.

He carried his copy up to the tower, cleared his desk and sat down to enjoy one of his favourite slack-hour occupations, that of observing the English through the lens of their Fourth Estate. He looked for no more than the usual generalisation of organised vice, according to the gospel of St. Stead, but had not read half a column before he decided that this was no ordinary diatribe, of the kind that had put a government in power on the strength of a few thousand butchered Armenians, and turned it out again by catching the flood tide of public indignation concerning that crank Gordon, who let himself be shut up and slaughtered in Khartoum. This was the scream of a soul in torment, so highly personalised and so fully documented, that it was obvious that the crusading editor had done his own reporting.

Even so, it was not until he saw a sub-heading *Child of Thirteen Bought for £5*, that the full significance of the article was apparent. He understood then the lengths to which this strange, dynamic man had gone to make his point, and what a journalistic triumph he had achieved, preparing the ground for a promised series of revelations that were designed to force the government to act upon the subject of child prostitution or make way for legislators who would. Every line, every word, was a barbed arrow, aimed at the complacency of the men who had swept this particular scandal under their Turkey carpets and the attack had been mounted with a degree of journalistic skill that was rare, even for Stead. Nothing was spared the reader save the child's ultimate violation, and even that was implied by a long row of asterisks. The virulence, and the recklessly stated detail of the article, almost took his breath away but what was even more unusual was the fact—obvious to all but the most cursory reader—that Stead had assembled the facts himself solely in order to vouch for them.

There was an account of an interview with a brothel-keeper in the Mile End Road, an even more graphic report of Stead's interview with a certain Mrs. Jarrett, a professional procuress of virgins, the oldest of them fifteen. And following that, as a horrific climax, the tale of 'Lily', the theme-bearing thirteen-year-old, whom Stead claimed had been purchased on Derby Day from a gin-sodden mother, conveyed to a house in Regent Street, and closeted with a would-be seducer. Stead must have been hard by at the time, for he wrote of the child's cry as 'the bleat of a helpless lamb'.

But that was only an opening salvo, fired on July 6th.

Adam Swann, half English, half Gascon, had fewer illusions about his fellow-countrymen than most men who did business with them. He had come to admire a great many things about the English, among them tenacity, inventiveness and buoyant self-confidence that Continentals mistook for arrogance but was not, for it stemmed from the heart rather than the head. He admired their steadiness and courage in peace and war, their deep and genuine concern for the basic freedoms of press and Parliament, and, above all, their almost mystical reverence for the law. But there was one aspect the English had that irritated and puzzled him ever since his return home after a youth spent in the East. He could never come to terms with English double standards as regards sex, and their gloomy habit of regarding it as an exclusively male function, locking the door on it socially and conversationally, and fostering the doctrine that any woman who found pleasure in it deserved nothing but social ostracism and a whipping at the hands of her natural lord and master or, failing him, the nearest available male.

It had always seemed to him that this attitude was not only at variance with all the noisy demands for fair play that the English voiced at home and abroad, but incubated a domestic tyranny that made a mockery of marriage, courtship and even debauchery, extracting the juice of human kindness from any legalised embrace and all the fun and frolic from unlicensed relationships. This double standard was not Stead's main target in his blistering 'Maiden Tribute' series. As a dedicated social missionary, self-righteous maybe but indubitably sincere, he was concerned, as always, with the under-privileged, and here Adam could applaud the fellow. If the man could beat some of the dust out of the hypocrisy of the English then Adam Swann, for one, wished him well, and made sure of the next instalment by reserving a copy at his regular news-stand outside London Bridge Station.

If he suspected that Stead had shot his bolt in the first broadside he was very much mistaken. Falling to with diabolical glee and reckless, it seemed, of the risks of libel or the label of public purveyor of pavement filth, the crusader warmed to his work in Instalment

No. 2, recounting dealing with two younger procuresses, Miss X and Miss Z, who were prepared to offer wealthy customers medical certificates of virginity with the goods supplied and had, in fact, delivered three of a promised five virgins to Stead himself on a wholesale basis and at a price that allowed a second profit.

There was ample evidence in this issue that Stead was not acting alone in his investigations, for he spoke of a group of eminent adjudicators known as the 'Mansion House Committee', said to include the Archbishop of Canterbury and His Eminence, Cardinal Manning. Stead wrote of agents prowling the country for Irish girls and country girls whom they could corrupt and sell on commission, and had somehow contrived to get these vultures to explain the methods they employed—a pledge of marriage, a good situation, enlistment on the staff of a respectable business house employing a hundred or more young girls, and the like.

In a sub-section of his third article published on July 8th (the *Gazette* was already banned from newstalls and selling on the streets at half a crown a copy) Stead wrote of a regular purchaser of children known as The Minotaur, who claimed to have debauched over two thousand working-class children. In addition, he all but named brothel-keepers, who freely admitted that Her Majesty's Judges and legislators at Westminster were among their most lucrative customers, and mentioned certain servants' registry offices and emporia as clearing houses for white slaves, alleging that some of the more spirited of the victims were drugged or strapped down for the initiation. In his final article, devoted to a summing-up, he described London as 'the greatest market for human flesh in the world'.

Adam, reading each successive article with the detachment of a man familiar with the stews of the Near East and India, was neither shocked nor surprised by the revelations. What did astonish him was the terrible furore caused by the campaign, for here, if one was looking for it, lay the hidden sources of the practices Stead had chronicled. Here, out on the streets, was the blatant hypocrisy of a society that conducted family prayers, prosecuted pioneers like Bradlaugh and Annie Besant for advocating contraception, and even went as far as to describe table legs as 'limbs' and adorn them with handsewn frills lest their curves should overheat the imagination of the young.

Slowly, but with a scorn that made him feel curiously isolated from his fellows, he watched the temperature of the capital rise day by day until it was at fever heat. Nothing in his experience had occurred on this scale before. It was as though London was in the grip of a steamy epidemic that advertised itself in the expressions on the faces of soberly-dressed men clamouring for copies of the journal, in the quips exchanged by his customers and workforce concerning Stead's latest revelations but, above all, in the mounting demand that this man, who had had the hardihood to lay the facts before them, should be exposed for what, in the opinion of a majority, he was—a lewd and scandal-mongering opportunist, prepared to go to any lengths to sell his newspapers, even if his articles enabled foreigners (who had no standards of decency!) to jeer at Britain as a whited sepulchre.

Adam saw this, but the issue was not really personalised until he read the savage counter-attacks made upon Stead in rival newspapers like *The Times*, *Lloyd's News*, and above all, the conservative *St. James' Gazette*, that took a high moral tone and branded the *Pall Mall Gazette* and its staff as pedlars of grubby fantasy. It was only then that he was able to gauge the extent of Stead's vulnerability, and it occurred to him, for the first time since the Maiden Tribute series had appeared, that Stead's danger surely extended to all his associates, particularly a woman associate like Deborah Avery.

It made him very uneasy then concerning her, especially when he recollected that he had not seen or heard from her in over a month, and prompted him to tell Tybalt he was likely to be absent for an hour or so and take a cab to her lodgings in Frederick Street, off the Gray's Inn Road.

It was here, standing on her doorstep and knocking repeatedly without being able to rouse anyone inside, that he had a curious sensation of having played the same role in the same setting a long time ago. The recollection was so vivid that he paused with his hand on the knocker, thinking back nearly a quarter-century to a time when, in search of her father, then his partner and financial sponsor, he had come seeking him in nearby Guildford Street, to be told that he was in flight from the bailiff's men and the Metropolitan Police.

He was a man not much given to premonitions but he had one then and it made his stomach cartwheel, so that he thought, irritably, 'Now what the devil ails me? What am I doing here, behaving as though the world was falling about my ears? Deborah is an expensively-educated adult and if she insists on associating herself with Stead that's her business, not mine!' and he turned away with the intention of hailing the cabby who had dropped him here before the vehicle merged into the flow of traffic moving towards King's Cross.

At the foot of the steps, however, he found his path barred, and in a way that increased his sense of unease. A young man was looking him directly in the face and saying, in the friendliest manner, "You won't find her, sir. The old dragon inside says she's gone abroad but we don't believe her. Are you a relative?" But Adam, now thoroughly alerted, growled, "No, I'm not, young man, although I fail to see what concern it would be of yours if I was! We haven't met, have we?"

"No, sir, I think not," the young man said, urbanely, "but if you're not a relative you must be press. It occurred to me we might work together tracing her. My name's Burbage. From Lloyd's," and he produced a card establishing him as T. H. Burbage, accredited representative of Lloyd's Newspaper, presenting it in such an engaging manner that Adam found himself admiring both his nerve and professionalism.

He used the card as a means of extricating himself from what came close to being a trap, one that a man of his experience should have anticipated, although it had never occurred to him that Deborah's lodgings would be picketed by the press. He said, carefully, "I'm not a newspaper man, Mr. Burbage. But I do have a message for Miss Avery, an important one from her solicitor," and enjoyed the glint in Mr. Burbage's eye.

Unexpectedly the door opened and Deborah's landlady appeared, but only for time enough to dart a single exasperated glance at Adam and shout, "One more knock and it's the police! There's a limit you know!" whereupon the door slammed shut and Mr. Burbage, with his infectious grin, said, "Quite hopeless, you see? I told my editor earlier on but he said don't give up. It's our only lead, you see, for she's almost certainly hiding Lily. Look here, sir, suppose we have a drink and lay out a plan? Not that I think Miss Avery is inside, but I've a suspicion the old girl knows far more than she admits. Vetch, of the *St. James' Gazette,* told me Miss Avery was here yesterday, but left again almost at once with luggage. It might have been one of the other tenants, of course, for four or five live there, but Vetch knows her by sight and swears it was her. He followed her to within a hundred yards of Victoria but lost her then in the traffic, so now he's off on a fresh tack, tracking down Mrs. Jarrett in Winchester. It's a damnably complicated story. All manner of red herrings are cropping up and no clear lead anywhere. What do you say to that drink, sir?"

It was as well Burbage was the talkative type. It gave Adam time to collect his thoughts, now in the greatest confusion. It was clear that Deborah was not only involved in Stead's campaign but had been identified by the press as playing a leading role in it.

He was glad then that he had read each successive article very carefully. At least it provided some kind of defence against Mr. Burbage's spirited enquiries, all couched in the friendliest banter but put with one object in view, to extract information from someone who might, conceivably, put him on the track of Lily's custodian.

It occurred to him then that he might turn the tables on the journalist, using him to discover what was known among pressmen about the unpublished background to the Babylon articles. Information of this kind might stand Debbie in good stead in the future, might even provide him with some clue of her present whereabouts. He knew pressmen sufficiently well, however, to offer a bait of some kind, so he said, resignedly, "Very well, Mr. Burbage. It's of little consequence to me one way or the other. My concern is a family matter, a legacy I believe, although naturally I can't discuss a client's interests with gentlemen of the press. Suppose we adjourn to the Red Lion? I might think of somewhere Miss Avery could be. I'm sure she wouldn't have gone abroad without telling my principal, for she was aware this matter was pending."

"Would you mind telling me your principal's name, sir?" said Burbage, taking Adam's arm and steering him through the swing doors of the nearest tavern.

"No harm in that," said Adam, twinkling, and beginning to fancy himself as an actor. "His name is Stock, of the firm of Stock, Frithlestone and Stock, London Wall. Very reputable people I assure you.

Er . . . sherry, if you please. Thank you. I can't spare more than a few minutes, for Mr. Stock will want to know more of this silly business. The late Mr. Avery, Miss Deborah's father, was an associate of his, long before you were born, young man," and he told himself he was doing very well, for Burbage, having paid for the drinks, at once became excessively respectful.

"I'm bound to say it's generous of you not to send me packing, sir," he said. "Most lawyers would. Lawyers think of journalists as very small beer, I can tell you, and really one can't blame them, when that chap Stead lets the profession down by strewing this kind of garbage all over London."

Aware that *Lloyd's News*, specialising in rape, society divorces and lurid crimes of every description was his cook's favourite reading, Adam jibbed at this, saying, "Oh, come, come, Mr. Burbage. There are some who would applaud Mr. Stead for rooting out evil." But Burbage replied, sourly, "Not if they knew the facts, Mr. . . ." and then smiled, adding, "You aren't obliged to give me your name, sir. 'Smith' will do, won't it?" and Adam said that it would, and admitted to having read *Lloyd's News* attacks on the *Pall Mall* stories but went on to say that he understood the main facts were not in dispute.

"Concerning prostitution they aren't," Burbage said, "although Stead is talking absolute rubbish when he compares London unfavourably to Continental capitals. We all know it goes on, sir, and that no Act of Parliament can stop it. But we haven't published all we know concerning Lily, the poor lamb Stead claims was bought for five pounds and sold for immoral purposes."

"Indeed? Well, that surprises me. I read the Babylon articles for possible libel actions, and it seemed to me that Mr. Stead was prepared to vouch for everything he set down as regards the actual abduction of the child. Is your journal denying that, Mr. Burbage?"

Burbage looked very thoughtful then and Adam made a shrewd guess at what was occupying his mind at that particular moment. He was weighing the worth of giving something away against the near-certainty of getting rather more in exchange. Finally he said, with studied carelessness, "There are certain things I feel you should know, Mr. Smith, as someone who presumably acts for Miss Avery. One is that 'Lily' isn't 'Lily'. Her real name is Armstrong, Eliza

Armstrong, and her parents, far from being the scoundrels Stead represents them to be, are not the type of parents likely to sell their daughter for five pounds. I've interviewed them and that's only an opinion, but a professional one. Certain facts have emerged, however, that don't fit Mr. Stead's theories at all. For a start, Mrs. Armstrong is plaguing the police to learn the whereabouts of her daughter. For another, we have certain proof that Mrs. Jarrett, the procuress, was in Stead's pay, that she got the child medically examined before passing her on and that Mrs. Armstrong was given not five pounds but one, as an advance on the girl's wages as a servant. She's a simple soul and pickled in gin, as most of her class are, but you can take it from me she was hoaxed. The whole thing is no more than a circulation stunt."

"Really," Adam said, trying to look shocked but feeling panic rise in his throat. "You surprise me, Mr. Burbage, but since you've been kind enough to tell me so much, and in view of information I might be inclined to give you, would you mind explaining Miss Avery's involvement in this unsavoury business? I've met the lady once or twice and she struck me as a respectable kind of girl, even though she does earn pin money writing for journals and magazines."

Burbage's expression of boyish charm had faded, replaced by the expression Adam often saw on the faces of some of his hard-bargaining customers. He said, "I'll tell you, certainly. Providing you'll tell me where Miss Avery is likely to be found."

"In Cumberland," said Adam, at random, and gave the address of his boyhood home, on the shores of Derwentwater, wondering a little that he could lie so easily, and on such slight provocation. "That mustn't go any further, Mr. Burbage. You people protect your sources of information, I believe, and I assure you if it got about that I had assisted you I should find myself out of a good billet without a character."

Burbage was now regarding him bleakly. "Why should you run that risk on my account, Mr. Smith?"

"I think I can answer that," Adam said. "I happen to think the same as you concerning Stead's motivation. And it looks to me as if he's been very cavalier about the people he engaged to assist him in the enterprise. Namely one of our lady clients. Does that satisfy you?"

Burbage relaxed again. "Perfectly," he said, "and now I'll keep my side of the bargain. My editor has it on good authority that Miss Avery actually participated in this so-called purchase and was present when the girl was certified a virgin by a bawd. We've established a direct link between Miss Avery and the procuress, Mrs. Jarrett, and both have now completely disappeared, together with Eliza Armstrong. For what it's worth, the Salvation Army is also involved—that fire-eater Booth has a finger in every pie baked in this kind of oven. One thing more that might alter your principal's views concerning Miss Avery. She doesn't earn pin money as a freelance. She's on Stead's staff, and writes exclusively for the *P.M. Gazette*." He finished his drink and smiled again. "You'll excuse me now, Mr. Smith. I've urgent business to attend to," and he winked so that Adam, watching him go, thought, "Can't help admiring the chap's professionalism . . . George would have made a good journalist . . . but he doesn't fool me with that high-toned attitude . . . Every editor in London is livid with fury at watching Stead's circulation soar, and trying his damnedest to jump on the bandwaggon . . ." But then his thoughts turned back to Debbie and he decided that Burbage's statement concerning her involvement in this mess was almost certainly true, and that she would need any amount of luck to emerge from it without worse damage than she had sustained on the witch-hunt in Brussels. And this made him angry with himself that he had not exerted himself to steer her away from these waters long ago, or at least extracted a promise from Stead that she would not be employed on work as dangerous as this. "Damn it," he told himself, as he crossed Gray's Inn Road in search of a growler, "it's no kind of job for a woman. Hetty's right. We ought to get her married off before it's too late for her to have babies and give her something more pleasant to think about!" and he snarled at a fat man wearing a topper a size too small for him, who skipped nimbly ahead of him and disappeared into the cab he had signalled.

3

He said nothing to Henrietta. He wanted time to think, to weigh every possible angle, but in the meantime he kept a close watch on the newspapers, snorting when he read, in the *St. James' Gazette*, that newsboys at Ludgate Circus were being brought before a magistrate for selling indecent literature. It was time then, he thought, to make a direct approach to Stead for news of Deborah's whereabouts, and he went round to the *Gazette* offices but despaired of getting inside, much less of locating Stead. The place looked as if it was under siege, so he returned to his turret and locked himself in, telling Tybalt he was not to be disturbed for an hour. In half that time he had written a forthright letter to the editor, demanding to know the precise extent of Deborah's embroilment in the abduction, where he could locate her and if she needed legal aid.

He read the letter over, deciding, regretfully, that it was crusty. He did not change it, however. Convinced as he was of Stead's sincerity, he did not value it much against the happiness of Deborah Avery, to whom both he and Henrietta owed a debt that had never been fully discharged by the provision of a home and family since childhood. For twenty years now they had regarded her as the family standby in times of stress and Henrietta's personal indebtedness to her went back to the time of the rail crash when she had played a woman's part in the crisis that came close to sending Henrietta out of her mind. He could even recall his wife's comment on Debbie a few hours after he came limping in with an artificial limb. She had said of her, at that time, "I can never look on her as anyone else's child after this . . ." And neither, he decided, could he, sealing the letter and blowing down the tube for a messenger to take it to Stead by hand, and wait for an answer. He marked it, in large, red characters, *Copy. Personal to Mr. W. T. Stead. Very Urgent.* It seemed the likeliest way of reaching a man all London was talking about.

The boy was back within the hour. In spite of his efforts he had been unable to deliver the letter personally but had given it to a sub-editor and with this Adam had to be content. Having warned his lawyer Stock that *Lloyd's News* might be in touch with him, and issued instructions that Burbage was to be bluffed as far as Cumberland if possible, he went on home, looking for a telegram from Stead but receiving none that day or the next.

On the day after that there was talk of warrants being issued for Stead and his associates. Mrs. Armstrong, now posing as an outraged mother deprived of her precious child by a trick, was making a great hullaballoo in *Lloyd's News* and the *St. James' Gazette*. In all the other journals, including the Continental and American press, the controversy continued to rage. It was time, he thought, to take Henrietta into his confidence and that same evening he did, telling her all he knew, and giving her back copies of both Stead's paper and those of his rivals containing attacks on his integrity.

He had looked for doubts, of the kind he himself entertained, but there was more than doubt in Henrietta's face when she emerged from her sewing-room with the bundle of papers under her arm. She flung them on his desk, stared at him unsmilingly and said, "Well, it's no more than I expected. You've failed her badly, Adam. The least you can do now is to find her and get her away from that dreadful man, do you hear?"

"Do you think I haven't tried to locate her?" he growled, but she made a gesture of impatience that reminded him of her father, once the terror of his factory floor.

"You haven't tried hard enough. Somehow Deborah has to be rescued from this awful business before she finds herself in real trouble, in gaol as likely as not. But that isn't the real point."

"What is then?"

"Your family is. *Us!* The boys particularly. How do you suppose a scandal like this would affect Alex and Giles? Alex is waiting on promotion, and Giles is hoping to marry one of the wealthiest heiresses in the land. Don't you think you owe them some consideration?"

He said, slowly, "I hadn't thought of that. But now that I do it doesn't seem to me relevant. You don't really believe Stead is doing this to boost his circulation, do you?"

"I don't care what his motives are. They don't concern me, or you either. The moment Debbie is found, and it's proved she helped to kidnap this child, her association with us will be broadcast throughout the land. She's regarded as a sister to Alex and Giles, and you'll be dragged into it too, mark my words. I don't often stand up to you, Adam, and I can't remember how long it is since I ran contrary to you but I do now, even if it means marching into that man's office and demanding Debbie is restored to us and her part in this hushed up, do you understand?"

"No," he said, stubbornly, "I don't. Why should I? Debbie isn't a child. She can do as she likes with her life, as I told you the last time she was in trouble . . ."

"Indeed she can't!" She circled the desk and stood over him threateningly, as though he had been one of the children in need of a whipping. "We've given her home and family, and she owes it to us to keep our name out of the mud! You won't ever accuse me of not having been a good mother to her, I hope. I was always very fond of her, and grateful to her for the way she stood by me when the others were too little, and you were at death's door. But that doesn't mean I'll let her drag any one of us down into this . . . this *cesspool!*" and she swept her hand across the desk so smartly that some of the papers she had thrown there fell to the floor. "There's another thing, too. I'd have taken it kindly if you had let me know about this earlier."

It was years, he reflected dismally, since they had fallen out on this scale, years since she had railed at him like a scold, or accused him, as she did now, of disloyalty to her and her children. How long ago exactly? More than twenty years, when he had taken her to task for allowing a brutal master-sweep to send a boy into one of her flues and choke to death on soot, touching off a quarrel that almost parted them. He said, deliberately, "You stand by that, Hetty? You don't give a damn what happens to any of these children Stead and Debbie are fighting for?"

"Not a pin!" she said, unblushingly, and it struck him then that, notwithstanding half a lifetime together, involving the raising of a family of five sons and four daughters, they were still as far apart on the wider issues of life as on the day they met a mile or so south of the wretched little town where her father had ridden a boy rioter into the ground.

He rose heavily and crossed to the window, looking out on the sunlit paddocks.

"Well, *I* care," he said, at length. "I care very much, and I'm no Holy Joe. I care because I'm British, and sometimes I've been proud of the fact, for at least we have the men and the courage to scour our privies in public now and again. That's more than you can say for most tribes."

He turned back to her. "See here, Hetty. You've led a sheltered life here in the country, and so, for the most part, have our boys and girls. You've done that on the money I earned, and I like to think every penny of it was earned honestly and decently. You've enjoyed comfort and security, and we've built something worth having right here where we stand, and up at the yard, and out along the network. But what the devil is any of it worth if we take our stand alongside the people crucifying a man like Stead, for the crime of making us aware of our social responsibilities? You quote my duty to Alex and Giles at me, as if they could be matched with the twelve and thirteen-year-olds sold to goatish old satyrs whose sexual appetites have to be whetted on virgins. I don't give a damn how closely my name, or Debbie's, or yours, or the children's are tied to those of Stead and Bramwell Booth in this instance. I happen to believe in those articles, even if he went about getting his material clumsily and recklessly. Someone had to do it, and it might interest you to know that because of him Parliament is already passing a law to extend the age of consent to sixteen. And not before time, God damn it."

She was unconvinced. He realised that before she replied, calmly, "Well, there's your answer. Leave it to Parliament."

But he burst out, "Good God, woman! Do you suppose Parliament would have lifted a finger if it hadn't been shamed into it by people like Stead and Debbie? You ought to be damned proud of her. I am, and I wish I could find and tell her so!"

He stumped out then, undecided whether or not he had made the least impression on her but not caring either, for suddenly the serenity of 'Tryst' became abhorrent to him and he felt a desperate need to submerge himself in the stink and clamour of the yard. He went out to the stables and saddled his favourite mare, brushing aside Stillman's startled enquiry as to where he could be going so late in the day. Five minutes later he was heading through summer lanes towards Croydon, and as he rode, scenting honeysuckle from the overgrown hedgerows, he remembered another time he had lunged out of the house in the same way, in search of a compromise between his public and private life. It was the morning after Henrietta had tried to solace him the only way she knew how, after that blear-eyed little eunuch had been dragged from his chimney and laid on his hearthrug and he thought, bitterly, "Twenty years ago, by God! Luke Dobbs then and Eliza Armstrong today, and neither one qualifying for the protection of the most powerful state in the world!" But then, remembering Stead, and the power that resided in his pen, his spirits lifted a little and he said aloud, "I'll go to him and offer to help, damned if I don't!" and maintained a mile-consuming trot through the darkness until he saw the lights of the livery stable where he stabled his horse.

4

Tybalt was at the weigh-bridge when Adam returned from his breakfast visit to the coffee stand, a regular port of call whenever he spent a night in his turret.

He saw at once that the little clerk was more than usually agitated, for he was peering up and down the street like an anxious mother awaiting an overdue daughter from a party. The moment he spotted him he came trotting across the pavement, exclaiming, "My word, Mr. Swann, I'm relieved you came straight back! He's here! He's been here twenty minutes or more!" and then, with a fearful glance left and right, "I . . . er . . . took the liberty of showing him up, before anyone in the yard recognised him. I mean, it just wouldn't do, would it?" But Adam, not in the best of humours, growled, "What the hell are you blathering about? *Who's* here? *Who* have you shown up?" and Tybalt's face went blank as he said, "You mean you weren't expecting him? I thought, naturally . . . well, in the circumstances . . ." and then he fell into step as Adam strode across the yard and said, breathlessly, "Mr. *Stead*, sir! He came into the counting house asking for you . . . fortunately I was there alone, so I hustled out and showed him upstairs at once. Did I do right, sir? It seemed to me the wisest course . . ."

Adam stopped short at the foot of the stair. "Stead's here? Stead came calling?"

"Just after you left. He said you'd written."

"I'd written, but I had no reason to think . . . Yes, Tybalt, you did the right thing. You say nobody else spotted him?"

"Nobody, sir."

"Then make sure I'm not disturbed and when I blow down have a cab at the foot of the stairs."

"Yes, sir. Certainly, Mr. Swann," and he darted away, as though the mere presence of W. T. Stead on the premises would infect him with plague or, at the very least, attract a crowd that would trample him and his clerks underfoot.

*　　*　　*

He was standing over by the window, looking down on Adam's favourite view, the broad curve of the river between the bridge and the forest of masts on the south bank. He looked, Adam thought, like a man near the end of his tether. Hunted, tense and drained of energy and yet, if you watched the eyes, defiant and undefeated, still able, as he turned extending his hand, to summon a smile of recognition.

"I'm afraid I rattled your head clerk, Mr. Swann."

"It doesn't take much to rattle Tybalt."

He found himself doing a mental sum and surprising himself with the answer. Stead, as he knew, was twenty years his junior but no one, seeing them together now, would have believed it. At thirty-six the man looked in his mid-fifties, his beard streaked with grey, the mouth firmly compressed, as with pain he was just able to bear. "The poor devil is killing himself . . ." Adam thought and suddenly he was ashamed. Ashamed for himself and Tybalt, for Henrietta and everyone who jeered and cavilled and sniggered at what this North Country parson's son was about. There was even something shameful about his circumstances here. Fleeting and furtive, like a convict on the run, seeking someone from whom he could beg a meal and a refuge.

He said, more to soothe his own conscience than reassure Stead, "You don't have to apologise to me. For being here, I mean. I already deeply regret the tone of that letter I wrote. I was concerned

for Miss Avery, for, as I said, she's more than a daughter to me."
Then, "Why did you come, Mr. Stead? You could have written or
sent a messenger."

"I have the reputation of doing my own dirty work, Swann."

He spoke with bitterness, a depth of bitterness that Adam would
have thought uncharacteristic of the man.

"You're getting plenty of support."

"At a safe distance, yes. You've read the articles?"

"Very carefully."

He moved round the end of the desk where lay a pile of yesterday's newspapers. *Lloyd's News* and the *St. James' Gazette*, two
journals heading the hue and cry, were on the top of the pile. He
turned and looked across directly at Adam.

"I didn't answer your question. You're a man in a big way of
business. I don't have to tell you where your business interests stand
in the matter."

"You're used to finding yourself in a minority, but it's my experience that you'll win everybody over in the long run."

"Not this time," Stead said, and seemed to stagger, so that Adam
said, "For God's sake, man. Take a seat and let me offer you a drink."

He crossed to his cupboard and took out a bottle of brandy, pouring two measures. It occurred to him then that the editor was probably a teetotaller but it did not deter him. If ever a man needed a
stiff drink it was Stead. He pushed the glass across to him. Stead
said, leaving the drink on the blotter, "Concerning Babylon, Mr.
Swann, I assume you're among the uncommitted. Like most of my
regular readers."

"That depends."

"On how deeply Miss Avery is involved?"

"No, not on that. As I reminded my wife last night, Deborah is
thirty. At that age one should have made up one's mind on most
issues, wouldn't you say?"

"Yes, I would." The thin smile came and went again. "But you're
getting on for twice that age and still 'havering' as the Scots say.
How do you explain that, Mr. Swann?"

How did he explain it? How did it come about that he had read
every word of the Babylon articles, and every counter-charge laid
against Stead, but was still unable to make a clear-cut decision con-

cerning what seemed, on the face of it, a festering sore on the body of a nation that prided itself on its Christian ethics, that claimed, almost, to have invented freedom, justice, and the rights of the individual.

He said, thoughtfully, "I met one of the bloodhounds. A man called Burbage, watching my ward's lodgings on behalf of *Lloyd's News*. He implied that what one read in your newspaper or his was no more than the tip of an iceberg. Does that apply to the 'Maiden Tribute' series?"

Stead stooped and heaved a briefcase on to the desk. "Having made your acquaintance I came prepared."

He unlatched the catch and upended the case. A shower of documents cascaded on to the blotter, most of them written transcripts and newspaper cuttings. Here and there was what appeared to be a dossier, bound in covers, the size of a school exercise book. "It would take a busy man like you too long to sift this much evidence. Take your pick and ask any questions you choose. The answers are all here . . ." he tapped his forehead, "and likely to stay there until the day I die."

He was on shifting ground and knew it. Stead was not here to answer testy enquiries concerning Deborah. He had a more specific purpose in mind, involving not so much Deborah's loyalty but his own, a man who, long years ago, had raised hell about a dead chimney-sweep. He picked a dossier at random and read the title aloud, *"Case of Elsie Griddle, aged fifteen (Comparative portraits)."* He was aware of Stead's Old Testament eyes watching him and was almost grateful to Elsie Griddle, whoever she was. As long as he could avoid Stead's eyes he was uncommitted.

"Compare the two portraits, Swann."

The voice seemed to boom from a great distance but there was enough authority in it to make him wince. "God damn it," he thought, "what am I doing here, standing like a schoolboy with a botched lesson . . . this is *my* office, *my* headquarters . . . Did I invite the fellow here to hector me?" But it didn't feel like his office so much as a courtroom, with himself in the dock.

Elsie Griddle was featured in both sepia photographs and this was clear from the captions. Without them one would have been unlikely to connect the pictures, for the one on the right, underscored *Market Harborough, aged twelve,* was that of a chubby, pigtailed child in neatly-pressed clothes, staring into the camera with the half-mischievous expression that children seemed to take with them to photographers' studios. The other photograph, captioned, *Elsie. Aged fifteen, Maida Vale, 1885,* was of a sallow, unsmiling young woman in a hitched up skirt that exposed one gartered leg bare to the thigh. The upper half of her body was naked, save for a kind of turban and she was holding a tray of fruit. Her small breasts, supported by the edge of the tray, made nine of a row of seven pomegranates. The pose was not so much lewd as silly. It braced him, somehow, to meet Stead's glance.

"You compiled this case-history yourself?"

"I spent nine hours interviewing her, before we sent her on to Booth's Salvation Army shelter. It's all there, if you've time to read it."

"I'll read it. But first I should like to hear it from you."

Stead sat and carefully crossed his legs, the gesture implying that he was now so sure of his audience that he could afford to make light of Elsie Griddle. "It's not untypical. Given time I could produce a thousand Elsie Griddles. I thought she deserved a dossier because the police traced her parents by means of that earlier photograph."

"She's in prison now, as a prostitute?"

"She hanged herself, more than a month ago."

Adam looked back at the photographs, closed the file and laid it down. The silence in the room was embarrassing. Over in the tideway a tug hooted, its sharp, fussy blasts emphasising the nonstop grind of traffic heading north and south over the bridge. Somewhere below a vanboy laughed and the sound, in that heavy silence, was charged with mockery. He stumped over and slammed the window shut.

"Tell me about her."

Stead half-closed his eyes. Behind the crackle of Old Testament fire and brimstone, Adam thought he detected a showman dressing the stage, positioning the players, setting up the old Aunt Sallies, and he was as sharply aware of this as if Stead had been ringing a handbell and shouting, "Roll up! Roll up! The finest show in Babylon!" But somehow it didn't matter. It didn't matter a damn. What mattered was Elsie Griddle, a suicide at fifteen. That, and Stead's superb journalistic flair.

His mind returned to the second Babylon article, in which Stead had cited methods used to recruit child prostitutes.

"Was she employed at one of those stores or hooked at one of the servants' registry offices you wrote about?"

"No, she was recruited on her own doorstep."

"Then somebody paid her parents money?"

"It wasn't like that either. Her people were decent folk. Very poor, of course, but church going. They probably still are. As I said, this is just one case in a thousand. To follow through half of them one would need a hundred trained investigators. Elsie's pander posed as a curate, so where was the harm in allowing him to take Elsie and two other girls to London to see the sights? She had never been to London. Her mother saw her off. She saw her again, after they had cut her down. A matter for the police? Yes, it was that, of course. But what chance do the police have of tracing a man travelling under a false name and posing as a clergyman, when the trail is a year old? And even if they did, how would they set about proving a charge of abduction the way they intend to prove mine?"

"She must have been around fourteen then and there were three of them. When they realised what was expected of them . . . there must be other factors."

Stead, all showman now, opened his eyes, sat upright and banged so hard on the desk that everything on it quivered. "Good heavens, man, of course there were other factors! The other girls were taken off on some excuse by two well-dressed women. Elsie stayed with the 'curate', who bought her a meal in a restaurant off Leicester Square. He gave her two glasses of wine and when she complained of giddiness he whisked her upstairs. His client was waiting for her, in the best room in the house. An Asiatic from a foreign embassy, who would pay as much as ten guineas for a virgin. Elsie cost eight. The agent had his own way with her after the client had left."

"She could have gone home . . . gone to the police . . ."

"After two experiences such as that, and at ten o'clock on a winter's night in a strange city? Come now, Mr. Swann, you didn't make a fortune using that kind of logic."

"After that she went on the streets?"

"After that she was trained as a decoy. She had a spell in hospital with venereal disease, and another in gaol for soliciting. In my opinion, it wasn't either experience that drove her to suicide."

"What then?"

"The fact that she had been the means of trapping other girls. That was brought home to her at the Salvation Army shelter, and I should have foreseen it. She wasn't ready for the impact. She needed time to adjust. You never think of these things until afterwards."

He stood up. "I still haven't mentioned what I came here to tell you, Swann. Miss Avery is due at Southampton this afternoon, with that child Lily there's been all the fuss about. I botched that too, as you'll learn when the warrants are out."

"Warrants? Against you?"

"Me, Bramwell Booth, Mrs. Jarrett, who was a procuress but has been working with us for years, and one of my reporters."

"Deborah too?"

"No. She played a walk-on part this time. They won't charge Deborah."

"They won't charge any of you. How could they? Your motives were never in doubt, not even among your most powerful enemies."

"They'll charge us none the less. The law has been passed now and they can't afford not to."

"But that's monstrous! You got the Criminal Amendment Bill on the Statute Book."

He seemed to expand momentarily. "Yes, I did. It's a beginning, I suppose."

He seemed indecisive for a moment. Finally he said, "Miss Avery and the child will come ashore without publicity. My information is they haven't traced their movements in France. If you wanted to accompany me to Southampton we could travel in separate compartments and the press wouldn't connect us. Would you care to do that?"

"No. I've correspondence to attend to . . . Would you trust this material in my charge for forty-eight hours? I could undertake to return it by registered post."

"Why not?" He smiled, bleakly. "The tip of the iceberg isn't the lethal part, Mr. Swann. Could your clerk find me a cab?"

"He's under orders to." He crossed to the speaking tube, blew into it and gave Tybalt the instruction. Stead watched him, his stance and expression still indicating a certain indecision.

Adam said, "It's my opinion that you still haven't said what you came here to say. Would it help if I told you that the correspondence I had in mind is concerned with what came out of that briefcase?"

"Possibly." He shifted his weight from one foot to the other. "See here. I'll appeal, if I have to, but I'm hanged if I'll beg! You said just now that I have plenty of support and so I have. But it's support from the committed, people who are already bracketed with me. The cranks, you understand, Mr. Swann? It's not the cranks who count in the end. This society is divided down the middle, as you'll have decided for yourself if you followed this controversy as carefully as I think you have. The cranks on one side, the laissez-faire battalions on the other. But there's a third group holding back and they're the people who'll decide this issue, and all similar issues in the future. I take it you are not a religious man, Mr. Swann? You don't believe in a Creator, in a spiritual purpose, an after-life?"

"I've never been sure, one way or the other. I'm resigned to uncertainty. Cheerfully, I might add, for there are enough problems here in all conscience."

"One of Bradlaugh's ilk," Stead said, "and I don't quarrel with that. 'There is more faith in honest doubt than in half the creeds . . .'" He was at the door now his hand on the latch. "I'm tired of leading the committed, Swann. The Booths, the Josephine Bakers. The Cardinal Mannings, even. The enemy has adjusted to them, you understand? They recognise their tactics and head them off without much trouble. We need back-stabbers now. Defectors, if you like, from inside the citadel. Men who have made their pile without compromising themselves. They exist but I only know one and I'm looking at him."

He raised his hand in farewell and then he was gone, descending the stairs lightly so that Adam was not sure of his departure until he heard hoofclops in the yard below.

He turned back to the desk, seating himself, swallowing Stead's

540

untouched brandy and then, methodically, sorting through the odds and ends the editor had tipped from his case. He read each of them carefully. Once, twice, three times. And every now and again he made notes on a scratch-pad. He sat there a long time undisturbed, having warned Tybalt to leave him in peace. Then, having sealed Stead's material in two large envelopes, he took sheets of headed note-paper and wrote two letters, one brief, the other covering three and a half pages of Swann-crested stationery.

The first, addressed 'Mr. Burbage, c/o *Lloyd's Newspaper*' was no more than a note. It said, "Dear Mr. Burbage, You may recall me as 'Mr. Smith'. We met outside the lodgings of Miss Avery, in Frederick Street. It would seem to me time to declare myself as Miss Avery's guardian and state in writing my position concerning her efforts on behalf of Mr. W. T. Stead. I am, as you will see from the heading, a regular advertiser in your publication. Or rather I was, for I no longer care to associate myself with a journal whose aim it has been over the last few weeks to denigrate a man who has my unswerving support. Sincerely, Adam Swann, Man. Dir. Swann-on-Wheels."

It was an easy letter to compose. The other, addressed to *The Times* as the most neutral of the London papers, occupied him the better part of two hours. He was never very relaxed with a pen in his hand. Composition demanded patience, and he had always been short on patience. At last, however, it was done, a forthright declaration of intent, set down without emotional stress of the kind one of Stead's 'committed' would be likely to use in respect of the contents of those buff envelopes. For he had taken Stead's point. Back-stabbers are not required to use ornamental daggers. A bread knife will do; or a butcher's cleaver. Only in the final paragraph did he allow himself the luxury of a flourish when he wrote, after five drafts, "Mr. Stead, by direct inference, has linked the capital of the British Empire with Babylon. After examining his evidence, much of it unpublished and unpublishable, it is my opinion he does Babylon an injustice. For Babylon, so far as I am aware, was free of cant. It flourished centuries before St. Augustine arrived in England."

For a man unfamiliar with the trick of putting his abstract thoughts on paper it had, he thought, a certain impact but he felt no personal satisfaction as he read it over, folded the sheets and addressed the envelope. He was only conscious, as never before, of needing a bath.

5

He was not much surprised to find Deborah waiting up for him when he returned home an hour after dark. Or, for that matter, to hear from her that Henrietta had gone to bed, after a restrained greeting and a somewhat embarrassing supper. Auntie was tired and upset, Deborah reported. Uncle Adam was having one of his moods. Uncle Adam had flounced off the night before. Auntie should be thoroughly used to this kind of display on his part, but she had discovered she was not. It was some time now since he had engaged in a sulk that properly belonged in the nursery, where the tantrums lived.

This at least coaxed a grin from him as he ate his cold veal and ham pie, and drank half a bottle of claret, topped off by what Deborah regarded as a very generous cognac. She said, watching him with a flicker of amusement, "I gather it was all on account of me," and he said it was, but added that since then the issue had broadened somewhat to include himself.

"How do you mean? You haven't seen her in twenty-four hours." And then as he went on eating, "Do you want me to tell you my part in it now? Where I've been and what I've been about? That was what Stead had in mind when he gave me my marching orders as soon as I stepped ashore at Southampton."

No, he said, her part in it could wait upon tomorrow's *Times*. "You'll realise then I'm in as deep as you are. Go to bed. You must be exhausted."

She took this as it was meant, a signal of dismissal and kissed him just above the right ear. "I'll keep out of the way in the morning. The last thing I should ever want was to come between you two."

"You'll never do that," he said, "for I'm still the gaffer here and don't any of you ever forget it! Apart from that I've got my strategy organised, and your aunt never had any to match it on big issues. Did you ever think otherwise, all the years you've lived here?"

"Never once," she said, "but you scared us sometimes by pretending to abdicate."

He thought about that, smiling as he went upstairs and taking no pains, as he usually did when she retired before him, to tread silently. It was not difficult to advertise his approach in this way. Every stair and every floor-board at 'Tryst' had an individual note of protest. Some, he was fond of saying, could play a madrigal.

She must have been sleeping soundly, however, for when he lit the dressing-table lamp he saw her lying with one hand pushed under the pillow and the bedclothes half thrown back. She was breathing deeply and regularly, so that he paused to look down at her, telling himself that it was remarkable how effortlessly she defied the years. She still had the pink and white complexion of a girl, and her tawny bedtime plaits, one spread across her shoulders, the other concealed in a dip of the pillow, held no traces of grey. Her lips were slightly parted, showing her small regular teeth, twenty-nine of them still perfect as she had boasted a day or so ago, when he complained about a forthcoming visit to the dentist. What was that Debbie had said? There were times when he pretended to abdicate in her favour? Well, it was a half-truth, he supposed, as far as 'Tryst' and the family were concerned, and they had even struck some kind of bargain about it that night at the George more than twenty years ago, when he had come home to her with a flea in his ear, put there by Edith Wadsworth, and learned from the Colonel that she had been playing the fool with that young gunner. But real abdication had never been thought of seriously, for she wasn't that kind of woman. When it came down to it she wouldn't have felt properly married if he hadn't bullied her now and again.

The sight of her lying there in that great Conyer bed soothed him, prompting a tenderness he hadn't felt for her downstairs. She looked so young and strong, and so—what was the right word—wholesome? He supposed he was the more aware of this because he had been grubbing about in the midden all day. He bent and kissed her on the nose and she stretched, rolled over and opened her eyes.

One of the things he had always envied her was her ability to emerge from a deep sleep into full wakefulness in a matter of seconds. It always took him ten minutes or more to come to terms with daylight.

He noted that she was pleased to see him and pleased to be awakened in that manner. It relieved them both of tiresome explanations, of the chitter-chatter most married couples would need in similar circumstances. She said, sitting up, "What time is it?" and when he told her an hour after midnight, "I didn't expect you back for a day or so. Debbie's here."

"I know. She waited up."

"You've had your supper? There was a veal and ham pie . . ."

"I've finished it. I was damned hungry."

She smiled then so that he thought, "Why the devil did I waste time working out an approach. People like us shouldn't bother with approaches . . . that's for courting couples, poor devils . . ." And suddenly her pertness and prettiness made a fresh appeal to him and he threw his arms round her and kissed her mouth, holding the kiss until she squirmed and gasped that he was badly in need of a shave. It was only her time-honoured way of teasing him, however, for even as she said it she levered herself into a kneeling position, put both arms about his neck and said, gaily, "I really think I might have been a little rude to poor Debbie. If she isn't asleep I'll go tuck her in," so that he laughed and said, "You'll do no such thing. For God's sake get it into your head that she isn't a child any longer. Besides, what passed was between you and me and it's settled now, as you'll see for yourself when Stillman brings *The Times* from the village tomorrow. Providing they print my letter, that is."

"*You* wrote a letter to *The Times*?"

"Supporting Stead, and no bones about it. I'm sorry if it annoys Alexander's colonel, and Giles has to apologise for me to his prospective father-in-law, but they'll get over it. If they don't they can keep their damned favours, the pair of them. I have enough trouble with my own conscience, and my wife into the bargain!"

She did not seem particularly interested in his commitment. Either she had had time to think about it, and had dismissed the entire subject as too dull to bother about, or her mind was on something more immediate. She said, with a shrug, "Well, I daresay you know what you're about. Blow out the lamp and come to bed. You needn't bother to shave, either. I'd sooner be sandpapered than lose myself in this great bed. It's like a desert when you're away. I was hours getting to sleep last night. I cried, too, after you'd stormed off in that way. It was like—well, never mind, do as I say."

He was tempted then to take her at her word but thought better of it. "I'll shave," he said, "while you take a quick look at this. I got it from Stead when he called on me this morning."

That did rattle her a little but he went on, quickly, "It won't take a minute to read, and might help you to understand why I broke my golden rule by writing to a newspaper," and he took Elsie Griddle's dossier from his pocket, laid it on the bed and went into his dressing-room.

She called, "You'll need hot water," but he called back, "It's luke-warm in the can. The temperature was still in the seventies when I left town."

After that there was silence, broken only by the rasp of his razor, the soft flutter of turning pages and once, as he stepped out of his breeches, a stifled exclamation from her, coinciding almost exactly with a nightjar's screech from the paddocks. She was still reading when he came back into the bedroom.

"Well?"

"It's awful," she said, "too awful to think about." Then, "Why did you have to give it to me now? I was so gay and happy when I woke up and found you were back."

"It'll save a lot of tiresome explanation in the morning. At least you'll have an attitude of mind when the children start asking questions. They'll surely do that when they see that letter I've written."

"Nonsense! I've never seen any of them except Giles open *The Times*, and he's sure to side with you."

"One of the servants will tell them. Then they'll all read it, take it from me."

"Suppose they do. If you're not there what on earth could I tell them if they did ask?"

"The truth, what else? We don't want them growing up as green as you were, do we?"

She said, looking at the two photographs again, "Fifteen. That's Helen's age. And I still think of her as a child. *Adam?*"

"Well?"

"What's wrong? In this way, I mean. Whatever makes some men find pleasure in . . . well . . . haven't they children of their own?"

"Some have. But they wouldn't be likely to confuse them with Elsie Griddle."

"I didn't know," she said. "That's all I can say. I just didn't know. Most women wouldn't, would they?"

"Most British women wouldn't. That was one of the points Stead was trying to make. If they had let him make it, without falling on him like a pack of wolves, I wouldn't have joined in, Deborah or no Deborah."

"But they wouldn't?"

"No. They're out there now, crucifying him and licking their slobbering lips over it. He seems to think they'll go as far as prosecuting him, though personally I doubt if they'll oblige him to that extent."

"If they did, would Debbie be involved?"

"No. He was man enough to guard against that."

"But surely . . . I mean . . . if a man publishing a newspaper gets hold of things like this, isn't it his job to make them public? To see everybody knows about it and stop it happening? What I mean is, those girls in houses and on the streets, the ones you've told me about, they're different, aren't they? I've always thought of them as women, old enough to do as they please, even though it always did strike me as quite dreadful that anyone could . . . well, sell themselves in that way, to a lot of different men, *all* kinds of men. I mean, it's hard to imagine anything worse from a woman's viewpoint and difficult too to imagine most men would want that kind of woman. It can't be the same, can it? Not like you and me, all these years?"

"No," he said, "not like that in any way at all. But we've been lucky in that respect. I've always told you so, haven't I?"

"Tell me something else, then."

"Yes?"

"Would *you* get any pleasure out of using a girl like Elsie Griddle? Would you?"

"Now? No, I wouldn't. But I might have once."

"When?"

"Before I learned about women from you."

She sat up, her mouth slightly agape.

"*You* learned anything from *me*?"

"A great deal."

She was deeply interested now, and flattered too, if the sparkle in her eye was anything to judge by.

"Tell me then. Tell me what difference I made, for I always thought of myself as a perfect goose in that way, and as ignorant as a baby about men. Sometimes I think I still am, in spite of having a long family. Is that what you mean about altering your outlook? Being a father, I mean?"

"No. The children are incidental."

"Then tell me. That's something I should like to hear. Any wife would, even after all these years."

He sat on the edge of the bed, looking down at her. As always on these occasions she seemed to him unchanged in any marked respect from the saucy girl he had hoisted into the saddle on the moor all those years ago, a little hoyden chock-full of impudence but capable of any amount of impulsive affection that she had used to light the lonely recesses of his heart. And even that was not all. She had brought him a loyalty equal to any he had ever enjoyed in the field, so that he had always been able to think of her, even on the many occasions she had infuriated him, as a comrade. Without her what would he have made of his life? Would he have survived those early years, when it was touch and go from one day to another? Would he have thrown it all over in a fit of pique, returned to soldiering and taken the easier road to half-pay and the sidelines, like so many Swanns before him? There were so many imponderables. He might have made a god of money, like most of his contemporaries. He might even have married some desiccated girl for her money and grown into one of those old goats who found a few moments' forgetfulness between the legs of strays like Elsie Griddle. None of these things had happened to him and it came to him now, not for the first time perhaps, that her gaiety, youth and steadfastness had given shape and sanity to his life, regulating the demands of his body and bringing so much warmth and willingness to the exercise that his spirit had been set free to range and develop in a never-ending quest for an identity. It would not be possible, of course, to explain this to her in those terms, but there was something he could tell her that might help her to understand the contribution she had made to his life.

He said, "You asked just now what kind of man would pay money for an hour or so with a half-grown child of that kind. Not necessarily the kind you imagine. The desperately lonely, maybe, with no aim beyond physical gratification. I should know, for I was one of them once. Years before I met you, when I was in Scutari after that shambles in the Crimea, I paid a Turkish pimp for the use of a Circassian girl no older than Elsie Griddle. It wasn't quite the same, perhaps. She had been schooled as a harlot before I met her. They have a different approach out there. Cruel and callous it might appear to Westerners, but kinder in the long run, if only because it's traditional. I tell you that now because I wouldn't care to have you think of me as a man incapable of such an act, and because it's important that you shouldn't undervalue your part in my life. If I've been faithful to you all these years it's to your credit, Hetty, not mine, for the plain truth is, in all that time, I've never wanted to bed another woman, a stranger. That's the most valuable byproduct of marriage, I imagine, a growing together so that ultimately, at our time of life, two people are virtually one. It's been that way with me at all events, and sounds pompous when it's put into words. A poet might make a soufflé of it but I'm no poet. I sense these things but I never find a way to express them well. I follow my instincts and instinct has governed my approach to you from the beginning. You had what I wanted and needed and were always prepared to give, freely and unconditionally. Why should a man with that need a harlot, trained or untrained? Do you follow that?"

"Yes, I understand, but there's more isn't there?"

"Aye, there is that. It wouldn't have worked if you had fallen back on that mock-modesty they've been cultivating in women, married and single, over here for the last couple of generations. Maybe that's the real root of the trouble. A full-blooded man wants a bit more from a woman than complacency, and when he doesn't find it at home he goes looking for it elsewhere. That's why, to my way of thinking, the British are less moral in the real sense of the word than other tribes. They expect prudery and carnality from the same woman at the same time and what the devil can that lead to but hypocrisy in a marriage? It was time someone like Stead opened the window."

He stopped, aware that he had been addressing himself rather than her, and feeling a little foolish when he realised that she could have understood no more than the drift of what he was trying to say. He was not surprised therefore to see her smiling, as though instead of struggling to enlighten her, he had set himself to amuse her. She said, "You do make it sound frightfully complicated, Adam. Even more than before I was married and had to rely on guesses. Put out the lamp and come to bed."

"Damn it, woman," he said, "you did ask me to try and explain, didn't you?"

"You paid me the nicest compliment," she said, "and I was fishing for a few more. All I seem to have hooked is a lecture and it's far too late for lectures."

He turned his back on her then, partly to unstrap his leg but also to hide a grin. "Twenty-seven years married," he thought, "and I still waste breath trying to teach her more than she cares to know," and was confirmed in the view when, as he balanced himself beside the bed preparatory to lowering himself, he heard her pulling her nightgown over her head. She had always done that when she needed him, ever since an occasion in the early days of their marriage when he had compared its rucked-up folds to a bundling bag.

Yet he misjudged her for all that. She had understood, more or less, what he was trying to say and might, indeed, have expressed it more directly, although only to herself, with whom she had held so many interesting conversations on this absorbing subject since the first night he had held her in his arms. She cared about the Elsie Griddles of this world. Anyone with daughters of their own was obliged to care, she supposed, but she was neither tempted nor equipped to cross parochial frontiers into the territory of the Steads and the Deborahs who, unlike Adam, seemed incapable of striking a balance between the general and the particular. On reflection, and in the light of that pitiful story he had brought home as evidence of his own commitment, she was prepared to admit she had been a fool to quarrel with him on such an issue. He was right, too, to dismiss repercussions that sprang to mind concerning Alex's promotion, and Giles' engagement to that predatory little miss, Romayne. If those concerned hadn't the good sense to see both as boys worth their salt then so much the worse for them.

He was beside her now and his arms were round her, but with

half her mind she was still able to conjure with fancies prompted by that extraordinary admission of his concerning her role in his life. In so many ways men were unbelievably dense and he was no exception, or not when it came to evaluating the mechanics of a partnership such as theirs. Was he really such a fool as to imagine that she was primarily concerned with solacing him when he had her in an embrace, with the door slammed shut on the Steads, the Deborahs, the choked chimney-sweeps, the ravaged Elsie Griddles, and even the long row of children that had resulted from their frolics in this bed? Did it never occur to him, for all his years of experience as her mate, that she had her own moments of exultation, that they were not merely physical but were nonetheless capable of transforming her into a person of tremendous consequence, who could patronise every other woman she had ever known or read about? He had his bonuses, she supposed, but they were paltry compared to hers. The act of possessing could surely never equal the act of being possessed, for how could it gorge the ego, as hers was gorged every single time she inflated him and emptied his mind of all those weighty concerns he lugged about with him all day and seemed unable to shed until the moment he could run his hand the length of her spine, fondle her buttocks, feed on her mouth and breasts and ultimately, usually too soon for her liking, spend himself between her thighs and slip away into his own world again, until the moment came when physical awareness of her would reduce him to the same state of servitude. That was real power, power of a kind no man born of woman ever had or ever could exercise, whereas she had it in abundance, would always have it so far as he was concerned, and wanted for nothing more.

Lying there, still locked in his embrace, she thought she could tell him things about marriage, and love within marriage, that would amaze him, but there it was, nothing would be gained by divulging her secrets, for one of the facts she had learned about men from him, and from his regular handling of her, was that they could never, ever, surrender the role of the aggressor, or regard themselves as anything other than the hunter and initiator. Why not let them live and die with this harmless fiction?

Part Four

ONRUSH

1

Time Miracle

It seemed to Adam, pottering doggedly about his concerns, that the pattern of his life was a long, uneven haul across a varying landscape, with an ascent here and a descent there, interspersed by long, flattish stages that could dull the senses and impair his judgement, so that a jolt, or a series of jolts, would leave him baffled and self-abusive, telling himself he had been a fool to lower his guard. For in his world, a world of catch-as-catch-can, to lower one's guard was to invite a bloody nose.

It had always been this way. He could look back on a dozen occasions when he had been caught napping on the box, and had had the devil's own job to prevent him and his concerns being run down or tumbled into a ditch. The financial crisis of the early 'sixties blew up out of a serene sky. So did the rail crash that cost him a leg, and after that, down the long, busy reaches of the 'sixties and 'seventies, there had been any number of rapids and collisions, cross currents and shoals. But always, being by nature a cautious optimist, he had backed himself to level out, adapting to new stresses in the way that had proved so successful when he shed most of his packload by making the managers custodians of their own pocket. As to the family, with the watchful Henrietta as his sergeant-major, he was still confident it could be chivvied along without much trouble and taught, in time, to look to itself, as he had had to do when he was younger and less wary.

The period between the late summer of 1885 and the early spring of 1887 was a passage over level ground. He was approaching his sixties then and inclined, more and more, to take the leisurely conciliatory course, prompted by his private philosophy that nothing mattered much, or not so long as a man retained his dignity and continued to trust his own judgement far beyond the judgement of others. Out along the network things prospered, and at home, after that one brush with Henrietta over Debbie's involvement in Stead's campaign, life went off the boil, nothing dire resulting from his enlistment in the social sanitary squad. Most people, he supposed, were getting a better social focus these days, were coming to understand that the counting-house was not the power-house of tribal concerns but only the repository. Tub-thumpers like Stead, Booth and that woman Butler were making a noticeable impact on the national conscience and this, in turn, was being reflected at Westminster, where some kind of compromise was emerging between the thunderers like Gladstone and the inheritors of Palmerston's *laissez-faire* society, men like Salisbury, who had just sent his rival packing.

In the meantime, in contrast to politicians who were obliged to promise miracles, the men of affairs, men of his ilk, occasionally achieved them. They had just driven tunnels under the Mersey and the Severn. A spread of new docks had been built down river at Tilbury, to handle the ever-increasing volume of Far Eastern trade. Catesby's dream of the 'fifties and 'sixties, the creation of a federalised workers' force strong enough and united enough to strike bargains with the captains of industry, was all but fact. The final nails were being driven into the coffin of the eighteenth-century pastoral economy by the arrival from dominions overseas of the first cargoes of frozen mutton. In short, after a frightening wobble or two, the British had resumed course, the only course open to them now if truth were told. For under the flag of Free Trade they could continue to smelt, delve and fashion for half the world, while the laggards of the era packed the holds of British vessels with the cheap food it would not pay home-based farmers to grow. Son-in-law Denzil Fawcett might rumble and grumble over this but, for himself, he faced up to it, had always faced up to it, ever since he had first read of Stephenson's iron road between Manchester and Liverpool, completed when he was a toddler.

As for the rest of the world, with its incessant clamour and its sporadic attempts to challenge British enterprise and British expertise, that was well lost so far as he was concerned. Sitting high in his truncated tower, overlooking the busiest river in the world, he had time, these days, to scan the foreign as well as the home news in the armful of journals that appeared on his desk each morning. What he read in them confirmed him in his belief that foreigners, one and all, were a noisy, clownish, posturing bunch, too occupied in striking attitudes to make a success of big-scale commercial pursuits. Sometimes their antics irritated him, exacerbating his impatience with the human race, but more often they amused him, so that he came to see them as a raggle-taggle assortment of anarchists, organ-grinders, sabre-clankers, peasants, pot-bellied, purple-cheeked trombonists and mountebanks of one kind or another who would rather spend themselves throwing double somersaults and quarrelling outside taverns than roll up their sleeves and settle to an honest day's toil.

At times like this his arrogance and self-sufficiency would inflate him to proportions when he could laugh at himself as well as at Continentals. There was that great land Russia, good for something, he supposed, although he wasn't sure what, for there it was, grinding along at the pace of a mediaeval cart, its progress punctuated every now and again with the crack of the assassin's pistol or the blast of a homemade bomb. How would that end, he wondered? In a modern Jacquerie most likely, with smoke rising from country houses, and Cossacks carving a path through street demonstrators. And then, nearer home, were France and Germany, still glaring at one another over the twitching corpse of Alsace-Lorraine, both taking out insurance against a renewal of the 1870 debacle. Well, the country would keep clear of that, he hoped. He had never expected much of France, with its out-dated conception of glory, and its tendency, every year or so, to rip up the paving-stones and proclaim a new constitution, but Germany was beginning to disappoint him. After all, the Germans were Anglo-Saxons, and Bismarck, Prussian boor that he was, had the makings of a statesman. Adam had even been impressed by his social reforms and even more by the Reichstag's recent refusal to give the military clique a blank cheque, but things had taken a turn for the worse since that ass Wilhelm had pushed his ailing father out of the limelight and taken to swaggering here, there and everywhere with that absurd eagle-crested helmet, and a gilded breastplate that wouldn't stop a slug from a Sikh's muzzle-loader. Further south the Habsburgs were on the way out, so they said, playing a muted second fiddle to Hohenzollern brass, and that meant the

Balkans were due to erupt any day and bring down the moribund Ottoman empire.

And then there was America, the up and coming country some said, but he wasn't so sure. There was plenty of space out there, and God knows how many mineral sources to be tapped once they organised their transport system, and stopped murdering one another. There was a sound Anglo-Saxon base too, with any number of thrustful immigrants, younger sons with their way to make flooding into the country, so they might do better than most; providing, of course, they standardised their language and banished the spittoon.

There was less stability to be looked for nearer home in Ireland, devil take the place, for who would have thought a bunch of ragged-arsed Paddies could split the British Liberal party down the middle and hold Parliament to ransom?

Well, thank God the country's real health didn't depend on what was said and done in that debating society a mile or so up the river. He knew and they knew that Britain's position in the world depended on men like himself and his customers within the square mile, and in a dozen or so cities dotted about the network between Clyde and Thames. The rest (with the exception of the Navy) was mere window-dressing, as he had often told young Giles, still inclined to take politicians at face value. Commerce and cannon. That was all that counted when it came to dealing with Russians and Turks, with men who strutted about in eagle-crested helmets and breastplates, with idiots who pulled up paving-stones when something was not to their liking. There was the Navy and behind the ironclads the Bank of England. And behind the Bank a trained reserve, as it were, a hundred thousand adventurers like himself, who had long since decided what made the world go round. As long as they attended to their business the peace of Waterloo would continue and foreigners might do as they pleased with one another, and with such tracts of desert and jungle as were going begging when the British had posted their 'keep out' notices.

There were some, Gladstone among them, who would have called a halt to overseas expansion and a time, Adam reflected, when he would have agreed with them. But that was before he had made his pile, and poked his long nose into half the factories and foundries of the land. He was a dedicated Imperialist now, he supposed, although by no means as starry-eyed about Imperialism as some, seeing it as a bazaar rather than a mission, and assessing each new slice of red on the map in terms of money in the bank ten or twenty years from now. Providing, of course, that the spoilers were prepared to take the long view, and put something in before milking it dry and making new enemies in the process. It was for this reason, he supposed, that he had sided with the Holy Joes over that Maiden Tribute business. An empire was like a firm. To yield a steady return it needed more than a planted flag, a few hard-bitten mercenaries, and a Bible-spouting general like Gordon. It demanded imaginative investment, well-guarded channels of communication and, above all, a trained work force that was aware, every hour of every day, which side its bread was buttered. That, to his way of thinking, was the prescription that had given Britain its place in the sun over the last fifty years. It had all begun as a sordid scramble, of course, with the weak going to the wall, but that hadn't lasted long. There had always been a sufficient number of clearheaded idealists on hand to scrape the maggots from the fruit, and encourage the penny-an-hour vineyard workers to think of themselves as potential shareholders, so that an idiot like the Czar, who declared strikes illegal, deserved nothing better than a bomb splinter up his backside, if only to teach his successor that you couldn't treat men like cattle and still expect the best from them. Even in Belgium, so Reuters told him, the military were shooting strikers in the street, whereas in Berlin those who 'spoke ill of the Kaiser' were slapped into gaol, as if everyone was living in the days of the Star Chamber and Holy Office. Britain's dominance of world markets wasn't simply a matter of Free Trade (although that was important) it was equally dependent on Free Speech and a Free Press, on the right of anyone with a grievance to air it, at the top of his voice if necessary. If you gave him leave to do that he would get the bile off his stomach instead of spilling it in an anarchist's cellar. This much had been learned over here a generation ago, and it was logical to assume that, given time, other tribes and federations of tribes would learn it. Until they did, however, they would continue to drag their feet, shaking impotent fists at the Channel, and short-changing any Englishman who was fool enough to cross it in the belief that he could learn anything to his advantage over there.

Meantime, with the Jubilee looming up, there was no harm in a bit of advertising, of the kind the event promised to provide in good measure. The thought reminded him to make a draft of a memo concerning it that he intended to send out to the regions. There would be a smart run on bunting, and red, white and blue ribbons come the spring, and he was advising the managers to buy in advance. He was no blind worshipper of royalty. Sometimes he thought of Victoria as an insufferable bore. But that was no reason why his waggons and Clydesdales should not make as fine a show as anyone's come the Day.

So he pondered, sitting tight in his eyrie looking down on the curve of the river. Obdurate, prejudiced, utterly self-sufficient, and thoroughly typical of all of his kind crowded into that vast, dung-smelling capital.

2

Sixteen or so miles to the south-east Henrietta was also stocktaking but her thoughts, as always, moved in a narrower circle. She was not much concerned with Romanoffs and Hohenzollerns, with trends in trade, or the scramble for Africa, and in this sense she was even more of an isolationist than Adam, her world being 'Tryst', and the brood that had been hatched there. For smugness, however, there was little to choose between them as the firm and family moved along the level stretch of 'eighty-five and 'eighty-six, and into the first weeks of Jubilee year.

The period began uncertainly for Henrietta. No sooner had she made her peace with him over that Maiden Tribute nonsense than she came to believe she had arrived at the menopause and the certainty of this, as summer gave way to autumn, caused her more initial worry than it need have done, for she had been exchanging gossip concerning its manifestations for many years now, The Change being a popular topic among the middle-aged marrieds the moment the men and children were out of earshot.

She soon realised, of course, that she could discount nineteen-twentieths of the tittle-tattle relayed to her by women a few years her senior. As always, in matters of this kind, they were soon seen to be liars or ninnies, with their ridiculous jeremiads of fainting fits, loss of memory, ungovernable fits of rage, depression, sleeplessness and even, God forgive them, mental breakdowns necessitating temporary removal from husband and family.

Not one of these dire prophecies had substance so far as she was concerned. All were seen to be as far-fetched as the old wives' tales fed her long ago concerning the alleged indignities of the marriage bed. Apart from a few hot flushes, and an increased impatience with the younger children and the maids, she hardly realised the change had caught up with her, whereas Adam, bless his heart, had been quick to notice and sympathise. No one could be more tolerant in this kind of field, as she had told herself many times over the last thirty years. Most women would have found it excessively embarrassing to raise the subject with their doctor, much less their husband, but he was prepared to joke about it, telling her it was years since he had seen her blush, and afterwards packing her off to the doctor, having smoothed the ground in advance.

That same night, when she showed him a bottle of the medicine old Dr. Birtles had given her, he sniffed it and said, gaily, "Well, I daresay you'll get through it with very little trouble. For my part I'm relieved to learn we've bolted the door on the stragglers. Nine is more than enough and I've heard they have a tendency to slip through at a minute to twelve." He looked at her fondly, "It wouldn't have bothered you if we had made it a baker's dozen, would it?" and she admitted that it would not, although it did occur to her that another baby, at her time of life, might have been a great nuisance, for it would have prevented their summer treks around the regions, an annual expedition she enjoyed immensely, especially when good weather enabled them to cover long distances in the waggonette.

She said, as she was getting into bed, "It isn't . . . well . . . it won't make any difference to us, will it?" and he replied, with feigned innocence, "Just how do you mean, dear?"

"You know perfectly well what I mean!" she snapped, and that made him laugh in the way he invariably did at any hint of modesty on her part.

"Well, it certainly won't affect me," he said, "for I'm spry enough, thank God. As to you, I can't say. I've not noticed any loss of interest lately," and she said he was beyond redemption but kissed him gratefully and went on to enquire if it was true that there was an equivalent change in men when they entered their fifties.

"I've always thought there was," he said, with a seriousness that took her by surprise, "but it's not a physical change. More of a change of heart, such as I had when I made up my mind I was carrying too much responsibility and passed some of it to those rascals in the provinces. You could call it a loss of drive, I suppose—no, not that exactly, more of a change of direction. At my time of life a man tends to look around and ask himself what he intends to do with what's left."

It was only rarely she had heard him talk in these terms, even in jest. Ever since she had known him, a matter of almost thirty years now, he had been utterly dedicated to that complex centred on the Thames-side slum. She said, doubtingly, "I can't see you devoting yourself to anything new, Adam. It'll always be that yard and those cronies of yours. If you turned your back on it all whatever would you do with yourself all day?"

"I'd start fresh right here," he said, unexpectedly. "I'd make this place something to set tongues wagging all over the south-east. A showpiece, that's what I'd make of it, and one of the most impressive of its kind in the land."

"You mean like Lord de L'Isle's place over at Penshurst, or Knowle House, in Sevenoaks?" But this only made him laugh.

"Good God, no! Nothing on that scale, woman. I haven't got that kind of capital lying around and even if I had it would go into the network. What I have in mind is something more intimate—cosier if you like, with landscaping and furniture and pictures typical of the English domestic arts over the three centuries the house has stood here. Something as unique as the network to hand over to Alex, or whoever takes on from us. Giles is the more natural heir, I suppose, for he's the only one among them with real taste to my way of thinking. Maybe Alex wouldn't care to settle here permanently, and George certainly wouldn't, so I daresay they could make some kind of arrangement after I'd gone."

"Well, don't talk as if you were in your dotage," she said. "Fifty-nine isn't old, and I've never known you spend a day abed since your accident."

"No," he said, "that's so, and I may even be good for another twenty years, given luck. But that isn't what I meant. It's not just a matter of furnishings, and keeping an eye open for good landscapes and portraits going cheap at the auctions. It's leaving something permanent. Trees, for instance."

"Trees? We've already got scores of trees, haven't we?"

"Yes, we have, but they're all English trees, oaks, beeches and elms mostly. I'd like to plant exotic trees, of the kind that do so well over here. Incense cedars, Hinoki and Sawara cypresses, Californian redwoods, Grecian and Himalayan firs, and Monterey pines. We could have a wonderful spread down at the foot of the paddocks and some of them are fairly quick growing. By the time I took my final look out of that window they'd be a rare sight, I can tell you."

That was one of the rewarding things about Adam Swann, she decided. You never stopped learning about him. Until this moment she had no idea he was even interested in trees and certainly none that he could talk about them knowledgeably. It took her a few moments to absorb his plan and assess the probability of him achieving it. She said, after a lengthy pause, "You really are the oddest man, Adam, but it's a pleasant thought. Do you know what? I think you ought to go about it at once. Where could you buy trees of that sort?" but, to her annoyance, he was asleep, and again she envied him the trick of slipping away so effortlessly, supposing it to be a legacy of his campaigning years, wasted years so far as she was concerned, for that was a time before she had the extraordinary good fortune to be thrown from a trap and abandoned on a moor in the middle of a thunderstorm. Did ever a few flickers of lightning bring a woman that much luck?

3

His talk of succession fired a train of speculative thought in her mind, so that she became a little absent-minded over the next few days, making an inventory of the family in a way she hadn't done for quite some time. Taken all round, she decided, it was as satisfactory a balance sheet as he was likely to cast up in that tower of his, and prospects, with one exception, looked very promising indeed.

Foremost in mind came George and Stella, both paired off and set fair for life she would say, at least in Stella's case. One could never be sure about anyone as free-ranging and unpredictable as George.

Whenever she thought of her eldest daughter (as a wife that is and not as a woman) she awarded herself full marks for her foresight, remembering that she had practically thrown the girl at that clodhopper down the valley. Since then, however, shocked as everyone had been at the time, Stella had never looked back and had certainly never pined for the days when she had every young buck in the county making sheep's eyes at her. She supposed, studying the marriage objectively, that something similar had happened to Stella as had happened to her, when she came within a hairsbreadth of being married off to that toad, Makepeace Goldthorpe, a piece of merchandise bartered for a strip of land adjoining her father's loading bays but in Stella's case, of course, the poor girl had to undergo the actual experience of a loveless marriage. It seemed probable that she was still drawing on her stock of relief at having escaped the clutches of that old goat Moncton-Price and his wretched son. Any woman, given those circumstances, could be expected to look on a man like Denzil Fawcett as a knight in rustic armour, but it was odd, Henrietta reflected, that this attitude should have survived the first transports of marriage. With the best will in the world nobody could call Denzil much of a catch and yet there could be no doubt at all that the girl had adjusted to him and his background in a way that was really quite astonishing when one thought about it. They had three sons now, and a fourth child on the way, so that there seemed every prospect (seeing that Stella was still only twenty-six) that she would fill the Fawcett farmhouse with children before she was done. Henrietta was sure, however, that the children were incidental and there was another parallel here if one looked for it, between the girl's attitude as a mother, and Adam's attitude as a father, something he had handed down to her like a birthmark. Stella's preoccupation was not with the children at all but with the farm, just as Adam's had always been with the network. And after the farm came the peasant who went along with it, as though the boy's adoration over the years had been absorbed, stored and then fed back to him in the form of glances and gestures that any experienced woman could recognise as the sign language of love, and a very earthy love she would say, noting the way her daughter's eye sparkled when he came stumping into the kitchen, threw his arm over her shoulders and paid her some commonplace compliment. Well, so be it, and good luck to the girl, for that was a byproduct of being happily married oneself. One found oneself wishing that every woman in the world took the same pleasure in the man who shared her bed and board.

Thus, in a sense, Henrietta was able to discount Stella whenever she did her family sums. There was nothing to worry about over at Dewponds. All one had to do was to sit back and await the arrival of grandchildren at brief intervals and if Stella became shapeless in the process, that was her business and Denzil's.

As to George, her source of satisfaction concerning him was twofold, for although he seemed settled enough with that pretty little Austrian girl hanging on his words, and trotting at his heels, his obsession, as she well knew, was not with Gisela, or the fat little boy Gisela had produced a few months after her arrival here but for that ponderous great engine he had assembled and was forever tinkering with over in the old stables.

Adam had given them the old millhouse, the house right of the drive entrance where the Michelmores had once lived, and with a little help from the Twyforde Green joiner, George had converted it into a comfortable home. Unlike any of the others, including Adam, he was an expert handyman and could have learned any craft that took his fancy, she supposed, apart from his overriding interest in engineering that must have come from Sam.

Aside from his absorption with the smelly old machine, however, George was more than pulling his weight at the yard, or so she gathered from odd remarks let fall by Adam. In addition to being clever with hands, it seemed, he was extremely shrewd when it came to dealing with customers and his command of three languages gave him unique advantages as a salesman, or so Adam said, although, up to that time, she had been unaware that merchants spoke anything but English.

So George, too, was settled, and Adam had what he badly needed, a son to take his place when he turned his back on that slum and addressed himself to planting 'Tryst' with exotic woodlands, making an Italian garden over by the fruit cage, and turning the house into a kind of museum that would find a place in Kentish guidebooks by the time they were coming up to their golden wedding anniversary.

There was even more abundant promise in Giles' future, for by now Henrietta had taken the measure of that Rycroft filly. Wild and wilful she might be, and a rare handful, no doubt, for a husband with a gentle disposition, but he had the advantage of her in one respect. Watching them clearly, Henrietta had made up her mind that she was madly in love with the boy and that, surely, was all that mattered in the long run.

They were to be married, so Romayne told her, on his twenty-first birthday, a date that had been selected by the lawyers arranging her settlement. It awed her a little to reflect that at least one of her sons would be marrying an heiress, and sometimes seemed too good to be true, for Giles had never struck her as a boy likely to attract luck in the way his brothers did, Alex by surviving that awful battle, George in lighting upon a dutiful little wife who was prepared to play second fiddle to an infernal machine. As regards Giles, in fact, Henrietta had only one source of disquiet these days and this was centred on the girl's impatience, almost publicly proclaimed at a 'Tryst' birthday party when, claiming a forfeit, she plumped herself on Giles' knee and gave him the kind of kiss that many young men would be lucky to get in private from a girl as richly endowed as Romayne. Had she been the girl's mother, instead of her mother-in-law elect, she might have had cause for concern. As it was, well, it was up to the boy, she supposed, and none of her business.

It was after that little give-away, however, that she began to watch them, and it occurred to her that a shorter engagement, lawyers notwithstanding, might have been wiser for all concerned. A year was a long time at that age and she found herself thinking, half-sympathetically, "I know precisely how she feels . . . but it wouldn't do to rush fences with so much money in the offing—might even create bad blood between the families." It made her think of her own waiting time, however, when she was a year younger than Romayne, and Adam was about his business and never on hand to court her. "I can remember a rash of goose-pimples when he touched me so maybe it was as well he wasn't, although nobody can tell me that little madam doesn't know far more about men than I did in those days . . ."

Stella . . . George . . . Giles. She could contemplate all three clearly and coolly, for they were out in the open, with their courses set. But the others, the younger ones, were still in shadow, so that her thoughts concerning them were more random. What, for instance, was one to make of Hugo, eighteen and already serving an apprenticeship at the yard. She remembered that curious letter Giles had written home from school, suggesting the boy made a career of athletics, and it really did begin to look as if Adam, so hard-headed in most respects, had been taken in by that gaff, for he seemed not to mind Hugo spending most of his time travelling about the country competing in sports events and even took a pride in his succession of triumphs and trophies. Already a dozen or more of the latter crowded Hugo's mantelshelf and when she went in there to give them a polish (Hugo did not like the maids to touch his paraphernalia) she wondered how on earth one conducted serious business on a cindertrack. Yet there was logic in it somewhere for Hugo, in high starched collar and dark serge business suit, looked no more than an amiable oaf, whereas Hugo, loping across the forecourt in shorts and singlet was quite beautiful. There was no other word for it and she had watched him until he passed behind the rhododendron clump. She knew nothing at all of athletics but it did not need a practised eye to recognise the grace of his movements, the long measured stride that set his calf-muscles rippling, the proud way he held his head, reminding her of a Greek god she remembered seeing in a catalogue of the Great Exhibition when she was a girl. Pride possessed her then, that she had given birth to such a specimen, so that she remembered something else from her girlhood—old Mrs. Worrell, who had known her Irish mother, telling her that the Irish were all the descendants of kings. Where would Hugo's path lead, she wondered. Many women, particularly the flighty variety, would go crazy over him, but Hugo, more than any of them, was going to need a wife with both feet on the ground. Where was such a one to be found in rural Kent?

Then there were the two younger girls, copper-haired Joanna, favouring her, and a saucy brunette, Helen, who favoured Adam, nineteen and sixteen respectively but showing no signs as yet of developing into girls likely to attract sober husbands. Oh, they were pretty enough, and great flirts into the bargain, but no man wanted a tomboy and neither of them, so far as she could discern, had a serious thought about anything, much less selecting a husband from the flock of lively young mashers who squired them at balls and tennis parties. Well, then, if needs be, she would do it for them, and go about it more judiciously than she had in respect of Stella, the first or second time round, for one farmer's lad was enough for any family, notwithstanding the domestic bliss that prevailed at Dewponds. A first step, possibly, would be to confide in Phoebe Fraser and seek ways and means of taking some of the bounce out of them.

She was less concerned about the two youngest, Edward, now eight, and Margaret, six, for both were young enough to keep under close observation. Lately, moving in and out of the nursery, she had noticed a curious thing about 'The Stragglers'. Each seemed to have taken on the looks and temperament of their grandfathers, in itself a very unlikely circumstance, for no two men could have been more dissimilar. Edward, strutting about house and garden with the air of knowing precisely what he was about, and getting his own way by a mixutre of brashness and truculence, not only behaved like old Sam but was beginning to look like him, with his solid, thickset frame, prominent blue eyes and hard-set jaw, as square and uncompromising as the butt end of a carpenter's plane. Margaret, on the other hand, had the old Colonel's colouring and his meandering gentleness too, so that everyone made a pet of her but she did not spoil easily and Henrietta had yet to see her in a tantrum. It was with a sense of shock that she discovered the child at work on a water colour one morning, a very clever little painting too if she was any judge, which she wasn't really, although she had always exclaimed over the landscapes the dear old man had hung about the house. There she was, sitting at the nursery window, trying to

capture the movement of clouds over the spinney below the paddocks, her little pink tongue peeping out in just the way the Colonel's
had when he sat in front of his easel in that old boat-shelter on the
bluff behind the house. It brought home to Henrietta, as nothing
had up to that time, the realities of heredity. There must be many,
many strains here but she could only identify four. The wide-ranging
Swann freebooters, the industrious d'Auberons from Gascony, the
Rawlinson roughnecks, and her own Irish strain from the far west,
of which she knew virtually nothing. It was rather wonderful, she
thought, how all four had combined to produce the latter-day Swanns,
bestowing a characteristic here, adding a trait there, so that each
child was touched by one or more of their four grandparents, just
as surely as by her and by Adam. The Irish peasant was showing
very plainly in Stella and the Swann military legacy in Alex. In
George she could identify her father's obsession with machines
and in Giles the gentleness that had been, according to the Colonel,
the one outstanding characteristic of his little Gascon wife. Hugo
had something of her own ancestors in him, or why should she remember that remark of Mrs. Worrell about Irish kings, whereas
both Joanna and Helen had Irish-Lancastrian sparkle, together with
a generous dash of Swann swashbucklers. Young Edward was predominantly Lancastrian, with that aggressive jaw, whereas Margaret reverted to the French strain again, reproducing not only the
gentle streak in some of the Swanns (so marked in all she remembered
of the old Colonel) but also the daintiness of Monique d'Auberon,
whose portrait still hung in the room that had been the old man's.
It was all very mysterious and some time, when he had a moment
to spare, she must discuss the subject with Adam.

In the meantime, there was so much to do. At 'Tryst', with so
many of them coming and going, there was always plenty to do.
She went downstairs, intending to finish some neglected work in
the sewing-room, but was brought up short at the bend of the staircase, for there stood Alexander, looking up at her from the hall, and
when he saw her he grinned, but nervously, as though caught out
in an act of mischief.

She began to descend then but he stayed her, holding up his hand
and glancing over his shoulder at the closed drawing-room door.
Then he moved up towards her and said, in a voice pitched so low

that it was close to a whisper, "Someone here . . . someone I want you to meet . . . You're not . . . not specially busy, are you?"

"No," she said, knowing somehow that this was an important moment in his life and hers, "I'm not in the least busy if you've brought a guest." And then, because he still looked a little confused, "It's a young lady, I presume?"

Improbably he blushed scarlet, saying, "Did one of the children see us arrive and let on . . . ?"

But she replied, soothingly, "Certainly not, it's written in large print all over your face, dear boy. Come, we can't leave her sitting alone," and she moved round him to descend the stairs.

She was two stairs down when he swung round and shot out his arm, grasping hers at the elbow, in a grip that made her wince. "Wait! I've something to tell you. Something important." He took a deep breath. "We're to be married. Quite soon."

"*Married?*"

"It has to be soon. I'm posted abroad . . . India . . ."

She had difficulty in keeping her voice low. "But, Alex! To someone we've never met, never even heard about?"

"It's all happened so quickly and I'm due to sail a month from today. Her name's Lydia, Lydia Corcoran, the Colonel's daughter. I did tell you he had a daughter. I'm sure I told you, that time I came on leave from Ireland."

She did not know whether to laugh or cry. He was so anxious and so hopelessly embarrassed that he was gibbering and it astounded her that a boy who had faced enemy shot time and again since that first hair-raising adventure of his should prove so unequal to a situation of this kind. His eyes, she noticed were slightly glazed, indicating that he had already been at the decanter, no doubt to fortify himself, and he was sweating freely at the temples. She saw him then as by far the most vulnerable of the flock, notwithstanding his seniority and battle experience. Maternal concern submerged her. She said, patting him, "There now, pull yourself together, lad. I'm not angry, just . . . well . . . bowled over, and you can hardly blame me for that, can you? Come now, introduce me, do," and she shook herself free of his restraining hand and moved down another three stairs before he dived in pursuit and caught her arm again, shaking his head and opening and closing his mouth but conveying nothing at all save a kind of agonised indecision.

They were level with the newel post then, ten feet or less from the drawing-room door and suddenly impatience got the better of her. She said, sharply, "Really, Alex, this is quite ridiculous! You bring home a guest, a young lady, and tell me you're to be married almost at once. Very well, then! You're twenty-five, and can marry whom you please. But I may meet her, mayn't I? For, if not, why did you bring her here?"

Her tone of voice rallied him so that his confusion ebbed a little and she saw him as she had seen him many times in her mind's eyes over the last few years, a lanky boy scared half out of his wits but determined to set an example to those under his command, so that he had learned the trick of holding himself poker-straight and making his face expressionless. He said, doing just this, "Er, before you go in, mother . . . She isn't pretty, like Stella and George's wife. And she isn't stylish, like you and the girls. She's older than me, too, three years older. But she's right for *me*, you understand? I'm sure of that. Quite sure."

She paused with her hand on the latch, wondering what it had cost him to make that little speech, but then a burning curiosity swamped every other emotion and she said, swiftly, "Leave it there, Alex. Now let me judge for myself."

He seemed to consider this and then nodded, circling her, opening the door, stepping back and half bowing, in a way that struck her, even then, as being dreadfully old-fashioned and quite unlike any gesture his brothers would have made, although people were always complimenting her on their manners. She went in, blinking in the strong sunlight that patterned the waxed floor, bypassing the small, grey-mantled figure standing over by the tall window looking out on the paddock, but before she was clear of the threshold he shot past her at the double, crying, "Lydia . . . my mother . . . mother, Miss Lydia Corcoran!" and the grey-mantled figure bobbed unsmilingly and raised a long, sad face to Henrietta, who at once thought of Gipsy the ageing, bottlenosed skewbald they had bought for the Colonel when he was too old and frail to sit a proper hack.

She knew why the skewbald came to mind. Horse and girl shared the same half-mournful, half-wistful expression and acknowledging this Henrietta's glance dropped, shifting from Lydia's face to her handkerchief dress, with its stiff cuirassed bodice, short basque and fanned throat screen. A dress like that had been all the rage in 1880, when Lydia and everyone else was six years younger.

It was the costume that struck her more than the girl's long, sad face, with squarish chin (Sam Rawlinson's kind of chin), much at odds with the rest of her features. For while one was obliged to accept the face and figure dispensed by Providence, one was surely at liberty to do something about clothes and posture. "Not stylish" Alex had said, and it was a lover's understatement. In her entire life Henrietta had never seen a woman with less claim to be called stylish, for even when it was in vogue the handkerchief dress was the last thing Lydia Corcoran should have chosen to wear. Its long row of buttons tended to flatten such curves as she had, whereas the lacy display at her throat drew attention to her short neck and rather angular shoulders. Even as she murmured a conventional greeting, directing Alex to pour sherry for all three of them, her mind was engaged in dressing the girl in a way that would enable her to pass in a crowd.

But then, telling herself she was rude and uncharitable, she pulled herself together and led Lydia to a chair, gesturing to Alex to hand round the sherry, and while Lydia reached for a glass at once addressed herself to the task of locating something—anything —to offset the poor little devil's lamentable lack of charm. Slowly and carefully her glance travelled from a middle-aged pair of buttoned boots, over the flattish chest, past the square, mannish chin, to the downcast eyes and here, at last, there *was* something arresting. It was the girl's eyes, grey and widely-spaced, with long curling lashes and a kind of steadiness one could look for in someone of authority, tempered by complete honesty. And perhaps, lurking behind the iris, there was courage for good measure.

She thought, wretchedly, "What *can* one say? What is there *to* say? None of them ever brought any one like this into the house, no one so . . . so *frumpish!*" but then, as she once again contemplated the creased, dusty pouches of the bag-plastron under the almost non-existent bosom her attention was deflected by a silvery glitter and her glance shot up again just in time to see two large tears drive parallel courses over Lydia Corcoran's prominent cheek-bones.

The tears humbled Henrietta as she had never been humbled in twenty-eight years as a wife and mother. Not because they told her, unequivocally, that the girl was fully aware of her rawboned awkwardness, but because they performed a time miracle on Henrietta herself, whirling her back to a day when she had stood in Lydia Corcoran's place, a travel-worn, tongue-tied stray, paraded for inspection in Colonel Swann's Derwentwater home and feeling even more inadequate than Lydia looked after a hundred-mile cross-country journey as Adam Swann's pillion-rider in the crinoline she had worn when she fled the embrace of Makepeace Goldthorpe.

Identification with the girl was so vivid and so compelling that she could have wept. Every nuance of that terrifying confrontation returned to her as clearly and faithfully as though she had been turning the leaves of a family album. For Alex, hovering nearby, was Adam, wondering wryly if he had just committed the crowning folly of his life by bringing her here, whereas she was Adam's sharp-tongued Aunt Charlotte, honking dismay at the prospect of receiving such a bedraggled fugitive into her house; and in Lydia's place was the forlorn little wretch Henrietta had been at that moment in time, so that pity welled up in her like some swift underground stream seeking the surface.

It made a difference. It made all the difference in the world. She no longer saw her as a drab, mousy little creature who, by means unknown, witchcraft possibly, had hooked her eldest son, but as she recalled herself nearly thirty years ago, in desperate need of love and, even more essential, what love might bring, absorption into a family unit, where she could hope to find an identity.

She reached out, took the sherry glass from Lydia's hand, set it firmly on the occasional table, and said, fervently, "He told me, my dear, and I'm glad for you both! Alex needs a wife badly. Someone like you, to watch out for him—*there!*" and she kissed her soundly on both cheeks, tasting a triumph that was salty but rewarding.

2

Lydia

THE original sponsor was Bonzo. Brash, toothy, open-handed, Bonzo Charteris, commanding A Company and reckoned an experienced ladies' man. For it was Bonzo who learned, in the course of a chance conversation as the port circulated, that 'Lucky' Swann, posted to them as supernumerary whilst awaiting passage to India, had not yet paid a visit to the Empire, Leicester Square, highly recommended by Bonzo as 'The resort of the most exclusive laced mutton in town'.

Alex, having spent more than five of the last seven years out of England, had not yet learned that 'laced mutton' was the fashionable word for 'harlot'. Last year, he recalled, it had been 'rig', and the year before 'bint', but one lost track of new slang on outpost duty and at advanced base, where laced mutton, if it was not off the menu altogether, was reserved for men who could outrank a captain, even a well-heeled one like Bonzo Charteris.

Bonzo, having extolled the bill of fare at the Empire, went on to say that the Colonel himself, (known by the subalterns as 'Bejasus', 'Fwat-Fwat' or 'Vorwarts') was himself a regular partaker of the Empire's laced mutton but took good care, as did any man with his wits about him, to go there in mufti.

"Met the old boy there half a dozen times," he said, "but we don't let on, y'know. Pass one another with half a wink."

It was this conversation that led to an invitation on the part of Bonzo to escort Swann to Leicester Square on their next weekend jaunt to town for Swann, reckoned a country cousin in the garrison town, was nonetheless respected as a man who had served three campaigns and been present, lucky devil, not only at Rorke's Drift but also at Tel-el-Kebir.

It would have amazed Charteris to learn that Swann had been far from lucky in other respects, and that, at twenty-five, he was still, technically, a virgin. It was naturally assumed that a man who had spent so long on foreign stations had enjoyed the favours of numerous oriental charmers and Swann was very careful to do nothing to correct this impression.

His continence, as a matter of fact, was not from inclination, although he took careful heed of the surgeon-major's dire warnings against contracting venereal disease when serving abroad. Rather it was from lack of opportunity, and the nature of the places where he had campaigned. Between times, in Deal, Cork and Malta, there had been three or four inconclusive encounters, but no sooner had he made a tentative lodgement than he found himself whisked away to some God-forsaken spot where the local women were off limits on account of the fact that medical supervision over them was impossible.

So it came about that Alex accepted Bonzo's invitation, travelled up to town on the four-thirty, booked in for an overnight stay at a private hotel in Dover Street and set out, in tails and opera hat, to do the town as Bonzo's protégé. His companion's air of genial patronage did not bother him, Charteris having served one campaign to his three.

They fetched up at the Empire round about nine, when the second showing of the tableaux-vivants was just beginning. Alex was excited by the colour, gaiety and frankness of the stage entertainment, forgetting for an hour or so that this was merely the hors-d'oeuvre and that the real purpose of the expedition was to seek out and price the best pieces of laced mutton on show.

The display, when it was at length presented to him on the promenades, made him gasp. Until then he had always taken it for granted that England was still a country of Puritans, and that the trade of harlotry, if practised at all on any scale, was confined to out-of-the-way corners in the seamier suburbs or that, where it did spill over into fashionable quarters, it was kept to the pavement. He soon discovered he was in error. Here, on the north side of Leicester Square, harlots plied in plush surroundings and under brilliant lighting, the promenades of the Empire being the regular resort not of prostitutes as he understood them but of haughty courtesans who could easily have been mistaken for young duchesses on the Sunday after-church parade in Hyde Park.

The very least of them was a most impressive creature, tricked out in the very latest fashions and smelling like an English garden in high summer, as they glided past (they seemed to move on runners) and basked—there was simply no other word for it—in the admiration of boulevardiers.

Bonzo proved an inspired compère but although he was obviously acquainted with many of the ladies he was careful to refer to them all in the general rather than the particular. To do otherwise, Alex gathered, would have been considered caddish, for the kiss-and-tell code of the mess seemed to apply here as much as in a garrison-town drawing-room.

"Some of them make a thousand a year," Bonzo told him, "and from time to time one retires, snapped up by some well-heeled Johnny and installed in a love-nest in St. John's Wood or Maida Vale. God bless 'em, I say, although one can't help feeling they must live to regret settling down with some balding old cove, who pops in Tuesdays and Fridays, spends the rest of the week behind his till and makes sure he never misses church on Sunday. I remember one who cut her losses and came back. The chap who kept her discovered she had never been confirmed and wanted to haul her off to church and get it attended to, before he paid her another visit. A place like this is a refuge as well as a high-class market. The police don't bother 'em here. They pay their five shillings entrance fee every night and they get a chance to look their clients over in the warm and dry. No risk of a dose with one o' these doxies. They look after themselves, and they can be particular, mark my words. Give 'em the eye but don't make a straight proposition. Let it be understood over a glass of champagne and leave me to talk terms. By the way, don't waste silver on chocolates, like some of the greenhorns, old boy. They sell them back over the counter the minute you turn your back. Seen anyone you fancy so far?"

Alex had, a fair, wasp-waisted girl, sitting at one of the round tables at the far end of the bar and looking a good deal less haughty than most of the mutton on show. Every now and again she laughed and showed perfect teeth whilst listening to the conversation of a dark-haired companion who had the dignity of a dowager and looked scarifyingly supercilious when a young man wearing a gar-

574

denia paused at her table and offered her a cigarette from a gold case.

"Ai don't indulge, thenk you!" she said, and her fair companion laughed again as though, like Alex, she was here to enjoy the fun and was in no mind at all to do business. He said, "Those two over there, do you happen to know either of them?" and Bonzo said he knew the dark one who was called 'Miss Montcrieff', and priced herself at around three guineas, exclusive of dinner, posing, champagne and any other incidentals. "Talking of names," he went on, "don't use your own, old son. Blackmail is rare here—wouldn't do the place any good—but it's not unknown, of course. I'll introduce you as Captain Teamster, of the Bengal Lancers, and you can call me Eddie, and let on I'm a gunner, for they're as sharp as needles here and would be sure to spot us for what we are if we tried to pass ourselves off as barristers-at-law or medical students."

They sauntered over and introductions were formally made, Miss Montcrieff maintaining her bleak expression even when accepting a glass of champagne, but the fair girl, presented as Miss Cecilia Royston 'a cousin of Miss Montcrieff's on a visit to London from the provinces', seemed jolly enough and glad of his company, so they sipped champagne and made elaborate small talk until Bonzo proposed they took another look at the tableaux-vivants, the show being about half-way through the second run.

It was like taking part in a saraband, where every move on the part of one's partner was carefully observed, and the level of conversation was more or less equivalent to that at one of his mother's croquet-parties at 'Tryst'. In fact, it seemed quite monstrous to imagine that the Misses Montcrieff and Royston were a couple of highly-trained whores hoping, indeed resolved, to turn an honest sovereign or two before sunrise. This illusion of gentility continued right up to the time they paired off after supper at an Italian restaurant Bonzo patronised in Frith Street. Bonzo and Miss Montcrieff (she never did relax sufficiently to divulge her Christian name) then entered a hansom and went off in the direction of Tottenham Court Road, Cecilia telling him that she had rooms in Long Acre, so near as to be hardly worth a cab-ride.

By then Alex had reached a state of some exhilaration, the food and wine having been excellent, and Miss Royston's company pleasantly undemanding, for Bonzo did most of the talking. Yet he felt a little shy when they were moving through a thinning crowd of West Enders and the late night snarl-up of hansoms and growlers chivvying their way through the busy streets now that the theatres were emptying.

The girl, however, seemed to make allowance for this and settled for the sisterly approach, dropping the slightly arch accent she had employed earlier in the evening and holding his arm in the friend-liest fashion as she chattered gaily of all manner of things in a way that reminded him of one of the numerous husband-hunters he had partnered at regimental soirées in Malta and Cork.

No sooner had they reached the tall, narrow-fronted house and climbed two staircases to her quarters, however, than she became very businesslike, saying, "Your friend made the arrangements with mine. It's for all night, isn't it? Would you like a drink? I won't myself, if you don't mind, for I only keep whisky here and whisky doesn't agree with me. Do make yourself comfortable. I should take off your boots if I were you."

He took off his boots, accepted a generous whisky and said, for something to say, that he had assumed she and Miss Moncrieff shared rooms, and was surprised to find her living here alone.

"Oh, I'm not really alone," she said. "Mr. Skilly, the landlord's agent, looks after a dozen or more rooms, all let to Empire girls, I understand, although I wouldn't really know, for I really am a new-comer to London and I'm still on commission, and likely to be until Christmas. That's the only way I could have possibly got on to the promenade. I was vouched for by Daisy—Miss Montcrieff—you un-derstand? I'm her protégée and she has a private arrangement with Mr. Skilly in the suite below, and the rent is paid by her every Saturday. It's nice here, I think, even though the market traffic does get noisy in the small hours, Covent Garden being no more than a stone's throw away. I was right lucky to run into Daisy, I can tell you, for I've had real gentlemen for the most part. Will you unhook me, soldier-boy? You don't mind me calling you soldier-boy, do you? I like soldiers. There's never any nonsense about them. I mean, they don't want to act stupid, and you can usually have a bit of a laugh with them, and they don't count the small change, do they? Lucy, that's the girl in the rooms immediately above, has a regular soldier at the moment, but he's very old and quite past it I'd say, although he's a rare trier, Lucy says, providing he hasn't shipped too much before he gets here. Mostly he has, of course, and then she has to call Skilly to help him down and pack him off home. That happened earlier in the week, and I had to lend a hand, for he was having the horrors, or so it sounded, the way he was carrying on and wanting to fight everybody. Quite harmless, of course, but not good for the house, which is quiet and very respectable as a rule."

While she was rattling on in this way she had, with a little assistance from him, slipped out of her evening gown and hung it on a hanger in a recess curtained by some bright-coloured chintz with a pattern that made his eyes hurt. He said, "We don't need this strong light, do we, Cecilia?" and she said, "Why, no, not if you don't wish it. I'm here to please. Most of them like it left on for some reason. I suppose to see what they're getting. Either that, or they're afraid for their pocket books. There," and she turned off the overhead gas-burner, leaving a tiny jet over by the door, so that the room was thrown into part-shadow, relieved by the glow of the gas-light in the street below. She said mildly, slipping out of what seemed to Alex half a dozen petticoats, "You're not a regular one for the girls, are you, soldier-boy? Oh, don't misunderstand me, please. It's nice to get a quiet one now and again, for a girl looks for all sorts in this line of business, doesn't she?"

Her naïveté, assumed or not, was very appealing he thought, and he answered that he supposed a girl did, adding that he had spent the last few years in places where one sometimes went months without even seeing a woman. This touched a chord of sympathy in her somewhere and she said, "Oh, dear, that must be awful for you! I see now why you're well . . . not in a tearing hurry, like most of the gentlemen, even the polite ones. I suppose . . . but there, it's none of my business."

"What were you going to say? You suppose what?"

"Well . . ." she gave a little chirrup of laughter, "I suppose after a time, months that is, you get out of the habit and have to work up an appetite when it's served up to you? Is that so, soldier-boy?"

"Yes," he murmured, "something like that, I imagine," and wondered whether she had blundered on the truth, for the fact was he did not feel in the least erotic, only intensely curious about himself and her, with all manner of strange, detached thoughts running through his head. For it did seem odd that he should be closeted here in a clean, comfortable room, with an attractive young woman stripped down to her corset and drawers, and yet find himself wondering what she earned, where she came from, how much she spent on those fashionable clothes, and the exact nature of the 'arrangement' that existed between her, the unsmiling Miss Montcrieff, and Mr. Skilly downstairs, who seemed to combine the duties of rent-collector, janitor and whoremaster of the house.

His three grown sisters, all interested in fashions, had familiarised him with the various items of her ensemble. He could tell that they were all run up from expensive materials and would not come cheaply. He wondered whether harlots of her class looked for some kind of discount from their costumier. The evening gown, with its straw-filled bustle sewn into the panels of the dress, had a long train and deep V-shaped decolletage, and might have been worn by a society hostess without occasioning much more than the lift of an eyebrow. Her underdress, worn over the fine linen petticoats, was of Ottoman silk, and the drawers were a riotous affair, made of cambric velvet and crossbanded with cornflower blue ribbons sewn on to the nainsook frills, with a red silk rose stitched to the seam of each leg. The sheath-like corset, shaped in wide curves and stiffened, he would say, with strips of steel, pushed her fine breasts very high and swept over the buttocks in a way that was obviously designed to emphasise the bustle she had hung in the closet. She seemed just the slightest put out by his scrutiny and said, with a smile, "A penny for them, soldier-boy!" and he replied, mildly, "I was only thinking how elegantly you dress, Cecilia," and she said, "But of course! How else would I get admitted to the promenade? The management doesn't let anybody in there, I can tell you. They have their reputation to think of."

"You mean the Empire is financially involved in what happens there?"

"Oh no," she said, laughing, "I say, you *have* been out of the swim a long time, haven't you? What I mean is, we girls *are* the Empire and far more important to them than the turns they book, and these tableaux-vivants we watched tonight. I mean, it's obvious, isn't it? Rich gentlemen wouldn't go there in such numbers if we didn't, would they? You get far better stage turns at the Star and a dozen other places if you're looking for straight entertainment. Mr. Skilly told Lucy, the girl above, the one with the regular, that last year the Empire shareholders drew eighty-three per cent on their investment, so naturally we're vetted before we're allowed to promenade. Why, even the police know that."

He said, suddenly, "Come and sit on my knee, Cecilia. It's years since I had a pretty girl on my knee."

"You mean, just as I am?"

"Well, that's up to you, Cecilia."

"Then I'll take off my corset if you don't mind. It's punishing me something cruel, I can tell you."

She reached behind her and tweaked the top bow so that the corset bulged outward as on a spring and her breasts, released from confinement, parted like a cleft pear, the resultant ripple giving him the first genuinely erotic impulse he had experienced in her company. She coiled herself on his knee, took his head in both hands and kissed him on the mouth. "You *are* an odd one, soldier-boy. But nice. I wish there were more like you. Are you married, soldier-boy?"

"Good God, no," he said, laughing. "Do I look as if I was?"

"No, you don't," she said, thoughtfully, "and I knew that before I asked really. Some girl is going to be lucky one day. Or maybe she isn't because it would be awful seeing you go off to war every now and again and not showing up for months on end. How do you feel about me now?" she concluded, improbably.

"Comfortable," he said, "and lucky, somehow. To have picked someone like you, I mean, for I can't imagine there are two of you down at the Empire."

"Oh, there's all sorts," she said, carelessly. "You'd be surprised, I can tell you. We've got to cater for a wide range and you never stop being surprised by the gentlemen."

"Are you surprised by me?"

"Well, so far," she said, "but there's time enough yet, isn't there? I realised straight off why you were shy but my experience is it soon wears off. It's beginning to already, isn't it?"

"I believe it is," he said, gaily. "Kiss me again to make sure."

Her second kiss was more amorous and she nibbled his lips in a way that told him her naïveté was almost certainly counterfeit, and she knew her business extremely well. He squeezed her bottom and she said, approvingly, "*That's* the spirit!" but when he tried to explore below the tight waistband, she said, laughing, "Here, you don't have to wrestle, love," and tweaked the tape so that he could prospect her in comfort, at the same time letting her hand pass lightly over his crutch and saying, "Well there! You got nothing to worry about, have you?"

He realised with relief that he had not and suddenly he felt very glad that he had accepted Bonzo's invitation and even more so that he had found an amiable creature like Cecilia, who combined humour with a tolerance and understanding he would not have looked for in a girl of her profession.

They cuddled there for what seemed to him a long interval, more like a couple of long-separated lovers in a cornfield than a man sporting with a hired drab in a house of drabs. The swift rattle of a market cart passing over the setts below seemed to recollect to a full sense of her duty and she said, slipping off his knee, "Here now, this won't do, soldier-boy. Let's go to bed, shall we?" and without waiting for his assent she began to pull off her drawers.

Then, as always with him, an outside agency stepped in, this time even more decisively than in Malta, Cork and Cyprus, where he was whisked away to a troopship at what always seemed to him a moment's notice. She had one leg free, and was stooping to ease the frills of the other over her stockinged feet, when there was a sudden outcry from the room immediately above, swelling, in a matter of seconds, to an uproar that could not possibly be ignored, for it included a woman's screams, a man's full-throated shouts, any number of heavy thumps and finally the crash of glass. Glass was still tinkling when he heard the rush of hurrying feet on the stairs and, a moment later, renewed outcry, as though a whole group of people were up there engaged in breaking up the furniture. The woman's yells continued, so that the entire house seemed to erupt and Cecilia shouted, above the cacophony, "It's Lucy and her regular again! He must be murdering her!" and darted across the room and out of the door, with Alex in hot pursuit just as the noise above shifted its centre from immediately above to the head of a flight of stairs rising steeply from the landing outside.

There was a relatively good light out here and glancing up Alex saw a trio of figures struggling together in confusion just beyond the top stair. Cecilia, now stark naked apart from her black stockings, headed up into the scrimmage, but before he could mount more than two stairs the banister rail parted with a long, splintering crack and the wedge of people descended in concert, bumping and rolling one upon the other, and giving him no opportunity to retreat and avoid making five of the group. All together, a confused mass of threshing arms and legs, they rolled on to the landing outside Cecilia's open door where Alex, the last to be involved, was the first on his feet, having jarred his shoulder on the post of what was left of the banisters. For a few seconds he was dazed by the impact but then, darting forward, with some idea of extricating Cecilia, he saw a grizzled head emerge from the mass of bodies and then a brown mottled fist, grasping about a foot of a broken walking cane, with a silver dragon's head as its handle.

He recognised face and walking cane in the same moment. Both belonged to Colonel Corcoran, alias Bejasus, alias Fwat-Fwat and Vorwarts. The old boy's mouth was open in a sustained roar of rage, or pain, or terror, directed at whatever monster figured in his current bout of delirium tremens and his rust-red whiskers stood out, giving him the appearance of a wild man at a fair. Above the gasps and moans of a middle-aged pot-bellied man (Mr. Skilly he assumed) and the muffled screams of Lucy, whose evening dress had bundled level with her chin, so that her bustle was acting as a kind of gag, he could hear the steady spate of oaths for which Colonel Corcoran was famous throughout half the garrison towns of the Empire, interspersed with volleys of his favourite expletive, 'Bejasus', that had won him his most popular nickname. Alone among them he seemed uninjured, for as Alex watched, too amazed to help, he fought his way free, striking out with the butt end of his staff. He was in full evening rig, but in the struggle above, or the tumble downstairs, the pearl buttons had been stripped from his waistcoat and his ruffled shirt, ripped across the front, exposed a mat of red hair that covered his chest.

His wild prancings, and the ineffectual blows he delivered, seemed to steady the others somewhat for they began to sort themselves out, massaging various parts of their anatomy that had come into contact with the treads or the splintered stair rail on the way down.

Skilly rose to his knees, his oaths entering into competition with the Colonel's but he was at a grave disadvantage for his high-crowned bowler hat was wedged tightly over his ears and until he could free himself he was all but blinded.

It was the most bizarre scene imaginable. Lucy, still unable to win clear of the press, waved her legs in the air, as though making despairing signals for help, but Cecilia emerged backwards, bent in an arc so that her broad bottom offered a splendid target to the enraged Bejasus, who dropped his near-useless walking stick and fetched her a tremendous slap that rang through the general din like the report of a Martini-Henry discharged in a canyon.

At that moment, when Alex had sufficiently recovered to grab Bejasus by the shoulders and haul him clear, there was a loud knocking on the front door and Lucy, sitting up and clawing the bustle from her face, shouted, "It's the police! Go down, Skilly. Go on down!" and to Alex's amazement Skilly scrambled to his feet and went off down the stairs at a stumbling run, both hands still raised in an attempt to free himself of his bowler. Then, mercifully, the Colonel stopped bellowing and hitting out, and seemed suddenly bemused, as though unable to get his bearings. Alex, steadying him against the splintered stair rail, shouted "I'll see to him . . . he's my colonel . . . nobody's hurt, are they?" but was aware, as he said this, of the rumble of voices below and a moment later an enormous police constable appeared on the stairs, with Skilly at his heels and Alex saw that the janitor had at last rid himself of his hat and was revealed as a florid man of about fifty, with cheeks as pendulous as a bloodhound's and a blue, watery eye that surveyed the scene with exasperated bewilderment.

He said, apologetically, "Touch o' D.T.s officer, same as las' time. 'Armless, mindjew. Better get a keb, 'adn't we?" And the policeman, who seemed excessively calm in the circumstances, agreed that this would be a good idea but added, very mildly, that this kind of thing wouldn't do at all twice in a few days, that somebody might have been injured in such a mêlée, and that it had better be kept from his sergeant with whom he had a point in a few moments.

Alex said nervously, "I know him, officer, and I know where he lives. Let me take him home. He'll be safe enough with me, I assure you!" and the policeman said, gravely, that he would be safe with anybody now so that Alex, turning towards Cecilia's room, saw that the Colonel was slumped against the skirting-board and fast asleep.

"Takes 'em that way, usually," the policeman went on, speaking more like a sympathetic doctor than an officer charged with keeping the peace. "In fits and starts, that is. That two-headed gorilla that was after him 'as been caught by the keepers. But he'll really have to start watering it more or he'll be a goner before he knows it. Best to get something on, miss." This to Cecilia, who was regarding the damaged stair rail with dismay and massaging her crimson bottom.

Skilly said, wearily, "Get yourself a drink, Lucy. You too, Cis. The young gentleman'll see to His Nibs so there's no call to worry. Would you give us a hand dahn with the old boy, officer? Can't manage him on me own," and the policeman nodded, saying, "I'll take his shoulders and as soon as we're on street level pop across to the cab rank and this young gentleman will take over. I'd like the colonel clear o' my beat before the sergeant shows up."

Between them they lifted Bejasus and began a clumsy descent of the stairs while Alex, glad to be out of it so cheaply, went back into Cecilia's room for his boots. He was lacing them when she reappeared, wearing a kimono bright as a Nile sunset. She said, "You really do know him, don't you? You didn't just say that to get us off the hook, for you needn't bother wi' P.C. Capley. He's on the landlord's payroll."

"Ah, so I gathered," Alex said, grinning, but then, recollecting that he had given her nothing, and that Bonzo had paid for her champagne and supper, he took out his purse, saying, "I suppose your friend will settle up with you, Cecilia, but I'd like to show what a pleasant evening I've had. Will you take this?" and shyly he offered a sovereign.

She looked at it without taking it and said, finally, "There's no call for that, soldier-boy. I haven't earned it, have I?"

"Oh, yes, you have," he replied. And she smiled, vaguely, saying, "Stuff an' nonsense, soldier-boy. It was only like I said. You fellows go long enough without seeing a girl and lose the knack for a spell. You aren't the first I come across. Will you be dropping in the Empire again?"

"If I get a chance before sailing for India."

"Ah," she said, sadly, "India now is it? Well, then, it don't look as if I'll have a chance to make it up to you, does it? Damn that old fool! You weren't just business to me, I can tell you that!" And she stood on tiptoe, leaned forward and kissed him softly and went out and up the stairs to Lucy's room. He laid the sovereign on the bed-side table and went downstairs where the policeman was peering anxiously up and down Long Acre, as though afraid of being caught with the recumbent Bejasus when his sergeant showed up.

A stream of carts was passing now, all laden high with produce for Covent Garden and among them, after an anxious moment or two, they saw Mr. Skilly, perched on the step of a four-wheeler. Skilly held the door whilst Alex and the constable bundled the colonel inside and the policeman said, "Where to, sir?"

"Smith Street," Alex told him. "I can't recall the number but I'll recognise the house. Tell the cabby it's on the left, just before you come to Park Lane." He got in, inhaling the stale, tobacco-laden atmosphere of the musty interior, and a moment later they were on their way.

2

It was a longish journey, for the horse was either very old or very tired and they were some time getting clear of the ever-increasing market traffic. Every time the cab paused under a gaslight he caught a glimpse of the Colonel's face, a pinkish blob fringed with fiery whiskers, deeply engraved wrinkles and a nose like the bowl of an old pipe. He was snoring now, with his mouth wide open and once, in a marginally stronger light, Alex saw a long white scar that ran diagonally from the right ear to the cleft in the double chin. He thought glumly, "A lance or a tulwar slash, poor old devil. He's been rough-housed all his life, and who gives a damn about what becomes of him now? Not the Government, certainly, whose battles he's been fighting since he was younger than me, for they'll be showing him the door if he carries on like this."

But then the cabby called, "About here, sir?" and he got out, rec-ognising the house where he had called a month or so before to collect some papers relating to his attachment.

The cabby, even more of an old ruin than the Colonel, served the office of Mr. Skilly, taking Colonel Corcoran's heels and between them they heaved him across the pavement and up the five steps to the front door. No light showed but looking through the letter box Alex saw a gleam reflected in a mirror beyond the stairs and when he rang the bell a third time there was movement in the shadows and he was relieved to see a gas jet flare, revealing a tall, broad-shouldered servant tucking his nightshirt into his trousers. He paid the cabby and dismissed him, supporting Bejasus, still snoring, by holding him against the pillar of the portico. A moment later the door opened and the servant was seen to be a middle-aged man, who held himself very straight, almost certainly a trained batman. No explanation was necessary. All he said was, "I'll take him, sir, if you'll be good enough to go ahead and open that door left of the stairs. Any message, sir?"

No, said Alex, no message, but recollecting that the Colonel might well have left some of his belongings in Lucy's room, added, "If he asks you could tell him he passed out in a house in Long Acre. I'm on his strength but don't tell him one of us brought him home. I daresay he won't recall a thing about it in the morning."

"No, sir," the man said, lightly, "he rarely does, but don't you worry. I can handle him, sir. I served through the Burma campaign with him."

Alex opened the heavy door and batman and burden passed in, the soldier servant kicking the door shut with his heel, as if to emphasise the fact that he was now in sole charge. Alex turned back into the hall, regretting now that he had dismissed the cab, for he was feeling very jaded, but then a light showed on the stairs and he looked up to see a small figure in a quilted dressing-gown, holding a candle above her head. For a moment he thought it was a child, but then he saw that it was a young woman, with her hair in curlers, and wished himself out of this, recalling suddenly that Bejasus had a daughter who kept house for him here. She called, sharply, "Wait! It's Captain Swann, isn't it?"

He was surprised to be identified so easily, for he had only been on the regimental strength a little over a month and as a supernumerary awaiting transfer to India had made few friends.

"Yes, ma'am," he said, diffidently, "I . . . er . . . I brought the

Colonel home. He wasn't feeling so well," and she said, evenly, "You don't have to lie about him to me, Captain Swann. He wasn't hurt, was he? And it wasn't in public, I hope?"

"No," he said, wretchedly, "it was at the house of some friends. We'd been to see the show at the Empire and he . . . well, he overdid it a little. No one else was involved. I brought him home by cab."

"How much was the fare and tip, Mr. Swann?"

"Fare and tip?" He gaped at her, a tiny figure, not much taller than his eight-year-old brother, Edward. "No more than a shilling or two. I really don't remember, Miss Corcoran."

But she said, drily, "I think you do. Anyway, I intend to pay you. I really don't see why you should be out of pocket on his account. Besides, you look tired, Captain Swann, so come below stairs and I'll brew you some coffee. I brew excellent coffee. I learned how to make it in the West Indies. I was born in Barbados and my mother died there. Please," and giving him no opportunity to refuse she pattered across the hall and through the green baize door used by the batman. "I expect Tilson will be down for coffee in an hour or so. It depends how much Father has shipped. Sometimes he won't stir until morning, but Tilson can handle him. Tilson won't stand any nonsense."

They were in a basement kitchen now, a spotlessly clean room, full of gleaming pots and pans and with every surface polished, as for company inspection. Someone, he suspected it would be she, had the servants well in hand. There was a fire rustling in the range and she set a large iron kettle on the hob. He said, "Could I . . . is there somewhere I could wash, Miss Corcoran?" She nodded towards the scullery and went about setting a tray and cups. There was a pump in the scullery and he flushed the trough, washing his hands and face with carbolic soap and thinking, wryly, "She's a colonel's daughter all right, and I wouldn't care to fall out with her, but it's odd she doesn't keep a tighter rein on the old boy . . ." He came back and stood about indecisively but she paid him no further heed until the coffee was made and he complimented her on it, thinking he had never stood so much in need of it, for his mouth was parched with all that champagne and his stomach sour with Cecilia's indifferent whisky. She said, briskly, "Take a seat, do," and he said, sitting at the scrubbed table, "I'm surprised you know my name. I'm only a supernumerary, Miss Corcoran."

"I know more than your name," she said. "I make it my business to know every officer and senior N.C.O. assigned to us and it's as well I do, for he'd never remember and there would be endless muddles. I even know who your father is and where you live. I know where you're going too, as soon as you can get a passage. You can smoke if you like, Captain."

It was more or less an order. He took out his cigar case and lit one of his cheroots. Slightly, very slightly, he began to adjust to her, looking across the table at the small earnest face, with those absurdly unflattering curling pins and huge, grey eyes. The eyes, he decided, more than compensated for the homeliness of the other features, squarish chin, heavy for so small a person, short, broad nose, compressed and rather prim mouth. He thought fleetingly of Cecilia and decided that there could have been no greater contrast between the two women who had held him in conversation that night. But then, neither did Miss Corcoran have anything at all in common with her rumbustious old father. He looked into the grey eyes again, fascinated by their authority. It was not so surprising that she knew so much about him. Eyes like that might hold half the secrets of the world. He said, "I should apologise to you, Miss Corcoran. For disturbing you this way, in the middle of the night. I ought to have managed it more discreetly."

"Nobody can be discreet with the Colonel in tow," she said. "But I prefer not to talk about him. Suppose we talk about you?"

"What is there to talk about?"

"A great deal, I'd say. Why, for instance, with a business as lucrative as Swann-on-Wheels, and you being an eldest son, you chose the army? And why you haven't made better use of your astonishing luck."

"My luck?"

"They call you 'Lucky' Swann, don't they? You got through Isandlwana, Rorke's Drift, Tel-el-Kebir and a sail down the Nile in a burning paddle-steamer. Don't you *want* to get on, Captain Swann?"

"Of course I do, but a company, at twenty-five—that isn't standing still, is it, Miss Corcoran?"

"Regimentally? No, I suppose not, providing you don't stick there and you well might, in India. I didn't mean that, exactly."

"What else can a man do except keep his record clean and hope for promotion?"

"Whatever you had in mind when you first went soldiering, I imagine. *Did* you have anything in mind?"

Against all probability he found her easy to talk to, easier than anyone he had met, so that his diffidence left him and he had a sense of enjoying her interrogation. He said, "I don't think I had anything specific in mind, other than travel and adventure. I soon had my fill of that but then something odd happened. I saw what could be done by training and discipline at Rorke's Drift, and it made up my mind for me in a way. I was ready to go home and be a haulier after that awful scare, but once I'd had time to think about it I decided to try again. This time as a regular."

"But that was seven years ago. What's happened since? I don't mean in the field, but your private attitude to the profession."

"I don't know . . . It's become routine, I suppose. One learns to adapt, to integrate, and as for personal ambition, well, one takes pot luck, the way one does under fire." He was suddenly aware of giving too much away. "Why are you asking me all these questions, Miss Corcoran? How can it matter to you whether I get on or don't get on?"

She said slowly, "I'm interested in people, in professional soldiers particularly. Like you I come from a long line of soldiers and it annoys me to see an honourable profession degraded to the status of a music hall joke. The kind of joke you and my father probably heard tonight at the Empire. Providing you went there for jokes, that is."

He had no idea how to reply to this. It was a clear indication that she was very well aware of the fact that he and her father had spent the evening in the company of whores, so he fell back on the main substance of his remark.

"How do you mean, exactly? How is the army being degraded by being made the subject of music hall jokes?"

"Do I have to explain that to a man who brought my father home tonight?"

"But he's terribly popular with all ranks, Miss Corcoran. I'm not just saying so. He really is. Everyone respects any man who has col-

lected a dozen wounds leading from the front. As to his private
life . . ."

"I don't give a damn about his private life," she said, savagely,
"it's his professional outlook that maddens me. His, and yours, and
that of every other popinjay who thinks soldiering is a matter of
wearing fancy dress, and mincing up and down the promenades at
a place like the Empire! It isn't, you know. It's a great deal more than
that. Real soldiering requires brains and I always did hate waste."

"Waste?"

"Wicked waste!" She looked at him levelly. "In twenty-five years'
time, providing you dodge the bullets, you'll be an exact replica of
that used-up old man in there, snoring his head off, watched over
by an enlisted man who has become a sort of keeper. Do you realise
that, Captain Swann? Does your father, who did something practical with his life?"

He was silent, and she respected his silence, giving him time, no
doubt, to absorb the impact of such an uncompromising accusation.
Finally, he said, "If you mean I should apply for a staff college va-
cancy I don't mind you knowing I haven't got the brains to pass the
entrance exam."

"I'm not talking about staff college but of specialisation. You aren't
staff material but you could be a great success as a specialist. In ten
years from now specialisation will be essential. Even the boneheads
in Whitehall will come to admit that. So far we've fought savages,
Zulus, Indo-Chinese, dervishes, but one day you'll have to face
Europeans, with weapons as good or better than yours. When you
do, without specialists in the field, you'll go down like partridges
and deserve to. That's what I'm talking about, Mr. Swann!"

Her drive, her lucidity and terrible singlemindedness reminded
him of his father. Almost everyone he knew spoke inconsequentially
and off the cuff, their thinking regulated, if at all, by some newspaper article or prejudice picked up in the mess or parade-ground
but she didn't speak like that at all. Every word she uttered was the
result of unremitting thought, so that it was like listening to someone with a crystal-clear set of convictions, with the directness and
experience of, say, the Duke of Wellington. He said, with a gesture
of bewilderment, "You're a young woman, Miss Corcoran . . . it

seems so strange, so unusual that you should bother your head about such things . . ."

But she replied, sharply, "Look at me! What else should I bother with? Fashions? Babies? Croquet-lawn tittle-tattle?"

He had a certainty then that he had been singled out and that concerning him she had something specific in mind; that his arrival here, in the middle of the night, was more than a stroke of luck on his part or hers and as he thought this caution and curiosity fought a duel over her in a part of his brain too remote to be located. As the minutes ticked by curiosity won. He said, "What kind of specialisation were you thinking of, Miss Corcoran?"

She smiled, as though relieved at his capitulation. "You're a crack shot," she said. "Oh, don't bother to be modest, for I know you are. With rifle and revolver. You've used a Gatling, too, and that's something most junior officers haven't done, save on the range. Well then, let's move on. Have you heard about the Maxim? Or are they still discussing archery and pike drill when the port passes in the mess?"

"They don't talk shop at all," he said, smiling, "but I've heard all about the Maxim. It's an improvement on the Gatling, isn't it?"

"It will put the Gatling out of business. In a year or less every army in the West will be chasing them. I'm offering you a headstart, Captain Swann."

His bewilderment increased. "But why? I mean, why me? And how does it come that someone like yourself should be in a position to offer me anything of the kind?"

"You're the right age, you're said to be lucky, you're a crack shot, and if you are your father's son you must have initiative in you somewhere. As to how I come to be drumming up support for the Maxim, that's a family matter."

"You're saying the Colonel selected me?"

She laughed. She had, he decided, a very infectious laugh, much at odds with her forthright way of speaking. "The Colonel wouldn't know a Maxim from an arquebus. No, no, it's an offer from my mother's side of the family, from my Uncle Hilary actually. The O'Neills are army too and Uncle Hilary served with the Federals in the Civil War in America. He stayed over there after the peace and began working with Maxim, and now he and the inventor are in London for a demonstration. It's to take place at Wimbledon, about a month from now. Not long, but time enough for a likely lad to get the feel of the gun."

He thought, "By God, I've never met anyone like her . . . there *isn't* anyone like her . . . She could sell coal in hell . . ." but said, "Well, that explains a good deal. But if the inventor himself is here, and your Uncle Hilary has been working on the prototype, wouldn't they be the obvious people to do the demonstrating?"

"No," she said, "they certainly would not. For one thing, they're both financially interested. For another they're civilians, and this test is a preliminary army test, and an unofficial one at that. If someone like you, a serving officer in a line regiment, with no previous training in gunnery, can put the gun through its paces, then it's as good as sold to the British Army. Well, Mr. Swann?"

"I'd back myself to do it, Miss Corcoran. I've always been interested in fire-power, but I'm not on leave, and I'm still on regimental strength at Deal. You ought to know that junior officers can't come and go, just like that."

"Oh, that is no problem at all," she said, cheerfully. "My father does what I say when he's sober, and I mean to keep him sober for as long as it takes to attach you to the Wimbledon range as an infantry observer. What are strings for if not to be pulled?"

She was, he decided, irresistible. There was something about her that put every other woman out of mind, that reduced handsome creatures like Miss Montcrieff and Cecilia to marionettes, and even hard-riding tomboys, like his younger sisters Joanna and Helen, to relative nonentities. "By George, you're absolutely amazing, Miss Corcoran! I think you could do absolutely anything you had a mind to do, and get anything you were determined to get. If you really can arrange that posting I'm your man. Shall we shake hands on it?"

"Surely," she said, and stood up, reaching across the table, but then, standing off and looking him up and down, "You know, they're right about you, Captain Swann. You *are* lucky. You were born lucky. Why else should you have walked in here the way you did, saving me the trouble of winkling you out when every day counts. Come, I'll show you to the door. You can get a cab at the Park rank, and as soon as you are transferred to Wimbledon I'll be on hand to make the necessary introductions. Don't bother to write to me. I'll know when you're expected."

They were standing on the top step of the porch flight looking down on an empty street in the first flush of dawn when a final thought occurred to him. "Suppose my sailing date comes through? It may, any day now, and if it did I should have to go no matter how many strings were pulled at regimental level," but she replied, with a shrug, "Ships are sailing for India all the time, Captain Swann, and I keep careful eye on the Colonel's correspondence. As a matter of fact that was where I did my vetting. Goodnight to you, Captain."

She extended her hand again but this time he did not shake it. Responding to an impulse that had never before been experienced in the company of a woman, he raised it to his lips. In the glow of the porch gaslight he caught her looking at him with a curious intentness. Then the door was shut and she was gone, and he walked the few steps into Park Lane in search of a cab. He was surprised to find himself whistling.

3

The gun itself dominated his daytime thoughts. The tubby little contraption mounted on absurdly high wheels, its single barrel snouting through a steel shrapnel shield and its pungent whiff of cordite as the belts of cartridges slipped into the breech to the accompaniment of the long dry rattle. The rattle itself was arresting. It was as though the Maxim was chuckling over its appetite and could never stow too many brassy little fish in its maw, or be fed them at a rate too fast to be swallowed.

That was how he saw the Maxim gun from the first day. Not as a sophisticated piece of equipment but as something alive, with a deadliness that made one think of the rattlesnake and the cobra. It was no more than an assembly of nuts, bolts and tubing, but one soon came to respect it as a piece of mechanism with the fire-power of a battalion in ambush. For all that it was not a hard taskmaster. All it required was a steady hand, an unwinking eye, and belt after belt of cartridges, that snaked between the wheels like the bandoliers of a dead giant.

Yet he grew to love the thing. Its feel, its absolute reliability, its awful concentration of power so that he thought, as he squatted astride the short trail, with his finger on the firing button, "With a weapon like this a man could have retaken Khartoum single-handed. With this, and a trooper to feed me ammunition, I could have stayed that rout under Isandlwana." These were the thoughts that occupied him by day, when he was on the range, or down at the butts from the first light to dusk. But on Sundays, and in the evening, quite magically it seemed, she had the power to banish all thoughts of the bewhiskered Hiram S. Maxim and his deadly tool from his mind, leaving it free to explore hers as they wandered here and there about springtime London, discussing everything from Swann enterprises to her childhood memories in sunbright garrison towns all over the world, from his adventures in the field to her curious obsession with the role of the army as the flag moved across embattled continents: To the greater glory of the Queen and her subjects he would have said a short while ago, but now was beginning to have different ideas, some of them approximating to his father's. For Adam had always held that trade did not follow the flag as a matter of course. It merely packed a flag in its grips and kept it handy in case the field looked promising.

She was down at the range every day in time for luncheon, usually eaten in the company of Maxim, her long-faced Uncle Hilary (who reminded him of the Twyforde Green undertaker) and field officers from all branches of the service, who stood about watching him demolish targets at ranges from four hundred yards to over a mile and then went away shaking their heads as though they could not believe what they had seen. These men seemed not to think of him as one of themselves, a mere captain of infantry, but as a young stray whom Hiram Maxim and his lugubrious American salesmen had picked up somewhere and brought along to do their donkey work, and perhaps clear up after they had gone. But when he mentioned this to Lydia during a Sunday afternoon expedition on the river, she said, with one of her pettish shrugs, "Don't let that concern you. Those old fools are in for a rare shock in a week or so and so perhaps are you. But you'll get no more than a hint out of me until I'm sure."

It was about a week after this that he received notice of yet another visitor. Her Uncle Hilary, a man of few words, impassive save when the gun was not giving a hundred per cent satisfaction, appeared one morning looking fussed and abstracted, and his unease seemed to communicate itself to everyone else on the range. It was coming up to the luncheon break, however, before Maxim announced that His Royal Highness Prince Edward was expected, and might even deign to fire a few rounds, in which case Alex was to expend all but the last few cartridges of the belt in order to reduce the chances of jamming to a minimum.

Ordinarily, he supposed, Alex would have been awed by the occasion but he was not, for he saw the gun as a great leveller. Behind it a keen-sighted crossing-sweeper, given a feel for the thing, could decimate all the royal houses of the world in a hundred and twenty seconds, so that when, around three, there was a stir behind him, and a portly, bearded figure looking like a prosperous rabbi emerged from a group to stand at his elbow, and Maxim ordered bursts at silhouettes over four hundred, eight hundred and twelve hundred yards, Alex loosed off a thousand rounds with complete unconcern. Then, standing and acknowledging The Presence with a bow from the waist, he moved aside and allowed the Prince of Wales to take his place at the trail, guiding the gloved hand to the firing-button and joining in the polite applause when the gun chattered its final rounds. Either the gun was particularly well-sighted or His Royal Highness had a sportsman's flair for firearms. The last silhouette went over and a gleam of satisfaction showed in the poached-egg eyes. "Remarkable, Mr. Maxim!" said the deep, fruity voice. "It seems that you have something reliable there. The point is, who else has? Or will have, eh?" It was a remark Alex was to recall in later years, when the Maxim was standard equipment for the British army and navy and had inspired Hilaire Belloc's tag:

> Whatever happens we have got
> The Maxim gun and they have not.

Alex never did discover how Lydia Corcoran managed to delay his posting to India for three months, time enough to introduce several minor modifications to the gun, and get his name included in a dozen or more reports as the marksman (including a piece in *The Times* naming him as 'the expert who had supervised the royal rattle at Wimbledon') but by then he had come to terms with her inscrutability, and even more with the dynamism reposing in her small, insignificant presence. Their friendship, at first wholly centred on the new weapon, began to ripen in the warm spring weather, and he discovered in her an ability to hold his interest and enlarge his estimate of himself that had never occurred in the company of another, man or woman.

She was, he soon learned, an accomplished raconteur, with an endless repertoire of amusing anecdotes, all concerned with army life in the Colonies, and she had what he had always lacked, a memory for trivia that distinguished his father and had contributed, so it was said, to Swann's success in business. In so many ways she reminded him of Adam, whom he had always revered without, somehow, being able to love, for his father never seemed to belong to any of them save, possibly, old George. And yet, in a curious way, Lydia *did* belong to him, almost exclusively one might have said, for she had no other intimates, male or female, so that he found the prospect of being parted from her increasingly depressing as the weeks went by.

Then, at last, his sailing date came through, and she gave him advance notice of it on a Sunday outing they made to Hampton Court gardens, adding that when the Maxim was officially adopted as an arm of the Services it was probable he would be recalled to Aldershot as an instructor. But that was unlikely to happen for a year or so. Government departments, she said, were notoriously lethargic and, in any case, time was required to put the gun into production.

The prospect of being separated from her was a sad blow to his confidence and he freely admitted as much, expecting one of her brisk interjections but she said nothing, continuing to stare glumly at the sliding Thames, where it ran between two enormous beds of yellow tulips. It occurred to him then that she too was contemplating the flatness of the months ahead after an experience that he was beginning to see as half an adventure, half a conspiracy.

He said, at length, "If I do get back here, as you say, and don't get overlooked, as I think more probable, will I see anything of you, Lydia?"

She replied, avoiding his eye, "That depends on you. I can make some of your decisions but not that one."

He said, gallantly, "Why, then, let me say this. I'll never forget your kindness in arranging all this on my behalf, even if nothing at all comes of it. I'll write to you, too. I'll tell you everything that happens out there, and you must promise to keep me posted about information you squeeze out of your Uncle Hilary . . ." But then he stopped, struck by her listlessness, so uncharacteristic of all he knew of Lydia Corcoran. He said, lightly, "Come now, cheer up! If what you say is right I'll soon be back, won't I?"

But she replied, dourly, "Aye, maybe. But it's the gun that'll bring you running, not me."

"The *gun*? You think that's all our partnership has meant to me? You don't realise how I've come to think of you, as a person."

She let her grey eyes play over him for a moment, then said, unsmilingly, "As a person, maybe. As a manipulator even. But not as a woman, Alex."

It wasn't true, or not in the sense she meant it, and not for the first time in a situation like this he yearned for the glibness of his brother George, or the subtlety of his brother Giles, neither of whom seemed to have the least difficulty in finding the right thing to say. "But that's . . . that's nonsense, Lydia! And it's not fair to either of us! I've never met a woman I admire half as much, or anyone I need as much for that matter. For the fact is I've never had confidence in myself as a man or a soldier. It was . . . well . . . meeting you, listening to you, knowing you were there, loading for me as it were, that made the difference. All the difference in the world, you understand?"

At the word 'need' her chin came up and her eyes seemed to expand so that they looked almost large enough to swim in. She took his hand, clutching it so fiercely that she dropped a glove on the gravel in front of the seat they occupied. He had seen that look of intensity once before, when she bade him goodnight on the steps of her home on the occasion of their first meeting. She said, fervently, "*Need*, Alex? You mean that? *Need*?"

And aware of gaining the initiative for the first time in their acquaintance, he said, emphatically, "Of course I mean it! I've thought of myself quite differently since that night we met. I couldn't make a success of anything without you in the offing. That's why I'm so damned low about sailing for India. I'll tell you something else. This last month has been the happiest of my life." And then, like a dissolving log-jam in the path of a torrent, all doubts concerning his future were swept away, for he saw her as a kind of bridge between himself and fulfilment and rushed on, heedlessly, "Why do we need to separate? If we married before I sailed I could get quarters, and you could come out on the first available boat, and India would be tremendous fun if you were there, for I'd know precisely how to tackle any job I was saddled with. Will you marry me, Lydia? Could it be arranged in such a hurry, because if not . . ." and he was going to say something conventional about her thinking it over, and perhaps discussing it with her father, but there was no trace of listlessness about her now as she said, with breathless positivity, *"Arranged!* Why, of course it could! How long do banns take? Three weeks, isn't it, and you've got twenty-four days, not counting today! Things like that—as important as that—why Alex, they've been arranged in half the time," and she threw both arms around his neck and embraced him with a fervour that made the playful approach of Cecilia seem anaemic. He noticed something else too, in that first, rapturous gesture on her part. Not only was she very pleasant to kiss but somehow her entire being had undergone a transformation in that she seemed, at that range, to contain more promise than any girl he had ever held in his arms.

*   *   *

Adam, watching them kneeling together at the altar of the garrison church in Deal, did not share his son's sentiments. He had always favoured chubby, well-rounded women, and had often told Henrietta that he married her on the strength of her shapely bottom, the first part of her anatomy he had seen as he rode over the skyline of Seddon Moor and surprised her washing herself in a puddle.

He conceded that Lydia Corcoran was an interesting little body, with a healthy complexion, large, soulful eyes, and any amount of spunk to judge by that square, resolute chin. He was even prepared to admit she was right for Alex, who had struck him, over the years, as being much in need of a qualified pilot, and maybe a barker to draw a crowd for him. But Lydia Corcoran's angularity, flat chest and overall boyishness made no appeal at all to his senses. And to interest him at all a woman had had to do that, from the moment he was required to tip his hat to them.

He said nothing of her deficiencies, however, not even to Henrietta, who seemed, improbably, to have taken a great liking to the funny little thing. Instead he congratulated himself on his own sagacity, as he invariably did at weddings, thinking back to the far off day when Henrietta, eighteen and as ignorant of men and men's needs as a Carmelite nun, had stood beside him in the parish church at Keswick, subdued for once. But happily not for long.

It was otherwise with Henrietta, sitting beside him, and contriving to look around thirty instead of forty-eight in a get-up that put every other woman present to shame. She was not witnessing the ceremony as a mother or a mother-in-law but as a kind of adjudicator in the eternal duel of the sexes and thus found herself prejudiced in favour of the bride. This was odd, she reflected, remembering that Alex had been her ewe lamb from the moment his sex was announced by Ellen Michelmore, her midwife, for she had felt badly about her first-born being a girl. She supposed, therefore, that she was applauding Lydia's David-versus-Goliath victory, and the courage and staying power of all women who went out to do battle with such modest equipment. For who would have thought a homely little pixie like her would have captured such a prize after so short a campaign? And with no bait save brains and a pair of soulful grey eyes. It really was remarkable, and had they been elsewhere she would have felt like applauding, for she saw Lydia Corcoran's victory as a victory for all women in their miserably handicapped battle against the lords of creation, although she might not have acknowledged it as such had she not been convinced, from that first encounter at 'Tryst', that the dear boy did not see Lydia as other men would. There was that old saw about love's blindness and she had made allowances for this at once, but it was the glitter of tears in Lydia's eyes that told her the girl had faced up to this from the first, and surely meant that she would go out of her way to compensate for her deficiencies. In Henrietta's eyes, this was a thumping good start to any marriage. Better than most grooms could look for, and better, to her way of thinking, than young Giles could expect come the spring, notwithstanding the looks, figure and dowry Romayne Rycroft-Mostyn would bring him.

As always at a family muster in church, she ran her eye proudly down the pews occupied by the Swann contingent and thought, seeing present one son-in-law, one daughter-in-law, and four grandchildren (a promising dividend in seven-and-a-half years if you thought about it). "Well, that's another of them off our hands, and before this time next year it will be Giles' turn. And after that Joanna's, maybe. Or Helen's. Or even Hugo's, and before we know it we shall be left in that great place with the two little ones, and I daresay the emptiness of 'Tryst' will take a bit of getting used to. But if Adam keeps his promise about spending most of his time there I shan't bother. One or other of them will always be coming back, and it will always be somewhere to dump the grandchildren . . ."

The thought was a reassuring one and worth a tear or two, so she reached in her sleeve for a handkerchief but suddenly thought better of it. She had never had the slightest desire to snivel at a wedding and only did it because people seemed to expect it of you. Instead, she did something that came far more naturally to her, sliding her hand along the leading edge of the pew until it brushed against Adam's. Taking the hint, he squeezed it, grinned, and at once put on his solemn face again.

3

Giles on a Seesaw

It was the most humiliating of their many quarrels. Not because, on that final occasion, it happened at an Oxford Street millinery counter, with a floor-walker and half a dozen assistants looking on, but because of all the unforgiveable things they said to one another on the way home, culminating in his rejection, on her door-step, of her peace terms. For Giles did not see them as terms but as an ultimatum, and because he was more of a Swann than he knew, an ultimatum that had to be rejected, even against his better judgement.

* * *

Henrietta's concern regarding the increasing roughness of Giles' ride was not misplaced. A long engagement, to a girl of Romayne Rycroft-Mostyn's temperament, was a marathon obstacle course and men older, wiser and warier than Giles Swann would have failed it. Few, for that matter, would have stayed half the distance, yet somehow, because he had learned to make generous allowances for all kinds of idiosyncrasies and inconsistencies in people, Giles hung on; helped by his books, maybe, certainly by his monumental patience. But in the main because his love for her was rooted in compassion.

He did not see her as all the others did, a spoiled, wayward brat, with a rich father who was far more interested in power than parenthood, but as a beautiful, desperately confused child who had touched his heart and learned, through her instincts possibly, to look to him alone for help.

He was not so much of a prig as to acknowledge this and yet, deep down, he knew that it was so. On the surface the love that blew hot and cold in him was no more complicated than that any impressionable young man might harbour for a girl as pretty as

Romayne Rycroft-Mostyn and there were times, many times, when he thought of himself as the most uniquely privileged male in the world. There were other times when he felt so bruised and battered by the contest that he was inclined to wonder whether he was equipped, mentally or physically, to accept such a challenge.

Then he would draw back for a day or so, to get his second wind he would tell himself, for he never seriously contemplated renunciation and usually, on her own initiative, she would bounce back into his life with all the gaiety and gusto of that first, idyllic month they shared together in the mountains. After that, for a period, she would conduct herself decorously until some ill-judged word, some fancied slight, some caprice or random manifestation of her eternal restlessness would promote yet another explosive situation and he would again retreat into himself, wondering if he had bitten off far more than he could chew.

There was simply no reasoning with her once she let her ungovernable temper erupt through the crust of her admitted need of him, a deep, personal need that sometimes appeared to him as an obsession rather than a normal relationship between a woman and man in love. Then there was nothing to be done but to stand clear and wait for the storm to blow itself out.

All in all, however, he was philosophical about the plunges, keeping his eye on the peaks and levels, for the poets had taught him that any woman worth her salt had to be wooed, and that the wisest woman in the world was short on logic. Once, after a particularly testing skirmish, he made a direct appeal to her father, expressing his doubts concerning his qualifications as a shrew-tamer. But Sir Clive, with whom his relationship had broadened to include humour, made light of his problems.

"The girl has always been exceptionally highly-strung," he said, offering his prospective son-in-law one of his best Havana cigars. "Growing up without benefit of a mother, in charge of rule-of-thumb pedants like those professional governesses and peasants like Maggie, in Beddgelert, hasn't done much to help her over the hump of adolescence. Come to think of it she's been slower than most girls about the business of growing up but I haven't much doubt that will be remedied the moment she acquires married status and responsibilities to go along with it." He looked at Giles shrewdly but kindly. "Sorry to counsel nothing but patience, lad," he added. "But then, patience is your strong suit, isn't it? That's why I realised from the very beginning you were the right man for her. If you can't tame the lass nobody can."

"I don't seem to be making much progress," Giles told him, glumly, but the industrialist dismissed this as excessive modesty. "You're not the one to assess that," he said. "I think you are and you're not suggesting Romayne is cooling off, are you?"

"No, sir. I'm prepared to admit that I mean a good deal to her but . . ."

"Mean a good deal to her? Good God, boy, face facts! She's head over heels in love with you and can't wait to call herself Mrs. Swann and have your babies! As for her temper, her damned contrariness —well, you have an advantage there that I never had. You've my permission to treat her as a wilful child if she tries your patience too far and don't wait until you're man and wife to do it. Do you or don't you intend to smoke that cigar you're fidgeting with?"

Giles said, with a smile, "I haven't your stomach for them, sir. I'll manage with one of these if you don't mind," and he took out a cigarette-case Romayne had given him for his twentieth birthday gift and puffed away at a Turkish cigarette, Sir Clive watching him with the genial expression he reserved for the few people he trusted.

"Glad you had the sense to come to me," he said. "Been meaning to broach something to you. I've already discussed it with your father as a matter of fact, and I daresay that was high-handed of me without sounding you first, but it's my way. How are you settling to that haulage business, now you've had time to assess it as a career?"

"If you've been discussing me with the Governor you'll know the answer to that," said Giles, having learned that Sir Clive and his father had that much in common. Both liked to come straight to the point when discussing business.

"Yes, I think I can say I do," Sir Clive replied, blowing out a cloud of smoke and watching it disperse in the draught from the window. "He was obligingly frank. Says you'll never make a salesman, and he wouldn't back you to get the better of someone who wasn't hamstrung by the theory and practice of a gentleman. He mentioned points in your favour, however."

"I'm glad to hear it. What were they?"

"That you had a way with people, work people. That you could get on their level without patronising them, and that's damned rare in a gaffer's son. Said you had a rare head for figures too, that neither of your brothers have, and that set me thinking. Towards selfish ends, I might add."

Sir Clive Rycroft-Mostyn had always interested Giles and he supposed he had respect for him, but he was not a man one could like, or not in the way it was possible to compromise between Adam Swann as man and adventurer. Giles had, from the first, seen his future father-in-law as a man wholly obsessed with money, and with the power money gave him. Closer acquaintance had done nothing to mellow this judgement. He said, politely, "What proposition did you put to my father, sir?"

"One that could give you scope, I should say. You've been concerned with the employees' Friendly Society, I understand."

"I have indeed and it's one of the best in being. I think the time will come when a scheme of that kind will be a statutory obligation for all big concerns. It already is in some parts of Germany."

"Inclined to agree with you," Sir Clive said, unexpectedly, "and that's where I think you could find a place in my concerns. Now don't shy away. Pay me the compliment of hearing me out, for I'm aware of your loyalty to your father and approve it. I wish to God I had at least one son I could fall back on but I haven't. You look like being the closest I'll ever come to getting one. Hold on a minute," and he moved over to his wall-safe and spun the combination.

He was a pioneer in this kind of gadget. Every contrivance that conservative merchants thought of as new-fangled, Sir Clive Rycroft-Mostyn made it his business to install, once he had satisfied himself it was likely to increase his administrative efficiency. He was one of the few businessmen Giles knew who subscribed to the London Telephone Company, and at his headquarters in Blackfriars he already employed two lady typewriters and their ungainly, chattering machines.

He came back to Giles with a typewritten document bound in strong, buff covers and tied with tape. "Run your eye down the first page. It's a privilege, I assure you. I wouldn't show it to anyone."

It was a list of all the Rycroft-Mostyn enterprises and although

Giles had always known they were extensive, he was astonished by their variety now that he saw them listed in their various categories. The tally included mines, iron foundries, a tinplate works, the cable factory Romayne had mentioned the first day they met, several Scottish export warehouses, that Giles recognised as regular ports of call by Jake Higson in the north, and over a dozen companies concerned with land and property development in London and north-country cities.

"How many men does your father employ?" asked Sir Clive, having given him a moment to absorb the list.

"Nowhere near as many as you, sir. Around two thousand, I believe. Concerns of this size must absorb almost double that number."

"More than double. Six thousand, eight hundred and sixty, to be exact. And what is more to the point nearly half that total are women. Tell me, does the initiation and maintenance of a provident scheme along your father's lines interest you?"

It had never once struck Giles that Sir Clive regarded his employees as people, certainly not in the sense that Adam did, and had done from the earliest days of the network. He said, carefully, "I don't think a provident society on our lines would survive long in your concerns, Sir Clive. The men run it themselves for the most part and on an area basis. You've always set your face against co-operatives of any kind. You've told me so, more than once."

"Aye, I have," Sir Clive said, blandly, "and I'm not going back on it, but there's more than one way to kill a cat. Having taken a close look at your scheme I can think of half a dozen variations. Co-operatives no. I can't see myself putting power into the hands of people I employ. Neither would I stand by and watch others play fast and loose with my capital. But suppose I was prepared to put pound for pound against employees' contributions, and invest the money accruing, profits to be ploughed back into a fund for sickness and accident benefits and a bonus based on increased output? Could you draft a scheme on that scale, involving over six thousand hands operating a dozen different industries?"

"Certainly I could, providing you supplied me with the information I should need."

"What kind of information exactly?"

"Rates of pay, annual turnover and profits on one year's trading for each concern."

He might have been mistaken but it seemed to him Sir Clive's expression hardened at the word 'profits' and it helped to resolve him. He thought, "Damn it, it's time I knew where I stand with him as well as his daughter . . . If he has something like this in mind it's prompted by prestige not charity . . ." and he went on, "There's one thing, however. My father's provident scheme is small fry compared with anything on that scale and I'm not saying I'm the man for the job. Any trained actuary could do it more objectively. If you're serious, that is."

"Oh, I'm serious, lad." The smooth, cherubic face assumed a genial expression so that Giles saw it as that of an intelligent, greedy baby. "I'm quite serious but you're wrong on one count. An actuary couldn't help me to come to a hard decision about something as momentous as this but you could, I'm persuaded of that. For one thing, you're a born radical, unless I am mistaken. For another you're of the generation touched by the hem of the worthy Doctor Arnold's gown. No, no, I'm not sneering, lad. You youngsters, products of the new schools, have been educated to apply Christian ethics to business practices. I didn't have that advantage and neither did any one among my managers. We all came up in the cut-and-thrust, devil-take-the-hindmost days of an earlier generation. The only academy I ever attended was the Academy of Midnight Oil, but I'm no stick-in-the-mud or I wouldn't have got as far as I have. Well?"

Giles considered. It was tempting, even if it meant turning his back on a man he understood and respected, and putting his future in the hands of someone he had never trusted.

"You want me to decide now?"

"Certainly not. Take as long as you please. We could shelve it until after you're married, if you prefer."

"I could give you an answer before that. I should have to discuss this with my father, and well . . . with . . . someone else, who I believe would encourage me to take it up."

"Romayne is in favour of it. I can tell you that now."

"Not Romayne, sir. Someone with practical experience of this kind of thing. But I'd prefer not to go into that now."

"Suit yourself. Consult whom you please. But I think you're the

man for the job. I also happen to think you would find . . . well
. . . let's say fulfilment in a task of that sort."

"Yes, sir, and thank you."

They parted on this note and there was little doubt in Giles' mind
at that time but that he would accept the post. But before he did
he meant to consult John Catesby, up in the Polygon. Of all people
he knew Catesby was the best qualified to give him disinterested advice on the wisdom or otherwise of accepting a position of referee
between Sir Clive Rycroft-Mostyn and the six thousand, eight hundred and sixty men and women in his employ. He thought, as he
made his way back to the Bermondsey headquarters, "He had that
figure off pat. Maybe a little too pat. I wouldn't put it past him to
know how many on his payroll were potential trade-unionists," and
it occurred to him that a paternally-based provident scheme might
be Sir Clive's way of insuring himself against industrial anarchy of
the kind men of his type were always prophesying as a result of
workers' participation in their affairs.

2

In the event he made up his mind almost at once. Catesby happened
to call in at Headquarters that same week and, somewhat to Giles'
surprise, enthusiastically endorsed the prospect of having a member
of the Swann family strategically placed in an industrial grouping
as powerful as the Rycroft-Mostyn enterprises. "Why, lad, you could
do a power o' good there," he said, as soon as Giles had outlined the
proposal. "Right here what are you doing but preaching to the converted? Your father has seen things our way for years, but that old
bastard, and the scabs he runs with, well, I'll be frank with you, I
took a knock when I heard you were to marry into that family! Rycroft has a bad reputation as an employer and maybe you knew that
from the start. But there, a lad doesn't pick a lass on the strength of
her folks, or not unless he's fortune-hunting, and that's not in your
line, is it?"

"Not in the least," Giles said, merrily. "As a matter of fact I always saw his money as a drawback, but a job like that gives point

to working for him and the Governor has left it up to me. After all, he now has two sons established in the firm and I've always regarded myself as expendable. I'll take it then, but I won't pay you the compliment of telling Sir Clive who will be likely to make the bullets I intend to fire."

"Nay," Catesby said, seriously, "for Christ's sake keep my name out of it, lad! I daresay I've been on Rycroft's private list of trouble-brewers for years. However, I would take it kindly if you kept me informed on the sort of scheme you intend to promote and how he shapes to it."

"I'll do that, John," Giles told him. "Maybe we could both learn something from the process." And he went off to tell Romayne that he had agreed to work for Sir Clive as soon as they were married.

The prospect of him being regarded as, in her eyes at least, her father's heir-apparent, kept Romayne in high spirits for weeks, and wedding plans were well advanced before another eruption on her part gave him a chance to put her father's advice to the test.

It was a cloudless day, and they were enjoying one of their expeditions up to the old military canal, a few miles south of 'Tryst', where the lock-keeper was always ready to lend them his skiff for a water picnic.

The canal was joined, a mile or so below the lock, by a small river that emptied itself into the reach at a point where the banks were screened by thick clumps of elms and poplars, and the inflow promoted a certain amount of current that spent itself the far side of the pack-horse bridge.

He noted a mischievous sparkle in her eye as he sculled slowly downstream and was, in fact, thinking how pretty she looked, sitting on the stern with the sun glinting in her red-gold hair, and her chin tilted so that the down-slanting brim of her spectacular hat (a creation known, so she told him, as 'The three-storey-and-basement' and the very latest in summer wear) threw a shadow across the lower half of her face. She said, suddenly, "Hi, let *me* row, Giles. Move back and I'll take one oar," but he said, glancing at the current, "Not until we can pull into the bank beyond the bridge. I can hold her steady there."

"No, Giles, now!" and she half-raised herself, grabbing the starboard scull to that the little cockle-shell swung into mid-stream rocking dangerously, shipping water in the bows and finally throwing her off balance, so that she sprawled face foremost across the thwarts.

She scrambled up and he was able to trim the boat somewhat by throwing his weight to one side but they lost an oar and began to spin in the current, heading into one of the buttresses of the bridge. The impact caused her to lose her balance again and this time they rolled together in the bows, with more water slopping over the gunwale as the boat rebounded, shot through the arch and grounded in an iris clump where a cattle path led down to the water.

"You damned little fool!" he shouted. "That water was deep and you can't swim a stroke! Don't you ever use your head, except as a post for silly hats?"

She was half-lying in the two or three inches of water they had shipped and her expression, as she raised her head and stared up at him, with her mouth open and her three-storey-and-basement hat half toppled, would have struck him as comical had he not realised how near she had come to over-setting them in a deep and turbulent patch of water. She said, rising to her knees, "How dare you swear at me! Nobody ever swore at me before!" And to his extreme indignation, she slapped him across the face with her wet glove.

It was not really a case of consciously following Sir Clive's hint. The exasperation of months went into his reflex action as he threw himself forward grabbed her by the waist, threw her half across his knee, and began to spank her so soundly that her struggles rolled them half out of the boat. Then he loosed his hold on her, so that she pitched half in and half out of the shallows where, despite the dry spell, there was still mud in hoof sockets left by the cattle.

She shrieked, despairingly, "You *beast*! You *wretch*! Look at me! My new dress . . . !"—But paying no further attention to her he went off along the towpath in search of the missing oar and presently spied it in a patch of reeds some three hundred yards beyond the bridge.

He took his time retrieving it and in ambling back, thinking, "If this is the end I'm not sorry—she'd try the patience of Job, and mine's about run out!" And suddenly the prospect of being free again, and no longer at the mercy of her moods, seemed to him almost desirable so that he approached the beached boat with a certain jauntiness that increased when, moving over the last fifty yards of towpath, he saw her hat floating in midstream.

He would not have been much surprised to have found her gone. It would have been like her, in one of these flaring tempers, to flounce off, no matter where she was, or what time of day or night it was, but she was still there, stooping over the canting boat and bailing with a tin bowl. She said, over her shoulder as he approached, "She's almost empty. We could tip her and drain the rest," but he replied, wearily, "Hang the boat, we've got to talk. Come and sit here," and he took a seat on a rail that divided the shillet from the open pasture.

She threw aside the bowl and came and sat beside him, her expression almost serene, saying, "You found the oar, then?" and when he made no reply, "I'm sorry, dearest. It was a perfectly stupid thing to do. I really *am* sorry. Both for that and hitting out when you swore at me. Am I forgiven?"

He said, dismally, "I'm hanged if I know, Romayne. You gave me a frightful scare. I daresay I could have fished you out if it came to it but it was a crazy thing to do in deep water and approaching the bridge on a current."

"Oh, I realise that," she said, equably, "and I got a spanking for it and now I've apologised, so we're quits, aren't we?"

"I'm not sure we are, Romayne."

"Why aren't we?" Her eyes opened as wide as a child's. "I don't mind in the least saying I deserved what I got and it hurt, I can tell you. You can hit very hard when you lose your temper." Suddenly she chuckled, an irrepressible chuckle that made him feel almost churlish for prolonging the quarrel. "I've never seen you lose your temper before. I wasn't even sure you had one. It was quite exciting to see it soar right out of you. Like a sky-rocket!"

"Well, God knows, it's a wonder you've never seen it soar before. There have been times enough. Or aren't you willing to admit that?"

"Oh, yes, I'm sure there must have been, but you always held on to it, didn't you? And that . . . well . . . nagged at me."

"Are you saying you deliberately provoked me just now?"

"In a way I did. Although I was the one who got the biggest surprise."

"But why? For heaven's sake, Romayne, you're not a kid running wild in Wales, as you were when you did something nearly as crazy to attract attention to yourself. Two months from now you'll be a married woman. In a year or so you might even have a child of your own. Doesn't that mean anything to you?"

She said, seriously now, "A great deal more to me than it does to you."

"Now what can you mean by that?"

"Just what I say, Giles. Marrying you, being your wife, having our children, means just about everything to me. You're the only person I care about in the world, the only one I ever did care about, although I don't think I could say why or not exactly."

"Well, then . . ."

"No, you listen, Giles. That isn't so in your case. Oh, not because you aren't in love with me, but because there's such a lot of you. There's *always* been a lot of you and you Swanns stick together as a tribe. If you lost me I daresay you'd mope for a spell but you'd soon get over it. One of your sisters would find you a nice, tame girl, and your mother would fuss over you, and if you cared to you could talk things over with that nice father of yours. You're just one of a clan, you see, whereas you are all I've got, for I don't count Papa, and he would admit to that if you asked him. There you are, and it's all fearfully lopsided, isn't it?"

How did one reply to this kind of plea, and in a way it was a plea. A minute passed before he said, carefully, "All right. But if I'm so important to you why the devil do you keep letting me see the worst of you? I can understand us quarrelling every now and again. Even people in love don't see eye to eye all the time, but hang it, you go out of your way to provoke scenes every so often, the way you admitted doing just now. What kind of reason can there be for that?"

"No one reason." She sat with her hands spread behind her along the rail, her eyes fixed on the further bank.

"Then tell me, if you can."

"One good reason is all this stupid waiting. Another is all the fuss everybody is going to."

"As to the waiting, it's nearly over, isn't it? And as to the fuss, you know I don't give a rap whether we have a spectacular wedding or a private affair, with just the two families. What are the other reasons?"

"They're about things you feel but can't put into words."

"Well, just try."

She turned her head then and looked at him, calmly and speculatively. "I suppose you could call it exploring, like men when they
climb mountains and cross jungles to see what it's like the far side of
a continent. What I mean is, you love someone, and you think you
know them, but you don't, of course. You go on finding out new
things about them all the time, the way I found out you had a
temper, and could act as Gilpin did provided you were goaded
enough."

"Who is Gilpin?"

"Gilpin?" Her eyes became vague for a moment but then cleared.
"Oh, no one special. A groom at a place we had in Hampshire, years
ago. He was the only other man who hit me but he did it with a
riding crop and I had bruises on my behind for nearly a month."

"Good God! What made him do that?"

"I took a mare out that was said to be dangerous. She wasn't
though, just weak-kneed and broke a leg, a hundred yards from
the stable. Gilpin came up and went for me with the crop. I suppose I deserved that too."

"What on earth did your father do to Gilpin?"

"He gave him a sovereign, I think. I'm not sure. He left soon after.
Where was I?"

He passed his hand across his brow. "You were trying to explain . . ."

"Oh, yes, I remember. Well, a girl thinks a lot about love and
husbands, long before she actually experiences either one of them.
I don't know how it is with boys. Not the same, I imagine. Then
you fall in love, the way I did that morning by the river, and naturally you're very curious to find out everything you can about the
man you're in love *with*, and want to spend your life with, but
to do that properly you can't just drift along hoping to learn things
by accident. At least, *I* can't. It's so boring, especially so in our case,
when we have to keep holding back all the time. Do you follow
me?"

"In a way," he said. "In a dim sort of way. But look here, Romayne,
haven't you ever asked yourself if it might be boring after we're
married?"

611

"I haven't needed to. I realised it would be exactly the opposite the moment I kissed you on the way home to breakfast after you fished me out of the river that time."

He sat thinking a moment. "Listen here, Romayne, at the risk of sounding terribly stuffy and pompous, I ought to remind you marriage isn't just a matter of kissing, and sharing the same bed. It's deciding things together, working things out together, giving way to one another now and again, all kinds of humdrum things of that kind."

"How do you know?" she said, unexpectedly. "You've never been married before."

"Well, of course I haven't, but damn it, I've watched other people and I've read and thought about it."

"Yes," she said, "and maybe that's the trouble. What I mean is you watch and read and think most of the time. The real *you* never comes out, except in flashes like just now. That was almost worth risking being drowned. It made me feel . . . well . . . important to you. For just a minute I had the feeling that, if it had happened somewhere more private, I would have had a chance to discover you as a person. You would have treated me as a woman ought to be treated by a man and I would have loved that. It would have made everything more real, if you see what I mean."

He had no more than a glimmering of what she was trying to say, sensing only that she was as primitive as a South Sea Islander, with all the instincts and appetites of a savage, hopelessly at odds with her environment and even more so with the times in which they lived. In the way that he had been able to see the Exmoor hills as he pictured them a million years ago, he caught a glimpse of her stripped of those fancy, flouncy clothes and removed from this sedate landscape, a woman effortlessly involved in the basics of existence, uncluttered by fads and fashions and prohibitions, groaning under him on the floor of some prehistoric cave, as she clamoured for seed representing continuity. In most ways more animal than human. He saw that much but what to do about it was something else, although it did cross his mind then that her real personality would never emerge until they were man and wife and lying in one another's arms. He said, at last, "We're right for one another, Romayne. I haven't the least doubt of that. And we could be very happy together, I'm sure of that too. It isn't long now, so why waste the rest of the day arguing the toss? Let's go on down to that spinney and picnic. We can light a fire there and boil up the kettle," and he put his arms round her and kissed her on the mouth.

3

It wasn't long certainly but, in the event, it was too long by more than a month.

Three weeks later, as they were bowling along Oxford Street some time after eleven o'clock at night, after dining with a maiden aunt of hers who lived in Bayswater, and wanted to consult them about a wedding gift, she called sharply to the cabby, telling him to stop outside a costumier's she was in the habit of visiting from time to time. It was a large, opulent establishment called McCready and Moffat, the place where she had bought the hat that ended its brief life in the military canal.

"Why, it's still there!" she exclaimed. "I made sure it would have gone. Oh, I must have it, Giles. It's adorable!" and as the cab stopped she pointed excitedly to a scarlet gable bonnet, perched on a stand in the centre of a recently-dressed window. "Isn't it chic? Wouldn't it just set off my going-away costume?"

"You can't have it now," he said. "It's eleven-thirty and they'll be closing."

"Rubbish," she said, skipping out on to the pavement before he could stop her, "it's Saturday night and they stay open until midnight on Saturdays. Besides, if I don't have it now it'll be gone by the time I get here on Monday," and without waiting for him to follow she sailed into the shop and approached the millinery counter.

He followed reluctantly, telling the cabby to wait. The shop was still open certainly but there were no other customers. At various counters yawning girls were folding lengths of material and draping dust-sheets over dummies. The girl at the millinery counter looked tired enough to drop, a very pale, red-haired woman, younger than Romayne, with hair parted in the middle and looped back over her ears. She wore a plain grey dress and was holding herself very straight, Giles noticed, but there was something about the turned-down mouth and drawn expression that suggested more than physical exhaustion. He saw another girl at the glove counter glance sourly across at them as a floor-walker, a paunched man with a mottled complexion and a walrus moustache, wiped the bored expression from his face and shot both cuffs. Romayne said, briskly, "The red gable bonnet in the window. How much is it?" and the pale girl said, with a strong Welsh accent, "I . . . I'm not sure, ma'am . . ."

He had a feeling of impending disaster. Out of the corner of his eye he saw the floor-walker glide forward and sensed extreme hostility in every girl within earshot, but the floor-walker said, sharply, "Then find out, Miss Davies! Don't just stand there!" and the girl's tired eyes flashed as she said, still politely, "In the centre of the window, it is, Mr. Bryanston. Mean taking everything out to get at it . . ." But then under his stern gaze she faltered, but went on, after an imperceptible pause, "Just finished dressing the window we have and it's gone closing time."

The floor-walker opened his mouth presumably to roar his indignation, but Giles cut in, "Reserve it, whatever the price. If you really want it, that is," and Romayne snapped, "Of course I want it. I know my own mind, don't I? And I want it now," and to the girl, "Get it!"

It was like watching a fuse splutter the last few inches towards a powder barrel. He knew, somehow, that the Welsh shop assistant was going to erupt, that everyone in the shop was watching and waiting for the eruption, as though poised to dive for cover. He heard the floor-walker gibber, "Get it . . . *get* it, you hear? The customer wants it now . . . *Get* it!" But suddenly the girl braced herself, seeming, in a curious way, to absorb the dignity that everyone about her had lost. Her knuckles gleamed white on the scissors she was holding and she seemed to rock a little, as though on the point of making a leap. Her complexion turned a shade paler. In the hard light of the overhead lamps it seemed the colour of cheese.

"No!" she said. "No, I won't get it! Sooner die, I would. Sooner die right her where I stand!"

Suddenly, for Giles, the images blurred and fused so that he had no more than an impression of several things happening simultaneously. The floor-walker raised his hands in supplication and the sound that emerged from him was not a roar but a squeak that might have been that of a child on whose foot somebody had trodden. At the same time Romayne swung round, moving towards the window, as though determined to help herself to the bonnet. The mousy-looking girl at the glove counter popped out from behind her barrier, grinning like an urchin who has just seen a barrel-organ monkey perform a somersault. Then the girl in grey let the scissors fall with a clatter and keeled right over, disappearing from sight behind the stacked counter.

Full awareness returned to him then and he grabbed Romayne by the shoulder, just as she had raised her hand to the catch that fastened the window backing. He spun her round, hissing, "*Out!* Out of here, before I cram the damned hat down your throat!" And then, to the floor-walker, "Look after her, you fool! Can't you see she's ill? Hasn't anybody got any damned sense . . . ?" And without quite realising how it was accomplished he whirled Romayne across the shop and through the door on to the crowded pavement, holding her tightly above the elbow while he lugged open the cab door and bundled her in so roughly that she pitched on her hands and knees in a flurry of skirts and petticoats. Seconds later he had followed her, shouting to the cabby to drive on and by the time Romayne had scrambled to the seat they were crossing the Circus and the shop was a hundred yards behind them.

*   *   *

He said, in a voice that went some way towards expressing the terrible anger he felt for her, "That was unforgivable! That poor little devil was sick! Sick and exhausted! She'd been fifteen hours on her feet, serving spoiled little brats like you, and they aren't allowed to sit on pain of the sack, do you realise that? My God, but I was ashamed for you! Right down in my stomach, you understand? How can you be so . . . so damned callous? How the hell would *you* like to stand there at the beck and call of every little bitch who fancied a hat, or a length of ribbon at this time of night? And for what, in God's name? I'll tell you! I'll tell you! Five shillings a week, and the mush they feed living-in girls at those places! Five shillings, and halfpenny in the pound spiffs if she's lucky. Less fines for 'refusing'. She's probably being fined now, the minute she comes out of her faint. Or sacked more likely. Turned loose without a character, with a choice of starvation or domestic service and someone like you holding the whip over her . . . !"

She said in a strangled voice, "Have you *quite* finished? Have you done humiliating me?"

"*Humiliating* you! By God, I'd really like to humiliate you! I'd like to peel off your drawers and take the skin from your backside in front of them all, just to prove you weren't God Almighty! This is the end, you understand? I can't stand any more of this. Not another day! Not an hour!"

In the dark interior of the cab he felt her stiffen. She said nothing for a moment and then, relatively calmly, "You really mean that, Giles? It isn't just another show of temper?"

"I mean it," he said. "I'll write to your father in the morning and you can sue me for breach of promise if you've a mind to." And he turned away from her, gloomily watching the reflection of the gas globes on the railings of the palace as the cab moved at a trot into Buckingham Palace Road.

There were no more exchanges after that. They sat in silence until the cab pulled up outside her father's house and he handed her out. She went up the steps slowly and he stood watching her from the pavement but as she raised her hand to the knocker he called, "Wait!" and ran up beside her. She turned then so that he could see her face in the subdued glow of the porch light. She was very pale but her expression, so far as he could judge, was blank.

"Well, Giles?"

"It wouldn't work. You must see that. We're different, utterly different. We see everything differently. All we'd succeed in doing would be to make each other wretched. You see that, don't you?"

"Yes," she said slowly, "as things are, I do."

"They can't ever be any different."

"You think not? Well, I don't. What happened back there wasn't as important as you make it sound. It was just that I didn't think, that it never once occurred to me I was doing anything other than buying a hat."

"But that's just it! You didn't think and you won't ever think. Maybe it wouldn't matter to most men but it matters to me. Things like that are important to me and if you haven't realised that by now you never will. You'd be much better off with someone more like yourself, someone who could have laughed that awful scene off." He paused. "I'm sorry. I'm desperately sorry for both of us. For your father too in a way."

"*Giles?*"

"Well?"

"Suppose . . . suppose we ran off? *Now.* This minute. To Gretna Green, where we could be married at once, with nobody but ourselves. Or not even that. Somewhere abroad where we'd be by ourselves."

"How would that solve anything?"

"But it would, I know it would. We'd be together all the time, we'd be lovers instead of showpieces for everyone we know, and it *would* make a difference. If we'd done that a long time ago this kind of thing wouldn't have happened. I'd have belonged to you. I'd have felt settled and . . . different. Different inside, you see? It's terribly hard to explain but I know I'm right. I *know* it, you understand? I . . . I'd grow differently. I'd change into the kind of person you want, that you wouldn't be ashamed of. Why can't we do that first and think about everything else afterwards?"

Her naïveté astounded him. That she could imagine, for a single moment, that intimacy and removal from all outside contacts would transform her magically into an entirely different person, seemed to him self-delusion amounting to hysteria. But he saw also that nothing he could say would persuade her that her thinking it was an illusion. He said, "No, Romayne. It wouldn't change anything. All it would do is to upset a lot of people. I'll write to your father tomorrow and make him understand somehow. You think about it quietly, and you'll understand too."

He went down the steps and turned towards the palace, having no clear idea where he was going or where he would sleep since he had planned to spend the weekend at her home. It was an airless night, with the street lamps burning steadily and very little traffic about. He felt numb, no longer able to think clearly and logically. He found himself listening to the sound of his own footfalls on the flagstones, as if he was walking alone down an endless corridor in a poor light.

4

Sunday passed and Monday. He said nothing of the quarrel to anyone, avoiding contact with all whom it was possible to avoid. When someone spoke to him he replied in monosyllables, pretending to be occupied with calls that took him away from home and Tybalt's counting house, where he had a small office of his own, used by George when he was about the place. On Tuesday he closeted himself here and made yet another attempt to set on paper to Sir Clive what had occurred but the words seemed banal and stilted and finally he tossed the page into the wastepaper basket and went out towards London Bridge, threading his way through slow-moving traffic without any clear idea where he was going until he found himself outside the Law Courts. There was a cab rank here and he stood hesitating beside it. Suddenly the prospect of writing to Sir Clive seemed cowardly and he said aloud, "God damn it, I'll tell him to his face. It's mostly his fault she's like she is," and he signalled a four-wheeler, giving the driver the address of Sir Clive's London office where he was likely to be at this hour of the day.

The silver-buttoned flunkey standing outside the revolving door recognised him and touched his rosetted beaver, saying that Sir Clive had returned from luncheon less than ten minutes ago and was almost surely in his office. Giles climbed the broad staircase to the heavy mahogany door that was the magnate's sanctum and around him, as he moved along the corridor, he could hear the muted hum of high-pressure enterprise; bells ringing, the heavy, hesitant clack-clack of Rycroft's new typewriter girls, an ambassadorial clerk treading softly to and fro carrying files and correspondence. He thought, bitterly, "All this, and the man can't raise one daughter properly . . ." and without waiting to be announced he knocked on the door at the blind end of the corridor and walked inside.

His man was seated at an enormous desk on which everything was neatly arranged and even the pen tray looked as if it merited a private auction. Sir Clive raised his neat head and smiled, extending his hand across the desk and saying, genially, "Ah, I wondered when we should see you. I had almost made up my mind to write but I guessed you would call here or at Eaton Place. Sit down, sit down, my boy. That one is the most comfortable. Cigar? No, you can't smoke them, can you? Help yourself from the box—Turkish, Russian or Virginian. I have to cater for all tastes up here."

It occurred to Giles then that he must know nothing of the broken engagement and this disconcerted him for a moment. But then he reasoned that it would be typical of Romayne to pretend it hadn't happened, to say nothing about it until she was convinced he was not bluffing. He said, quietly, "Clearly Romayne hasn't told you I broke our engagement, sir?" but the man did not even blink. "Haven't seen the minx," he said. "Haven't set eyes on her since luncheon, Saturday. All I know is that she's gone off somewhere, and she hasn't paid me the compliment of saying where. Have you any notion where she might be?"

For a moment Giles was too astonished to comment. He had always known Sir Clive Rycroft-Mostyn was an exceptionally cool customer, but this casual approach to his only child's abrupt disappearance was almost beyond comprehension. He said, falteringly, "Romayne isn't at home? You say she's run off somewhere? When? When did she go?"

Sir Clive did not answer at once. He was occupied getting his cigar to draw. When it did he said, with a lift of his shoulder, "Couldn't say for sure. Early on Sunday, probably."

"Three days? Did you suppose she was with me? At 'Tryst', maybe?"

"Oh, dear no, I knew about your tiff, dear boy. She left this letter for you on her dressing-table. It was sealed but one doesn't have to be Sherlock Holmes to guess what's in it."

He took a sealed envelope from his inside pocket and handed it across the desk. On it was written Giles' name in Romayne's childishly round hand, and as his fingers closed over it he felt the outline of his ring, a single sapphire mounted on a high shank. He thumbed open the envelope but there was nothing inside save the ring wrapped in a wisp of tissue paper. He stared down at it, saying, "You're not worried about her? Where she is? What she could be doing?"

"Not in the least," Sir Clive said. "Would you be, if she was your daughter?"

"Yes," he said, slowly, "I would be. I'd be very worried indeed in the circumstances."

"What circumstances?" But then, carefully, "You don't have to tell me if you prefer not."

"I came here to tell you. We had a particularly bad quarrel. It doesn't matter what it was about. I don't think that would interest you in the least, but it was one of many and this finally decided me. I told her if we went ahead with the wedding we should only succeed in making one another miserable. And in disappointing you too. So I broke it off, outside your house, about midnight on Saturday. I told her I'd write to you but it seemed a shabby thing to do after all the kindness you've shown me, and the fact that I was going to work for you."

For the first time the man looked concerned. "So you've decided to welsh on that too?"

"Welsh on it?" He fumbled for one of his own cigarettes but made a bad job of lighting it so that Sir Clive pushed matches in his direction. He said, taking the cigarette from his mouth, "How could I work for you in the circumstances? You must see that isn't possible. She could bring a breach of promise action against me if she wished. I've no kind of defence, for it wasn't a mutual decision. She wanted me to run off to Gretna Green on the spot, without telling you or anyone else. She seemed to think marriage would transform her into somebody quite different."

"Now that's quite original," Sir Clive said. "It's generally a case of the lady making up her mind to transform us."

Quite suddenly Giles had difficulty in restraining an impulse to walk round the desk and do something positive. Hit Caesar over the head with his ebony ruler, for instance. Or empty a bottle of green ink down his shirt front. Anything to bring to the man his personal involvement in the situation. He said, between his teeth, "This isn't a joke, Sir Clive. Hasn't it occurred to you that she might —well—that something awful might have happened to her running off like that? Without a note or message. In the middle of the night?"

"Indeed it hasn't. She took a change of clothes and that dog of hers. Jilted brides don't clutter themselves to that extent if they have it in mind to jump off Westminster Bridge."

In a way it was a relief. He had no idea at all, if one ruled out

North Wales, where she could have gone or why, but there was logic in her father's assumption. She was extremely attached to Prune, the floppy black Labrador that had trotted at her heels ever since he had known her. It seemed likely, in the circumstances, that she had returned to the Beddgelert holiday home, perhaps in the hope that he would pursue her there. Sir Clive seemed to guess his line of thought.

"I wired Wales this morning," he said, offhandedly. "Not because I'm bothered to any great extent but because I thought it likely you might want to know. She isn't there at the moment. If she turns up there will you go after her?"

"No, sir. I've made my decision and I think she understands that."

"I see. Well, then, where does that leave us? With an obligation to put a cancellation notice in *The Times* I suppose. And I understand a few of the invitations have gone out, so I daresay your people will want some kind of explanation. But let's take all that as read, eh? So far as I'm concerned the arrangement between ourselves still stands. I don't make important decisions of that kind as lightly as my daughter. I still say you're the right man for that job."

"I told you it was I who broke the engagement, Sir Clive."

"Oh, I daresay, technically."

"I don't think I follow you there, sir."

Suddenly Sir Clive pushed back his chair and stood up, moving clear of the desk and over to the window, where he planted his feet with his back to Giles, puffing thoughtfully at his cigar. He said, finally, "How much did she admit of earlier pranks, Swann? Did she ever mention, say, a stable lad called Gilpin? Or a music-teacher called Bellocq?"

"She mentioned someone called Gilpin once. She said he thrashed her with a riding-crop, for riding a dangerous horse when you lived in Hampshire."

"And the foreign chap, Bellocq? Or a young manservant called Dodge?"

"No, sir. And she only mentioned Gilpin in passing."

"How did his name come up?"

"I took your advice and gave her a spanking after she took a crazy risk when we were rowing on the canal. She didn't resent it. As a matter of fact she admitted she had acted stupidly and apologised."

"I see. And since?"

"We never had a cross word until late Saturday night. Then, to my mind at least, she behaved outrageously in a shop in Oxford Street, and it came to me that we were hopelessly incompatible."

He moved back to the desk, puffing steadily at his cigar.

"If you want my opinion, free of bias, that is, you're well rid of her."

"*You* can say that?"

"Who has a better qualification to say it? I was obliged to suffer her tantrums until she was of age last January. Then she came into a small income from her mother's estate, enough to keep her off the streets. But she'll gravitate there, given time, mark my words. Did you ever hear of homesickness for the gutter?"

"Yes, I did. But she never once struck me as suffering from that. The reverse, I'd say."

"She generally made a good job of concealing her tracks and that must mean something, I suppose. Possibly that she has a deep affection for you. Saw you as a lifeline perhaps. As I did, and freely admit to it."

The sensation of lightheadedness that had troubled him ever since the doorstep parting returned. It was as though he was looking across the desk at Sir Clive through a slightly distorted glass. He was conscious of a persistent buzz in his ears and his stomach rumbled, reminding him that he had eaten practically nothing in the last forty-eight hours. When his head cleared somewhat he saw that Sir Clive was offering him brandy, taken from a cabinet from behind the desk.

"Drink it," he said. "You look as if you need a drink, boy," and Giles took the goblet, swallowing half the contents in a gulp.

"I'm not renowned for making my motives public," Sir Clive went on, "but as regards yourself I think I owe it to you. If only because I admire staying-power, particularly in the young, and you've shown it, God knows. There's a streak of madness somewhere in that branch of the family. Or maybe it's in mine, for I was never one for excavating ancestors. Anyway, it's there, and in her it takes the form of wantonness, coupled with extreme indiscipline, hatred of any kind of restraint. I daresay you've noticed that and I'm not going

into details. What's the point now? There was this young manservant, Dodge. I surprised him fumbling her in a guest-room when she
was around fifteen. There was a far more serious affair with the
music-teacher. He was married, and I had to pay him off and ship
him back to Belgium. And finally, a year or so before you showed up,
there was Gilpin. Up to then she had a penchant for brutes. That's
why I was surprised when she stuck to you for so long. Well, I paid
Gilpin off, too, but there's a limit to this kind of recklessness. As I
say, she's reached her majority now, and is well aware I'm not to
be counted on any longer." He flicked the ash from his cigar and
looked at Giles shrewdly. "I imagine you acted the gentleman
throughout and you never became lovers. Well, that wasn't wise, but
how could you be expected to know that? If you had we might at
least have got her married. And divorces are easy enough to come
by these days, provided you'd wanted one."

What puzzled him far more than the account of Romayne's
string of lovers was the detachment the man was able to bring to a
discussion of his own daughter's follies and deficiencies, as though
he had been making a brief, factual report on the shortcomings of
a scullery maid concerning whom somebody had called seeking a
reference. His cold-bloodedness was as chilling as standing neck-
deep in a barrel of ice, and as repugnant, in another way, as handling something dredged from a drain. In yet another way, however,
it had the effect of rallying him, for he thought, "He talks of her
as if she was a consignment of spoiled goods that had been returned
to one of his damned warehouses . . ." and with this rage mounted
in him so that his resentment was switched clear away from Romayne and concentrated on this bland, bloodless merchant, who
thought of everyone, including his own flesh and blood, in terms
of marketability. He said, cutting into the man's smooth, rambling
talk, "Suppose she isn't in Wales? Will you mount some kind of search
for her?"

"Not I! That's up to you, young feller-me-lad, if you feel so inclined. I tell you I'm done with her. I've got other and far more
important things to think about."

"You don't regard yourself as being responsible for the way she
ran wild? For the silly scrapes she got herself into?"

"No. And don't give me that fool's talk. People are what they are, or so I've always found."

"But, God damn it," Giles burst out, "she needed help! She's always needed help."

"Then find her and give her help if you feel so disposed. But don't look to me for backing. I hate weaklings. I always have, and your father would say 'Amen' to that, I daresay."

"No," Giles said, slowly, "my father wouldn't. He's enjoyed making money, but he's never made a god of it the way you have. And with him flesh and blood have always had a certain value, apart from what they were worth to him in hard cash."

He never discovered what Sir Clive Rycroft-Mostyn made of that for he was not looking at him when he said it, and the moment it was said he turned away, tugged open the heavy door and walked out into the corridor. The typewriter girls were still slamming away at their machines. The ambassadorial clerks were still padding about with files and memoranda. The silver-buttoned flunkey at the door had not forgotten how to convey the impression that it would be a pleasure to be stepped on by anyone with personal access to Sir Clive Rycroft-Mostyn. This, he reflected, was big business as most city men recognised it, and everyone involved in it was a cog or a screw. Dehumanised, sealed off from the mainstream of Christian civilisation. It was comforting to reflect that Swann-on-Wheels was not run on these lines. It never had been and it never would be. It was still, and would always remain, a family concern, no matter how many and how varied were those involved in its practice and policy-making. Goods and capital investment and profits counted, but neither one of them so much as people. He turned his steps towards the Thameside slum, a drunk instinctively making his way home.

*   *   *

Adam was in the tower, Tybalt said, and had been asking for him, so he went up the narrow staircase to find his father sitting at his littered desk, with his gammy leg stuck out at the familiar angle, and his long chin supported by his right hand, as if he was assessing the imponderables of some complicated cross-country haul of fish, fruit or hardware. His eyes lit up when Giles entered but he still looked tired and curiously dispirited, for Giles had noted that up here, immersed in his own concerns, he was almost invariably brisk and cheerful. He said, gruffly, "Tybalt tell you?"

"No, sir," said Giles, momentarily forgetting his own wretchedness, "tell me what?"

"About George."

"What's happened to George?"

"He's gone. Walked out. Thrown in with Sam Rawlinson, your grandfather, of all people. We haven't seen eye to eye on a number of things lately but there was nothing we couldn't have ironed out, given time. It was that damned machine of his. Seems to have taken possession of his senses, to the exclusion of everything else, including his wife and children. Well, so be it, and to the devil with him and his thunderbird. But I don't mind admitting I was badly upset by your mother's attitude."

"What's mother got to do with George's Maximus?"

"What indeed?" He never recalled his father sounding so embittered. "I daresay that will emerge but the short answer is she backed him to the hilt. It was at her insistence that he threw in with his grandfather for, believe it or not, the old fool sees yet another fortune in that contraption. You'd think he knew better at his age. You'd suppose he'd had enough of fortunes and what they cost a man to make. However, there it is." He paused a moment, toying with a paper-knife made in the shape of a cavalry sabre. "It's hit me damned hard, son. Particularly with you going too."

"I won't be going. For what I'm worth I'm your man, not Rycroft's, from here on." And then, carefully, "Can you stand another buffet, sir?"

He was relieved to see Adam's grin, the grin he had always associated with an overgrown schoolboy planning a practical joke.

"Why not?" He cut the air with the paper knife. "I survived a good many when I earned my keep with one of these. A straightforward business that. Sometimes I think I should have stuck to it. You're the brandy man. Alex is port, George is beer. You *are* the brandy man, aren't you?"

"I'm becoming one," Giles said, as Adam rose and stumped over to his cellarette beside the ready-reckoner that the network knew as Frankenstein. "I've just had a double from my ex-father-in-law."

He saw his father's face narrow as he paused in the act of pouring, "Well?"

"I walked out on Romayne and she walked out on him. Then I made it a treble by throwing his job in his face. I'm glad about that part of it at least."

"You want to tell me?"

"Eventually. Not now."

Adam came forward with the drinks. "To abdication, then."

"We'll survive, sir."

"By God, we will."

A shaft of late afternoon sunshine stole through the little Gothic window and picked out the dust that always gathered up here, no matter how often Tybalt sent the yard men up with their brooms. To Giles, to Adam also possibly, it brought a little warmth into the turret.

4

Henrietta as Broker Again

THAT was the summer of the first Jubilee and the tribes as a whole, half-exiled Celts, ponderous Saxons, predatory, far-ranging Scandinavians, and methodical, hard-fisted Norman French who had travelled this far together, were aware of a sense of fusion and common purpose that had eluded them (save in widely-spaced moments of peril) for more than eight centuries. There were still dissidents, of course, but their voices were muted, submerged in the thrum of national breast-beating, lost in the flutter of unfurled flags and the drift of bonfire smoke. For this was a time when the nation made ready to pay ritual homage to the dumpy, toothy little widow who had come to see herself, not merely as a queen and queen-empress, but as the power-house of a new centre of gravity sited somewhere between the Pool of London and Windsor. Or perhaps carrying it about with her, like a celestial seal of office, on her annual migrations to country houses in Norfolk, the Isle of Wight and the banks of the Dee.

But for Swann-on-Wheels and for Adam Swann particularly, who had always identified with the epoch, there was an anomaly here. For that same summer, the summer of 1887, was a period not of fusion and closing ranks but the reverse, with the network showing unmistakable signs of stress, and a feeling of unease and uncertainty at the very hub of the thirty-year-old venture that had seemed, less than a year since, as durable as the monarchy and far more adaptable to external pressures. Or so he would have claimed.

Yet it was not so. From his truncated turret above the curve of the brown river he could sense the tremors of dissolution and they frightened him, for he was turned sixty now, aware of the ache of old wounds, and that sense of doubt that accompanies shortness of wind, rotting teeth and, above all, a hazing of that clarity of

627

thought and diabolically accurate memory that had proved so invaluable in his triumphant years.

Somewhere—he took his time locating its source—there was grit in the axle and it did not stem from the regions, now enjoying a devolution of power that he himself had initiated but from much nearer home, from the very foundations of the tower in which he sat, and the knowledge of this, notwithstanding his enormous experience, made him less sure of himself than he had ever been since he first came here in his thirty-first year to play chuck-farthing with destiny. Around him, sometimes seen but more often heard as a rustle in the dark, was a spirit of near-mutiny and he came at last to identify its storm-centre as George, the heir-apparent. But identification enabled him neither to scotch it nor adapt to it, for it was too nebulous a thing to be defined and studied in the way he had tackled successive crises in the past. It centred on George certainly, drawing inspiration from the boy's tremendous thrust (so like his own in the very earliest days), from his easy affability with staff and customers that Adam had never really acquired, from the boy's outward-looking optimism or arrogance, however you were disposed to view it, from his ready command of three languages against Adam's one, but, above all, from his expressed certainty that the horse and cart era was nearly over and along with it the patriarchal tone and regional autonomy of the enterprise. It was a view that Adam was too long in the tooth to share.

George Swann, at twenty-four, had not only succeeded in astonishing his father's acolytes, he had also astonished himself. More than three years of free-ranging abroad, with no real necessity to work, and the emphasis, if he was honest with himself, on diversion rather than furthering his technical education, had made him wary of the disciplines inherent in a permanent position at the yard, where he had perforce to adjust to the rhythms of men like Tybalt, the clerk, and Keate, the waggonmaster. Yet he did adjust, and in a matter of weeks, making a unique place for himself as a powerfully-placed referee, to whom the younger men began to defer and to look to for support of any change in regional policy that smacked of modernisation.

Nor was this all. As a young man, with first-hand experience of important Continental firms, he discovered that middle-aged customers were willing to give him a hearing and, having heard him, to follow his advice. In this way, aided by his natural enthusiasm and amiability, he soon emerged as the most successful prospector of new business Swann-on-Wheels had thrown up in its thirty years' handling of the nation's goods. In the first six months he landed thirty-eight new contracts, all in the Headquarters' area, but when Adam, applauding his initiative, suggested he should go out into the regions and break fresh ground he did not take kindly to the proposal. Instead he fired his first warning shot across the provincial bows. He did not see Swann-on-Wheels as drawing its inspiration from the shires, he said, or even from territories as large as Jake Higson's beat in the North, that included several industrial centres. The future, he hinted (and it was scarcely more than a hint at that time) lay right here beside the Thames. In other words, with improved rail services and faster hauls, centralisation was imperative. He went even further down a road the old stagers would be likely to see as heresy. To his mind the regions already enjoyed too much autonomy, were already too parochial in their thinking. What was needed now, what would have to come in the near future, was some form of centralisation and, more particularly, the appointment of managers each responsible for a particular branch of the system. Devolution, that is, based not on geography but the nature of the goods hauled and vehicles used in performance of a specific job.

Adam challenged this at once, pointing out that a change of policy as revolutionary as this would embitter relations between Headquarters and the regions, particularly men like Lovell and Ratcliffe, who were very jealous of their frontiers and had never taken kindly to Headquarters' writ, although they had always been ready to abide by policy decisions carried by majority vote. Semi-independence of the regions, Adam insisted, had always been a cornerstone of the firm's policy and when George had moved about a bit, and taken the measure of old hands scattered about the shires, he would tread warily as regards the imposition of London decisions on men who, whatever their other failings, knew their customers and territory far better than anyone beside the Thames.

"My line was always to pick a local man and give him a free hand," he argued, but George, with one of his infectious chuck-

les, said that here and there, unless he was much mistaken, free
hands were twiddling thumbs, as in the case of that old peasant
Ratcliffe in the Western Wedge, who was beginning to regard himself as wholly independent west of the Dorset-Somerset borders. "I'm
not advocating any diminution of their powers," he urged. "In some
ways I'm giving them more. Centralisation would take some of the
work-load from their shoulders, give them an opportunity to get into
the four corners of their beats, exploit their local knowledge, pull
in more customers and increase turnover and dividends, the way I've
been able to do in the suburbs. They can't do that when so much of
their time is occupied in paper work, in running repairs, in scratching around for the right type of vehicle at the right time. The fact
is, Guv'nor, if you talked to some of the younger men out there you
might find my views regarding a breakdown of hauls under
Headquarters-based specialists, might be welcomed. Why don't you
try it sometime, if only to prove to yourself that I'm talking through
my hat? I'll withdraw if I'm proved wrong!"

That was the way of George. He put forward his views and then
invited the opposition to test them, and this was what Adam did,
in the autumn of 1886, when they were still coasting along the level
stretch. He learned to his secret chagrin that George was indubitably right, that the regional thrusters, men like Godsall, of the Kentish Triangle, Rookwood, of the Southern Square, and even the
Scottish viceroy, Jake Higson, would indeed welcome the appointment of specialist managers based on London, who would accept
responsibility for distinctive hauls such as house-removals and the
holiday-brake traffic that threw a heavy strain on their teams
throughout the summer months. He learned something else, too.
That some of the older men, notably Hamlet Ratcliffe, in the West,
and Bryn Lovell, in the Mountain Square, were ageing faster than
he had been led to believe and that, here and there among their senior staffs, were some who were well past their prime and by no
means up to their work.

Grudging admiration for his son's prescience did battle with his
own obstinacy and also with his loyalty to old friends. But what
really prevented him from a frank admission that there was something to be said for centralisation and the appointment of specialists to handle traffic outside the regional bread-and-butter categories,

was a reluctance to tamper with a system that had proved so successful over such a long period. Something deep inside him mistrusted
any rigid form of centralisation and stemmed, possibly, from the
memories of all he had suffered in the field at the hands of high-
ranking nincompoops operating ten miles outside the range of enemy's shot and shell. At all events, he did nothing beyond ponder his
findings, promising himself that he would take another look at the
situation in the spring.

Then winter closed in, a savage winter, with all its attendant vex-
ations and unforeseeable contingencies, and everyone was working
round the clock, feeding reserves to every region as snow, frost and
mire strained resources right across the board.

Reserve capital dipped badly that winter, with a heavy outlay
on new pinnaces and expensive Cleveland Bays to pull them, mostly
to cover the flood of new business George had drummed up in and
around the capital. The long spell of bad weather also exposed weaknesses apparent to him in his autumn tour and by March, when
everyone was drying out a little, he was ready to compromise. He
said, tossing George a spring balance sheet and the latest returns
from the regions regarding vehicles and teams, "Take a long look at
them, lad. Then draw up a scheme to include those policies you
advocated in the fall. But make it conservative, mind. I shall have to
lay it before a special conference in any case, and I don't want a
mutiny among those rascals now that we've weathered the winter
and can take a breather right across the country."

George took the papers, together with others he coaxed from Tybalt and Keate, and was not seen for more than a week, so that Adam
had all but forgotten his directive when, on the first day of April,
George appeared in the tower looking a little less sure of himself than
usual. He said, with a nonchalance that did not fool a man with
thirty years' experience in dealing with juniors, "Are you specially
busy, Guv'nor? Could you give me an hour this afternoon? After
you've had time to study this?"

'This' was a file containing a score of closely written foolscap pages
in George's rather dashing hand. Recognising it as a detailed breakdown of what he had learned to think of as 'the state of the poll'
Adam said, "By thunder, you took me seriously, didn't you? Damned
if I hadn't forgotten all about this memorandum. When your mother

asked where you were I said you had been out drumming up new customers all the week. Yes, I'll look into it right away. We'll do it together if you've a mind to," but George jibbed at this, saying he had a backlog of calls to make in and about the city and that it was better that Adam should study the recommendations alone.

"You could make notes as you go along," he added, guardedly. "I've left a wide margin for that purpose," and he ducked out, whistling his way down the stairs—'to keep his pecker up', thought Adam, grinning, but his heart warmed towards Old George (he had always thought of him as 'Old George', even when he was a toddler) for here, if he needed it, was evidence that the boy was settling to the collar like a thoroughbred.

His expression hardened, however, before he had progressed beyond the second page of the report. By the time he was halfway through he was bewildered and resentful. By the time he had caught the general drift of the report he had an unpleasant certainty that they were on collision course. For running like a thread through the pages of the report was something far more comprehensive than a straightforward championship of centralisation, and a reasoned argument in favour of relieving the regional managers of responsibility for specialised traffic. It was no more no less than a relentlessly argued case for re-structuring the entire enterprise and some of its more telling paragraphs made him gasp. For here was George, at twenty-five, calling his entire system to account for the winter's muddles and losses, for its needless drain on capital, for any amount of blunderings on the part of men who refused to see Swann-on-Wheels as a national concern but persisted in regarding it as a shire-based enterprise, men so parochial in outlook, so dedicated to methods they had used over three decades, that they were quite unable to make an unprejudiced assessment of their responsibilities to Headquarters, to colleagues in other regions and even, in the final analogy, to their own customers.

George had obeyed the letter of his instructions. He had devoted several pages to a thesis on the advantages of centralisation, and the appointment of specialists to take charge of excursion traffic, house-removals and the like. But his real purpose, as was immediately apparent, was to strip away the dead wood of the network by wholesale retirements, made compulsory at the age of sixty-seven, and optional at sixty. He then went on to advocate a system of promotion by merit, with no sentimental nonsense about seniority, a closer tie-in with railways along the lines of some of Swann's most successful competitors, the downgrading of two or three less prosperous areas into sub-regions, and the expansions of others, among them Northern Pickings, to take in several industrial cities in the West Midlands. He gave it as his opinion that the Scottish territory was too unwieldy in its present form and that, good as Jake Higson was—and he stressed this—no one man could be responsible for territory including so many industries. He outlined a plan for breaking out of the Dublin Pale and establishing a service clear across Ireland to Galway and Cork, with a second depot at Belfast.

All this was far-reaching enough, both from the point of view of investment and its likely effect on personnel, but there was a paragraph in the summing up that gave Adam the key to George's thinking and raised his hackles at first reading. It ran: *"Many of these changes may well be forced on the company by circumstances in a year or so, but even where they are no more than desirable they would be likely to give the network a clear lead when, as is virtually certain to my mind, the horse begins to be replaced by mechanically-propelled vehicles of one sort or another. I see this happening in ten to twelve years and it would seem to me advisable to restructure well in advance, and steal a march over competitors. For when it does happen it will happen almost overnight, like the introduction of steam."*

Adam sat there a long time before he had succeeded in swallowing his bile. Time enough to force himself to look at this deluge of truths, half-truths and what he saw as downright fantasy objectively, perhaps as something more than a display of arrogance by a lad still wet behind the ears. Whatever one said, George clearly possessed abundant faith in himself, so that if he was to be deflated (and if Swann-on-Wheels was to continue as a going concern this seemed inevitable) then it would have to be done tactfully. Tact was not one of Adam Swann's specialities. All these years he had had to manage without it.

Yet George was the Crown Prince, designated by himself, and whilst it did not do to give a Crown Prince licence to overset the throne, it was almost as dangerous to humiliate him, to dismiss every suggestion he put forward as hot-air generated, most likely, by that hissing, humming, clattering juggernaut that occupied so much of George's time and was beginning, it seemed, to regulate his entire thinking.

There was room for compromise here, for a formula that would save the boy's face when he learned that no proposals as revolutionary as these could be put before a conference of men who had devoted their lives to road-haulage. He could yield a point here and there, perhaps softening the blow somewhat by pleading poverty, but this would only postpone confrontation. Somehow the boy must be made to understand that he, Adam Swann, had never seen his creation as an impersonal, endlessly proliferating venture, taking people and using their strength, like some half-crazed Pharaoh raising a pyramid. He had no patience with the soap-boilers, matchmakers, biscuit manufacturers, who used a work-force in the way they used their machines. That had never been his way. Not because it ran counter to his religious convictions (he had none worth speaking of) and certainly not because he saw himself as one of these fashionable theorists, who made a cult of universal brotherhood. Mainly it was because he saw everyone of those men out in the shires as a friend, someone who had agreed to join him in a half-humorous conspiracy to milk a living out of the men dedicated to the making of money. Under a scheme such as George's this easy camaraderie would disappear overnight.

He took a pen and went to work on the report, annotating it paragraph by paragraph, sometimes with a word, sometimes a paragraph, and when he was done he sent for Tybalt and told him to give it to George as soon as he returned for the afternoon appointment. "I'll give the lad an hour to mull it over," he told himself and went out, drifting down towards the docks and watching the steady bustle there, remembering a time when every ship about here carried sail and there was very little of the fug and clatter that overhung the whole area now. The reflection linked itself to George's final paragraph and he wondered if there was anything in the boy's prophecy and whether, in his lifetime, he would see horses disappear from these congested streets and the acrid stink of dung superseded by

the fumes that filled the old stable at home where George, who would
be thirty-seven when the century had run its course, tinkered and
tinkered with that juggernaut he had shipped home from Vienna.

2

George had gone by the time he returned, leaving a curt note to
the effect that he had read his father's comments and needed time
to consider them before making any constructive counter-proposals.
Not knowing what to make of this Adam returned to routine work
and caught an early train back to 'Tryst' but George was not there,
and when he looked in at the mill-house Gisela said he had not yet
arrived home. Adam said, "He'll be late, I shouldn't wonder. Don't
worry if he stays over in town for the night. Why not join us up at
the house for dinner?" But Gisela declined and he thought he detected a little stiffness in her attitude, so that he went away thinking,
"She'll stand by him and that's as it should be. He's probably already
talked her into believing I'm a backward old buffer, bogged down
in the eighteenth century, but that's the way of things, I suppose.
I thought it of my father at his age, but then I was right—the old
chap never did a damned thing but lop the ears from Frenchmen
and paint a few water-colours . . ." And he sought out Henrietta
with relief, feeling drained by the demands of the day.

He said nothing of his passage of arms with the heir-apparent
and it was not until they were on their way to bed that he noticed,
or thought he noticed, the same reserve about her as he had spotted in his daughter-in-law. The thought crossed his mind then that
both women were privy to George's brutal assessment of his life's
work. He said, casually, "Did George mention that he was working
up terms of reference for a special conference down at the yard?"
and she said, uneasily, "He told me something on those lines a few
days ago. Gisela and I were discussing it yesterday, as a matter of
fact."

He was quite sure then that they had been conspiring, that
George had briefed his wife, who had then approached Henrietta,
almost surely with a view to enlisting her support, and maybe the

promise of a backstairs campaign. Somehow it accounted for George's cancellation of their appointment that afternoon. He said, half-jestingly, "What's going on, exactly? Have they been getting at you, about the kind of changes that boy has in mind?"

"They told me about the report. They even let me read it. Gisela said George was going to give it to you this morning. Did he do that?"

"Yes, by God, he did!" Adam said. "And I'm not sure that I care for this hole-in-the-corner way of going about things. Why do you suppose he took you into his confidence before I knew of the existence of the damned thing?"

"Is that how you think of it?"

"Of course it is, how else? If I went ahead with a plan like that half the regional managers would throw in their hand and the other half, Godsall, Rookwood and the like, would set about talking me into early retirement, so that they could convert Swann-on-Wheels into a kind of mobile factory."

"What does that mean exactly? That you've thrown his report out?"

"Of course I've thrown it out."

"*All* of it?"

"Practically all of it. I'll concede a few of his points but as to re-structuring on that scale, why it's mad. I wouldn't consider it at any price."

"You've told him that?"

"I haven't had the chance. We had an appointment to discuss it this afternoon but he preferred to mooch off with my marginal comments burning his ears." He looked at her reflection as she sat brushing her hair in front of the dressing-table mirror. Her expression, he thought, was very serious, unusually so for an occasion when they were alone up here. She said, deliberately, "I think you're making a very big mistake, Adam."

"Oh, you do, do you?"

"Yes, I do. I went over that report twice. Here and there it seemed to me to take too much for granted but, by and large, I thought it clever and long-sighted." He was amazed at her perfidy. If anything it hardened his attitude to George. He limped across the room and glared down at her.

"You mean you believe in that stinking contraption he plays with out there in the stable?"

"Yes, I believe in it, and so does Gisela. I would have thought you would too, for I never did see you as a stick-in-the-mud. Quite the opposite, in fact. You always struck me as a person with his eyes very much on the future. You were when you were his age, I'll be bound, even more so than when I met you and you started the network."

"So I was," he exploded, "but I dealt in facts not fancies! I started a family business and kept it going as such. If I carried out half his proposals we should lose all personal touch with those chaps in the regions and become just one more London-based, money-making concern. You know me well enough to understand how I should react to that, don't you, Hetty?"

She said, softly, "There's very little I don't know about you, Adam Swann. Enough to know you've got it all wrong now, for instance, and that you aren't being honest with yourself." She laid the brush aside and stood up. "You want me to go on?"

"Say what you have to and let's bring this whole thing out in the open."

"Very well. Your opposition is personal. In your heart you know very well that Swann-on-Wheels needs gingering up, and that George is perfectly right about shedding dead wood and modernising. And I'm not talking about that machine or any machine that'll likely replace horse-power in the years ahead, the way the railways drove the stage coaches off the roads when you were a lad. That's a side issue and you're using it as a red herring. I'm talking about your approach to the firm as a whole. Yours and that of the old hands, like Ratcliffe, Lovell, Catesby and even comparative go-aheads like Edith and Tom Wickstead."

"How do you mean 'personal'? What's so personal about it? We've done pretty well as a team these years, haven't we? We've gone on expanding and stayed on the map, despite all the competition."

"Of course. But you're sixty now, and having a lot of trouble admitting it, Adam. That's partly why you defend conservatism on grounds of loyalty to the old stagers."

"Damn it, woman, doesn't experience count for anything at all?"

"It's not a matter of experience. Experience belongs to the past. It's adapting to the future that George is concerned about."

"Has he got the prerogative to look into the future?"

"His generation has. He's seven years younger than you were when you started out. Besides, you trained him with that in mind, didn't you?"

"Aye, I did, and it looks to me as if I've been sowing dragon's teeth!" he growled.

But she said, sharply, "That's rubbish and you know it's rubbish! The root of your objections lie in the fact that, when it comes to bedrock, you can't bear the prospect of stepping aside, not even for one of your own sons and the one you always planned to take over. The network is too much a part of you. In a way it would be like dying and I can understand that. But it has to be done, sooner or later. You, and all those old cronies of yours, can't hand over in name and still keep control of the policy. If you do you'll fall apart, like any other worn-out machine."

He was outraged now, for her deadly logic touched his manhood at a raw spot. "So you think of me as a worn-out machine?"

She looked very troubled then, and seized his hand. "No, no . . . not as a person, not as a man . . . But you must understand that a thing as big and complex as the network needs new ideas all the time, just as it did through all the years you ran it virtually alone. If I were in your shoes I should be proud of George, and go out of my way to encourage him. After all, he's the only one among them who has inherited your gambling instinct."

He thought, "By God, she's right, and that's the trouble. Maybe there is a personal element, but my loyalty isn't just to him. It's to all the men of my generation, and most of us aren't ready to step down . . . not yet . . . not for a year or so . . ."

He said, gruffly, "We ought to be able to arrive at some kind of compromise. He's got support in the network, I'll admit that, but all this is a leap in the dark, involving every bit of capital we have and frankly I'm against it, and that's a fact. He'll have to see it my way until I put my feet up. Then he, and those other youngsters like Higson can take their chances, sink or swim."

"But you won't ever put your feet up, Adam. That's what bothers them I think. Sooner or later it'll come to a straight choice. You or them."

"Don't lose sleep on that account," he said, grimly, "they all know which side their bread is buttered!"

But she countered, swiftly, "Men like Jake Higson and Godsall do, but George occupies an entirely different position. He isn't absolutely dependent on you, and even if he were there's far too much of you in him to admit it. He'll go his own way, and Gisela will stand by him. And that's something I shouldn't care to see happen."

"I can assure you it won't," he said. "And now I've had about enough of George for one day so blow out the lamp and let's sleep on it."

*　　　*　　　*

He was obliged to admit, as weeks passed without any real relaxation of the wary attitude between father and son, that Henrietta appeared to be right and a compromise might be difficult to achieve.

They discussed aspects of the report together but George was apathetic in his responses, as though he judged further reasoning on his part a waste of breath. And yet, something had to be done, for as the enterprise emerged from the long winter Adam sensed dissatisfaction from the Grampians to the Channel coast, as though the firm was entering upon another prolonged wobble and needed a firm touch on the tiller before it could resume course.

He could not have said how he knew this. His perception, as regards the tautness or slackness of the network, had always been keen, and perhaps he sensed trouble in a variety of ways, a word or two in a regional report, a surly look, a sharp exchange between Keate or Tybalt with one or other of the viceroys when they looked into Headquarters. Anyway it was there, an overall pettishness that was not solely the hangover of a long, tiresome winter and he could not help but feel it was linked, in some way, to George's claims of weaknesses in structure and personnel.

By late spring he was tired of guessing and ready, in a way, to make terms. He said to George, without the face-saving preamble most men in his situation would have found necessary, "Listen here, son. I daresay I was too hasty over that report of yours. It's plain things aren't as they should be, here or in the regions. We've run out of steam and need a tonic. Suppose you go the rounds on the pretence of drumming up trade, and put some of your remedies to the managers and their deputies? On the strength of what you report I'll call a midsummer conference and we could at least get general reactions."

But George, to his bafflement, said, civilly, "That would be a waste of time and travelling expenses, Guv'nor. I already have their reactions."

"How could you have?"

"I've seen or written to every one of them in the last month or so."

"You're telling me you canvassed their views before you penned that report?"

"I'm not such a fool as to use my position as a basis for a palace plot, if that's what you're thinking."

"I don't know what to think," Adam growled, "except that things aren't as they should be out there, and it's nothing to do with turnover. Last year was the best we ever had. My guess is it's a slip in morale. Well, you hinted at allies. Who are they?"

"A disgruntled minority," George said, with a flash of his old humour, "too divided to stage a coup, believe me."

"But your report touched on weaknesses in every region."

"Yes, it did, and everyone out there has at least one rotten tooth. If you take my advice you'll pull them one by one in private. Certainly not at a conference."

"Suppose you're right? Where does that leave us?"

"With three factions; yours, mine and neutrals with private grouses. And even mine have axes to grind."

"Who takes your line that the depots ought to be resited, and frontiers merged on grounds that the days of horse-power are numbered?"

"Only Godsall, in the Triangle. Rookwood, in Southern Square, is wavering."

"And the rest?"

"There's your group, the old stagers. Ratcliffe, in the West, Lovell over in Wales, Catesby in the Polygon, and the two Wicksteads in the Crescent. Their loyalty is to you and I don't quarrel with that. It's as it should be. You've all come a long way together."

"Who do you regard as those sitting on the fence?"

"Jake Higson for one. He's forward-looking, and would have stood in with us if I hadn't felt obliged to warn him his territory would be split up. That made him think twice. Then there's Morris, in Southern Pickings. He's too well-heeled to take risks, and Vicary, of The Bonus, who is any way for a pint, and O'Dowd, over in Dublin, who is keen enough to break out and cover the country but sees a Fenian with a bomb behind every bush."

Because he knew every man so well his picture of the regional pattern began to clarify. He sensed too that, had George been ready to make concessions, such as dropping his plans to resite depots and break up the ancient frontiers, he could have rallied enough support to win a majority at conference, enough to wash the Diehards right out of their seats. But he had not made those concessions, and it followed that his dedication to that stinking machine of his was more complete than even Henrietta had assumed.

He said, "Why wouldn't you compromise, George? Why wouldn't you take one fence at a time and carry a majority with you?"

George replied, levelly, "Because I'm not interested in patching, Guv'nor. I want to make a major contribution when I'm good and ready."

"And when will that be?"

George hesitated. For the first time since he had handed in that report he looked unsure of himself. He said, at length, "That could depend on you."

"You mean when I'm ready to retire?"

"No. That's irrelevant." He thought a moment longer and then took the plunge. "It's tied to Maximus—'That stinking contraption' as you always refer to it. The future of all of us is there, however much you deny it. You and those older men have earned your bread and salt with horses all your lives, and can't be expected to recast your entire mould of thought overnight. But it's different with someone my age, who has worked alongside men like Gisela's Uncle Max—'that crazy old Austrian' as you think of him. Well, he wasn't so crazy. Gottlieb Daimler was written off as a crank but he'll live to see the carriage horse put out to grass and nothing will convince me I won't see transport revolutionised long before I'm your age."

"But, good God, boy, we're dealing with practicalities. That machine of yours hasn't even been road-tested. And even if it was successful you'd be breaking the law of the land to drive it over four miles an hour, the pace of a broken-down cart-horse. Can you honestly see Swann-on-Wheels hauls preceded by a chap waving a red flag?"

"Acts of Parliament can be repealed," George said, stubbornly. "Most are, given time."

It was odd, Adam thought. Suddenly he saw himself as old Tim Blubb, the ex-coachman he had hired thirty years ago, who never ceased to lament the passing of the stage-coach, and consistently referred to the railway as 'that bliddy gridiron', and locomotives as 'they stinkin' tea-kettles'. He wished then with all his heart that the boy could convince him, if only so that they would find themselves in accord again. He said, "It depends on me, you say. How does it? I don't know a damned thing about oil-driven vehicles. I've watched yours work but I find it absolutely impossible to see it hauling a ton of goods up a one-in-ten incline. Some of our routes are one-in-five, and unsurfaced at that."

"It's only half a prototype," George said. "It needs redesigning and stripped down to half its weight. That means a year's concentrated work, and ten times the capital I've put by, in spite of pouring half Gisela's housekeeping money into it all this time. Listen, Guv'nor, you backed your own dream once, why can't you bring yourself to back mine? Give me a year off, and two thousand to play with, and you'll own the patent. It'll make you more money than the network in the long run!"

It was tempting to buy peace at this price and for a moment or two he hesitated. Then his old hatred and mistrust of favouritism stirred, warning him that the network, such as it was, had been spun on principles of equity and impartiality. He said, "You're welcome to take a year off, George, but I couldn't pay you for staying in that stable tinkering with that machine. Neither have I the right any more to invest the firm's money in a venture of that kind unless a majority vote sanctioned it. You see that, don't you?"

"Yes," George said, "I see it. I knew it would be that way and I don't quarrel with it. Everyone looks on you as a just brute."

He went out then, swiftly but peaceably. At least he's no door-slammer, Adam thought, and would have liked an hour or two of solitude to think through all the implications of the discussion, but Tybalt summoned him on the speaking tube, reminding him that he had promised to travel west before the Jubilee break and interview a replacement for old Hamlet Ratcliffe, who had at last announced his intention to retire. He picked up his overnight grip and went down the winding stair into the yard. George was standing by the smithy with his back to him, watching a Clydesdale being shod. He thought, briefly, "If he's right that's another trade that will go the way of coaching . . . I wonder what old Blubb, bless his pickled old heart, would have had to say about horseless carriages?"

3

It was Friday morning when he had this conversation with George and he was not back in London until Monday afternoon, the selection of a Westcountryman to replace old Hamlet having taken longer than he had anticipated. Ratcliffe had made up a short list of applicants, that included a number of relatives. Adam finally picked on one, a shambling, rather lugubrious nephew of Hamlet's amiable wife, Augusta. He was not surprised to learn that 'Bertieboy', as Augusta introduced him, had served time as an undertaker, the traditional trade of her family. The young man impressed him, however, with his knowledge of horseflesh, saddlery, and all the byroads of the west, for as well as an undertaker he had been a corn chandler's drayman, serving a wide range of agricultural customers, the backbone of the carrier's trade down here.

He left Exeter on Sunday midday, with the intention of stopping off and spending a couple of days with Rookwood, in the great slab of territory known as Southern Square, but the wily Rookwood had the answer to all his questions at his fingertips. By Monday afternoon he was through, and able to catch the three o'clock out of Salisbury that got him home to 'Tryst' by early evening.

To his astonishment Henrietta was not there to greet him. One of the younger girls told him that her mother had gone off to Manchester early on Saturday, the day after his own departure for the west, and was assumed to be paying a call on Grandfather Sam. This puzzled him even more, for Henrietta and her father had never been close, and he could only suppose that Rawlinson's second wife, Hilda, had wired saying the old chap had been taken seriously ill.

He could get no confirmation of this, however. The big house seemed unresponsive and semi-deserted. Joanna and Helen were rushing off on one of their seaside jaunts, and even Giles was not to be found, Phoebe Fraser, the governess saying she believed he was staying with the Rycrofts in town. Hugo, he knew, was at a meeting of the Amateur Athletic Association in the Midlands, so there was absolutely nobody to commune with but the two youngest children. Feeling slightly disgruntled he ambled down the drive to the mill-house, with the intention of inviting George and Gisela up to supper. Another surprise awaited him here. The door was shut and locked, and he wondered where they could have gone with the two babies, concluding it must be to spend a night with George's principal ally, Godsall, who lived in Bromley, and whose wife was a great friend of Gisela's. He thought, grumpily, "Damn it, a man raises a family of nine and comes home expecting a bit of company, but the place is like an empty barn . . ." and thinking he would wire Henrietta at Sam's, asking her how long she would be away, he went round to the stableyard to find someone to ride into the village.

Here, however, he paused by the pump, his mouth agape. The doors of the old stable quarters were standing open and George's machine had gone. The place was empty, save for some discarded mounting blocks and a pile of evil-smelling rags.

He almost ran up the steps to the kitchen, bellowing for Phoebe, who was seeing the two youngsters to bed. She came running, and in response to his breathless enquiry said, "That old engine, sir? Why, it was carted off Saturday afternoon. There were two waggons up here, with Mr. George handling every crate, as though it was full of eggs. Did he no' tell ye it was being taken away then?"

"He never mentioned a damned word about it!" exclaimed Adam, wrathfully, feeling himself the victim of a conspiracy and ignoring Phoebe's Calvinistic grimace at what she would regard as strong language. "What the devil *is* going on around here? That's what I'd like to know!"

Phoebe said, guardedly, "Mrs. Swann didnae think ye'd be home until tomorrow. Those were my instructions, 'Look for him around late afternoon, Tuesday.' She said that as she was going off and, to tell the truth, sir, I had the impression she'd be back ahead of ye."

"She actually said that?"

"No, she didnae gi' me more than ten minutes' warning. Did I get it wrong then?"

"No," he said, thoughtfully, "for I didn't expect to be back until tomorrow and told her so. But I got through my work quicker than I expected. Come to think of it, I recall telling her I wouldn't be back until around tea-time on Tuesday. That'll be all, Phoebe. And I apologise for bad language!"

He said this seriously. Everyone at 'Tryst' had been taught to respect Phoebe Fraser's prejudices in this respect and he was no exception. She withdrew then and he dined alone. Having so much to think about he no longer hankered for company.

There was a pattern here somewhere. Henrietta, who, in all their married life, had never once failed to greet him on his return from one of his trips, had rushed off to Manchester within hours of his departure, so that if she had gone in response to a message it must have reached her between eight and nine on Saturday and nobody here seemed to have any knowledge of the reason behind her trip. Then George and his family were missing, with their house locked up, and again no message left with Phoebe, or with any of the older children. Finally, Maximus had been dismantled, crated and carted away, and that within a few hours of his refusal to endow the brute, and this in itself seemed ominous, although what it had to do with George and his family leaving the mill-house was more than he could say. It occurred to him, although not very seriously, that George might have taken his refusal so much to heart that he was selling the machine. But if that was so it seemed unlikely that he would encumber himself with a wife and two babies on a visit to the scrap-yard, or wherever one disposed of several tons of junk. On the whole, however, George's erratic course did not bother him so much as Henrietta flitting out of the house like a fugitive, and going so far afield without so much as writing him a note, or telling anyone the purpose of her trip. He thought, irritably, "I'll be damned if I send a wire . . . she should have wired me. Whatever has happened to that old rascal Sam it won't cause her much concern. I daresay she only posted off for the look of the thing!"

He carried his coffee into the library and idled there until past

645

midnight, drinking more than twice his brandy ration, and smoking half a dozen Burmese cheroots. For all that he slept badly, remembering, when he woke up in the small hours, Henrietta's complaints concerning the size of the Conyer bed when one had it to oneself. He dropped off again finally and sat up with a start about nine, two hours past his usual hour of rising. He had an aching head and a furred tongue, and to add to his troubles stubbed his toe on the way to his wash-basin in the dressing-room that gave him a good excuse to use some of his favourite Hindustani oaths. A glimpse of his youngest child, seven-year-old Margaret, riding her pony across the paddock, failed to lift his spirits. It reminded him of his age and he thought, wryly, "I can remember Hetty telling me that child was on the way, a month or so after we buried the old Colonel. Seems the day before yesterday. At this rate I haven't so long left to do everything I plan to do . . ." and that made him think of George again, and regret that he hadn't been more generous with the boy. Taken all round, and judged commercially, George was the flower of the flock.

He felt more cheerful with coffee and eggs and bacon inside him and had one of his rare impulses to play truant, telling himself it was a long time since he had taken time off to enjoy an early summer's day about here. There was no word from Henrietta or Giles, so he told Phoebe he would not be going up to town as usual and went off down the drive, admiring the haze of bluebells that grew under the copper beeches and the riot of campion and dandelion about the margin of the paddocks.

At the gap opposite the old mill-wheel he cut through the pine and larch wood to the road, leaning there with his back against a tree and feeling peace steal over him as his headache lifted and his thoughts crystallised on the straight stretch of carriageway that led to the main road a mile to the north-east.

It was down that strip, more than twenty-seven years ago, that he had driven Henrietta one soft April evening an hour or so before their first child, Stella, was born. Time was a curious thing when you thought about it. Sometimes, as when he was shaving only an hour since, it telescoped, the years running into one another. At other times, as now, it unrolled like an endless length of ribbon, and gaily-coloured ribbon so long as you didn't let your eye dwell too long on the dun patches. On the whole they had been good and fruitful years, better than he deserved when you took his late start into account, and more rewarding, he would judge, than those of most of his contemporaries. For those who weren't already dead were paunched and short-winded, and preoccupied with things like stocks and shares, and saddled, for the most part, with old hags and a straggle of dull, querulous children, whereas Henrietta was still fresh and comely at forty-seven, and each of the children was as much a character as the regional managers when you contemplated them individually and not, as he usually did, as a gaggle.

There were the two eldest, Stella and Alex, both rather solemn and set in their ways. There was Old George and Giles, both original but temperamentally as disparate as a Chinaman and a Zulu. There were the two younger girls, Joanna and Helen, the handsome extroverts of the family, Edward, who was beginning to look like a pocket version of old Sam Rawlinson, Hugo, a great handsome oaf who yet moved round a cinder track like a Greek god and still had trouble with spelling two syllable words, and finally Margaret, who reminded him somehow of the picture he had formed of his own mother, based on the one portrait that had come down to him.

He thought, lazily, "Now why the devil did I work myself up into such a lather over Old George, and that daft notion he had of pouring money into that engine of his? What the devil is money for but to fool around with, the way I have all these years? Most men of my standing would have a hundred thousand invested by now, but I should have a job to lay hands upon ten, unless I parted with the house and everything inside it. How much would George have wasted before he admitted it was going down the drain? A thousand? Two thousand?" But then, coming to him as a sustained rattle from beyond the tree-lined bend, he heard the approach of a light vehicle and thought, joyfully, "It's Hetty! . . . I'd know that jingle anywhere," and climbed down from the bank just in time to see the yellow gig swing round the bend into the straight, with Henrietta perched on the box, moving at a spanking trot as though she was in a great hurry to be home.

He called, waving his arms, "Hi, there! Where's the fire?" and she pulled up, looking quite startled for a moment, after which she at once set to work to compose her features, an exercise that always afforded him amusement, for in all his comings and goings over the years she had never liked to be caught at a disadvantage.

He had not been mistaken about her hurry, however. The pony was lathered and glad to pull up. She said, "And what are *you* doing here at this time of day? Is anything wrong?"

"Not my end," he replied, cheerfully, "how about yours?"

She looked, he thought, very unsure of herself for a moment and took her time answering but then, squaring her shoulders, "Climb up here. I'll tell you before we go home, though I'm dying for some tea. I got into Euston very early, took a cab across to Charing Cross, and then on to Croydon. I've made good time." She glanced at the little heart-shaped watch pinned to her corsage. "Fifty minutes from the livery stable. It was a lovely drive on a morning like this."

He could not help chuckling. She was so like the girl he remembered. She never changed, or not in any important particular, and the remembrance of this caused him to throw his arm round her and kiss her.

"Come Hetty, out with it. Is it to do with Sam?"

"In a way. And George too. Mostly George."

"Well?"

"I'll get it over and done with, and explain motives later. George has left here, Adam. For good, and his family with him."

"*Left here?* You mean, left the mill-house?"

"Left the firm. He said there was no other way. He said he'd put a proposition up to you and you turned him down flat. You had it out, didn't you, before you left for the West Country?"

"Well, yes, you could say that. But we didn't quarrel and I got the impression he saw my viewpoint. More or less."

"I'm sure he did. But it didn't help. That engine is everything to him, just as the network was to you in your early days. The fact is he couldn't pretend any longer."

"Pretend to devote himself to Swann-on-Wheels?"

"To Swann-on-Wheels as constituted. With you, and most of the others, determined to jog on in the same old way. He said he had to go about it his way or no way at all."

"He's taken a job with someone else?"

"No! He wouldn't do that. He isn't disloyal. It was a personal decision. He made up his mind somewhere between the yard and getting back here on Saturday to strike out on his own."

He was amazed. "Great God! Does he realise what's involved? To start up in our line of business needs fifty times as much capital as he has, even beginning in a small way, smaller than I did. He's not such a fool as to imagine he can sell that idea of his to someone with capital, is he?"

"He isn't going to sell it. He means to go on working on it until it is marketable."

"But what about Gisela and the children? They have to eat, don't they? And have somewhere to sleep nights?"

"Sam is attending to that."

"*Sam!*" The first hint of her treachery—and he saw it as that under the initial impact—was like a stab in the belly. "You're saying *you* arranged it? That's what took you to Manchester?"

"Yes. It was either that or see him pack up and leave with no prospects at all. He was absolutely determined and began to talk wild when I raised the same questions as you raised concerning his responsibilities to Gisela and the babies. I never saw him so determined about anything. He kept talking about a man called Pal something . . . a Frenchman I believe, a man who invented something and burned his wife's furniture for some reason."

"*Palissy?* Bernard Palissy?"

"That was it! Who was he? And why on earth did he burn his wife's furniture?"

"He was just such a crank as George only his obsession was enamel-processing. He burned the furniture to keep his ovens at a certain temperature."

"Has he made an awful lot of money since? Is he well-established now?"

He was very grateful to her for having said that. It took a little of the strain out of the situation. "Palissy lived in the sixteenth century. Yes, he did succeed in making enamel-ware and none better. But he died in the Bastille for all that. George should have picked someone else to inspire him. He's going to need more luck than Palissy."

"No," she said, "not luck exactly. I've been able to take that element out of it. Sam is backing him."

"Sam Rawlinson backing a nonsense like that? You're joking! Sam's a gambler but he only backs odds-on chances, like Suez Canal stock." And then, watching her, he understood that she had been rather more than an intermediary. He said, sharply, "Just how deeply are you involved in this? Apart from passing him on to Sam, I mean?"

"I never pretended to you I didn't believe in George, did I?"

"No, you didn't. But believing in him is one thing. Encouraging him to pack his traps and walk out of my life and my firm is something else. I'm damned if I understand how you could have brought yourself to do such a thing, Hetty."

"Well I did," she said, "and I'm not sorry for it. I'll tell you why if you have the patience to listen."

"I'll listen," he said, grimly. "What choice do I have? He's gone, hasn't he?"

"Not necessarily for good."

"Don't deceive yourself about that, my dear."

"But I'm not deceiving myself. It seemed to me the only possible compromise. Sam is still one of the family, isn't he? In a sort of way, I mean. It was a determination to keep us in touch that made me nerve myself to well . . . to go about it behind your back. I hated doing it. It seemed mean and shabby, for I know how much George meant to you. But it was better than losing him altogether, better than seeing him go off and work for strangers and maybe end up as a rival to you. Can you understand that, Adam?"

He was beginning to. In a way he could see her dilemma and also sense the strain it had put upon her loyalties. His family or hers? Swann-on-Wheels, or the Swanns of 'Tryst', sired by him but always taking second place in his list of priorites? A straight choice, he supposed, and one that he himself had been called upon to face three days ago. But he had chosen the other alternative, letting George go in favour of the network. He said, presently, "Very well, I see your problem. How did it resolve itself in the end?"

"I was going to give him a letter but then I thought, 'Sam's old, and getting woolly, and a letter won't do. I'll have to go to him and explain,' and that's what I did, as soon as George had taken that engine to bits and packed it up. I took Gisela and the children. We caught the six o'clock north and stayed overnight in the Midland Hotel. Early on Sunday we went out to Sam's, and I told him he could use any money he was intending to leave me for George's family and George's ideas."

"And where was George himself while you were doing that?"

"He came up on a Sunday train with the crates. He wouldn't let them out of his sight. He joined us late on Sunday and I hoped to get back before you showed up but I couldn't. There was signing to be done at Sam's lawyers, so I stayed over and took the early morning train south. Even then I thought I'd be in time, for you said you wouldn't be back until today. That was bad luck on my part, for how many days a year do you stay home anyway?"

He began to warm towards her, inexplicably it seemed to him, for, despite George's vehemence, he found it difficult to believe the boy would have put his family and future at risk without her connivance. Yet there was logic about her actions, and a certain ruthlessness too, of a kind that he understood very well. She was fighting for what she regarded as her paramount interests, just as he would have fought for the network, and for the first time in all the years they had been married he saw them as having pursued different goals, often in different directions, but with the same steadiness of vision and the same obstinacy. The family unit was what mattered to her, taking precedence over everything else, even him.

He said, mildly, "Right. Let's get you home and brew that tea. But between here and the teapot tell me how Sam Rawlinson reacted to the arrival of that damned contraption on his doorstep. To say nothing of its inventor, his wife and two babies, still in long clothes."

"He was absolutely splendid. Once I made him understand that is, and so was Hilda, and that was even more surprising."

"It isn't all that surprising when you think about it," he said, picking up the reins and chivvying the pony between the pillars into the drive. "It's a late score for him. Two in one when you look at it. He's got you back after half a lifetime, and he's coaxed my likeliest entry into his stable. I wouldn't put it past the old devil to pour money into that bottomless pit of George's, out of pure cussedness. It's the kind of challenge that would likely appeal to a man who began as a bale-breaker in a ratty old mill, and went on to make three fortunes in a row. It makes me wonder why he underestimated his most promising investment all those years ago."

"What investment was that?" she asked, innocently.

"You," he said. "Damn it, woman, if he'd played his hand better he could have married you to real money, and would have been in the House of Lords by now. Lord Rawlinson, of Seddon."

"I had my own ideas about that," she said, "but maybe you've forgotten."

"I haven't forgotten a thing about you," he said, pinching her thigh as the pony toiled up the slope at a snail's pace. "Not a thing, d'you hear? I was telling myself just that down by that copse and if you hadn't needed your breakfast I might have played you at your own game down there."

"I could have waited," she said, calmly. "It would have been the quickest way of getting you off my conscience," and he laughed.

They ambled into the yard and he handed her down, calling to the lad to bring her bags inside and give the pony a rub down before turning him out to grass. She moved ahead of him up the steps to the kitchen and this was just as well for he was chuckling and she would have found too much satisfaction in that.

5

Jubilee

IT was like a dynamo switched on to warm up long before it was required to run at full power, that had then somehow got out of hand, generating current that pulsed far and wide across the length and breadth of the country, quickening everything within its orbit, so that mundane concerns were forgotten as everything and everybody was caught up in the swirl and thrust of the runaway engine.

Or like a placid hay ride that had developed into a raucous free-for-all outside the alehouse, where dignity was forgotten in a wild, tribal orgy involving chants, dances and merrymaking of a kind ordinarily discouraged in a nation dedicated to the till and family prayers.

It was licence to get roaring drunk after a lifetime of sobriety, amorous after a life of celibacy, spendthrift after years of parsimony and, within it all, an awareness amounting to certainty that, in the decades leading up to this magic moment, the human species had subdivided, a minority (that was British) hiving off to occupy the seats of the elect, a majority (foreigners, poor devils) standing off to admire, much as Sunday morning loiterers watched the parade of the privileged after church in Hyde Park. But with a qualification. The loiterers, given British citizenship, were now numbered with the carriage folk.

*   *   *

Its effect upon the network was uneven, the regions responding according to the men who reigned there. In the past the meeting of a crisis caused by bad weather, shortage of cash at Headquarters, a trade recession, could be gauged to some extent by reflection on the several temperaments of the viceroys and their key men. But there was no gauging this, so that no specific directive went out advising the satellites how to celebrate, how much money to spend,

653

how to go about using the occasion as an excuse to project themselves and their concerns. It was left to each of them to caper or to stay at home, taking advantage of the national holiday to put their feet up, so that the Jubilee meant different things to different men; a splendid occasion to some, an extra Bank Holiday to others.

To a degree reaction was governed by geography. The regions within excursion range of the capital, where the national celebrants operated, made no significant contribution of their own, executives and small fry alike preferring to travel up to town overnight and scramble for kerbstone vantage points along the royal route from Buckingham Palace to St. Paul's. Thus, Godsall, of the Kentish Triangle, Vicary, of The Bonus, north of the Thames estuary, and Headquarters personnel, who lived in the very hub of the rituals, looked to officialdom and flunkeydom for a free spectacle, not even bothering to spend their regional allocation on rosettes for the teams and bunting for their premises. On the day itself their employees and customers were left to their own devices, to let off a few firecrackers and sing a few music-hall ditties round bonfires.

Adam himself was among this idle group, standing with Henrietta and his four youngest children at the office window of a customer within fifty yards of St. Clement Danes in the Strand, the three girls getting very fidgety during the interminable wait, for they had to be in position long before breakfast-time.

When, at last, the glittering cavalcade passed below, Henrietta and the children judged it had been worth the effort to get here but Adam had his doubts. He had never cared very much for the plump little woman, whose longevity had touched off this hullaballoo. His allegiance, and that was qualified, had been to her German husband, one of the few surrounding her who had foreseen the technical revolution and been able to isolate trade from trappings. But Albert had died long ago, when the network was in its infancy, and hardly anyone remembered him now, looking upon his sixty-eight-year-old widow as the catalyst of the new imperialism. He watched her pass, with her jingling escort of Household Cavalry, her horde of relatives, and her scarlet-clad janissaries, and it struck him that this whole affair was an anachronism, for both she and they represented an England that belonged more to his father's day than his. He said nothing of this to Henrietta. For her, somehow, the pageant was the enactment of a girlish dream that had been concerned with moustached warriors and the panoply of conquest, and in this context it was a pity that her single contribution to the set-piece was far away in India, with his homely bride, the Colonel's daughter. It crossed Adam's mind then how her eyes would have sparkled if Alex had been numbered among the royal escort.

After that there was nothing to do but go home and preside over the local celebrations at Twyforde Green, where there was an athletic meeting, a public tea, the distribution of mugs and, as darkness fell, the discharge of sky-rockets to light a sky already reflecting the glow of hilltop beacons. Personally there was not much to celebrate just now. George was lost to him, and with George went the sense of continuity, whereas Giles, poor chap, was all dressed up with nowhere to go, save as coat-holder for Hugo at the Crystal Palace sports rally.

It seemed very quiet when, around midnight, they saw the two youngest to bed, Joanna and Helen having already changed and left to dance the night away at one of their country-house balls, occasions that were always promising to lead to a double engagement and double wedding at Twyforde Green parish church but somehow never did. For the Inseparables, although by no means short of suitors, put an impossibly high price on youth and freedom.

It was around one in the morning when he came stumping out of his dressing-room to find Henrietta asleep, her Jubilee finery strewn about the room. He stood by the window a moment, counting the twinkling points of light on the Kentish hillsides, trying hard to identify with the national occasion. Alone among them, save for an elderly servant or two, he could remember a time when the adjective 'Victorian' had no significance, and it seemed to him, standing there counting the beacons, almost as long ago as the day the first Conyer built under this wooded spur. He had a sense of hurrying time, and no compensating sense of achievement that he had so often experienced in this house, where so many of his plans had been laid and all his children had drawn their first breath. Somewhere along the line, he supposed, he had taken a wrong turning that was threatening to run him into a cul-de-sac in his old age but maybe he was not alone in this. He had an intuitive sense that the nation had made a similar miscalculation and that backtracking, for man and tribe, might prove a long and tiresome business. Pride in one's achievements was well enough. But pride was no substitute for a compass.

2

Albert Rookwood, forty-three years of age, and Gaffer of the Southern Square since he was a lad of twenty and rubbing Howarth's Moustache Oil on his upper-lip, had no such misgivings.

Alone among Swann's viceroys (with the possible exception of Jake Higson, his fellow ex-gamin in the network hierarchy) Rookwood had seen profit in using the national mood as a springboard for promoting an advertising campaign clear across his territory, from the Solent to the southern slopes of the Cotswolds. He was very careful, however, to ensure that dignity was not sacrificed to vulgar display, of the kind they seemed to be encouraging among hucksters and back-street shopkeepers. Whatever he did by way of telescoping the House of Windsor and the House of Swann would be characterised by the sobriety and restraint that had sat upon Rookwood like an undertaker's frock-coat ever since he had married his landlady's daughter, raised a family, taken his place among the city worthies, and erased from his mind any lingering doubts concerning his obscure origins.

He lectured his sub-depot managers, marshalled and inspected his teams, doled out his Union Jacks and rosettes, and issued a stream of crisply-worded bulletins concerned with shining brasswork, well-oiled saddlery, decoration of premises and general deportment on The Day. Then, as a final concession to the national mood, he gave orders that every vehicle that left one of his yards bore on its tailboard a sedate cut-out of Windsor Castle, and that waggoners' whips could be decorated by a neatly-tied bow in red, white and blue silk. The general effect of all this was a stunning uniformity.

Having, as it were, dressed a colourful window, he gave careful thought to what he could offer the customers who stepped inside. Broadsheets were distributed offering ten per cent cuts in rates during Jubilee month, and notices were placed in the local press to the effect that, in the week leading up to the day itself, Swann waggons, free of charge, would be placed at the disposal of any municipality in the territory concerned with organising loyal festivities. A gesture such as this, he reasoned, would get him and Swann-on-Wheels talked about and he was right. Almost at once he was co-opted on to the Salisbury Jubilee Committee, where his opinion was solicited on a variety of matters, by no means all of them concerned with transport. Already a city councillor, people began to see him as a future mayor, so that even those in the network who remembered him as a lad came to forget that he was the very first jewel the evangelist Keate had dredged from the Rotherhithe mud, or that he had paid good money to have South Bank parish registers searched in an effort to discover his identity.

But there was one person about him who did not forget, who marvelled as she heard him booming responses at the Cathedral thanksgiving service on The Day. This was Mrs. Gilroy, his mother-in-law and onetime landlady, who had always seen 'Young Rookwood' as the son she longed for but never had. To her, grandmother to the quiverful of handsome children who surrounded her on that occasion, Albert Rookwood was the living embodiment of the Whittington legend.

The thought remained with her all day, warming her old heart as she recalled the occasion when That Dear Boy (she never thought of him under any other title) had been on the point of leaving them, having fallen hopelessly in love with her pretty, flighty, over-educated daughter, and being unable to imagine that such a splendid creature would look favourably upon the suit of a spillover of a baby farm or worse. But Mrs. Gilroy had had her own ideas about that. Within no time at all she had made her dispositions and had the extreme satisfaction of seeing That Dear Boy walk down the aisle with Little Madam on his arm and now, praise God, Little Madam was as tame in his presence as the latest local chawbacon, signed on as an off-loader at the Swann yard. And dutiful to boot, judging by the biennial proofs of affection she offered.

She stood very close to the Dear Boy during the last event of that memorable day, when a set-piece of Her Majesty, forty feet high, red-eyed, blue-haired and veiled with golden rain, coaxed a long, satisfying *Ahhh* from the onlookers, whereupon Councillor Rookwood, never at a loss for an original phrase, murmured, "God Bless

Her! She's come a long way, mother!" And mother was moved to reply, sharply, "No further and not so fast as you, Albert!"

He did not deny it. Why should he? It was undeniable.

His waggons, wherever they rolled that summer, caught and held the eye in a way that somehow suggested Swann-on-Wheels teams and vehicles had the right, had they wished to exercise it, to display the royal arms, and the legend 'By Appointment to Her Majesty the Queen', but modesty dictated that they adhered to the nationally-recognised insignia of a swan with a waggon-wheel in place of a port wing.

3

Rookwood's realm was patriarchal. It was otherwise with another Swann manager who decided to make hay of the loyal harvest.

Four hundred miles to the north, where Jake Higson administered the largest of the Swann regions between Hadrian's Wall and the Grampians, hirelings close enough to the Gaffer to know how things stood at the Edinburgh depot thought of him as henpecked, and under the thumb of his volatile Scots wife, Mary. In the broadest terms they were right. Jake never made an important decision without consulting her, but this was not because he adored her, or thought of her as an oracle. It was because, being a McKenzie of the Jedburgh branch, she was his direct channel of communication with all his customers, Lowland and Highland. She told him what to say and how to say it and, what was more important, whom to seek and say it to. Thus, when Jake, who had retained his cockney opportunism whilst shedding every other Sassenach trait, decided to follow that stuffy chap Rookwood's suit and carve himself a slice of Jubilee cake, he naturally consulted Mary, who promised to give the matter careful thought. In a day or so she presented him with what he regarded as a masterly approach to the problem.

She pointed out that anyone seeking commercial exploitation of the event should take into account the fact that Her Majesty favoured Scotland far beyond any other sector of her domains, and, moreover, made no secret of the fact, for London-based Cabinet

Ministers were now resigned to making the round trip to Balmoral and back simply in order to get her signature on a document. And as though to underline her preference, she had employed John Brown, a gillie with a known liking for good Scots whisky, as her body servant for time out of mind, and even gone so far as to excuse his staggers in the Royal Presence on the grounds that 'poor John was not well'. All this surely pointed in one direction. Whatever steps Jamie took to identify the firm of Swann-on-Wheels with fifty-years-a-queen, had better be directed towards Scotland, dismissing England, Wales and Ireland as mere appendages to the Crown. For herself, she would make a special contribution, writing and staging a royal pageant, to be acted by a combined cast of children drawn from the western districts of Edinburgh where she had once taught school.

They both set to work at once and it would be difficult to say which of them displayed the liveliest imagination. Mary managed to produce a seventy-page script depicting the history of Scotland's royal family without once mentioning the word 'England', rounding it off with a delightful epilogue portraying the many happy sojourns of Albert, Victoria, and all the little princes and princesses beside the Dee in the dear yesterday, when Her Majesty was wont to walk abroad in tartan and widow's weeds, her costume for so long now.

Jake, himself working round the clock on his own display of loyalty, took time off to watch the dress rehearsal, and if he was slightly puzzled by a diminutive Albert addressing the ten-year-old starlet in the broadest Scots dialect, and Victoria answering in the same, he did not say so. Instead he told his wife that dramatic authors had been ennobled for less.

By then, of course, his own endeavours were beginning to be noticed in the city, and in all the highways and byways of the Lothians and the Border Counties. Unlike Rookwood, Jake Higson had never set much store by dignity but he had a cockney's love of display. Swann waggons, hauling coal and pig-iron south, hardware north from the Tyne basin, fish, fowl and vegetables citywards from sources as distant as Saltcoats in the west and Tayport in the east, might easily have been mistaken for units in the victorious army of Douglas-led moss-troopers, laden with Sassenach plunder. Each of them bore, in addition to the Swann insignia, a plywood, weather-proofed shield depicting Britannia robed in Stuart tartan and, on the nearside, a stencil of the Royal Family at Balmoral. Floating proudly above a diminutive and apologetic Union Jack (wedged low down in the whip socket) was the proud banner of St. Andrew.

The stencil, measuring some five feet by four, had been limned by the yard carpenter, who fancied himself as a landscape artist but it was his first essay into portraiture. Even so, the early roll-offs were recognisable likenesses of the late Prince Consort and the Queen, but as some three hundred were required, and the creator was working under constant pressure, the later stencils had a woolly look and the royal visages tended to become fuzzy, suggesting to the hypercritical an impressionist's version of blear-eyed clansmen, assembled in front of a keep and a pile of pink cannonballs resting on mounds of snow. Peering closer, however, bystanders got the correct impression. The clansmen were male and female, and the pink cannonballs were the heads of royal children wearing long, white mantles.

Finally, hearing over the network grapevine that Rookwood had decreed that all his waggoners wore red, white and blue cap cockades, Jake approved the notion. Instead of red, white and blue rosettes, however, he persuaded a sempstress to make him three hundred good Scots thistles.

Garish it may have been but the display made the news. A reporter, seeing a Swann waggon pass under his office window, persuaded his enterprising editor to offer a prize for the best-decorated vehicle plying in Edinburgh that week. The loyal committee naturally awarded it to the Swann yard.

It was a day or so after the celebrations had ended, and the debris (burned by the improvident English) was being folded and laid aside in anticipation of the Diamond Jubilee, that Jake happened to ask Mary why it was that Her Majesty spent so much of her time at Balmoral, when she was known to possess two royal palaces and so many splendid English houses. Mary said, drawing close to him, "Why, man, she and Albert were very happy up here when they were first married. Wouldn't I feel the same about Rothesay, if you were taken from me, Jamie?"

His eyes misted at that for Rothesay, in Bute, was the place where they had spent their first three days as man and wife, and Mary had taught him bridegroom's manners in much the same way as she had put him on the road to becoming one of the most influential merchants in Scotland.

4

There was no gainsaying it. Indeed, Adam Swann had once remarked on it when discussing monthly returns from the regions. Wherever a viceroy was bedded down, so to speak, with the right kind of wife, his region prospered, whereas bachelors, however young and pushing they might be, did not seem to possess the stamina to hoist them to the top flight of a Swann progress chart.

There was Young Rookwood and there was Jake Higson, consistently vying with one another for the end-of-year accolade and bonus. There was Bryn Lovell in the Mountain Square, who had never made much of Wales until he married a half-caste and adopted her coffee-coloured children. There was that old dodderer Hamlet Ratcliffe who, so long as his wife Augusta was around to prod him, still held his own in the Western Wedge. There was Morris, of Southern Pickings, who had married money and was said to extend the same elaborate courtesy towards an elderly wife as Disraeli had shown the Queen in his heyday. There was Godsall in the Kentish Triangle, whose wife was a cut above all the other vicereines, and whose social contacts had kept the Triangle in the upper bracket for twenty years. And finally (all the other, more laggardly regions being ruled by single men) there was Tom and Edith Wickstead, who now managed the areas once designated, Crescent South and Crescent Centre, based on Peterborough.

Married or single, the managers of all the regions, exclusive of Rookwood's and Higson's, made no special effort to use the Jubilee as a trade festival. At Peterborough, however, Tom and Edith contrived, almost by accident, to convert it into a personal anniversary, for June the twenty-first happened to be the day they had married, in 1866, within a week or two of Adam Swann's return from the dead.

Tom Wickstead had had his hands full in the period leading up to the event and it was not until the morning of the nineteenth when, throwing wide the bedroom window, he watched the band of the Northamptonshire Volunteers march by playing 'The British Grenadiers', that he said, gaily, "Have you forgotten we have our own celebrating to do on Jubilee Day? Damn it, woman, it's *our* coming of age, as man and wife! Twenty-one years of it, and nobody's offered us the Dunmow Flitch. Why don't we take a trip somewhere and get away from this brassy uproar?"

She joined him at the window, still occupied with her hair, long enough (as Tom would tell anyone prepared to listen) to sit on.

"No matter where we go on the day," she said, "we won't escape crowds and noise." And then, smiling, "No, I hadn't forgotten. Have I ever forgotten, as you do, sometimes two years running? As a matter of fact, I've got a present for you. Seeing it is a rather special anniversary."

He said, reflectively, "That first time I had a little something for you, remember? And it caught you on the hop, by God! I never did see a woman look more confounded come to think of it."

It was an old joke, qualifying as a family chestnut by now, but today it sparked off a chain of happy memories in her mind so that she exclaimed, "But there *is* somewhere I would like to revisit, Tom! Somewhere we've never been since. Can you guess where?"

"Aye, I can at that," he said, "and we'll celebrate by going there tomorrow. Once there I daresay we'll find our own formula for travelling backwards, the way everyone will be doing on the twenty-first," and her answering laugh left no doubt in his mind that they were sharing thoughts of a little country inn called The Garland on the outskirts of the Welsh border town of Ludlow, whither she had gone to lie in ambush for him on the eve of her thirtieth birthday.

It was a simpler journey nowadays. Then, she recalled, scared half out of her wits by what she was resolved to do, it had been a tedious cross-country traipse, with any number of changes but now, with special trains running over every stretch of main line in the country, they were outside the inn long before sundown, and looking up at its half-timbered façade, as if it stood for something very meaningful in their relationship.

He said, eagerly, "Do you suppose we could get the same room?" and she replied, gaily, "We could try, Tom," and marched in, remembering as she did how forlorn and desperate she had felt when she approached that same desk more than twenty years before, signing herself in as 'Mrs. Wickstead', with him not even aware she was this side of England. And after that there had been the long nerve-wracking wait until he returned, with her entire future balanced very precariously on the moment of recognition, and how he was likely to regard this extreme impertinence on her part. But then, almost effortlessly, the drama had resolved itself into farce, for, seeing how it was, he had produced the ring she now wore, bought with the first honest wages he had ever earned in the whole of his life. A month later she had the right to sign herself Mrs. Wickstead.

They were lucky. The inn was half empty, despite the blare of the town band and the gala trappings in the streets. Almost everyone, it seemed, had gone to London on a cheap excursion, or to Shrewsbury, where there was a pageant and sports meeting, or to the coast for a breath of sea air, and local celebrations looked like being parochial. They were not here on a public occasion, however. From the window they watched traps and market carts making their way towards the castle green, where the Morris dancers were assembling, and presently a troop of cavalry jingled by, in dazzling dress uniforms that Edith felt obliged to admire, saying they looked like a party of latecomers hurrying to Waterloo. He said, half-seriously, "I wore the Queen's uniform myself once. But it wasn't a good fit!" and she replied, in the waspish tone she always used whenever he referred to his convict past, "That's enough of that, Tom Wickstead! You didn't wear it for the reasons most lawbreakers do, and today is not the day to remind me of them, even in jest!" But then, seeing him look a little nonplussed, she kissed him, saying, "Dear God, it was *me* who was lucky to run into *you*. Sooner or later you would have straightened yourself out, without my help! Come, let's see what they have for dinner, for I'm sharpset and I'm sure you are."

"Not for food," he said, unexpectedly, "and certainly not in here, remembering," and he drew the chintz curtains so that the pleasant, low-ceilinged room was rosy with filtered sunlight.

Lying in his arms she remembered (as she often did on these occasions) the two other men in her life, Matt Hornby, drowned off Holy Isle on the eve of their wedding, and Adam Swann, who had half-resolved to make her his mistress but had thought better of it on her advice, for she had sensed, somehow, that he would regard the price paid for her too high for his peace of mind. And after that, thank God, Tom, stronger and more masterful than either of them, yet gentler, much gentler, and more in need of her, so that they had set out as partners and had remained partners all this time.

He sat up presently and smiled down at her, reaching out his hand as though to establish some kind of order in the tumult he had made of her hair, wondering a little at her youthfulness, and the joyful gusto of her responses, very rare, he would say, in a woman turned fifty. He said, boyishly, "It was a good idea of yours to come back here, Edith. Sentimental, maybe, but encouraging at our age," and she replied, "Not as encouraging as my original expedition, I think. For I'm quite sure, ring notwithstanding, you would never have got round to proposing, Tom. You really did need some positive encouragement that time. Will you admit to that after twenty-one years?"

"Aye," he said, "perhaps, for what the devil did I have to offer a bonnie little baggage like you? I wanted you the moment I laid hands on you, but I wasn't eager to press my luck. I owed you too much already and that's a fact."

"You never owed me anything," she said, hoisting herself up and reaching out for her hairbrush. "Except maybe, the excuse to stop lying to myself that I was engaged on missionary work. I wasn't, of course, not even the night I caught you looking for Solly Beckstein's diamonds in a Swann mail sack. I daresay I thought I was, but I wasn't. I was man-hungry and all I was looking for was someone who wanted me as a woman and not a yard gaffer willing to accommodate him after business hours."

"Is that how Adam Swann thought of you?"

"More or less," she said, "but don't hold it against him. He didn't know his own wife in those days. If a man as dedicated and lusty as Adam Swann was finds a woman he can use as workmate and bedmate as fancy takes him can you blame him making the most of it?"

"You said 'was'. Does that mean disenchantment setting in for Swann?"

"I think it is. He's had his disappointments, along with the rest of us. Besides, when a concern goes on growing, as his does, there comes a time when it becomes too bothersome to manage. He'll step down soon, mark my words. And the moment he does the fun will go from it for all of us."

From the castle yard the strains of the Morris dancers' accompaniment reached them, a very English sound, she thought, that invoked the essence of all that had happened to them under the Swann aegis. Not merely herself and Tom but the long muster-roll of men who had driven over every foot of the country, hauling British goods that were the sinews of the nation and the touchstone of the orgy of chest-beating that had no parallel in history, not even if you looked back two thousand years to Imperial Rome. She heaved herself clear of the bed and began pulling on her clothes. "What are we doing, lying here discussing the future of Swann-on-Wheels, as if we still had our way to make in the world? For heaven's sake let's eat, man. I could have lived on love in the old days but not at my age. Besides, we're supposed to be on holiday, aren't we?"

5

Less than a day's haul to the north of Ludlow, another Swann manager was using the occasion to take a private holiday, and one that had as little do with Victoria's longevity as the Wicksteads' sentimental journey. Yet, again like their expedition, it had its roots in the past. More than twenty years before, Bryn Lovell remembered taking his four coffee-coloured stepsons on the same expedition as he now led three of his grandsons. To the mountains that is, to see a Wales that owed no allegiance whatsoever to the House of Hanover, or to any of its predecessors either. For, as he was careful to point out when the little party looked up at a cloud-free Snowdon, this enclave had never sworn fealty to anyone but men like Llewelyn and Glendower. And after Glendower, perhaps (stretching it a little) to the evangelist John Wesley, who had checked the drift back to paganism.

In a way his presence here was an expression of that same independence, a thumbing of the nose at all that glitter and martial music in the streets of the English capital three hundred miles to the south-east. He had no quarrel with the English but he had never seen himself as one of them. Indeed, he had always considered it his duty, as a conscientious step-father, to inculcate into these dark-skinned little Welshmen an awareness of their true heritage. He must have succeeded. The fathers of these boys both spoke Welsh, even though their grandparents had been born on a Caribbean island where nobody had ever heard of Llewelyn. It had seemed to him that Jubilee Week was a unique opportunity to pass the lesson on to the next generation, so here he was preaching the gospel he had preached to their fathers, Enoch and Shadrach, years before anyone had ever dreamed that Victoria would become a legend.

"As I once told your fathers," he said, "the English took the plain and built their castles there but they never reached us here. Never forget that. As good Welshmen it is important to you." It was Shadrach's boy, the nine-year-old David, who had a pertinent question. "In the villages everyone speaks Welsh, Grandad. But down south, at school that is, nobody does. But where we live is still Wales, isn't it?"

It was a poser and he had to think about it a moment. Finally he said, "Yes, indeed, Davey boy. Geographically it's Wales, but that's as far as it goes. Down south they made their peace with the English long since, having no choice in the matter. Where could they hold out against men better armed, better led and twice as many? But up here, as I say, they never did more than harry us. We rolled stones down on their columns and we stuck them full of arrows until they stole our longbows, learned to use them and started shooting back. But you can't goad an Englishman into attempting the impossible, boyo. He holds on to the passes and builds his castles close to the sea and there's a lesson there, too. The sea, to the English, is what the mountains are to us, if you follow me?"

It is doubtful if they did but always they liked Grandad Bryn's stories, and he had done his duty as a Welshman. He said, opening the straps of his knapsack, "I bought souvenirs for you at that little shop in the village. Here, boys, take them and keep them," and he gave each of his three grandsons a flag, emblazoned, it was true, with the obligatory legend, '*God Save the Queen. June 21st 1887*', but stencilled on a background of the red dragon of Wales.

6

By early evening, beacons were beginning to twinkle up here, those who fed them taking their cue from the thin pillars of smoke already rising from Brecon Beacons, and the rounded hills of Montgomeryshire and Radnorshire. Then, against an orange sunset shot through with heliotrope, the first of them showed in Flint and on across the Dee estuary and the Wirral to the Cheshire plain.

The South Lancashire sky was violet, tinged as always by the vomit of a thousand chimney stacks that today trailed no more than token plumes, this being a national holiday. But they still belched for all that, as John Catesby noticed going his rounds on his barrel-chested cob; "To see the sights" as he told himself, wondering at the inconsistencies of the English, a nation that could still make a fetish of royal occasions after deposing so many kings and removing the head of one who refused to be deposed.

He poked about all day on his patient, barrel-chested nag, for it was quite impossible to drive a trap through the congested streets. By sundown half the celebrants were tipsy and it needed a steady hand on the rein and plenty of tact to return from St. Peter's Square where, earlier in the day, he had watched five thousand people eat a public meal at municipal expense. Irish labourers weaved under the cob's nose and every now and again he had to pull up short to avoid a fight. By dusk, he supposed, the constabulary would be filling their Black Marias, as they often had up here, but with far less tolerance than they would show tonight. He would have liked to discuss the phenomenon of British royalty-mania with someone intelligent and sober. That likeable boy of the Gaffer's, for instance, who had spent some time up here with him and had, according to the network grapevine, jilted a millionaire's daughter. But no one with the necessary qualifications was on hand, so he had to answer his own questions and they were many and various, probing deeply into the maw of a society with such a colourful political history, with so many deeply-rooted prejudices, and a capacity, matched nowhere in the world, for compromise, for holding on, for adjusting to each new pressure, social and industrial, any one of which would have raised the barricades in Paris, Petrograd and Vienna.

Barricades had been up here, of course, from time to time, but had always been taken down again, not by police and military but by men persuaded that there were more practical ways of defending their rights. People hereabouts still talked of Peterloo as a massacre and perhaps it was technically. Yeomanry sabres and charging horses had claimed a few dozen victims on those same setts where, only an hour or so ago, he had seen five thousand Mancunians stuffing themselves with municipal pies and popcorn. But Peterloo was more than sixty years ago, when he had been a toddler waiting to be taken on at a mill for fourpence a day. 'Remember Peterloo' was no more than an archaic rallying cry these days—days of craftsmen's alliances and a Trades' Congress. They had come a long way since then but not far enough, by God, not by many a mile. Revolution had been averted somehow. The monarchy, deucedly shaky in those days, had survived to become a kind of religion, not merely for those enjoying a living wage and three square meals a day in their bellies, but for every Jack and Jill in the islands save a tiny minority of hard-core republicans, whom nobody took seriously.

Well, if that was how they wanted it he was not prepared to take issue with them. He had always thought of himself as a people's man, a majority man, and if that gibbering drunk, propping himself in a corner and waving his penny Union Jack preferred a hereditary symbol to an elected president on the American style, then John Catesby had no wish to persuade him otherwise. What point was there in doing so, anyway? Old Vicky was harmless enough now, pruned of most of her power, shorn of royal prerogatives, and obliged to suffer an anarchist if one was returned to Westminster. Things were moving in the right direction and it was time they did. Was it too much to hope the pace of reform would quicken a little in the thirteen years left of the century? Well, hurry along or not, it didn't concern him much nowadays. He was pretty well used up. Youngsters like Giles Swann would have to take his place if they had a mind to. He pulled the cob aside to avoid a strapping rogue in corduroys waving a bottle of stout and said, genially, "Nay, lad, drink it yoursen, an' then home to sleep it off. You'll have a rare head on you in t'morning!"

668

7

An ageing man standing by a Kentish window, contemplating his own arrogance and that of his tribe, and wondering where both would lead; an ex-gamin, masquerading as a civic worthy, basking in the sun of his own success and seeing, or believing he saw, precisely where it would lead; an ex-chimney-sweep, with an eye on the main chance; an ex-highwayman and his wife, deeply in love at fifty-plus; a kindly old scholar, instructing coloured grandchildren on a mountain slope; an industrial warrior, riding his cob through a sea of drunks and seeing some kind of progress in the exercise . . . This was the copper coin of the Golden Jubilee so far as Swann-on-Wheels was concerned. Passed and forgotten as soon as it changed hands. But there was one region of the network that had cause to remember the day with awe and wonder. Down in the far west Hamlet Ratcliffe was not concerned with small change that blazing June but with all he possessed. And he in his eightieth year.

*   *   *

They brought him the news about midday on the twentieth. Bertie-boy, heir-apparent in the Western Wedge, was temporarily out of action, and at a time when his presence on the road was imperative if Swann's reputation for speedy deliveries was to be maintained.

In the weeks leading up to the Jubilee, Swann's waggons had hauled a wide variety of goods directly associated with the event. In Northern and Southern Pickings, that is to say between Worcester and the Potteries, where china sold all over the world was manufactured, they had carried hundreds of thousands of celebration mugs to be distributed to schoolchildren in the form of municipal largesse. Similarly, thousands of Imperial flags and a hundred miles or more of bunting, spun and dyed in Polygon mills had been hauled south and east, to float over a thousand town halls and along ten thousand High Streets. But only Ratcliffe's beat in the West had the privilege of actually hauling a queen. Here, as the day approached, a frantic mid-Devon mayor made a personal appeal to

Hamlet to deliver by the twentieth of June, at the very latest, an eight-foot bronze statue of Her Majesty cast to fit into the frontal niche of the town's new clock tower, a monument upon which mayor and colleagues had staked capital and dignity in order to go one better than their neighbours.

The mayor poured out his tale and Hamlet listened in impatient silence. The statue, he learned, had been cast in Devonport, finished well ahead of schedule, and despatched by rail on the seventeenth. That was cutting it fine, but there had been some inexplicable blunder concerning arrangements for the final stage of the journey from Exeter, a matter of twenty-eight miles up the river valley. Now, unless Swann-on-Wheels was prepared to step into the breach, the Jubilee would pass into history unmarked by the community. Flags draping the new clock tower would be pulled aside to reveal— a clock, a fountain, a horse-trough, and a large, empty niche, so that ever afterwards the monument would be classed as a folly and its sponsors would go down in local history as buffoons.

Hamlet, his rheumy eyes slightly bloodshot, his girth so enormous now that, given his short stature, he looked like Humpty Dumpty in a frock coat that Augusta had twice let out in the last three years, viewed the commission thrust upon him as a confounded nuisance. Most of his waggoners had been given the week off, and he was short of heavy vehicles that would be required to haul such an awkward load over unsurfaced roads. Yet he was still peasant enough to see the mayor's point of view. An anticlimax on this scale would almost certainly enlarge itself into a legend in the locality. Local wags would set to work manufacturing jokes about it, jokes that would pass from mouth to mouth and generation to generation. Hamlet knew village life and could even conjure with some of those jokes in advance—"Arrr, that was the day 'Er Majesty got left behind in the goods yard, and old Mort Wonnacott (Mortimer Wonnacott was the mayor in question) messed his britches waiting on 'er . . ." That kind of thing, the heavy, savage irony, of which the Devon peasant is a pastmaster, shamefaced authority having been his favourite target since the days of Norman overlords.

He said, at length, "Vair enough, Mr. Mayor! Now lemme think, will 'ee? For 'ow can I think on it when youm tellin' me 'ow to run my bizness?" Whereupon Mayor Wonnacott, seeing a gleam of hope in the haulier's gruffness, clamped his jaws shut and waited, as upon the jury's verdict in a capital trial.

Hamlet said, at length, "Us c'n do it. But it'd cost 'ee over the odds. A vower-horse team it'd need, over a twenty-eight mile run from St. David's goods yard to that there clock o' yours. Well, us'll have to measure the distance, but suppose us takes your word for it? Twenty-eight mile you say. So what do 'ee zay to twenty-eight pun'?"

The mayor made a sound like a whippet at the receiving end of a welt but then, noting the baleful gleam in Hamlet's eye, he changed it to a gurgling sound, signifying virtual acceptance of the quotation. "I'll have to look vor it in me orn pocket," he said, gloomily, but Hamlet replied, steadily, "Ahh, mebbe you will. But that's your conzern, bain it? You should 'er come to me in the virst plaace, and had no truck wi' that bliddy railway. For I wouldn't ha' left 'ee with your breeches down, and your arse waiting to be kicked, Mr. Mayor! As tiz you c'n leave it to me. I'll undertake to have that statue off-loaded by mid-night on the twentieth. Mebbe before, depending who hauls it there, and whether or no us can lay hands on some heavy transport. Shall us shake hands on it?"

They shook hands. Down here in the far West money was not often wasted on lawyers and contracts. Westcountrymen diddled foreigners every summer. They did not make a habit of diddling one another.

But then, when the bargain was struck, and a four-horse team had been selected and harnessed to the one serviceable dray in the yard, Bertieboy, chosen as the only possible man on the yard's muster-roll equipped to deliver such a load at short notice, had to put his foot down on a patch of ground a split second before a Clydesdale hoof descended, pinning it there. His shrieks of agony brought Augusta Ratcliffe running, to proclaim, at the top of her voice, that Bertieboy had broken two toes and was *hors de combat* for a fort-night.

Hamlet viewed the scene of the disaster with pitiless irritation, a kind that had settled on him increasingly with old age. He said, sourly, "On'y a bliddy gurt vool would get between Floss an' where she's a mind to put her veet! 'Er's alwus bin 'andy with 'er favours. A man who bin workin' 'er as long as Bertieboy should ha' knowed it!

Now us is in a rare vix, bain us? I promised that there statue delivered by midnight the morrow, and it looks as if I'll 'ave to haul
'un there meself. There's no one else I'd trust wi' royalty aboard.
Pack me a foo sandwiches, Gussie, an' dornee forget my flask o' sloe
gin. Then zend the boy round for Doctor Ambrose to make what
he can o' that bliddy vool's voot. But leave that till last, do 'ee hear?"

It was useless to argue with him. Useless to point out that he
was within four months of his eightieth birthday and that this was
a job for stronger, steadier hands than his. He rejected the notion
that anyone, least of all Gussie, should imply that he was past his
work, and when Augusta wailed, "Dornee do it, my luv! Youm not
up to 'andlin' a vower-team. Tiz all you c'n do nowadays to manage a pair . . ." he snarled, "For Chris' sake, dornee talk so daft,
woman! I'm the Gaffer, bain I? What's more, I give Mayor Wonnacott my word an' I mane to keep it!"

So she made him his sandwiches, bringing them out to him just
as he was being hoisted into the driving-box by two yard boys and
an interested stableman of The White Hart, a hostelry adjoining
the Swann yard.

Down at the Great Western depot there were plenty of porters
to manhandle the statue on to the flat surface of the man-o'-war
and lash it there under its yards of canvas wrappings. Hamlet, aware
that descent from the box was a complicated manoeuvre, had perforce to superintend the loading from where he was and this was
not entirely satisfactory. He found it very difficult these days to
look over his shoulder on account of arthritis in his neck. He assumed
they knew their business, however, and it seemed they did. By four
in the afternoon he was on his way, moving at a walking pace up a
river valley that ran parallel with the valley down which, in the
prime of his life, he had hauled Dante, the lion he recaptured single-
handed beside the river Bray.

The recollection of this legendary feat afforded him the greatest satisfaction, affirming as it did that he was indestructible. For
here he was, twenty-five years later, performing a task that he dare
not entrust to anyone else on Swann's payroll, and doing it, moreover, in the finest possible style, that is to say behind a four-horse
team that caught and held the attention of everybody he passed.

By the time he had traversed the village of Stoke Canon, a few miles north of Exeter, he had mellowed sufficiently to reply amiably to those who asked what it was he was conveying. "Why, the queen," he would say, enigmatically. "Who else, seein' what day tomorrow be?", and when this statement was received with incredulity he would pull up and ask the questioner to lift a corner of the wrappings shrouding the royal face, or feel the outline of the angled sceptre that protruded level with the ponderous shoulders. These investigations delayed him somewhat but he had time in hand. It would be light until very late at this season of the year and he was well on his way and likely to arrive at the base of the clock tower by ten, two hours inside his deadline.

He had reckoned without Barley Dip, however, where the byroad marked out as his quickest route took a steep plunge down to a stone bridge crossing a tributary of the Exe and then climbed again, at a gradient of about one in six over a loose, gritty surface. Halfway down the descent the terrible weight of the waggon began to hurry the wheelers, despite Hamlet's manful application of the brake, and there was a particularly nasty moment when the clumsy equipage levelled out to cross the bridge, passing between the stone parapets with no more than a couple of inches to spare on either side.

He managed it, however, and without mishap save for the loss of a hubcap. After a long and satisfying pull of sloe gin, he moved along the flat and stopped at a cut-out, taking a look at his map in the fading light, and using the interval to demolish the wedge of ham and cheese sandwiches Augusta had cut for him.

It was very pleasant down here, in a long green tunnel of summer foliage, with the last rays of the evening sun slanting through the great umbrellas of cow-parsley atop the hedge, and the distant murmur of the brook running swiftly through the slimed arches of the pack-horse bridge he had just negotiated. Drowsiness stole upon him, bringing with it a benediction that was a compound of some of his most satisfactory memories. Half-asleep and wedged firmly between the box rails, he had a vision of Augusta as a bride, the very last of the seven Bickford sisters, who was twenty-eight on her wedding day and so vastly relieved when twenty-two-year-old Hamlet had married her that she had fallen upon him, as one of her ribald relatives had put it, "like parson's wife on parson at the end o' Lent".

He remembered other things, failures as well as successes. Moments out of his life as a corn-chandler's clerk in Barnstaple, and an auctioneer during his spell of servitude in the brick wilderness of London, whence he had been rescued by Adam Swann to achieve triumph as the captor of the Bamfylde lion. Sitting here and nodding off, as the leaders cropped the sweet grass of the verge, and the scent of honeysuckle came to him on the lightest of summer breezes, he reasoned that his thirty years as a haulier had obliterated all his earlier failures. Somehow that lion-catching incident had made him a man of substance overnight and now, whenever anyone in Devon thought of transport, it was Hamlet Ratcliffe not Swann who sprang to mind. If it were not so would he be here at this moment, within a mile or so of the parish border, where Mayor Wonnacott had agreed to accept delivery of an eight-foot bronze statue of Queen Vic?

The jeering cackle of a jackdaw roused him, reminding him of his duty, and he called, "Giddon up there!" to the team, moving forward to tackle the long, steep haul to the top of the ridge where, no doubt, Wonnacott's sentries were already posted to pass word of his arrival. The big vehicle slowed to about two miles an hour, then one, and then half a mile, its wheels grinding the skittering surface of the track as Hamlet, raising his voice to a high, quavering pitch, called *"Giddon* there! *Up*, me booties! Lay to it, Floss! Lay to it, Margy!" as the leaders heaved and strained and sweated, their hooves striking showers of sparks from the flints and causing the wheelers to throw their heads about in a way that alarmed Hamlet, for the dray was now progressing at a rate of about five yards a minute.

Then, within fifty yards of the crest, an unforeseen thing happened. The tilt of the waggon-bed put too much strain on the fastenings under the royal neck and the statue stirred under its taut wrappings, the plinth and two slippered feet sliding out towards the tailboard and canting to the right in a way that upset the entire balance of the load. In the ensuing moment of panic Hamlet cursed the railway porters aloud, twisting his arthritic neck in a way that enabled him to see precisely what was happening back there, as the canvas folds rucked up under the box and more and more of the queen began to show like a corpse emerging from its shroud, a movement that suggested levitation of the kind witnessed by Hamlet

as a boy visiting Barnstaple Goosey Fair. At the same time the shift
in weight caused the wheelers to falter, so that the waggon not only
stopped but began to slip back at an angle of about forty-five degrees
that would land its rear wheels in the ditch unless it could be arrested.
Once there, as Hamlet's experience told him, there would be no
getting it back on the road short of an additional team harnessed
ahead of the sweating Floss and Margy. And if this happened to
whom would the credit go? Not to him and Swann, but to chaw-
bacons up yonder, who hurried to his assistance.

It was not to be thought of. He knew then what he should do,
what *must* be done if he was to avert disaster and disgrace. The
leaders must be steadied by hand, must be given active encouragement to make one final effort to win the crest, and without giving
the matter another thought he heaved himself out of the driving
seat and flung himself down to the road, lurching as he landed but
saving himself by clutching the leading edge of the shaft and clawing his way along it until he could duck under Margy's head and
grab her bridle with both hands, bellowing, "Come *up*, me booty!
Hup, hup, *hup! Hold* there, for Chris' sake! *Hold*, will 'ee, you bliddy
gurt brute!"

And Margy did hold, somehow managing to brace her hind legs
against a ridge in the flinty surface and thereby steadying Floss
who, in turn, steadied the floundering wheelers.

He hung there for more than a minute, spattered with Margy's
foam and glaring sideways at the slithering load. About half of
Victoria was now visible, stripped of wrappings certainly, and
liable to slide altogether free, but still in place, for the corner of
the plinth on which she stood had run up against the metalled ridge
surrounding the waggon-bed, so there seemed no certainty of a royal
descent into the ditch. Or not providing he could restart the team
and reach level ground.

He could not see clearly now. Sweat and dizziness blurred his
vision but he could sense what was required and began to back up
the hill, all the time calling piteously to the team. Slowly, and with
a kind of ponderous grace, they responded to his tugs and exhor-
tations. Inch by inch they struggled forward into what seemed to
Hamlet a blackness, shot through with exploding rockets, so that
he could only assess the gradient by the soles of his boots. Statue

and waggon did not part company, miraculously so it seemed to Hamlet, for in their efforts to get a purchase on the gritty surface, all four of the Clydesdales began to weave, Margy carrying Hamlet with her so that more than once his feet swung clear of the ground. Then, somewhere out ahead, he heard shouting but he could not identify its source. The sounds seemed to reach him from a vast distance, like the cries of men drowning in the darkness marking the end of the long, green tunnel. Then, with a great sense of relief, he felt the momentum of the team quicken. His last conscious thought was being whirled upwards and outwards like a nosebag attached to Margy's head. And after that, nothing, or nothing but the axle squeak of the tormented dray.

*　　*　　*

He was dead when they reached him. As dead as a doornail someone said but he was unmarked. Hooves and wheels had missed him in their erratic passage over the crest to the gentle downslope above the town.

It was getting dusk then and people came running with lanterns, buzzing round the halted team like a swarm of grey-brown flies, asking one another what this could mean, and how such a bizarre tragedy could have occurred on their doorstep. Then Mayor Wonnacott rattled up in a trap, the doctor beside him, and there was an expectant silence whilst the latter knelt, unbuttoning Hamlet's frock coat and holding a watch glass to the bluish lips. "Heart," he announced, "grossly overweight. No business at all to be driving at his time of life!" The doctor was a man of few words but Mayor Wonnacott wasn't. He was quick, as most politicians are, to see human drama in such a sacrifice to duty and after he had dwelt on the theme for a few moments he gave orders that the corpse be lifted up and laid beside the queen, who had been edged back between her timber parallels but left uncovered, for her wrappings were now a tangled ball of canvas and twisted ropes.

Thus it was that Hamlet Ratcliffe, lion-catcher, and courier extraordinary to Her Majesty the Queen, shared the final stage of the royal progress to the foot of the new clock tower and in a way Hamlet took precedence for, whereas the Queen entered the town uncovered, Hamlet had the benefit of a horse blanket. Criers went before them, yelling the news, so that upwards of a thousand people surrounded the bier when it halted, and Mayor Wonnacott had another opportunity to make a speech, extolling Hamlet as a man who had died at his post rather than disappoint the rate-payers.

And so he had in a way. When, at first light, a local carter back-tracked on his progress up the one-in-six incline, and saw the angled ruts cutting into the verge fifty yards or so below the crest, he was able to deduce what had happened and this gave Mayor Wonnacott yet another inspiration. After the unveiling ceremony he called the local stonemason on one side and said, "Us'll have words, Ben, when tiz all over. But say nothing yet, for I'd like to think on it. Commemoration, that is, for I knowed Hamlet Ratcliffe as a boy . . ." and then he wandered off, leaving the stonemason scratching his head.

They came for him that same evening, a dry-eyed Augusta, fortified by half a dozen of his Exeter cronies, who had always known somehow that he would leave them in some such fashion, for he was, as one of them put it, 'the greatest little varmint yerabouts'. But that wasn't the end of it, or not quite. When all the tumult had died away, and the Devon river valleys had resumed their timeless rhythms, Mayor Wonnacott wrote to Augusta and asked her to make the journey north while the good weather held. He had, so he said, something very special to show her. Bertieboy drove her up in the gig and when, once again, they stood before the blue granite clocktower, where a vexed-looking Victoria was wedged between drinking fountain and Gothic apex, they saw, low down on the coping alongside the inscribed foundation stone, a second legend. It read ". . . And to the memory of Hamlet Ratcliffe, aged 79 years, who died helping to erect this monument. June 20th, 1887." Then, at last, Augusta wept.

6

A Study in Substitution

THEY came down Spout Hill hell for leather, Helen thirty yards in the lead, much faster, it seemed to Joanna, than either of them had ever travelled since the new safety bicycles had been stripped of their wrappings in the stable yard and the first cautious circuits made in the forecourt.

The exhilaration of a rushing descent, the sensation of coasting along at what struck her as approaching the speed of a train, with the wind whipping at the binder holding her round sailor hat in place, prompted Helen to shout for joy. Joanna, knowing the hill rather better, lost her nerve halfway down, applied her spoon brake, and screamed a warning as they rushed onwards towards the brick pillars of Addington Manor. Helen did not hear her shout, of course, but if she had she would not have heeded. More and more these days she was inclined to assume the leadership of the pair, a fact that only Henrietta noticed and thought upon, finding it strange that Joanna, now almost of age and by far the prettiest of the Swann girls, should be led into mischief by a chit of seventeen and a half.

Yet it was so and here was proof of it, Helen applying no more than a touch on her brake as they whirled down the gradient towards the Keston crossroads, travelling, Joanna would have thought, at twenty miles an hour and heading straight for disaster if horseman, haywain or milk float happened to be using the junction leading to West Wickham and the main road to Croydon.

It happened about fifty yards short of the crossroads. Joanna, braking hard, sensed the approach of the horsemen before the first of them showed beyond the curve of the stone wall enclosing the paddocks. Perhaps she heard the scrunch of hooves on the gravel or perhaps she saw, out of the corner of her eye, the gleam of a stirrup iron through the chink in the lodge gates that stood wide open. Whatever it was it caused her to scream again but it was then too late and a spill or head-on collision was inevitable.

The leading horse reared as its rider sat back in the saddle, applying what must have been a merciless jerk at the reins, and the following horse, brought up short, wheeled and sidled, butting the grey in the rump, so that it bounded forward as the bicycle shot directly under its nose, swerving madly towards the nearside bank, half mounting it, careering down again, and projecting its rider over the handlebars in a flurry of skirts, petticoats and flailing arms and legs.

Joanna was quite sure then that Helen had broken her neck. No one, surely, could survive such an impact, even though the ditch was full of last year's beech leaves, sodden by yesterday's thunderstorms. She jumped off somehow, bringing the machine to a halt midway between the two cavorting horsemen and heard, through her panic, the curses of the young man on the grey, now fully occupied with keeping his seat. She noticed other things too in that first fearful moment, when she ought to have been mourning Helen—odd, inconsequential things, like the firm seat the young man had on the scared grey, the barley-gold glint of the sun in his whiskers, the blueness of his eyes and sleekness of his mount, clipped shorter than she would have expected at this time of year, when most horses were out to grass. She paid little attention to the other man, who was clearly less expert a rider and was draped around his bay's neck like John Gilpin halfway to The Bell, at Edmonton. Then, in a second or so it seemed, the young man with the golden whiskers had brought his horse under control, dismounted and was running across the road to where the flurry of skirts seemed to be making good time down the hill.

Several things happened simultaneously then. The following rider, having quietened the bay, was half out of the saddle and the man with the barley-coloured whiskers (who looked much younger dismounted) had overtaken the flurry of skirts and lifted it, bracing himself against the angle of the bank and cradling Helen in his arms. Then his companion had his hand on Joanna's arm and was enquiring, very calmly considering the circumstances, if she was hurt, and when she gasped out that she was not he took her machine and leaned it against the wall, saying, "I say, I'm most fearfully sorry . . . Our fault entirely . . . Should have come out at a walk, for that's a brute of a hill for a bicyclist . . . !" Then he called, urgently, "Is she hurt, Clint? I'll fetch Mallow . . . hold on!"

But by then Clint was halfway back to them, still cradling Helen in his arms and the look on his face was in great contrast to the stricken expression of his companion as he said, gaily, "No bones broken! Just a scratch or two, I'd say. Soft landing . . . those leaves are two feet thick over there. Get the bicycle off the road, Rowley!" And he strode away with his burden, passing through the lodge gates and across a strip of garden to the door, which he kicked open before disappearing into the lodge.

Joanna said, shakily, "Is he right? . . . Is it possible . . . ?" and the man addressed as Rowley smiled and patted her reassuringly, saying, "I'll make sure just as soon as we get her bicycle. It's a danger to others lying there. I'm a doctor . . . well, almost a doctor. Give me a hand with the machine," and they walked over to where Helen's bicycle lay in the middle of the road and dragged it under the wall.

It was impossible to wheel it. The handlebars were askew, one pedal was missing, and the front wheel was bent into a figure eight, with spokes projecting like arrows from a target. He said, ruefully, "I say, that's a goner. Come, let's see to your sister, Miss Swann," and she said, astonished, "You *know* us?" Whereupon he laughed, saying, "Why, of course I do. Who doesn't around here? We even knew you had safety bicycles. My brother Clint told us about it yesterday and Mamma was annoyed he mentioned it in front of the girls. Now they've started clamouring for them. This will put a stop to that, however. Come into the lodge and I'll clean and bandage her cuts. Clint is too ham-fisted for that kind of thing."

They went through the little sitting-room to a scullery at the back where Helen, still dazed with shock, was slumped in a kitchen chair and Clinton was working the pump in what seemed to Joanna a lackadaisical manner considering that Helen's palms were bleeding through shredded gloves. At once, however, the man called Rowley took charge, telling his brother to see to the horses. Peeling off his coat he said, "Work the handle, Miss Swann. It's a deep well and needs a minute or two. Your sister will be more comfortable on the sofa," and while he was talking he rolled up his sleeves, lifted Helen from the chair and carried her back into the tiny sitting-room, leaving

Joanna to work the pump-handle until water gushed into the trough
and she could fill a bowl she found in the sink.

It was fascinating to watch him work. Clinton was right, it seemed.
Helen's injuries were trivial, despite the distance she had rolled
but her new bicycling costume was in ruins. Every button but one
had been ripped from her waistcoat bodice and the blouse underneath was also ripped, showing an inch or two of pink chemise.
The heavy pleated skirt, however, had cushioned her knees, and the
hard straw hat, split across the crown, had protected her head. For
all that, she seemed to be dazed for when Joanna brought the bowl,
and Rowley began washing the blood from her hands, she opened
her eyes and asked, vaguely, "Where am I . . . what happened?"
And Clinton, returning at that moment to say he had sent Mallow
for the dogcart, said irreverently, "Not in Paradise, I'm afraid, Miss
Swann! This is only Addington Manor, and we're called Coles. I'm
Clinton and that's Rowland. Don't be shy. He's a doctor, or will be
in December."

"I'll need my bag," Rowley said, briefly. "Ride up and fetch it
and tell Mamma there will be two more for luncheon. This young
lady has had a bad shaking and can't ride back yet."

"She can't ride back at all," Clinton said, grinning. "That so-
called safety bicycle of hers is for the scrap-yard. All right, all right,"
as his elder brother looked severe, "I'll get your bag, but there's a first-
aid box on that shelf above your head. Mallow keeps it handy for
the saw-mill staff." He smiled engagingly at Joanna. "Why don't you
come along with me, Miss Swann? I'd like you to meet my sisters and
I'm sure they'd be enchanted to meet you. Your family is a legend
round here. We're newcomers but we've all heard about you!"

"Go and get that bag, confound you," Rowley growled, and
Joanna thought, "He's so terribly earnest but the good-looking one
is the exact opposite . . ." And suddenly she was glad things had
turned out this way, and that little goose Helen was being fussed
over leaving her an open field with Clinton, for that was something
that would not have happened if Helen hadn't been too dazed to
make her grab. She paid lip-service to convention, however, saying
doubtfully, "I ought not to leave Helen here alone . . ."

But at that, surprisingly, Helen spoke up quite sharply, saying,

"Don't be stupid, Jo! You've just heard, he's a doctor—*Owww!*"
as Rowley pressed her lacerated hands into the bowl.

Clint said, still grinning, "I'll send Mallow down with the bag
and dog-cart. Meantime make the most of it, Rowley. You won't
get many patients as fetching as Miss Swann once you're in practice."

They went out then, leaving them, and began to climb the drive
that ran under an arch of beeches to a pretty Queen Anne house
perched on the crest. Clinton said, "You'll be wondering how we
know you but there's no mystery really. We were with the Phillimore party at the Tonbridge Jubilee Athletic meeting and saw
your brother Hugo win the open mile at a canter. Your family—
you and your sister especially—were pointed out to us, and Rowley
plagued Jock Phillimore, who said he knew you, to introduce us.
I remember being surprised by that for Rowley is the serious, dedicated type, not much given to showing interest in pretty girls."

She was going to reprove him for his sauciness (this was the second
time in five minutes he had commented on their looks) but he went
on, gaily, "However, you disappeared, the whole lot of you, during
the tea interval. We searched the ground and poor old Rowley was
desolate. He's always lucky, however, for here you've fallen right
into his hands."

She decided then she liked his impudent approach. She was an
uncomplicated person, like Hugo. Helen was a romantic, and was
probably greatly impressed by Rowley's bossy show of professionalism, but Joanna had always encouraged her beaux to make the running and not too many of them had. Mostly they seemed to approach
a flirtation as if it was a gavotte. She said, "I remember now. We
left the sports rally early, to dress for a ball over at Maidstone. But
I always thought Colonel and Mrs. Walters had Addington Manor.
Nobody told us new people had moved in."

"That isn't surprising," he said. "We're trade, and people are stuffy
round here, aren't they? My father is a chemist. Doesn't the name
Coles mean anything at all to you?" and he gave her a saucy, sidelong
glance.

"I'm afraid not. Should it?"

"That depends on whether you are a hypochondriac," he said.
"Coles' Cough Lozenges. Coles' Instant Headache Powder. Does

your hair fall out? Do you fear the winter chills? The Governor has something for everyone. It's rare to find someone who has never had to turn to him."

She knew the firm, of course. Their advertisements could be seen on hoardings and omnibuses. It was just as he said. Coles' products claimed to cure everything overnight, from constipation to house-maid's knee, and privately she thought some of their boasts vulgar. She said, "Well, it's nice to know other people get looked down on because they're in trade. It's happened to us more than once and if you got my father on the subject he could discuss it for hours. Without malice though, for it never did bother him in the slightest. Or Mamma either, for that matter."

"Ah, but there's a difference," he said, in a way that made her think he was making gentle fun of her, "the time element enters into it. Your father's carrier's business was going before you were born, and your Mamma has had time to put down social roots, like all the local families who made their pile out of the slave trade or French smuggling or holy relics, and heaven knows what else. We're newcomers to the fair. My father started his business in a little phar-macy in Norwich only twenty-odd years ago. Rowley, the eldest, was born over the shop. Advertising put us on the map and nothing else, believe me. Most of the poison we sell is straight out of the witchdoctor's wigwam!"

She laughed, thinking how refreshing it was to meet a young man who did not mind saying things like that. Almost all the trades-men's sons who had attended garden-parties and soirées at 'Tryst' adopted fancy airs and tried to speak (as her father would say) with plum stones balanced on their tongues. She said, "Well, your brother Rowley seems to take himself very seriously. You aren't at all alike, are you?"

"No," he said, "we aren't. But we all like Rowley, despite his terrible earnestness. He's deeply interested in his profession, you see, and he'll make a first-class doctor. He might even be famous, or so Mamma thinks."

"And you, Mr. Coles? What are you studying for?"

"How to live on my father's money," he said, promptly, "and I'm sure I shall be very good at it. But don't keep calling me 'Mr. Coles'. I'm 'Clint' to my friends, and you'll join them, won't you?"

"I should like to," she said, laughing, "so I'm Joanna, number Five on the Swann muster-roll. Helen is the next girl down. Hugo comes in between. Are there a lot of you?"

"Four," he said. "Rowley, me and two girls, Melie and Nell, who likes to be called 'Eleanor'. The girls are nineteen and seventeen. Rowley is years older than any of us. Sometimes I think of him as being of the Governor's generation. Well, here we are. You'll like Mamma. She's fun, and the girls aren't so bad when you can stop them talking about clothes. They'll enjoy meeting you, I can guarantee that."

She stopped him as they passed through the stable yard arch. "Just a moment . . . before I do meet them . . . *Why*, exactly? I mean, how does it come about that you know so much about us. Your folks don't think of us as . . . well . . . notorious, do they?"

"Good Lord, no! Just liberated. That's an accepted fact about here, it seems. 'Papa Swann lets his sons and daughters do as they please, instead of how it pleases him.' At least, that's how I've heard it!" He was serious for a moment. "That's rare," he added, "rare enough to make other girls jealous."

2

He could hardly have taken more trouble had he been treating a patient with a severed artery. Every movement of his hands was controlled and deliberate, and his expression did not vary at all from one of grave concern, so that she had the impression of being someone of tremendous consequence. Visiting royalty, perhaps. Or someone world-famous, like Jenny Lind, the Swedish Nightingale.

She soon realised it was useless to flirt with him in the accepted manner and abandoned her ailing Elizabeth Barrett Browning pose within minutes of Joanna and Clinton leaving them alone. Instead she lay back and relaxed, watching him roll bandages on to her lacerated palms and bring to the task the neatness and precision of an old maid at her embroidery frame. And yet, in another way, he was very masculine, more so than anyone she had ever known, save her father. He had a trick of proclaiming, without a word of self-praise, that he knew precisely what he was about and although, in a way, this made him slightly forbidding, his eyes were as kind and gentle as a girl's. He had, she noticed, beautifully-kept hands, the kind of hands she imagined a concert pianist might have, but his features, beetling and rather craggy, suggested austerity, even severity, as though, in some way, he was at war with himself, and having as much as he could do to subdue a livelier, more reckless Rowland Coles. It even occurred to her that he was monkish, and possibly shy of women, as when he asked her gravely if she had any other injuries apart from her stinging palms, now blissfully soothed by the ointment he had applied. She said, doubtfully, "I've bruised my knee, I think. The left one. It isn't bleeding but it feels very sore and stiff."

It was fun watching him work that one out, his professional concern at odds with his notions of propriety, but then Mrs. Mallow, the lodge-keeper's wife, came bustling in and he said, gravely, "Would you like me to examine it, Miss Swann? I daresay it was badly jarred, and will stiffen up before you can get to your own doctor. Be so good as to wait, Mrs. Mallow."

She nearly giggled at that, telling herself that the prospect of displaying her knees to him pleased her, for she had always been proud of her slender, shapely legs, the prettiest legs in the family according to her mother, who took a lively interest in such things. Carefully she lifted her muddied skirt, revealing a grey stocking shredded at the kneecap. The flesh below was tender and already an area of blue-black bruising was visible.

He said, "Er . . . roll down your stocking, Miss Swann," and stared hard at an atrocious water-colour hanging above her head while she slipped her garter and quietly disposed of it, placing it in her pocket. He said, impersonally, "I'll use arnica. I have some here," and probed in the box, while the plump Mrs. Mallow stood watching, holding herself as straight as a sentinel. He applied the arnica and gave Mrs. Mallow the stocking, telling her to burn it. "One of the girls will have a change of clothes for you," he said. "Then, after luncheon and a rest, Clint or I will run you home in the dogcart. Take it quietly for a day or two. Luckily that bruise has come out, and I don't think you'll have trouble with it. Leave the bandages on the hands when you go to bed tonight. Your own doctor will apply fresh, no doubt."

The prospect of passing out of his orbit and submitting to the gruff ministrations of old Doctor Birtles was depressing. She said, quickly, "I'm not obliged to go to another doctor, am I? I mean, since you were the first one to treat me, couldn't you keep the case until I'm healed up?" And at that he smiled and said, "Your injuries aren't that serious, Miss Swann. They might have been but fortunately they aren't."

He went through into the scullery then to wash his hands and she thought, irritably, "He must be made of stone! He's the first young man to see my pretty legs above the ankles but he might just as well have been looking at a couple of dumb-bells!" And it occurred to her to pretend to have a relapse, so that he would lift her and carry her up to the house, but common sense told her he was not that gullible and she would have to think of something more original. But before she could apply her mind to it the dogcart arrived, driven by Mallow, and Rowley offered his arm on which she leaned half her weight as they crossed the little garden to the drive.

He was very slow, it seemed, at taking hints, for when she staggered all he did was to brace her with his forearm, instead of taking the opportunity to encircle her waist, and she thought, glumly, "He acts just as if he were married but I'm sure he isn't. Maybe that's the way of young doctors. They're afraid of getting compromised by women patients . . ." But then, like administering a slap in her face, he made a direct reference to Joanna, saying, anxiously, "I do hope that idiot Clinton looks after your sister properly. He's good-hearted but a regular clown, and I got the impression she was very shy. Would you say she was shy, Miss Swann?"

It was at once a rebuke and a confession. For years now, she and Joanna had worked as a team, perfecting the technique of passing young men between them like shuttlecocks. And a very stimulating game it had proved, ever since Helen had put her hair up and Joanna, then eighteen, had given her the benefit of all her experience, so that Helen had started out with an enormous advantage over all the other junior belles, extracting the maximum fun and excitement from romance without once getting into a serious scrape, or having her name erased from a local Mamma's invitation list. Together, in their shared bedroom when the house was asleep, they had pooled their experiences night after night, giggling and descanting over this beau and that, but always with a sense of holding on to the initiative, and generally regarding their admirers as puppies, good for a romp, and a little spoiling maybe, but aware, at any given moment, they could be called to heel. In all this time they had never once fallen out over a beau and there had never been an occasion when she felt a pang of jealousy for Joanna. She felt one now, however, and it baffled her, for something was telling her that this beetle-browed, craggy, gentle, rather prim young man was aware of Joanna in a way that he certainly wasn't aware of her, even though he had touched her bare knees, a privilege, she would have thought, that would have reduced most young men to a state of servitude.

She said, sulkily, "Joanna can look after herself, Mr. Coles. None better, believe me!" But having said it regretted having given herself away, and would have fallen back on the time-honoured technique of praising her sister had they not arrived in the stable yard at that moment, to be engulfed by the entire Coles family, all talking at once, all regarding the accident as the highlight of the week.

She was right about Rowley, however. On seeing Joanna standing between his sisters Amelia and Eleanor, he forgot her entirely, and it was left to the brash Clinton to hand her down and introduce her to his parents and sisters.

Coles père, she decided at once, was a pet and looked as if he had been the model for Cruickshank's Mr. Pickwick. Mrs. Coles was a red-faced, excitable little woman, who at once began to fuss over her as if she had recently undergone a major operation. Then Eleanor, the younger of the two girls, screamed that she had a change of clothes ready, and mother and daughters dragged her into a sewing-room adjoining a large room where a table was set for luncheon and everybody continued to talk at once and she wished that Rowley would reappear and tell everyone she was suffering from nothing more than a few scratches and a bruise. But it was Clinton who presented himself, announcing that luncheon was served, and when she went out into the long, low-ceilinged room, gleaming with silver, she caught a glimpse of Rowley through the open door of the conservatory. He was standing beside Joanna who was pretending to admire the fuchsias. His expression reminded Helen of a cud-chewing cow in the pasture adjoining the 'Tryst' paddocks.

3

That was the way of it. Somehow, no one could say how exactly, they all got off to a wrong start, and there were many times during the next six months when Helen Swann, and Joanna too for that matter, wished they could rewind time and set it going again at the moment they began their breakneck descent of Spout Hill.

When they were adolescents, and given to childish games, they had often taken part in a game known as 'The Jolly Miller', in which everybody formed a ring around the player chosen as miller and circled him, chanting:

> There was a jolly miller
> And he lived by himself
> As the mill went round
> He made his wealth;
> As the mill went round he filled his bag,
> As the wheel went round he made his GRAB!

At which point the miller would select his favourite for a wife and kiss her before the circling would begin all over again.

The memory of this silly kissing game coloured Helen's reflections on the developing situation between herself, Joanna, and the two Coles boys. They had each, as it were, made their grab, but the circle had stopped moving too soon or too late, with the result that all four—to Helen's mind at all events—had grabbed the wrong partner.

The spill at the foot of Spout Hill, and the luncheon party at Addington Manor that followed it, began an association that would have been very rewarding in happier circumstances, for the Coles family were excessively jolly and hospitable, and she got along very well with Papa Coles (whom she could never disassociate from Mr. Pickwick), his excitable wife Letty, their rather homely daughters,

Amelia and Eleanor, and, above all, with the livelier of the two boys, Clinton, who squired her here, there and everywhere throughout that winter and the subsequent spring. This was well enough, and had it not been for an unforgettable moment in her life—opening her eyes in the lodge parlour and looking up into the face of Rowland Coles—she would have made the most of it and enjoyed a protracted flirtation with Clinton, as well as the company of his sisters, both of whom, it seemed, had fallen madly in love with her brother Hugo.

But moments like that, she discovered, could not be erased like a squiggle from a nursery slate. This one would return to her, unbidden, every time she saw Rowland's spare, upright figure, pacing the 'Tryst' terrace, or the gravelled paths of Addington Manor, beside an impassive, untroubled Joanna, whereas Rowland's total indifference to her, as anything more than an appendage to Joanna, had the effect of undermining all the confidence in herself assembled during the years when she had regarded herself (along with Joanna) as one of the most sought-after belles in Kent. The cuts on her palms and the bruise on her knee healed in a matter of days. The injury to her self-esteem festered, promising to sour her existence.

This might not have happened, of course, had she been able to bring herself to admitting the facts to Joanna, or even to herself, but she was unable to do this, falling back on a general prickliness that was uncharacteristic of her, so that her temper would flare over trivialities. Anyone less preoccupied than Joanna, or more discerning than Clinton Coles, would have noticed something was amiss when the three of them, accompanied by Rowland whenever he could spare time from his studies, dashed about the countryside to meets, soirées, a ball or two, and when the better weather came round, picnics into the countryside adjoining 'Tryst', or the home of the boys five miles nearer London.

They were not always a foursome. Sometimes a whole group of the country-house set would join them at a gymkhana or a birthday party at one or other of the towns or villages about here. Then, if Rowland were present, Helen would try to capture his attention by a display of excessively high spirits, or an exhibition of reckless flirting with any young man who gave her encouragement but it was to no avail. Rowland, it seemed, had eyes for no one but the strangely subdued Joanna, mooning after her everywhere she went, hanging on her lightest words, blundering forward to open doors or set chairs for her, so that sometimes Helen's resentment was half-submerged in amazement that nothing final emerged from this spectacular display of courtship, and Joanna dropped no hint that Rowland Coles was on the point of proposing or had, perhaps, already proposed and been refused in the certainty that he would go on doing it until Joanna judged he had been kept dangling long enough.

Now that Helen was eighteen the two sisters no longer shared a room so that their cosy, after-dark confidences were not so readily available. Nonetheless, she did manage to make it clear to Joanna that she, of all people, would be extremely interested to learn what, if anything, was moving in this direction and was indignant when Joanna hedged and seemed disinclined to confide in anyone. Helen could only assume from this that there was really nothing to tell, and asked herself (for possibly the hundredth time since that crash outside the Manor gates) whether her obsession with Rowland Coles was rooted in pique at his indifference, or in some deeper emotion, deep enough to scare her a little. For while it was agreeable to fancy oneself in love with a beau who was only awaiting a suitable opportunity to declare himself, it was humiliating to love someone who looked past you at your elder sister every time you crossed his path.

Then, in a single moment of time it seemed, Helen's worst fears were confirmed and she had proof that the Jolly Miller game had indeed gone very much awry. A slightly bewildered Joanna appeared on the threshold of her bedroom after midnight one night and asked if she could discuss something very important. Helen, opening the door wide and almost bundling her sister inside, was aware of a dragging sensation in the pit of her stomach. She had no doubt at all that Joanna was here to tell her Rowland had at last made his intentions clear and she said, eagerly, "Why, of course. Everyone's asleep. Come in and tell me, do! It's Rowley, isn't it?"

"Yes, it is," said Joanna glumly, and Helen thought it strange that a girl who had just received a proposal, however long delayed, should look so indecisive and woebegone. There was a coal fire in the grate and Joanna seated herself in the wicker chair before it, leaving her sister to perch herself on the edge of her bed.

"Well? Go on, go on!"

"He asked me. He asked me tonight, when you and Clint and his sisters were in the stables looking at Clint's new mare. He said he would have proposed long ago if he hadn't been waiting upon his examination results."

"Oh, never mind his dratted examinations, get to the point Joanna! What did *you* say?"

But at that Joanna looked amazed. "What did *I* say? Well, what could I say but no?"

"No? You mean you . . . you *meant* no?"

"Well, of course. I wouldn't dream of marrying Rowley, nice as he is in many ways."

One of Helen's ears popped and for a moment she could hear nothing but a loud, unpleasant buzzing sound that made her feel dizzy and slightly sick.

"You're as definite as that?"

"Certainly I am. I simply said I wouldn't dream of marrying him because I didn't love him and anyway, I was quite wrong for him. I certainly can't see myself as a missionary's wife, living in some awful jungle or faraway island, full of creepy-crawlies and cannibals. I mean, it's a positively ridiculous notion, isn't it? I'm not even religious, or not really. I believe in God of course, and all that, but devoting one's whole life to it . . . well, it would be like being a nun. And even if I was in love with him I should have to be absolutely sure he did his doctoring right here in England, where we could keep our friends and entertain, and I could come home whenever I wished." She broke off, as if suddenly aware of Helen and Helen's stricken look. "Whatever's the matter with you? You look quite ill. Are you bilious or something?"

It was understandable that Joanna should forget Rowland Coles for a moment, and switch her mind to her sister, still perched on the edge of the bed, mouth open and gaze fixed on a point level with the mantelshelf that supported a single ornament, a bucolic-looking shepherd embracing a reluctant nymph, one of the many porcelain figures Adam had scattered about the house. Instinctively Joanna followed her sister's gaze but could find nothing in the group to

691

account for her sister's expression. She got up, crossed to her and shook her by the shoulder, by now convinced that Helen was sickening for something.

"What *is* it, Helen? What on earth's come over you, girl?" The shaking, or perhaps the edge on Joanna's voice, had some effect. The somnambulist's gaze did not fade exactly but wavered, as Helen gave a shudder, raising both hands to her face and pressing them there as she wailed, *"Why didn't I know? Why wasn't I sure?* One is supposed to be sure of something as important as that but I wasn't . . ." and she turned a despairing gaze on her sister. "All this time! Ever since he bandaged me in the lodge after that spill. Why, it's quite monstrous, for I was in love with him from the very beginning, from the moment he touched me. And now he's proposed to you, and you've turned him down! Don't you see what an awful fix we're in, Jo?"

It seemed, however, that Joanna did not, for after contemplating her sister a moment longer she began to laugh, quietly at first but soon so immoderately that she had to grab the corner of her dressing-gown and hold it against her face, reasoning no doubt that laughter of that volume would awaken the household on both corridors.

"Oh, dear . . . !" she managed to gasp, at last. "Oh, dear, what geese we are, Helen! And both of us believing we were so artful, and could make things happen any way we wanted to." But then, because there was no sign of Helen appreciating the humour of the situation, natural affection reasserted itself and she grabbed her sister's hands, dragged her upright and over beside the fender, saying, "For heaven's sake, don't *take* it that way. See how much worse it would have been if I had accepted him! Why, if you really mean what you say, if you aren't fooling yourself that is, you could quite easily make him fall in love with you."

"Oh, no I couldn't! Do you think I haven't tried? Nobody could make Rowland Coles do anything, and anyway he's obviously in love with you and was, even before we met that time."

"Rubbish! Just listen to me, Helen. I've got to know Rowley and it's not me he wants so much as a wife to keep him company in those awful places he intends going to, and as I told him—for his own good that is—no girl I know will take kindly to that prospect, even if she's dying for a husband, as most of our set are."

"You said *that* to him?"

"In as many words. Wouldn't you have?"

"*No!*" She almost screamed the word. "No, I most certainly wouldn't, Jo! Because it wouldn't be true. Not of me, and not of any girl who wanted . . . well . . . wanted adventure, something exciting to happen, something to take her out of the round of parties and dances and shopping expeditions and fox-hunting, and all the silly things we've thought of as important since we got out of the schoolroom! Why, if Rowland Coles had asked me to marry him I wouldn't have hesitated a minute. I would have gone *anywhere* with him, anywhere at all. Among cannibals, even, because that's just the kind of man I admire and respect, and I see now I must have sensed this about him all the time, without actually knowing it, or maybe because I couldn't bear to admit that he wasn't in the least bit interested in me." But at this point misery engulfed her like a vast, soggy blanket and she subsided on to the bed, her mouth puckering and tears of frustration welling, so that Joanna found herself remembering the irrepressible Helen of the days when they shared a bedroom and discussed beaux with the indifference of a couple of drovers speculating beside a bullock pen at a market.

She said, briskly, "Oh, cheer *up*, Helen! It isn't the end of the world! You've got time to change his mind for he isn't going for months. Why, the London Missionary Society has to approve of him . . ."

But love, it appeared, had transformed Helen, for she jumped up at that, saying, in withering tones, "How *can* you talk like that? What kind of person do you think he is, for Heaven's sake? Do you think he's like . . . like Clinton, out for all he can get, without committing himself, and without a serious thought in his head? Do you think someone quite splendid like Rowley would change his mind about who he wanted to marry, like changing trains at a station?"

"Yes," Joanna said, calmly, "that's exactly what I do think. And if you'll calm down a bit, and condescend to listen instead of carrying on like a hysterical housemaid, I'll explain why. He's been long enough coming to the boil and I've had plenty of time to find out everything about him, so there!"

693

This at least had the effect of checking Helen somewhat, so that Joanna saw no reason, at that stage, to enquire further into her sister's tacit admission that Clinton had been exceptionally venturesome. Not that it surprised her. She had thought him very saucy from the moment she first met him, but it was interesting to learn just how saucy in this roundabout way. She wondered momentarily how far Clinton had ventured with Helen and how much encouragement he had received in return. They were neither of them without experience in these matters and it occurred to Joanna that it would be a more rewarding occupation to resist Clinton than to wear oneself out attempting to stimulate Rowley, a task that had occupied her, intermittently, for more than half a year. She said, "Now listen to me, Helen. We could do something about this providing you're serious and don't get put off by a lot of silly nonsense about Rowley's highmindedness. He isn't any more highminded than the next man, and this missionary business is no more than an adventure to him. The fact is, he sees a doctor's life in an English country town as too dull for his taste . . . no, *listen*, I can assure you I *know* what I'm talking about . . . Oh, he's kind and well-meaning, and he'll make a splendid doctor, and a good husband too, I've no doubt, but if you made up your mind to catch him you could, I'm quite sure of that! And why not? You're brainier than I am, just as pretty and you've got a better figure!"

"He doesn't think so," Helen said. "He put arnica on my knee that time and saw most of me but it didn't impress him the slightest bit."

"Why should it? He was looking at you as a doctor, wasn't he? Listen, just you leave this to me. I'll really put my mind to it and I've already got an idea of how to go about it. But before I decide there's something I've to know about Clint and I'm not just prying, you understand? How fast *is* he? I mean, when there's just the two of you?" and she was intrigued to see her sister colour.

"About as fast as a man could be, I imagine. If a girl gave him the slightest encouragement, goodness knows how it might end. But what's Clint's forwardness got to do with it?"

"More than you suppose," Joanna said, smiling, "so now just go to sleep and Don't Worry! It'll turn out just as you want, so long as you let me plan it for you. There now!" as she kissed her and

gathered her dressing gown about her, "Not a word of this to anyone, you understand? Not one single word!"

She went out, closing the door softly and slipped along the corridor to her own room. It was some time since she had felt so light-
hearted. Seven months of lugubrious courtship on the part of an
embryo missionary had given her a feeling of already having joined
the married set, women who had put fun and frolic behind them
and did all their gossiping and scandalising behind fans.

4

The characteristics of two parents and a mixed foursome of grandparents had been carelessly scattered among the children of Adam
and Henrietta Swann. Here and there traits could be spotted but
mostly they remained hidden, revealing themselves occasionally as
a flash, a salmon leaping a weir, a chink of light beaming from a
suddenly opened door. Adam's singlemindedness; Sam Rawlinson's
preoccupation with machines; the old Colonel's gentleness; the Celtic gloom and compensating high spirits of Henrietta's Irish mother.
All filtered down, one way or another, to the second and third generation, and possibly Joanna Swann's sensuality, coupled with her
artfulness, was another by-product of mixed blood, that could be
traced back to Irish and Gascon ancestors, whose names she had
never known.

Alone among the Swann girls Joanna had her mother's propensity
to contemplate the male animal as a mate rather than a husband.
Marriage, as such, had never occupied a prominent position in her
thoughts but this did not mean that she was not absorbed in the
mating process, and had been, ever since an enterprising sixteen-
year-old had slipped his hand inside her bodice after catching her
in the broom cupboard during a hide-and-seek game at a Christmas
party. Phoebe Fraser's unremitting efforts to alert her charges to the
terrible risks of rousing the half-slumbering beast in men had, to an
extent, backfired in Joanna's case. Like her mother before her, she
was intensely curious about men and men's appetites concerning
women, and this curiosity had added spice to her many flirtations,

from the age of about fifteen upwards. The exciting incident in the
broom cupboard had gone some way to explain the reckless ardour
of the average male, whenever he was given an opportunity to indulge it, but several other incidents of a similar nature had been
withheld or watered down during discussions on the subject with
Helen or other intimates, for she had a private conviction that most
women were boobies when it came to handling a man. Now, faced
with a direct challenge that promised to exercise her wits to the full,
she began to formulate a plan that promised more fun and more
excitement than had ever come her way in the past, but it occupied
the better part of a week to enlist Helen as an accomplice. Once
committed, however, she thought her sister could be relied upon to
play her part with the dash she had shown in earlier conspiracies
between the two girls.

By then mild spring weather had arrived and there was no difficulty in persuading Rowley, recently freed from the tyranny of his
finals, to organise a railway picnic to the village of Hildenborough,
down the line from Tonbridge, where a couple of traps could be
hired for a drive out to Penshurst Place.

The temperature favoured the plot. It was as warm and sunny as
June when the four of them collected the traps from a local stable
and set off down the winding road to Penshurst, the village selected
by Joanna for the complicated manoeuvres she had planned.

They paid a yawning loafer to turn the hacks loose and let them
graze while they had their picnic, Joanna leading the way up the
long slope "to see the spread of primroses", she said, "that grew more
thickly here than anywhere else in Kent." As regards the primroses,
no one was disappointed. The entire hillside, a mile long and a
quarter-mile deep, was starred with them, and the view from the
ridge, taking in the splendours of the great Sidney mansion in its
park of three hundred and fifty acres including the wood-fringed
mere and the famous Penshurst oaks, was very impressive.

Joanna said, briskly, "Put the hamper down here, Clint, and begin laying out, Helen. First I intend to show Rowley the haunted
oak. I know just where it is," and before either one of them could
comment she put her arm through Rowley's and walked him purposefully over the crest and down a narrow path leading to a copse
some two hundred yards nearer the fenced, cultivated land.

This was supposed to be Helen's cue but now that the moment had arrived her heart began to beat almost painfully, for what had seemed so subtle in rehearsal now appeared to her as something grotesque and farcical. She remembered her briefing perfectly, however. She was to encourage Clint to be forward, more forward than he had ever been, Joanna had urged, and everything would follow on from that and there had seemed no special difficulty about this, for Clint had never needed encouragement in this respect.

She said, sitting back from the hamper, "Let the picnic wait. I'm not hungry, are you, Clint?"

And he replied, smiling, "Not in the least, my dear," and at once, just as she anticipated, he put his arm round her and kissed her, holding the kiss for that much longer than was considered permissible. Gently, as though it was no more than a part of the accepted ritual, she raised her hands and pushed him off, saying, "That's the trouble with you, Clint. You never pay the girl the compliment of asking first, do you?"

"Not when I find myself with one as tempting as you," he said, cheerfully. And then, looking at her in a way that made her feel uncomfortable, "After all, you did set yourself out to turn a man's head today, didn't you?"

Thinking by this he must have an inkling of what was going on she replied, quickly, "Why do you say that, Clint?"

"Oh, for no special reason. It's meant as a compliment. You and Jo always dress well but everything you're wearing is first time on, isn't it? I notice these things. My mind isn't cluttered with people's insides and visions of the next world, like poor old Rowley's."

"I'm not sure I follow you, Clint."

"You don't? Well, put it this way. I'll take this world. It's good enough for me," and he embraced her again.

It occurred to her then that she ought to contribute something positive to the switch, apart from the purely passive role that had resulted in leaving Joanna an open field with Rowley all this time. After all, with the other two out of sight beyond the hill there was no risk at all in letting herself go and she had to admit that Clinton was far better at kissing than most of the young men she had embraced. Deliberately, and now beginning to enjoy the fun of the occasion, she let his weight incline her against the bank but she was unprepared for developments resulting from this overt encouragement. At once, it seemed, he was more or less on top of her, and kissing her in a way that was quite new to her, so that it occurred to her that things were happening at a speed neither she nor Joanna had anticipated, and that this was likely to interfere with what Joanna had called 'the split-second timing' of the plot. Crushed under him, and without the slightest opportunity to see whether or not the others were in view, it was all she could do to hold him off, for he soon became very much the man in possession. Before she could utter a word of protest he had undone three of the jet buttons of her jacket bodice and slipped his hand over her breast but outside her chemise, although she knew very well it would not stay there for long.

The Swann girls, who regarded themselves as experienced flirts, had a scale in male licences and its application depended upon a variety of factors, including the degree of privacy, the amount of light available, the seriousness of the young man involved, and the degree of physical appeal a particular beau exercised. The scale began with the chaste kiss on the cheek or brow and advanced progressively to the point Clinton had now reached, in a bound, as it were, and moreover in the open and in broad daylight, with the prospect of being overlooked from the top of the ridge. This was not part of the plan. In fact, it struck Helen at once that the plan was beginning to miscarry, and might well end in a moment of frightful embarrassment, so she brought both arms down, caught Clint's adventurous hand at the wrist, squirmed her head free and said, firmly, "No, Clint . . . Not here . . . please!"

To her surprise he seemed to regard this protest as no more than formal. Without removing his hand he said, "Nonsense. Why do you suppose they went off and left us?" and at once began kissing her again, his range extending to that section of her neck and shoulder exposed by the unbuttoned bodice.

It was not that Helen resented this as too outrageous on his part. In more propitious circumstances, in the back of a cab returning from a dance of a winter's night, for instance, she had allowed her escort privileges that amounted to the same thing, particularly when wearing a low-cut evening gown, or when, full of cider-cup at a hunt ball, she had allowed one of the Arscott twins (good-looking boys both) to pinch her bottom. It was the hovering presence of Rowley that scared her, so that she forced herself half out of his embrace, tore his hand free and shouted, "No, Clint! You mustn't! Stop it at once!"

It was at that moment that disaster swept down on them both, just as she had feared. There was a sudden rush of feet and Clinton was plucked from her and sent staggering ten yards further down the bank, and there was Rowley, looking down at her with an expression she could only think of as outraged as she began fumbling madly with the fiddling little buttons of her bodice, her cheeks flaming, her hair, shorn of half its pins, falling over her shoulders.

At that moment it was not of Clinton she thought but Joanna, feeling that she could have strangled her with bare hands for embroiling her in such a degrading situation. But Joanna, strangely, was nowhere to be seen.

When the last of the elusive buttons had been pushed into its buttonhole she scrambled up, ignoring her new bonnet that had slipped off in the struggle and now lay in a clump of primroses at Rowley's feet. Clinton, a few yards down the slope, was looking almost as embarrassed as she felt but truculent too, as he faced the glowering Rowley. But then he obviously decided to brazen it out, saying mildly, "Oh, don't be such an ass, Rowley! It was nothing. Ask Helen if you don't believe me. And do stop looking like the wrath of God!"

His brother, improbably, seemed to consider this statement, as though weighing its authenticity, and Helen was so absorbed in the interplay between the two brothers that for a moment or so she almost forgot her own embarrassment. Rowley said, at length, "She was telling you to stop. I heard her quite clearly from back there. Damn it, I knew you were selfish, Clinton, but I didn't reckon on you being a cad. Do you know I've a good mind to punch your nose here and now!"

But the threat seemed to put Clinton on his mettle, for the last of his embarrassment faded and he grinned as he said, "No harm in trying, old boy. You've never succeeded in the past, have you?" and on that they began squaring up to one another so that a sparring match seemed inevitable.

But then, with a rush, Joanna appeared, quite out of breath, crying, "*Stop* it! Stop it, both of you! What on earth *are* you? A couple of schoolboys?"

"He isn't at all events," Rowley said, quietly. "Ask Helen how he was behaving."

"I don't have to," Joanna said, coolly, adjusting to the situation with what seemed to Helen amazing speed. "What on earth got into you, rushing away like that and tearing them apart . . . She didn't scream for help, did she? For Heaven's sake, Rowley, do stop being so . . . so stuffy and self-righteous and pompous!"

It was the look that Rowley directed at her that reminded Helen of her own involvement in this ridiculous scene, played out between the four of them on an open hillside overlooking the great grey mansion below. It was the expression of a trusting child, struck by a parent for the first time, or that of a spoiled puppy at the receiving end of a beloved master's boot, so that she thought, "By God, she's hard! . . . And this crazy plan wasn't hatched for my benefit, as I supposed . . . All she's about is to show herself to Clint as the easygoing one of the pair," and the recollection of her careful briefing returned to her like a sour taste, Joanna sitting in her basket chair beside the fire prophesying, "Within five minutes of me taking him away Clint will kiss you and all you have to do is to protest, as loudly as you like . . ." and when Helen had asked how this was likely to steer Rowley her way, Joanna had hugged herself with glee, saying, "Don't you realise, you little goose? Rowley has seen himself as a knight in armour since he was six. The very fact of you having to defend your honour against his brother will make him see you in an entirely different light . . . After that, of course, it will be up to you, but at least he'll be *aware* of you. Apart from that, if I take Clint's part, he'll begin asking himself what he saw in me in the first place!"

It had all seemed so clever and artful but logical too she would have said, having regard to the diverse temperaments of the brothers. But somehow it hadn't worked out that way and now, the memory of Rowley's glance at her unbuttoned bodice returning to her, she felt so wretched and degraded that she could have burst into tears. She managed to restrain herself, however, sufficiently to turn away and begin walking along the lip of the escarpment in the direction of the village, aware only of the need to put distance between herself and the scene of an incident that involved the sacrifice of her dignity and his.

She had gone, perhaps, two hundred yards before Rowley caught her up. He was holding her bonnet by the strings and looking, she thought, very composed considering the circumstances. "You forgot this," he said, in level voice. "Put it on before we pick up the trap and drive back. You'll want to go straight home, I imagine."

"I don't care where I go," she said, savagely, "so long as it's a long way from here!" but she took the bonnet and rammed it on, pulling the strings taut with such a jerk that she bit her tongue. He said nothing but fell into step with her as they reached the hillside path that led down to the façade of the Sidney mansion. In silence they passed through the lych-gate to the spot where the loafer they had hired to watch the horses was fast asleep, his back to the churchyard wall.

She busied herself with her hair and the removal of traces of bracken from her skirt and jacket whilst he was harnessing the pony to the trap. Then, still without a word, he handed her in and they set off, not towards Leigh and the Tonbridge road, as she had expected, but up a narrow, leafy lane in the general direction of Sevenoaks.

They had gone about a mile when the lane broadened out and he pulled over on to a verge under some mature beech trees. It was a pretty spot, the bank starred with dog-violets and wild daffodils, fallow land stretching away to a belt of woods on the horizon. Blackbirds sang and a startled hedge-sparrow whirred from her nest in a moss-lined cavity of the bank. Seeing the bird he smiled and moved on fifty yards or so, saying, casually, "She'll be sitting. Pity to scare her off. Hedge-sparrows often desert if it happens a lot and it will here on a road." And then, letting the reins go slack so that the pony could crop, "Right. Now tell me what happened, Helen."

She was very confused now, not knowing in the least what to make of his calm and relaxed mood.

"I'll do no such thing. You saw what happened."

"Oh, yes," he said, genially, "but I mean *before* I arrived on the scene. According to plan, that is."

It occurred to her then that Joanna must have been so indiscreet as to give him a direct hint of how Clint was likely to behave the moment he was left alone with a girl, so she compromised, saying, "I'm sure I don't know what you mean. I wasn't looking for help. I had no one but myself to blame. It wasn't Clint's fault, not really."

"I didn't think it was. But something in the way of a rescue was looked for from me, wasn't it? All I'm interested in knowing is why."

She was silent, realising what complete idiots she and Joanna must have been to assume he could be taken in so easily.

"Well?"

She said, sulkily, "I'd prefer not to say. Let's drive back to the stables, and take the next train home."

"Not on your life," he said, "or not until I discover exactly what you were up to and what Joanna was up to. Not if I have to sit here all night, with you beside me. Then you really would be compromised and no mistake."

She was amazed that he could threaten her in those terms but had no doubt at all that he meant what he said and that made her regret having separated herself from Joanna, whose fault it was that she had landed herself in such a scrape. She decided to see what could be done with bluff. "If I told you the full truth," she said, "you would be more embarrassed than I was the moment you pounced on us back there. Just leave things as they are, Rowley. I made a fool of myself and so did Joanna but it won't help anyone to discuss it, least of all with you."

"No," he said with a half-smile, "I suppose not, but it might teach me something about women and I'm beginning to think that part of my education has been very neglected. Let me clear the air for you. That detachment on Joanna's part was planned but I was meant to come running back at a given moment. That's true, isn't it?"

She was silent, biting her lip and wishing the Kentish landscape would erupt like Vesuvius, or that a herd of mad elephants would come stampeding round the bend ahead, but he went on relentlessly, "Well, at least you don't deny it, so from here on I'll rely on guesses. Clint got down to business sooner than either of you anticipated. And also went further than you were prepared to tolerate. That's true also, isn't it? What I don't understand is the real reason behind the charade. Were either of you trying to compromise Clint? Has he been too slow in coming up to scratch? Something of that kind?"

She blushed to the roots of her hair. This was far worse than being caught full-length on the ground with one's bodice half-unbuttoned and it stunned her to think he could suppose she was so much in love with Clinton that she was prepared to snare him like a desperate scullery-maid. She said, indignantly, "Do you suppose I'd throw my cap at anybody as stupid as Clinton? Do you suppose I'd marry him, if he compromised me fifty times over? You really don't know much about girls. That's very obvious."

"But there was a reason, wasn't there?"

"No."

"And if there was you wouldn't tell me?"

"No."

"I think you'd better. We've left our lunch behind and you'll be very peckish by tea-time."

His coolness maddened her but then so did his blindness. He could reason this far but the main point appeared to have escaped him completely. She said, suddenly, "You insist on knowing?"

"You owe me that, Helen."

"I don't owe you anything," she snapped. "You've neither looked at me nor spoken two consecutive words to me since you patched me up after that spill I had at Addington last September. You've been mooning after Joanna ever since that first day and you still are, although she's told you she isn't in love with you. Just how does that leave me in your debt? You're so anxious to ferret everything out so go to work on that, Rowland Coles!"

She had not meant to be so explicit but now she was glad he had goaded her into losing her temper. The blank expression on his face—until then anything but blank—was worth what amounted to an admission that she was in love with him and had been since the moment he bandaged her after that brother of his had picked her out of the ditch outside their home. He looked so startled that she could have laughed. "Well?" she taunted him. "Are you satisfied now you know? Shall we turn around and go back to Tonbridge?"

"Good Lord," he said, at last, "I really am an idiot! When it comes to people, that is. And I'm supposed to be the brainy one, the chap who walks through exams and takes all the prizes. Now Clint never won a prize or sat an exam in his life but in a situation of this kind he wouldn't even have to think on it, not for a second! I mean, he'd *know*, wouldn't he?" And he turned to her desperately, as though her corroboration was vital to his peace of mind.

"Yes," she said, "he'd know all right. He probably has known, from that first day we had luncheon with your family. Joanna knows too, for that matter, because I told her the minute she told me you had proposed to her, and I daresay your parents, and certainly your sisters guessed long ago. But all these people knowing that I would give everything in the world to *be* Joanna doesn't help, does it? I see that now very clearly. If I had the sense I was born with I'd never have let her talk me into taking part in such a silly, stupid novelettish situation."

She leaned over to lift the reins from the rest but he caught her hand, checking her. The pony went on cropping. The hedgesparrow, after a cautious circuit or two, decided there was nothing to fear and flitted back to her nest in the hollow. He still looked as if he had been struck on the head with a croquet mallet but there was a hint of laughter at the corners of his mouth. He said, wryly, "There would be no point in wishing you were Joanna now, Helen."

"Why? Because she refused you? Don't believe it! I know men better than you know women. Rejection only puts them on their mettle. You'll ask her again. And again after that, and in the end she'll be so flattered she'll accept."

"I won't ask her again," he said. "Both of you can be sure of that."

"Why not? Just because she played a silly trick on you?"

"No, not really. Because the trick worked. In a queer sort of way."

He said it quietly and without much conviction, so that it made no immediate impact on her. Yet some kind of reply was obligatory, so she said, with the same offhandedness, "Oh, there's no call for you to act the gallant any longer. I made a frightful fool of myself and I'm quite prepared to admit it, even if Jo isn't."

He smiled at that, a slow and very engaging smile, the first she had ever seen on his long, solemn face.

"Gallant? Who the devil said anything about being gallant? You and Joanna aren't the only two who can play charades."

"What can you mean by that?"

"I'll tell you something. I came back to you and Clint *before* I was supposed to. I came because I was curious and for no other reason at all. I knew Joanna was up to something but I couldn't fathom what, except that it had to do with you and with Clint. Well, I've found out now and, as I say, the trick worked to some extent. At least it showed me that you and I have something in common."

"And what's that, pray?"

He dropped his reasonable tone and flashed out, "Oh, don't sound so damned priggish! It's nothing to be ashamed of. You and I, we both make up our minds what we want and go straight at it. We aren't easily turned aside by what stands in the way." He looked at her speculatively. "What did Joanna tell you of what I have in mind now that I've qualified?"

"That you intended to become a medical missionary overseas."

"And what did you deduce from that?"

"That you were convinced you 'had a call', I suppose. That's how they refer to it, isn't it?"

"Yes, that's what it's usually called. But it wasn't what I had."

"I don't understand."

"How could you? You would have had to have known me a long time ago. You would have had to have known my father and grandfather when they were my age. It's in the blood, like your brother Alex following the drum, and your father starting that business of his. To make something out of nothing. My grandfather rolled pills for a druggist in a country town until he was nearly forty, but he always had two rooted ambitions. To own a shop of his own and to come to London. He achieved both. My father had a different ambition. He had it in mind to make a fortune, and set up as a country gentleman and that's just what he's done."

"And you set your mind on becoming a missionary?"

"No, I didn't. I wanted to qualify as a doctor and I've done that, as I knew I should. But I'm only twenty-six, and I want adventure. I'm not much interested in saving souls but I'd like very much to take a crack at tropical diseases. If I have to do it by teaching them to stop eating one another I don't mind taking that in my stride, for that way I'll get official status and financial backing wherever I go. You ask your father how the flag and the Bible travel as partners to all these out-of-the-way corners."

She was listening to a very different Rowland Coles. She had never suspected that he would reveal himself as a tradesman, a man with something to sell, of the kind her father took pride in being. Yet she could discern similarities between them now. They had the same arrogance, the same prickly self-sufficiency, the identical 'I'll show you' and 'Take-me-as-you-find-me' approach to the world. But he had a surprise in reserve for her. Before she could adjust to the new Rowley he said, "I daresay Joanna implied I was stuffy, didn't she? No, that's not fair, you don't have to tell me what she said. But the fact is, looking back, I see now she made it pretty clear I didn't appeal to her. As a man, I mean, as well as a future medical missionary in Patagonia, or Sierra Leone. Well, that's her privilege. Clint is more her type but it took me time to admit that. All the same, I'm not *that* stuffy, and I'll prove as much after we've had tea at a place I know in Hildenborough, just up the road. They serve rum butter, with home-baked scones and apricot jam. We'll go there in a minute but first I should like to prove I'm as much flesh and blood as Clint—" And he put his arm round her, holding her in a grip that made her wince and lifting his other hand tilted her chin and kissed her on the mouth. It was not what you would call a lover's kiss but it had about it a very definite air of proprietorship.

7

Henrietta as Matchmaker

It was the time she came to look back on as The Family Exodus. A time when the tempo and rhythm of 'Tryst' faltered, changed, and reasserted itself yet in a way she could never have foreseen.

She had always known, of course, that such a time would come and had, in a sense, looked forward to it, seeing it as part of the pattern of fulfilment. The children, even the youngest of them, would grow up and scatter but this was of no consequence. Progressively marriages would take place and by the time little Margaret was tormenting her first beau 'Tryst' would be half full of grandchildren. This was one of the hidden bonuses of producing a long, carefully-spaced family. But it didn't happen in quite that way. Instead there was a trickle and then a rush of weddings and abdications that succeeded one another at such a speed that it sometimes seemed to Henrietta she was moving from early middle age to the evening of her life in a matter of weeks. It was enough to make any woman look over her shoulder for creeping shadows.

Alex, and his stocky little bride Lydia, had sailed for India in September but she was well-accustomed to Alex's migrations by now. This time she resigned herself to a separation of anything up to five years and looked for his reappearance with two or more toddlers in tow. A glance at Lydia's hips suggested she would have little or no difficulty in this respect.

Then, overnight George, Gisela and his two babies decamped, leaving the millhouse empty and uncared for and she could not bring herself to advise Adam to let it. This would be to set the seal of George's abdication, making it more final than she was prepared to admit, even to herself.

A few months later, Helen came romping into the house, shrieking that she had become engaged to the elder of the two Coles boys, the serious-looking one who was already a doctor, and was going to be a medical missionary and whisk her off to some God-forsaken spot halfway across the world. This had given Henrietta a jolt, for it made nonsense of her private predictions. Until then she had been convinced that Rowland Coles had no eyes for anyone but Joanna yet here he was, fidgeting about in front of an embarrassed Adam, asking for Helen in the most formal manner imaginable! Adam, the poltroon, hastily shuttled the stammering young man on to her, which was most inconsiderate of him. He must have known that she was disinclined to encourage Helen, younger than Joanna by three years, to jump the queue in this slapdash manner.

There was absolutely nothing she could do about it, however. The couple had clearly made up their minds about one another and were not disposed to wait the three years or more that Rowland would be away on his first assignment. And in support of haste (almost indecent haste to Henrietta's way of thinking) Helen was saucy enough to quote her own words at her, reminding her that she had often expressed strong disapproval of Giles' long engagement to that Rycroft girl, and events had proved her right. The silly girl had tired of waiting, run off in a tizzy, and had never been heard of since.

Helen and Rowland (somehow Henrietta could never learn to call such an earnest young man 'Rowley') were married in July. Ten weeks after that they followed Alex and Lydia overseas and were lost to her almost as surely as if they had gone to the moon. How long did it take a letter to come from Papua, granted that a place as outlandish as Papua had a postal service?

They had been gone less than a fortnight before the kaleidoscope was given another violent shake, this time by someone whom Henrietta had thought incapable of surprising her. Deborah, thirty-one if you please, suddenly announced her intention of quitting the London scene and marrying a penniless young man no one at 'Tryst' had heard of until his moment of presentation.

Luckily for all parties, Adam was on hand to act as buffer on this occasion. Indeed, it was Adam, shamelessly enjoying the joke, who broke the news to Henrietta. Unlike all the other children (not excluding George) Deborah had always maintained direct access to the titular head of the family. On this occasion the hussy made full use of it.

2

It happened towards dusk one blustery October afternoon, when Adam, watching the slate-coloured storm clouds over Wren's dome, decided to make an early start for home and blew down the speaking tube to ask Tybalt to send a lad for a cab. Tybalt said, apologetically, "Er . . . excuse me, sir—if you've time, that is—you have a visitor. Miss Avery, sir . . ." and when Adam said he was to tell Miss Avery to wait, pending his descent, and that she might as well accompany him to the station, Deborah spoke into the tube, saying, with laughter in her voice; "What I've to say to you can't be said in a five-minute cab-ride, Uncle Adam! I'll come up if you don't mind!"

He had, it seemed, no choice in the matter for the click told him the speaking tube stopper had been replaced and it was this that put him on his guard, implying that Deborah was taking no chances with counting-house eavesdroppers.

A moment later she appeared and he saw at once that she was very elated about something. Her eyes sparkled and she was very breathless, as though she had run the length of the spiral staircase.

He said, with the counterfeit crustiness he reserved for enthusiasts of all kinds, "Well, what is it now? An assignment to look into the sanitary conditions of the gaols? Or my blessing on a trip to the leper colonies in the South Seas?"

But she kissed him on both cheeks, perched herself on the corner of his desk nearest the window and said, gaily, "Don't be such a bear. It doesn't become you, but I'll put your mind at rest right away. What would you say if I told you I was to be married this day week?"

She had her revenge if she had looked for one. His jaw sagged and he half-rose, bringing both hands down on the letter trays and upending one of them so that a Bradshaw lying there spun and fell with a thump on his sound leg.

"Oh, come now, not you! *You're* catching it from Alex and Helen . . . ?" but then, more seriously, "It's a proposition I take it, not a fact."

"A fact, I'm afraid," she said, laughing at his confusion, "but it's been a near-certainty for several months now. For Heaven's sake, Uncle, don't look so astounded! It really is most unflattering. Oh, I'm well aware that both you and Aunt Hetty have resigned yourself to having an unclaimed blessing on your hands, but claimants do show up from time to time, even for leftovers."

"Who is he?" he managed to say. "Do I know him?"

"Not personally. Though you must be acquainted with him by remove."

"Now what the devil is that supposed to mean?"

"It means you have read his articles. You must have done, since you're a regular subscriber to the *Gazette*. His name is Jeffs, Milton Jeffs, and he asked me to marry him when we were working on the dock strike in the summer. I refused then but we've both had a change of heart."

"You've both had?"

"He's going to buy and run a local paper in the West, where I can be more than a pencil-sharpener to him, all I've been so far. So I said yes. *Please*. And soon!"

He had to laugh at her. She was a feminist of the deepest conviction but there was little about her that characterised all the other feminists he had met and read about, aggressive young hoydens or sour old biddies for the most part, making a lot of noise about what they called their back seats and second-class citizenship. He knew Jeffs too, now that he came to think about it, a cool and very precise journalist, who dealt in facts rather than sermons, itself an unlikely qualification for a post on Stead's journal.

"How old is he? Around Stead's age?"

She swung her legs to the floor and crossed to the window. "See for yourself, Uncle."

"He's here?"

"I very much wanted you to meet him. I want your approval too. It's very important to me."

He was glad she had said that. Their relationship had always been close and suddenly he realised that her happiness was something he cared about very much. More than the future of any one of them, if he was completely honest.

He glanced down into the yard and saw a tall, hatless young man standing beside a half-laden frigate outside the warehouse. He had curly hair and was not, he would have said, as old as Deborah. His loose-jointed stance, together with the expression of profound concentration on his face as he watched the warehousemen, made him look boyish.

Deborah said, "I won't be coy with you, Uncle Adam. Milton is five years younger than I. But he's the kindest, the most discerning and the most intelligent man I've ever met. I love him very much."

"I suppose I should say 'That's all that matters'," he said, "but it's a phrase that always sticks in my gullet. The one thing Continentals arrange much better than us is their marriages. Has he got any money?"

"Two thousand pounds. And every penny of it has gone into his newspaper."

"Does he know about your father and how we stand in relation to one another?"

"He knows as much as I know."

It was not a rebuke but perhaps it could be interpreted as a query, so that he thought, "And that isn't so much either! But now isn't the time to rake over Josh Avery's middens!" and he threw the casement open and called, "Mr. Jeffs! Come up and take the chill off the evening!"

The boyish face looked up and smiled. "At your service, sir!" as Adam, turning back into the room said, "I'm going to like him, Debbie. Don't ask me why. Just a feeling here," and he patted his stomach.

*   *   *

The conviction stayed with him even when he learned that Milton Jeffs came from a Quaker family and subscribed to many of their beliefs. There was something about him that reminded Adam of the gay young men with whom he had shared hard tack in the trenches before Sebastopol, and on long, dusty marches across a sub-continent at war. The type, he told himself, was common enough in the field, and even here in the city. Youngsters who made no bones about their worth in the open market, who were prepared to grab joyously at any opportunity for advancement that came their way.

Jeffs' ethos was a blend of idealism and realism, with a generous dash of humour thrown in, so that it was easy to see what attracted him to a woman like Deborah Avery. He approved the way the man looked at her, with laughter behind eyes that were shrewd as well as kind and found himself thinking "I'm glad she took her time . . . In a way she reminds me of Edith in the presence of her Tom. But in another way he reminds me of myself, when I was around his age, although I never harboured his expectations of human decency."

The age gap between them did not worry him as it seemed to worry Henrietta. What was five years at their age, particularly as they had both knocked about a bit? It was not, of course, Hetty's type of marriage, with the emphasis on mutual physical appeal, but a match between two young people who had their instincts under control, who were looking for something more than physical accord, of the kind that had proved so important to her all these years. Privately, he suspected, Henrietta would have reservations about it, particularly after that embarrassing, Quaker-type wedding, where a prayer-meeting free-for-all replaced the traditional marriage service. For himself, he was equipped to probe a little deeper, assuming that Milton Jeffs' participation in the ceremony—if it could be called a ceremony—was no more than a warm-hearted gesture towards his elderly father and mother, two very gentle creatures, overawed by what they would think of as Henrietta's grand manner and his own wealth and social position. But Milton wasn't, thank God, and set to work to charm Hetty from the moment he met her. Soon there was no more talk of his marrying the girl for what she was likely to inherit, either from her foster parents or that seedy rascal Josh.

There was no point in inviting Josh Avery to attend. Apart from all other considerations, he was hardly a man to grace a Quaker wedding. But he heard about it, as Adam knew he would, and wrote care of the bank, enclosing a draft for five thousand pounds made out to Adam, together with a request for a personal report on young Jeffs.

Adam invested the money, without telling Debbie too much about it. He was determined to keep Avery's secret as long as he could. For ever if possible. He wrote back briefly, giving it as his opinion that Debbie had made an excellent choice and that he thoroughly approved the match, leaving Avery to make what he could of this. He had a feeling that Josh would be relieved after that unpleasant business in Brussels. Transition from Stead's controversial journal to a tin-pot newspaper in the West meant that there could be no repetition of what had happened when the girl was out scavenging for the Lord's Anointed.

His insight into Jeffs was carried a stage further whilst they were hanging about waiting for Debbie to change and catch the boat train for Paris. He said, suddenly, "Why a small-town newspaper, Milton? You've already make your mark in Fleet Street and done very well for a chap your age. If you prefer the provinces why not one of the big dailies up North?"

Jeffs replied, "Two reasons, sir. In the first place, we've decided we want to shape our own editorial policy, even if it is limited to the design of the parish pump."

"And the second reason?"

"A private statute of limitations. At twenty-one both of us believed ourselves capable of shifting the Alps. Now, after several years with Stead, we're ready to settle for a few tons of topsoil from the Mendips."

"Something in that," Adam grunted, "but I daresay Debbie will say I'm the wrong man to admit to it."

3

Alex and Lydia, Helen and Rowley, Debbie and Milton Jeffs, George and Gisela. Four couples paired off, three couples moved out of reach all in little over a year, yet the house was not noticeably empty on their account.

Giles looked like developing into a confirmed bachelor but Henrietta, for one, did not underestimate the bruises left on him by that madcap Romayne, still mustered among the missing.

Hugo was living at home when he wasn't plunging all over the country collecting cups and medals. The two younger ones, Edward and Margaret, were growing fast and filling the house with pony-mad friends. There remained Joanna, rising twenty-two, and Henrietta was not at all sure what to make of Joanna nowadays.

It was natural, of course, that she should miss Helen more than any of them. They had been closer than any two of the children since their nursery days but she had seemed lively enough up to the time of the wedding, and through the fag-end of the summer after Helen and Rowley had sailed. Latterly, however, particularly since Christmas, she seemed to droop a little and Henrietta, quick to notice such things, detected what she could only describe as a loss of the dash and sparkle for which Jo had always been famous, particularly among the hearty hunting set she and Helen had favoured. She was still very much in demand but Henrietta had the impression she was beginning to tire of the nonstop round of hunt balls, soirées and bicycle picnics that had been her steady diet for so long now, and wondered if Helen's marriage had set her thinking about the advantages of settling down. There was no real evidence of this. She saw a good deal of that jolly, rakish brother of Rowley's, Clinton Coles, but showed him no particular preference, continuing to flirt with half a dozen other young bucks, none of whom, in Henrietta's opinion, merited more than a kiss or two under the mistletoe. She might have spoken to Joanna about prospects of marriage but she did not. She had never enjoyed the confidence of the Inseparables. All the time they were growing up they seemed to turn to one another rather than her. In some ways she felt more at ease with Alex or Giles than with either of them. She was certainly closer to George's Austrian wife, Gisela.

So she said nothing but kept her eyes and ears open. It was the latter that served her in the end, one windy night towards the end of March, when Adam was away in the North seeking a replacement for O'Dowd, his Irish manager, who had suddenly decided to emigrate to the United States.

It was by the merest accident that she stumbled on the cause of Joanna's loss of appetite and partial withdrawal. Nine-year-old Margaret, down with a feverish cold, had been sleeping in Phoebe Fraser's room for a week and had run a temperature three nights in a row. Phoebe had seemed tired out at luncheon and readily acceded to Henrietta's suggestion that Margaret was now well enough to go back to her own room at the far end of the corridor, where she could keep an eye on her until Doctor Birtles pronounced her fit to come downstairs.

Henrietta was late to bed that night. She usually was when Adam was away, preferring to sit reading into the small hours, always half-hoping that he would reappear out of the darkness, as he often had in thirty years of coming and going. It was thus around one o'clock when Henrietta went the rounds and trudged upstairs, remembering to look in on Margaret before she went to bed. The invalid was sleeping quietly so she turned back along the corridor and was passing Joanna's door when she heard what she took to be a cough and paused to listen, thinking irritably, "So now Jo has taken it." But then, as the sound was repeated, she realised it wasn't a cough but a muffled sound like a sob and unrestrained enough to be positively identified as such if you stood there a moment or two.

She followed her instincts then and went in without knocking. Joanna might be of age but if something was causing one of her daughters that much distress, and in the middle of the night, then she regarded it her inalienable right to know what it was.

She was concerned but in no way prepared for what she saw when she pushed the door shut and moved across to the bed where Joanna was lying with her head half-buried in the pillow, her lovely, tawny hair spread like a flame. She was half undressed and the bedside lamp, turned low, threw elongated shadows across the patterned wall in a way that caused Henrietta, now deeply disturbed, to remember another night long ago, when she had heard the paddock oak crash down and had gone downstairs to find Denzil Fawcett at the door with news of Stella's flight from the Moncton-Prices.

There was no special reason why she should remember that wretched incident but she did and it sharpened her perceptions. She understood at once that this was no mere tantrum on Joanna's part, and that the girl was in real trouble of one kind or another. She said, gently, "What *is* it, Jo. What's upset you?" but then she had another shock.

Joanna, who seemed not to have heard her entry above the rush of the wind outside, suddenly jerked herself out of range of her mother's outstretched hand and blurted out, "You've no *right*! This is *my* room! You always said . . ."

" 'All of us should have somewhere no one else has the right to enter without invitation.' Yes, yes, I know that, and I've always held to it and still do."

The girl said nothing to this but continued to crouch there like a sick animal so that Henrietta, running an eye over her, saw that she had not imagined her strange loss of vitality since Christmastide. Even in this subdued light it was all too evident, so that she thought herself a perfect fool not to have made a direct approach long ago.

Of all the girls Joanna had been the liveliest and, in some ways, the most original. She had Stella's self-sufficiency and Helen's daring, tempered with a cool judgement, of a kind Henrietta associated with Adam. Her rare pink and white prettiness, however, was all her own. As she passed from childhood to adolescence and then to womanhood she had ceased to suggest a Swann, a Rawlinson or even a D'Auberon, but one of the elegant models in the fashion journals Henrietta studied; the type of girl most people thought of as typically Anglo-Saxon, with strong features that would serve her well until she was past thirty when they might need regular massage.

The change, now that she looked for it, was quite startling. Her face was much thinner, almost pinched, and her eyes, red with weeping, looked as if they would never sparkle again. Her mouth, so full and generous, was drawn down at the corners, like the mouth of a nag, and suddenly, amalgamating and assessing these manifestations, she cried, "In God's name, what *is* it? What's the matter with you? Why are you crying like this?" but Joanna's reply was limited to a sullen, "Leave me alone! You make rules, then break them. Go away, *do!*"

It was all Henrietta could do to prevent herself boxing the girl's ears. It would not have been the first time by any means. All the children, at one time or another, had felt the weight of her hand, although Adam had never laid a finger on any of them. She controlled herself, however, for it suddenly occurred to her that she might know a possible reason for Jo's wretchedness. It was linked, she was sure, to Helen's abrupt removal from the scene and also, perhaps, to Helen's husband Rowland, for Henrietta now recollected her own astonishment when the young doctor had turned up demanding Helen's hand after squiring Joanna all over the county for months. The conviction grew on her then that she was looking at a jilted bride, the victim of a scurvy trick on the part of her closest confidante, and with this she felt a rush of sympathy for the girl. She said, "Tell me, Jo. It'll surely help to tell someone. Is it because of Helen? Helen and Rowley?"

"*Rowley?*"

She mouthed the word as if it was all but incomprehensible to her. "You think I'm crying for Rowley?"

"Why not? He was your beau to begin with. You saw a rare lot of one another before Helen . . ."

"It's nothing to *do* with Rowley! Rowley was . . . was dull, and it was I who helped Helen get him! But I don't want to talk about it. Stop nagging me, please."

It was not often Henrietta felt as baffled and helpless as she felt in the face of this. Instinct told her that Joanna, in so far as Rowland Coles was concerned, was telling the truth. She was not concerned for her pride and therefore had no interest in her brother-in-law. She said, quietly, "Very well, if you say so, but I would have thought you could talk to me since you're obviously extremely upset over something," and she turned to leave.

She had her hand on the latch when Joanna called and the urgency in her voice spun Henrietta round, as if in response to someone crying out in fear of death. "*Mamma! Please . . . !*" And then, in a voice not much above a whisper, "Don't go. Shut the door. Is everyone asleep—Phoebe, the children?"

"They've all been in bed for hours."

She came back into the room and stood close to the bed, aware that Joanna was making a great effort to control herself, to contain a fresh storm of tears and talk rationally and coherently.

"Well, Jo?"

"It isn't Rowley. It's nothing to do with him and nothing to do with Helen. In the beginning it was. But now . . . it's Clinton, Rowley's brother."

"You mean you're in love with Clinton Coles and he doesn't love you?"

"That's a part of it." Her teeth, whiter and stronger than the teeth of any of the others, clamped over the heavy underlip. "Yes, I'm in love with Clint. I told myself I wasn't over and over again but I am. I must have been . . . *must have been*, you understand?"

Henrietta did not as yet. The girl was making no more than partial sense and all this time hysteria was trying to raise the key of her flat, impersonal tone.

"He's marrying someone else?"

"Not him. Clint won't marry in a hurry. He isn't the marrying kind."

"Very well then, put him out of mind. You're nearly twenty-two and you've been racketing about long enough . . ."

But the girl seemed not to be listening. She was sitting on the very edge of the bed with her head bowed so that her hair was a copper screen masking her face. Her hands fidgeted with the ruin of a pocket handkerchief, twisting it and tugging it, as if it had been the knot on a parcel.

" 'Put Clint out of mind'? How can I? I'll be having his child in six months."

Henrietta's first reaction was not one of shock, or even extreme indignation. It was something more practical, for at once her glance moved from the girl's head to her figure, searching out evidence of this appalling announcement. She found none. Joanna had always inclined to plumpness and there seemed no sign of pregnancy about her rounded, sturdy figure, although that might be because she was still wearing her corset.

She said, in a voice that seemed to come from the back of her head, "Stand up! Stand up and look at me!" and Joanna stood very slowly, like someone responding to a hypnotist's command.

"In six months? You're sure?" and Joanna nodded, wordlessly.

"Dr. Birtles knows?"

"No one knows."

"Then you can't be sure. You *can't* be!"

"I am sure. There's no doubt about it."

"Wait a minute . . . don't say anything . . . let me think . . . *think* . . ." and Joanna subsided slowly on the bed, resuming her former position. There was a long silence in the room. The small fire shifted, rustling like a handful of dead leaves. Outside the wind gusted down from the spur to lose itself in the avenue beeches. Henrietta, with an insignificant part of her mind, reminded herself yet again how much she hated wind, of the kind that tormented 'Tryst' at this time of year.

718

"You say 'no one'. Does that include him?"

"Yes."

"You've told him nothing? Not even hinted?"

"No. I was only sure myself earlier in the week. I've not seen him since . . ."

And at that Henrietta's speechless indignation boiled over so that she wailed, "How *could* you be such a fool? How *could* you . . . ?" But then, to her own surprise, fury ebbed from her and she rallied on something more fundamental, some hidden force that came hurrying up like a reserve, very late and very much out of breath but infinitely welcome. Sooner or later they all had need of her. Sooner or later every single one of them, from Adam downwards, came to her to solve their complicated, personal problems, to make sense out of their muddles and misjudgements, their acts of thoughtlessness and bad guesses, that persisted far beyond the time when each and every one of them should have learned to stand on their own feet, as she had done when Adam lay helpless and mutilated more than twenty years ago.

There had been him, and after him Stella and Alex, both fugitives from their own impulsiveness. There had been George and Gisela, with their complex concerns, and soon afterwards Giles with his. And now here was Joanna, who had never once sought her counsel, telling her she had Clinton Coles' child in her belly, and that he wasn't likely to marry her. Well, something would have to be done about it. At once. Before a whisper of it passed beyond these four walls. But before anything could be done she would have to have a clear, unequivocal picture of the situation and common sense told her that the least likely way to get it was storm or rave at the girl, taking the stand most mothers took when faced with a domestic problem as old as civilisation that never offered a cut-and-dried solution.

She said, "Very well, tell me everything. *Everything*, you understand? For I can't help if I have to guess and I mean to help, do you hear? I mean to sort this out before your father hears about it and before we're all in disgrace again, the way we were over Stella."

Joanna's chin came up slowly. "There's not much to tell. I began flirting with him after Helen told me she was in love with Rowley. Rowley had proposed to me then but I didn't tell anyone save Helen because I wasn't going to accept. But I helped switch him to Helen and it worked."

"When *was* this?"

"Almost a year ago. One day when we were over at Penshurst on a picnic."

"Well?"

"After that Clint and I paired off. I didn't take him any more seriously than Rowley, although I was always much fonder of him. We were alike, I suppose. I didn't want to settle and neither did he."

"He seems to have had his fill of fun, nonetheless." It slipped out and at once she was sorry for it. "Never mind. Go on."

"We went everywhere together and I grew more and more fond of him after Helen and Rowley married and went away. I missed Helen a lot but Clint made up for it. Sometimes I thought he would propose but he never did. If he had I would have accepted but I wasn't surprised that he didn't. He just isn't that kind of person."

"What kind of person is he?"

"He's weak in many ways. He doesn't intend to work if he can help it. He keeps refusing to go in his father's business but over there they all spoil him, his father, his mother, his sisters. I can see why. He's so gay and . . . well, *likeable*. Wherever he goes people like him. He could have any girl around here and not simply because his father's so rich but because . . . well, because he's always fun to be with. He laughs at everything and makes everybody else laugh, even at serious things, if you follow me."

"Right. Now tell me how he came to make such a little fool of you."

"It was more my fault than his. As much, anyway. I think it always is really . . . the girl's fault, I mean. I was perfectly aware what I was about. In a way it was deliberate . . . well, half deliberate."

"How can you say that? Good heavens, you're not a child, you must have known . . ."

"I wanted him so much. It seemed a way to make certain."

With a part of her mind she found herself admiring the girl's devastating honesty. In a way it was a matter for pride, she supposed, that a girl in her situation could bring herself to admit as much, refusing to take refuge in whining complaints about being betrayed.

Until now she had never seen anyone look less dignified but there was dignity, of a kind, in Jo's frankness and Henrietta found herself responding to it.

"It happened more than once I take it?"

"Yes. Several times, until lately."

"You mean you stopped seeing him?"

"Not exactly. I saw much less of him. When I finally decided he wouldn't make up his mind one way or the other I was angry, especially if he paid the least attention to other girls."

"He's not attached to anyone else? You're sure of that?"

"I'm quite sure."

"When did you last see him?"

"Nearly a month ago. We had a quarrel . . . well, not really a quarrel, more of a tiff. We were coming home from the Volunteers' Ball in Sevenoaks and he began . . . well, I put him off, and since then I haven't set eyes on him."

"How did you 'put him off', exactly?"

"I told him he was selfish, that he was all take and no give, and that I was sorry I'd let him treat me that way and wouldn't again, ever."

"You didn't mention marriage?"

"No. I wanted to but I couldn't when it came to the point. It seemed . . . well, degrading, and besides, I had a feeling it would scare him off altogether and I didn't want that to happen. Was that the wrong way to go about it?"

"Every single move you made was the wrong way and I would have thought any girl of mine would have known that instinctively. A village oaf can be caught that way but not a man like Clinton Coles. But you don't need telling that now, do you?"

Joanna said nothing and Henrietta, glancing at her saw there was nothing more to be said, or nothing that would help. She had her brief and it was as comprehensive as she was likely to get. She said, "Right. You're in a rare fix, girl. We're all in a fix, so it's up to me to do what I can to get us out of it, and with as little damage as possible. But you'll have to help so I don't want any nonsense about pride and dignity. It's far too late for that. From now on you'll do as *I* say, and behave as I say, and not a single word of this to anyone. Is that clear?"

"What can be done? Are you saying I should go to him, tell him . . ."

"Not *you*. I'll do the telling."

"*You* will? But . . ."

"Hold your tongue and listen. Where would I be likely to find him? In private. Away from his house and this house. Somewhere we could talk and come to an arrangement?"

She looked so bewildered that Henrietta felt her profound irritation returning as she thought, "She's quite the silliest of the whole string and that's a fact! No wonder she let that young rascal take advantage of her and still think she was being so damnably artful . . ." But then the sense of urgency returned and she snapped, "Don't sit there gaping like a goldfish! Where can I find him? In the morning. As early as possible. I'll call on him if I have to, but it would be far better if I didn't at this stage. I'd sooner . . . sooner waylay him and find out where we stand—you, him, all of us!"

Joanna said, uncomfortably, "He's training a horse for the flat. He goes out early most mornings, up to that long, level stretch, our side of Cudham."

"Alone?"

"Usually, but . . ."

"What do you call early?"

"Soon after it's light. About seven o'clock by the time he's up there. I thought of going there myself."

"You'll do no such thing. You'll get your packing done."

"Packing?"

"Packing! And only take what you have to. Two bags at the most, you understand? I want you out of here before twenty-four hours are past."

"But where am I going?"

"That," said Henrietta, "depends on a number of things. Right now, wash your face and go to bed."

She crossed to the door but paused, her hand on the latch. "There is one other thing."

"Yes?"

"Don't beat about the bush. Tell me as simply as you can, providing you have an answer. Is there any possibility he loves *you*?"

Thirty seconds ticked by as Henrietta stood waiting.

"I think he does. In his own way."

"Ah, and what way is that?"

"After himself he loves me."

She went out then, remembering to close the door softly.

4

She saw him first as a silhouette against a clear, windswept sky, horse and man rising out of the dip and moving into a smart trot as they breasted the slope to the level stretch where she rode her cob in the centre of the hammered track.

The wind had dropped but it was cold up here and she was glad of the steamy warmth of the cob's flanks against her legs. His horse scented hers and whickered so that he reined in, sitting well back in the saddle. When he saw who it was he came forward at a sidling walk, as if he was having difficulty holding in his grey. His easy manners came to his rescue and he called, touching his steeple-chaser's hat, "Top of the morning, Mrs. Swann. I didn't know you were in competition with me. I look on this stretch as mine!" and laughed.

He had, she decided, a musical laugh and thought at once of his solemn brother, Rowland. She did not recall ever having heard Rowland laugh, although he had smiled when Helen's eager response went off key at the wedding last summer.

There seemed no point in mincing matters and the nip in the air put a particularly fine edge on her voice as she said, "You'll know why I'm here if you think about it, Mr. Coles."

In some ways he seemed even more stupid than Joanna for it was manifestly clear that he did not know. She thought, studying his handsome but unremarkable face, "They should suit one another . . . not a ha'porth of sense between them," but said, in the tone of voice she had used to prise the facts from Joanna, "Don't just sit there, help me down. Any minute that great beast of yours will run away with you and the cob will follow suit."

He made a great show of dismounting, hooking his bridle over his arm, steadying the cob with the engaged hand and using the other to lift her from the saddle. His touch was firm but gentle. "It would be!" she thought, sourly, "he's a lady's man and no mistake," as she heard him say, "Is anything wrong, Mrs. Swann? Can I be of service to you?"

She could have laughed at that and almost did. Resisting exploitation of the irony, she said, "Yes, there is something wrong, Mr. Coles. As wrong as can be, so far as I'm concerned. As to whether you can put it right that's up to you, I imagine. Or your folks, whichever you prefer."

She saw then that 'the penny had dropped', as old Mrs. Worrall, her father's Lancastrian housekeeper, had been fond of saying. He took a step backward, his eyes widening, his mouth crumpling like a child's. For a dreadful moment she thought he was going to add his tears to Joanna's but he pulled himself together more briskly than she would have expected, and said in a low voice, "It's about Jo then?"

"Who else?"

"You'd best explain, Mrs. Swann."

Her North Country forthrightness flashed out. "I didn't ride out here on an empty stomach to pass the time of day, lad! Joanna tells me she's expecting your child. You're not going to deny it, I hope."

"No," he said, flushing, "I'm not a cad, Mrs. Swann." And then, his head coming up, "Did Joanna tell you I would?"

"No, she didn't. And she was ready to shoulder more than half the blame. That's rare in the circumstances, wouldn't you say?"

"It's like her. Does Mr. Swann know?"

"Mr. Swann is away, thank goodness."

"Then why didn't Jo tell me herself? Why did she send you?"

"She didn't 'send' me. And she wasn't sure herself until a day or so ago. I happened to pass her room very late last night. She was crying and naturally I wanted to know why. I don't imagine she could have kept it from me much longer in any case."

Nothing stirred up here. With the two horses they might have been the only creatures astir in the whole of Kent. The air was so crisp and heady that it made her nostrils smart. He was not looking at her. His eye seemed to be fixed on a glistening pebble lying near the grey's nearest hindleg. He said, at length, "You don't have to worry, Mrs. Swann. And it won't be another case of 'having' to get

724

married, as they say. I'm very fond of Jo, and I think she's fond of me. I would have proposed anyway sooner or later. Without this happening, I mean."

The strange thing was she believed him, so that her opinion of him began to rise with every moment that passed, every word he uttered. Joanna had said he was weak but he wasn't as weak as all that. She fancied she had learned something about men in more than thirty years of marriage to Adam Swann and it seemed to her that Joanna's instinct had not led her far astray. She said, briskly, "So far, so good, then, but I'm not here to 'bring you up to scratch' as the saying goes, or not entirely. I've got a plan that will save us all a peck of trouble and embarrassment if you'll agree to go through with it. Will you listen to my advice?"

Improbably, and in a way that robbed her of all initiative, he smiled. He had a very nice smile, as infectious as George's, and as wry as Adam's when he was enjoying a joke against himself.

"I'd rather take it as read, Mrs. Swann. We'll elope. In the traditional manner. Tonight if that isn't rushing things too much. Was that what you had in mind?"

"Yes, it was," she said, somewhat taken aback. "As I see it there's a great deal to recommend it and I should know. I eloped with Mr. Swann before you were born. Did Joanna tell you that?"

"No," he said, "but I'm not the least bit surprised to hear it, Mrs. Swann. What time shall we say?"

"Around one a.m. would be best. Don't come up to the house, wait down by the spinney." Then, curiously, "Where will you head for? Gretna Green, as couples in your situation usually do?"

"They don't any more. Irregular marriages there were stopped by Act of Parliament about the time you ran away with Mr. Swann. Romance is becoming unfashionable, Mrs. Swann. Lovers have to hang around up there for three weeks, and it's no kind of weather for the Border. You see that I must have given some thought to the matter."

She had to smile at that and to cover up said, "What makes you fight shy of hard work, Mr. Coles? You don't strike me as lazy. A lazy man wouldn't get up at crack of dawn to train horses, would he?"

"He might, if horses were the only thing he knew about. I'm not bright, like Rowley, and I draw the line at devoting my life to marketing pills and potions. Whatever I do will be done in the open air. Maybe this will make up my mind for me, and I'll stay in Ireland and take up training seriously."

His talk of horses touched a chord in her memory. Adam had said something like that when she first met him—"Horses are the only thing I know about," and this, together with his reference to Ireland, gave her yet another idea. It seemed an outrageous one in the circumstances and too vague to mention to him now, but she meant to think about it as soon as they were clear away.

"How will you explain things to your parents?" she asked, and he replied, gaily, "I'll leave them to draw conclusions, Mrs. Swann. They like Jo and that's a good start."

There seemed no more to say. It was lonely up here but at any moment somebody might chance along and it would never do for them to be seen together, so she said, extending her hand, "Well, good luck, lad. I'll get in touch with you somehow. Maybe to your advantage but I can't go into that until I see how Mr. Swann takes it."

"You'll tell him then?"

"As to why you've run off? No, I won't. I'm not that much of a fool. I'm going to be as outraged as everyone else this time tomorrow."

"What will you say. I mean, what *can* you say?"

"I'll think of something. When occasion demands I'm the best liar in Kent. You have to be when you're saddled with a family of my size."

He helped her mount, swinging her up as if she had weighed a pound or two instead of almost nine stones, and she thought, sensing his vigour, "I can find excuses for Jo now that I know the boy . . . in one way at least she's her mother's daughter."

He called, when she was ten yards off, "Don't fret, Mrs. Swann! I'll take very good care of her!" and she lifted her hand in acknowledgement.

"He will too," she told herself aloud. "He mightn't be clever but to my way of thinking Jo got a far better bargain than her sister."

* * *

She had resolved to stay awake and listen for signs of departure, sharing to some extent the excitement and relief that would surely be Joanna's when she slipped out of the house and went to him down by the spinney at the foot of the drive. The loss of one night's rest, however, claimed its toll. Long before one o'clock she was asleep, remaining so until eight when she woke up with a start and hurried along to Joanna's room to collect the note she had dictated.

She had all she could do to subdue a giggle or two when she read it, reflecting that here was an eloping couple unique in the history of runaway matches. But then it occurred to her that perhaps she was taking too much for granted. It might well be that many anxious mammas had written the part for their erring daughters and no one a penny the wiser. All the note said was *"Have run away to marry Clint Coles. Please don't worry. Very happy. Joanna."* It wouldn't fool most fathers but it would fool Adam, she was sure of that. Meantime she rehearsed an explanation concerning Jo's absence at the breakfast table that would likely satisfy Phoebe Fraser and the younger children. Jo had been called for late last night to stand in as bridesmaid for Sophie Turnbull's wedding in Maidstone, Sophie's sister having gone down with measles. Sophie was a niece of Godsall's, who was getting married shortly, so that everyone accepted the story at face value, although Phoebe sulked because she hadn't been invited to help Joanna pack.

About eleven she told the stable lad to harness the trap for her drive over to Addington, to confer with the Coles and this was a mission she did not relish. Rowley's parents, whom she had met briefly at the wedding in September, had struck her as fussers, who were likely to ask a lot of awkward questions.

She need not have bothered. A red-eyed Mrs. Coles practically dragged her over the threshold, jabbering something about a letter Clint had left. Then Mr. Coles and his two plain daughters appeared, and she was given the letter, together with a glass of sherry but she found it difficult to read for Mrs. Coles kept repeating, over and over again, "Such a *silly* thing to do! Why couldn't they have waited? Why couldn't we *share* in their happiness . . . ?"

Mr. Coles, thank God, was more discerning, and Henrietta was in no doubt at all but that he suspected the truth and was determined not to admit it, even to himself. He kept patting his wife's shoulders, saying, "There now, don't carry on so, my love. Mrs. Swann is the injured party and see how calmly she's taken it." And then, to Henrietta, "What *can* I say, Mrs. Swann? The boy's a fool and that's a fact! Your husband will have every right to be extremely angry about this as soon as he hears about it."

"I don't think he will be," Henrietta said, feeling rather sorry for him. "After all, he married me very much against my father's wishes, and we're already relations of a kind. What little Mr. Swann and I have seen of Clint, we like."

It wasn't true, of course. Adam, as she well knew, would have difficulty in recalling the boy's name, but what was one more white lie among so many? She went on, "Would you mind if I borrowed Clinton's letter and read it in private, before I showed it to Mr. Swann? It will embarrass all of us if I read it here, in front of you," and both Mr. and Mrs. Coles agreed, so eagerly that it was obvious they couldn't get her out of the house quickly enough and looked to her to break the news to Adam in their absence.

The two girls followed her out to the trap and she realised then that the furore at Addington Manor was largely counterfeit. Amelia, the younger daughter, whispered, "Don't mind mother, Mrs. Swann. She was delighted when Rowley married Helen and she'll be just as pleased about this, once she's got over the shock."

Halfway home, in a cutaway on the edge of the Downs, she pulled in to read Clint's letter. The handwriting was sprawling, more that of a schoolboy than a man who could hoist a woman into the saddle with one hand, but the artful composition confirmed her in her opinion that Clint Coles was not as stupid as he looked.

"My Dearest Mother and Father," it began dutifully, "When you read this I shall be a long way off, having persuaded Joanna Swann to elope with me. We hope to be married almost at once and I owe you an explanation of what you will be sure to think of as unkind and unfilial behaviour on my part. The fact is, as I am sure you will have guessed, Joanna and I are very much in love, but both of us shirked a wedding that would have entailed, besides a lot of fuss, a long and tedious wait. That is one reason but it isn't the real one. You remember I agreed that when I married and settled down I would make Father happy by taking charge of the firm? Well, I've given thought to this a great deal lately, and come to the conclusion, however much disappointment it might cause him, that I couldn't honour the bargain and spend the rest of my life in the city. So this seemed to me the only thing to do—that is, marry Jo and make a place for ourselves, somewhere fresh, perhaps in one of the Colonies, where I can stand on my own feet and stop being a charge on your purse. The sensible thing to have done, of course, would have been to try first as a single man but that would have meant years of separation that neither one of us cared to face. Please tell Jo's parents not to worry. I'll look after her in every way, and I hope both you and they will forgive us in time. Your loving son, Clint."

She folded the letter and put it back in its envelope, thinking, "He knows about people as well as horses, the young rogue. I hope she can manage him, for I'm sure I couldn't." And then, seeing the road was deserted, she had the laugh that had been bottled up for long enough.

5

She had enjoyed, she would have said, more than her share of luck but more awaited her. Adam, informed of the situation, was inclined to dismiss it as an elaborate prank that hardly merited a serious thought, much less the loss of a night's sleep. "The more you clear a path for these youngsters the more determined they are to strew boulders along their route," he grunted, when Henrietta showed him Jo's note and Clint's letter. "A yokel and a scullery-maid would have shown more sense. And more dignity too, I wouldn't wonder! Why the devil couldn't he come up here and ask for the girl in a civilised manner? Does he take me for an ogre? And that's not the truth of the matter either," he rumbled on, giving Henrietta a bad moment. "It wouldn't surprise me to learn that the idea originated with her, not him. She probably saw herself as the wilting heroine in one of those trashy novelettes you fed her!"

"I fed her no such thing," Henrietta protested, with genuine indignation. "You weaned me off those books before she was born! To tell you the truth, I don't think either she or Helen ever read anything heavier than a *Bentley's Magazine* serial in the whole of their lives."

"Well, there's a bonus in it for me, I suppose," he continued, preparatory to dismissing the subject, "it'll save me the outlay on another wedding. Do you have any idea where he might have taken her?"

"None at all," she lied cheerfully, "and neither have the Coles. I shall know when they're man and wife, however."

"I wouldn't wager on that," he said, beginning to enjoy his displeasure, a habit that had been growing on him since the Rycroft debacle and George's abdication. "If she can slip off like that she'll take her time writing, you can be sure of that. Let me see that correspondence again. No, no, not that silly note of hers, the letter the young idiot left on *his* mantelshelf!"

She gave him Clinton's letter and watched him knit his brows over it. "Funny thing," he grunted, laying it down, "I wouldn't have thought a young chap with his seat on a horse would let himself be talked into a frolic like this by a chit of a girl, with her head full of hogwash. But there it is, you never can tell what a man will do when a saucy little baggage bewitches him. He had a rare future as a steeplechaser. I saw that when I watched him win the Sidney Cup, over at Tonbridge last spring. It'll be goodbye to his hopes in that direction."

On the whole she was relieved he took this line, preferring to see the escapade as something Joanna had engineered, probably with the object of getting him away from a rival or rivals. It was further proof of Edith Wickstead's dictum that, while he was admittedly an excellent judge of man's potential, he had never learned anything important about a woman's. She was careful to say nothing to disillusion him but listened patiently to his grumbles concerning his inability to find a reliable substitute for O'Dowd, at the Dublin depot. This was her extra piece of good fortune as it happened, for it fitted into a plan that had been maturing ever since she met young Coles up on the Downs. When the first letter arrived bearing a Cork postmark, informing them that the runaway couple had been married by special licence in Belfast, and were honeymooning in Kerry, she took her courage in both hands and confronted him. "If you haven't filled that Dublin post yet why don't you keep it in the family by offering it to Clinton?"

He stared at her as if she had said something very stupid but she had been prepared for this and went on, before he could explode, "Well, *why not?* I mean, he's young and strong, wants an open-air life and has good commercial connections. And you've admitted yourself he's a first-class horseman. He's also your son-in-law, like it or not. From the little I remember of him I think you'd get along with one another."

"Do you imagine I pick my depot managers on the strength of their steeplechase performances? Good God, woman, they don't act as outriders on the waggons. A man handling that job in a place like Ireland needs nerve, cool judgement, imagination."

"Well, as to that," she countered, "I would have said he's shown proof of all three. Nerve to ride his fences straight. Judgement to pick one of our girls, instead of getting hooked by one of those ninnies they've introduced into the house from time to time. And imagination enough to turn his back on a readymade pill business where he couldn't hope to be anything more than a figurehead!"

She saw at once that her broadside had taken effect, raking his prejudices and all but demolishing his private conviction that Clint Coles was a weakling manipulated by a woman. That was another rewarding aspect of Adam Swann. Presented with a line of reasoning that ran directly contrary to his own, he was never too proud or too obstinate to change his mind on the spot. He said, slowly, "There might well be some sense in that, Hetty. I confess I hadn't looked at it in that light. I'm sometimes inclined to forget that you ran the business for a year that time I was laid up. It must have taught you something about people's potential."

"Bringing up your tiresome family has taught me that," she said, briefly, "so pooh to your patronage, Adam Swann! I know my sons and daughters well enough to be certain the silliest of them wouldn't hitch themselves to an idiot!"

"Stella did," he reminded her, but she was ready for this too. "Stella had the good sense and courage to backtrack and try again, so don't quote her at me. It's my belief Joanna knew precisely what she was doing and meant to get the boy by hook or by crook. You owe it to her to go over and decide about him for yourself, before you hold this against both of them for the rest of their lives!"

"That's something I should have to think about," he said, but he

731

didn't think long. Forty-eight hours later he was on his way to Fishguard to catch the Irish packet. One week later he was home again, with young Coles established in Dublin as viceroy-elect of the Irish bridgehead.

His mood was in great contrast to that of his previous homecoming, admitting that her instinct had served her well and that young 'Jack-o'-Lantern' (he had coined this name for his new son-in-law on the homeward crossing) was a lively young spark who might inject some much-needed ginger into the Irish beat. "Don't mind saying I took to the lad," he said, "once he'd made me a handsome apology. Did you know he has a lot of influential acquaintances over there?"

"Most horsey men have," she said, trying to conceal elation that came bubbling out of her like a pudding on the boil.

"Well, it decided me," he said. "He's no great shakes at paperwork, and never will be, but clerks are two a penny. What I was looking for in Dublin was someone who could match the Irish at blarney. He's on six months' trial at all events. Flat rate, plus commission."

It was typical of him, she thought, to let business prospects completely cloud the family issue so that finally she had to make a point of asking him if he had seen Joanna during his visit. He seemed surprised at the question. "Seen her? Good God, of course I saw her! What kind of father do you think I am? Young Jack-o'-Lantern brought her to breakfast at the Gresham before I showed him over our yard."

"Well, how was she, for heaven's sake?"

"Oh, bonnie," he said vaguely. "Stars in her eyes, and not much to say for herself. Seems to be putting on weight."

She had to beat a precipitate retreat on that, spluttering something about having forgotten to give Phoebe the shopping list, but once the door was closed on him she took refuge in the darkest corner of the hall, where the gallery overhung a passage they used as a broom store. Once here she hugged herself, shaking with laughter that was prompted less by his innocent remark than the congenital blindness of all males, particularly those who, immersed in large concerns, prided themselves on their perspicacity.

8

Landfall

GILES had never really abandoned hope of a re-encounter. To some extent that hope ordered his approach to his comings and goings about the network in that he was aware, at the deepest level of consciousness, of a never-ending search that would set him studying the faces of pedestrians as his cab ran alongside crowded pavements. Or while his train stood at a terminus ready to leave a platform. Or when, on foot, he picked his way through the streets of provincial cities between the southern limits of Rookwood's beat in the south, and the northern outposts of Higson's territory in Perthshire.

Sometimes, catching a fleeting glimpse of a tip-tilted nose, or a shaft of lamplight alighting on a woman's neck or shoulders, his heart would miss a beat. But then, when he had taken a closer look, he would see that he was mistaken, or that his imagination was playing tricks with him, or that some conjunction of light and shadow had made a fool of him yet again.

His work, as the firm's provident society superintendent, plus complaints investigator (Adam had decided he was by far the best man to make the initial approaches in both fields) took him into every region at all seasons of the year. He seemed always to be travelling, rushing through the darkness, rattling over the skein of lines at the approach to some murky wilderness of brick, slate and stone, breathing the stale air of a growler or hansom in a traffic jam between station and depot, or between depot and customer. Only occasionally could he escape into open country to renew his old friendship with Gray, John Clare, Blake and Wordsworth. When he did it was like returning home after a period of exile and seeing a landscape through the eyes of a man revisiting scenes of childhood.

Yet he was not unhappy. His work, work that he took very seriously, absorbed him from dawn until dusk and often far into the night compiling reports on claims and missing freight, all manner of occurrences relating to employees who had suffered some injury, or gone down with a prolonged illness that entitled them to payments from the provident funds. But at night, and particularly when he was in Bryn Lovell's beat in the Mountain Square, his thoughts would return to her in a way that caused an ache under the heart. Then he would seek to cure it by concentrating on the happier memories of their association, some incident that recalled her ringing laugh, her scrambling response to some proposal he put forward, or the memory of what it was like to hold her close and inhale the scent of her hair.

He never once thought of her as dead, or even very far away and out of reach. She was always just over the horizon, waiting to be rediscovered and perhaps—who knew?—reclaimed and reassured. For he understood now that if he lived to be a hundred, and she led him a nonstop dance to the moon, he could never put her from him altogether and take some other woman for a mate. He could never begin all over again from that first impulsive kiss she had given him as a reward for her 'rescue' at Aberglaslyn.

*　　　*　　　*

The heat-wave had continued all through June and into the first days of July, day after day of brassy, blazing sunshine, with the sun moving at a snail's pace across the cobalt sky, with hardly a trailer of cloud and no breath of wind until dusk, when fugitive eddies would slip between the cliffs of warehouses and many-storied dwellings of the England the money-men had ravaged, a land that was left after the contents of fifty thousand corporation dustcarts had been emptied on the once-green farmlands and coppices of the north.

The heat hung over the Polygon like a greasy dosshouse blanket, discouraging movement, stifling creative endeavour, so that all who could dozed through it and a majority who could not counted the seconds until sunset brought about some amelioration of the stench of Catesby's beat, whither he had gone to follow up a report concerning the shipment of a marine engine off-loaded at Fleetwood and now, it appeared, missing some vital parts.

He had never previously visited this particular stretch of the Lancashire coast but had heard about it from Catesby, who had watched

Blackpool emerge from its fishing-village chrysalis to become the gaudy butterfly it was today. When his work at Fleetwood was done he moved down to the holiday centre, expecting to find a larger, noisier edition of Southend or Margate but noting at once that it had an identity of its own, with its formal esplanade, its fleets of sighing trams, its teeming beaches and uniform rows of drab, red-brick houses where bathing costumes and towels hung from window-sills, the banners of a beaten army awaiting the terms of the enemy.

He stood at a junction of roads named after half-forgotten victories won in the old Colonel's heyday, wondering why so many sought recreation in such a labyrinth of brick, asphalt and cast-iron. Crowds jostled him and he was wondering what a painter like Frith, the first man to find subject matter in such a scene, would make of this spectacle, when suddenly his eye recorded the approach of a panting dog that came slouching across the esplanade, seeking a way between the feet of a hundred idlers, most of whom were absorbed in demolishing yellow liquid that dripped from cones of ice-cream, dispensed by a stall-holder a few yards nearer the junction.

With one part of his mind he recognised the dog instantly, but with another he rejected the coincidence as monstrous. For a moment he dithered, bracing his palms against the baking brick façade of a boarding-house that occupied the corner site.

The dog was her black Labrador, Prune. There was absolutely no doubt about this for, although he acknowledged that one black Labrador looked much like another, Prune had a singular personality. He had always been an overtly fatuous dog, with the tempera-ment of a crafty but lazy clown, and his habitual expression, Giles always thought, was that of a canine police informer trading on counterfeit affability and equally counterfeit stupidity. He had a lumbering, half-hesitant walk, as though it was his business to pre-tend he wasn't going anywhere special. Indeed, the only occasion he showed animation was when Romayne rattled his feeding bowl on the kitchen floor of their holiday home at Beddgelert. In all kinds of ways Prune was a unique dog and Giles soon learned to come to terms with his uniqueness, for it explained Romayne's devotion to her pet.

He saw the dog meandering towards him and he identified it in a flash. Prune's presence meant Romayne's and for a few seconds he was so startled and so confused that he remained stock still, eyes riveted to Prune as the crowd drifted this way and that, buffeting and bewildering him in the blinding heat of the afternoon.

Then, simultaneously, three things happened. A German band struck up a mazurka. Prune found an exit through the mainstream of pedestrians and moved into Talavera Road, that ran at right-angles to the sea-front. And Romayne, in hot pursuit, passed within yards of him as he stood under the white signboard of The Balmoral.

Had it not been for the dog he would have had some difficulty in recognising her. Less than eighteen months had passed since he turned his back on her outside her father's town house in Eaton Place but the interval might have been years, so changed was her appearance. In those days she had a rosy complexion, subdued by a light tan, the result of all those months running wild in the mountains. Her glance, and her gait too, had animation and her wide, full-lipped mouth was either laughing or petulant, so that it was always possible to judge her mood by looking for puckers at the corners. The young woman crossing the road in pursuit of the dog was nothing like the lively girl he remembered so vividly and with so much affection, despite their bitter parting. Her shoulders were bowed and she was much thinner about the face. Her complexion was pale, with no sign of pinkness or tan but a pallor that suggested she had spent the intervening months indoors. Her expression was neither gay, mischievous nor sulky. It was what he would have described as wooden, reminding him sharply of his sister Stella's depression when she was between husbands, and the memory of this, as much as the shock of seeing the deterioration, aroused in him a sharp pang of compassion. His instinct was to call out to her, to put his arm about her and comfort her in some way but the German band's eruption prevented any such gesture. The moment the brass began to blare the tempo of everyone about him changed, idlers converging on the bandstand from all sides so that he was swept halfway across the esplanade. Before he could extricate himself and regain the junction she had disappeared.

He went tearing down the street and was just in time to see her and Prune pass through an iron gate giving access to one of the featureless houses some way down on the left-hand side, and when he drew level with it he saw that it was a boarding-house, with dingy lace curtains and an immense aspidistra occupying the central bay of the room facing the street. By then he had checked the impulse to hail her, reasoning that any reunion would be best achieved in private. The boarding-house had a 'Full' notice on a grubby card set in the fanlight.

He stood there riding out the shock, aware of a dampness under his arms and at his temples that was not caused by the glare of the sun or the airlessness of the street. And then, before he could collect his thoughts, she came out again, walking swiftly, turning inland towards the main shopping centre and disappearing in a matter of seconds around the first corner.

There was no immediate urgency. He knew now where she lived and could make some kind of attempt to examine his emotions and discover how they related to the prospect of presenting himself and perhaps making a fresh start with a girl who looked, for all the world, a complete stranger to the Romayne of Beddgelert and Eaton Place. He sauntered back to the sea-front, entered a crowded café and ordered a pot of tea, surprised to discover that his heart was still hammering at his ribs and that the entire scene of the town at the height of what was apparently a Wakes Week had a curious insubstantiality, as though it was the backdrop of a dream. He noticed tiny, inconsequential actions that had no meaning and seemed to be performed by automata. A blowsy woman giving change. A tired waitress swaying under the weight of a pyramid of dirty crockery. A middle-aged man in a tilted boater laughing and showing gold-plugged teeth and pink gums. He thought, desperately, "What the devil am I doing here drinking stewed tea now that I've found her? How could I leave here without knowing how she was and whether she has been able to put me out of mind, in a way I've never been able to do with her . . . ?" and at last he jumped up, paid his bill and almost ran from the café to the house in Talavera Road. Without giving himself time to reflect he pulled the bell-chain that set off a discordant jangle somewhere at the far end of the passage.

The landlady took her time answering. When she appeared she was a stringy woman in her fifties, wearing a plain dress of bombazine, hung about with a variety of heavy, jangling accessories that included jet earrings and pince-nez glasses slung on a gun-metal chain. Her irritable expression faded when she had had a chance to look him up and down. She said, "I'm sorry, sir. I've nothing, not even a share-up. It's Wakes Week, you see—Rochdale an' Burnley. You'd think they'd plan it better, wouldn't you? The on'y thing I can suggest is . . ."

But he said, touching his hat, "It wasn't a room, ma'am. I wondered if I could talk to you a moment about one of your guests."

At once the woman's eyes narrowed, indicating hostility and she said, crisply, "Police?"

"No, no . . . nothing like that. It's just that I thought I recognised someone I knew, an old friend. My name is Swann—here's my card —and the person I'm referring to is a young lady, Miss Rycroft."

She took the card and studied it carefully.

"Swann the removal people?"

"Yes."

The woman moistened her lips. "A Miss Rycroft, you said?"

"Yes."

"No one here by that name."

"But I saw her come in here. She had a dog, a black Labrador."

The woman's expression changed again. She smiled and for some reason looked relieved as she returned his card. "Oh, *her!* She's not called Rycroft, or not so far as I know. You mean Miss Mostyn."

"She might use that name. It was her mother's. Look, could I come in? It's important and I . . . I've an important message for her. I've got to see her as soon as she comes back."

"She won't be back, not until Sunday between chapel services. She doesn't stay here. Just the dog."

"The dog?"

"Come inside. It's rude to keep a gentleman like you on the doorstep. I'm sorry, it's just that I'm fair clemmed up this week and don't know which way to turn," and she led him into a passage that smelled strongly of linoleum and boiled cabbage, motioning him into the room with the drab curtains and the aspidistra.

"Take a seat. Over there's the most comfortable," and she indicated a leather armchair, the only one in a room stuffed with furniture and bric-a-brac, a place that was obviously off limits to boarders, for it had a fusty, unused smell. A dozen or so studio portraits of relatives, framed in fumed oak, crowded the walls, and assorted ornaments, dominated by a blue and gold Staffordshire group of Victoria and Albert in Highland dress, stood on the draped mantelshelf.

"Look, I don't want to seem inquisitive but I'm thinking I've a duty to a girl who pays me seven shillings a week to board a dog and never gave me the least trouble. If you know her, and you saw her come in an hour since, why didn't you step up and say how-do-you-do?"

His experience handling diffident and evasive clerks and employees' dependants came into play. He said, sizing her up, "I really don't see why I shouldn't confide in you, Mrs. . . . ?"

"Rawson," she said. "I'm a widow. That's Rawson up there," and she waved a heavily ringed hand at a pop-eyed man in a Derby hat standing half-sideways and glaring down at them, his hand on a plaster pedestal in a manner that implied he had just discovered the North Pole and was proud of it.

"Miss Rycroft . . . Mostyn, and I were engaged to be married until the spring of last year. We quarrelled and she ran away when I broke it off. I don't think even her father knows where she is or what she's doing. I haven't set eyes on her since. Nobody has and naturally I feel responsible."

She said, her eyes meeting his with bafflement but intense curiosity. "That card you gave me. Is the gaffer o' that great concern a relation of yours?"

"My father. I work for him."

"*Your father!* Good grief!"

"Why should you be so surprised, Mrs. Rawson?"

"Why shouldn't I? That lass works as a pay-desk clerk at Birley and Cookson's, the drapers. My guess is she gets under fifteen shillings a week, plus board. Why is she at a place like that if she's the kind of girl who hobnobbed with young gentlemen of your standing?"

"Romayne works in a draper's?"

"Aye, and a sorry place it is from all I'm told. None o' those living-in cribs are what you'd call home from home, but yon Birley's a real slavedriver, for all his chapel-going. I wouldn't work there, not unless I had to, I can tell you that, Mr. Swann. It's no business of mine, of course, but if there are no hard feelings, and you were once that friendly, get her a place where she can live out and feed

739

up. Slops, Birley feeds 'em, and she's proof of it. She's not so bonnie as when she first came here."

"When was that, Mrs. Rawson?"

"Getting on for a year now. Early autumn of last year. She showed up with a chit from Mrs. Corbie—she's next door but one, and shuts between seasons. Wanted somewhere to leave that dog and offered me a shilling a day, if you please. I thought it was daft and I still do, with her earning next to nothing, but she's attached to the old rascal and I know how it is. I had my cat Sam fifteen years before he got run over by the watercart. I never cared to get another after that."

"But when does she ever see the dog, Mrs. Rawson?"

"When? Twice a week. On her half-day, which is today, Thursday. After three-thirty, that is. Trust that skinflint to hold 'em to the minimum. And Sundays, after chapel, same as I said. All Birley's girls have to attend his chapel or they're turned off, make no mistake."

"Has she ever talked to you, told you about herself?"

"Precious little. She's a strange lass. Offered her many a feed, I have but when she's accepted she's only pecked at it. Never seen her smile either. Not that she's got much to smile about down at Birley and Cookson's." She hesitated again. "I don't know as I should be telling you all this. She's never let on, as we say up here, and keeps herself to herself. She did tell me she had a hard time getting a billet, having no experience or character, but she's ladylike and that'll be why Birley took her. He's got a good class of trade, you see, so it pays him to be particular!"

His mind juggled clumsily with the factors in the woman's story as Mrs. Rawson ran on, outwardly with a show of reluctance but inwardly with a relish that was rooted, no doubt, in her burning curiosity concerning someone who would pay half her weekly wage to board a dog she saw twice a week. On the face of it the situation seemed monstrous, a girl with a millionaire father hiring herself out to a tight-fisted bully for fifteen shillings a week, and submitting to all the humiliations that attended servitude at any of these establishments. His mind returned to that tongue-lashing he had given her in the cab, the last evening they spent together. She had admitted then to knowing nothing of the conditions under which most people were required to work and had seemed, on reflection, quite shocked by his brutal summary. There would be difficulties getting a situation without a trade and without references, but she could have managed better than this, even if she was determined not to apply to her father. She could have been a governess or a companion, and the sale of her jewellery and clothes would have kept her in comfort for a long time. There was something here that he did not understand and he had an uncomfortable certainty that it related, in some way, to him and to her father's wealth. He said, suddenly, "Look here, Mrs. Rawson, I think she's doing this out of pique. I mean to talk her round and send her back home. If I succeed could she stop here overnight? I'd gladly pay you a sovereign."

"A sovereign? Nay, lad, there's no call to do that, for she'll have to bed down on cushions in here." She smiled a tired but knowing smile. "Aye, if I can help out I will. You've come looking for her, haven't you?"

"I've been looking for her for sixteen months, Mrs. Rawson. Although I don't think I was really aware of it until today. Since it's her half-day where would I likely find her?"

"I can tell you that. At her quarters, for where else could she go on her money? It's a big place, five minutes from the tram terminus. You can't miss it. The staff entrance is at the side. A good view of the gasworks, she told me once. But even then she said it with a straight face."

He thanked her and left. The heat was beginning to go from the day but the air was stale and full of dust, rising from the baking pavements like vapour over a marsh. He found the place easily enough and went down a cul-de-sac between high brick walls. A door marked 'Employees only—private' stood ajar and he passed through to find himself at the foot of an iron staircase, giving access to narrow corridors. It reminded him uncomfortably of a prison he had visited at Knutsford recently whilst seeking information from a former employee. Even on an evening such as this there was a bleakness about the place and it struck him that it must be a cheerless lodging in winter. A persistent sound came from a room on the ground-floor, the soft, uncertain plucking of a banjo, played by an earnest amateur. The banjoist was trying to play the air of 'Allan Water' and the melancholy song seemed to Giles a perfect accompaniment for the setting. He knocked and the music stopped at once. Hesitant steps approached the door that opened a few inches and a youth about nineteen stared at him through the chink.

"Yes, sir?"

The young man, whoever he was, seemed scared, as though anticipating a rebuke connected with his banjo-playing, or possibly on account of his appearance. His grubby shirt was open at the neck and his soiled cuffs were attached to shortened sleeves by threads of elastic.

"I'm looking for a young lady who works here, a Miss Mostyn. I wondered if you could show me her room?"

The young man now looked quite terrified. "Her *room*? You . . . you mean to *visit* her? To go up to the girls' dormitory? You couldn't possibly do that, sir. She'd be sacked on the spot and so would I for not reporting you to Mrs. Pedlar."

"Who's Mrs. Pedlar?"

"The housekeeper, sir. Young ladies' followers aren't even allowed in the shop, much less inside the crib."

"Where could I find this Mrs. Pedlar?"

"You can't, she's out."

"Well, then, since she's out I'll give you half-a-crown to tell me how I can get a word with Miss Mostyn. You can come along with me if you're not prepared to take me on trust."

The youth washed his hands. Giles had seen this gesture performed by male assistants in shops of every kind and it had always struck him as rather comic. It did not seem comic now but abject and pitiful. He said, taking a coin from his pocket, "You don't have to tell me anything. Just nod, or shake your head. Is it one floor above here?"

The youth shook his head.

"Two?"

The youth nodded.

"Left or right at the stairhead?"

The youth lifted his left shoulder an inch, and then, pocketing the coin, whipped back into his room and slammed the door.

Giles went up two flights of iron stairs to a long corridor that ran left and right from an uncurtained window. Through the dust-coated glass he could see the gasometer, silhouetted against an orange sky. The place seemed empty and silent. Only one door, also ajar, broke the long expanse of the facing wall to the left and he approached it, pausing on the threshold and peering through the crack into an austere high-ceilinged dormitory, containing about a dozen beds, each fitted with a deal locker. Despite the brilliant sunset outside the light was bad up here and already the big room was in half-shadow. There were two sash windows, each half-obscured by cheap, dun-coloured curtains. A strip of coconut matting ran between the iron cots but the floor spaces were bare boards. On top of each locker was a case or grip of one kind or another and at the far end was a fixed plank, supporting a row of washbasins and ewers.

He did not see her at once. She was sitting by the furthermost window, looking out over a wide expanse of roofs that lay between the butt end of the building and the great, grey gasometer that brooded over this part of the town. There was a book open on her lap but she was not reading. Instead there was a kind of listless repose about the way she held herself, as though the preceding hours had drained the dregs of her energy and expectations. He had a conviction that if the landscape below had erupted like Pompeii she would have continued to sit there, watching and waiting, with no wish to do more than witness the catastrophe. Her demeanour indicated nothing beyond mute acceptance, as though she had come to terms with every probability, including the Apocalypse.

It cost him a great effort to intrude upon her thoughts, whatever they were. More than a minute passed before he could nerve himself to advance into the room when the sound of his footfall on the boards caused her to turn her head. He saw her stiffen, saw her blink half a dozen times, then raise one hand and pass it slowly across her brow, as though she found it impossible to believe what her senses recorded.

He said, hoarsely, "It's all right, Romayne . . . it's me . . . Giles. I've come for you. Come on home, dearest," but she continued to hold herself rigid and stare fixedly at him, just as though he had been a ghost.

He crossed to her then and took her hand, finding it cold and unresponsive. He said, "It isn't a miracle, and I didn't hunt you down. It was pure coincidence. I was up here on business and saw

743

Prune and then you. I watched you go into Mrs. Rawson's. I don't know what you're doing here but whatever it is it's over. I won't have you living like this, in this awful place . . ."

But then, at last, she spoke, speaking his name in a low voice and with a note of query.

"Giles?"

He was sorry he had been so impulsive. It would have been wiser, perhaps, to have written and asked her to meet him somewhere. Or demand some explanation from her employers as to what she was doing here and what, if anything, she had told them about her identity. The shock of stealing up on her in that way seemed to have stunned her. She let the book fall and he stooped to pick it up, noting that it was a paper-backed edition of Tennyson's *Idylls of the King*. It told him something, not much, but enough to see her presence here as a kind of penance, lifting the corner of a curtain on one of the root causes of their incompatibility, for he had often nagged her to read verses that he himself loved. He saw, however, that she was in no kind of state for an involved discussion of any kind and said, authoritatively, "Get your things together. You're getting out of here. Tonight. *Now.*"

She stood uncertainly. "That isn't possible . . . Mr. Birley . . ."

"Damn Birley. You don't owe Birley a wave of the hand. I've heard all about him and his kind and I'm not leaving you here. Get your things."

"There's Mrs. Pedlar, the housekeeper . . . If I'm missing they'll notify the police . . . One of the girls ran off and there was a great commotion . . ."

"I'll pay Mrs. Pedlar the compliment of telling her where you've gone and why. Is this your locker and bag?"

She nodded and he swung the grip down and opened the locker. There was very little inside. A shop dress, a pair of shoes worn through the soles, a pair of black woollen stockings, some clean underclothes and a workbox with its hinges broken. As he stuffed the box into the bag its lid fell off and he caught a glimpse of a bundle of his own letters, together with some sixpenny editions of anthologies.

She seemed incapable of making the smallest decision but stood by, neither helping nor hindering him. But when he snapped the bag shut she said, looking along the row of empty beds, "I would have liked to have said goodbye. They were wonderful people, Giles." Somehow the remark told him more about her pilgrimage than anything he had learned so far. He kissed her, saying, "You can write to them. As soon as we're married."

He had the impression then that she wanted to re-open the inquest on their relationship, perhaps harking back to all they had said to one another during that final confrontation in Eaton Place, but he gave her no chance, sensing that the only way to prise her loose from this dismal place was by giving her no choice in the matter. He took the bag in one hand, her hand in the other and led the way out on to the landing.

From the stairwell the hesitant melody of 'Allan Water' could be heard, as though the youth with the grubby cuffs was playing to keep his courage up. He said, "Wait one minute," and setting down the bag took out one of his cards and a pocket diary containing a pencil. Using the banister rail as a rest he tore a page loose and wrote, "*Mrs. Pedlar. Please accept this as Miss Mostyn's notice and inform Mr. Birley that she left in my charge. Any further communication between us can be conducted through my firm. Faithfully, Giles Swann.*" After a moment's reflection he added, "*I think you should know Miss Mostyn's father is Sir Clive Rycroft-Mostyn, the well-known industrialist, also that she is my fiancée and her father is aware of this.*"

He found a paper clip attached to some correspondence in his wallet and clipped card and note together. At the foot of the stairs he knocked on the same door and again the music stopped abruptly but this time there was no movement inside the room. He went in, finding a smaller dormitory, almost identically furnished, if furnished was the word. The youth, now wearing a collar and jacket, was sitting on his bed beside an open window. He said, "Give this to Mrs. Pedlar the moment she comes in. Say that you tried to stop me and if they ask questions I'll back you up."

"It don't matter what I say I'd get the push," and he locked his hands behind his back, as though to touch the note would involve him in irretrievable ruin.

"Listen, you must have heard of Swann-on-Wheels, the carriers?"

"Yes, but . . ."

"If you're sacked come to me at this address. I'll find you a job and it'll be a damned sight better job than you've lost. I'm Swann's son, Giles Swann. Now take the note."

He took it, handling it as though it would bite and laying it down very carefully on the top of his locker. Giles thought he had never seen a human being look more desperate as he said, "That's a promise, Mr. Swann?" and when Giles said it was, "Then I'll do it. She never really belonged here, not with people like us. We all knew that." He called, through the open door, "Good luck, Miss Mostyn. Run for it!"

He piloted her into the stifling alleyway, then down to the tram terminus and through the side streets to Talavera Road. With his free hand he held her arm above the elbow. She said nothing, walking like someone in a trance.

*   *   *

Mrs. Rawson had made ready for her. Cold supper was laid on the parlour table and from some attic or cupboard she had excavated a battered truckle bed, pushing the chairs back to clear a space on the hearthrug. Prune was there, lying with his head between extended paws, and when Romayne came in he wagged his tail but did not rise. She sat down and patted him absently as Mrs. Rawson said, "I saved you some supper. Make her eat it, Mr. Swann. She needs fattening up. I'll bring cocoa later, when the others are back. Where are you booked in, Mr. Swann?"

"Nowhere," he said, "I was only passing through. I'll get a room at one of the hotels."

"You won't. There isn't a bed in the town. I could let that old truckle ten times over."

"Then I'll stay here, with Miss Rycroft, if you'll permit it."

She hesitated, common sense and compassion doing battle with her notions of propriety. Finally she said, "All right then. You're a gentleman, I can see that," and went out.

Very slowly, like a wax figure in a peepshow coming to life, the extreme rigidity of her posture relaxed. A trace of colour came back to her cheeks and finally, after making what seemed to Giles a tremendous effort, she smiled. He said, "Mrs. Rawson's right. Try and eat something," and was encouraged when she got up, crossed over

746

and sat at the table, picking up knife and fork and nibbling at the edge of a slice of steak pie. Prune, true to form, rose at the rattle of cutlery, stretched himself, and moved over beside her, lowering his head on her lap and turning his mournful eyes upward. She said, without looking at the dog, "He kept me sane. It was a kind of link. Can you understand that?"

"Yes," he said, "that's easy to understand."

She went on eating, slowly but determinedly, and when Mrs. Rawson came in with two cups of cocoa she took the drink and sat musing, her hands clasped round the mug as though the temperature in the room had been below zero instead of in the seventies. A muted uproar reached them from unseen areas of the house, feet stumping on floors, children crying, men calling out in strong Lancashire accents, a high-pitched laugh that ended in a spluttering cough. Still they sat in silence over the ruins of the meal, the dog waiting for the occasional piece of crust that Romayne popped into its mouth. She fed Prune without looking at him. Her thoughts seemed to be concentrated on something outside the range of their present circumstance. He said nothing to prompt her. Instinct told him that a resolution, of one kind or another, would have to originate from her.

At last she said, in a quiet, level voice, "I couldn't begin again, Giles. Not without telling you, not without your knowing. That would be an unforgivable thing to do."

"There's no need to go into it now. You're shocked and tired. We've got the rest of our lives to talk."

"*No!* That was how it was last time. I won't go through that again."

"You love me?"

"More than ever."

"Well, then, there's nothing more to be said. I'll never let you go again."

"I think you might. Most men would, if they knew."

"Knew what?"

"What I'm really like. Or was when we were to be married. I'm not talking about running away but—other things, things that happened before I met you."

He began, dimly, to understand. The crazy segments of their

erratic association began to make some kind of pattern. He said, "Whatever it is, now isn't the time. Later . . ."

"*No, Giles!*"

She was suddenly very emphatic. Her vagueness, that he had half-mistaken for a kind of drowsiness due to shock and despair, left her. A little more colour came back to her cheeks and there was something of the girl he remembered in the way she jerked herself up and thumped the table so that the crockery rattled.

"Well, then, tell me if you have to."

She faced him. Prune, sensing he was unlikely to get more scraps, lumbered away and flopped down on the hearthrug, head between paws, eyes still watchful.

"It's about the kind of person I am—was. If you'd known you wouldn't have wanted me. No man would, except as a woman he could . . . use!"

He could see the tremendous effort it was costing her to say this but all it did was to increase his compassion to a point where he wanted to hold her close, stifling anything she felt impelled to say.

"I know about all that. Your father told me."

The disciplines of the drapery trade had left their imprint on her. She was able to absorb this without a great deal of difficulty. He saw her throat muscles contract as she swallowed. Her glance, that had been level with his, dropped.

"Father told you? About Gilpin, the groom who thrashed me? About Mr. Bellocq, and that manservant, Dodge?"

"All of them. It was then I decided I could never work for him."

"Well?"

"It doesn't matter."

"Three lovers before I was eighteen and you say it doesn't matter? It *must* matter. I was only fifteen when . . ."

"It doesn't. I love you more than anyone in the world. We can get married at once. I'll take you to my sister-in-law and my grandfather in Manchester. We can be there by noon tomorrow and I'll make all the arrangements."

She began to cry, very quietly and without altering the level posture of her head so that the tears ran a straight course down her cheeks, dropping from her long jawline and splashing on to the backs of hands folded on her lap. She let them fall unchecked.

After a minute or so he took his handkerchief and passed it to her. It was soiled with sweat he had wiped from his forehead earlier in the afternoon, when he had pursued her and Prune across the esplanade. She pulled herself together as he knew she would, sniffing a little and dabbing her eyes. "That's the first time since the night I tried to buy the hat. There were plenty of times when it would have helped but you can't cry to order. That's another thing I found out."

Her defencelessness, so manifest and so childlike, was terrible to watch. And yet, in a way, it drew them closer with every passing second.

He said, "Why the drapery trade? You must have known it was the worst of all. Why not one of those posts for a governess or a companion that people advertise for in the Home Journals?"

"It wouldn't have been the same."

"The same as what?"

"That Welsh girl, the one who refused to serve me and then fainted."

"You're saying you deliberately inflicted this kind of life upon yourself *because* of her? Because of what I said that time?"

"Not entirely . . . that was what prompted me, but there was much more than that. It was the only way to find out. To really find out."

"About people like her, about those other girls in Birley's dormitory and that poor devil with the banjo?"

"In a way. But even that isn't all the answer."

"Tell me then."

She got up and went over to the armchair, seating herself on the arm and beginning, in some indefinable way, to recapture a little of the vivid personality he remembered.

"To find out why people like you cared. Why you were interested enough to care. Without understanding that, there was no real hope of belonging to you as I wanted to belong, ever since the first minute I talked to you that morning at Aberglaslyn. Does that sound silly? Something I've made myself believe?"

"No."

Neither did it. Somewhere—it might take him years to define— but somewhere behind this extravagant, exculpatory gesture was logic of a kind he had never hoped to find in her, or in anyone like her. It made up for so many things. For her wildness, perverseness, selfishness and promiscuity; for all the wearisome dances she had led him over the past four years; for inhuman calculating machines like her father and Birley the draper; for all the injustice and ignorance and stupidity he had encountered since that day he had stood on the grass verge outside a labourer's cottage at Twyforde Green and watched an aged, ailing couple evicted and despatched to separate workhouses like old slaves being sold down the river. It gave him not merely hope but an access of strength and courage, for it surely followed that if she could set herself to learn then anybody could. Even her father. Even Mr. Birley, who housed his staff like convicts, fed them on slops, and sacked them for not using their one rest day to worship in his tin tabernacle.

He said, "You must have learned a very great deal. Far more than I. More than anyone like me could learn. Books can't teach you that kind of thing and what you've learned I'll learn from you. Go to sleep now. I'll pull up another chair and make do with a shake-down. I should take your dress off. You'll be too hot to sleep if you don't."

He moved into the window bay and drew the calico blinds and when one of them flew up again he heard a sharp brittle sound that made him swing round. She was laughing and said, through her laughter, "It's a kind of honeymoon, Giles. Unhook me, there's a dear."

He unhooked her, stooping to kiss the back of her neck. She reached up and seized his hands, pulling them down and pressing them hard against her breasts. Her hands, he noticed, were warm again.

The touch did more than anything else to clarify his complex feelings concerning her essential place in his life, if it was to be the life he had contemplated in happier days and not the drab, day-to-day existence that had been his ever since he had turned on his heel in Eaton Place. He had to make a decision for both of them then, whether to claim her here and now, in this stuffy, cluttered room, or exercise an entirely different kind of restraint from that of the past, when she had done her utmost to make him run contrary to his instincts concerning their association. He wanted her most desperately but not solely in the physical sense. He wanted to exorcise any lingering doubt in her mind that they had somehow attained new levels in their awareness of one another as man, woman and, above all, comrades. Her insistence that possession of her could achieve this did not seem extravagant and fanciful now but logical and necessary, so that he was on the point of telling her this between kisses when his eye met the steady gaze of the late Mr. Rawson, staring down at them from his fumed oak frame over the mantel. Then, most improbably, humour took a hand, the kind of humour that had never been absent from their relationship and had played its part in repairing so many ruptures up to the moment of their parting. He said, kissing her lightly, "Not here. Not in front of Rawson," and magically she laughed, the familiar dancing light returning to her eyes as she looked from him to Rawson and back again. She withdrew from him then, sitting and unlacing her dusty boots. Through a threadbare patch in the blind he watched a last gleam of evening sunshine light on a copper curl behind her ear. He left her to get into bed, gathering the crockery and cutlery from the table and taking it out into the narrow passage.

9

Adam in a Holly Bush

BETWEEN the posts, when one sheaf of correspondence had been reviewed, annotated, mulled over and either consigned to the waste-paper basket or tossed into Tybalt's tray, Adam would sometimes spare an hour or so to make an objective survey of that other family of his, the British tribe, in whose concerns he was still involved although he had no means of regulating them other than by writing letters to *The Times* and his Member of Parliament.

He would see British concerns as extra-European. That is to say, in no way related to the junketings of other tribes across the Channel and the Atlantic, but this did not mean he ignored what was occurring elsewhere. On the contrary, he regarded foreign news columns in the stack of newspapers he read each day, as his light relief, a splodge of jam on the rice pudding of relevant, national affairs.

The post had been exceptionally light that morning, so that by ten thirty he was free to turn to his newspapers. He read first of the continuing dock strike over what they were calling 'The Dockers' Tanner', telling himself he knew precisely how it would end. The dockers would get their tanner, and the furore would evaporate, with the fire-eating Ben Tillett, organiser of the dockers' union, getting himself canonised. Just like old Tom Paine. Just like Sam Bamford of Peterloo fame, the Tolpuddle Martyrs, and all the other saints in John Catesby's calendar. All of which was only one more shred of evidence that he, Adam Swann, had been more prescient than others when he started out in business, writing his labour force into the order book as an ally, not a potential liability to be set against profits.

He read a thousand words or so of the interminable Parnell Commission wrangle, making a private bet with himself that the Irish leader would come out of it unscathed and be judicially vindicated of complicity in the Phoenix Park murders. Lately he had come to regard Ireland as a fractious near-relative all but excluded from the inner councils of the tribe and occupying, say, the position of an alien who had acquired the protection of the flag but did not regard it as a privilege.

His Irish concerns were prospering under that saucy young spark, Jack-o'-Lantern, who had run away with his daughter, following a seduction that Henrietta obstinately refused to acknowledge. But Adam never viewed his Irish bridgehead with the permanence he attached to regions like the Polygon and the Western Wedge. Sooner or later the Irish would hive off and seek their own way to perdition, and the sooner the better so far as he was concerned. Their affairs had a habit of clouding all manner of more important issues at Westminster and claiming too much space in the national journals.

After reading that the Act of Parliament to prevent cruelty to children was at last on the Statute Book he turned with relief to European affairs, much as a man stirs his coffee after enjoying three courses of solid fare. There was a column and a half dealing with the frightful clamour aroused in the Habsburg capital over the death, by shooting, of the Austrian Crown Prince Rudolf and his eighteen-year-old mistress, Marie Vetsera, in January. The handling of this affair, he thought, was typical of methods employed by foreigners when something went awry in high places. Unable to face the music they at once worked themselves into a lather in egregious attempts to lie their way out of the social and diplomatic consequences. He could spare sympathy for that bewhiskered old pedant, Franz Josef. At least the old chap was showing remarkable staying power, concerning the troubles that rained down upon him year by year, but he had no patience at all with the official versions that were being leaked by palace flunkeys. The fate that had overtaken Rudolf was predictable, a young man enmeshed in a tangle of protocol and given nothing constructive to do whilst waiting around for his father to die. Rudolf, clearly, had killed the girl and then himself and that was that. What on earth was gained by all this drivel about accidents and terrorists and assassination by Hungarian nationalists? Nobody was likely to miss a Habsburg. There were more than enough of them to go round.

He studied the faces of the leading players in the tragedy, finding in Rudolf's features the pop-eyed blankness he found in portraits of all highly-placed Continentals. Inbreeding was the trouble, of course, and it was even beginning to show over here. But there it was, these royal popinjays were scared stiff of new blood, preferring to entail their physical and psychological weakness as if they were priceless heirlooms. He found the portrait of the girl more interesting. A sensual little partridge with her rounded face, dark fringe, soulful eyes and well-developed bust. He could understand a rake like Rudolf finding pleasure in her and made a mental note to show the newspaper to Henrietta as soon as she returned home. It was the kind of story that would interest her more than Ben Tillett's tanner.

He read an item dealing with Italy's protectorate over Ethiopia, reflecting that the Italians were welcome to that slice of the African continent. The British had been there twenty years ago and had come away again, and the British never did that if there was anything worth having. Portugal was losing its grip on Brazil, he noticed, and this too was to be expected. You couldn't hold on to an empire of that size without sea power, of a kind that Portugal had once had but had no longer. He turned to news from Paris, noting that the French were going to extraordinary lengths to ensure that no one overlooked the centenary of the fall of the Bastille come July. Well, much good had come of *that* fracas in the long run. After a hundred years of street riots and short-lived autocracies and republics they were still, to his way of thinking as politically immature as England about the time of Magna Carta. Gouty old Louis and his tribe of pensioners were said to have learned nothing and forgotten nothing when they returned from exile during his father's youth and this applied to the French as a tribe. They still made a practice of solving their problems with brickbats and there was precious little evidence of the famous Gallic logic one heard so much about. Gustave Eiffel's tower interested him, however, and he told himself he would take a look at it if he ever went to Paris again, which was very unlikely. He was getting more and more insular these days, less and less inclined to try anything new. Tybalt, confound the man, was always urging him to become a subscriber to the new London telephone exchange but he resisted the old clerk's importunities. It was the kind of innovation Old George would have installed within days of settling in here. But George, it seemed, was lost to him, so the new telephone could wait upon whoever succeeded him as managing director.

He was still thinking ruefully of George when the speaking tube whistled and he lifted the mouthpiece, learning that he had a lady visitor who was on her way upstairs, without so much as a by-your-leave. It must be Edith Wickstead, he thought, or maybe the newly-married Debbie. They were the only two women Tybalt would pass on without his permission.

When the door opened, however, and he rose stiffly to his feet, angling his tin leg round the corner of the desk, he saw that it was neither Edith nor Debbie, but his Austrian daughter-in-law, Gisela, and this, he thought, was odd, seeing that he had been thinking of George at that precise moment. He welcomed her, however, for he had always liked Gisela, ever since that impulsive son of his had brought her back from the Danube, along with all those crates containing his infernal machine. Gisela, to his mind, was all that a wife should be. She was pretty, shapely, mild-mannered and dutiful, so that sometimes he thought George didn't deserve her, and should have married someone like Alex's Lydia, who would have tossed that machine of his in the dustbin.

She said, with a shy smile, "Do I disturb you, Father? Is it convenient?" and he said, motioning her to a chair, that it was not only convenient, but that he was delighted to see her looking so well and pretty.

She blushed at the compliment but he saw that it pleased her, telling himself that she did not get all that many. George would reserve all his gallantry for the gizzards of that damned machine. He said, eagerly, "Are you on your way to 'Tryst'? Hetty will be happy to see you, my dear," but she said she was not and had made arrangements to catch the afternoon train back to Manchester, having promised the children she would be home in time for supper.

"Ah, then," he said, with a touch of masculine patronage, "it will be shopping, no doubt, although I had the impression you made your own clothes, except for special occasions. Don't tell me George leads a social life up there for I wouldn't believe you. Would you care for some coffee? I brew it myself and can recommend it."

She said gravely that she would enjoy a cup of his coffee and he set about making it on his stove, noting as he did so that she seemed more than a little nervous. She had always been diffident and had needed, Hetty would say, 'bringing on a little', but there was more than natural shyness in her manner today. She sat primly on the edge of his visitor's chair, her neat little hands fidgeting with her gloves, her face frozen in a smile that had to be kept there by will-power.

She said, carefully, "I came to confer with you, Father. George does not know I am here. I think he would be much displeased if he found out. I would be happy if you would promise not to inform him."

He liked her quaint, didactic English, and the pretty, lisping accent she had never succeeded in discarding. Handing her the coffee he decided he liked everything about her and that she qualified as his favourite daughter-in-law. Lydia, Alex's doughty wife, was all right in her way but she reminded him of the tubby daughters of the regiment he had been compelled to squire in India during his mercenary days. Romayne Rycroft, that madcap Giles had married in such a hurry last autumn, was very fetching, and said to be tamed, but a girl who had run out on her wedding, and had to be rescued from a draper's sweatshop in Blackpool, was surely capable of anything. He did not wholly credit Giles' assurances that she had done this crazy thing with a specific purpose in mind—that of discovering how the poor lived, if you please!

When he had resettled himself at the desk he said, trying to prompt her a little, "Is it about George, my dear? You want my advice on something?" and at that she looked flustered but replied, after a pause, "Yes, indeed. Or perhaps not advice. What is the word I seek? 'Alliance'?"

"Co-operation," he suggested and she nodded eagerly.

"That machine of his, the one my Uncle Max gave him. After two years' toil it is ready. He is about to try it on the road. At a place near Altrincham, in Cheshire."

She spoke, he thought, remarkably good English, even though Altrincham emerged as 'Alshingham', and Cheshire as 'Seshire'. It must be difficult, he reflected, for the girl to get her pretty little tongue round these English place-names. An English girl would have made heavier going of, say, 'Szeged' or 'Ischl'.

She went on, with a rush, "I would much like for you to be there, father. No, no—" as he opened his mouth to protest, "not for him to see but as a spy. Is that right? 'Spy'?"

"Hardly," he said, chuckling, and now thoroughly intrigued. "I think you mean as an observer. An uninvited guest, who keeps out of the way. Behind a hedge, for instance."

She clapped her hands like a child. "Ach, yes! That is what I came here to say! That is very much how I would like it!"

"You came all the way to London without George's permission to ask me that?"

She nodded, her eyes sparkling with excitement or pleasure. She really was an extraordinary girl and suddenly he felt very drawn to her, and very sorry for her too, in a way. It must have demanded a great deal of resolution to bring her to the point of coming here as a secret advocate of the boy. He said, thoughtfully, "How can you be sure he wouldn't regard this as a piece of unwarranted interference on my part and yours? He's a hot-headed chap, as obstinate as the pigs in Ireland as we say here. He might be very angry with you for suggesting it."

"Perhaps," she said, giving him the impression that this prospect did not bother her overmuch, "but I was determined to ask you, nevertheless. This . . . this quarrel between you. It is very stupid. It makes me unhappy. You too, I think."

"Ah," he said, grumpily, "that's neither here nor there. The point is, how does George regard it?"

She was more at ease now and had stopped fidgeting. "He is unhappy, too. He loves you very much. He has much respect for you, I think. It is just that he is . . . how did you say? Like an Irish pig?"

"Not exactly," he said, chuckling, "but you've got his measure and that isn't surprising. You should have by now." He went off at a tangent. "You get along well, don't you? As man and wife, I mean."

She drew herself erect and it struck him he had touched her pride. "George is a genius," she said. "Uncle Max was a genius too, and he understood George from the beginning."

"But I didn't?"

"It is more difficult for a father. You see him still as a little boy, I think."

He pondered this for a moment. Did he? Not really, for somehow George had never qualified as a little boy, or not in the manner of Alex, Hugo and Edward. In a way, in a very different way, he was closer to Giles, someone who had skipped the intervening stages between infancy and a sort of precocious maturity. But in George's case development seemed to have stopped at around twenty, so that he remained an intelligent youth, with a youth's lack of balance. He said, "Where is this test to be? Precisely, I mean. Could you show me on that map?" and he pointed to the wall-map of the Polygon.

She got up and crossed the room, standing back with her little blonde head on one side as she studied the Lancastrian and Cheshire complex, drawn up by him so long ago and overwritten, here and there, with all manner of markings in red and blue pencil. She pointed to a spot two or three miles west of Altrincham, where the river Bollin wound its way across the plain. There were one or two villages marked alongside the railway and one of these, where her finger rested, was called Dunham.

"Here," she said, authoritatively, "between here and a farm a mile along the road. I have listened to his discussions with Grandfather Sam and the engine that has already been taken there. It is against the law, of course, but George, and Grandfather too, make their own laws. The spot was chosen because it was secluded and level. It is to be very early in the morning, as soon as it is light. The crates went there by rail and are being assembled in one of the barns. They have measured a mile and will make two journeys, one to the station and one back to the farm. It is planned for next Friday, three days from now, and I wish very much for you to witness it. Then I will have done my part and will be satisfied. Will you do this small thing for me?"

It was impossible to refuse her, even if he had been inclined to, and he was not. The stratagem appealed to his sense of fun and adventure. The very idea of lying in ambush, and watching Old George try out his stinking engine on a deserted stretch of road at crack of dawn, was like a return to his venturesome youth when he had made a habit of this kind of frolic. He said, laughing, "Why, of course I will, with all my heart. And if I don't like what I see I'll

758

go away again, without showing myself. What time does your train leave Euston? Do you intend to catch the three-twenty express?" and when she nodded, too pleased with herself to speak, "Then I'll give you lunch at the George. And talking of the George I'll let you into a family secret. That headstrong husband of yours was conceived there, one hot summer night in 1863, and that's how he came by his name. That's something you didn't know, I'll wager."

"No," she said, "I never heard it. But neither, I think, did George." Then, shyly, "Some news for you. You are to be a grandfather again in September and I will promise you something. I will ask George to call the boy Adam. Because of this kindness you do me."

"It might not be a boy. What then? Shall we say Eve?"

"It will be a boy," she said, with some of Henrietta's assurance on the same subject. "All my children will be boys."

2

It was, he thought, one of the coldest mornings he was ever abroad in, the knife-edge wind boring through his topcoat and setting him squirming with discomfort in his cramped, uncomfortable ambush, a holly bush that formed part of the hedge dividing the local rectory appropriately called The Hollies, and a straight stretch of road that ran between a large farm and Dunham Halt on the Liverpool branch line.

He had been obliged to get there under cover of darkness and send his cab away, walking briskly along the stretch until he came to the farm and could peep through a chink in the gate and satisfy himself that her information was correct. It was. Several figures moved to and fro in the yard, although it was not yet light enough to identify any one of them. But there, under heavy tarpaulin wrappings, stood George's engine, looking smaller and more compact than he remembered, as though it had shrunk during its sojourn in the North. He did not dare wait until the wrappings were stripped away but back-tracked towards the station, peering about for a place of concealment and remembering, as he did so, that it was the first time he had done this in pre-dawn murkiness since his Mutiny days, thirty years ago.

His instinct for cover seemed to have survived. Five minutes after leaving the farm he was tucked away, with a good view of the road, thanking his stars he had remembered to bring his brandy flask and fortifying himself with a noggin whilst he waited.

Mercifully they were not long making their preparations. A steady, throbbing mutter shattered the early morning silence as the engine came to life some three hundred yards east of where he sat and he cocked an ear to the note, comparing it to the uncertain, heavier stutter he remembered when the engine was running in the old stables at 'Tryst'. He thought, "He's done something to harness that thrust. Regulated it somehow. Sounds more like a factory belt, without that harsh, metallic clatter it once had . . . It's only half its original size too . . . I remember it reminded me of Trevithick's iron carriage that Keate told me about . . ." And feeling a little sheepish on account of the sense of occasion that had invaded him, he chafed his hands and blew on them, seeing his breath cloud the air like the trail of exhaust gases of George's machine.

Then, hearing the throbbing sound increase, until it had attained an insistent rhythm, he forgot to feel like a schoolboy mounting an extravagant practical joke and surrendered to excitement fortified by all the brandy he had swallowed, inching forward until he could poke his head clear of the prickly leaves.

When it came its rush and clatter stunned his senses. It was almost light now, with a heavy ground mist evaporating over the fields opposite, a million frost-points glittering on the hard-packed flints of the road, as if someone had passed by scattering diamonds. He caught no more than a glimpse of it, a solid, compact mass of iron, brass and planed timber lunging out of the mist like a gross primeval monster swooping on an enemy. Instinctively he cowered, feeling the rush of air strike his face as it passed, but he saw old George sitting up there like a mahout herding a laden elephant down an Indian forest track, save that no elephant had ever moved at such a speed or with such a sense of purpose.

The apparition passed in a flash. He had just time to notice that the carriage of the machine was piled with what looked like squarish packages of one sort or another. Then, as it slowed down nearer the station, the note of the engine changed again, rising to a snarling roar, so that he thought, "Great God! He'll have everyone out of their beds screaming that there's been an earthquake . . . !" But the windows behind him remained curtained. It was clear that George had squared the locals and had almost certainly used this same level stretch for earlier tests.

Then, again taking him by surprise, the thing rushed down on him again, so that he wondered how on earth the boy had reversed such a cumbersome vehicle so rapidly. It was now travelling at what he estimated to be something over twenty miles an hour and this time the passage of man and machine introduced into him a sense of wonder and humility, so that he thought, ruefully, "God help me, I've been wrong all the time! That vehicle was carrying freight and nothing I possess in the way of waggons and teams could cover the ground at half the speed."

In his excitement he quite forgot that he was an uninvited spectator and burst out of the bush, stumping up the road to the point where he could see the machine at a standstill, trailing a plume of blue gas that was poisoning the air around. George was still aboard but at road level were several other people, one of them a thickset elderly man, muffled to the eyes in a coat with an astrakhan collar, and waving his stick to proclaim a schoolboy's glee.

He was within twenty yards of the group when they recognised one another. The topcoated man was Sam Rawlinson and Adam was so surprised to see the old chap here at this time of day that he stopped dead, but Sam waddled forward, shouting above the raucous *tut*-sk-*tut* of the engine, "By Gow, see who's here! George lad, it's your father!" and George, who had been bent over the mechanism, jerked himself upright and stared over his shoulder, so that Adam suddenly felt miserably self-conscious concerning his presence and a little fearful of repercussions on Gisela.

He was relieved, therefore, to see a broad grin split George's face as he jumped down and came running, shouting, "Why, you secretive old . . ." but then he stopped, himself somewhat embarrassed, so that Sam expressed what was surely in the boy's mind, saying, "Eeee, but he's a knowing one, is your dad! No flies on *him*! There's nowt goes on anywhere *he* doesn't hear about, and that's summat I decided long ago!"

Then they all shook hands with the utmost cordiality and George said, pride showing through his excitement, "Did you see her go? Did you see that turn of speed back along the road?"

"I did indeed," Adam said, "and I'm more than half converted. No hedging, lad, I had no idea . . . it's nothing like I imagined . . . nothing like it used to be and you've freight aboard. What is it? What have you stowed there?"

"Setts. Road surfacing blocks," Sam said, with some of George's elation. "Aye, an' near half a ton of it, not counting cement! I said to George, after he'd made first test run over Blackley way, a month since, I said, 'Where's t' damn sense in running her empty again? Load her up, lad, and show she'll do t' job she's built for!' Aye and she did, didn't she? Dammit, boy," turning back to George, "she ran better loaded nor unloaded to my reckoning!" and he joggled a stop-watch he was holding.

"What was the average over the half-mile?" Adam asked, after measuring the distance with his eyes and Sam said, "Twenty-two mile an ower. And don't tell me you've owt in your stables to hold a candle to that!"

"No," said Adam, "I haven't, and neither has any other haulier, for that's racetrack speed. And you say there's half a ton aboard?"

"Half a ton plus," George said, so that Adam thought, "He's pleased to see me but he wouldn't be human if he didn't enjoy rubbing it in," but for the first time since George had arrived home with his twelve crates of junk he could look at the machine with respect, noting that he was right in his assumption that it had been reduced to half its original size. It now looked more like a big, shaftless waggon than a crackpot's fantasy. The tyres, he saw, were steel-studded rubber and great attention seemed to have been paid to springing. The steel leaves inserted above the rear axle were more than six inches thick and the body of the vehicle, half-full of setts and cement, fitted snugly over the frame, giving the thing a grace it had never possessed in its experimental stages.

"Come aboard while I drive her into the yard," George said, and Adam hauled himself into the cushioned seat beside the driver's, looking in dismay at the complicated array of knobs and levers protruding from the angled dashboard like flatheaded pins from a pincushion. Under him, as George adjusted two of the controls, the machine vibrated, so that Adam had the sensation of sitting a horse

762

with a bad reputation and experienced identical qualms. He said
nothing, however. Indeed, anything he might have said would have
been lost in the engine's roar as George released the heavy brass
brake-lever and twisted the steering spokes hard left, after which the
machine moved forward at a walking pace, passing between the
gates to the cobbled yard. A flood of questions suggested themselves
but now, he decided, was not the time to ask them. How much did
it cost to build a mechanical carriage of this size and power? How
skilled and experienced did a man have to be to propel one on an
open road? What guarantees were there that it would not break loose
and go thundering across country like a juggernaut? All kinds of
queries and uncertainties but the sum total of them seemed frivolous
when measured against the boy's achievement.

He climbed down and men hurried forward with tarpaulins, draping them over the machine like grooms of the bedchamber. He noticed something else too, that perhaps everyone else took for granted.
Respect for the vehicle was inherent in their approach and in Sam's
too but some of it, a good deal of it he would say, rubbed off
on George, who stood about issuing orders like a young Napoleon.
Observing this he remembered Gisela's claim concerning the boy,
voiced in the tower three days ago. A genius, she had called him,
but not with any emphasis in her voice. She said it as a simple statement of fact, as though assuring him categorically that the earth was
spherical and not, as he had long assumed, flat.

They all trooped into breakfast at the farm where Adam discovered
he had a schoolboy's appetite, addressing himself ravenously to
ham, eggs, marmalade and a quart of coffee, but he was not so occupied as to overlook the genial relationship that had developed between George and Sam and it made him a little jealous. "The old
rascal has resisted fossilisation better than I," he told himself glumly
and said, as soon as Sam was safely engaged in conversation with a
sallow man in overalls, whom Adam took to be a mechanic, "What
are your plans, George? Are you going to patent the machine?" and
George, looking him straight in the eye, replied, "It is patented. In
your name."

"In *my* name?"

But before he could exclaim further George went on smoothly,
"There are all kinds of possibilities. We should have to talk them over

in great detail but first I should want you to see the workshop and blueprints."

He said, quietly, "I couldn't butt in like that, son. Not at this stage, when you've justified yourself in the face of all I had to say about that monster out there. Any credit left over belongs to your grandfather for he backed you. I didn't and I'm not the man to wriggle out of it at this stage."

"Oh, to the devil with niceties," George said, gaily, "we're a family and if you're convinced there's a future in Maximus, that he's more than a complicated toy, then we can move on from there. As a matter of fact, I've already discussed it with Gramp and he isn't disposed to exercise his rights as sponsor. He's nudging eighty and has all the money he needs, and half his pile is willed to mother in any case." He smiled and looked at his plate. "I'll let you into a secret. Sam didn't back me because he believed in its commercial future any more than you did. He did it for fun. It gave him a new interest in life, when all his others were going stale."

"Suppose that's true. Where does it leave us, exactly?"

George was silent for a moment. Finally he said, diffidently for him, "I don't know, Governor. Where you want it to leave us, I imagine." And then, suddenly stretching his mouth in a way that reminded Adam poignantly of his very first glimpse of him, when he came home to 'Tryst' to learn the boy had been born in his absence, "It was Gisela who got you here, wasn't it? All right . . . you don't have to admit it, and I won't press her. It was a good idea in the circumstances but will you tell me something that doesn't concern her? What would you have done if Maximus had let me down, as she has times enough over the past couple of years?"

"I can answer that," Adam said. "I should have climbed out of that damned holly bush down the road, caught the milk train from Dunham, and gone home without a word to any one." He paused, wondering how much he should give away concerning the void George had left in his life. "Something else. I would have gone wishing you luck. I flatter myself I've mellowed that much in the last couple of years."

3

He saw himself in the next few days as having gone full circle. Tagging round after George, coming to terms with the boy's easy mastery of this new, clamorous and rather frightening world, he felt diminished but not uncomfortably so. There was no sourness left in him and certainly no envy. Why should there be? George was only himself, thirty-odd years ago, when he had plunged into the business of building the network on limited capital, sailing over most of the hurdles that intervened between him and his dreams and demolishing those he was unable to jump so that his work force, men like ex-coachman Blubb, the missionary Keate, Catesby, Lovell and all the others, could stream after him, tormented by all manner of doubts that had never troubled him.

And at the same time he was conscious of an accelerated ageing process that he had never felt in the tower overlooking the Thames. Up here there were any number of Georges thronging to occupy the citadels of their fathers and ready, if need be, to swarm south in the new decade, a young and victorious army, coveting a capital still dominated by the shellbacks of his own generation.

Yet an understanding, a full acknowledgement of this did not bother him. Somewhere there was a rightness about it, a logic that he had never accepted as valid until the moment that engine thundered past the Dunham Rectory at twenty-two miles per hour. In his youth and middle age he had been vain concerning his perception and adaptability, seeing himself as one of the very few eager to explore the vistas opened up by pioneers like Stephenson and Brunel. But time, confound it, knocked everyone off their perches in the end, and here he was, standing in the discarded top-boots of old Tim Blubb, who had never been able to speak of railways without a curse.

The workshop and George's yard (where the original Maximus was already regarded as a museum-piece) did not interest him much from the technical viewpoint but its portents did. He had been a transport man long enough to see that there was some substance in George's claim that the horse and cart days would not long survive the turn of the century, now only eleven years away. If George, virtually an amateur in the field, could build a machine capable of hauling half a ton of road blocks over a flint road at twenty-two miles an hour, then it followed that the professional engineers would soon be moving in with all manner of prototypes. Indeed, according to George they already had in France and Germany, where the horse was not a national fetish and where there was no Red Flag Act.

The option was open but it was a very narrow one. He could hang on and adapt, he supposed, with George as his preceptor, but he knew himself well enough to understand that this was an uneasy compromise. He had always thought of himself as an innovator, a pioneer and a winner. Never as a runner-up, entering races he could never hope to win. He did not understand much of George's technical jargon. It seemed that words like 'induction', 'transmission' and even 'drive' had other meanings for the boy and his overalled acolytes. The phrase 'variable speed' made sense in its literal form but not when it was applied to the function of cogs and flywheels.

And yet, in a way, he was fascinated, not so much by George's assurance and technical ability, as by his sense of restraint that many might have mistaken for modesty. Yet George was not modest. Deep down he was completely sure of himself, as sure as Adam had been in the very earliest days of the enterprise. For all that he held himself in, spoke guardedly of the machine's future, soft-pedalling his own achievement and the inevitability of dramatic changes in the world of road transport.

Perhaps, Adam thought, two years of trial and error had taught him patience, but this was only partially responsible for his attitude. There was a more emotional reason behind his reticence and he suspected that it had to do with their relationship, always cordial but ever watchful, a couple of gladiators each aware of the other's strengths and weaknesses. It was this more than the engine's spectacular performance that helped Adam to his decision.

*   *   *

They had gone into the yard's office, hardly more than a lean-to shed, in order to say their good-byes over a drink. The hansom that was to take Adam to London Road was already at the yard gates and it was natural that the moment should have significance for them. It was the counterpart of their last private meeting, a few hours before George, with Henrietta's connivance, had struck his tents and abdicated. Adam said, "Will you be staying up here indefinitely? Are there modifications to be made before you're ready to go into production?"

And George replied, ruefully he thought, "Not on this model. I've taken her as far as I can without finally committing myself." He smiled. "Does that sound like a recantation?"

"No. Should it?"

"Perhaps. After all, I burned one lot of boats when we parted company two years ago."

"Yes, you did, and showed a profit on it."

"That isn't what I meant, sir."

"What did you mean?"

George braced himself. "Mechanisation, represented by the old Maximus, was just the mainspring. I had other ideas, remember?"

"Indeed I do. Some of them good ideas, I recall."

"They were all good ideas and I've never renounced one of them. I should be obliged to, however, if I took the plunge, and devoted myself full-time to the kind of specialisation I've been about up here."

The admission surprised him. By now, he supposed, he had come to think of George as a dedicated man who had renounced all thoughts of being anything but a mechanic.

"You're saying you're still interested in road haulage in the wider sense? In deliveries, as well as the means of delivery?"

"Did you ever suppose otherwise?"

"Why, naturally I did. And so did your mother."

The boy looked a little disconcerted, thrusting his hands deep into his trouser pockets and hunching his shoulders, a trick he had when anyone faced him on an issue.

"Then you're both wrong. I came up here, and worked nonstop on that brute in the yard, simply to prove to myself I could solve at least one complicated problem. Well, I solved it. To spend a lifetime fiddling with variations of it would be too dull for my taste."

"Am I to understand from that you'd like to come back, under certain conditions."

"It isn't for me to lay down conditions. I always maintained you were the Gaffer. You built that network from nothing and it was a far tougher job than getting Maximus moving. I've had time to think since I wrote that long-winded report on how the firm should be run, and one thought I've had was that I was too cocksure by half. That's something that doesn't strike you until you find out how damned lonely it can be out in front, with everyone looking to you for answers you haven't got."

Adam said nothing for a moment. He had a feeling that it had cost George dear to come this far in search of a peace formula. Through the window of the lean-to he saw two of George's team working at a portable forge, one man beating, the other holding a glowing bar to the anvil. Sam Rawlinson waddled slowly across his view and there was something to be learned from the old chap's uncertain gait. He thought, "There's someone who has never learned when to call 'Whoa'! He'll die down here in the muck and maybe that's how he wants it, but not me, by God!" He said, suddenly, "Suppose there aren't any terms?" and the boy's head came up sharply. "Suppose I had other plans, entirely unconnected with Swann-on-Wheels. Do you feel qualified to take over at Headquarters?"

"You mean . . . retire? Hand it over? *All* of it?"

"All of it. To back out, and to the devil with grace and dignity."

"But that . . . that isn't *you*, Governor!"

"How can you say it isn't me? I'm almost sixty-three, and I know when I've had a bellyful. I'm not your grandfather, without a thought in his head save money and how to make it. He was born and raised up here. Foul air, grime and clatter are meat and drink to him. But I'm a countryman at heart and I've a notion I'd like ten or twelve years left to me at 'Tryst', along with your mother and the younger children. Well?"

"You're asking me to take over? In a single jump?"

"It's the only way to do it. You're too much like me, George. Neither of us could work with the other without a weekly display of fireworks. Occasional fireworks are well enough in any concern, but not when two men are competing for the honour of lighting all the fuses. Don't tell me you couldn't do it, either. I know damned well you could and so do most of the regional managers, particularly the thrusters. How long would it take you to pack and come south?"

"A few days. No more, but . . ."

"Then do it. As to the scratch team you've got together for putting that engine on the road, bring them along if you care to. Set up a workshop in London, somewhere close enough to the yard to keep an eye on them. How you divide your time is your business. Yours, and the men from the regions who are your partners." He took out his watch. "That train of mine. I mustn't miss it. I promised your mother I'd be home tonight."

They shook hands and Adam noted, with sardonic amusement, that Old George seemed lost for words. The boy's bewilderment was something of a sop and as George followed him across the yard to where the cab waited he thought, with a tinge of malice, "That's his first lesson in overall responsibility any road! It's one thing to dream of it but quite another when it falls on you like a ton of bricks!" But then, as the cabby cracked his whip, and he caught a final glance of George standing by the kerb he had a more generous thought. "He'll rise to it, nonetheless. If my lease is a long one I might even live to see every damned vehicle we own moving at twenty-two miles an hour!"

ANOTHER VIEW OF THE RIVER

May–December, 1889

He would have imagined that it would take him a long time to pack up and go when it came to the point. Thirty-two years of his life had been based on this octagonal remnant of a mediaeval nunnery and there was more up here than personal files and mementoes, scattered like a trail over three toilsome decades. And yet, when the final week ran out, and George wrote saying that he would begin his tenancy of the tower on the first Monday in May, the clutter of his life was stowed away in a couple of crates in two hours, leaving him something in excess of seventy minutes before he made his last, almost ritualistic descent of the spiral stair to the yard, stumped the seven minutes' walk to London Bridge, and caught the five-forty for home.

He soon disposed of Keate and Tybalt, who had been fussing about him like a couple of over-zealous soldier-servants equipping a testy brigadier for a campaign. They were jointly charged with the job of dismantling Frankenstein, the outmoded ready reckoner, and carting him piecemeal down to the frigate chartered for his private exodus. He could not have said what he wanted with such an unlovely antique but it seemed a shabby trick to abandon him to the mercy of George's caprice. Frankenstein, the apparatus that every visitor mistook for a postcard-stand made from a tailor's dummy, belonged to the very earliest days of the adventure, conceived in a single night and assembled by the master carpenter in a five-hour stint. Something peculiarly Swann's, for surely nobody else would have invented such a means of equating routes and distances with time-tables and the idiosyncrasies of a thousand shire-based customers.

They got him down somehow and from the narrow window overlooking the river Adam saw him stowed aboard, alongside the cardboard folders containing the original maps, a stack of box files, the swivel chair that had adapted itself to the awkward seat of a man with an artificial leg, some framed newspaper cuttings recording the feats of Hamlet Ratcliffe, lion-tamer, Bryn Lovell, mine-disaster hero, and Tim Blubb, slayer of Fenians. There were two other relics of Blubb's in that waggon. One was the blunderbuss with the shattered stock that the ex-coachman had used to break the skull of a highwayman. The other was a printed replica of Dickens' letter to *The Times*, acknowledging the old drunkard's heroism the day of the rail smash at Staplehurst, in June, 1865. One or two other curiosities were carried down and stowed away. A faded photograph of Dockett's first furniture pantechnicon, with its saucy slogan, '*From Drawer to Drawer*', painted under the trademark; a piece of coal in a labelled jar, evidence of Fraser's first foray over the Border at the time of the wreck of an Eyemouth collier; the copy of Longfellow's poems, given him by Edith Wickstead at the end of the momentous conference when he first shed the overall load, together with other private curiosities he had never cared to discard. One relic of the past he would entrust to no one but had wrapped to carry under his arm. It was the silver model of a Swann-on-Wheels frigate, bearing the names of all his regional managers that had been presented to him on his return here in July, 1866, after a year in hospital. It was something that epitomised his intense personal pride in having learned to walk again at the age of thirty-nine.

Keate, essentially a practical man and lacking even a thin streak of sentimentality, said, "What will you do with all these odds and ends, Mr. Swann? Will Mrs. Swann care to have them lying about in that fine place of yours?"

No, he said, Mrs. Swann would not, but Mrs. Swann was unlikely to see them. They would be consigned to one of the attics as soon as the frigate arrived at 'Tryst'.

"Then why not let me dispose of most of them now, sir? I could get the scavenger squad to . . ." but he stopped, sensing that he was treading on corns. He had liked and respected this spare, dark-browed man ever since they had taken their first Dockside stroll together, recruiting wharf rats as vanboys in 1858, but he could not honestly say that he had ever come close to understanding him. He went away and left him to his thoughts, grumbling to his friend

Tybalt that things wouldn't seem the same with the Gaffer gone, and young Mr. George sitting up in that tower.

He had gone the rounds by then and said his private farewells. If he ever did return here, which he doubted, it would be as a visitor, with a careful guard on his tongue. By then, no doubt, most of the old hands would be dead or retired, with strangers in their places. He doubted if George would renew the lease on the ratty old place when it ran out in a year or so. Doubtless he would shift his Head-quarters to some more salubrious spot, away from this fume, grime and racket, somewhere in an outer suburb maybe, where the inflow of waggons was not at the mercy of traffic jams that made nonsense of delivery schedules. As for him, he could never do anything so posi-tive. The view of the river had imprinted itself on his inner con-sciousness by now, so that he saw the ebb and flow of the tideway as a graph of his own progress and the nation's. As for the reek of the soap factory and the adjacent tannery, he had long ceased to bother about it. It was the smell of challenge and what was unsavoury about that?

Less than an hour to go now and he felt the weight of his de-cision for the first time as he glanced around the uncluttered room. For the first time in his long reign here it looked like a belfry again. He fancied he could almost hear the soft patter of the nuns' feet, the swift rustle of their habits, the monotonous, one-note clang of the bell that had hung from the blackened crossbeam. The place was full of ghosts and he was already one of them.

He got up, his eye searching for something to exorcise his touch of melancholy and found it, as always, in the booming traffic of the river beyond the sea of slate and tile outside the yard boundaries. It never stopped. It never had stopped in all his years here. Not even on Christmas Eve or New Year's Day. Not even when Ben Tillett had all the dockers out on strike. Strings of barges, tugs and wherries went shooting through the arches and down beyond the forest of masts that marked the Commercial Dock. Over on the far bank, a square whitish tower, brooding over a hotchpotch of greyish round ones, stood eternal guard over the busiest reach of the river. Eight hundred years it had stood there, planted by a taciturn Norman with a flair for administration. Eight hundred years against his own thirty-two. It would still be there when George drew stumps forty years from now. So would the river traffic, no doubt, but by then sail would have disappeared altogether. Every vessel in the Pool would be sporting funnels and screws, as half of them were today. In a way it was a comforting thought. It meant that he was not alone in growing old and hidebound. The whole way of life was changing at a prodigious pace, much faster than it had changed in his youth, when Stephenson and Telford and Brunel delved and blasted their way into every corner of the land, and set blood pressures soaring in every English fox covert.

Twenty minutes to go. Down river a ship's hooter honked, and closer at hand, in the cavernous street leading to the bridge, a coster's barrow was overset by a passing dray. He was too far off to hear the lively altercation that followed but he could imagine it as coster and drayman squared up to one another and were parted by an officious policeman.

The tiny incident touched off a train of memories that came running like beggars to pocket their Maundy Money, some of them old and bedraggled, others young and sturdy. Tim Blubb, sitting on the box of the first three-horse man-o'-war, about to drive into the Kentish Triangle, in 1859. Edith Wickstead (not Wickstead then) in 1863, here on some trivial pretext to tell him she was emigrating to Australia. Edith here again on that fabulous St. Valentine's Day three months later, demanding a managership as the price of her *not* going to Australia. Little Tybalt feeding Frankenstein with county statistics, pending their first real breakout in the spring of 1860. Sam Rawlinson home from Egypt, telling him to invest in that bloody great ditch that was now the Suez Canal. Himself flexing the muscles of two sound legs one frosty December night in 1861, before walking as far as the Mall to hear of the Prince Consort's death from typhoid.

And one deeply personal memory, of a summer afternoon in 'sixty-three, when Henrietta, fresh as a rose, had come sidling in here with that drooling young gunner on her conscience, to be whisked off to the George, fed, wined and propositioned as regards the new articles of their alliance—he to his work, and she to hers at 'Tryst', providing she had the capacity to command. He had an odd thought then. When, as it were, the treaty was signed, he had made love to her twice within a few hours and out of that rollicking encounter came George, to initiate this renunciation on his part. He had always wanted continuity and here it was, but he wondered, briefly, how the men of the regions would take it. Doubtless Old George would set himself to retire the originals, replacing them with youngsters of his own generation. Well, that was the way of the world, he supposed, and he no longer quarrelled with it. He was sure about one thing. He was not going home to vegetate. He had his own ideas about the way he would take up another entirely different challenge.

He looked at his watch again, took his hat, stick, gloves and the parcelled presentation frigate, and lumbered down the narrow staircase to the yard. Nothing much had changed here but changes were surely on the way. In place of those half-laden pinnaces, frigates and men-o'-war, with their sleek, patient teams, vehicles approximating to George's vapour-trailing engine would trundle in to receive and discharge freight. But that, surely, would not be for a long time yet. For the time being the overriding smell of dung and sweating horseflesh would persist hereabouts and from over there near the warehouse would come the musical clang-clang of the smith's hammer on the anvil. He moved out into the April sunshine and over the weighbridge to Tooley Street. He carried his head high and why not? In a way he was beginning all over again.

2

He knew, more or less, how he would go about it. The project had been in his mind for some years now, growing from a seed planted there during a chance conversation with Henrietta about how he would occupy himself if and when he turned his back on that Thameside slum.

The project divided naturally into two separate endeavours, or three if you included landscaping on the scale he had decided upon. There was the house and its fabric and furnishings. There were the immediate surroundings, including the drive, laurel plantation and walled garden. And there was the general setting, made up of the paddocks, the wooded hill to the north, the coppices to the south, and that stretch of the river that touched his property to the east, a reach he meant to use as a source for his ornamental lake.

As a man who, in his time, had handled virtually every product every type of merchant bought and sold in the Western world, he knew precisely where to go for his labour and materials. He would need hundreds of tons of stone, hundreds of seedlings and young trees that would survive transplantation, a thousand or more shrubs, an army of diggers and an ironmaster who knew his business when it came to forging the decorative work that he had in mind.

He knew how to draw up his plans too, the way he had set about conjuring an enormous volume of traffic out of a few maps, some county almanacks and gazetteers, and a handful of stolen rubies as capital. That first summer, when he was largely prospecting, he used identical methods to organise his ideas, jotting them down in a fat red notebook filled with figures, estimates and sketch-maps. Particularly sketch-maps.

He had always been an excessively neat cartographer and soon the rearward pages of his notebook were filled with detailed sketches of how he saw the new 'Tryst' and its environs in his mind's eye. All the big, initial changes were here. The diversion of a short arm of the river. The rectangular lake, with its island folly south-east of the drive. Two levels of greensward, Cumberland turf if it wasn't too costly, and a long, stone balustrade, broken by niches for urns and statues he had acquired from a bankrupt importer of Italian masonry.

Lower down, where the larch coppice now stood level with the road to Twyforde Green, the pinetum would be planted, imported trees supplementing the many conifers down there, some fifty or so, planted at sixty feet apart. That clump, following through from the lake, lawns and an islet, would give a focus for the eye to anyone looking south and south-east from the terrace but the two supplementary gardens, one on the Italian style, the other laid out as an English Hermitage-style enclosure, would fill the existing areas of meadow and woodland right and left of the pinetum. He would have to take professional advice on the Italian garden but he knew what he would make of the Hermitage. Down there, west of the coppices, was a fine stand of oak and beech, self-seeded from trees the first Conyer had planted high up the slope. Here he would build the summer house and thinking this he had an idea that made him smile. It linked up with Keate's question as to what Henrietta would make of the clutter he had taken out of the tower. He knew now that it would not, as he had told himself, be consigned to one of the attics but would form the basis of a transport museum, a *Swann-on-Wheels* museum, housed in a commodious bower built under the oaks and beech and occasional elm growing there. Here would be the final resting place of Frankenstein and all his other mementoes, so that anyone who wanted to trace the history of the enterprise, when he was safely tucked away in Twyforde Green churchyard down the road, could come and potter among the flotsam of his youth. The notion made an immediate appeal to his vanity and he noted it down, on the page following that containing the detailed sketch of the Hermitage.

The lake would be a straightforward job. All that was necessary was to dig a canal behind a group of willows, linking the backwater to a natural depression in the left-hand paddock, a place that had always cried out for a sheet of water. Lilies and water-iris would do well down there and fish too, no doubt, with a fountain on the islet but no provision for a boathouse. What he was seeking, what he meant to have from here on was tranquillity, of a kind that had escaped him all his life. Beauty and colour certainly but the singular beauty he had always associated with English landscapes. Order imposed on natural contours that were predominantly green all the year round.

He turned then to the herbaceous borders nearer the house. He had never liked laurels or, indeed, the Teutonic formality McCready, the gardener, had brought to the circular and half-moon beds fronting the house. To his mind they were beginning to look like part of a city park and he had other, more ambitious plans, that included a small forest of rhododendron, any number of lilacs, forsythia, clematis, camelia, acacia, magnolia and flowering cherry. In the spring, say from late March until early June, there would be a riot of colour out here, supplementing the carpet of yellow provided by the primroses, daffodils and narcissi that already ranked themselves by the thousand under the copper beeches of the drive. He half-closed his eyes and had a swift, satisfying vision of the place ten years from now. "By God," he said aloud, "I'll make 'em sit up around here, just the way I did thirty-odd years ago! I'm not done yet by many a long sea-mile, and they'll all have to acknowledge it . . . George along with the rest of them, although I doubt if George knows the difference between a Japanese maple and an Irish yew!" For a pleasurable moment he conjured with a string of names in the pages of his notebook devoted to imported trees—giant silver fir, Korean fir, Algerian fir; bitter nut, king nut and cow's-tail pine; Leland cypress, Sawara cypress, Monterey cypress and Arizona cypress; red spruce, Honda spruce, Norway spruce, weeping spruce; cider gum, spotted blue gum and white Sallee.

He made his approximate dispositions and turned his steps to the wooded spur. Ever since he had lived here this had been the rendezvous of wildflowers of every species but dominating, throughout the summer, were the serried ranks of foxgloves, his favourite periwinkle, and wandering convulvulus wreathing itself among the spires of rosebay willow herb that marched all the way up the slope to the heavy timber at the summit.

He would not disturb this overmuch, despite old McCready's annual grouse that it was a source of weeds that bid fair to ruin his kitchen garden below. He knew that Henrietta liked this corner of the estate and the old Colonel had liked it too. All that was needed was a careful rearrangement of rocks and the cultivation of rock plants in all the crevices. He went down again and into the house, where Henrietta was hearing young Margaret at a lesson. "Turn her loose and do the rounds with me," he said. "I've finished planning outside and I'm about to make a start in here."

She came willingly enough. It had taken her a month or two to get accustomed to seeing him about at all hours of the day but now that she had she liked it well enough, for he never interfered in her domestic schedules.

It was mid-June then, with sun flooding the whole southern façade of the house and exposing corners where the maids had scamped their dusting. He said, moving into the big drawing-room, "I never did subscribe to this passion for clutter in rooms one uses as much as we use this one, the study, and the big bedroom upstairs. Most of the houses I've entered in the last twenty years have been crammed with furniture and trumpery knick-knacks. Rubbish, most of it, and dust-traps galore. Nowadays it's the fashion to embellish everything.

I don't know why, unless it's the trademark of the Johnny-Come-Lately. The English once had a reputation for clean, straight lines and spaciousness, and kept their rooms in period. Mind you, one can be too pedantic. This place, built in the fifteen-eighties, was once furnished almost exclusively with black oak, but this eighteenth-century mahogany, walnut and rosewood I've introduced looks at home here," and he trailed off, stopping here and there to make notes, for he had plans to buy more furniture and pictures and porcelain, so that she could see herself enlisting another maid or two to keep it waxed and gleaming.

Aside from clothes she had no kind of taste herself and freely admitted it. She was content to leave the arrangement of the rooms to him, not only because he had always been deeply interested in English craftsmanship but because it gave him a lasting excuse to stay at home and keep her company. She needed his company more than ever now. All but two of the children had flown and three of them, Alex, Joanna and Helen, were as good as lost to her, together with the offspring they had produced and were likely to produce. Alex and Lydia appeared occasionally, for he was back in the Western hemisphere now, with a roving commission to Imperial garrison posts queueing up to be initiated into the mysteries of that new gun Lydia had foisted on the British army. Joanna, based on Dublin, came less often, and none of them had seen Helen since the week of her wedding. Young Hugo drifted in from time to time, sometimes once or twice a week between business trips and athletic meetings, and George had returned to his mill-house so that she had the company of Gisela and the babies. Stella she saw once a week and Stella's tribe were always in and out of the place, borrowing ponies, building wigwams and fishing down by the islet that she always thought of as Shallott. Giles, and that handsome wife of his, lived nearer London and spent their holidays in Wales, a part of Wales she had never visited, although Giles said it was the most spectacular part of the British Isles. Young Edward was here throughout his school holidays and Margaret was here all the time but she was a solitary child and not much company to a fifty-year-old woman whose main interest, apart from the family, was in clothes.

She said, as she trailed after him, "You don't really want my opinion, Adam. It isn't worth having, anyway, not about this kind of thing. I can run a house as well as any woman alive, but I can't re-create one, the way you seem bent on doing. Won't that landscaping, added to what you intend doing in here, cost a great deal of money?"

"Practically all we have to our private credit," he said, cheerfully, "but it will appreciate, mark my words. One or other of them will doubtless reap the benefit. There'll come a time when connoisseurs will pay very high prices indeed for some of these oils and pieces I've picked up in my travels. The rubbish most cabinet-makers are turning out now will be used for firewood, as it richly deserves." He stood back and looked at her whimsically. "Are you telling me you really can't appreciate the difference between the kind of furniture your father has in that red-brick monstrosity of his in Wythenshawe, and that Derby comport over there, or the Pembroke table it's standing on?"

"Not really," she admitted, "to me it's just a pretty bowl and a nice table and Sam's house is stuffed with china and tables, isn't it?"

"Yes," he said, "it is indeed. Mostly Staffordshire fairground prizes, and great bulbous-legged pieces tortured into fantastic shapes and smeared all over with layers of varnish. To say nothing of yards of drapery tacked up everywhere. The place has no kind of welcome for anyone but a junk-dealer."

"Well," she said, "Sam never cared for anything but money-making and you've done your share of that. Like it or not, you left me to run this great place singlehanded for long enough."

"I'm not complaining," he said, smiling and gave her one of his playful but heavy-handed slaps on the bottom, so that she skipped nimbly away from the bed and slammed the door on Phoebe Fraser, who happened to be passing down the corridor.

"Complaining? I should think not indeed! But while we're on the subject do have some regard for the servants about the place. I'm sure I don't know what you'll say or do next since you came home and left George to get on with it. Just then, for instance, whatever will Phoebe think . . . ?" But he only threw back his head and laughed, so that she felt a little spurt of pleasure that he was so content here and showed no signs of pining for the business that had absorbed him so completely over the years.

All their married life they had been adjusting and readjusting to one another and this, she supposed, was no more than another phase in their relationship. He beckoned her over to the window and stood to limn for her the southern vista he planned but she was less concerned with his prattle of ponds and pine plantations than the fact that he put his arm round her waist and then, almost absent-mindedly, turned his head and kissed the back of her neck. It was all at one with his mood these days, as if, finally off-loading that fearful burden he had carried, he felt younger and more hopeful of the future. He showed it in the way he talked about George and George's impending spring-clean, about Lydia's salutary effect on Alex, about Joanna's young Jack-o'-Lantern (he invariably referred to Clinton by this name) currently reorganising the Irish sector, about the regeneration of 'poor old Giles' since he had taken the bit between his teeth and finally married that madcap, Romayne. But, above all, it showed in his attitude to her, for although he was in his early sixties he made love to her more than occasionally, and always with the same gusto. It established beyond any doubt that he still found her personable, was still able to find extreme pleasure in her body, as he had from the earliest days of their marriage. Standing here, his arm about her waist, she had one of those sudden insights into the girl she had been when he had dumped her at his father's lakeside house and rushed south on his very first foray. She remembered then how she had been assailed with doubts as regards her appeal to him as a bride, wondering, as she stood looking at herself in Aunt Charlotte's swing mirror, whether a man of his worldly experience would find her as pretty as she found herself as she playfully measured her eighteen-inch waist with a blue hair ribbon. Well, there was nothing to worry about on that score, even at this late stage. Only a few hours before he had held her in his arms and made her feel like a bride again.

She said, unable to restrain her exultation, "You do just whatever you've a mind to do with the place. I'm sure I won't care, so long as you don't go traipsing off again."

*   *   *

He took her at her word. By midsummer the place was a hive, with seemingly every labourer for miles around making inroads into the paddocks and coppices. McCready, poor man, was dragged from his beloved vegetables, saddled with a couple of boys, and set to work on the rockery behind the house. From the oak and beech clump west of the right-hand paddock came the sound of hammer and saw as the Hermitage took shape, and almost every day one of his pinnaces or frigates arrived to unload something he had picked up somewhere and dumped in a warehouse to await collection. A brace of carpenters invaded the house to make brackets and niches in unadorned corners, and when he unpacked his crates and shook the shavings from a piece of Rockingham or Spode, or a statuette of an armless Venus or a dying gladiator, he reminded her of one of the children opening presents on Christmas morning.

The fine weather broke in August and the violated left-hand paddock, where they were deepening the depression and digging the feed channel for the lake, took on the appearance of a field under the walls of a besieged town, with trenches, sapheads and ramparts connected by plank runways for the stream of barrows. Autumn, however, was dry and sunny, so that the ground soon hardened again and progress speeded up. By late October the transformation could be seen, if only in outline, and she could make some kind of sense out of a master-plan spread out in her sewing-room, confound him, where she had once grappled with administrative work during his absence after the imminent arrival of Giles had compelled her to abandon the yard.

By a happy chance everyone save Helen and her missionary husband was on hand for Christmas, Gisela's third son (christened, to Henrietta's delight, Adam) having been born in early autumn. At supper that night, when they were all gathered at the long table set in the drawing-room where there was space enough to accommodate them, she had one of her Queen-Empress impressions, especially when George, bottle-merry by then, proposed a toast to her and the eight grandchildren asleep in various parts of the house. There were now nine, in fact, but Joanna's daughter, Valerie, had been left in charge of a nurse at home, 'too young to take her chances with the Irish sea' as Jack-o'-Lantern put it. And soon, if her observation was as accurate as it usually was in this respect, there would be ten, for Giles' wife, Romayne, was looking tubbier and a good deal more complacent than Henrietta recalled, in the days of her long, stormy courtship. She never had known what to make of that young scapegrace but Giles, poor wight, was obviously enslaved by her and the best of luck to them. If Giles was anything like his father, it wouldn't be the first and last and a tribe of children would steady her down. From what Henrietta recalled of her she needed steadying.

Deborah, and that nice young man Milton she had married, turned up on Christmas Eve to Adam's special delight and Henrietta, calculating her age, wondered if it was too late now for her to present 'proofs of affection' as they used to say. She hoped not. Any child those two produced was sure to be biddable and they were clearly as pleased with one another as the besotted Giles and that sensual little baggage he had tracked down and married.

All in all it was less of a family than a clan and she wished very much that Helen and her husband could have been here to complete the tally. She found herself hoping that the earnest young doctor who had come asking for her so unexpectedly (and at once whisked her off to Papua of all places) would soon have a change of heart, abandon what must surely be the unrewarding task of teaching head-hunters the creed, and buy a nice, comfortable practice in Sevenoaks or Tonbridge.

She managed, in her way, to have a private word with most of them concerning Adam's latest obsession of converting 'Tryst' into a beleaguered fortress. Their responses were interesting. Alex replied gravely that he supposed Father knew what he was about. He usually did and invariably came up with a profit. George's response was more predictable. He said, lightly, "It'll keep the Gov'nor out of mischief," and she knew very well that this was precisely how he thought of it. He was the very last man in the network to want Adam turning up at the yard proffering unwanted advice.

Giles, the only one among them who shared Adam's interest in pictures, porcelain and what Henrietta thought of as 'secondhand furniture', was enthusiastic, saying that none of them would know the place when it was tidied up and all the workmen had left. And here, to Henrietta's surprise, he was enthusiastically supported by Romayne, who said that Adam Swann was a very remarkable man in his way. She knew that, of course, and did not have to be reminded of it by a flighty daughter-in-law, but what surprised her much more was her daughter Stella's espousal of the changes. She remembered then that Stella had taken a lively interest in the landscaping during the summer and autumn, and had popped over to watch progress whenever Dewponds could spare her. Perhaps it wasn't all that surprising. Stella had once helped to rebuild a burnedout farm with her own hands, thus emerging from her long trance after that frightful experience in Sussex. Maybe building something was a kind of medicine and Adam was now dosing himself, to ease the heartache caused by the surrender of his network.

She had a pleasant, gossipy session with the girls late on Christmas night, when the men were still at their port, the first time she could remember enjoying the segregation of the sexes the moment dinner was over, a custom she had always thought excessively dull and stupid.

She had a chance then to note that hardening of alliances between them, of a kind that had existed within the family before they began to scatter. Joanna seemed to confide in Romayne and this was something else that made sense for they had, Henrietta thought, a good deal in common. One had been silly enough to get herself pregnant before she was safely married. The other had succumbed to panic and run off somewhere (Giles had never disclosed why, exactly) when her wedding day was a few weeks off. Stella and Gisela had formed a firm friendship a long time ago. Each approved the other's practical approach to men and marriage, although Gisela was never likely to influence George to the extent that Stella had moulded Denzil. Lydia, to a lesser degree, inclined towards this faction, whereas Margaret, her youngest daughter, who walked alone for the most part, had always looked upon Deborah as a special kind of person. More and more Henrietta began to see her youngest child as a female equivalent of the gentle old Colonel.

It was thinking of him that sent her out into the hall on the excuse of getting a breath of air. It was a very mild night for December, so she took a shawl and opened the front door, slipping out on to the forecourt and looking up at the stars. A merciful darkness shrouded the ugly diggings, contrasting with the blaze of lights that lit up the front of the house.

Standing here she could catch the sound of male laughter from the dining-room, and supplementary giggles from the eastern end of the house. She had, at that moment, an awareness of intense, personal achievement, telling herself that she was the source of all that health and vitality in there. Not for the first time she acknowledged it as a very remarkable accomplishment on her part, and one that, in the real sense, had been achieved single-handed. For what had Adam brought to it, apart from a few moments of zest and affection? He had kept them housed and fed and clothed, certainly, but all the really important decisions had been hers. It was she who had been the first to judge the effect Lydia would be likely to have upon Alex's character and his chances of promotion; she who had resurrected Stella and promoted the match with Denzil; and she who had intrigued to keep George inside the family circle. It was she who had extricated Joanna from her awful dilemma and she who had nursed the entire brood through all their turbulent patches. Now, she supposed, her influence would lessen year by year, but this was not a prospect that dismayed her. She would be fifty-one next birthday and it was time to look about for a bit of peace, and perhaps some cautious foreign travel if she could talk Adam into breaking his resolve never to quit Britain again.

She felt extraordinarily happy and hopeful standing here inhaling the night air and almost as young and romantic as the girl who had waited outside that shepherd's hut on Seddon Moor for her White Knight to ride over the skyline and hoist her on to the rump of his mare at the very beginning of the adventure. Remembering this, she felt a familiar surge of gratitude for the tall, dark-browed sixty-two-year-old, currently swapping coarse jokes, no doubt, with his buccaneering sons and sons-in-law. Acknowledgement of her affection for him was so definite that she looked forward to bedtime, when they would withdraw from all the chatter and badinage and put their arms about one another in that great Conyer bed they had shared since they settled here and their partnership had properly begun.

She took another look at the stars, sniffed the dampish air, drew her shawl about her, and marched back into the house, closing the door gently so that no one would scold her for exposing herself to the risk of catching cold. She rarely did catch cold. Apart from lying-in periods, she could not recall ever having spent a day abed and she still had—what?—twenty to thirty years ahead of her.

The drawing-room door opened while she was replacing her shawl in the cupboard and the men trooped out, a little the worse for wear some of them, but not Adam, who came last, his left hand flexing the muscles of his truncated leg, something he could always be seen to do when he had been seated for any length of time. The boys made for the sewing-room in a body, and from the uproar that greeted them she concluded there would be any amount of private junketing when they finally separated and went to their beds, for all the girls save Margaret had had their share of hock and Burgundy at dinner.

But Adam hung back seeing her standing there, and seemed to be reading her thoughts, for he winked and then stumped across the flagstones and took her hand. He said, conspiratorially, "We'll leave 'em to it in half-an-hour or so, shall we?" and she nodded, so eagerly that he chuckled, drawing her forward into the storm centre of conviviality across the hall.

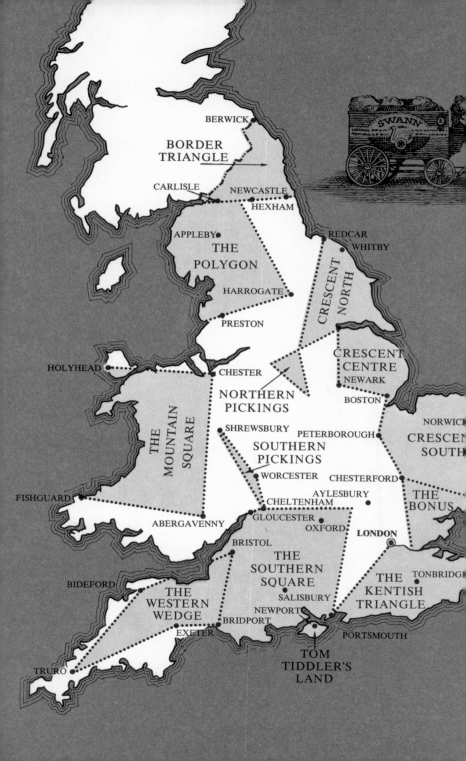

BERWICK

BORDER
TRIANGLE

CARLISLE
NEWCASTLE
HEXHAM

APPLEBY
THE
POLYGON

REDCAR
WHITBY

CRESCENT
NORTH

HARROGATE
PRESTON

HOLYHEAD
CHESTER

CRESCENT
CENTRE
NEWARK

NORTHERN
PICKINGS

BOSTON

THE
MOUNTAIN
SQUARE

SHREWSBURY
PETERBOROUGH
SOUTHERN
PICKINGS
WORCESTER
CHESTERFORD

NORWICH
CRESCEN
SOUTH

FISHGUARD

AYLESBURY
CHELTENHAM
ABERGAVENNY
GLOUCESTER
OXFORD
LONDON

THE
BONUS

BRISTOL
THE
SOUTHERN
SQUARE

BIDEFORD
THE
WESTERN
WEDGE
SALISBURY
NEWPORT
BRIDPORT
EXETER

THE
KENTISH
TRIANGLE

TONBRIDG

PORTSMOUTH

TRURO

TOM
TIDDLER'S
LAND